D1736955

SHE HAD LEFT HOME A GIRL.
SHE WAS RETURNING A WOMAN.

Bristol Adams was returning from over the seas to the town of Salem that she had left under a cloud of shame.

Behind her she was leaving the splendors of London and the seductions of the lover who had conquered her body and soul, only to betray and almost destroy her.

She was going back to the man who had first taken her innocence, and whom she now surpassed by far in knowledge and need of the flesh.

Bristol Adams was coming home . . . back to a love that might be no more than a memory . . . back to a place where the passions flaming within her might lead her to a different kind of fearful fire. . . .

SALEM'S DAUGHTER

Big Bestsellers from SIGNET

☐ ALEXA by Maggie Osborne. (#E9244—$2.25)*

☐ MAGGIE'S WAY by Martha Barron Barrett. (#E9601—$2.75)*

☐ THE BOOKS OF RACHEL by Joel Gross. (#E9561—$3.50)

☐ EMPIRE by Etta Revesz. (#E9564—$2.95)

☐ LORD SIN by Constance Gluyas. (#E9521—$2.75)*

☐ THE PASSIONATE SAVAGE by Constance Gluyas.
(#E9195—$2.50)*

☐ THE WILTONS by Eden Hughes. (#E9520—$2.75)*

☐ THE RAVISHERS by Jeanne Duval. (#E9523—$2.50)*

☐ TAMARA by Elinor Jones. (#E9450—$2.75)*

☐ LUCETTA by Elinor Jones. (#E8698—$2.25)*

☐ LOVE IS NOT ENOUGH by Ruth Lyons. (#E9196—$2.50)*

☐ LET THE LION EAT STRAW by Ellease Southerland.
(#J9201—$1.95)*

☐ STARBRIAR by Lee Wells. (#E9202—$2.25)*

☐ FOREVER AMBER by Kathleen Winsor. (#E9234—$2.95)

☐ DAYLIGHT MOON by Thomas Carney. (#E8755—$1.95)*

* Price slightly higher in Canada

Buy them at your local bookstore or use this convenient coupon for ordering.

THE NEW AMERICAN LIBRARY, INC.,
P.O. Box 999, Bergenfield, New Jersey 07621

Please send me the SIGNET BOOKS I have checked above. I am enclosing
$_____ (please add 50¢ to this order to cover postage and handling).
Send check or money order—no cash or C.O.D.'s. Prices and numbers are
subject to change without notice.

Name _____

Address _____

City_____ State_____ Zip Code_____
Allow 4-6 weeks for delivery.
This offer is subject to withdrawal without notice.

Salem's Daughter

by
Maggie Osborne

Ⓢ
A SIGNET BOOK
NEW AMERICAN LIBRARY
TIMES MIRROR

PUBLISHER'S NOTE

This novel is a work of fiction. Names, characters, places, and incidents are either the product of the author's imagination or are used fictitiously, and any resemblance to actual persons, living or dead, events, or locale is entirely coincidental.

NAL BOOKS ARE AVAILABLE AT QUANTITY DISCOUNTS WHEN USED TO PROMOTE PRODUCTS OR SERVICES. FOR INFORMATION PLEASE WRITE TO PREMIUM MARKETING DIVISION, THE NEW AMERICAN LIBRARY, INC., 1633 BROADWAY, NEW YORK, NEW YORK 10019.

Copyright © 1981 by Maggie Osborne

All rights reserved

SIGNET TRADEMARK REG. U.S. PAT. OFF. AND FOREIGN COUNTRIES REGISTERED TRADEMARK—MARCA REGISTRADA HECHO EN CHICAGO, U.S.A.

SIGNET, SIGNET CLASSICS, MENTOR, PLUME, MERIDIAN, AND NAL BOOKS are published by The New American Library, Inc., 1633 Broadway, New York, New York 10019

First Printing, February, 1981

1 2 3 4 5 6 7 8 9

PRINTED IN THE UNITED STATES OF AMERICA

To my dearest friend George with love

1

ONCE each week, on market day, Salem Town square filled to the hedges with dark-clad curiosity seekers. They arrived by cart and wagon to trade goods and replenish supplies and remained to taunt the unfortunate men and women clamped in stocks and pillory, jeering those who dared transgress the common good.

Until today Bristol Adams hadn't suspected the crowd's mockery might be as severe a punishment as anything the church fathers had devised. But until today Bristol Adams had never earned public punishment. In the past she'd been a part of the crowd, adding her scorn to theirs, never dreaming she'd one day be the object of their ridicule.

Now, facing the crowd, Bristol drew a halting breath and glanced toward the multitude of stony faces, pretending a bravery she didn't feel. It seemed each set of accusing eyes fixed on her, every whispered laugh was meant for her.

Deep inside, Bristol understood this wasn't true; others awaited punishment and received their portion of scorn as well. Only when the constable focused his attention on one person alone did the crowd swing and direct eyes and accusation in a centered manner. But in her fear and the shame of standing here, Bristol Adams imagined all eyes pierced her soul and found it wanting.

She shifted uneasily and turned slightly to follow where the crowd pointed. Behind her, an incorrigible blasphemer drew a din of loud snickers and mockery, providing the crush of onlookers exactly the entertaining spectacle they most relished.

Taunting voices rose and hooted as an obese constable muttered beneath his breath, circling, slipping, struggling to catch the blasphemer's wet tongue between his fingers. Even strained heads jutting from pillory boards grinned as the heavy constable and his man slid in the snow, grappling

1

toward an inevitable end. Finally, as the crowd had known he would, the constable succeeded in snapping a split birch branch upon the tip of the blasphemer's tongue. The man's dark eyes bulged above his protruding tongue, and he struggled with the ropes securing his hands behind his back.

The constable frowned and wiped his hands on a long coat. He spit in the snow and bent to the fire pit.

Knowing what was to follow, Bristol squeezed her eyes shut and turned her head to one side. She winced when the man's strangled scream reached her ears. In a moment, the constable stepped past, triumphantly brandishing the fiery poker he'd thrust through the man's tongue.

The eyes of the crowd followed the glowing poker, and a murmured hum of approval swept the square. Goodman Willis Moxon would never again disgrace the community with offending words. No God-fearing man or woman need risk hearing the Lord's name defiled in the lanes of Salem— not by Goodman Moxon.

Now expectant eyes swung toward Bristol Adams, to the whipping post and her lush trembling figure. And with a sinking heart Bristol understood her turn had come. Her mouth turned dry as summer dirt, and her shaking hands rolled her apron into damp balls.

Bristol wet her lips. She blinked at the sea of faces, frantically seeking her father's features within that wave of austerity. But she saw only staring eyes, waiting and judging.

If only she could locate Noah Adams! Her father could step forward even now and withdraw the charges. It wasn't too late! Bristol's green eyes darted from face to face. "Please," those eyes despaired, "Please, Papa!" She scanned hard expressions, feeling the desperation in her gaze, and she heard the quickening beat of her heart. Where was he? Please, God, let Papa step forward.

Her darting eyes moved and settled and moved again. Sober disapproval met her gaze, but Bristol didn't see Noah's red hair among any of the nodding steeple-crowned hats. Instead, she recognized friends and neighbors, harsh and unfamiliar when viewed from the perspective of shame and humiliation.

"Weren't you ever young?" Bristol wanted to shout. "Didn't any of you ever speak or exchange a glance without your father's permission?" But such an act was unthinkable, and her voice had turned to sand. Her defiance seeped away like water through fingers.

Suddenly Noah Adams' weathered face appeared to leap

from the thicket of faces, and Bristol stared, imploring him to forgive with the emerald eyes so like his own. For an instant their gaze locked; then Bristol lowered her face with a hopeless groan. No softening eased her father's stern expression. He would hold to the charge he'd stated to the magistrate. Bristol's pride and defiance must be publicly whipped away. She would learn to obey as all dutiful daughters must; she would behave for the common good. Bristol could court Caleb Wainwright only when and if Noah's prior permission were obtained. And Noah had granted no such permission.

"Oh, Caleb," Bristol moaned inwardly, licking dry lips. "Why didn't we talk to Papa? Why didn't you speak out for me?"

But she knew the answer, had thought of little else for months. Caleb Wainwright would not be eligible to receive his inheritance until next month, April 1690. Only then would he be welcomed as a suitor by any self-respecting father. Until then, Caleb had nothing to offer but himself.

A small cry escaped Bristol's lips as rough hands gripped her wrists. She averted her face from the constable's sour breath; he sweated heavily despite the chill air and drifts of snow rippling the ground. Grunting, the constable knotted her wrists with hemp and lifted both hands above her head. An elbow brushed her dust cap to the ground, and a tumble of brilliant red curls cascaded over Bristol's small shoulders. Deep within the crowd, a man's voice murmured appreciatively, and the constable paused for a threatening glare. Then he secured Bristol's hands to the iron ring above her head.

Angry, frightened tears sprang into Bristol's eyes, and she battled to prevent them spilling down her cheeks. Grinding her teeth, she repeated the vow she'd made earlier. No one would have the satisfaction of hearing her scream or seeing her cry. The town could whip her, but she promised herself to bear the lash with dignity and pride. Her crime was small, and she didn't regret it. Hers was an error of the human heart, and when she thought of Caleb Wainwright, she knew she'd speak to him again, look at him again, with or without Noah Adams' permission.

Never having experienced an angry blow, Bristol had no measure by which to judge the realities of her vow. And even if she had, her mind felt numb, deadened to the actuality of her situation. To be whipped publicly seemed so unbelievable, Bristol continued to think Noah would surely intervene.

3

He might allow the constable to scare her, but he'd not let his daughter actually be lashed. She swallowed. Would he?

Her wide green eyes sought Noah; if her father intended to rescue her, it must come soon. At sight of the suffering in her father's face, a terrible doubt fluttered through the pit of Bristol's stomach, and she sucked in a deep breath. He was clearly in pain . . . and she was in pain . . . why didn't he step forward? Noah stood with his large hands clasped before him, his eyes resolute.

Anxiously Bristol glanced to Noah's side, and a prick of worried tears moistened her eyes. Her mother sagged at Noah's elbow, her eyes closed and her hands folded across her breast. Bristol blinked and choked on the lump clogging her throat. Her eyes moved to her sister.

Charity leaned on Hannah's shoulder, an arm around her mother's waist and her carroty curls bright against her pale face. Seeing Bristol's stricken plea, Charity dashed a hand across her eyes. She attempted a smile of support, but the weak effort wavered and cracked.

Bristol bit down on her lip as the constable's thick body blocked her family from view. Her heart leaped in apprehension. "Papa, please, Papa," she murmured through dry lips. He wasn't going to save her. Shock tingled through her suspended body. Closing her green eyes, she swayed from the iron ring. If Noah allowed the constable to rip her dress, her terrified mind understood, the whipping would take place. It would happen!

The constable's hand shot forward and tore away the old gown Hannah had insisted she wear. First from the front, then from behind. Bristol's face blazed in an agony of scarlet heat as her full rounded breasts fell free, pink and white in the winter sun. A startled gasp blew through the crowd, deepening her shame, and Bristol's head dropped, sending a shower of red hair curling past her shoulders, partly covering her nakedness. But not enough. No, she thought in rising despair, not enough.

Somewhere in the shifting ocean of scorn, Bristol felt Caleb Wainwright's eyes. And she shriveled at the thought of Caleb seeing her shame. Of all the stares examining her nakedness, Caleb's cherished blue gaze weighed heaviest.

Closing her brimming eyes, Bristol tried to control the fear pounding in her temples like drums. The constable strutted before the crowd while the town crier read her offense: disregard for the common good through parental disobedience and rejection of custom.

4

The words flowed past Bristol in a meaningless stream; all she heard was the rhythmic smack of a thick black whip handle striking the constable's palm. Staring through a shadow of long lashes, Bristol saw nine rawhide thongs, each an inch wide, dragging the ground before her horrified gaze.

". . . six lashes, well laid on." The crier cleared his throat with importance. "Let all children observe and remember!"

Dutifully parents nudged their children forward for a clear view, then folded their arms rigidly across their bodies. Waiting. The constable's sour grin approved, and he crunched through the snow until he stood in position behind Bristol, staring thoughtfully at her smooth white back.

Bristol's glazed eyes swept the crowd, familiar faces seeming to jump forward, then recede. Martha Cory, village busybody, whispered furiously into Elizabeth Proctor's ear. Old Rebecca Nurse leaned on her cane, shouting at Ann Putnam as if Goodwife Putnam were as deaf as Rebecca. Reverend Samuel Parris held his mouth in a tight line, but his small eyes focused on Bristol's ripe young breasts. Abigail Williams shoved her little cousin against Bridget Bishop. Bridget paid no heed, her sensual lips forming a semblance of pity. They all appeared frozen in place.

Bristol swung pleading eyes toward Hannah, and a brackish taste welled in her throat. Hannah's faded blue eyes examined a point above Bristol's head. As Bristol watched, her mother stiffened and shook away Charity's hand. Hannah Adams refused to bow her head before the community. Bristol was and would always be flesh of Hannah's flesh, blood of her blood. For Hannah Adams, the bonds of motherhood transcended any shame. She met Bristol's anguished eyes with a smile of encouragement, communicating her love and strength across the distance separating them. Bristol's heart ached.

A crack snapped in the crisp air, the nine tongues of fire seared across Bristol's bowed shoulders. Her face collapsed in shock, and her spine arched away from the heavy blow, her quivering breasts jutting forward. Agony burst from her lips, scattering any foolishly brave intentions.

A roar deafened Bristol's ears, whether from the crowd or from her own exploding mind, she didn't know or care. Her heart felt as if it would burst through her body, and her pulse fluttered wildly in throat and temples. The pain was staggering, beyond all imagining.

The next lash burned into her naked back before she'd fully comprehended the first. Heavy rawhide bruised into ten-

5

der flesh that had never known a rough touch. Bristol gasped and sagged from the iron ring, her swimming vision seeing but not seeing the glowing eyes that judged each swing of the whip, sternly appraised every twitch, measured each cry of pain. Bristol Adams' mind narrowed to the whistle of the lash and the fiery torment flaying her shoulders.

Nine fingers of agony crashed across her bare skin, cutting into the previous stripes swelling up on her back. Something wet dripped along the curve of her spine, and through the red haze clouding her thoughts, Bristol wondered wildly if blood rivered into the waist of her torn gown, or if icy bits of melting snow trailed from the leather thongs. Cold and heat were no longer distinguishable.

A high scream sounded above the next crushing blow, and Bristol blinked rapidly through a scald of blinding tears. Her ashen face twisted. Who screamed? Who mocked her in a voice so like her own?

Bewildered, she tried to look into the staring crowd. But faces melted and shifted in a montage of dark color. Cloaks and hoods and aprons and hats blended into a swaying black wall.

"Mama?" Bristol sobbed, swinging from the iron ring. Her arms twitched and ached, her back was a single open wound. "Papa?" She could no longer remember why she hung from the ring or what was happening to her. But there was pain. Terrible searing pain. If only she could find her parents, they would help, they always had. An image of worried faces flashed into her screaming mind, showing Noah and Hannah as they'd looked bending above her bed when she tossed in a delirium of yellow fever. Two years ago? Three? "Help me, please!" Bristol cried, her blank eyes darting along the black wall.

Another whistle of fire branded into her flesh, slicing a pink trail in the milky field. Sticky wet flowed freely down her back and sides, pooling in the damp waist of her oldest gown. Bristol's head fell toward a frayed hem, and she blinked in confusion. Why was she wearing such a ragged dress? She shook her glossy curls at the heart-wrenching sound of sobbing, uncertain who uttered those raw gasping sobs. "Someone is crying about my gown." There was a reason she'd chosen it, there must have been, but . . .

Her thoughts dissolved into a blinding shriek as the lashes ripped across torn flesh. "Sweet God in heaven!" Bristol screamed, lifting a tortured face toward the sky. "Please!"

6

White-hot agony flamed along her back, black dots spun before her eyes.

Finally, rough hands reached to cut her free, and Bristol fell, her limp quivering body caught in Hannah's embrace. Before her lids closed, she saw Noah rush to cover her nakedness with his cloak, and Charity bathed her streaked face with a handful of cold snow.

Bristol fought to remain conscious. Desperately she tried to focus on the blur of breeches and hems moving rapidly toward the pillory, where it had been promised the constable would next nail the ears of a notorious liar to the pillory boards.

"Can ye walk, girl?" Noah's strained voice filtered past a buzzing in Bristol's ears.

"Papa! Oh, Papa, my back . . . it hurts so much . . ." Every nerve shrieked protest, her knees rattled like twigs in a high wind.

Hannah's warm hand brushed at the damp red tangle obscuring Bristol's face, and Bristol felt the tremor in her mother's fingers. "Shhh," Hannah soothed. "It's over now. Stand tall."

Tentatively Bristol staggered forward, crumpling to the frozen ground at the first jarring step. Excruciating pain jolted upward into raw flesh. "I'm sorry, Mama, I . . ." A black wave rolled over her vision, then Noah's stocky arms swept her up and his arm against her open back was more than her mind could withstand. Mercifully, the darkness closed, and Bristol fell into a faint against Noah's wide shoulder.

Agonizing awareness rose intermittently throughout the eight-mile journey to Salem Village and home. Noah's wagon bounced over rutted roads, shaking Bristol awake to find herself cradled in the warm straw of the wagon bed, covered with thick quilts. Even so, violent shivering racked her body when green eyes fluttered open.

"Oh, Brissy," Charity whispered, her freckled face wet with tears. On the high seat above Charity's head, Bristol blinked at Hannah's stiff back and Noah bent over the reins, his gaze fixed on the horses' backs. Bristol groaned and closed her eyes.

As the wagon bumped through the Adamses' gate, Bristol again battled past gray mists of pain. She stared with relief at the weathered boards and a wisp of smoke curling from the chimney. Here was safety, a haven from the world's ills. Teeth chattering, she anticipated the cheery warmth of Han-

7

nah's kitchen. Supper would be waiting. Perhaps a fragrant stew bubbling in the iron pots beneath the lug pole, filling the house with steamy good smells.

Slowly, drops of pain leaking from her eyes, Bristol struggled up on one elbow and lifted her face toward the tall pines rimming Noah's fields. The forest rose in green silence, shrouded in snowy majesty. Quiet. Peaceful. No scorching heat. No blazing lacerations. No . . . Bristol toppled forward, washed in a tide of brutal pain.

She awoke to wincing agony when Noah laid her facedown in her bed.

"Careful!" Hannah's voice was sharp. "Be careful with her!"

"Aye, woman! Do ye imagine I like this any better than ye do?" Noah's work-hardened hands lifted Bristol's mass of red hair, gently dropping the long curls upon her pillow. His whisper sounded harsh and pained. "'Twas for the girl's own good! She has a willful pride as fiery as the hair on top her head. Ye know as well as I, Hannah Adams, self-will has no place in a community. The common good, not self, is all-important! The girl must learn obedience to the common good! And humility."

Hannah's lips thinned into a line. "If she lacks humility after this disgrace, then milk pails can fly!" She fisted her hands on narrow hips and glared at her husband. "I'll not be needing you for the healing," she announced tartly, watching Noah stamp from the bedroom. "Charity, fetch the water and salt."

"Aye, Mama." Charity's freckles stood starkly against a white face. She untangled her hands from her apron folds and scurried to do as her mother ordered, returning with a bucket of well water and a basket of tiny salt chips Hannah had prepared before dawn.

Hannah's chest rose in a deep breath, and her faded blue eyes flinched. She dreaded what must be done. Sighing, Hannah gently removed the cloak from Bristol's flayed shoulders. As the cloak peeled away, Charity gasped and pressed a hand to her mouth before fleeing the room.

Hannah stared.

"Mama?" Bristol's sob-choked whisper was nearly inaudible. "Mama, can I bear it?"

Hannah's breath released in a rush, and she squared her shoulders. "Of course you can. You're an Adams! Bite down." She inserted a smooth oaken oval between Bristol's teeth. "I've seen worse," she added grimly.

Indeed she had. In her rounds as occasional midwife, Hannah Adams had observed all manner of human suffering. But Bristol was her firstborn, and that made all the difference. She wiped her hands on a long white apron and tucked an errant strand of graying chestnut hair beneath the edge of her dust cap. Further hesitation only invited infection and fever.

Bristol watched through blurred eyes, her mother wavering and fading as Hannah poured part of the salt chips into a cracked basin. Hannah sloshed the water until the chips dissolved, then immersed a clean rag and wrung it carefully.

"I'll be brave," Bristol vowed, trying to be convincing, but she couldn't hold back a scream when the salt-soaked cloth touched the edges of her wounds and passed in cleansing circles over the rusty stains streaking her sides. Her teeth bit convulsively into the oaken oval; then she shuddered and sank into feverish oblivion.

Hannah's eyes lifted briefly, and she nodded. Working rapidly, she took advantage of Bristol's faint. She cleaned the oozing strips of pulpy flesh, then filled her palms with chips, trickling salt directly into the long crisscrossing wounds. If God willed it so, the scars would be slight, but scars there would definitely be. A lesson forever seared into flesh.

Finished, Hannah covered Bristol's back with light bandages, then sank to the cold plank floor and folded her hands. Her prayer was one of thanks. As Noah said, God was for thanking, not asking. And Hannah thanked God the damage to her daughter's back had not been worse. She thanked God for a caring husband and a snug house. She thanked God for her surviving daughters, forcibly turning her mind from the row of gray stones in the village cemetery where her sons slept. She thanked God for good health and a plentiful larder. And lastly, she slowly but firmly thanked God for giving her a temperate tongue.

Hannah struggled to her feet knowing her last words of thanks constituted a questionable maneuver. By thanking God for a temperate tongue, she fervently hoped he would grant her one—that she would bear her daughter's suffering without casting words of recrimination at her husband. Sighing, Hannah stepped into the kitchen and propelled a pale-faced Charity toward the evening chores. To ease her own aching thoughts, Hannah busied her hands by stirring the pots. Then she poured flour from a stone crock and made biscuits. Regardless of trouble, her family still must eat.

Except Bristol. Nearly a week passed before Bristol could accept solid food without vomiting. During these dismal days

9

she tossed and groaned in her bed, spiraling between painful cognizance and blissful black emptiness. However, each time her feverish green eyes blinked open, the pain seemed a little less, the healing begun.

On the eighth day, she was able to bear pillows against her back, and she sat up, sipping a tepid nourishing soup.

"How do you feel?" Charity inquired anxiously, a frown puckering her forehead.

Bristol adjusted her sore back with a grimace. "Better," she answered. "I don't know which pains more, the stripes or the salt Mama rubbed into them." Bristol attempted a weak smile.

Quick tears sprang into Charity's eyes. "Oh, Brissy, Mama wouldn't dream of hurting you. She had to use the salt to—"

"Charity, you goose! I know, I know. I was only trying to coax a smile from you." Bristol sighed. She should have known better. Charity, like Hannah, lacked any hint of humor. Frivolity didn't align with Puritan thought patterns.

Bristol frowned at her hands. Somewhere along the years, a deficiency had developed in Bristol's growth. Despite discouraging faces, moments occurred when she felt compelled to laugh or smile. She didn't always see life as the dour, serious affair others determined to make of it. Caleb often told her the twinkle in her eye attracted him more than anything else. Her full lips twisted. She wouldn't allow herself to think of Caleb just yet.

Charity blinked rapidly. "Were you being . . . uh . . . humorous, Brissy?" She colored with embarrassment and dropped her eyes. "I'm sorry. I never know if you mean what you say or . . . I try, but I just don't see much to laugh at most of the time. And I . . ."

Bristol patted Charity's hand, thinking affectionately what a dull stick poor Charity had become. Unless the conversation dealt with crops and rainfall and livestock and farm concerns, Charity tended to remain silent. In another year, Charity would be the same age as Bristol, seventeen, and ready for courtship. In Bristol's view, few desirable swains were likely to appear asking for Charity. With a look of genuine concern, Bristol studied her sister in the dim wintry light.

Shy and meek, Charity Adams shrank in the shadow of her vivacious sister. Like Bristol's, Charity's head was topped with Noah's hair. But the curls tied at Charity's neck gleamed a carroty orange rather than the striking red shimmer spread across Bristol's pillow. On Charity, Bristol's deep emerald

10

eyes became watered green glass. And her freckled skin darkened to a spotted patchwork each summer, while Bristol's creamy face remained clear.

Absently Bristol patted Charity's hand. If only Charity possessed a whisper of humor to spark those serious eyes; if only a small fire of spirit lifted her thin chest, then perhaps Charity's future would hold a brighter promise.

Uncomfortable being the center of such intense scrutiny, Charity cleared her throat. "Would you like to play Wish?" Her face brightened. The rules for Wish were simple. One player stated a wish, the other guessed true or false based on his knowledge of the player. The game was both revealing and entertaining.

Bristol sighed. They had played at least one hundred games of Wish in the past few days, it seemed. "Very well." She smiled. Wish was Charity's favorite pastime.

"You first," Charity urged.

"Hmmm. I wish I could live in Salem Village all my life," Bristol said. She felt a twinge of guilt, as the truth seemed all too obvious.

"False!" Charity crowed, clapping her hands. "I've seen how you stare at the ships in Salem harbor and heard you wonder where they're bound for." She smiled. "My turn."

Annoyed and surprised, Bristol shook her head. "Wondering is not wishing. I really do want to live here. This is home! Why on earth would you think I'd want to leave?"

Confused, Charity gave an apologetic shrug. "I'm not sure. Except . . . I sense a restlessness in you, Brissy. I don't know. I always imagine you marrying a wealthy merchant or maybe a sea captain or . . . someone important." Her cheeks pinked. "I think maybe you'd like to sample more of the world than Salem Village can offer."

Bristol laughed. "No merchants or sea captains, Charity. I only want to marry Caleb and be a farmer's wife." Her face sobered at the mention of his name, and she glanced miserably at the quilts. After the whipping, would Noah ever agree to allow Caleb to court?

Charity lowered her voice and darted a glance at the closed bedroom door. "Caleb Wainwright rode over to talk to Papa," she whispered.

Bristol's head snapped up, and arrows of pain shot along her shoulders. Eagerly she leaned forward, her heart quickening. "He did? Why didn't you tell me sooner? What happened? What did Caleb say? Oh, Charity, tell me!" Her emerald eyes glowed, and her thoughts whirled. If only Noah agreed to let them court! If only! She'd bear her lash marks proudly if she could be with Caleb openly!

Charity's eyes darkened with sympathy. "Papa told Caleb"—she stumbled over his name, her cheeks turning pink—"Papa said Caleb must never ride here again. Papa said Caleb's father should have insisted Caleb be whipped as well."

Bristol stared, unable to believe what her ears heard. "But . . . but Papa couldn't have sent Caleb away like that! He just couldn't!" Her voice rose in dismay, her green eyes brimmed. "Why? Why would Papa do such a cruel thing?"

Shyly Charity reached for Bristol's cold hand. "Papa doesn't mean to be cruel, Brissy, he's only doing what he thinks best. Papa believes Caleb is the cause of your troubles. He told Caleb he dishonored you by engaging in public conversation, enticed you to disobey the rules of common good." Charity's color deepened. "Papa said Caleb seduced you into a . . . a flirtation!"

Helpless tears spilled past Bristol's long lashes. "But Caleb couldn't speak out for me! He won't receive his mother's land parcel until next month. He has nothing to offer until then!" Her heart ached. Despite having nothing to offer, despite knowing Noah would refuse, still Caleb had courageously confronted Noah and asked for her even now. He dared this for her sake. And he had been refused. Bristol shook her red curls. It was unthinkable.

Bitterly she struck the quilts, sending a sharp tremor of pain up her spine. "It isn't fair! All this for a few words! A few words!" A guilty inner voice reminded her this wasn't a strict truth, but she ignored it. "Papa hates me, he doesn't care if I'm happy or not!" Tears flowed down her cheeks.

Shocked, Charity took both Bristol's trembling hands. "You, don't mean that, Brissy, you're upset now, but—"

"I do mean it! Charity, I . . . I love Caleb Wainwright! And now Papa's told him never to come back!" She sobbed against Charity's shoulder, not seeing the wince of misery pinching Charity's face.

"Caleb . . ." Charity arranged her expression. "Caleb Wainwright is a good man." She hesitated over the next words, her tone not convincing. "But Salem Village is filled with fine men." She stroked Bristol's shining hair, careful not to touch the wounded back. "As beautiful as you are, Brissy, you can have your pick of all the men in Salem Village, and Salem Town too."

Bristol sobbed, her heart cracking into fragments. Next to

12

the pain of losing Caleb, the ache along her back dwindled to nothing. Nothing! "But I love Caleb, only Caleb!"

Charity patted Bristol's head until Bristol sat up, sniffing and wiping her dripping eyes. Charity lifted a helpless hand. "In time . . ."

"In time I'll feel exactly as I do now! I'll always love Caleb Wainwright! I'll live and die an old maid, a thornbark, before I'll have anyone else." Fresh tears pricked her lids. A picture of Caleb Wainwright shimmered in her mind; she saw his strong young face, the set of his broad shoulders, the thick sandy hair curling at his neck. "Oh Caleb!" She buried her face in her hands, her shoulders shaking.

Sympathetic tears glistened in Charity's pale eyes, and she wrung her hands in her apron. "Maybe you could ask Pa to reconsider," she offered haltingly, not believing for a moment that Noah would weaken. "He always listens, Brissy. Maybe . . ."

Bristol's lovely wet face lifted, and she stared at Charity with rising hope. "Aye!" Desperately she seized on the idea. "When this has calmed over, maybe Papa will hear reason. Aye, of course he will!" She nodded slowly, sniffing and dabbing her eyes. Her full lips firmed with determination. "Aye." Bristol's wavering smile lit the wintry room. "That's precisely what I'll do! But first, I need my strength."

Feeling instantly better, as she always did when she had a purpose, Bristol attacked the soup bowl as if each eager bite brought her closer to Caleb Wainwright.

And each day she grew stronger and felt better. Healthy enough to experience a pang of guilt when the rooster sang in a new dawn and she remained idle while her family rose to the chores of a new day. She felt restless, anxious to resume her place in the family. Anxious to confront Noah.

Beyond the wall next to her pillow, Bristol heard early stirrings from her parents' bedroom, the soft sounds of Hannah moving in dawn darkness, then a whisper of the bedroom door opening and closing. Curled near Charity's warmth, Bristol listened to her mother's firm footsteps moving purposefully across the kitchen, rattling the wood box, poking a carefully banked fire into morning life, stirring the kettles, and lighting oil lamps. These sounds knit the fabric of Bristol's life; each morning her day began with these comforting homey noises. She smiled and snuggled deeper into the feather bed, glancing at Charity's carroty curls tumbled at the top of the quilt.

In a moment, Noah dropped to his knees on the cold

13

planking and Bristol heard a low murmur of morning prayer. She strained to hear, as she had most of her life, unable to distinguish his words, but knowing for a certainty that Noah requested no favors from God.

God charted each individual's life from birth to death, and the path could not be altered. Thus, asking help or favors was a futility; one could only thank the Lord for charting a favorable path. Regardless of how favorable or unfavorable the path might appear at any given moment.

Bristol sighed and stared at the dark ceiling beams overhead. She herself was guilty of slipping in a request now and again. She thought of Caleb Wainwright. If God was in a happy mood—that is, if God were subject to moods—then perhaps he'd hear her pleas and alter her pathway just enough to include Caleb. Bristol shivered, hoping these weren't blasphemous thoughts.

The bedroom door interrupted Bristol's morning prayer, and she peeked through a sweep of lashes to see Hannah tiptoe into the room. Even in the faint dawn light there could be no mistaking Hannah's tall form. Smiling into the quilts, Bristol decided she would recognize Hannah's ship-mast-straight figure anywhere.

Hannah Adams' erect posture reflected an indomitable nature that years of hard work and the loss of five sons had done little to diminish. She faced life squarely, long ago stripped of any fanciful illusions. The gray threading Hannah's chestnut hair had been earned.

But Bristol seldom noticed the gray. Hannah's energy made it difficult to concede she was no longer a young woman, even though her blue eyes blurred and squinted over her close work. To Bristol, Hannah would always be . . . well, Hannah. Steady, unruffled, diligent in all duties; Hannah Adams embodied the practical spirit of work and thrift that John Calvin's teaching sought to instill in all the Puritan women.

And Hannah strove to inspire such attitudes toward work and accomplishment in her daughters. She leaned over Charity, her callused hand gently moving the sleeping girl's shoulder. "It's dawn, missy," Hannah murmured. "Time to be about."

Charity sat up, yawning and scrubbing her pale eyes. "I'm awake, Mama, thank you."

Hannah straightened her back, as stiff and erect as the lodgepole pines crowding the forest. "We'll allow Bristol another day of sleep." She turned to the door.

14

But Bristol wriggled from her cocoon of warm quilts, gasping at the cold bedroom air. "I'd rather get up today, Mama." She stretched, testing her back. "You and Charity have been doing my chores long enough." She smiled, ignoring a small soreness between her shoulders.

Narrowing her eyes, Hannah studied Bristol in the faint light filtering past the crystals frosting the window. "Are you certain? We can manage. The important thing is to regain your strength. You needn't rush, missy." Her voice hesitated, pleased at Bristol's progress, but unwilling to hurry a recovery.

"I'd like to try, Mama."

"Aye. Very well." The door closed.

Bristol smiled happily. Today, she thought. Maybe today she'd talk to Noah. She pinched Charity playfully. "Out of bed, goose, the chores are waiting!"

Charity returned a timid smile. "I do believe you're actually anxious to empty slop jars and fetch wood and water, Bristol Adams! As I live and breathe!"

Bristol's full mouth fell open. Was Charity actually teasing? Laughing delightedly, she tossed her pillow at Charity's dodging shoulders and then swung long shapely legs over the edge of the bed.

Both girls dressed hastily in the frigid air, pulling long gowns over homespun petticoats, then fastening their collars and white aprons. Charity cracked a thin layer of ice capping their water pitcher, and each gasped as icy water splashed her cheeks. Reaching for their dust caps, they dashed for the warm kitchen.

Pewter porringers of corn mush waited on a long oaken table, and Hannah poured each girl a steaming mug of beer before returning to a lump of satiny dough she kneaded across the end of the table. She squinted at Bristol, noticing the girl's wince when she sat. Hannah frowned. "Nothing strenuous for you today, missy. You'll do best to take it slow."

Bristol nodded. Helping herself to a second portion of mush, she recognized approvingly that her appetite had returned in force. Later today, if she continued as strong as she felt now, she'd convince Noah to allow Caleb's courtship. She could convince her father, she vowed confidently. And she would.

At the buttery door, Charity waved and departed toward the corral to shoo the cows into the barn for milking, and

15

Bristol turned her steps toward the well near the gate, a wooden pail swinging from her arm.

A sharp breeze caught her breath, and Bristol bent her head against the wind, avoiding mounds of soiled snow with an unconscious grace, her ripe young body moving with the assurance of an older woman. Beneath a heavy cloak, her gray camlet gown molded a figure impossible to hide, generous curves that drew envious glances from women and hidden moisture to men's palms.

But observers first noticed Bristol Adams' brilliant hair. The rich curls tied below her dust cap glowed in fiery tones of red and gold. Parted in the center, her shining hair flowed back to frame a face not easily forgotten once seen. Emerald eyes fringed with surprisingly dark lashes sparkled above Bristol's high cheekbones, and beneath them curved a full mouth sculptured for laughter and kisses. Her appearance whispered of a different time, far removed in thought and deed from the somber austerity of Puritan discipline.

Occasionally Bristol herself sensed the irony of her physical form. Beneath the drab Puritan garb, she suspected a most un-Puritan sensuality simmering beneath the surface. She'd noticed a certain glow in men's eyes when she entered a room, and if she was truthful with herself, the glow wasn't entirely offensive. As she thought about it, a deliciously wicked color fired her cheeks.

Bristol gave herself a little shake. This wasn't the moment for such bold thoughts. But a smile lifted her lips. She definitely felt better.

Passing the house, Bristol regarded the weathered boards with a soft look of affection. Regardless of what Charity thought, Bristol cherished her home, her roots.

She'd been born in this small house. And Bristol remembered toddling behind Hannah when her mother first set out the rosebushes that surrounded the walls in waves of pink and red throughout summer. At six, she'd cut her lip falling against the rain barrel near the front door. At ten, she'd crashed out of the maple tree, nearly breaking a leg. Her favorite brother, Noah Junior, had died over there, near the barn, crushed by a collapsed hay wagon. Swallowing, Bristol hastily averted her eyes.

Behind the house lay Hannah's kitchen garden, then a young and thriving orchard. Between the fruit trees and the forest edge stretched Noah's fields—not the best in Salem Village, but fertile enough to yield a living. Her home.

A sudden lump constricted Bristol's throat. No matter what

happened in life, no matter how harshly the world might treat her, or how far away she and Caleb might one day live, so long as this house and this patch of land remained to come home to, then nothing would defeat Bristol Adams.

Bristol dashed moisture from her eyes and her smile turned wry. Some picture of bravery she made! The mere thought of leaving home wrested tears from her eyes.

Still smiling, she lifted the bucket to a stone ledge circling the well.

Then she saw it. A scrap of white cloth tied to the well bucket, nearly invisible against the white ground and pale dawn sky.

Caleb's signal!

Bristol spun, her long skirts billowing. She squinted against an early sun turning the fields to shades of pink snow. Her heart thudded wildly, and she peered past the house and fields, intent on the rim of forest, searching for any sign of movement. She saw nothing, but Bristol sensed that Caleb Wainwright watched.

Lifting a shaking hand to her throat, Bristol squeezed her green eyes shut. After all that had happened, after enduring the lash, she dared not sneak off. At least not until she'd spoken with Noah. How could Caleb imagine that she would?

She drew up a pail of sweet icy water, pretending not to see the excited tremble in her fingers. She poured the water into her house bucket and untied the scrap of white cloth.

Slowly Bristol returned to the house, her emerald gaze fixed on the edge of thick pines and winter brush. "Dear Caleb," she whispered. Her heart ached to see him. "I dare not. I can't!" She stumbled, catching herself before she fell. "When I've convinced Papa, we'll have all the time in the world. The rest of our lives."

But she hesitated at the buttery door, and her hand rose toward the beckoning forest. She knew Caleb would see. And he would be waiting.

2

THE Adamses' narrow kitchen steamed with spicy scents of cooking and a tang of herbs drying on strings above the fireplace. Above these familiar smells hung a faint odor of polish and pine soap. Several fire-blacked caldrons suspended from the lug pole bubbled and hissed under Hannah's watchful eye.

Bristol hung her cloak on a buttery peg and carried the bucket of fresh water past shelves laden with stone crocks and small barrels and baskets of foodstuffs. For a moment she paused to watch Hannah divide a ball of dough into four parts, then rapidly shape the rounds into mounded loaves.

Thoughtfully Bristol placed the bucket away from the heated hearth. Perhaps she should talk to Hannah before confronting Noah. She sensed her mother's ear would be more sympathetic. Bristol chewed her lip doubtfully. Publicly Hannah always supported Noah's position. On the other hand, many times Bristol had overhead low angry murmurs emanating from her parents' bedroom—they didn't always agree privately. It might be wise to have Hannah soften the path before Bristol committed herself to the discussion with Noah. "Mama, there's something I'd—"

"Sit ye down, girl."

Bristol jumped, startled by Noah's booming voice. She hadn't noticed him sitting in the shadows near the spinning wheel, away from the heated cheer of the hearth. Noah rose slowly, favoring the leg that pained in damp weather. Limping, he carried his morning beer to the table.

At sight of his face, Bristol's heart sank. Stern lines ran alongside his mouth, and the sun-baked streaks cracking his forehead were deep and forbidding. An odd hurt flickered at the depths of his green eyes, whether from his leg or something else, Bristol couldn't guess. And he would not mention it; Noah Adams was no stranger to pain or hardship.

18

Born the second son of a simple English cobbler, Noah had never had an easy life. Being a second son had limited his hopes for a prosperous future, never great in any event, and he'd chosen to sail to the colonies at the age of sixteen. Landing in Boston, Noah Adams immediately sold himself into bond service, accepting near-slavery as a first step toward a better future. Throughout the following seven years he had worked hard and shrewdly, hoarding every coin that passed his way. When the bond was fulfilled, Noah had amassed enough cash for a plot of precious land, and soon after, a wife. Over the years he'd added to the land, land he could not have aspired to own in Mother England.

And in achieving his dream, Noah Adams had worked harder than a man should be expected to. Life was hard in the Bay Colony. Especially for a man with no surviving sons to offer strong backs and willing hands. But Noah Adams didn't dwell on the might-have-beens; he did what had to be done, cheerfully performing the work of four men and optimistic that the Lord would see him through.

Today Bristol found no trace of that good humor in the eyes so like her own. In his steady gaze she saw only the odd pain and a grim resolution.

Hannah exchanged a sharp glance with her husband and placed her bread to rise near the hearth. She joined Noah and Bristol at the table, her mouth clamped in a thin line.

Nervously Bristol arranged the folds of her gray skirt. An apprehension grew in her mind. She felt something momentous in the atmosphere, saw it in her parents' tight expressions. Never could she recall anyone in the Adams family sitting without some type of piecework. Her parents looked incomplete, and her own hands felt empty and awkward.

Staring at her parents in the uncomfortable silence, Bristol quite suddenly perceived them with fresh perspective, not as the energetic vital people she saw them as being, but more as they actually were—a middle-aged man and woman worn by disappointment and hardship. Two people bending under a heavy weight.

And their troubled eyes hinted that easing the burden would bring pain to all. Bristol drew a breath and clasped her hands tightly in her lap.

For a long moment no one spoke. Noah ran stubby fingers through a thatch of graying red hair, and he stared into his beer as if the words he sought might be floating there. Hannah perched stiffly on the edge of her chair, gazing stonily

19

into the fireplace. As she looked slowly from one to the other, Bristol's anxiety increased a hundredfold.

Finally Noah began. "Our lives are mapped by God from the moment of birth." He continued to stare into the mug he turned between his fingers. "Sometimes we pretend we have free choice, but ye know this isn't true, merely a vanity of men. Our lives are cast by God." He lifted his head, and pained eyes met Bristol's. "The whipping ye endured was scheduled when first ye popped into the world. Nothing could alter it. And nothing could alter the events leading ye to flirt and earn the lash."

Bristol bowed her head, Noah's old speech patterns echoing in her mind. With a flash of deadening insight, she knew—absolutely knew—that he would never allow Caleb to court her. She'd delayed too long, his mind was set.

Stunned, Bristol blinked rapidly at her clenched hands. For days she'd planned each careful word, mentally framing the speech to bring her and Caleb together. And now, Noah prepared to sweep her dreams out the door forever. She felt it coming, read it in her father's lined face, heard it in the finality of his tone. She attempted to raise her mug to quivering lips, but the beer splashed her fingers, and she returned the mug to the table, hiding her hands in the pleats of her apron.

"Looking backward, I see the signs pointing ye toward the whip. And looking ahead, I see a pathway of return." Noah lifted his beer and drank, setting the pewter vessel hard against the table. He wiped his mouth with the back of his hand. "God doesn't chart a course, then leave us to flounder, wondering what that course might be. He sends a providence to guide the way. And the providence in yer case is clear."

A tension charged the kitchen. Now, Bristol thought helplessly. It's coming now. Her eyes widened, and unaware of doing so, she balled her apron into damp knots. Tiny breaths burned past her throat. She could not have looked away from Noah if her life depended on it.

Noah leaned forward over hands that tightened into fists. "Young Wainwright found the arrogance to ride here and ask for ye. After his conduct brought disgrace on the heads of this family." Noah's voice was harsh. "I refused him. If ye were intended to wed young Wainwright, there'd be no lash marks crossing yer back. God does not set such obstacles in the true path. No, the signs point another direction."

Hopeless tears spilled from Bristol's eyes and dropped to her clenched hands. A wind whistled through her head, and her heart splintered into shards. No nightmare ever felt as black and numbing as the awful words pouring from her father's lips.

A deep, painful sigh rattled Noah's chest, but Bristol's hurt and bewilderment cut beyond noticing.

"There's more," Noah said, as if anything else might matter. "I ordered young Wainwright not to speak or look at ye. He refused a promise." A grudging admiration crept into Noah's voice, quickly replaced by anger. "He'll not be giving a promise that can't be kept, he said. I respect the man his truth, girl. But I despise his intent." Noah's green eyes glowed, and his voice soared. "His glances and his words seduced ye once to the lash, and I'll not be seeing ye there again!"

Her father's angry face swam before Bristol's eyes. Something terrible worked at Noah's features, his face twisted with pain. Bristol covered her mouth, and her brimming eyes widened in fright.

She'd thought the hurt of losing Caleb was the worst thing that could occur in her life, but Noah's strange expression announced worse to come. "Papa?" Bristol breathed in a weak voice. Her nails cut crescents in her palms, and tears ran unnoticed down pale cheeks.

"Noah . . ." Hannah's hand reached to cover her husband's fist. A plea lay in her voice, and her face had assumed the color of paste.

Noah shrugged her away. "No, woman, it's decided!" His battered hands knotted into tight balls, and the intense green eyes appeared feverish.

Without realizing, he shouted, his booming voice filling the kitchen. "Hear me, girl! I'll not suffer ye at the lash again!" Noah drew a deep breath, passing a hand over his eyes. With an effort he softened his tone. "Young Wainwright refused to allow ye peace, and ye've shown yerself susceptible to his eye and tongue. The providence is clear. Ye must be sent away. 'Tis God's will and direction."

Bristol choked. "Sent away? Papa?" She stammered in disbelief, a stone lodged in her throat. Sent away? This was not possible . . . this could not be happening! She was living the worst nightmare of a lifetime!

Noah stared into the fireplace. He waved a sheaf of papers. "Here is God's providence, girl, as clear as ye'll ever see. I prayed for a sign as to where I might send ye, and this arrived yesterday."

Bristol's horrified gaze fastened to the crabbed writing fill-

21

ing the pages. "No!" she whispered. "Oh, Papa . . . no!" Bristol covered her streaming face with her hands, her small shoulders shaking.

"Aye," Noah answered firmly. "My sister, yer Aunt Prudence, will take ye in hand. A more upright and godly woman ye'll never find. In her cottage ye'll learn whatever it is yer Mother and I failed to teach. Ye'll learn discipline and humility and the way of the Lord. And ye'll be safe from Wainwright's seduction." He added the last softly, in the tone of an afterthought, but everyone at the table understood that here lay the crux of the problem, all that mattered.

"But, Papa, Caleb isn't a seducer, he always intended to ask for me . . . he was only waiting to receive his inheritance. Until he had something to offer. It isn't that he's trifling with me." Bristol sobbed through her fingers.

He should have waited until then before breaking the community way and seducing ye to the same." Noah's voice was unyielding. "Had ye both behaved properly, in the common good, I'd have no objection to young Wainwright. But I see an improper influence here."

"Don't send me away!"

"Yer Aunt Prudence raised me like she was my own mother, and her but two years older. The lessons learned at Prudence's side have served well for nearly half a century. So will it be with ye. Ye'll see the wisdom of tradition and the community way."

"Please, Papa!" Bristol sobbed. "I've learned the lessons! Don't send me to England. Please!" Nothing on earth represented a worse punishment than being expelled from home. One hundred lashes would be preferable to that. Racking sobs strangled her voice, slurred her words.

"Ye must go," Noah said in a low voice. "In my heart, I recognize yer good intent. But Wainwright won't allow ye to follow squarely, he refused his promise. I can't send Wainwright away from ye; all that's open is to send ye away from Wainwright. Such is the providence."

Hearing the finality of his decision, Bristol threw herself across the table and buried her face in her arms, weeping violently. She'd rather die than sail to a strange land where no person knew of Salem Village, where no familiar face smiled, where nothing was safe and known. England would be devoid of memory. How could she live with no past, no shared memories, no safe place in her world? With a stranger.

"Papa, I beg you, please . . . please!"

Noah stood abruptly, his chair crashing behind him. Bristol

felt his touch, hesitant on her heaving shoulders, then the buttery door slammed behind him, and the only sound was her anguished sobbing.

Hannah slowly rose from her chair. She bent and gathered Bristol into her arms as she hadn't done since Bristol was a small child. Hysterically Bristol flung her arms around Hannah's neck, clinging in shock and pain.

"Shhh." Hannah rocked back and forth, patting and stroking Bristol's hair, crooning in her ear. "Shhh. Everything will work out right. Shhh."

But nothing could ever be right again. Never!

As the storm gradually wore itself out, Hannah pressed a clean linen into Bristol's fingers for nose and eyes. She curled Bristol's limp hand around a fresh mug of steaming beer. Bristol stared at the golden foam with dull eyes, deep shuddering breaths shaking her whole body. No. Oh, no, her mind repeated senselessly. No.

Hannah frowned, squinting to see. She did the only thing she knew to do. Hannah set a slab of Indian pie near Bristol's elbow, even though she knew the girl couldn't swallow a bite. It was Hannah's offering, all she had to give.

Sinking to the settle, Hannah gazed into the fire, listening to Bristol's quiet weeping. Five sons she'd given to the village cemetery, and with each went a piece of herself. Now she must surrender another slice of body and soul. Hannah listened to the moist noises choking her daughter's throat and heard them with a mother's heart. No one else would have noticed the subtle change, that slight alteration of despair that signaled the assertion of youthful resiliency. A resigned acceptance hovered near the edge. Pain, aye, there remained a deep pain, and it would be long before the hurt eased, but thankfully, the girl refused to be broken.

Hannah rose, her spine erect, her shoulders tall. After a gentle touch for her daughter's cheek, she tied her cloak and opened the buttery door. The chips of heart and spirit that rested in the cemetery and those that would sail to England with Bristol were not Hannah's alone. Another felt a pain as deeply as she. She hurried through the drifts of snow, calling Noah's name.

To be alone in the silent house, surrounded by all she held dear, was more than Bristol's aching heart could tolerate. But her dazed mind refused to move her body. She remained at the table, rigid with shock, moving only when a convulsive breath shuddered past her dry throat.

Aunt Prudence. England. It all seemed unreal and terrifying. Any moment she prayed to wake beside Charity's orange curls. They would smile at each other and laugh over Bristol's nightmare.

Bristol closed her eyes, fresh tears leaking beneath her dark lashes. Would she ever laugh again? Her eyes opened and crept to the crumpled pages scattered over the table. If that letter was anything like the others Aunt Prudence posted each month, not a hint of gaiety would be found. No laughter existed in Aunt Prudence's austere world; her letters were gray tracts reading like sermons.

Bristol called up all she could remember about Aunt Prudence. And the picture tallied with the cramped tight handwriting. Such terms as autocratic, somber, stiff, colorless, hollow, self-righteous, and juiceless—these images surfaced to taunt Bristol's thoughts.

Such a woman could write sermons like the one before her eyes. Such a woman could choose to remain unmarried after all the years. Such a woman could take a young niece under her dark wing and mold the girl into a dry replica of herself.

Distraught, Bristol shoved at the tangle of red curls falling past her eyes. How would she breathe in such a choking atmosphere? She would wither like a flower plucked before its time. The barren woman of those long godly letters—what could she remember of young love? Did Prudence Adams recall how a pair of eyes could quicken a heart? Had she ever cherished a tender word or a stolen glance?

No. The fingers penning those rigid unbending letters knew nothing of gentle touches. Aunt Prudence's cottage would be cold and astringent, loveless and stifling.

Drawing a deep shivering breath, Bristol searched her apron pocket for a linen to blot her eyes, and her shaking fingers touched the scrap of white cloth. Tremulously she withdrew the fabric and pressed it to her cheek. Caleb's hands had touched this strip, his fingers had tied it to the well bucket.

Caleb, Caleb. A heart-tearing sob caught in Bristol's throat. "Oh, Caleb." When would she ever see him again?

Bristol's head jerked up; her green eyes popped wide.

Caleb waited in the forest! Sweet heaven, she'd forgotten! Every thought in the last hour had centered around Caleb Wainwright so intently that she'd forgotten that the object of this storm waited patiently in the woods!

Springing to her feet, Bristol dashed into her bedroom and splashed icy water over her eyes. She peered into a small

24

hand mirror. Her eyes looked red and swollen, but it couldn't be helped.

She paused with her hand on her cloak. Running off to meet Caleb secretly was exactly what Noah most feared, she was being sent to England to prevent this very thing. Being exiled from home. Her emerald eyes stung, and Bristol passed a hand across her face. Wouldn't it be best to forget that Caleb waited for her?

She leaned against the buttery wall, pressing her face into the folds of her cloak and touching the scrap of cloth in her pocket. This might well be her last opportunity to be with Caleb; almost certainly she wouldn't have another chance. Bristol groaned. She hated deceiving her parents. But it was Noah who denied her Caleb, Noah who sent her to the lashes in punishment . . . and it was Noah who planned to ship her across an ocean. She couldn't bear to think of leaving; her heart clutched in a spasm of anguish.

Everything was Noah's fault. Abruptly, her mind made up, she lifted her cloak from its hook. If this opportunity with Caleb was to be the last, then she would seize what she had. She would treasure his beloved face, the last sound of his quiet voice.

She ran to the musty warmth of the barn and saddled old Brown. Digging her heels into Brown's sides, Bristol raced across the snowy fields toward the towering forest edge, toward Caleb Wainwright.

She guided old Brown into a dangerous jump, the wind stinging her cheeks, pulling at her hair. Then Brown landed with a jarring thud, and she shouted him on, racing like a leaf before a storm, galloping furiously toward another storm she couldn't foresee.

One last fence separated field and forest, and rails rushing toward her. Bristol urged old Brown forward, leaning over his mane and soaring into space, her desperate heart as wild and reckless as the jump.

3

EARTH and sky spun in a crazy tumble. Brown's forelegs slid and stumbled in thick snow; his head lurched down, and Bristol flew forward. She cried out, feeling herself hurtling past Brown's bent neck, spinning, then landing hard and deep, plunging into a bank of wet cold.

For an instant she held herself perfectly still, her only movement the wild hammering of her heart against her ribs. Slowly her dazed mind cleared, and gingerly Bristol righted herself, testing first one arm, then the other. Nothing seemed broken, although she suspected she'd ache with bruises tomorrow.

She pulled upright with a frown, assessing her situation. She stood buried to the waist in a drifted snowbank. Beneath her shoes, an embranglement of snow-clogged branches strained under her weight, not feeling the least secure. Carefully Bristol attempted to free a foot, and discovered she could not. Thorny twigs held her fast, her efforts succeeding only in cracking a few slender branches and causing her to slip deeper into the snow. She drew a calming breath, willing herself to quell a rising sense of alarm.

And there was Brown. Her eyes narrowed. If she'd hurt poor old Brown with her foolishness, she deserved whatever punishment Noah would devise. With a whispered prayer she turned her green eyes to the right.

Brown's quivering body stood quietly, his head down, great plumes of silvery vapor blowing from his nostrils. Thank God, Bristol breathed silently, squeezing her eyes in gratitude.

She studied the horse thoughtfully. Now, if she could only coax Brown closer, she might be able to catch hold of his mane. He could drag her out of the snowbank before she sank farther. Thank heaven Brown hadn't broken a leg—he easily might have!

"You can thank God you didn't kill that horse with such a foolish stunt!"

The words tracked so closely with Bristol's thoughts that it was an instant before she realized she hadn't spoken. Her startled movement drove her deeper into the snow, and she heard small branches breaking beneath her shoes. Now she stood thoroughly wedged, unable to wriggle, her young breasts nearly resting atop the snowdrift.

"Who's there?" Carefully, hoping not to disturb the uncertain sprigs beneath her feet, Bristol swiveled her head, but she couldn't turn enough toward the trees to find the voice.

"Such rash acts are the very events that earn you colonists your heedless reputation. Are caution and sense unknown qualities in the Bay Colony?"

An embarrassed flush rose from Bristol's neck. This unseen man with the rich, lightly accented voice had obviously witnessed her failed jump. And was rude enough to berate her. She bit her lower lip. Bad enough to have such a foolhardy act observed by a neighbor who might grin and tease, but to have a stranger happen on her predicament, and one with such brash manners—it was humiliating.

Bristol sighed heavily, and her shoulders sagged. In the last weeks she'd experienced enough humiliation to endure for a lifetime. And humiliation was not a condition that sweetened with repeated exposure.

"I need assistance, sir," she called in a small voice, resigned to the fact that, humiliating or not, she'd been granted a stroke of good fortune in having assistance nearby.

The man laughed. "Indeed you do! Some patient soul needs to take you in hand and teach you something about horses. That aging specimen has long passed his days of sailing over fences." Behind Bristol, twigs snapped, and she heard a horse move forward. "And young ladies of your age should be past such antics as well."

A sharp retort sprang to Bristol's lips, quickly repressed. She was in no position to argue. For one thing, the man's opinion was correct; and for another, she doubted she could extricate herself from the snowbank without aid. She shivered uncomfortably in the cold and wet. Fervently Bristol hoped the embarrassed pink coloring in her cheeks would diminish before the man rode into view. She doubted it would. Sighing, she waited quietly.

A magnificent black stallion pranced from the forest rim, drawing to a halt beside Brown's bowed head. Two wild turkeys

27

swung from an ornate saddle, their bound feet tied near a musket across the man's knees.

The man leaned to stroke Brown's neck. "*Courageux cheval*," he murmured soothingly, clicking his tongue. Bristol's mind raced, placing the accent underlying his excellent English. The man was of French origin.

And obviously wealthy. While he carefully examined old Brown, Bristol studied him from beneath her lashes, gaping at the expensive fabric and cut of his clothing. Only those able to prove an estate in excess of two hundred pounds were allowed by law to wear such clothing. Heavy silver buckles gleamed at his boots and on the band of his hat. Beneath his cloak she saw a repeating flash of silver buttons. Fine lace frothed from his jacket sleeves, and his white collar appeared to be of the best Holland linen. A satin bow tied his dark hair at the neck.

Only a handful of village people dressed as richly, and Bristol knew them all by sight, if not personally. She guessed the man to be a guest of the Porters or the Caines, the village's wealthiest residents. Or perhaps he came from Salem Town, larger than the village and less familiar to Bristol.

As she watched him, her cheeks burned with rising anger. There he sat atop the finest mount she'd seen, dressed in an impressive array of expensive finery . . . and he wasted his attention on a horse! He fussed over Brown as if old Brown were comparable to the stallion. While, for all he knew, Bristol might be lying in a broken heap, racked with terrible pain. If she'd been capable of stamping a foot, she'd have been tempted to do so. As it was, all she could do was wait and fume. What sort of person valued animals above people? she wondered angrily.

At last he appeared satisfied that Brown had sustained no permanent injury, and he turned to study Bristol, leaning casually on his saddle, not the least hurried.

Beneath a broad-brimmed felt hat, his gray eyes examined her with a twinkle of amusement. Looking into those bold eyes and the grin widening his generous mouth caused the pink in Bristol's cheeks to deepen. In her heart, she'd hoped the man atop the stallion would reveal himself to be much older than this man. Finding her rescuer to be under thirty somehow added to her embarrassment.

With sinking dismay she suspected he relished the scene before him. She sensed his laughter. Her chin rose, and she opened her lips for a curt word, then halted at closer examination of those gray eyes. Beneath his amusement flickered a hard center, a hint of ruthlessness. Quite suddenly Bristol could imagine this man pointing his musket at another man as unfeelingly as he'd discharged it at the hapless turkeys dangling from his saddle. Her eyes focused upon an old scar running jaggedly along a strong jaw and disappearing into his white collar. Instinctively Bristol sensed he'd given as well as received in whatever altercation had produced that wound. Her eyes darkened to emerald, and her brows came together. All in all, he was startlingly handsome.

The man's grin widened at Bristol's unconscious frown. "With the color in your cheeks and your hair tumbled about your shoulders, you look like a poppy blooming in the snow." He narrowed his gaze, mimicking a limner, one of those painters who traveled from village to village painting barns and an occasional portrait. "No, I believe you remind me of a figurehead. Aye, you belong on the prow of a noble ship, exactly as you look now."

Bristol's face flamed scarlet. For the first time she became agonizingly aware that her breasts above the snow did indeed jut forward, emphasized precisely as those of the exotic figureheads decorating the ships in Salem harbor. Quickly she wrapped her arms over her chest, the sudden movement bending fragile branches below her feet and sending her another inch into the snow. Now her breasts carved twin nests in the chill bank.

Face burning, she lifted her chin and glared at a point above his head. "Are you going to help me or not?" she demanded coldly.

He laughed, a rich delighted sound that made Bristol furious. "A 'please' might be in order, do you not think so?" The French accent, faint but definite, lent an intriguing enigmatic quality to his resonant voice. Bristol ignored it. "Ah." He smiled. "You think not."

She maintained a stubborn silence, gazing steadily above his head. Her heart raged at his insolence and lack of common basic manners. He played with her! Well, she'd stand here and freeze before the word "please" passed her lips. Not to him. An icy trickle melted into her shoe, and Bristol shifted uncomfortably, but her lips remained pressed into a tight line.

He clicked his tongue softly, and the stallion obediently pranced forward. In no hurry, the man swung from the saddle and holstered his musket. He stood before Bristol, his hands spread on his hips. He grinned into her face. "If you are this lovely when you're angry . . . *Mon Dieu*, what a

29

beauty you must be with a smile on those lips!" His gray eyes touched the curve of her mouth. "I have half a mind to steal a kiss while I have you helpless," he teased.

Shocked and appalled, Bristol stared. No one spoke like this! No one did such things as he suggested! The man was an outrage, an utter outrage!

For the first time she felt acutely uneasy, and her wide green eyes slid past his shoulder for a quick glance at the deserted fields. She swiveled toward the stallion, her eyes flicking to the musket, but it lay so far out of reach it might as well have been absent entirely.

Following her gaze, the man laughed. "I see I am confronted with a maid of virtue." His tone implied a doubt, as if anyone foolish enough to stick herself into a snowbank would also surrender virginity as foolishly. Bristol glared at him as if he were a strange new species of animal. His grin widened. "A pity. But, as you wish. I prefer my women to be willing." He shrugged. "It appears there's nothing for it but to pull you out and send you on your way."

He stepped closer, grinning when Bristol drew back. "Put your arms around my neck." He spoke with easy authority, accustomed to being obeyed.

Bristol blinked. If Noah sent her to the lash for a glance, what might he do if he glimpsed her arms about a man's neck? She saw no trace of Noah or anyone else in the snowy fields, but Bristol didn't dare take the risk. "I . . . I can't do that. Don't you have any rope?"

Now it was the man's turn to stare in disbelief. *"Mon Dieu!"* He lifted an exasperated eyebrow. "Mistress Whatever-your-name-might-be. Had I known when I set forth this morning that I'd be lassoing idiots from snowbanks, I would most certainly have included a coil of rope. Unfortunately, such an eventuality did not occur to me. Now, if you wish to place your feet on firm ground, put your arms about my neck!"

"I . . . I . . ."

He roared, "Around my neck!"

She jumped, slid, and reached for his neck, blushing to the roots of her hair.

Powerful hands reached beneath the snow, found her waist, and swung her up and free, as if she weighed nothing. For an instant Bristol's face passed within inches of intense gray eyes, and she felt a rush of warm breath on her cheeks. A dizzying sensation swept her mind, and her hands on his wide shoulders trembled. Never had she imagined herself in

30

such intimate proximity with a strange man. Hot color warmed her face.

He set her firmly on the ground, his hands remaining at her waist a fraction too long. Angrily Bristol bent away, hiding her face beneath a curtain of red hair while she brushed furiously at the snow clinging to her skirts. He watched steadily, and Bristol felt his grin without seeing it. The man was impossible! And tall. Standing beside him, she realized she could have stood under his chin with room to spare.

She slid a glance toward the silver buckles flashing on his boots. She should thank him. His lack of manners would not excuse an omission of her own. Bristol sighed and opened her lips, pausing at the sound of a woman's laughing voice floating from the forest.

"Jean Pierre? Jean Pierre! Where have you disappeared to?"

Smiling at Bristol, the man called, "Here!" Immediately the forest crackled with sounds of several horses moving toward them, snapping low branches and plunging through snow-covered underbrush. Voices called back and forth, and laughter echoed from the pines.

The man answering to "Jean Pierre" continued to study Bristol openly, not bothering to disguise his admiration. "The figurehead has feet. Altogether, I'd say I've uncovered a sunken treasure." He grinned approval, a glint of interest sparking the smoky eyes. "And you are Mistress . . . ?"

"Adams," Bristol snapped. If he imagined these remarks to be charming, he was wrong! Such personal comments might earn him a flirtatious response in decadent France or old England, but in the colonies, suggestive banter brought fathers with horsewhips. Hearing the riders' approach, Bristol hastily pushed her streaming hair beneath her dust cap, dismally suspecting another humiliation on her horizon—she couldn't possibly be presentable, her hair dripping from her cap in damp tendrils and her skirt clinging wetly to her thighs. She bit her lips and looked toward the woods.

The woman emerged from the forest first, smiling beneath a crimson hood and lifting a fur muff in greeting. Behind her followed several men, only one of whom Bristol recognized. She knew Mr. Morgan Caine by sight and reputation; few did not. Morgan Caine controlled nearly all the lumber trade in Essex County and surrounding counties as well. Mr. Caine and the others all wore the exquisite clothing of the very rich.

The dark-haired woman reined in a few feet from Bristol and the man she called Jean Pierre. Her sculptured brow

31

lifted in surprise and her dark eyes swept Bristol. The woman's smile hardened. "And what is this?" she asked coolly.

Her voice would have sounded the same if she'd discovered vermin in her kitchen, Bristol thought angrily. She felt an acute awareness of her simple plain clothing and disheveled appearance. Well, she'd not bow her head to folk as uncivil as these! She glanced at the woman's crimson fur-lined cloak, mentally comparing it to her own worn cloth wrap. No matter. The Frenchman had proved that wealth guaranteed no excellence in breeding or manners.

Bristol's green eyes flashed, and her chin rose. The Adams line was a proud one—more than the woman staring so disdainfully could claim. Bristol had placed the pretty face on the horse. The woman dismissing her so openly was a young widow from Salem Town. A woman of unsavory reputation, if Bristol recalled correctly. And no wonder. Who but such a type would ride in the woods in the company of several men?

Jean Pierre laughed. "This snow goddess is Mistress Adams. The young lady met with a slight accident. To my honor, I was able to offer assistance." He swept his hat across his chest and mocked Bristol with a bow worthy of royalty. Several of the men chuckled, but Goodwife Sable Horton's eyes remained cold.

"How charming," she said icily, her eyes moving from Bristol to Jean Pierre and back. "Adams . . . Adams." A knowing smile touched her lips, but not the dark eyes. "Ah, yes. I thought you looked familiar. Didn't I see you recently in the square?" Now her voice purred, and she glanced archly at Jean Pierre.

The color in Bristol's face deepened. Obviously Sable Horton saw Bristol as a rival. Though Bristol sensed the man at her side was more interested in hunting than in women, clearly Sable waged her flirtation regardless. And she chose to combat Bristol with insulting innuendo.

Bristol's hands clenched at her sides, and her eyes narrowed to green fire. She'd not submit meekly to this attempted humiliation. "Perhaps you did, Goodwife Horton. I'm flattered you remember me. Unfortunately, I know you only by reputation." Bristol smiled sweetly. "I don't recall seeing you before. One sees so many people on market day, it's impossible to remember anyone in particular unless she's remarkable or outstanding, don't you think?" The implication that Sable Horton was of no consequence hung in the air.

Goodwife Horton's cheeks turned as crimson as her cloak,

and her pouting lips clamped into a line. She stared at Bristol with flaring eyes.

Throwing back his head, Jean Pierre roared in delighted laughter. "I don't pretend to follow this discussion," he said, "but I judge the encounter to end in a draw. Or perhaps you've been bested, Sable?" Before Goodwife Horton could spit an answer, he turned to Bristol and took her hand. His warm lips brushed across her fingers, and he murmured, "Enchanting."

Bristol jerked her hand away. But before he released her, Jean Pierre bent near her ear and whispered, "Your cap is crooked and you look like a wet cat." Grinning, he swung into his saddle, and the party moved into the woods, laughing and shouting to one another.

But before they entered the forest, Sable Horton stared over her shoulder with eyes that promised Bristol she would not forget this exchange. Then the forest swallowed them, and the only sounds were old Brown's snort and Bristol's pulse pounding in her ear.

Angrily she slapped at her snowy skirt. She felt childish and provincial—a shabby example of prudish Puritanism without having shown any of the finer qualities also associated with such a background. Bristol fumed. No queen had ever examined a serf with more disdain and contempt than had Sable Horton when her dark eyes dismissed Bristol. And the Frenchman!

How did he dare address her like he had! Like she was an ill-bred serving wench quivering for his notice. Bristol ground her teeth at a wave of heat starting near her toes and flowing upward. The encounter both infuriated and confused her.

Suddenly she wanted nothing more than Caleb's gentle, familiar smile. With Caleb she didn't feel hot all over, she felt sure of herself and comfortable. Dear Caleb.

Bristol mounted old Brown, patting his neck affectionately. Poor Brown, he'd been ill-used today. And so had she. But enough of that. Bristol's forehead creased in concentration; she needed a plan . . . everything seemed better with a plan. If this was to be her last meeting with Caleb, then the moments must not be wasted. They needed to decide their future today. Now.

Listening intently, she satisfied herself the hunting party had truly departed; then Bristol guided Brown's plodding steps toward a hidden pathway. Faint and overgrown in summer, now the trail lay beneath a snow pack and a sprinkling

33

of animal tracks. She would have missed it entirely had she not known of the path's existence.

In the snowy stillness of the winter forest, Bristol heard the steady beat of her heart, quickening in anticipation with each swaying step old Brown placed. Gradually a plan took form in her thoughts, and she urged Brown forward, frustrated when he refused to be hurried.

She knew what must be done. Caleb had to be convinced. Noah might not bend to her entreaties, but Caleb would do as she suggested. Wouldn't he? Bristol studied the reins thoughtfully. If Caleb proved stubborn . . . Well, the Frenchman had unwittingly pointed the way; he had revealed a plan that could not fail. Brazenly Bristol lifted her wind-stung cheeks. If words failed to sway Caleb, the Frenchman's rude gaze had reminded her of the power in a woman's body.

Shamed by these thoughts, Bristol carefully examined her alternatives. She could see none. All she held dear in life was threatened, and she had to fight with whatever weapons she possessed. And never mind Reverend Parris's teachings, she told herself grimly, surprised at her daring in this arena. But surely God condemned no one for the courage to battle for home and the man one loved!

Anxiously Bristol peered over Brown's head as they wound deeper into the thick pines and bare-branched skeletons. When she spotted the abandoned settler's cabin, Bristol released a vapory sigh of relief. The logs blended into the encroaching forest so well that discovering the cabin was always a surprise. She looked at the thin wisp of smoke curling up from a sagging thatched roof. Caleb still waited!

Reining Brown to a halt, Bristol stared at the log structure with an expression composed partly of eagerness, partly of dread. Her plan was sweeping. She'd made a momentous decision both in outcome and in method of persuasion. Once she was committed, there could be no turning back.

A tiny voice of sensibility warned her to remount and leave, reminded her of the dangers in disregarding providences. Bristol shook her glowing curls stubbornly. Providences could be misinterpreted. Besides, this was Caleb! How could her plan be wrong? They loved each other . . . and Caleb was her last hope. Her only hope.

The cabin door burst open, and Bristol stared at the large man filling the doorway. Her heart melted as did any nibbling thoughts of abandoning her plan.

Caleb Wainwright's broad shoulders touched the doorframe on either side, and a tumble of sandy hair brushed the top of the jamb. He wore leather breeches and a leather doublet over a rough shirt straining to cover muscles hardened by years of heavy farmwork. Bristol swallowed. Below thick sandy brows, Caleb's pond blue eyes touched the curves of her face.

"Bristol! I was afraid you couldn't come."

"Oh, Caleb, I have so much to tell you!" She pushed back her hood, and the dim winter sun fired the red curls escaping her cap. His blue eyes followed each movement.

"You're wet. Did you have a fall?" He pushed open the door, and Bristol looked past him at the inviting fire warming the small cabin. "Quickly, Bristol, before you take cold."

Her thoughts had been so concentrated, she hadn't taken notice of the wet chill of her skirts until now. A shiver rippled her small frame, and she hurried inside, feeling the heat of his large body as she passed.

Long ago abandoned by the settler who had built it, the one-room cabin was constructed of logs and mud. Much of the crumbling mud pack had fallen over the decades, allowing weak lines of light into the windowless room. If the builder had possessed any furnishings, they too had disappeared with the passage of time. The only furniture consisted of two wooden stools placed before the fire.

Bristol extended her cold hands to the flames, looking at the stools from the corner of her lashes. One stool bore a carved B and the other a C on its top. Last summer Caleb had etched their initials in the stools; a hot still day, lazy with the scent of honeysuckle and a drowsy drone of insects. He'd finished with a proud flourish, holding out the stools for her admiration. And his sober young face had studied her seriously. "Someday, Bristol Adams, I'm going to marry you." Then he'd leaned forward and pulled her into a quick, awkward kiss, and Bristol had been surprised into laughter.

Perhaps a wounding laughter, Bristol thought, as he'd never kissed her again or mentioned that moment. And he'd had opportunity. Bristol was able to sneak a few moments alone with him about once a month. She lowered her head in a spasm of guilt. The lash marks crossing her back were deserved.

Caleb spoke near her ear, bringing Bristol forward in time. "Bristol, when I saw you in the square, I wanted to tear that whip from the constable's hands and turn it against his own back! If I could have offered myself in your place, I would have!" His voice was anguished. "Your pa is right. I should have been whipped at your side. I'm more to blame than you!

35

If my own pa wasn't dying, he'd have put me there. I should have taken the responsibility myself!"

Bristol smiled into his troubled blue eyes. "Caleb, that's all behind us now . . . I need to talk to you." She sat on the B stool and waved Caleb toward the other. She leaned forward and peered intently into that cherished face. "Caleb, I . . ." Bristol swallowed hard, the words clumsy and halting on her tongue. "Do you love me?" She said it in a rush, blushing. They had never spoken the words aloud.

Caleb's hair gleamed sandy bright against the red flooding his cheeks. He stammered. "Bristol . . . you know I do. I—"

"Papa's sending me away from home!" she cried, unable to withhold the news another minute. "He's sending me to England, and we might never see each other again!" The words spilled from her full lips, and quick tears brimmed, sparkling like green diamonds in the firelight.

Caleb's mouth fell open. "England?" He looked staggered.

"Caleb! Caleb, if you truly love me, help me!" Her lovely features came together, matching the desperation in her voice. "Don't let Papa do this to us!"

Caleb touched his forehead, shaking his sandy hair. "England?" England existed in another universe, across an ocean, impossibly distant. "Bristol, are you certain?" He slid from the C stool and knelt by her side, staring into her wet eyes in disbelief.

"Aye!" She told him about the talk with Noah, about Aunt Prudence. "Oh, Caleb, I can't bear it! I can't bear it!" She hid her face, embarrassed to cry in front of him but unable to stanch the flow of tears. "I don't know what to do!"

Awkwardly Caleb patted her shoulder, then stood and stared into the crackling flames. "Bristol, I . . ." His jaw worked, and then he turned to face her, his mouth firm. "Your pa's idea won't work! I'll wait a lifetime for you if I have to. He can't keep us apart forever. If he tries, I'll . . ."—his arms waved wildly—"I'll come fetch you. We'll be wed without his permission. Let me think . . . I receive my inheritance in April, and the harvest should be in by . . ." He frowned, mentally calculating the seasons. "If you haven't returned by October, I'll come for you, I swear it!"

"No, Caleb." Bristol sniffed, wiping her eyes. He wasn't saying what she wanted to hear. "You don't understand. I don't want to leave home at all!" She rose and lifted her face to him, her cheeks streaming tears and her eyes begging. "There's another way! Couldn't we elope? Run away now?" Shamelessly she pressed on, ignoring the surprise in his expression. In her original plan, Caleb suggested this solution, but she realized he needed to be nudged. "We could elope to Boston. Oh, Caleb, it's all I thought about, riding here. We'd be together, and I won't have to leave. Don't you see?" Her voice rose in excited persuasion.

Caleb's strong face clouded in astonishment. "Bristol, we can't!"

Bewildered, Bristol stared up at him. "But . . . but you said you loved me!"

"I do! Enough to want the best possible future for us. Eloping won't provide any future at all." Caleb captured her hands and looked down into her wide eyes, anxious that she understand. "Bristol, how would we live? Have you considered that? I'm a farmer. Farming is what I know, all I want to do and all I'm suited for. If we wait a month, one month, I'll have my own land . . . rich bottomland that will yield a living good enough for any man. If we run off now, we'll leave our future behind us. Ma's will stipulates I must be single to receive the inheritance. If we wait, we'll have it all, everything we want."

Bristol choked, her hands turning to ice. "But . . . but if we wait, I'll be shipped to England! Away from home!"

Caleb gently stroked her hands. "If we elope to Boston, you'll be away from home," he pointed out softly. His anxious eyes searched her face.

"You don't understand! At least in Boston we could be together." She felt a surge of rising frustration. She felt like grabbing his shoulders and shaking him. "There's more to life than farming!" Drawing a calming breath, Bristol detailed her plan, the plan she'd hoped Caleb would suggest. "So you see, all we have to do is wait in Boston! Papa can't turn his back on us forever . . . he won't! Then we'll come home. The important thing is that we'll be together, and we'll be here in the Bay Colony. Not an ocean away!"

"The important thing, Bristol, is that I can't earn a living in Boston. And I'll—"

"I could be a serving wench and . . . and you could be a cobbler!"

"—and I'll lose my inheritance."

Unable to understand why each continued so obstinate, they glared into each other's flushed faces. The fire snapped in a heavy silence.

Caleb dropped her hands, as if suddenly aware he held them, and he turned his face toward the flames, running a hand through his thick hair. His jaw knotted. "Bristol," he

37

said in a quiet, reasonable tone, "if we display only a little patience, we'll have a good solid future. If we act hastily as you suggest, we have each other sooner, but we lose the land and a chance for your pa's goodwill." He frowned, thick eyebrows meeting. "You're upset now, and not thinking clearly."

Bristol's teeth clenched, and she clasped her hands tightly, hiding a tremor beneath her long white apron. Walking angrily away from the fire, she paused at the cabin's back wall to stare at Caleb's silhouette and allow the cold to freshen her mind.

He vowed he loved her, but he refused to elope. She turned his reasons in her head. Aye, she understood his concern. But wills could be broken, unreasonable conditions set aside; remaining single to receive his inheritance was an unreasonable condition. Why wouldn't Caleb see this? Bristol's breast rose in a deep sigh.

Very well. She'd hoped it wouldn't be necessary to put the second part of her plan in force, but there seemed no alternative. Let him refuse her after this! Grimly Bristol untied her hood and cloak, folding them near the wall. She smoothed her gown over lush breasts, tugging it tight. Next she removed her dust cap and shook the brilliant curls loose around her shoulders.

For an instant she paused, staring at Caleb's stiff back. This wasn't remotely the romantic encounter she'd envisioned for her first experience with a man, but desperation drove people to desperate acts. And her future was at stake. If she was destined to perform with cool calculation instead of great ardor . . . well, then, so be it.

Pasting a smile on her lips, Bristol stepped forward and touched Caleb's arm lightly. "I'm sorry, Caleb. You're right . . . I am upset. So much has happened . . ." She let her voice trail, touching her back with a grimace and allowing her eyes to brim. Tears clinging to her lashes, Bristol lifted her face with a tremulous smile, turning slightly toward the flames, knowing the firelight would display her to best advantage.

Caleb stared. His blue eyes swept from her flowing mass of shining hair to the tears sparkling in her long lashes. And his gaze steadied on the brave smile wavering about her full mouth. His face dissolved.

"Poor Bristol. It has been hard on you, hasn't it?" he whispered.

Stepping into his arms and pressing her face against his

shoulder seemed a natural response. Caleb stroked her hair, sucking in his breath at the soft silkiness beneath his fingers.

Smiling into his shoulder, Bristol relaxed in Caleb's embrace. She'd imagined this moment for so long. No matter that his warm arms circled her in a contrived arrangement; he was here and she was here, and he held her in his arms. Her heart soared; she believed she could spend the rest of her life with his arms holding her.

She felt unsure of her next move, but she needn't have worried. The warmth of his body pressing against her own drove all previous calculations from her mind. The unfamiliar sensation of a man's hard-muscled body was explosive enough to sweep away the set of motivations that had drawn her into his embrace. She felt his body next to hers and became not a thinking being, but a feeling one.

She felt the power of his strong arms, and the tensing muscles of his chest beneath her palms. The hand on her back burned as though the fabric of her dress did not lie between his hand and her skin. A peculiar weakness churned in her lower stomach, sending a tremble to her legs, then flooding upward to confuse and quicken her breathing.

Outside girlish dreams, no man's arms had tightened around Bristol Adams, and the effect was dizzying. It seemed as if an immense wave of heat flowed from Caleb's tall hard frame, encircling her and turning her bones to jelly.

Lips parted, she lifted her head to see if Caleb experienced any of the confusing sensations racing through her small body. Her ears rang with the pounding of a rapid heart, and her breast rose and fell in quick shallow breaths.

Caleb's eyes met hers with a strange stricken expression, as if he wanted to step away but could not. Helplessly Bristol's green gaze dropped to the firm broad line of his lips, lingering there to recall their first clumsy kiss. If he kissed her now, she thought, it would not be an awkward brushing of the lips ... and she would not be tempted to laugh.

And she knew Caleb would kiss her. His blue eyes devoured her face, settling hungrily on her moist parted lips. Trembling in anticipation, Bristol wet her mouth with the tip of her tongue and heard Caleb groan.

"Bristol . . ." The choked voice sounded hoarse and unfamiliar. His arms tightened, and she felt his hand cupping her head, guiding her mouth to his. Then his lips covered hers with sudden bruising force.

The kiss seemed to endure forever; they frantically pressed to each other, years of pent-up emotion burning in that long

kiss. Vague longings that Bristol only now began to understand crystallized and grew, swelling until every thought, every tingling nerve cried urgently for the release that rushed
toward them with each hesitant touch, every slight adjusting
movement.

Tearing his lips from her mouth, Caleb buried his face in
the firelit gloss of her hair, whispering her name again and
again. Then his hand slid to cover her breast, and something
like a sob ripped from his throat.

Bristol's head fell back, and she lifted her breast to his
hand, feeling the heat of his fingers scald through her gown
and into the trembling flesh beneath. A terrible fever swept
her body, sapping her strength and turning her thoughts to
mindless need.

Not in her wildest fantasies had she imagined a man's
touch would rouse her to such blinding passion. The hard
muscles of his chest, the strong thighs pushing into her
softness, enflamed Bristol's mind and body, and she met his
crushing embrace with a responding pressure of her own,
moving and seeking to fit her body to his.

She moved her hips, and for an instant her body tensed at
the swelling tension between his legs, pushing, pushing against
her stomach. Then his mouth found her lips, his searching
hands stroked her breasts, and she responded with flaming eagerness, pressing against the hard demanding swell of his
body. Hot moisture flowed to ready her secret place, and her
arms circled his neck fiercely, her fingers curling in the sandy
hair at his collar.

A sound wrenched from Caleb's throat, and he pulled her
roughly to his straining body, his erection throbbing insistently against her. His large frame shook with an intensity of
desire, and his exploring hands moved in increasing urgency.

"Caleb . . . Caleb?" Bristol whispered against his lips, not
knowing what she asked, but feeling the need to repeat his
name. Damp heat shone on her forehead, matched by the
gleam on Caleb's face. Her legs shook, possessing no strength,
and she knew her nerveless body would fall if he released
her. Between her legs, a startling tingle pulsed and swelled,
turning her stomach to straw, sweeping her body with a fiery
urgency both frightening and overwhelming. Something dormant had awakened; she could not have stepped away from
him.

Sweeping her into his arms, Caleb lowered her gently to his
spread cloak, his ragged breathing hot in her ear, equaled by
the gasping sounds from her own throat.

Green eyes wide, she stared into his flushed face as Caleb held her cheeks, bruising her lips with his kiss. The man crushing her mouth was a stranger, his face swollen in desire. For a brief instant a chill of fear sobered Bristol's mind. What they did was wrong. There could be no going back; the act, once committed, was irrevocable.

This Caleb Wainwright wasn't the quiet, gentle man she knew. His probing hands fondling her breasts had forgotten any touch of gentleness. But would he find her face familiar if he opened his eyes this minute? Had he suspected her of this moaning sensuality?

His demanding body pressed her backward on the cloak, and she felt the ground rise to meet her trembling flesh. This was Caleb! The man she loved. The man with whom she would build a life. She had nothing to fear.

Closing her eyes, Bristol surrendered to his kiss, offering herself willingly. His deep groan filled her heart with aching need.

At last, at last, his large rough hand slid from her panting breast and rushed up under her skirt. He fumbled at the string of his breeches.

"Aye, aye," Bristol urged, her head back, her buttocks lifted to him.

She gasped in shock when his hand suddenly found the red silk curling between her legs. He stroked her reverently, and Bristol moaned, her wild body moving beneath his tantalizing fingers.

Abruptly Caleb halted. An agonized sob tore from his lips, and his head dropped, sandy hair brushing her dry lips. "Caleb?" she cried. He lifted his face and stared into her eyes. Then he tensed upward, and a searing rod of fire thrust into her body.

A scream of pain and surprise tore past Bristol's lips, and her green eyes flared wide. After the urgency of desire, the throbbing need, an agony of hot flesh jolted into her with pain she hadn't expected.

A dark wave obscured her vision, the firelight flickered in and out, glowing upon sandy hair, then gone. Caleb pushed forward twice, three times; then his damp hands clamped convulsively upon Bristol's shoulders, and he shuddered, his face a firelit mask of pain and ecstasy.

Dropping his head to her shoulder, Caleb gasped and gulped for breath.

Stunned and aching, Bristol stared unseeing at the smoky thatch of the ceiling. A small stone pushed painfully into the

41

small of her back, and her shoulders felt sore where his fingers had bruised across the lash marks.

Is this all there is? she thought blankly.

Stroking his heaving back absently, Bristol listened to her heart quiet. He lay against her, depleted and limp. But she . . . she swelled with a frustrated tension that could easily be mistaken for deep anger. She'd expected, even hoped, that the mystery of men and women offered more than just searing pain, provided more than a few seconds of thrashing discomfort.

She held herself very still, daring to hope that Caleb might rouse himself and do . . . What? She couldn't guess, but there must be something! Something to ease the tensions continuing to boil through her body and mind. She felt empty, somehow deprived, still needing an elusive something that had not happened. Could not possibly happen in so brief an encounter.

Caleb stirred, and Bristol felt an overpowering tide of vast disappointment. He groaned and pushed up on an elbow. In his eyes she saw there would be nothing more. Nothing for her.

Blinking, Caleb stared around him blindly, finally turning dazed blue eyes to meet Bristol's steady gaze. His lids opened and closed, and he shook his head stupidly. He stared.

"Oh, God," Caleb whispered. "Oh, my God, what have I done?" He rolled away and stood, turning his back while he hastily fastened his breeches. Then he swiveled, and stricken eyes stared as Bristol tugged at her rumpled gray skirt. "Bristol . . . oh, God!" His voice cracked, and Caleb sank to his knees before the fire, burying his sandy head in large hands.

Now, Bristol thought, forcing her disappointment aside, now was the right time. She went to him, placing her arm tenderly around his neck, turning his tormented face into her shoulder. "It's all right," she soothed, thinking how like Hannah she sounded. "It's all right." A wave of love softened her face. She could imagine him as a toddler, bringing his small hurts to be kissed away. "Shhh."

"Bristol, I . . . I'm sorry! I don't know what to say. I can't explain. I . . ." He whispered into her shoulder, his hands forming into fists on her waist. "I'd give anything to undo these minutes, to take back the dishonor I've done you! It's only that I've dreamed for so long, loved you for so long . . ." He raised his head and stared into her green eyes. "You know I love you, don't you? As God is my witness, I do love you!"

Bristol smiled and rested a gentle hand on his cheek. "I know, I know." A teasing sparkle twinkled in her emerald eyes. "The blame can't be laid entirely at your door, Caleb Wainwright. It was I returning your kisses, and I don't recall giving you much of a struggle." A blush tinted her cheeks, but a welling rush of happiness overrode any attempt at modesty. She didn't want him spoiling her happiness with remorse. What had happened between them was predestined, was right. Everything would work out now; she felt it, believed it.

Caleb smiled uncertainly. "You're being wonderful, Bristol." Impulsively he gathered her into his arms—but carefully, the passion replaced by a cautious tenderness. "And so beautiful," he murmured. Lifting a shining red curl, he watched it twine around his finger. "So beautiful!"

Seeing his strong young face in the firelight, Bristol felt a flood of heat and again experienced a rush of frustration. Her eyes darkened and dropped to his wide mouth, and she wished she could turn back the clock to that moment when first his lips covered hers. Only, this time, when the moment of mystery came, he would . . . he would . . . Angrily Bristol wrenched away from such thoughts. They had a lifetime to explore each other; her turn would come.

Gently she moved from Caleb's embrace and sat on the B stool, combing her fingers through her hair and pinning the long spill of red beneath her dust cap. She smiled happily, her heart swelling with confidence at the love shining in his eyes.

"We'll have to be married, of course."

He nodded and smiled. "Of course. My responsibility is clear."

Bristol's heart soared. She'd done it! No more threats of the lash; and most important, no England, no dried-up Aunt Prudence! An elation filled her to bursting, and she sprang to her feet, dancing around the small settler's cabin, her skirts swirling about her shoe tops. Over! All the worries and tears were over! She wouldn't have to leave her home. In that moment she loved Caleb Wainwright with a grateful intensity unmatched by anything else in her life.

He watched her spinning about the small cabin, and soft lights smiled in his eyes. "I'll cherish this picture of you while I'm waiting," he said softly. "When you're happy, Bristol, I swear you light up the room." He waved his hands expansively. "The whole world."

But Bristol didn't hear. Her dance spun to an abrupt halt,

the gray skirt billowing around her ankles. "Waiting? *What* waiting?" She felt breathless, her eyes wide and confused.

Blinking, Caleb frowned uneasily. "Why, until you return from England." His frown deepened. "Bristol, what's wrong? You do agree we're to wed, don't you? We must. After what's happened . . ."

"Aye," Bristol choked in disbelief. "But now! Now! I mean, after . . . I thought . . ."

Caleb stood slowly, looking at her across the room. "Bristol, what happened between us alters nothing," he said gently. "I can't support a wife until I receive my land parcel next month. And I'll not be eligible, as we discussed, if we're married." He shrugged, his voice patient. "That was Ma's condition, Bristol, not something I welcome, but something I cannot change."

Bristol stared at him, appalled. She couldn't be hearing correctly, not after what she'd done. "Caleb," her voice pleaded. "Caleb, you must understand! We have to be married. Now!" She blinked furiously at angry tears. "Pa is sending me away! Oh, why can't you see? After what we've just done, how can you refuse me? Don't you love me enough to help me?"

His face was blank; his mouth fell open. Bristol stamped her foot and bit back a cry of utter frustration. At this moment Caleb looked like a simple farmhand, incapable of comprehending any but the plainest logic. She felt like flying at him and striking that obstinate face, slapping him until she saw reason flicker there. Lifting a shaking hand, Bristol pressed her forehead. She'd never wanted to strike anyone in her entire life. If proof were needed of how strongly she felt about her home, here it was.

When she opened her eyes, Caleb's face had hardened, a conviction growing in his eyes. "Bristol," he said tightly, "did you lie with me because of love, or because you thought to save yourself the trip to England?"

"Both!" Bristol cried. "Both! Is that so wrong? Aye, I wanted your kiss and your . . ." She dropped her head and bit her lip. "And I want to wed you and not leave home. My home, Caleb! Is that so terrible?"

His eyes darkened almost to black. "And I flattered myself it was me you wanted, when all the time . . ."

"And I flattered myself you truly loved me! That you cared enough to marry me now, when I need you!"

They stared across a tense room.

"I'll marry you, Bristol Adams, and gladly," Caleb said,

44

breaking the silence, his body stiff and his tone formal. "But we'll wed in the right time. I'll not destroy a profitable future to indulge a whim. In the years to come, you'll thank me for keeping a clear head."

A flaring hope died. "Whim!" Bristol spit the word. "It was a whim to think I cared for you or that you cared for me!" Swiftly she bent and scooped her cloak into shaking hands. Her eyes glittered with furious tears. "Well, I'll never marry you! Do her hear? Never! I hate you, Caleb Wainwright! I hate you!"

She whirled and stumbled blindly from the cabin as he turned to the coals, his broad shoulders sagging.

Running to old Brown, Bristol flung herself into the saddle. Hand pressed to her mouth, she urged Brown into the snow-covered pines and away from the settler's cabin. Away from Caleb Wainwright and away from the ruin of her innocence, leaving behind the shattered remnants of her dreams and her girlhood. In her mind she saw a drop of bright blood staining Caleb's cloak, and a sob of betrayal broke from her lips.

She did not look back.

4

THE days flew, gathering speed like an avalanche, piling one atop the other with frightening finality. Noah's letter sailed to England. In it, he informed Prudence Adams of her niece's forthcoming arrival on board the *Challenger*. Noah's broad handwriting presented Prudence with a fact, allowing no time or possibility for his sister's refusal. Before Prudence scarcely had opportunity to accustom herself to the startling idea of an unknown niece's visit, Bristol would arrive—welcome or not. The *Challenger* was scheduled to sail within days of Noah's letter, as quickly as her cargo of lumber and Caribbean sugar could be fully assembled and loaded.

Each miserable day bringing Bristol nearer to departure also brought her face to face with the shame and irony of her situation. At times, she felt half-mad with frustration and guilt.

When she wasn't berating herself for her needless actions in the settler's cabin, Bristol mentally composed pleading speeches for her father. Repeatedly she approached Noah, trying to explain that her drastic exile wasn't necessary . . . Noah need fear no longer regarding the despicable Caleb Wainwright. Through a storm of anguished weeping and pleas, Bristol swore her lack of interest, her total disregard for Master Wainwright. His imagined power to seduce had ceased its effect. She swore herself cured of him forever.

"I loathe the very thought of Caleb Wainwright!" Bristol insisted. "I'd not consent to marry him, Papa, if you suggested it yourself!" Even as the words rushed from her lips, Bristol realized her mistake—the phrasing could not be worse. All she'd accomplished was another example of willful disobedience. Changing direction, she sobbed through a fresh line of reasoning. But as she didn't dare admit to having seen or spoken with Caleb, her arguments carried no strength. Noah nodded grimly and turned a deaf ear.

Accordingly, Bristol's dispirited world narrowed to the word "last." The sands of time ran ever faster, speeding her toward the moment of departure. And with the passing of precious days, even the most hated chores assumed a new significance when performed from the vantage of "last." Bristol emptied slop jars and carried in heavy loads of wood, discharging each task with a sad smile. She churned butter, polished kettles, carded wool for Hannah, made cheese, wove candle wicks . . . and each chore shone with a bittersweet aura of farewell.

The word "last" blew through her mind like a chill wind. Everywhere Bristol looked, each item her hands touched—all assumed a cherished and precious value. Would Aunt Prudence's drab cottage have soft yellow paint above the wainscoting? And would a single woman have need of seventy-pound kettles as fine and deep as Hannah's? Could Aunt Prudence offer Bristol a feather bed, or, more likely, would her simple cottage be furnished coarsely?

Bristol turned her face from the bed she shared with Charity and blinked fiercely at the mist over her eyes. She'd spent so many hours with a shimmer of tears just behind her lids that she began to feel she'd passed most of her life fighting sobs. Angry with herself, Bristol dashed a hand across her face and shoved a pewter mug deep into the trunk she was packing.

46

The mug wasn't hers to take, but she'd used it for years. Her own carelessness had produced the scratch on the handle. Hopefully Hannah would understand when she discovered the mug missing. It would be something of home in a strange distant city when she needed a reminder of home. As if she'd need any reminder!

Tilting her head, Bristol listened to the familiar ring of faint bells drifting from the Coopers' farm, and in a moment the slam of the buttery door as Noah rushed to pull the bell in the Adamses' yard. Almost immediately, William Grigg's bell answered Noah's, and the buttery door banged again.

Each sabbath dawn, Reverend Parris began the Sunday pealing by tugging the bell fronting the parsonage, until responding bells sounded from each direction. Those answering neighbors rang their bells in turn, until the next-distant farm heard and replied. Thus the call to worship traveled out to the villagers.

"My last meeting," Bristol murmured, her heart squeezing. Listlessly she brushed her red curls and tied them at her neck. She wouldn't mourn the loss of Reverend Parris and his dry, complaining sermons, but she felt desolate at leaving the weekly gathering of friends and neighbors.

Heart as heavy as her cloak, Bristol climbed into the wagon bed and settled next to Charity in the warm straw. Hannah handed the girls thick wagon quilts to combat the chill, then took her place on the high seat next to Noah. The horses pulled from the Adamses' yard.

Sad eyes peeped over the quilt edge, and Charity asked, "You'll leave this week, won't you?"

"Aye."

"Oh, Brissy!" Charity's lower lip quivered, and her pale eyes moistened. "I'll miss you with all my heart!"

"I'll miss you too, goose." Bristol reached for Charity's glove under the quilts, and she tried to smile, wishing Charity wouldn't cry. Her own tears bubbled too near the surface to withstand an outburst from her sister.

Bristol's full mouth curved in a wry smile. All she needed to complete her disgrace was to arrive at meeting with red and swollen lids. Every eye in the village would be watching. She doubted a single soul in Salem Village remained unaware that she was being sent away.

She sighed. "I'll write, Charity, and you must, too." She patted Charity's hand. "Tell me everything that happens, no matter how small it seems."

Charity nodded, glancing quickly at her parents' stiff spines above her head. She leaned close, cupping her hand, and whispered, "I'll send word of Caleb."

"No!" Seeing Charity's startled expression, Bristol softened her tone. She too flicked a hasty look toward her parents' backs. "I never want to think about Caleb Wainwright again!" Deep inside, she wondered if she could actually live up to such a vow. He'd been only a whim, she reminded herself.

"But, Brissy . . ." Charity frowned, puzzled.

"That part of my life is over. I despise Caleb!" Stonily Bristol stared at patches of melting snow dotting the fields. Spring's first tentative breath lay in the air. And she would not be here to smell the buds blossom in the apple trees. Or watch the honeysuckle unfurl. Did honeysuckle grow in London?

"Brissy, what's happened?" Charity's eyes rounded, and the quilt dropped from her chin. "You saw him!" Amazed, then anxious, Charity darted a glance toward her parents. But the swaying backs above took no notice.

Not daring an answer, Bristol stared at the passing fields, but a reply showed in the set of her jaw, in the angry betrayal deepening her eyes to jade.

Charity's thin mouth fell open. Timidly she leaned forward and touched Bristol's sleeve. "Brissy, are you certain? You really . . . *despise* . . . Caleb Wainwright?" Her voice was incredulous.

"I do!" Bristol answered emphatically. "I hope I never see him again!" Because of him, she'd lost her last chance at home. A dismal existence in England would be largely his fault.

Charity's face lit with a soft glow, and a rose-colored wash bathed her freckles. "Are you very certain, Brissy?"

"Aye!" Bristol said between clenched teeth. Let Caleb tempt someone else to the lash. Let him use another's body and turn the trust to betrayal. But not hers, not Bristol Adams'. Never again!

Stammering and blushing furiously, Charity spoke in a rush. "If you're certain . . . I mean, I think that I . . . that is, if you and Caleb aren't . . ."

Bristol stared. "Charity! Are you saying you feel something for Caleb Wainwright?" She was astonished. Perhaps a small flame of passion burned in Charity's breast after all. But Caleb!

"Aye," Charity whispered, plucking at the straw.

Bristol turned the information in her mind. Caleb's refusal to elope stuck like a thorn in her heart. She'd never forgive him . . . would she? Why should she care if Charity wanted him? Bristol didn't want anything more to do with him. He'd cost her the home she cherished.

That wasn't all he'd cost. Bristol's cheeks flamed scarlet, and she hid her face. Dark smudges shadowed her eyes from lack of sleep; each night she tossed in a quagmire of guilt and shame, regretting those moments in the settler's cabin.

Her first impulse was to warn Charity of the lash and the cabin in the woods, but she saw no way to speak of these things without revealing more than she could bear to. Or without sounding jealous of Charity's interest.

Charity's timid eyes watched anxiously, containing a flickering hope which Bristol recognized. How often her own face must have looked like that! Poor Charity, she thought sadly. She couldn't imagine Caleb courting Charity; the girl had set her heart for the moon.

Impulsively Bristol squeezed Charity's hand. "Beware his eyes and tongue. Papa is right, neither are to be trusted."

An inner radiance spread across Charity's face. "Oh, Brissy, do you mean it?" she breathed. "You don't mind?"

Smiling, Bristol shook her head, submitting to Charity's elated hug. Gently she disengaged herself, feeling a pang of guilt at Charity's response. Bristol didn't believe the remotest possibility existed that Caleb might be induced to court Charity. For one thing, Noah's opposition stood in the way, and for another, Charity was . . . well, such a pallid little thing compared to Bristol.

Ashamed of such vanity, Bristol shifted in the straw, feeling disloyal and contrite toward her sister. But, a devilish voice persisted, a vast difference *did* exist between the two.

Uncomfortably Bristol realized she counted on this difference. It only appeared she made Charity a generous parting gift; in truth, she offered Caleb in full belief that her own position would not be weakened. If she chose to forgive, Caleb would be waiting.

Changing her mind, Bristol turned to Charity. But she closed her lips at sight of Charity's beaming happiness. No, she'd say nothing. Charity's hopes would be punctured soon enough in the natural course of events. There was so little to brighten the lives of the village's young girls, it could do no harm to allow Charity her dreams.

Still, Bristol felt strange thinking someone else wanted Caleb, would be watching him in that special way. Noah reined the horses before the meetinghouse, putting an end to Bristol's confused thinking. How could it be that she'd sworn to hate Caleb and now had second thoughts when she learned Charity wanted him? She brushed any tender thoughts out of her mind. All she need do was recall where she'd be spending next sabbath to refresh her anger.

Lifting her small charcoal foot warmer, Bristol held up her chin and followed her parents into the frosty meetinghouse. She slid into the children's pew next to a starry-eyed Charity and settled her feet near the little stove. The service began. Bristol lifted her face, resolutely refusing to glance toward the men's side of the room. However, she fervently hoped the tithingman found cause to strike a certain sandy head with the hard knob at the end of his long cane.

Reverend Parris had chosen the book of Job for his morning text, and hearing, Bristol sighed. There could be no mistaking whom Reverend Parris cast as the modern-day Job. She fixed her attention on the pulpit, knowing today would stretch long, with more than the usual bickering and number of altercations during the noon break.

From the beginning, Salem Village had been divided in opinion regarding Reverend Samuel Parris. The strutting little preacher's supporters backed him solidly, but nearly half the village viewed their reverend as a pompous fraud. He lacked previous preaching experience, they pointed out, he had no history of notable success in anything, and scant leadership ability.

Nevertheless, his supporters countered, Reverend Parris was the best Salem Village had been able to entice, and they defended him staunchly. For his part, Reverend Parris fought the defectors with increasingly bitter sermons.

Today, Bristol correctly guessed, the great firewood controversy would surface, thinly veiled, before the afternoon sermon. Her shoulders dropped. Not a person shivered in his pew who had not suffered countless firewood allegories many times previously.

Reverend Parris continued to insist that each villager personally deliver firewood to the parsonage door, paying direct homage to the importance of the reverend. The Village Council, however, stubbornly viewed this demand as an imposition. Particularly as most of the congregation would be required to spend an entire day traveling nearly eight miles round trip to deliver their portion, and particularly as Reverend Parris had only to step from the parsonage door, walk one hundred yards into the forest, and pick up all the firewood any man might require.

By way of compromise, the Council voted a six-pound increase in the reverend's yearly salary, deciding to settle the matter by providing funds to purchase firewood, generous funds. Thus the reverend would have his firewood, stacked and split, at no inconvenience to himself, and no parishioner would be forced to a long cold ride. An equitable settlement, most felt.

With the exception of Reverend Samuel Parris. The fight raged on. Any congregation worthy of calling themselves saints should be willing, even eager, to deliver their pastor's firewood in person. The issue was a question of respect. Such deference was a pastor's just due.

Weekly, some accusing reference surfaced in the words flowing from the pulpit. "God," shouted Reverend Parris, "allowed his chosen one to suffer, to be spit upon and defiled and abused by Satan."

Not a person in the congregation mistook who assumed the role of Job and who acted Satan. Satan deprived Job of firewood. Several chins firmed along the pews, and more than one pair of eyes took on a steely, defensive glint.

"And where is Satan today?" Reverend Parris paused dramatically and hefted the paunch above his breeches. His small raisin eyes bored into the shuttered faces. "Look about you! See Satan hiding behind self-satisfied smiles, jeering the saints in this very house of God! See him here! I assure you, Satan walks in Salem Village as surely as the pines stand in the forest!"

Goodman Giles Cory jumped up to announce noon break, and a breath of relief fogged the frigid air in the meeting-house. Everyone sprang to his feet gratefully, stamping away cramped muscles, smiling hesitantly at neighbors. Everyone knew the reverend referred to those depriving him of firewood when he shouted Satan dwelled in Salem, but . . . one couldn't be absolutely certain; unexplained events did occur. Hadn't Goodman Thomas Putnam's crops been blasted last summer, burning in the fields, when all around him the plots yielded bountiful harvests? An ounce of caution and a watchful eye were clearly indicated, firewood or no firewood.

One watchful eye cared more for a head of sandy hair than speculations about Satan. Carefully Bristol averted her face from the men's side of the room, lingering with friends until the meetinghouse cleared. Only then did she submit to Charity's impatient tug.

She'd glimpsed Caleb from the corners of her lashes, but she refused to meet his eye. Each morning, to her shame, she'd run to the well, her heart leaping with hope of discovering a white scrap tied to the bucket; and each morning she'd been disappointed. Caleb would not alter his decision to let her sail. Bristol tied her hood with angry, jerky movements.

Only when she was certain Caleb and his ailing father walked enough ahead to prevent a chance encounter did she wave to her friends and follow a small group of Parris supporters to the parsonage.

Pausing at the door, Bristol looked briefly toward Ingersoll's tavern across the lane. There the majority of the congregation fled for warmth and a steaming mug and a fortifying bite. Did Caleb stare from those steamed windows, or did his blue eyes scan the room in search of a new pretty face? Bristol's mouth set, and she stepped into the parsonage, giving the door a little slam behind her.

As always, the conversation focused on local politics, with each man offering an opinion to explain the ruptures within the village. Bristol folded her hands in her lap, prepared for a lengthy redundant discussion.

"We need to be a town in our own right," Thomas Putnam insisted, his open rural face intense. "Only when Salem Town grants us autonomy can we hope to solve the village problems fairly!"

Old Francis Nurse rumbled agreement. "Everyone here is suing someone else, and we have to look to Salem Town to settle the issues, when they know nothing of underlying causes." A lively discussion of Goodman Nurse's property disputes followed; then Reverend Parris deftly turned the conversation to the merits of parishioners delivering firewood. A few eyes hardened. Even among this small group of like minds, serious differences of opinion simmered below the surface.

Bristol sighed. Sometimes Salem Village reminded her of a sleeping volcano, tempers and animosities held temporarily in check but rumbling and bubbling just out of sight. The political and personal ground appeared to be always shifting, always uncertain, always threatening eruption.

To the relief of most, Reverend Parris hefted his stomach and offered the noon prayer. Table conversation would be of a lighter nature.

All the women contributed dishes to Elizabeth Parris's sabbath table, not cooked on Sunday of course, but diligently prepared the evening before.

Bristol eyed the groaning table without interest, knowing no matter how tempting the food, each bite would stick in her throat. She lacked the heart for this last meal at the parsonage. Dinner chatter rose around her, and hands reached and bowls passed along the long table. A lavish array of food passed beneath Bristol's nose: hot pumpkin soup, fried eel, cold mutton, cornmeal pudding, slow-cooked baked beans, buttery squash, whortleberry swish, venison pasties, and flaky white sheets of roast turkey.

Staring at the slab of turkey on her trencher, Bristol recalled the Frenchman in the woods. Had she known her efforts with Caleb to be wasted, would she have allowed that Jean Pierre his stolen kiss? She pictured him sitting atop the black stallion, wild turkeys swinging from his saddle. And she remembered the odd feeling in the pit of her stomach when he pulled her from the snowbank. Circles of hot color dotted her cheeks; now she understood her own response. The Frenchman had been strikingly handsome.

Of course, I wouldn't let him kiss me, she told herself vehemently, wondering why she'd had such a thought. Still . . . At least the Frenchman made no pretense of his intentions. Whereas Caleb . . . Recalling that day reminded Bristol of the attendant humiliations. First Jean Pierre's teasing laughter sounding in her ear, then Caleb's refusal after she had . . . Bristol shook her head angrily and stabbed the suddenly offending turkey.

"My, my," Martha Cory murmured, lifting an eyebrow. "Aren't we testy today!" She spooned a bite of corn pudding into her mouth. "If you want my advice, you'll submit to your punishment gracefully. You brought this grief upon yourself. You should thank your pa the punishment wasn't worse!"

Shoulders sagging, Bristol listened to Martha Cory's unwelcome flow of advice. Goody Cory took it upon herself to be the village conscience, dispensing judgment and advice with equal vigor.

"Children today haven't an ounce of sense! At least most." Martha paused for breath, her snapping eyes pointedly telling Bristol which child she meant. Bristol dropped her eyes. "Some folks could learn a lot from little Ann Putnam over there." Goody Cory nodded toward quiet, sober ten-year-old Ann Junior. "Ann is such a comfort to her mother! Why, that child runs the Putnam house like a woman three times her age. There's a lesson there!" Martha leaned forward, squinting at Ann Junior. "I believe I need to mention Ann's hair. She has more of it pinned under her cap than is decent in a young girl. I'll speak to her."

"Hmmm." Bristol chewed at the sawdust turkey. Ann

Junior *had* to run the Putnam house, like it or not. Ann Senior proved generally incapable, falling into continual nervous depressions. Bristol glanced down the table toward Ann Senior. Ann Senior toyed with the food on her trencher, her distracted gaze directed out the frosty window toward the village cemetery.

Bristol sniffed. Hannah had lost as many babies as Ann Senior, but you didn't find Hannah Adams wandering the lanes in a strange demented state looking for the witch responsible. A lesson to be learned, indeed!

Her last meeting was proving a large disappointment. None of the girls her age had been invited to the parsonage, and Goodwife Cory was her dinner partner. The day sank from bad to worse. Grimacing, Bristol decided to try her luck with old Rebecca Nurse. She swiveled and shouted into Goody Nurse's ear.

Rebecca's little face lifted with a quick smile. She reminded Bristol of a withered brown apple left in the sun to ripen into a thousand cheerful wrinkles. "What?" Rebecca answered in a loud voice. "What is it, dear? I'm a tad hard of hearing, you know."

Bristol smiled. "I said, do you like the baked beans? Mama made them."

"Do I take greens? Aye, dear, when we have them, but I don't believe Elizabeth has any today. Wrong season, you know." Goody Nurse patted Bristol's knee with her soft veined hand and returned to her trencher. Bristol's breast rose in another sigh, and she gave herself up to Goody Cory's persistent stream of complaints and admonitions.

When the meal ended, the adults congregated before the reverend's hearth, which contained a feeble parlor fire—one more reminder of his continuing battle on the firewood front. The children were dismissed to the kitchen. In Puritan New England, children included all unmarried girls regardless of age, a restriction the girls resented, but not today.

Immediately, five young faces brightened, and the girls gladly excused themselves in favor of the reverend's large warm kitchen.

"Thank heaven!" Abigail Williams breathed loudly the moment she stepped into the kitchen. "They're all so boring! Everything is boring. There's nothing around here for sport! And Sunday is the worst."

Ann Junior smiled at the reverend's niece. "You make your own sport, Abigail. I saw you pinching Betty all through the text."

"Pish! I never saw such a crybaby!" Abigail snorted in contempt, and shoved her cousin, scorning the tears rising in Betty Parris's blue eyes.

"That's enough, Abigail Williams!" A sharp voice cut through the kitchen, and the girls turned toward a dark woman rocking near the fireplace. Tituba removed a corncob pipe from her mouth, and her chocolate eyes stared hard at Abigail. "The reverend and Mrs. do a kindness to take you in. You want me telling himself how you treat this baby?" She extended stick-thin arms, and little Betty Parris scrambled into Tituba's narrow lap, burying her bright head in Tituba's neck. Tituba leaned back in the rocker and stroked Betty's blond curls. "There, there, baby. Jest rest. Jest rest." She glared at Abigail.

Abigail shrugged, flouncing golden curls beneath her cap. "Betty's seven years old, she's not a baby anymore." Abigail spun toward Bristol. At ten years old and developing a respectable bosom, Abigail aligned herself more with the older girls. "Would you like a walk, Bristol?" Adroitly Abigail sought to change the subject.

"Not today," Bristol answered, more tartly than she'd intended. Generally she enjoyed the younger girls of the village, but Abigail Williams' unpredictable behavior was unnerving. No one could trust what the girl might do or say.

Turning aside from Abigail's glowering frown, Bristol joined Charity near the fire, taking a stool and turning expectant eyes toward Tituba. Occasionally Tituba could be coaxed into remembrances of her native Barbados, and she would spin wonderful tales of a sunny land where snow never fell, where odd plantings grew, and where dark-skinned people walked with no shoes and no cares. Or so Tituba chose to tell. Sugarcane grew as high as a man's head in Barbados, and rum flowed as plentifully as sunshine. Even babies sucked on sugar tits soaked in rum. Tituba and the reverend's man, John, had toiled in the canefields until Reverend Parris bought them and converted them from pagan superstition to the true path.

"Will you tell about the summer place?" Bristol asked. Tituba's stories made the reverend's kitchen a favorite gathering place for the village girls.

"Please?" Charity begged.

"No, no!" Abigail objected. "I'm sick to dying of hearing about Barbados! It's boring. Tell our fortunes instead!" she demanded.

Bristol frowned. Abigail truly exceeded the bounds of rea-

55

son. She'd seen Goody Martha Cory lecturing the girl, and Bristol thought in this case Goody Cory's ministrations were sorely needed. "Abigail! You know better than to suggest fortunes! That's forbidden. It's witchcraft!"

Abigail flared. "Stop this, stop that! Don't do this, don't do that! I'm sick to dying of it all! Don't any of you want a little excitement? Besides, fortunes are fun . . . and it's only white witchcraft, not the bad kind!"

"Witchcraft is witchcraft!" Bristol snapped. "One kind is as unnatural as the other."

Ann Putnam Junior shook her finger and clicked her tongue. "What you want, Abigail Williams, is to have the world spin just around you. The moment no one pays any attention, you're up to mischief!"

"You're a fine one to talk, Ann Junior! That's not . . ." Abigail's angry retort broke off as Betty Parris gasped.

Betty bolted upright on Tituba's lap. "Tituba? Tituba?" She leveled wide teary eyes at Abigail. "Now, look what you've done! She's gone away again." Betty slid from Tituba's rigid lap and ran to fling her arms around Charity's neck.

Every eye swung to fix on Tituba's stiff body. The old woman rocked in her chair, the pipe dangling from bony fingers and her dulled eyes staring blankly at something no one else could see.

Nervously Bristol glanced at the others. She guessed her own face to be as white as theirs. She'd heard whispers that Tituba had the sight, but this was the first time Bristol had observed for herself.

The fire popped, and all the girls jumped in a charged silence. Tituba's chair squeaked back and forth, backward then forward. Tiny hairs rose along the back of Bristol's neck, and she shivered. She imagined that despite the crackling fire, the temperature abruptly dropped.

Suddenly Tituba's body jerked and appeared to coil in on itself. The chair rocked to a standstill. Tituba's taut throat worked convulsively, and a strange voice emerged, split and cracking. "Four are and one is not," she croaked, her chocolate eyes staring blindly into space. The girls' pale faces turned, counting five. "The one who is not, departs by water."

Bristol gasped, and her hand flew to her throat.

"Blackness on the land. One shall escape. One destroyed by flesh. One destroyed by thought. One destroyed by hemp. And the one who is not, shall stand in dark flames. Fear and darkness level the land. Many are no more."

Tituba's glazed eyes blinked and cleared. She shook her grizzled head once, then leaned back in the rocker, drawing on her pipe.

"Tituba!" Bristol's breath released past dry lips. "You said . . . But what does it all mean? What . . . ?" Her hands shook within the folds of her apron, and her face felt white as chalk. She glanced quickly at Charity, seeing the freckles standing out like painted dots. "Tituba?"

But Tituba answered nothing. She reached her thin arms for Betty Parris, and the little girl ran happily to climb into Tituba's lap.

From the parlor drifted the voices of departing adults calling for the afternoon sermon.

A sermon Bristol scarcely heard. She fidgeted beside Charity in the children's pew, Charity no calmer than she. The entire episode was nonsense! A dangerous toying with forces best left untouched; catering to Satan's minions tempted the hangman, invited spirits into a God-fearing home.

And this in the parsonage! At another time, Bristol would have appreciated the grim humor, but she was too upset to enjoy the humorous ramifications of witchcraft in the reverend's own kitchen.

". . . Four are and one is not. . . ." The words spun over Reverend Parris's drone. Bristol's frightened gaze found an unbending head of sandy hair. A crimson stain fired her cheeks, and she dropped a shining head in earnest prayer.

If Tituba could see into the settler's cabin, did that mean the other upsetting words were true as well?

"Heavenly Father," Bristol began, but the whispered words lodged in her throat. A cracking voice cut above, repeating in her mind. ". . . And the one who is not, shall stand in dark flames. . . ."

5

THE *Challenger* rocked at anchor near the mouth of Salem harbor, her masts majestic against a clear cold sky. Deep within the cargo holds, acting as ballast, lay a fortune in lumber and sugar, secured by heavy knotted hemp. God willing, this fortune would be delivered intact to English buyers. To ensure God's will, the *Challenger* mounted twenty-four guns, twelve to a side, as protection against pirates prowling English shipping lanes. The *Challenger* would not surrender her cargo easily; the guns were no idle threat. She'd faced battle before and was furbished to do so again.

The groups of people onshore prayed the voyage would prove uneventful, but all eyed the cannon and felt privately assured. As they watched, a longboat splashed into the waves, knit caps bent over the oars. The *Challenger* required only her passengers to be under way.

Noah shifted and cleared his throat, his broad-brimmed hat circling in his fingers. "Well, girl . . ." Green eyes watched the longboat rowing toward the pier, and his voice faltered.

Bristol's mouth felt as if dry stones clogged the passages. She lowered her head. All had been said that could be; she wouldn't waste these precious minutes with another futile plea. She smoothed her brown dress with trembling hands.

"Oh, Brissy!" Charity wailed. She flung herself on Bristol, arms clasping her sister with fierce strength. "Oh, Brissy!"

The girls clung to each other. Over Charity's shoulder, Bristol's swimming eyes noticed the second group on the wharf watching, but she didn't care. Wiping a hand across her eyes, she stepped from Charity's frantic hug.

"Mama?" Bristol whispered haltingly. Hannnah extended her hands, and for a long moment they stared into each other's eyes. It seemed to Bristol that Hannah's eyes were moist, but that couldn't be; her mother never cried. Hannah leaned forward, offering herself in a stiff, awkward embrace.

Hannah bit down on her lip and her strong chin quivered. "Mind your manners, missy." Her voice emerged tight and choked. "I . . . I'll miss you," she murmured, and gently pushed Bristol away, dropping her eyes.

I can't bear this, I can't! Bristol thought wildly. She battled an irrational urge to fling herself on the rotted wood and beg her father to reconsider. *I'll do anything,* her mind screamed. *Anything, just don't send me away!*

The longboat bumped against the wharf, and a hard-eyed man climbed to the dock, standing a short distance from the two groups. His shaggy head dippped in a short nod toward the longboat, and he crossed his arms over his chest.

Bristol swallowed a giant lump. "Oh, Papa." All the

despair in her world lay in those two words. She pulled forward the edge of her hood to hide her eyes.

" 'Tis for the best, girl. Ye'll come back stronger than when ye left." His eyes sought his daughter's face, but she wouldn't look at him.

The other group stepped past, and a slim, sober-faced woman of middle age accepted assistance into the longboat. The hard-eyed man stared pointedly at Bristol.

The tears Bristol had vowed not to shed rivered down her pale cheeks. So many things remained unsaid; there was so much more she wanted to tell them all.

Noah thrust out his hand, his green eyes memorizing her face. "There's a small purse in yer trunk," he said roughly. "Yer ma and I thought ye should have it." He pumped her hand, reluctant to release her fingers, wishing she would look at him.

Slowly Bristol lifted her streaming eyes and for an instant she wanted to throw her arms around her father's neck and kiss his leathery cheek. But he was the one sending her away. Instead, she spun and ran blindly toward the hard-eyed man, and his hands lowered her to a jumble of feet and oars. The man jumped lightly into the boat and shouted. Sweating men bent to heave the long wooden oars, and the longboat shot through the water toward the waiting *Challenger*.

Bristol faced the *Challenger*, her eyes wet, but her spine rigid as she knew Hannah would expect. Dimly she felt the other woman's curious gaze, but Bristol ignored it. What did it matter that she'd made a public spectacle of her leave-taking? All that mattered were the people on the wharf behind. Her family . . . her home! Self-consciously she searched her apron pocket for a linen and blotted her eyes, certain she'd never been so alone in her life. In the deepest corner of her mind she hadn't let herself believe this moment would actually arrive. Always she'd believed something would intervene to spare her.

But the grunting men straining at the oars were real, not a bad dream. The salt spray stinging her cheeks was real. The *Challenger*, immense and armed, was real.

The longboat nudged the oaken hull, and a pair of disembodied hands tossed a rope ladder over the side. The hard-eyed man scrambled upward, waving for Bristol and the other woman to follow.

At the top, quick rough hands tugged her forward, then turned to the woman behind. Uncertain and disoriented, Bristol waited near the rail and looked around her, chewing her lip at the sheer size of a sailing ship. It appeared to stretch endlessly, intricately rigged with maze after maze of soaring rope. A pungent scent of pitch and tar filled her nostrils.

To Bristol's surprise, the sound of animals joined with the noise of men's shouts and groaning rigging. Cages and pens lay scattered about the spar deck, filled with hens, turkeys, ducks, geese, and pigeons. Two cows, several calves, a few pigs, and two dozen sheep bawled from penned enclosures. The ship was a floating barnyard!

A man rushed past Bristol, nearly toppling her onto the undulating deck, and she hastily stepped backward, removing herself from the frenzied lane of activity. Beside her, the second woman passenger seemed as confused as Bristol. The woman's heavy-lidded eyes stared with perplexity and a faint disapproving look. Neither knew where she was expected to go.

And no one appeared inclined to offer instruction. Every hand on board was occupied. Dark shapes swarmed up the ropes; more men hung in the rigging high overhead. A man's voice shouted, and the sailing master's crisp commands cut across the ship. Immediately sheets of canvas began dropping from the yards. Slowly the canvas filled and cupped with wind, until it snapped full with a sound like a pistol shot. At each sharp crack, the *Challenger* shuddered and strained like a tensing racehorse.

Forward, a high squeal sounded from a turning crank, and the anchor, trailing mud and weed, broke from the sea with a sucking noise.

Then slowly, amid a shouting, cracking, squealing, bawling din, the *Challenger* swung to port side, turning half-circle to face the open sea. She fired a deafening cannon salute, white puffs of smoke drifting across the decks. Overhead, the sails snapped and caught the wind, billowing into cups of cloud. The *Challenger* slowly moved through Salem's difficult harbor mouth, gathering speed, the leadsman's loud voice singing out fathoms.

A tingle raced through Bristol's blood, and her pulse thudded painfully in her throat. Frantic, forgetting everything but the desperate need for a last glimpse of home, she gathered her skirts and ran heedlessly over the ropes netting the deck. She dashed toward the stern, scrambling up a short flight of steps to the quarterdeck, and she stood gasping at the rail. Her knuckles whitened against the wood.

Across a widening stretch of rolling water, she yearned toward the figures on the wharf. She couldn't distinguish their faces, but Charity's carroty curls and Noah's red hair stood clearly against the drab, weathered shore buildings. Bristol waved wildly. Behind them, a horse skidded to a halt, the rider a dim male form.

Bristol's hand froze in the air. Caleb? A sob wrenched from her lips. Had Caleb come for her? Only to be too late? She dropped her head into her hands, the wind tearing her hood away. "No! Oh, no!" She bent away from the shoreline, unable to tolerate the despair of watching, and her hair lifted in the chill sea breeze, a brilliant red river flowing away from her ravaged face. The wind tugged and rippled the long silky strands, molding her gown to breasts and thighs, but Bristol felt nothing. Had the rider been Caleb?

Without warning, iron fingers gripped her wrists, yanking her hands from her face. Startled, Bristol lifted her wet eyes.

"You little fool!" a familiar voice hissed, the accent heavier in anger. "Is it your intention to run us aground before we even clear the harbor?"

"You!" Bristol gasped. She stared into the flinty-gray eyes of the man called Jean Pierre. Her hands leaped to her throat as her mind made the connection. She'd met him in Morgan Caine's company . . . Morgan Caine owned Salem's largest lumber industry . . . the *Challenger*'s primary cargo was lumber. Of course.

Hard angry eyes swept across her breasts and hips, lushly outlined in the freshening wind. He took her by the shoulders, his fingers bruising into her flesh. Jean Pierre turned her roughly out of the breeze. "Fool! There are over one hundred men on this ship, every one of whom is staring at you this minute! Pray they don't mistake your idiocy for an invitation!" He glared the length of the ship and roared, "Back to work, you bastards! If you've energy to spare, Mr. Aykroyd will find a use for it!" His fingers curled on the hilt of his sword, and his face was thunderous.

Bristol stammered, her cheeks coloring, "I'm sorry . . . I wasn't thinking about—"

"You weren't thinking," he stated flatly. "A condition which appears chronic with you, Mistress Adams!"

Bristol stared. No hint of amusement softened his hard face; she saw the naked ruthlessness she'd suspected when first they met. She lifted her chin. However slight their acquaintance, at least his was a somewhat familiar face in a strange and unknown landscape. She swallowed fresh humiliation and tested his name. "Jean Pierre?" she said haltingly.

"Captain La Crosse," he snapped. His voice was cold.

"And the person responsible for delivering you in England in the same condition as I received you." His stormy eyes swept her body. "I'll thank you to cooperate in making that task as easy as possible." He cupped his hands and shouted, "Mr. Aykroyd! Get these fool women below decks! *Stupide!*" He ran toward the forecastle, his steps light and certain across the rope-littered decks. "You, there, on the jib! Ten lashes if that canvas is too tight!"

Bristol gaped after him, her face hot with embarrassment. She dared a longing gaze toward the receding shoreline, wishing with all her heart and soul that she stood there and not here. If she must share the voyage with a familiar face, why couldn't it have been someone of pleasant associations?

"Mistress Adams? I'll thank ye to follow."

Bristol whirled, her skirts flying and her heart jumping to her mouth. The voice sounded so like Noah's that for an instant she deceived herself it might be her father. Instead, she looked into the face of the ugliest man she'd ever seen. Thin wisps of white hair, stiff with salt, protruded from a grimy knit cap of uncertain color. Beneath the cap jutted a face so pocked and crisscrossed with scars that Bristol's hand jerked to her mouth in revulsion, restraining an involuntary gulp. In addition to the scars, deep lines etched the man's mouth and forehead, outlining a nose folded in some long-ago brawl.

He waited patiently, accustomed to stares. "I be Mr. Aykroyd, mistress. Ye're to come below." He smiled then, the scars and welts pressing into one another. Bristol focused on the only feature in that face she didn't find repellent. The bright blue eyes smiling out from his incredible face were surprisingly kind and gentle.

Blinking rapidly, keeping her eyes fastened to his, Bristol responded with a hesitant smile of her own.

Delighted, Mr. Aykroyd gallantly offered his arm. Immediately hoots of derision and mockery rose from the decks and floated from the high rigging. "Such beauty is wasted on this scum," Mr. Aykroyd said scornfully. His knotted fingers tightened on a knife protruding above his faded breeches. "Shut up, you whore-sons! This be a lady!"

The calls quieted, but every man watched as Bristol accepted Mr. Aykroyd's arm with a wavering smile. She stepped carefully, eyes fixed steadily on a blank space before her. She felt the men's eyes strip away her gown, and a tremor ran through her limbs. Acutely aware of the danger La Crosse had mentioned, she dug her fingers into Mr. Aykroyd's arm.

He held her rock-certain, guiding her toward a yawning black opening. "Filthy lusting beasts!" he muttered.

Bristol didn't dare look around her. She felt them breathing, felt the weight of leering eyes, felt the pull of her gown across her full breasts. Every step was agony; the swing of her hips felt exaggerated and emphasized. She stumbled over a wooden peg, and Mr. Aykroyd's arm instantly stiffened in support.

He spoke from the corner of a twisted mouth. "If ye show this scum ye fear them, they'll be on ye like a pack of rats. Stare 'em in the eye, gel, show 'em the iron in yer backbone!"

She sensed he was right. Bristol lifted her chin and squared her shoulders. She was an Adams, and she bowed to no one! Steeling her nerves, she swung her eyes to the left, sucking in her breath at the raw animal lust she saw devouring her body. A savage face, one eye hidden beneath a sunken black patch, grinned and exposed a mouth of gapped and rotted teeth. The man's dirt-blackened hand moved slowly across an enormous lump bulging in his breeches. He rocked his hips lewdly toward Bristol, his grin widening and his hand moving faster.

Bristol stopped, her face white and stony. She stared contemptuously into the man's one good eye; then she leaned and deliberately spit at his feet. A howl of laughter erupted around them, and the man turned a threatening face upward, raising a finger in a rude gesture.

"Aye, gel! Ye have the spirit to match yer hair!" Mr. Aykroyd nodded approvingly and pulled her forward.

Bristol's heart sank at sight of the narrow steps leading down into blackness. "There?" she asked in a faint voice. A dank, musty odor wafted from the opening.

"Aye." Mr. Aykroyd rattled a ring of keys dangling from his belt. "Ye and Goodwife Able will be safe down there."

Bristol hung back, inhaling the fresh ocean breeze. The dark opening did not look promising. She frowned into the blue eyes of Mr. Aykroyd's ruined face. "Must I?"

"Aye," he answered firmly, his eyes flicking to the leering men.

Sighing in resignation, Bristol preceded him with reluctant steps. The staircase led down to a narrow hallway, doors opening along its length. A wall-mounted oil lamp threw bleak flickering light, the end of the passageway remaining in darkness.

"I don't be having all day, mistress." A note of impatience crept into Mr. Aykroyd's voice.

"Aye. I'm sorry." All she'd done since boarding was apologize, Bristol thought glumly. She stepped past the dim light and into shadow, walking past what appeared to be a galley and then a storeroom.

A man's shape loomed in the black passageway, and Bristol halted abruptly, her heart leaping.

But Mr. Aykroyd prodded her forward. "That be Mr. Speck. He's to guard ye and Goodwife Able." Mr. Aykroyd glared into a face nearly as scarred and mapped as his own. "Guard, Mr. Speck! Nothing more, or the captain'll take the hide off yer back!" Mr. Speck's bearded mouth lifted in a sly grin, and he stepped aside to allow Mr. Aykroyd's key access to the door.

The door pushed open, and Mr. Aykroyd stood aside, allowing Bristol just room to pass. Inside, a woman sprang from the edge of a narrow cot, hands flying to her throat, her dark eyes wide in a pale round face. "It's you," she breathed in obvious relief, and sank back to the cot.

Behind, Bristol heard the key turn. She sighed and leaned against the door, examining the quarters that would serve as home for the next two months. There wasn't much to see.

Two small cots bolted against both walls, a narrow aisle between them. Bristol's trunk and that of Goodwife Able nearly filled the aisle, leaving only enough room to wriggle sideways to the cots. The walls were of stained dull wood; a dim oil lamp emitted a feeble light. They weren't passengers, Bristol thought, they were prisoners.

Goodwife Able waved a hand before her round face. "I . . . I don't feel well. The rocking . . . I wish this infernal rocking would stop!" She talked through her nose, each word a nasal scraping sound.

The ship lifted in a slow roll, and Bristol swayed over Goodwife Able, then dropped suddenly until Goodwife Able appeared to be sitting on the wall above her.

"Oh, dear Lord!" the woman wailed, falling back on her cot and clutching her stomach. Dark eyes implored Bristol's understanding. "I'm sorry. This is a terrible way to meet." Tiny beads of perspiration dotted her forehead, dampening the dark curls hanging from her cap. "I'm Jane Able, and I know you're Bristol Adams. That hideous Mr. Aykroyd informed me."

"Are you ill?" Bristol asked, remaining by the door. Immediately she felt foolish. Of course Jane was ill. Bristol watched Goodwife Able uncertainly, her own stomach reacting to the queasiness she read in the woman's moon face, a face that didn't match her slender body. Bristol didn't know whether to approach Goodwife Able and offer assistance, or negotiate the trunk-filled aisle to her own cot, or tap on the door for help.

"No, I'm not ill," Jane Able snapped, "I'm dying!" Her side of the room rose, and she clamped her hands onto the cot, eyes wide and frightened. "Oh, dear." The ship dropped, and she squeezed her eyes shut. "I'm sorry to be sharp. I just want this to stop! Even just for a minute! If everything would just be still for . . . If it would just *stop*, I'd be all right!" The ship rocked and shuddered, and Jane Able uttered a strangling sound. "Oh, dear . . . oh, dear . . . oh dear." She jerked to the side of the cot and vomited into a slop basin, lifting miserable embarrassed eyes when she'd finished.

Bristol swallowed hard, and squirmed past the trunks to her cot. She sat down and untied her hood and cloak. A sour odor permeated the tiny room.

"This will pass," Bristol offered weakly, not at all certain, but feeling compelled to say something. "I'm sure you'll feel better in a few days." She placed a shaky hand on her stomach, the odor affecting her own stability.

"Days!" cried Jane Able. "Days? I can't survive this for days!" Her round face turned an alarming shade of green, and she bent over the slop basin.

Turning aside, Bristol lay back on her cot and stared at the sliding ceiling, trying not to listen to the gagging noises an arm's legnth away. A feeling of utter desolation crept through her mind. It was unsafe above deck and intolerable below. She could scarcely breathe in the close sour room. Even if Jane Able were well and hearty, Bristol dismally suspected the woman's company would not be a cheering influence— Jane's pinched disapproving expression wasn't encouraging.

Sitting up, Bristol rummaged in her trunk until she found the pewter cup. For a moment she turned the cool metal in her hands, then pushed the mug beneath her pillow, where her fingers would touch it first thing in the morning and last at night.

Lying back, she turned her thoughts to the figures she'd left standing on the wharf. A tear slid from her lashes and fell to the cot. Had the rider been Caleb? Had he come to fetch her after all? No, not with Noah there. What, then? And her family . . . when they sat to the evening meal, would their eyes stray to the empty spot beside Charity?

Her defenses crumbled, and Bristol gave way to a deep-stabbing grief. She buried her face, smothering the sound of weeping in her pillow, her hands clutching the pewter cup. This wasn't fair; it was all so unfair!

Gradually the storm passed, and she gasped weakly, her red-rimmed eyes fixing on the dipping ceiling. Across the jumble of trunks, Jane Able moaned and splashed into the basin. Bristol ground her teeth and pretended not to notice.

Slowly an anger built in her breast and grew to strain the capacity of heart and mind, an anger directed toward herself.

I've cried a lifetime of tears in the last weeks, she admitted to the roof. And all the tears have changed nothing. Not one single thing. Images raced through her mind, showing her a teary face and weeping green eyes. Bristol's hands clenched into fists, and her cheeks burned with humiliation. Never again . . . I'm better than that! she thought fiercely. I've cried for the last time! She blotted her eyes, and her mouth set in stone. I'll waste no more time crying over things I cannot change!

She'd wept from anger, from self-pity, from frustration, and her tears had gained nothing but internal misery. Bristol's eyes hardened to jade. Tears had not averted the lash. Tears had not altered Noah's decision. Tears had not influenced Caleb. And tears would not magically return her to the Salem dock.

"I . . . will . . . never . . . cry . . . again!" she whispered past clenched teeth. "*Never!*" A granite shell formed around her heart, and Bristol knew this time the vow would be kept, the tears were sealed forever.

She sat up, repeating the oath. "No more tears!" The torture of wondering about Caleb, about her family, disappeared. No logic existed in tormenting herself over the figure on the dock. She had no way to discover the man's identity or purpose. The ship would not turn back. Clearly tears accomplished nothing whatsoever. "Never again," Bristol vowed, her fists striking the edge of the cot. She had her memories, and she'd treasure them, but they'd not turn into items for self-pity.

Her resolute gaze fell upon Goodwife Jane Able, and Bristol stood, new strength in her stance. Gone was the lethargy that had blunted mind and action since she first stepped into the longboat.

Squirming past the trunks, she set about doing what little she could for Jane Able. Holding her breath, Bristol cleaned the mess around the slop basin, her own stomach churning, and she bathed Jane's stricken face.

"Thank you," Jane Able murmured. "I misjudged you.

When I saw you weeping on the dock, I thought you had no grit. I thought . . ." She groaned.

"Later," Bristol soothed, not wishing to recall the scene on the wharf. "We'll talk when you feel better."

The minutes passed like hours, filled with the stench of vomit and sour perspiration. And Jane Able's nasal tone complaining bitterly of the rocking motion. Jane prayed in a shrill voice to either die or recover.

Bristol pushed loose strands of hair beneath her cap and continued nursing the woman with a secret conviction that hell could be no worse than a tiny room and a violently sick person.

When a knock sounded, Bristol wiped her forehead and glanced up eagerly; any diversion would be a welcome relief. With all her heart she hoped the rasping key signaled a reprieve from the dark malodorous cell.

Mr. Aykroyd leaned his scarred face into the doorway, Mr. Speck's bearded leer above his shoulder. "Good evening, ladies," Mr. Aykroyd sang cheerily. "I've brought ye a candle. One a night is permitted, no more." He placed the candle in a wall sconce, securing it carefully. Added to the dim light of the oil lamp, the candle made the room appear warmer and more cheerful.

"Thank you," Bristol said, her shoulders dropping. No trick of light would make the cabin less depressing. She listened to Jane's moan, then sighed. It appeared no reprieve would be forthcoming. She waited for Mr. Aykroyd to close the door.

Instead, he sniffed the foul air, his folded nose wrinkling in distaste. His steady blue eyes fastened on Goodwife Able curled in her cot. "Her don't be having her sea legs," he said contemptuously. Such a person merited no further consideration. He turned to Bristol. " 'Tis custom on the first night out of port for the passengers to take supper with the captain. I be escorting ye, if ye be hungry."

Bristol's spirits rose. She had no desire for Jean Pierre's company, but remaining here with the stink and the groans had no appeal at all. She felt desperate to escape this small choking room, but . . . Uncertainly Bristol looked at Jane. The woman moaned and clutched her stomach; then she emitted a little scream and hastily leaned over the cot.

Bristol's decision was made. "Thank you, Mr. Aykroyd," she blurted, feeling instantly guilty and elated. She straightened her dust cap, recalling Captain La Crosse's teasing criticism the first time they'd met. Tonight, she vowed, he'd find no cause to criticize.

Before following Mr. Aykroyd into the dark hallway, Bristol cleaned Jane's face. "Shall I bring something for you?" she asked solicitously. Guilt shadowed Bristol's voice; Jane had to remain here, while Bristol would breathe fresh air again.

An inarticulate moan of revulsion erupted from the writhing figure, and Bristol hurried from the room, biting her lip in dismay. Behind her, the door cut off the sound of splashing.

On deck, all was dark and secured for the night. Reedy notes of a melancholy flute drifted across the planking, and men's laughter wafted faintly from below decks. At the helm, a bearded figure turned a sand glass and relit the glow of a pipe. Overhead, soft murmurs called back and forth in the shadowy rigging.

Bristol gulped the cold crisp air, filling her lungs gratefully. Instantly she felt better. Above, stars twinkled like distant chips of ice, and below, black waves lapped the hull with a mother's rhythmic pat.

"It's beautiful!" Bristol said softly, awed. A sliver of moon broke from a bank of scattered clouds and ribboned across the water. As she watched, something glided across the dark waves, a graceful shadow, and then gone. The *Challenger* rocked and swayed, and it seemed to Bristol as if a wooden cradle lay beneath her feet, creaking with comfortable night noises.

Ignoring the chill, she paused at the rail, enraptured by the vista spreading before her wide eyes. "I had no idea," she murmured softly.

Mr. Aykroyd leaned beside her, his ugly features turned toward the blending horizon. "Aye," he said, and Bristol heard a pleased approval in his tone. "They be a beauty to the sea like no other. She enchants and seduces. But she be a fickle mistress, gel, tempting men to a watery grave. Many a ruined suitor lies in the arms of the sea, brought there by arrogance and vanity, having forgotten that none do conquer." He fell silent. "The sea is like a vain woman; she demands constant attention and tribute."

Bristol stole a surprised glance at his face, marveling at such poetic thoughts emerging from such a visage. Beauty blooming amid ugliness. She decided abruptly that she liked Mr. Aykroyd; liked him very much. Smiling, she accepted his arm, and he guided her around unfamiliar tarred objects toward the distant stern. There they descended a flight of stairs and followed a flickering passageway to an oiled door. Mr. Aykroyd knocked once and pushed the heavy wood.

The captain's cabin proved unexpectedly large. Each wall contained full bookcases, protected by a thin rod to hold the books in place during inclement weather. A curtained bed was bolted to one wall, the cutains open and revealing a large comfortable mattress. Behind a desk covered with books and rolled charts rose a bank of windows looking out at the night and the ship's silvery trail.

Jean Pierre La Crosse lifted his dark head from the piles of maps he examined. Tonight he wore a flowing white shirt open at the throat, a dark doublet, and blue breeches. Shining dark hair gleamed in the glow of his desk candle, tied at the neck with a thin cord. He frowned at Mr. Aykroyd. "Goodwife Able?" he asked in the rich, lightly accented voice.

Mr. Aykroyd's lip curled. "Her be indisposed." He gave Bristol a forward push. "But this one be fit company for any man."

Captain La Crosse leaned back in his chair, his gray eyes sweeping Bristol. A slow smile lifted his generous mouth. "Indeed. Inform Master Boyd we'll dine whenever he's ready."

"Aye, sir." Mr. Aykroyd stepped into the passageway, closing the door with a solid click.

"Oh, but . . ." Bristol looked at the door with a sense of alarm. She hadn't considered that she would be alone with Captain La Crosse. Uncertainly she stole a look at him, her hands smoothing the edges of her long apron. Jean Pierre La Crosse filled the room with a prowling energy, a rugged maleness that made Bristol acutely uneasy. She fiddled with her apron, shifting uncomfortably. Unreasonably she wished he weren't so handsome; even with the scar disappearing into his shirt, he was a striking man. She rushed past this thought, unwilling to dwell on his physical appeal.

La Crosse grinned as if reading her thoughts. Gracefully he rose from the chair and bent over a chest, removing a bottle of wine. "I can assure you of the quality," he said easily, opening the bottle and talking to Bristol as if continuing a conversation begun some time ago. "No self-respecting sea captain leaves port without the best wines stocking his personal supply. To do less would disgrace the profession." He poured two glasses and extended one to Bristol.

She accepted the wine, his warm fingers brushing her own. Startled, Bristol jerked, spilling a few drops across her hand. La Crosse lifted a dark brow and smiled, but he refrained from comment. All of which made her feel very young and very inexperienced and very foolish. Not a good beginning, she thought angrily. What was it about this man that brought out the worst in her? She frowned into the wineglass.

"Now," La Crosse said, reclining on the bed and raising a knee, "tell me why a young girl risks a long journey unaccompanied." He rested a wrist on his knee, the wineglass elegant between his fingers.

Young girl! He made himself sound so old, and he couldn't yet be thirty! Nevertheless, Bristol felt like an awkward colt standing in the center of the room offering herself for inspection. Her chin lifted and she walked to the vacated desk chair, raising her hands to the strings of her cloak. The last time she'd been alone with a man . . . But Caleb and Captain La Crosse were like an ox and a racehorse, totally dissimilar. Still, she couldn't help drawing comparisons. When she realized how poorly Caleb compared to the vital, elegant captain, she blinked in irritation and ended the game.

"I'm traveling to London for an extended visit with my Aunt Prudence," she answered. She tried and failed to inject any enthusiasm into her tone. Daring a quick look at him, Bristol hastily dropped her eyes. Crisp dark hair curled from the throat of his snowy shirt.

"Prudence?" he mused. A spark of interest lit his gray eyes. "I'm acquainted with a Prudence in London. Could she be your aunt, I wonder?" He lifted his glass to sensual lips, but lips with a hint of cruelty in the contours, Bristol noticed.

With a frown, she decided his manners had not improved. On the one hand, she resented his prying questions; on the other, she dreaded a silence between them. In a silence, his eyes . . . She lowered her head, confused by the thoughts and the flush of warmth in her cheeks. This was maddening; she bit the inside of her cheek. "I doubt it," she finally said. Truthfully, she couldn't conceive of any situation in which this man might encounter her aunt. "Prudence Adams isn't likely to frequent such places as you." Her face flamed; she'd insulted him without intending to do so. "What I mean is . . ."

La Crosse threw back his head and laughed delightedly. "Prudence Adams. And you don't see her frequenting the same degenerate haunts as I."

The color in Bristol's face deepened to scarlet, and frustration and anger clogged her throat. "No! I . . . I base that opinion on having seen the richness of your clothing. My aunt would not move in the circles of the wealthy." She wanted to drop through the floor. Now she was discussing a man's clothing. She felt embarrassed and infuriated, believing herself maneuvered into an area of questionable respectability. And so easily. Her inexperience galled her.

"Ah. So this . . . Prudence Adams is of reduced circumstance?"

Bristol's green eyes flashed. He passed the limits of polite conversation. "I can't see how my aunt's financial status is of any concern to a stranger!" she snapped. She'd not set aside her pride to the extent of tolerating such personal probing. His manners were appalling.

Grinning, Jean Pierre watched her, not the least perturbed and appearing to enjoy her discomfort. "You're quite correct, of course. May I make one further observation regarding your unfortunate aunt, then we'll leave the topic?" Supremely confident, he continued without waiting for Bristol's assent. "I'll venture a wager that you have not met the lady."

Taken aback, Bristol narrowed her eyes. How he guessed, she couldn't imagine. Thinking furiously, she could see no harm in admitting he was right. She relaxed somewhat in the chair and felt an easing of the tensions between them. "I can't imagine why you'd think so, but as it happens, you're correct. I've not met Aunt Prudence."

"Perhaps she'll prove a pleasant surprise."

Bristol stared curiously. "I don't recall mentioning any apprehensions," she said finally. He said nothing, but his steady gray gaze indicated he sensed her dread. Bristol drew a breath and sipped her wine. Perhaps she'd misjudged him, perhaps he possessed a keener insight than she'd first suspected. "I . . . I hope you're right about that too," she answered in a less guarded tone. Captain La Crosse confounded her. Hard one moment, charming the next. She wondered if others found him as perplexing as she did.

"Enter," he called in response to a knock at the door.

A young boy, perhaps twelve years old, pushed through the doorway, balancing a tray on one thin shoulder. "Supper, sir."

Jean Pierre waved his glass toward a table glittering with silver. "Mistress Adams?"

Bristol stepped forward, waiting while the boy cleared Goodwife Able's place and lit a wax candle. She slid into a chair bolted to the planking and looked at the table, trying not to gape. The table setting was richer than any she'd imagined.

Instead of wooden trenchers, decliate china plates gleamed before her, and each person was provided a fork of polished silver. Awed, Bristol thought of the solitary china saucer in

Hannah's cupboard, a treasured item. What would Hannah think of this rich display? Bristol shook her curls, dry-eyed. She refused to dwell on thoughts of home.

Young Master Boyd snapped a square of linen and draped it across Bristol's lap, doing the same for Captain La Crosse. Wide-eyed, Bristol studied the table and inhaled the scents of better food than she'd expected to taste on board ship. Captain La Crosse lived very well indeed. After a moment she shifted her attention to the casual flow of conversation between Captain La Crosse and the boy.

". . . any appointments tonight?" Jean Pierre teased, pouring more wine into his glass, then Bristol's.

"Aye, sir." The boy brushed at a lock of blond hair falling across his forehead.

La Crosse laughed. "One would think shore leave had satisfied the men for a while. I'd have supposed business would be slow for at least a week."

The boy grinned, his fresh scrubbed face angelic beneath a knit cap. "No, sir. I'm much in demand," he answered with a hint of pride. Master Boyd served a platter of roast capons in orange sauce and added an array of additional dishes, all steaming deliciously.

Bristol smiled. Had the boy been red-haired, he would have resembled her second brother, Josh. "How nice," she murmured, wishing Josh were alive and proud of something.

The boy started, then dropped his eyes with a blush. Captain La Crosse's brow rose, and he smiled at Bristol curiously. "I'd have expected a scowl of disapproval Mistress Adams."

Uneasily Bristol lifted her wineglass, wishing she'd paid greater attention to the start of the conversation. She felt a growing sense of discomfort. "I'm afraid I misunderstand. Would you be kind enough to explain, Captain?" She stressed the word "Captain," reminding him of his earlier instruction.

La Crosse ignored the implication. He flicked a glance at the boy, who fled the room. A sardonic smile played about La Crosse's lips. "The boy is a whore," he said flatly, refilling his glass.

Bristol choked, wine spilling into her lap. She looked quickly toward the closed door, then back to Jean Pierre. Her wide green eyes registered disbelief. "A . . . a . . . ?" She couldn't say the word.

"A whore," La Crosse finished for her, amusement in his eyes. He shrugged and tore a capon in two. "Master Boyd is a most enterprising young lad. Most cabin boys are subjected to certain . . . indignities . . . by force. Master Boyd submits

72

willingly. But for a price, and on his own terms. The lad makes a handsome business of it." La Crosse laughed. "By the time he reaches his majority, Master Boyd will be a wealthy young man."

Bristol sputtered. "But . . . that . . . that's terrible! How can you allow such an abomination?" She set her shaking glass on the table. Suddenly she lost interest in the food. An unbidden picture leaped to the front of her thoughts: Master Boyd's sweet face and the sailor with the black eye patch. She pressed her linen hard against her lips.

Leaning back in his chair, La Crosse studied her with an expressionless face. "Mistress Adams. You're speaking from youthful innocence. The world is not a pretty place. Nor moral, according to the concepts you've been taught. These things occur . . . and worse."

"But . . . but . . . that little boy and the others . . ." She fought a lump of revulsion. "They can be hanged for . . . for . . ." She waved a helplesss hand, hating herself for a prudish reluctance to say the words; but never had she imagined herself discussing such topics. The words stuck in her Puritan throat.

"Homosexuality," he said in an amused tone. "However, you are speaking of New England. Other countries aren't so rigid." His broad shoulders rose and fell. "Why concern yourself? One person cannot change a hundred years of custom. Besides, the arrangement is agreeable to all involved."

"But it's wrong! A hanging offense!" Her voice rose. "You must stop this at once. As captain of this ship, it's your responsibility to save Josh . . . I mean, that boy!" She leaned forward, meeting his gaze.

La Crosse stared, and his eyes darkened to flint. "Mistress Adams, I do not need you or anyone else to interpret morality on board my ship, nor to dictate my responsibilities." His voice turned to ice. "Master Boyd would defend his right of choice to his dying breath. What he does is of his own choosing. Would you prefer him raped? The path he's chosen will one day ensure a comfortable future he would not otherwise have."

Bristol lifted her hands, dinner forgotten. "But how can you look at that little boy and show such inhuman disregard? You should—"

"That is quite enough, Mistress Adams." His voice was soft and dangerous, cutting to bone. His eyes glittered. "I did not invite you to share my table with any thought of enduring a lecture. Don't meddle in things you know nothing about."

Bristol's face colored, and she dropped her eyes, feeling about ten years old. Her hands curled into tight balls. How could she have thought for a moment that Captain Jean Pierre La Crosse possessed any charm? He elevated himself above morality and church law and state; outside everything Bristol understood. If God were indeed merciful, then this would be the last she saw of Captain La Crosse during this voyage. And the meal couldn't end quickly enough to please her.

They ate in strained silence. Bristol yearned to leave; even her sour cell was preferable to sitting in Captain La Crosse's company. She was appalled by his libertine attitudes and shocked at seeing the results. Each bite stuck in her throat, and her chest constricted with disgust.

Once she lifted her face, determined to say more, but seeing the warning in his stormy eyes, she stopped the words on her lips. Why didn't he close the collar of his shirt or wear a cravat? The dark hair curling from his chest was oddly disturbing. She resented the sheer maleness of Captain La Crosse, the lack of softening qualities. And his clear gray eyes unnerved her, causing a tension in the pit of her stomach. She stabbed at her capon, irritated by the confused jumble of conflicting emotion.

The instant she'd eaten what she could, Bristol threw down her linen and slid from the chair. "Thank you, Captain," she said curtly. She tossed her head and reached for her cloak. "I'll be leaving now."

His eyebrow rose, and he smiled. "As you wish. I'll ring for Mr. Aykroyd." He tugged a rope near the table and stood.

"I'd rather not wait," Bristol snapped impatiently. She wanted a breath of fresh air; she wanted to be away from his eyes and his authority. Her hand touched the door latch.

"Foolish little girl," he said softly. A blush climbed Bristol's neck. "That is not only idiotic but also dangerous."

Each time she'd encountered Jean Pierre La Crosse, he'd called her a fool. It was not to be borne. Bristol's chin rose in defiance and pride; her green eyes flashed fire. "I assure you I can take care of myself."

"Can you?"

Suddenly she was in his arms, iron bands pressing her body tightly against his. His steady eyes laughed into her face.

Outraged, Bristol squirmed against his lean, taut body, struggling in his arms. "Let me go!" she hissed, her fists striking his chest. She thrashed, her body moving against hard,

74

unyielding flesh. Her eyes flared wide as she felt the quick hardening response growing between his legs. A sure hand cupped her buttocks and pressed her against that demanding heat.

"Can you?" he repeated, his eyes on her mouth.

A bolt of lightning shot through Bristol's body, and her lips trembled helplessly in a hot face. She felt the fire between their bodies, and her expression froze in horror.

His hand lifted her chin, and smoldering eyes stared into her wide green gaze. "Can you take care of yourself, Mistress Adams?" he asked softly. "So beautiful," he murmured. His eyes lingered on the curve of her lips. Pushing against his arms, Bristol wrenched her face violently to the side. Her breath spurted in short frightened gasps.

He stroked her cheek with his thumb and pulled her roughly to his body, molding her to his hard frame. Then, laughing lightly, La Crosse stepped away, releasing her. He'd succeeded in demonstrating her lack of power.

Bristol staggered against a row of books, her breath emerging in ragged whispers of fright and outrage. "How dare you!" Her voice was embarrassingly shaky. "How dare you!"

Her rebellious body burned where his flesh had pressed hers, and she hated herself for this revolting and confusing response. Frightened at her helplessness, she wondered what might have happend if La Crosse had decided to press his advantage. He was master of the ship; there was no one to beg for assistance, no one who would dare help her.

"You . . . you . . ." Words eluded her in the rush of fury at the slow grin lifting his mouth. "I'll never come here again!" Her cheeks burned at the pallid threat, but it was all she had. Bristol smoothed her brown gown with trembling fingers, fighting for a semblance of dignity.

Behind her, the door cracked, and Mr. Aykroyd called.

But before Bristol could respond, La Crosse's hand shot forward, capturing her wrist. His eyes touched her breasts and thighs, a dark flicker in the depths. "It's a long voyage. You will be back," he said softly. "There are depths in you that you don't yet recognize." He pulled her against his body, letting her feel the hard readiness of his need; then he released her. Bristol heard him laugh as she fled into the passageway.

6

A WEEK out of Salem harbor, Jane Able felt well enough to sit up and attempt solid food. Mercifully, she held it on her stomach. Bristol watched each bite with tired eyes and drooping shoulders. Goodwife Able's seasickness had been an ordeal. In her heart, Bristol felt if Jane cried out in her nasal voice, "I want to die," just once more, Bristol would be tempted to oblige her.

Sighing, Bristol pushed at a strand of limp red hair. She'd reached a point of desperate longing for one uninterrupted night of sleep—without the assault of moans and retching. And fighting.

Nearly every night had been interrupted by midnight scufflings outside their locked door. Each time, Bristol and Jane had bolted upright in their cots and stared at the door, wide-eyed with fright, listening to muffled swearing and the clash of brawling along the passageway. Even when a creaking silence returned, neither woman could sleep. The wakeful nights had resulted in smudged eyes and frayed tempers.

But, Bristol thought gratefully, at least tonight she could rest without listening for Jane, as Goody Able seemed on the mend. Jane had proved out as Bristol first suspected. Not a warm woman, but a pious one. Even throughout the worst of her sickness, Jane prayed twice daily, and her pinched disapproval drove Bristol to the planks as well. Jane seemed determined to use the voyage to better Bristol's soul, both in conversation and prayer. Jane and her family had witnessed Bristol's whipping, and she felt it her Christian duty to lecture Bristol at every opportunity.

Bristol heaved another small sigh. Even so, Jane's company was better than none. Not by much, she thought, but enough.

These gloomy thoughts needed interruption, and Bristol raised a hopeful face toward the knock at their door.

Mr. Aykroyd leaned inside with a cheerful smile, delivering

a message from Captain La Crosse. "Now that ye be hale, Goody Able, the captain requests the presence of both ye ladies at his table this evening."

"No, thank you!" Bristol said vehemently.

"Aye!" Jane answered.

Each looked at the other in surprise. Jane spoke first, her nasal tone grating across Bristol's ragged nerves. "Why, Bristol Adams . . . you've spoken of little else but escaping this cabin. Now you refuse a perfect opportunity. Such contrary attitudes are not becoming." Her tone was acid, and the crease deepened between her eyes.

"I'd rather stay in this stifling cabin than eat with Jean Pierre La Crosse!" Bristol leaned wearily against the bulkhead and folded her arms across her breast. "And I'd advise you to refuse as well."

"Whatever for?" Jane's round face studied Bristol with reproof. "You forget, I've not had a breath of fresh air in a week!"

Bristol didn't answer. Let Jane go. To be alone, blessedly alone, without Jane's nasal voice rasping in her ear—the prospect sounded wonderfully welcome. But she should say something. "He's a monster," she snapped. Her conscience was salved; at least she'd given Jane a small warning.

Mr. Aykroyd chuckled from the doorway. "Then the captain be the finest monster I ever hope to see!" He waggled a teasing finger toward Bristol. "Ye'll be eating crew's fare while the other lady dines on roast mutton." Bristol notched her chin higher and stubbornly looked away. "Very well, gel. When ye glimpse yer supper tray, don't be thinking I didn't warn ye."

During the next hours, Jane pressed for an explanation, but Bristol remained obstinately silent. "Form your own judgment," was all she'd say.

"Very well," Jane sniffed. "If you propose to be unreasonable, I'll do just that." She rummaged under her pillow and withdrew a well-worn copy of the Bible. " 'Tis time for evening devotions," she announced, managing to sound pious and disapproving at the same time.

Bristol sighed heavily and bowed her head. She'd grown up in a devoted family atmosphere, but nothing as dedicated as Jane Able. Instead of attending to Jane's long, rambling prayer, her mind flew ahead to the captain's cabin. An impish grin played at her full lips, and Bristol quickly lifted her folded hands to hide her mouth.

She could vividly imagine prudish Jane Able dining with a

libertine like Captain La Crosse. The contrast delighted her. Bristol peeked over her tented fingers with sparkling eyes. She wagered Goodwife Able would not remain in the captain's cabin until dinner, let alone endure an entire meal in his company. And what of the insolent La Crosse? Bristol's small shoulders shook with repressed mirth.

She suspected no amount of protests or icy words would silence Goodwife Able—Jane wouldn't halt a sermon, once begun. And Captain La Crosse's life-style provided ample material for Goody Able's critical eye.

With these delicious thoughts diverting her mind, Bristol felt Goodwife Able's ritual prayer passed more quickly than any since she'd boarded the *Challenger*.

After prayer, the women picked up their hoops and embroidered in silence. Occasionally a wicked little grin earned Bristol a hard glare. Which only made her hidden amusement more compelling. She had only to glance at Jane to feel a bubble of laughter welling in her throat.

When Jane compressed her thin lips in disapproval, as she did continually, it seemed that acres of fleshy cheek stretched along her face. Jane's features were small, squeezed together in her round face, as if God had erred and given her the wrong eyes and nose and mouth for that face. Bristol stifled a giggle. She had an idea La Crosse would see a great deal of Jane's cheek tonight. Jane's lips would certainly pinch constantly throughout dinner.

When Mr. Aykroyd arrived, Jane threw down her sewing, looking as relieved as Bristol felt. She shrugged her cloak over a spotless white collar and tied her hood. "You won't change your mind?" she asked Bristol. Her tone was scrupulously polite, but under the nasal twang lay a clear hope that Bristol would not alter her decision.

"No, no. I hope you enjoy yourself." Bristol managed to speak before collapsing across her cot in gales of laughter.

Jane Able's mouth opened, then snapped shut. "Most unseemly," she sniffed, sweeping grandly from the small cabin.

After the door closed, Bristol repeated the words, "Most unseemly," mimicking Jane's nasal pinch. She fell on her cot, laughing until she felt weak, letting go the dismal emotions of the previous week. Pious, prim Goodwife Able was about to receive a generous dollop of "unseemly." It was small revenge for the hours of cleaning slop basins and mopping Jane's acid face—definitely unworthy of an Adams, Bristol thought—but she enjoyed the moment immensely.

The smile still lingered at her lips when a knock sounded.

Bristol's smile widened. The confrontation between captain and saint must have been worse than her wildest imaginings for Jane to be returning this soon; she'd scarcely had time to walk the length of the ship and back. Bristol wasn't to have her time alone after all. And that was to be regretted, but worth it, she decided. She looked up expectantly, struggling to keep a straight face.

Mr. Aykroyd pushed open the door. Peering behind his shoulder, Bristol looked for Jane's outraged face, but saw no one. She lifted her brow. "Where's Goody Able?"

Mr. Aykroyd's eyes widened in surprise, his face a tortured map of scars and deep clefts. "Why, her be with the captain, of course. Have ye turned daft, gel?"

"But . . ."

"I come to fetch ye for a turn on deck. Captain say it be all right to take ye up at night for a piece of air."

Bristol sprang to her feet, an eager smile transforming her tired face. "Oh, aye! You can't imagine what it's like being cooped up in here!" She threw on a dark cloak, even smiling at the bearded Mr. Speck in her enthusiasm. Mr. Speck hung over Mr. Aykroyd's shoulder, watching hungrily.

Mr. Aykroyd grinned at Bristol's delight, the effect on his ruined face enough to turn weaker stomachs. "Ye can't imagine what ye'd face if ye didn't be locked in. Isn't that so, Mr. Speck?"

Mr. Speck stroked his beard with a grimy hand; he nodded, his staring eyes never leaving Bristol's breast. Suddenly Mr. Aykroyd's arm flashed, and the hilt of his knife struck deep at Mr. Speck's ribs. Mr. Speck howled and doubled over, clutching his chest. "Ye don't be staring at a lady with lust in yer black heart!" Mr. Aykroyd hissed dangerously. He hauled Mr. Speck upright by the man's filthy collar and glared into his eyes. "Don't be forgetting that, Mr. Speck," he said softly. "Or ye be finding yerself swabbing animal pens instead of sleeping peaceful outside this door."

"Aye, sir," Mr. Speck answered sullenly. He rubbed his ribs, resentful eyes on the planks.

"Now, then"—Mr. Aykroyd shoved his knife into his breeches and offered Bristol his arm—"we'll be taking a breath of air."

Bristol smiled into her hood. It seemed the incredible Mr. Aykroyd was capable of lightning changes in mood. She suspected Mr. Speck would feel a painful bruise for several days. Gratefully she pressed Mr. Aykroyd's arm, allowing him to lead her on deck.

The night sea took Bristol's breath away. A light breeze chased the waves, and Bristol wrapped her cloak tightly about her body. After a turn of the spar deck, they climbed to the rear quarterdeck and leaned against a wooden rail out of the wind. Bristol felt a deep reluctance to return to the cramped cabin.

Watching the moonlit foam marking the ship's trail, she realized that beneath her feet, below decks, Captain La Crosse now dined with Goodwife Able. Bristol found it inconceivable that the two had endured one another this long. She glanced toward Mr. Aykroyd, his face dim in the moonlight. "Tell me about Captain La Crosse," she asked, giving way to an overwhelming curiosity. "What is he really like . . . what's his background?"

Mr. Aykroyd removed a clay pipe from his coat pocket and lit it. He leaned his elbows on the railing and blew a stream of blue smoke toward the water. "What do the captain be like?" He shrugged. "I've known him most of his life, and I can't answer ye fully. The captain be a man of many faces, many depths. But I promise ye this: Captain La Crosse be the finest man I ever hauled canvas with or ever expect to meet."

Dismayed, Bristol turned from the night waters and leaned her spine against the rail. She gazed out over the dark, creaking ship. Somewhere inside, she'd hoped for Mr. Aykroyd as an ally; she'd hoped Mr. Aykroyd disliked Jean Pierre La Crosse as deeply as she believed she did. A frown soured her voice. "He lacks manners, and he's rude and patronizing and of doubtful moral character!"

Mr. Aykroyd chuckled. "Oh, the captain has the most elegant manners when he chooses to use them. His ma, rest her soul, saw to that." He glanced at Bristol's profile and added, "As to his moral character . . . he be a man, Mistress Adams, not a saint."

Bristol pressed her lips together, deciding not to comment. Instead, she keyed on a different point. "Then you knew the captain's mother?" A note of surprise lifted her voice.

Mr. Aykroyd looked into the glowing bowl of his pipe, answering softly. "Aye. Marie La Crosse be the finest woman ever drew God's breath."

"She's dead?" Bristol found herself interested, not only in Jean Pierre's history but also in Mr. Aykroyd's responses. There was something in his tone . . . a tenderness Bristol hadn't suspected. He delayed so long in answering that Bristol wondered uncomfortably if the question had upset him.

"Aye," he said finally. "There was an agreement with Jean Pierre's father. At the age of fourteen, he was taken from Marie, lest she soften the lad with a woman's influence. She sent the boy to his natural father . . . and then Marie died. Some say she died of a broken heart; the boy was her treasure, her life."

Bristol considered the information. Night sounds of groaning rope, faint laughter, and the sliding whisper of the waves floated around them. "His natural father. Then Jean Pierre is a . . . a bastard?" Perhaps she had grown since boarding the *Challenger*; the word wasn't as hard to say as it would have been two weeks ago.

"Aye." Mr. Aykroyd's voice hardened. " 'Tweren't Marie's fault! Many a country lass has lost her heart to a dandy with gold in his purse, and then lived to regret it. Young girls without protection stand at the mercy of a man's will!" He paused, and a defensive pride crept into his grizzled voice. "But Marie carried her head high, she did."

Bristol tilted her face, puzzled. "But . . . how do you know all this? And was Jean Pierre's mother French, or his father?" She touched Mr. Aykroyd's sleeve in sudden consternation, embarrassed. She'd been furious with the captain for prying; now she was doing it. "I'm sorry, Mr. Aykroyd. I'm prying, and I don't mean to. I . . ."

Mr. Aykroyd stared at the black water, lost in a private memory, unaware of Bristol's interruption or touch. "Jean Pierre's father commissioned me to stay with the boy from the first. And to help Marie as I could. 'Twas me that took the boy away." His tone lowered to a whisper. "I didn't be there when Marie died. She died alone." His hand tightened around the pipe bowl until Bristol thought the clay would shatter. "All alone. I should have been with her, but I was in England with the boy and his father."

Bristol blinked nervously at the fierce emotion drawing Mr. Aykroyd's mangled face. She tugged his sleeve, breaking the chain of painful memory. "Where in France did Jean Pierre and his mother live?" This seemed a safer subject, less bruising, she hoped.

Mr. Aykroyd slid an embarrassed glance toward Bristol, then away; his fingers loosened around the pipe, and he stretched, standing erect. "Where? In a cottage in a small village called Eze. On the southern coast of France." Composed again, he tucked Bristol's arm in his and propelled her toward the steps. "A prettier village ye never saw, thatched cottages nestled in a valley, and an old castle crumbling on top the

81

mountain, looking out to sea. Just the place for a boy with dreams to fancy himself a sea captain." He drew on his pipe, then knocked the ashes over the side. "Or a woman with no dreams to be buried."

Bristol stared at him, moonlight glowing on her high cheekbones. "You cared for her. Very much." It wasn't a question, but a statement. She too knew the pain of leaving someone she loved, and she recognized the ache in Mr. Aykroyd's face and voice.

For a moment he said nothing. Then Mr. Aykroyd laughed, a short, pained bark. "Care? Open yer eyes, gel! Caring for the likes of me? Him what looks like this don't dare to love." He tugged her forward. "I was paid to look after Marie La Crosse and her son, and that I did." Mr. Aykroyd prodded Bristol down narrow stairs, not allowing her time to ponder the sadness in his voice. "I still be looking after him," Mr. Aykroyd muttered. "They be some tasks what have no ending."

Bristol glanced at him from beneath her lashes. "The captain won't let you go?"

Surprised, Mr. Aykroyd halted. "I won't let *him* go! He looks like . . ." He stopped and frowned. "The bloody fool bought me a cottage in Southwark. For my retirement, he said. Thinks he'll be giving me a hearth and a bit of garden and I'll not be peering over his shoulder. A garden!" Mr. Aykroyd spit over the rail. "I promised Marie I'd stay with the boy, and so I will until these old bones wash off the decks."

They walked the length of the ship and entered the stairway leading down. As they passed beneath the flickering light in the dim passageway, Bristol stole a glance at the wisps of white hair peeping from under Mr. Aykroyd's knit cap. She wondered how old he was; with his ridged face, it was impossible to form an accurate guess. Sighing, she pressed his arm sympathetically; life had dealt hard with Mr. Aykroyd.

A soft shuffling noise sounded from the shadows near Bristol's cabin door. Moving closer, she saw Master Boyd step quickly away from Mr. Speck. A grimace turned down Bristol's mouth. The young boy's flushed face smiled up at her, his blond hair shining in the feeble light.

Hastily he bent to the planks and retrieved a bottle of red wine. "This is for you, mistress," he said, extending the bottle. "With the captain's compliments. He asked that I express his regret at your absence."

She looked at him, trying not to think what he might have

been doing in the shadows with Mr. Speck. La Crosse was right. One person could change nothing. "Thank you." She frowned, turning the bottle in her hands.

The captain bested her in a belated show of manners. But still she found his choice of messenger uncomfortable. Annoyed, she struggled with the paradox of the captain's character. "Thank Captain La Crosse on my behalf, please." The words came slowly, sticking to the roof of her mouth.

"Aye, mistress." The boy didn't move. He stood on one foot, the other raised and rubbing along his calf.

Puzzled, Bristol glanced at Mr. Aykroyd. The way the boy stared caused her to wonder if she overlooked something. Did he sense she felt uneasy with him?

"Off with ye." Mr. Aykroyd grinned. He patted the boy's thin shoulder and gave him a little shove.

Master Boyd's head swiveled for a last glimpse of Bristol. "I never saw a prettier lady!" he blurted. Then he disappeared, running down the dark passageway and bolting up the stairs.

Mr. Aykroyd laughed, pulling out his ring of keys. "I believe ye've made a string of conquests on board this ship!"

A wry grin tugged Bristol's pink lips. "If so, I'm only aware of that one." She shook her head, fiery curls bouncing along her shoulders. "That poor child." She glared at Mr. Speck, but not a trace of shame humbled his yellowish eyes. Bristol shuddered and carried the wine inside.

"Good night, gel." Mr. Aykroyd pulled at the door.

"Oh, wait!"

"Aye?"

Bristol leveled beseeching green eyes toward Mr. Aykroyd. "This was so pleasant . . . couldn't we do it in the daylight? I'd so like to see everything in the sun. Could you speak to the captain for Goody Able and me? Please?"

Doubtfully Mr. Aykroyd pulled at a wisp of white hair. "Ye be asking a lot, mistress. Wouldn't be a man on board able to steady his hands after one look at that flaming hair of yers."

"I'll pin it under my cap and wear a hood. Please?"

Mr. Aykroyd chuckled. "Yer hair don't be the only part of ye apt to drive a man mad, gel."

"I'll wear my loosest apron and my cloak over that." She smiled impishly, holding out the wine bottle. "Would you accept this wine in trade for asking Captain La Crosse?"

Mr. Aykroyd pushed back his cap and ran a knotted hand through the puffs of thinning hair. "It's persuading, not asking, that ye mean to trade for." Bristol grinned and nodded. Mr. Aykroyd shook his head and slapped his cap into place. He accepted the wine bottle, and a rueful smile rippled the scars and valleys. "Gel, either I be too old for sense, or ye can count two in yer conquests." He sighed. "If ye don't beat all, gel!"

Bristol clapped her hands, green eyes sparkling. "Oh, thank you! Thank you, Mr. Aykroyd!"

He wobbled a finger, and his blue eyes sobered. "Now, mind ye, they's no guarantee! The captain might not agree. He don't warm to hauling women passengers in the first place, and having 'em on deck be courting trouble!"

Bristol smiled confidently. "You'll persuade him, Mr. Aykroyd, I just know you will." Her eyes twinkled.

Mr. Aykroyd stared. "Gel, ye be a natural-born flirt! Ye live in the wrong age. Ye belong in a time where such talent be put to better use than bargaining for a bit of sunshine!"

Blushing, Bristol dropped her eyes, but she felt pleased. From anyone else, such talk would be familiar and offensive, but from Mr. Aykroyd it was a compliment.

He hurried through the door. "I best be fetching Goodwife Able before ye bargain me out of my key ring!" He smiled over his shoulder. "I'll talk to the captain."

Bristol's spirits rose a hundred percent. Humming under her breath, she removed her cloak and hood and sat down to the tray waiting atop her trunk. Immediately her pleasure diminished.

Scouse again. The concoction of finely pounded biscuit, bits of salt beef, and potatoes boiled in pepper appeared to be a great favorite of the crew's, but Bristol regarded it with distaste. She wondered what Goody Able had eaten for dinner; definitely not scouse. Nor duff, that awful sabbath dish which the crew treated as a savory delicacy; as nearly as Bristol could determine, it consisted of a mound of flour boiled in seasoned broth, then drowned with thick molasses. She made a face and stirred the scouse with her spoon, her appetite vanishing.

She pushed away the tray when Goody Able returned, unable to force another bite. Jane Able swept into the cabin, her moon face glowing with high color, and her small eyes lively. She glanced at the half-eaten scouse and wrinkled her nose.

"We had roast mutton and goose and ham slices. Delicious!" Jane swirled out of her cloak, ignoring Bristol's open-mouthed stare. "I can't imagine why you refused such a delightful evening . . . the captain is quite charming!" Jane inched past the trunks to her cot. "And so educated," she enthused. "Look!" Jane brandished two heavy books. "Jean Pierre was kind enough to lend us these from his personal library."

Jean Pierre? Goodwife Able was permitted first names, but Bristol was restricted to "Captain La Crosse"? Bristol's lips thinned and her eyes narrowed to angry slits. La Crosse appeared determined to humiliate her at every opportunity.

"Now we'll have something to occupy our minds while we sew. One can read while the other embroiders. We'll take turns." Jane examined the titles. "I believe we'll begin with this one. It's a persuasive argument against papist doctrine. The other presents arguments for and against kneeling to receive Communion. Jean Pierre promises both are excellent and elevating."

Bristol swallowed. "That's what . . . Jean Pierre . . . claims, is it?" This was astounding. Jane looked ten years younger. "You . . . you found Captain La Crosse *charming?*" Helplessly Bristol wondered if they were speaking of the same person. A charming Jean Pierre La Crosse did not tally with the man she'd shared a dinner with.

"Indeed! I do hope the dear man invites us again soon." Jane lay back on her cot and turned serious eyes to Bristol. "I only wish Herman could meet Jean Pierre. They have so much in common."

Bristol couldn't imagine what that might be. Jane's husband emerged such a meek, mild creature in Jane's descriptions. "I thought Herman was a farmer," she replied incredulously. La Crosse must have bewitched Jane; there didn't seem any reasonable explanation for what Bristol's ears were hearing.

"He is, he is." Jane waved an impatient hand. "But when I return from England, Herman and I intend to invest in a small business." Jane traveled to London to receive an inheritance from a distant uncle. Her nasal voice sounded wine-drowsy. "Perhaps some form of shipping," she mused aloud. In a few minutes a rousing snore rose from Jane's cot.

Bristol extinguished the lamp, brushing her long hair in the darkness. How in all of heaven could Jane possibly have thought the captain anything but vulgar and boorish? What had they discussed to produce such a glow in Jane's pinched cheeks? Bristol frowned in irritation. A twinge of something very like jealousy pricked her heart. "What nonsense!" she muttered, flinging her brush into the trunk and tossing herself onto the cot. Sourly she wagered Jean Pierre La Crosse hadn't taken Goody Able into his arms when she attempted to depart.

Bristol flung herself onto her side, pressing her face against the rough pillow. Her fingers reached to touch her pewter cup, and she tried to imagine how the fields in Salem Village must look now, with the snow melted and spring in the air. But she couldn't concentrate. Jean Pierre's image teased her mind, and she remembered his lean, hard body pressing against her breasts and hips. Abruptly she pounded the pillow with a fist.

She loathed him, so why did his face appear to haunt her night after night? This wasn't the first time she'd tossed awake thinking about the handsome captain. An embarrassed flow of warmth rose along her body, and suddenly she discovered herself remembering Caleb and the settler's cabin. A confused tumble of feelings whirled through Bristol's head. She didn't know how she felt about Caleb. Enough time had passed that she realized how unreasonable she'd been, demanding that he give up his inheritance. Still, the ugly words had been spoken, and she didn't know how deep a rupture she'd caused. Or whether she still cared for him, or how much.

As usual, Bristol drifted to sleep thinking about Caleb Wainwright. But a different man dominated her dreams. He stroked her quivering dream flesh, his searching mouth bent to her parted lips . . . but the face was not Caleb's. The man warming Bristol's sleep stared into her face with gray eyes . . . and a scar streaked his jaw.

She awoke with an irritated sense of vague longing and frustration, producing an annoyance that lasted until Mr. Aykroyd unlatched the door. He offered the women their morning beer and slabs of bread and cheese. Then he placed his hands on his hips and looked at Bristol with a twinkle in his blue eyes.

Bristol's mouth flew open, and she cried out in happiness, "You did it!" Had the trunks not obstructed her path, she'd have flung her arms around his neck no matter what Jane thought. "Oh, thank you! Thank you!"

Jane lifted a quizzical eyebrow. "For what, if I may ask?" Her tone was stiff. Mr. Aykroyd's appearance ruffled Jane's nerves. She'd confided to Bristol that she fully expected Mr. Aykroyd to knife them in their cots before the voyage ended.

"We can go up on deck!" Bristol almost shouted, her excitement pinking her cheeks. "We haven't seen sunshine in over a week!" Immediately she began stuffing handfuls of red curls beneath her dust cap. She loosened her apron sash, pleased at the sudden eagerness lighting Jane's face.

Mr. Aykroyd lifted a hand. "Now, slow down, little gel. They's conditions." Bristol froze. "Ye aren't to speak to any of the men. Ye are to stay put on yer stools and not walk about. Ye are not under any circumstances to interrupt the captain unless he addresses ye first. Understood?"

"Aye," they chorused.

His face cracked into a smile. "Then what be the delay? I haven't got all day."

Gratefully they followed Mr. Aykroyd through the passageway and up the stairs, Mr. Speck hovering behind, his sword in hand. On deck, a brilliant sky opened overhead, and the water sparkled as if strewn with diamonds. Bristol sucked in her breath and stared, only gradually becoming aware of an unnatural silence.

She heard the creaks and groans of the ship and the whisper of sail puffing beneath the yards. Animal sounds drifted from the hatches and on-deck pens. Below, a cook roundly cursed an assistant. But not a single man's voice sounded above deck.

Uneasily Bristol glanced to the side. Two men leaned against the foremast, their hard narrow eyes devouring her body as a brisk breeze toyed with her cloak. Bristol snatched the cloak ends and jerked them close. Everywhere her eyes darted, she met hungry stares. It seemed that every man on the ship stood frozen on deck or leered down from above. Beside her, Jane nervously cleared her throat and inched closer to Bristol.

One of the men moved, stepping back when Mr. Speck growled and shifted his sword to a more visible position. Mr. Aykroyd's face tightened into an ugly scowl, and his fingers knotted around the hilt protruding above his breeches. The small group moved toward the elevated quarterdeck, and their shoes striking the planking seemed the only human sound on deck.

A harsh voice roared, "Back to work, you whore-sons! Do you beg for the lash? Have you never seen women before? Scum!" The captain waited at the top of the quarterdeck stairs, his face dark as thunder. He looked into Bristol's eyes with a tight expression, letting her see he understood she had instigated this foolishness and he did not fully approve.

"Captain!" Goodwife Able gushed into an awkward silence. "What a generous gesture. I do appreciate it!" She lifted her hand expectantly.

If Jean Pierre La Crosse felt an additional annoyance at this intrusion into his anger, he did not show it. Instead he swept off his cap and bowed, touching his lips to Jane Able's hand. Jane's cheeks warmed with pleasure. Watching, Bristol hid a smile. Surely no other man had kissed Jane's hand. Mr. Aykroyd was right—Captain La Crosse could indeed be charming when he set his mind to the task.

However, he did not reach for Bristol's hand. Releasing Jane's fingers, he waved both women toward a curtained area behind which waited two stools. The curtain was arranged to afford a magnificent view of waves and sky while concealing the women from the balance of the ship. Jane settled herself and fussed with the folds of her skirt. Bristol's smile widened. To her knowledge, this marked the first incident of vanity Jane had displayed.

Eyes twinkling with droll merriment, Bristol's glance slid toward the captain. For an instant their gaze held, and Bristol recognized an answering flicker in the captain's gray eyes. So, he was not immune to Jane's apparent infatuation. Not that Jane recognized it as such, Bristol thought with a smile.

Holding her lips steady and fighting a bubble of mirth, Bristol lowered her eyes, fearing if she looked at Jean Pierre any longer, she would burst into teasing laughter. The sunshine, the snap of sail above the sparkling water—all combined in a soaring lift of spirits. She felt almost drunk; nothing could spoil this glorious day.

Happily Bristol took her stool and folded her hands demurely in her lap, resisting an urge to arrange her own skirt. She dared an impish glance at La Crosse, who leaned against the rail watching her. He grinned as if he'd read her mind.

Surprising herself, Bristol returned the smile of secret communication. With a slight flush she realized this was the first time she'd smiled at him. The color in her cheeks deepened. What had he said the day they met? "If you are this lovely when you're angry . . . what a beauty you must be with a smile on those lips!" She wondered if he too recalled those words.

Annoyed with herself, she tried to drop her eyes, but his gray stare held her. And as Bristol looked into those smoky depths, her heart quickened, her mouth parted. His eyes were like gray mist, drawing her toward a moist center.

The smile faded slowly from her lips. How long they might have stared at one another, she couldn't guess. A voice drifted from overhead, and the moment was broken. La Crosse peered toward the upper reaches of the mainmast, shading his eyes.

"Sail to starboard! Sail to starboard!" The lookout's shout floated from a canvas-shrouded perch high above.

Jane touched Bristol's arm, her thin lips rounded with curiosity. She'd observed the look between Bristol and Captain La Crosse. "I think . . ." But Bristol shook her head, not wanting a lecture and unable to explain what she did not understand herself. She nodded toward the rail and the activity there, directing Jane's attention from herself.

La Crosse tensed against the railing, extending a hand for the spyglass Mr. Aykroyd slapped into his palm. Pulling the glass full length, he fitted it to his eye and scanned the watery horizon in a slow sweep. The glass fixed. After a moment, La Crosse handed the glass to Mr. Aykroyd, his own eyes remaining on the horizon.

Bristol held her breath, her emerald eyes widening. Don't let it be pirates, she prayed silently, knowing Jane's thoughts matched her own. Both women strained forward, waiting anxiously.

"Do you make her?" La Crosse's rich voice asked quietly.

Mr. Aykroyd lowered the glass. "Aye, sir." He returned the spyglass to La Crosse.

"The *Cadiz*," La Crosse said. He lifted the glass and stared at a distant white patch. His jaw worked, the scar moving rhythmically. A twitch rippled down his thigh.

"Aye," Mr. Aykroyd affirmed.

La Crosse telescoped the glass into his palm, and both men stared silently across the waves. A heavy stillness descended upon the ship; even the animals seemed muted. Every pair of eyes fixed on the distant horizon. Nervously Bristol felt a thickening tension, growing even as the white square grew.

"Are we on schedule, Mr. Aykroyd?" La Crosse's voice cut crisply through the quiet, thoroughly professional, thoroughly businesslike.

"Aye."

"The wind?"

"In our favor. Six knots out of the west, sir, with a light sea running."

La Crosse nodded, smacking the glass softly into his palm. Once, twice, then a pause. Once, twice, then a pause. And again. "We can outrun her," he said, as if speaking to himself.

Mr. Aykroyd agreed, his face expressionless. "That we can, sir."

Nothing on deck moved; not a man spoke. The only sound was a screak of rope and the flutter of overhead canvas. Bristol's eyes ached from staring, and she leaned forward, hardly daring to breathe. She'd overheard enough to understand the *Cadiz* must be a pirate ship. What she couldn't grasp was La Crosse's hesitation. If the *Challenger* could outrun the pirates, why didn't every hand leap to do so?

Jean Pierre La Cross stood at the rail like a stone statue. He might have been alone, unaware of the nearly tangible tension mounting across the ship. He stood wide-legged, lost in private thought. His stony eyes focused on the square of approaching sail, and those eyes looked into memory.

Beside Bristol, Jane lifted a shaking hand to her throat and shifted on her stool. Mr. Aykroyd turned from the sea to the captain, his blue eyes patient. The entire ship quivered with expectation. Everyone held his breath and waited.

The pressure built to fill hearts and lungs to bursting. Bristol's nails cut into her palms. Every eye focused on La Crosse's hand, slowly rising to trace the ridge of scar disappearing into his collar.

"Sanchez," he murmured. Listening, Bristol heard something in his whisper of a caress, almost the eagerness of a denied lover.

Abruptly La Crosse turned and strode to the stairs of the quarterdeck. Slate-colored eyes stared over the silent decks, gauging the multitude of waiting faces. Then he lifted both arms and shouted, "We engage!"

Instantly the tension split in a deafening cheer bursting from every throat. The deck exploded into activity. The planks came alive beneath running feet, and the air vibrated with a hiss of rope and shouting, swearing voices.

Jane Able slid to the deck in a silent faint. Bristol blinked at Jane's crumpled form, the sight not registering.

La Crosse had chosen to fight the pirates! He chose to risk all their lives, and every man on board cheered him. It was unthinkable. And terrifying.

7

"REEF and furl!" La Crosse stated evenly, and Mr. Aykroyd cupped his hands to his mouth, shouting the orders. But the men anticipated the command; already they swarmed the shrouds, climbing aloft. High above, they threw themselves across the yards, hauling at the sail.

By waiting, the *Challenger* gained a vital advantage: she had time to stow canvas, whereas the *Cadiz* needed her sail to catch them. The *Cadiz* would present a far greater target exposure.

"Store spare rigging in the scuppers, batten the hatches, sand the decks," Mr. Aykroyd echoed La Crosse's steady commands. "Arm the guns!"

Shouted orders followed hard one on the other; Mr. Aykroyd's voice boomed above the melee of sound and frantic activity.

Skilled forms swung from the yards, heavy muscles straining and bulging; slowly the sails disappeared. Animal cages and pens vanished into hatches, loose objects were lashed into place. Movable bulkheads came down, mauls and short plugs for leak repair appeared. Men scattered tubs of water over the decks and laid out boarding grapnel both fore and aft. From the gun room came ammunition, and someone passed muskets to all the men.

Distracted, Bristol helped Jane to her feet, and both women watched with white faces. In the excited burst of preparation, they seemed to have been forgotten. A man appeared to strip away their curtain, and another grabbed up their stools, but neither man spoke. They huddled near each other at the rail, uncertain what was expected of them.

"We should go below and pray!" Jane advised, wringing her hands.

Bristol couldn't stand the thought of staying in the

cramped cabin, of not knowing what happened above. She swallowed hard. "I can't do that, Jane."

"I don't know. I don't think we should . . ." Jane broke off, her eyes wide and frightened.

"You go if you like," Bristol said stubbornly, her eyes darting across the activity swarming the decks. "But I have to stay here." Despite a hard kernel of fear, Bristol felt a part of herself swept up in the excitement. She scanned the ship, her eyes focusing on the flurry about the cannon.

Under the gun master's harsh eye and screaming voice, the long guns moved inboard for loading. Men slammed woolen bags of powder into brass muzzles, and a loader tamped the bags home with a long-handled rammer. Next, someone secured the powder by stuffing cloth wadding into the barrels. All along the deck, men juggled twenty-four-pound balls to the barrel mouths, then rolled them into position. Another wadding pack followed the balls into gleaming muzzles.

Now the gun crews leaped forward to man tackle, and they heaved and grunted, hauling the heavy weapons into firing position. Shoving the men aside, the gun master pointed higher or lower, directing the men with hand spikes in raising or lowering the guns, leveling them to fire true.

When the guns met the master's exacting satisfaction, he ordered the powder cartridges pierced. At each cannon, fine-grained, fast-burning powder was poured through the touch hole, and extra balls lashed in place. The guns sat ready for firing.

"Why are they pouring sand on deck?" Bristol spoke more to herself than Jane, but Jane answered.

Bristol's cheeks paled to snow as Jane explained that sand scattered spilled powder, lessening the danger of fire. And sand absorbed blood. "So the decks aren't slippery," Jane finished, her nasal voice a whisper.

Bristol's hand flew to her throat, and she stared blankly at the naked fear in Jane's small eyes. Sand. Blood. Guns. The words raced through Bristol's numbed mind. She blinked and tried to clear her head. Above, the canvas had been cut to short sail and trimmed. The decks were sanded and clear. All waited in readiness.

Bristol whirled and looked out across the water. Across a narrowing distance, she could see men running over the *Cadiz*'s decks as both ships maneuvered cautiously, jockeying for advantageous position. An awareness jolted into Bristol's brain, slicing through the inertia she'd experienced since La Crosse first shouted, "We engage!" She and Jane stood in the open, exposed and vulnerable on the quarterdeck, with no protection.

Her paralysis broken, Bristol grasped Jane's wrist and half-dragged her down the stairs. "We need a place to hide!" Furrowing her brow, Bristol scanned the decks, her green eyes settling on a stack of folded canvas near the stairs leading to the captain's cabin. "There!" she cried, tugging Jane forward. The solid pack of canvas offered an ideal spot; only their heads showed above the pile. From this vantage, they could observe all that happened, with some degree of safety.

In truth, Bristol doubted any space on ship afforded complete protection; a barrage of ball and shot would make the entire ship unsafe. She drew a calming breath and searched for La Crosse, her narrowed green eyes dark with anger. How could he justify this decision? This was an unconscionable action, without defense in her viewpoint.

She couldn't see him, but his crisp orders could easily be heard throughout the ship, shouting over the charged silence of the men. The men waited quietly, clustered around the big guns, touching piles of ball and shot. The fighting would take place to leeward, and additional cannon had been moved accordingly. Those not assigned to the cannon leaned against the rail stroking their muskets or fingering the hilts of glinting swords.

The *Cadiz* closed distance, and she fired, white puffs exploding from her side, the sound reaching the *Challenger* a split second later. Too startled to duck behind the canvas, Bristol watched a scatter of balls hiss into the waves short of the *Challenger*'s bow.

"They're testing for range," the gun master shouted.

"Lie steady," La Crosse commanded. "Hold fire."

Bristol stared at the maneuvering ship. Figures on board the *Cadiz* took form and faces; malevolent-eyed men strained at her cannon, working strenuously to reload. Bristol held her breath until her sides ached, without realizing she did so. Her lip mangled beneath her teeth.

Aboard the *Challenger*, an eerie silence thickened the air. The only noise emanated from groaning rigging and the muted sound of penned animals in the hatches below.

Sudden footsteps jarred into the quiet, and La Crosse ran past the stack of unused sail where Bristol and Jane crouched. He took the quarterdeck steps two at a time and extended the glass, training it on the *Cadiz*' forecastle. "There he is." La Crosse spit. "Sanchez! May he rot in hell!"

He lowered the glass, continuing to stare intently at the

Cadiz. His fists clenched and opened at his sides, curling around the hilt of a curving cutlass. La Crosse turned to Mr. Aykroyd, gray fire burning in his eyes. "This time we'll send that sea vomit to the bottom! No prisoners!"

"Aye, sir." Mr. Aykroyd wiped a grimed sleeve across his brow. His eyes expertly measured the lessening distance between the ships, and he flicked a questioning glance at La Crosse.

"Bring her around, Mr. Aykroyd. Prepare to fire." La Crosse's eyes never left the forecastle of the *Cadiz*. A tall man paced there, dressed in a flamboyant scarlet coat and yellow breeches, a cutlass in one hand and a short knife in the other. A stream of Spanish oaths drifted the distance, spit from a mouth hidden beneath a shaggy black beard.

Mr. Aykroyd's face opened in relief and joy. His voice rang across the silent ship, heightening the tension. "Prepare to fire!" The *Challenger* swung into position, presenting her guns full front, leveling a broadside toward the *Cadiz*.

But before the *Challenger* could fire, a shower of balls whistled overhead, two striking the main deck in jarring explosions of flying splinters. Immediately, half a dozen men ran to douse the smoking holes before surfaces thick with pitch and tar could burst into flame.

Bristol's eyes flared, and the salty taste of blood seeped from beneath her teeth. Inside, her stomach churned in sick dread. Why didn't La Crosse fire? In the name of God, why didn't he fire? Would he wait until the *Challenger* erupted into a ball of flame? She stared toward the *Cadiz*, watching a drift of smoke clear to reveal the concentrated faces of the men working the cannon. Bristol's heart rolled in her chest. They were so close! So close!

Jane's fingers clawed into Bristol's arm, but Bristol felt nothing. Her ears pounded with the drum sound of her pulse, and a wall of dark fear closed on her mind. Her knees turned to water, and she sagged against the pile of canvas like a sack of wet straw. For the first time in her life, it occurred to her that she could die. They could all die.

". . . And the one who is not, shall stand in dark flames," a phantom voice whispered in her head. Unbidden, the words rose, to hang like an omen in her thoughts. Was this the meaning of Tituba's prediction? Would the *Challenger* sink in tarry flame? Bristol's breath tore past sandy lips, and her fingers whitened on the edges of canvas.

"Fire!"

Thunder and flame erupted from the *Challenger*'s leeward

deck. Thick clouds of acrid white smoke enveloped the deck and gunners. Choking, their eyes streaming, the men leaped to reload and aim.

Bristol staggered backward, clutching at the stiff canvas for balance. She blinked through the smoke, scrubbing her eyes and peering frantically toward the *Cadiz*.

As the smoke floated clear, a massive cheer burst from the decks of the *Challenger*. The gunners had scored a direct hit on the mizzenmast of the *Cadiz*. The tall mast rocked and wobbled, then crashed amid snapping strands of hemp tearing free as the mast fell. It smashed across the stern, trailing rope and wood into the waves.

The scarlet figure on the forecastle screamed outrage, and the *Cadiz* answered. A rain of shot and ball whistled toward the *Challenger,* and the top third of the foremast ripped away, falling to the deck with a crash that sent a shudder throughout the entire ship. Beneath the heavy mast top, two men lay in a red pool, crushed beyond recognition.

Bristol bit back a scream. Wherever she looked, devastation met her eyes. Before her horrified gaze, a man spun and clutched his cheek, covering a gaping hole where a musket ball had torn a path. He choked and coughed, spitting blood and teeth across the front of his shirt.

Bristol covered her mouth and turned away, only to see another man shriek and bend to his ankle. A flying splinter had sheared into flesh, ripping it away and piercing bone, exposing a gleam of white and red.

Across the ship, flowers of red blossomed on men's clothing. A loud splintering screech sounded above the din, and all eyes swung upward. Another piece of the foremast tottered and crashed down, landing near the first and bringing a flying trail of rope and splinters. The mast piece crushed down across the thighs of a fallen man. The man struggled to sit up, staring in horror at the red pulp that once had been his legs. His screams faded in the splintering crashes jarring the ship, but someone heard.

The man wearing the black eye patch ran forward, kneeling beside the shrieking creature whose life soaked into wet sand. He shouted something in the man's ear and touched his hair. Then the man in the eye patch lifted his musket and neatly blew away his friend's head. The torso rocked forward, then fell to the deck, and the man in the eye patch raced back to the rail.

Bristol gagged and pressed her hands to her lips, not seeing La Crosse dash forward to the foredeck. But she heard his

95

shouts cutting above the smoke and confusion and saw men leap in response to quickly throw tubs of water on flickering smoky holes. Under La Crosse's relentlessly driving voice, the *Challenger* swung in front of the *Cadiz*, moving across her bow and away from the murderous pirate cannon.

"Fire!" La Crosse screamed, and the *Challenger*'s cannon spit fire and fume before she moved out of position. When the smoke lifted, the *Cadiz*' sail hung in shreds, her foremast neatly halved, with only snapping rigging holding the mast to the deck. The *Cadiz* was mortally wounded.

On the *Challenger*, raw throats cheered and the men crowded the rails, sweeping the decks of the *Cadiz* with musket shot, reloading as fast as humanly possible, and aiming again.

"Fire!" La Crosse shouted, his voice hoarse. "Fire!"

The cannon roared, and when the white cloud of stinging smoke drifted free, a jagged hole appeared, piercing the hull of the *Cadiz*. On her decks, men lay dead and dying. Those able, fired their muskets blindly through wisps of smoke.

Safe now from the aim of the pirate cannon, the *Challenger* rocked closer to the *Cadiz*, men standing ready with grapnel and boarding hooks. Mr. Aykroyd ran the length of the decks, shouting, his hands waving. "The bowsprit!" he screamed against the shriek of splintering wood, popping rope, and musket fire. Men on both ships staggered and fell, others taking their place. "The bowsprit!"

Twenty men sprang to help Mr. Aykroyd capture the sprit of the *Cadiz* as it passed along the *Challenger*'s starboard. With frantic haste they lashed the bow fast to the mizzenmast of the *Challenger*, coupling the two ships. Turning, the men scooped up knives and cutlasses; grapnel and hooks flew to sink into the pirate ship's deck.

With screams of triumph the *Challenger*'s men swarmed down the bowsprit and dropped to the decks of the *Cadiz*. Instantly the air vibrated with a clang and whistle of meeting swords.

Bristol watched with heart in mouth as the battle surged back and forth. The bowsprit connecting the ships served as a bridge, and grim, shouting men fought across the sprit and spilled onto the *Challenger*'s decks. They raged across both ships, the decks running red with blood, the air ringing to the sound of clanging metal. Every space Bristol's wide gaze touched churned with spinning, thrashing fighting men.

She looked down in horror as a hand, lopped at the wrist, spun across the sanded planks, coming to rest inches from her hem. Gasping, worrying her bleeding lip, Bristol squeezed her eyes shut, opening them to fix anxiously on the two men battling back and forth across the forecastle of the *Cadiz*.

Staring intently, her breath burning in her lungs, Bristol imagined she could hear the ring of those two particular swords. She followed the parries and thrusts, staring sickly at the flashing arms and glittering metal. This was the only fight that mattered. If La Crosse fell, Bristol sensed, superstition and fear would turn the tide of battle. Even though each man fought fiercely with his own opponent, she understood that the men on both ships all tuned an acute awareness to the duel on the *Cadiz*' forecastle.

Both captains fought with deadly concentration, as if unaware of the thrashing mob around them. They were well-matched. Sanchez, fierce and powerfully large, met the skilled thrusts of La Crosse with weighty expertise. La Crosse, lean and agile, countered Sanchez with polished lightning thrusts. Their arms rose and fell, slashing, plunging, and they fought with fury up and down the forecastle deck.

Sanchez' scarlet arm lifted and dropped, the power in each stroke driving La Crosse back, back against the railing. The black beard split in a hideous grin of determination and triumph. Straining against the rail, his spine arching, La Crosse moved his sword in swift defensive arcs. The two swords met and held; then La Crosse twisted deftly and spun free of the rail, having turned Sanchez' point from his throat. Gracefully La Crosse whirled and faced Sanchez, cutlass swinging in one hand, his dagger threatening with the other.

Sanchez met the blow with furious effort, his face murderous. But slowly Sanchez appeared to give way, driven backward by the frenzied skill of La Crosse. The swords whistled and quivered at impact.

And held. Both men leaned their weight against the straining metal, the cutlasses tight. Above the swords their eyes met in blistering hatred. Then Sanchez screamed and wrenched the hilt of his cutlass, heaving La Crosse's sword from his hand. The cutlass flew up and over the railing into the waves below.

Bristol shrieked, her scream lost in the cacophony of sound. Faint with dread, she gripped the canvas edges until her fingers ached. Sick inside, she saw the pirate leader smile.

A lazy, evil smile, pink in the midst of shaggy black. Sanchez lifted his arm, slow and deliberate in victory.

Seizing the split second available to him, La Crosse lunged forward, under Sanchez' arm. He gripped Sanchez in tight embrace, allowing no space to maneuver. La Crosse's left hand shoved deep forward, then ripped upward, and a look of vast surprise filled the pirate's eyes. They swayed together, locked in a waltz of death. Black eyes stared deeply into gray eyes. Then La Crosse pushed away, glaring at the dagger hilt protruding from Sanchez' scarlet coat.

The pirate lowered his bearded face, growling and roaring at a deepening wet spreading across his scarlet coat. He blinked and raised cloudy eyes to La Crosse. Then his arm flicked, and the tip of his cutlass slid lightly across La Crosse's chest, opening a pink trail through the flowing white of La Crosse's shirt. Slowly, moving in twitching jerks, Sanchez brought his sword to his forehead in a mocking salute. Then he crumpled to the planks, and a gush of dark blood spurted between his lips.

Bristol fell weakly against the canvas pile, her breath releasing in a dry rush. Thank God! Surely it would end now. The men of the *Challenger* cheered, imbued with fresh spirit, and their yells and cutlasses sounded across the decks of both ships. Wearily Bristol lifted her head.

Instantly a fiery sting gazed her cheek, and her hood blew back from her hair, tearing her dust cap away. Brilliant curls spilled past Bristol's shoulders, catching the slanting rays of a late sun. A shaky hand leaped to her face, then lowered, and Bristol caught her breath at the smear of blood staining her fingers. Dear God! She pressed the torn hood to her cheek, a surge of nausea flooding her mouth. Another fraction of an inch and the musket ball would have ripped open her face instead of merely grazing her cheek.

Stunned, she turned to Jane. "Jane! Did you see . . . ?" Bristol's words died in a strangled gasp. Jane Able sprawled half on the sanded planks and half against the pile of canvas. A wedge-shaped splinter gouged the hollow of Jane's throat, her white collar slowly soaking red. A look of fear and distaste froze Jane's round face. Her empty eyes bulged outrage.

Bristol retched and clutched her stomach, vomiting until her throat burned and rasped. Jane. Jane Able dead? She stared at Jane's limp body in horror, her hand pressing her mouth. When? Bristol had seen nothing, heard nothing. Yet a three-inch splinter had punctured the throat of the woman standing not a foot away.

Trembling violently, Bristol bent and closed Jane's staring eyes, her fingers moving stiffly. She didn't sense the figure behind her until a powerful arm circled her waist with bruising force, dragging her up. A wave of fetid breath blew against her cheek as the man jerked her hard against his chest, holding her like a shield.

For an instant Bristol was paralyzed with shock and fear; then she screamed and beat at the circling arm with her fists, kicking backward as hard as she could. Blood roared in her temples, and her body quivered.

"Help!" Bristol screamed. She couldn't see the pirate's face, only a tar-blacked hand waving a cutlass in front of her body. The man dragged her toward the bowsprit as if she weighed nothing, her thrashing struggle slowing but not stopping him. Above her flying hair he yelled a stream of Spanish boasts, calling attention to his prize.

"No!" Furiously Bristol scratched and struck the rock-hard arm crossing her waist. Through a gap in the fighting she saw Mr. Aykroyd start toward her; then a grinning bloody Spaniard leaped in his path with flashing sword. Desperately Bristol searched the sea of shifting men, looking for La Crosse, anyone to help her. She saw no one.

Above her soared the bowsprit, and she recognized the scent of victory in the man's sour breath and triumphant muttering. Dear God, Bristol prayed, does my path lead to a pirate ship? Her eyes closed in terror, imagining what the Spaniards would do to her. Increasing her struggles, she lashed out, kicking and clawing, thrashing violently against the man's hard body.

Without warning, a hissing whisper sliced past her ear, then a dark head fell against her shoulder, dropped to her breast, and bounced onto the deck, rolling to rest against the mast. A fountain of blood pulsed over Bristol's back, wetting her hair and gown and the side of her face. The arm at her waist fell away, and the pirate's headless torso slid to the deck.

Screaming, both hands pressed to her bloodless lips, Bristol ran to the rail and spun to stare at the jerking body draining into the sand. "Oh, God," she panted. "Oh, my God!" Over and over. She lifted an ashen face and met Jean Pierre La Crosse's steady gray eyes. He saluted her with the bloodied tip of his sword, grinned, and dashed past. Immediately he hurled himself into battle.

Bristol passed a shaking hand across her forehead. Gasping and panting, her wide eyes drained of color, Bristol leaned her weight against the rail. Small fires flickered on the decks of both ships; rigging dangled, wooden splinters littered the planks. And above everything rang the clang and clash of grinding metal, above the moans of wounded men, above the shrieking of splintered ships. Both ships swarmed with a fighting mob. And the smell of powder and sweat hung thick in the air.

Bristol couldn't guess how long she clung to the rail, but when her mind began to thaw, she understood the *Cadiz* had been thoroughly looted and the pirates had been driven back across the bowsprit into the wallowing *Cadiz*.

As the last snarling Spaniard fled the *Challenger*, Mr. Aykroyd rushed to the mizzenmast and lifted a bleeding arm. "Cut her away!" he shouted.

Stained swords hacked the ropes, and the ruined *Cadiz* began a slow drift from the *Challenger*. Men sprawled on her decks, growing fires gnawed her wood, and the jagged hole in the hull yawned black and wet.

Bristol watched with dull eyes. It was over . . . finally over. The sun rested like an orange ball just above the waves. Blinking in amazement, Bristol stared at the dying sun and realized the battle had raged for hours.

But it was not over. Not yet. "Load!" La Crosse's hard voice roared from the forecastle, and the gun masters hastened to rally their men at the cannon. Tired, bleeding bodies grunted, hauling in the big guns.

La Crosse's voice floated to the *Cadiz*, and the pirates waved frantically. Assessing their situation, they sprang to the rail, screaming an outburst of Spanish pleas and curses.

"Aim!" La Crosse shouted.

The remaining pirates rushed to the longboats, wounding each other in a frenzied attempt to lower the boats.

"Fire!" La Crosse screamed.

A wall of flame and smoke erupted from the deck of the *Challenger*, rocking the ship in the water. Streaming eyes stared through a drift of smoke and evening gloom; then every raw throat on board the *Challenger* opened in hoarse victory.

The enemy mainmast cracked, swayed, and toppled with a deafening crash. Fire raced along the decks of the crippled ship, moving closer to the powder magazine, with its store of ammunition and powder and guns.

Every able hand hauled at the *Challenger*'s sail, widening the distance between the two ships. Overhead, a crisp wind fluttered, then caught at the canvas, and the *Challenger* cut through the sea.

Suddenly a tremendous explosion blew up from the *Cadiz*, sending waves of scorching heat to wash the *Challenger*'s decks. Wood and canvas and writhing figures lifted into the air, dark against roaring orange flame, then fell into the water like hailstones.

Bristol leaned against the railing, watching with a dull face. The bow of the *Cadiz* dipped lower and lower. Slowly at first, then gaining speed, the *Cadiz* sank into the water, her stern rising. At the last moment, another explosion belched from the rear decks, lighting a night sky; then the *Cadiz* slipped beneath the waves in a roaring sizzle of flame.

And now it was over. Bristol pried her hands from the railing and turned slowly to survey the wreckage along the *Challenger*'s decks. Trembling fingers reached to touch the scrape along her cheek and felt a line of dried blood. That she had survived with only this minor scratch seemed a miracle; so many lay dead or wounded.

On all decks, men moved slowly, quietly, binding bloodied limbs, dousing the remaining deck fires, taking count of dead and injured. The ship surgeon moved rapidly from man to man, doing what he could, then moving on.

Bristol stepped forward aimlessly, her eyes sickened at the torn cheeks, the missing limbs, the slashed faces and bodies. Her feet slipped in red sand, and her nostrils choked on a thick smell of powder, blood, and fear. "Oh, my God," she whispered, appalled at the utter devastation. "Oh, dear God!"

Stumbling past the pulpy horror beneath the mast top, she stopped to catch a gulping breath. She glanced down, her teeth grinding as she met the gaze of young Master Boyd. The boy's eyes strained from the sockets, and he'd bitten through his lower lip. A thin mewling sound hummed in his throat. Bristol staggered backward, her fists pressed to her mouth. She choked, then screamed, "Doctor! Doctor! Over here!"

An expressionless man smelling of liquor and old sweat rushed forward, his expert eyes sweeping Master Boyd. "Pitch!" he shouted. Someone ran toward them with a boiling pot and set it beside the boy. The boy's wide eyes swung to the doctor, and a thread of spittle leaked from the corner of his mouth.

"My arm . . ." he gasped through bloody lips. "Can you save my arm?" The arm hung by a shred of flesh, severed below the elbow.

"Here, boy." The doctor lifted Master Boyd, ignoring the boy's shriek of agony. "Drink this!" Master Boyd sputtered and strangled. The doctor lifted a quick glance and found Bristol. "Hold him up like this," he commanded.

Bristol stepped back, her face colorless. "I can't!" She

wrung her hands, and sour bile gushed into her mouth. Black dots speckled her vision.

"Do it!"

She sank to her knees in the wet sand and reached shaking hands to prop the boy's back. Blinking frantically, she tried to clear her eyes.

"Steady! Hold him steady!" The doctor yanked a heavy knife from his belt.

Bristol's violently shaking hands refused to steady, so she pulled the boy against her breast, cradling his thin body in her arms, supporting him. "Help us, God," she prayed aloud, "help us now."

The doctor's arm lifted and swiftly dropped, slicing through the string of flesh; Master Boyd's lower arm dropped into the sand. Moving quickly, the doctor's fingers clamped on the boy's shoulder and jerked him forward, plunging the red stump into the pot of boiling pitch.

Master Boyd screamed and screamed, the sound an assault on sane men's souls. Then his small body fell limp against Bristol's breast. The doctor lifted his head toward a hoarse voice calling from the bow, and he struggled to stand.

"Wait!" Bristol pleaded, gasping. "Is he . . . is he dead?" The boy's thin, weightless body didn't move.

The doctor's hard eyes flicked over the boy, and he took a long pull from a bottle before answering. "No. He's fainted." He nodded toward a bandaged man, and the man scooped Master Boyd up. He headed below decks, the boy dangling from his arms.

Bristol dropped her head. Her fists clenched into aching white balls. "I . . . will . . . not . . . cry!" She brushed a furious hand over her damp eyes. "I . . . will . . . not . . . cry!" Gradually she conquered the strangling ache in her throat and pushed to her feet, brushing damp sand from her skirt. Looking up, she glimpsed Jane's shoes protruding from behind the pile of canvas. So many . . . there were so many.

Deep shaking anger choked her breath, rising to consume her mind. This needn't have happened! These people, all of them, could be alive and whole! If . . . Her glittering green eyes swept the deck, this time with purpose, settling on the rear quarterdeck.

Lifting her blood-spattered skirts, Bristol darted toward the stern. She took the steps two at a time, bursting onto the deck in panting fury. She halted, her eyes burning into La Crosse.

"Murderer!" she screamed, pointing a trembling finger. "You killed them as surely as if you put a gun to their heads!" She waved toward the littered decks. "You did this! You could have escaped, but you wanted to fight, and now they're dead! Or maimed!"

La Crosse's head snapped up from the chart he examined with two other men.

"Murderer!" Bristol ran forward and hurled herself on him, mindless in animal fury. Her nails racked his face, digging parallel trails of pink. "You killed Jane and all the rest!" Dry sobs tore her throat.

La Crosse's hands caught her wrists and held her fists against his chest. His slate eyes bored into hers, and the lust of battle and blood smoldered in his stare. For an instant their bodies met, and she felt a quick, hard response thrust into her, the touch of his body searing past her ripped gown.

"Monster!" Bristol screamed, thrashing wildly against him, striking out with fists and feet.

His hoarse voice lashed the men beside him. "Take this wildcat to my cabin!" he ordered.

"No!" Bristol screamed. "Never!" She kicked at the grinning men and spun, her hair flying. Lunging for the rail, she tried to escape. "Never, you hear me? Never!"

The men captured her easily.

The last thing she saw before they dragged her into the dark passageway was La Crosse. He leaned against the inner rail, watching . . . and those flaming gray eyes stripped her clothes away and ravished the tender flesh beneath.

8

FULL darkness descended with the suddenness of night at sea. Deep shadows cast by deck lamps undulated across the torn planking and splintered rigging, illuminating a continuing cleanup operation. All hands labored in the uncertain light, scrubbing decks, restoring items to normal places, cleaning the cannon and locking them into position, assessing damage and beginning minor repairs. Everyone moved with tired steps, but few complained—this too was part of battle; they had been through it all before.

Captain La Crosse ordered tins of rum for every man and double portions of sea biscuit and salt beef. The men ate and drank and worked and recalled the fight with hard-eyed pleasure. Those unable to participate strained to hear and sorely missed the camaraderie of work and battle tales.

The man chosen to guard La Crosse's cabin leaned against the door and cocked an envious ear toward the noise above deck. He flipped his dagger idly, wishing he was topside to hear the stories and work with his hands instead of standing in the silent passageway. He didn't like guard duty. It was one thing to use his knife against a bastard pirate, another thing entirely to turn that knife into the ribs of a mate.

Two of the mates already had tested him, creeping down the dim passageway as if drawn to the woman by an invisible rope. No blood had spilled, but it had been a near thing, and the night had just begun. The man sighed and stroked a stubbled chin. No good ever came of having women on board a decent ship.

His head froze at a whisper of footsteps, and he coiled into a crouch, straightening when he recognized the captain.

"All quiet?" La Crosse passed beneath a flicker of smoky light, weary shadows beneath his gray eyes.

"Aye, sir," the guard answered, standing tall. His hard eyes sharpened with respect and admiration.

"You'll be relieved when the watch changes." La Crosse paused with his hand on the latch. "Have you eaten?"

"Aye, sir."

La Crosse nodded. "And the lady?"

The guard kept his face carefully impassive. "Her sent the tray back. Her say she not be eating in a devil's nest."

La Crosse's smile was tight. "Very well," he said shortly.

Inside the cabin, Bristol listened to the murmur of voices beyond the door. During the passing hours, she'd achieved control of the raging emotion that had sent her running onto the quarterdeck. What was done was done. Nothing could undo the damage or return the dead. She thought of her attack on La Crosse with dull helplessness. He wasn't a murderer, he was a hero. He'd rid the seas of barbarous pirates. But at what cost. At what terrible cost. Could anyone live through the hell on deck and ever again be the person he had been? Bristol couldn't conceive of it.

At the sound of the opening door, Bristol's heart raced and her muscles tensed. Whatever changing emotions she felt toward the battle did not alter her own position. She vividly recalled the lust glowing in La Crosse's eyes. That question could not be resolved by a few hours of rational thought.

But she was ready for him. No one had appeared to light the lamps, but a silvery moon shining in the bank of windows had provided ample light for a search. She'd found what she wanted, and Bristol waited tensely before the windows, both hands curled tightly around the hilt of a cutlass.

From the moment the men pushed her into La Crosse's cabin, she'd known what to expect. And she'd listened to the scuffles outside the cabin door, knowing without question what they signified. Every man on board the *Challenger* would ravish her in an instant, fired by blood and victory. Even the *Challenger*'s captain. Bristol's fingers gripped the sword hilt painfully, and she stared toward the door.

La Crosse paused just inside the cabin, allowing his eyes to adjust to the dim light.

"Don't come near me!" Bristol hissed. She lifted the sword, tilting the blade to catch the moonlight. She wanted him to see that she'd kill before submitting to his rape. She prayed the killing was over, that the elapsed time had deadened his lust. But she would run him through if he forced her.

La Crosse blinked, then laughed.

Nervously Bristol shifted. She didn't know what she'd expected, but definitely not amusement. Angry and uncertain, she frowned toward the rich roll of laughter.

When he could speak, La Crosse shook his dark head, holding the wound on his chest. "Ah, little girl . . . you play the fool once more. *Jeune fille! Mon Dieu!*" Ignoring Bristol's glare, he lit the wall lamp. In total unconcern he moved to the lamp at the desk.

Quickly Bristol stepped back, jerking up the tip of the sword, her heart thudding against her ribs. But La Crosse didn't glance at her. He lit the desk lamp and walked to the door, ordering the guard to send for a meal.

"I'll not eat in this room," Bristol spit.

La Crosse's dark eyebrow rose. "Did I say the meal was for you? Even devils must eat. The food is mine." Impatience tightened his deep voice. Wearily he sank to the edge of the bed. Bristol's wary stare did not leave his face. He rolled his head on his shoulders, stretching with slow tired movements. Lifting a foot to his knee, La Crosse struggled to pull off his boots. He glanced up with a slow grin. "I don't suppose you might offer assistance?"

Bristol's knuckles whitened on the sword hilt. He was beyond rational comprehension—like a chameleon, changing from one mood to another, and each more offensive than the last. She struggled to reconcile the man of the flashing sword and lustful eye with the tired man wrestling his boots. "Never!" she shouted.

His grin widened. "I rather thought not." The boot slid off, and he tossed it to the planks, reaching for his other foot. When both boots lay on the planking, La Crosse sighed. "So. You still see me as a murderer." Extending his feet, he wiggled his toes luxuriously.

Bristol bit her lip. These normal homey actions confused her weary mind. Would a man contemplating rape wiggle his toes? Thoroughly bewildered, she swung suspicious eyes to stare at La Crosse. He didn't seem to expect a comment, and she offered none.

When he stood, she lifted the sword, and her eyes flashed. But La Crosse paid no attention. Instead, he stripped off his shirt, peeling it carefully from his wound, and threw the torn bloodied shirt toward a wooden chest. He walked to a basin of water near the bed.

Bristol chewed her raw lip, the sword heavy in her moist palms. Protesting nerves quivered on edge. Why didn't he get this confrontation behind them? She could not tolerate the waiting. She'd seen the look in his smoky eyes, she'd felt the hard urgency between his legs. That he would come for her, she didn't doubt. The question was when.

Vigilant, her muscles tensed and ready, Bristol watched him through a narrowed sweep of lash. Strong sinews rippled along his back as he leaned over the basin, wringing a cloth in the water.

She shifted uneasily. Despite her fear and loathing, a glimmer of fascination sparked her green eyes. She cleared her throat. La Crosse was the first man she'd observed at close range who was not wearing a shirt, and the sight of his naked skin pulled her eyes like a magnet. She stared at broad, well-developed shoulders and an upper body that tapered to a lean waist. Angry with herself, revolted at her thoughts, Bristol wrenched her eyes away.

Then back. La Crosse winced and uttered a soft sound as the cloth moved over his chest. Silently Bristol watched as he cleaned the wound, unreasonably feeling a twinge of guilt. That is ridiculous, Bristol thought wildly, not understanding her own confusion of emotion. If he needed assistance, wouldn't he call to the guard? Aye, of course he would. Still, she wished he'd turn so she could see for herself how bad the wound was. Not that Bristol cared, she assured herself hastily, but . . . but what would happen to the crippled ship if La Crosse were severely injured? More important, what would happen to her? Would the men respect her safety? No.

She wiped damp palms on her skirt. Her nerves grew more ragged by the minute. Swallowing, Bristol made a noise in her throat. It galled her to satisfy her curiosity, but she had to know. "How . . . how badly are you hurt?" Her voice emerged weak and petulant. Annoyed at her tone, she felt a spot of color appear on her pale cheeks.

La Crosse turned then and smiled, his eyebrow arching in amusement. "So, you can still talk. Your concern is touching, Mistress Adams." Bristol ground her teeth and dropped her eyes to the slash of red cutting through a thicket of dark hair. "I think you'll be disappointed to learn that I will definitely survive. The wound is troublesome but not serious."

Despite herself, Bristol felt a weak tide of relief. She pulled her eyes from his muscled chest and up to the strong face, noting with satisfaction the faint marks of her nails along his cheek. Her gaze lingered on the scar tracking his jaw. He wouldn't have sounded this casual following that wounding.

"Did Sanchez give you the throat wound as well?" she asked abruptly.

La Crosse's smile vanished. His brows met. "Aye," he answered sharply. "Long ago. Hardly a man in these waters hasn't felt the bite of those cutthroats." His voice hardened to grim pleasure. "But never again." He tossed the pink cloth into the basin and touched his chest gingerly.

"But at what cost!" Bristol said bitterly, not looking at the crisp hair curling on his body. "So many men . . . and Jane Able." She shivered, thinking of Jane's torn throat.

La Crosse's smoky eyes darkened. "Goodwife Able's death is to be regretted." He shrugged gracefully. "For the men . . . they understand the risks when they sign on. A certain amount of loss is to be expected. It was far less than it might have been. The men fought bravely and well."

"But it was so unnecessary!" Bristol fought tears of despair pricking her lids. Her fingers tightened on the sword hilt. Glancing down, she suddenly felt vaguely ridiculous. She threatened an imaginary enemy. Here they stood, conversing like normal people. La Crosse hadn't shown the slightest inclination toward raping her, either by word or glance. Still, pride wouldn't let her back down, and a sense of security existed so long as the hard metal lay in her grasp.

Her head jerked as La Crosse called, "Enter."

Mr. Aykroyd carried a tray inside the cabin and set it on the desk. A spotted bandage circled one arm; an earlobe was missing. Bristol offered him a wobbly smile of sympathy, refusing to think about the young boy who normally served the captain's tray.

"Thank you, Mr. Aykroyd." La Crosse summoned a tired smile. "Is it still too early for a complete report?"

"We be knowing more by daylight, sir. I dispatched most of the men to their hammocks, and we be keeping a short watch." Mr. Aykroyd slid a concerned glance toward Bristol, visibly relaxing when he saw she was unhurt. "The *Challenger* be limping, sir, but she don't look to set anchor for repair." His eyes returned to Bristol's tight-lipped glare, then dropped to the cutlass she gripped. Making no comment, he turned an expressionless face back to the captain.

La Crosse had moved and taken his seat at the desk before Bristol realized what he intended. Angrily she stepped against the windows and stared at his naked back. Calmly La Crosse lifted a fork from the tray. "Thank you, Mr. Aykroyd, that will be all."

"Aye, sir." Mr. Aykroyd's blue eyes looked behind the captain at Bristol's stormy expression; his eyes lingered on the cutlass; then he smiled and stepped through the cabin door.

Seething, Bristol felt a resurgence of hot anger. Mr. Aykroyd's smile dismissed her like an impotent child. He wasn't the least concerned that his precious captain might be in danger. And La Crosse! She glared at the flow of muscle along the ridges of his back as he bent to his food. He, too, didn't seem troubled by having a sword pointing at his neck.

She stared at his shining dark curls. She could swing the sword and lop off his head. And he would be as dead as Jane Able . . . as Master Boyd's arm . . . as many of the men from his own ship.

Bristol stared at his neck until her eyes ached. And all the while, La Crosse behaved as if he were alone in the room. He ate with relish, consuming every bite of the steaming mutton and pearly mounds of rice. Wishing she could neither see nor smell the food, Bristol yearned toward a small dish of orange sections that emitted a tangy scent so tantalizing she felt faint. Her stomach growled, and abruptly she recalled she hadn't eaten since last night.

Sighing, Bristol quietly lowered the sword point. Aye, she loathed him; she hated him. But this man had saved her from the pirate. This man's skill had won the battle. And Bristol Adams was not a killer. Not unless he threatened her, attempted to take her against her will. Green eyes lingered on the dish of oranges. If La Crosse made a single motion toward her, just one, she'd run him through in an instant. The oranges smelled of a spicy heaven. And she'd kill him without a pang of remorse. None.

La Crosse swallowed his wine and bit into an orange slice, the delicious aroma drifting back to tickle Bristol's nose. She choked on a burst of moisture watering her mouth.

"Please!" Her voice was too loud. "Give me a slice of that orange!" Her mouth watered unbearably, and her stomach growled so loudly she knew he must hear. How could she have refused the earlier tray with such lofty disdain?

"No," La Crosse answered calmly. Deliberately he finished the remaining orange wedges.

Bristol blinked at the rough cord tying his dark curls. She stared at the empty dish and fought to control a biting disappointment. Frustrated and hungry, she shifted the cutlass between her palms. "Why not?" she blurted in a small voice, sounding foolish even to herself. The oranges were gone; he truly had eaten them all.

La Crosse swiveled in his chair, examining her with steady gray eyes. "Mistress Adams. I grow weary of your childish demands." He studied her, the eyes hardening. "Little girl, it is time you grew up." Blotting his lips with a square of linen, he rose from the chair to tower over Bristol. A hard center leaped in the smoke-colored eyes. He extended a hand. "Give me the sword," La Crosse commanded softly, but there was nothing soft in his face.

"No!" Instantly Bristol's mind sharpened and her eyes narrowed. "No." She looked up at him, tightening her grip on the hilt and catching her breath at the expression on his face.

The smoky eyes turned to slate. "Give me that sword," he repeated, soft danger in his voice.

Bristol stepped backward, the sword heavy in her shaking hands. "No," she whispered, and her voice cracked. As long as she commanded the cutlass, she believed she had a chance.

La Crosse advanced a step, forcing her back. He extinguished the desk lamp, plunging his face into shadow while Bristol's features shone in the light of the wall lamp. Nervously, eyes wide, Bristol retreated around the desk, waving the cutlass in sweeping arcs before her torn skirt. Now it was she who stepped into shadow and La Crosse's strong hard face that leaped forward under the illumination. Bristol chewed the inside of her cheek. La Crosse was staring at the rapid rise and fall of her breast, his eyes flat and hungry.

"Never!" she spit, her throat dry. "I'll kill you first. I mean it, La Crosse!" She grasped the sword with both hands, stepping backward. "I mean it," she repeated in a strangled whisper.

La Crosse followed steadily, step for step, forcing her back. Without removing his eyes from the swell of her breast, he lifted an arm and snuffed the wall lamp, throwing the room into sudden darkness. Bristol blinked frantically, willing her eyes to rapidly adjust to the wash of pale moonlight flooding into the cabin.

She screamed as powerful hands shot forward in the darkness and caught her wrists, whirling her hard against the wall. The cutlass clattered to the planks, and Bristol's hope shattered with the sound. Fear and dread shocked her mind as he pinned her arms above her fiery head, his lower body crushing her into the wall.

"No!" Bristol gasped. She fought to jerk her hands free and could not. Bucking her hips foward, she desperately tried to throw his body away from hers. Instead she met a solid, unmoving scald of heat. A hard bulge strained his breeches, growing against her. "No . . . oh, no." Bristol sagged in despair. Then, frantic to escape, she increased her efforts against him, fighting, trying to arch away from his touch. Helplessly she kicked out, but his body held her fast, and she felt his erection, stiff and demanding, press into her body. Against her cheek, his breath beat in short bursts, warm and smelling of wine. Then searching lips covered hers, bruising her mouth with savage force.

Gasping, panting for breath, Bristol wrenched her head violently to the side. She screamed, "No! Please!"

La Crosse was past hearing. Sweeping her into powerful arms, he crossed to the bed and dropped her into a patch of silver moonlight. He stepped back, his hands tearing at his breeches string.

Desperate and terrified, her heart a thundering drum in her head, Bristol scrambled toward the edge of the bed, her knees sliding in a tangle of skirts. La Crosse's hand bruised into her shoulder, and he tossed her back onto the bed, his fingers catching the throat of her soiled gown and ripping down, tearing away her gown and apron as if they were sewn of paper. Shamed and frightened by her sudden nakedness, she fluttered her hands in a vain effort to cover herself; a dry sob broke from her throat, and she trembled like the last leaf of summer, terrified by his strength and purpose.

La Crosse halted, standing over the bed, his naked body

catching fingers of moonlight. He sucked in his breath and stared. *"Mon Dieu!"* His voice emerged in a hoarse whisper. His hungry eyes devoured Bristol's lush body bathed in moonlit tints of ivory shadow. *"Mon Dieu!* Even bloody and soiled you are a beautiful woman!"

Bristol's pleading eyes closed, shutting out his face, and her fingers curled into helpless fists. Nothing she did or said could prevent what he was about to do. A desperate mind raced through a wild jumble of thought. She could not match his strength and lust-driven power. Terrified with shame and fear, Bristol squeezed her eyes. How could she endure this? How?

Suddenly she recalled the settler's cabin. In less than a minute, La Crosse would finish with her—so it had been with Caleb, so it must be with all men. Thinking of this steadied Bristol's churning mind. Anything could be borne for one minute. Even this. Even this terrible horrifying violation of everything decent and private . . . even this could be endured for one small minute.

La Crosse knelt on the bed and bent over her, capturing her wrists and pinning them above her head. Bristol's eyes flared and her heart pounded wildly in her breast. Remember, she screamed within her mind, lie quietly, and it will all be over in a minute. One tiny minute!

Clenching her teeth, she forced her body to go limp. The longer she resisted, fought the inevitable, the longer this nightmare would continue. Resolutely she stared at the ceiling, her naked body shivering in revulsion and fright.

For an instant La Crosse paused, his gray eyes hungering over her quiet curves; then he lowered himself beside her. At the shock of his heated body stretching along the length of her own, Bristol drew in a sharp breath. She felt his erection throbbing against her bare thigh, and she bit hard on her lower lip, but she ceased her attempts to wrench away from him.

Still holding her helpless, La Crosse peered into her resigned face, and he murmured into the darkness. "Ah, so that's how it is," he whispered softly. "But Jean Pierre La Crosse does not take an unwilling woman."

Instantly Bristol's heart leaped with hope, and she looked into his eyes, the beginnings of gratitude shining from beneath her lashes. But she'd misunderstood his intent. His hand lifted, and then she felt the searing touch of his fingers cupping the soft mound of her breast, stroking her skin with a light warm caress. Bristol gasped and writhed on the bed.

Caleb Wainwright had done nothing like this! Her green eyes widened and her breath seemed to stick in her throat. "Don't!" she breathed harshly, trying to wrest from his hand. Instantly his gentle touch disappeared, and La Crosse caught her roughly, pulling her hard against his naked chest.

The shock of their naked skin meeting swept her body like wildfire. The warm strength of his broad chest sent Bristol's heart thudding wildly, her pulse hammering in her ears. She fought desperately for control. Quietly! her mind shrieked. Lie quietly and let this abomination finish! Shaking, her mind off balance, Bristol forced herself to lie in rigid stiffness.

He laughed softly, his face hidden in shadow. His hand returned to her quivering breast, warm and light. Then, holding her wrists securely over her tangled hair, La Crosse lowered his head, and Bristol gasped as his warm lips found her nipple. Her mouth fell open in shock, and her green eyes squeezed tightly. A bolt of tingling sensation shot through her body as his wet tongue circled her breast, teasing, coaxing.

A choked sob tore from Bristol's throat, and her breath came in shallow, rapid gulps. "Don't. Don't," she pleaded. But his dark head brushed her chin, moving. A skilled tongue caressed her breasts, tantalizing, coaxing, calling forth a responding heat from her trembling limbs. To Bristol's horror, she felt her nipples harden, rising pink and ripe to his lips.

A frightening weakness flowed through every muscle in her suddenly flaming body. His naked chest brushed her stomach, moist and strong and burning where he touched. Beneath his stroking fingers, her breasts tingled, and a bewildering sense of urgency began in her thighs and swelled, sweeping her breath away.

"No," she moaned. "No." His lips and tongue whispered to her skin, and she wasn't certain if she resisted La Crosse or her own rebelling flesh. Something overwhelming and scalding and mind-sweeping fired her body, intense and demanding release. Her breasts rose to his expert lips and hands, lifting as if of their own accord.

She whimpered into the damp pillow as La Crosse rolled onto her, his knee guiding her legs wide apart. And her breath caught in strangling noises when his hand discovered the silky forest between her legs, moving in a slow, teasing search. Her body dampened in a sheen of fire as his fingers probed and stroked, and her mind darkened to blind thrashing need. Vaguely Bristol realized her hips moved in a primitive rhythm of instinct, an inborn awakening to ancient mystery.

His face rose above her, and for an instant she met his smoldering gray eyes; then his mouth burned against her lips and his naked chest crushed against her breasts. When his bruising mouth released her, Bristol's breath was as ragged and gasping as his own.

Suddenly her arms were free, and they dropped to circle his neck. Her lips opened to his with the urgency he'd created; her frantic body strained against hard flesh with the plunging need he'd drawn from every trembling nerve. Blind yearning filled the very fiber of her aching body. Bristol's sensual nature exploded into life, wakened by his skilled touch with all the intensity of a long-dormant instinct craving expression.

He stroked her shuddering body and kissed her hard nipples until Bristol's body writhed in mindless abandon. All the tensions and frustrations of that empty moment in the settler's cabin burst from her mind and body. She moaned helplessly, her moist body flaming beneath his fingers, a damp fire rising on satiny skin. His warm hand curved over her stomach and dropped between her legs, exploring, teasing, searching, until Bristol fought for each gasping breath and believed her heart would race from her breast.

In her ear, La Crosse's rich husky voice whispered in French, his lips moving against damp tendrils. His warm, panting breath on her cheek turned Bristol dizzy with need. Her lips sought his, and her arms tightened around his neck. She strained against his lean hard body, pushing her breasts against the mat of crisp dark hair.

"Now?" he whispered, moving against her, holding her to his body.

"Aye," Bristol gasped, "Oh, aye, aye! Please!" The whispered groans tumbled from her aching lips. Every rational thought melted, and she understood nothing but her own demanding emptiness, the urgency to fill herself with this man, to take what her body craved.

Only when her need had risen nearly to a scream did La Crosse lift himself over her and thrust into the throbbing honeyed space.

"Aye," Bristol screamed, her mindless hips rising to match his rhythm. "Oh, aye," she groaned. Her tangled hair fell back and her eyes closed, and tortured breath rushed past her parted lips.

Her fingers tightened on La Crosse's rippling shoulders, and some buried part of her mind recognized that he paced himself, moving in deep rhythmic strokes, adjusting to her

113

own instinctive cadence. And then faster and faster and harder and more urgent. Until an expanding universe spun behind Bristol's lids, pouring color and sensation, rocking and glowing. And then her universe narrowed and cracked into a mind-sweeping explosion. Her body shuddered and contracted and erupted into ecstasy.

Panting for breath, her breast heaving, Bristol fell limp, and La Crosse's dark head dropped to her shoulder. Together they lay tangled in the damp bed, bathed in a shimmer of cooling perspiration. Waiting for racing hearts to quiet.

Bristol held his head to her breast. She drifted in a warm sea, her mind empty, her body heavy and sated. This was the true mystery of men and women, she mused drowsily. A blissful draining of tensions and need . . . an explosive rapture.

Gently La Crosse shifted. He blotted his seeping wound, then stretched wordlessly beside Bristol, gathering her soft yielding body into his arms and cradling her head on his shoulder. In a moment she felt the deep regular rise and fall of his chest and knew he slept.

Gradually, as if awakening from a warm clinging dream, Bristol's senses cleared. Her eyes widened in the darkness, her nostrils aware of the man and a musky scent of love. Dear God! What had she done! Her body stiffened in his arms, rigid with shock.

In the shadowy moonlight, her cheeks burned in hot shame. She bit the back of her hand to keep from crying out. She'd paced this very room for hours fearing La Crosse and his lust. But La Crosse had not raped her . . . Bristol had *begged* him to take her, to use her quivering body.

She moaned softly, shaking her head in denial. But years of truthful upbringing refused to allow her comfort. The truth accused. How could she ever again live with herself, knowing she'd called out to him, knowing she'd wanted him like nothing else in her life? Bristol groaned and rocked on the bed.

Then slowly, careful not to disturb La Crosse's even sleep, she inched from his arms and out of the bed, unable to bear his closeness another minute.

Shivering and offended by a blaming nakedness, she bent and held the shreds of her gown to the dim window. Heart sinking, Bristol dropped the gown to the planks. She searched in the darkness, finding La Crosse's wardrobe and pulling at the wooden doors. Taking the first shirt her fingers touched, she hastily covered her nakedness. The shirt hung to her knees, and cuffs dangled below her hands.

She pushed at the sleeves, a thousand shamed accusations burning through her mind. How did this happen? She bowed her head. How?

A sliver of moonlight glinted on the blade of the discarded cutlass, and Bristol bent, lifting the sword with trembling hands. She touched the cold metal, pressing the edge against her finger until a bright drop welled in the pale light. Moving in numbed jerking movements, Bristol touched the point of the sword between her breasts. The carved hilt rested solidly against the planking, and the tip pressed sharp to prick her tender flesh. She stared down. All she need do was fall forward.

Bristol stood very still, staring at the cold gleam of metal, listening to the rising noise of her heartbeat. Her mind refused to function; she couldn't unravel the full meaning of what had passed between La Crosse and herself, but she knew this day—the fighting, the killing, and Jean Pierre La Crosse—had altered everything she had believed herself to be.

She lifted her eyes to the slumbering form in the bed, seeing a glow of moonlight on La Crosse's shoulder. Because of him, she now recognized that moment with Caleb in the settler's cabin had been a mockery. There was more—so much more—than Caleb could give. But she'd lain with Caleb in love. At least for a while she'd thought it was love.

The man in the rumpled moon-washed bed represented no tender feelings—only blind desire. And yet it was he who had awakened a deep sensuality, he who had shown her the woman she could be. Bristol's face paled, and she battled a misting of tears.

How long she stood frozen in the silent darkness with the sword at her heart, she didn't know. What Bristol finally understood was that she would not kill herself; the will to live beat too strongly. She would endure a lifetime of guilt and regret. Knowing that once her rebellious body had lifted to La Crosse's thrusts, had longed for his lips, had cried "Please"—this knowledge would burden her soul all her days, would signal a break with her Puritan background that might never heal. In the hours since morning, she had changed, had begun to grow up, and the process was painful.

Blinking rapidly at the cold sword, Bristol quietly lowered the cutlass and stumbled aimlessly toward the bank of windows. I will not cry, she reminded herself. Her fists balled and her jaw knotted. Tears solve nothing! Change nothing! She rubbed her aching eyes until the unshed tears receded, leaving a tight pain in their place.

Sinking into the desk chair, Bristol curled her legs under her, blanketing her body beneath the long ends of La Crosse's shirt. It smelled like him, clean and mannish and faintly salty.

Bristol closed her eyes. "What I cannot change, I will accept," she repeated under her breath. Opening her eyes, she stared dully at the black water outside the windows. She couldn't change this new sensual image of herself—could she accept that? Bristol dropped a pounding head into her hands.

Dear heaven, had she ever endured a more destructive day? She couldn't recall one. Drawing a deep shivering breath, Bristol pushed at her hair, feeling clumps of dried blood matted between the long strands. On her cheek streaked a crusty line of her own blood, in her hair clung a pirate's dying blood, and across her breasts the blood from La Crosse's wound. So much blood!

Brooding, her emerald gaze stared moodily at the moon-silvered waves beyond the window. Her mind spiraled back in time, drawn by thoughts of blood, and she saw the bright smear staining Caleb Wainwright's cloak in the settler's cabin. A lifetime ago, it seemed.

She tried to sort out her feelings for Caleb, but already he seemed a shadowy memory figure, dim and pallid next to the man sleeping across from her. What did that mean? She had genuinely thought she loved Caleb; had it been only a girlish infatuation? The thought of him had the power to pain, but was it love or guilt?

There were no answers. "I want to go home," Bristol whispered. Caleb had said he would come for her—would he still, considering the way she'd left him? "I want to go home, to the world I understand," she whispered to the rolling waves trailing the ship. "Please, Caleb, come for me and take me home." She watched the black water until her eyes drooped; then she shifted in the desk chair, her head dropping into her arms. "Come soon," she murmured, her eyes closing.

Wild dark dreams of fighting figures spun in her tired mind, sleeping visions of swords, and thundering guns and terrifying danger. Once again Bristol bent above Jane Able, gagging at the bloodied throat. Once again a pirate's arm circled her waist and dragged her backward through a mob of ringing swords. Bristol opened her mouth and screamed,

116

but no sound emerged. No one saw the pirate's hand roughly fondle her breasts as he dragged her inexorably toward the bowsprit. Not a face turned when the pirate threw her to the deck and ripped away her clothing. Bristol moaned. Not one person glanced toward her silent screams or remarked the dirty hand reaching toward her body.

Groaning, Bristol fluttered and opened her eyes. Immediately an evil-smelling hand clamped hard across her lips. She jolted awake, her eyes flaring in terror. The fingers bruising into her breasts were not a dream! Fetid breath blasted her face. The leering, drunken man tearing at La Crosse's shirt was very real.

9

THE drunken man swayed and stumbled in front of the desk chair. His rum-rancid breath grunted into Bristol's face. One hand muffled her screams, the other crawled along her inner thigh, digging into soft flesh. Bristol clawed and scratched and clung fiercely to the chair. If he succeeded in dragging her to the floor, she would be lost—he'd be on her in an instant.

Her terrified eyes rolled toward La Crosse's sleeping figure, praying he would wake; she despaired of winning this silent battle without help. But La Crosse's chest rose in even breaths.

Wrenching violently in the chair, Bristol fought to draw away from the brutal searching fingers. Thrashing, hitting; her efforts to protect herself only served to excite the man further.

He dropped to his knees, panting wafts of rum-soaked breath, and his bearded face darted toward her breast. Rotten teeth tore savagely at La Crosse's shirt. Bristol yanked backward with a stifled scream, a scream not audible a yard's distance from the chair. The man's dirty bruising fingers climbed higher inside Bristol's leg, and a sense of hazy white

117

panic blew through her mind. Her pulse thundered so loudly, it seemed impossible for La Crosse not to hear. Jean Pierre! her mind shrieked. The man's teeth ripped open the shirt, and one pale breast fell forward, exposed to his glittering eyes. A dark-stubbled face split in a grin.

No! Bristol's silent mouth screamed against his reeking palm.

Blindly she stretched her hand along the desktop, groping across the polished wood until her fingers found La Crosse's meal tray and touched the cool silver of his fork. She grasped the fork tightly, and swung her fist with all the force she could muster. A flash of silver arced down, plunging into the man's fleshy shoulder.

The man screamed in surprise and pain, one hand leaping to the quivering fork, the other smashing across Bristol's face. Red agony exploded near her right eye, and Bristol's head snapped to the side, her hair flying.

Following the motion of the blow, she scrambled from the chair with a shout of pain and terror, spinning toward the bed.

The man lay sprawled at her feet.

Bristol froze in a crouch and looked upward, meeting smoky eyes. La Crosse stood above the crumpled man, a wooden pin in his hand. Even in the dim moonlight, she saw the thunderous outrage on his face.

"That man . . ." Bristol panted, "he . . ." Everything had happened so quickly, it took her a moment to understand it was over. She lifted the torn flap of shirt, covering her breast, and she touched a shaking hand to the edge of her eye, already beginning to swell where the man had struck her.

Swiftly La Crosse stepped into his breeches and threw open the cabin door. The guard lay unconscious in the passageway. "Watch!" La Crosse roared up the steps leading to the decks. He returned to the cabin and lit the lamps, then cast a hard searching look at Bristol. "Are you hurt?" Nodding at Bristol's babbled assurances, La Crosse threw a blanket over her shoulders, covering the tremor shaking her body.

Then he lifted her face with a thin smile. "Thank God you weren't armed with a fork earlier in the evening." He gestured toward the silver handle protruding from the man's shoulder. "Or that might be me. Swords, I know. Forks are another matter."

Understanding he tried to cheer her, Bristol managed a wobbly smile of gratitude. La Crosse stroked her cheek with his thumb and returned to the doorway, leaving Bristol to stare at the fallen man. She touched the lump rising near her eye, mentally comparing it to the knot bubbling up on the man's head. Shivering, she turned toward the sound of running feet filling the passageway.

Several men crowded the doorway, staring down at the battered guard, then swinging toward the man stretched on the planks inside the cabin.

La Crosse gestured with the wooden pin. "Take the guard to the hold and put him in irons. When he wakes, tell him he'll stay there three days with no food or water." The wooden pin pointed to the man on the cabin floor. "Put that one in irons." La Crosse's tone was ice. "When he wakes, tell him he'll receive twenty lashes at noon tomorrow."

Expressionless, the men dragged the limp body from the cabin.

Bristol watched, and her eyes glittered like emerald chips. While La Crosse assigned a new guard, her mind pulled up the memory of her own lashes. And she estimated the damage twenty strokes would do. Her anger peaked, and she shuddered.

Weak, she sank to the desk chair and accepted the glass of wine La Crosse pressed into her fingers. She gulped it, welcoming the explosion of warmth in her stomach. Gradually her heart began to quiet.

From the depths of her soul, Bristol Adams yearned for home, for the safety of Noah's snug house and her own secure place in it. She violently rejected what she'd seen of the bigger world. The world seethed with evil undercurrents. There wasn't a safe place. If only she could be home now, nothing would ever again tempt her to jeopardize that security. She didn't understand this larger sphere; she wanted Salem Village. Bristol desperately wanted to be home. Home!

Guessing the emotion that pinched her expression, La Crosse touched her hair lightly. "Back to bed," he said. "You'll be safe there." His rich voice was gentle, but allowed for no argument.

Bristol's troubled eyes rose. She'd nearly fallen on a sword from shame of sharing his bed. "I . . ."

"Get into that bed, or I swear I'll throw you in!" La Crosse roared, his patience evaporating. "I've had enough trouble for one night!" He advanced a step, the wooden pin still in his hand.

Bristol's wide eyes lifted from the pin to his stern face. She didn't believe he'd actually strike her, but . . . She scuttled

119

across the room and scrambled over the bed, pressing herself flat to the wall on the far side.

La Crosse looked at her before extinguishing the lights, seeing the torn shirt and the dark swell beside her eye. He smiled and shook his head, then climbed into bed. "Come here," he said softly, opening his arms.

Bristol hesitated, waging a losing battle with herself. She was frightened and longing for the warmth and protection of his strong arms. Still . . .

"Come," he whispered in the darkness.

And she went to him, breathing a tiny sigh of secret relief as his arms closed around her, gentling her against his body.

But she didn't sleep immediately. She stared at his moonlit hand, feeling the weight of his arm where it crossed her body. In sleep, his tapered fingers lay relaxed and open, like a child's, and Bristol found this simplicity oddly disturbing. His open hand, the fingers curled, seemed vulnerable somehow— an attitude Bristol did not associate with Captain Jean Pierre La Crosse.

Bristol pressed his hand flat, feeling awkward at touching him.

Surprised, she kept her hand on his for a moment, confused by the tightening in her stomach. Burning memories deviled her mind, and she was suddenly acutely conscious of his smooth naked body along her back.

Bristol's mind whirled, and she battled a wave of sensual images lapping the rocky shores of her thoughts. Quickly, as if she touched hot embers, she snatched her hand away and closed her eyes, shutting out the sight of his skin.

Never had she experienced such wild swings of emotion in so short a period. A few hours ago she'd been ready to kill herself; now she lay spooned against La Crosse's body, grateful for his warmth and protection.

Distraught at being unable to sort out her emotions, Bristol chewed a thumbnail and glared into the darkness. Only gradually did she give way to a deep exhaustion and the comfort of the softest bed she'd slept in since leaving home. Dear God, she longed for home!

She awoke to the dim light of predawn tinting the cabin in shades of pink and gold. Momentarily Bristol forgot where she was, blissfully aware only of the softness beneath her body and a comforting warmth curled around her back.

Her green eyes snapped open in jolting memory. Carefully she peeked at a smooth, hard shoulder. What was warm and protective in the darkness became a hideous embarrassment when exposed to daylight.

Hastily Bristol squirmed from La Crosse's arm and rolled against the wall, opening a space between them. But the heat of his naked body and his rich male smell still reached her.

La Crosse groaned and stretched awake. He rubbed a blue sheen on his chin and opened his eyes with a smile. Looking at her from his pillow, he said, "Good morning, Mistress Adams." His smile turned to a grin. "Or may I call you Bristol? It seems a bit stiff to stand on formalities now, doesn't it?"

Grinning at the flame of pink springing to Bristol's cheeks, he rose and flexed his body, the muscles rippling smoothly. Filled with the purpose of a new day, La Crosse strode across the cabin and tugged a rope, then set out a basin and long razor. Seeing Bristol's averted gaze, he laughed and tugged on his blue breeches.

Only then did Bristol dare to look in his direction, watching as he slid into a fresh white shirt with flowing sleeves. La Crosse appeared totally unselfconscious, as if waking beside a woman were nothing out of the ordinary.

Finding this thought vaguely irritating, Bristol frowned. An image of Goodwife Sable Horton and the arch look Sable had directed to La Crosse drifted into Bristol's mind to annoy and perplex. Obviously Captain La Crosse did not lack for female companionship. And why should he?—he was strikingly handsome. For reasons she refused to examine, Bristol pushed away all thoughts of Sable Horton, giving her head an angry toss.

Mr. Aykroyd responded to the rope tug, bringing hot water and two mugs of steaming beer. For an instant his sparkling blue eyes strayed to Bristol, who sat in the bed, lost within La Crosse's floppy shirt.

She accepted the foaming beer with downcast eyes, scarlet burning on her cheeks. But if Mr. Aykroyd thought it strange to leave a furious woman gripping a sword, then discover her in the morning sitting in bed wearing the enemy's shirt, he gave no outward sign other than the twinkle in his eye.

Bristol stared into her beer. She noticed Mr. Aykroyd had brought *two* mugs without being told to do so. Unreasonably she felt an intense need to make an explanation of some sort to Mr. Aykroyd. But she could think of no way to adequately explain the evening's events to herself, let alone anyone else. She clutched a handful of sheet and made herself sip the hot beer with an outward pretense of calm.

121

La Crosse splashed his face in the hot water and lifted his razor, giving Mr. Aykroyd orders as he shaved. The list was lengthy. Much needed to be accomplished to repair the limping *Challenger*. When La Crosse finished, he wiped his cheeks with a linen square and added, "I want every man assembled at noon to witness the lashing."

"Aye, sir. They don't be a hand on board what doesn't know the tale." Mr. Aykroyd darted a flicker of sympathy toward Bristol, his eyes touching the aching swell near her eye.

La Crosse tied dark curls at his neck with a thin piece of cord. "Have a tub filled for Mistress Adams. I think the lady would like a bath."

Bristol looked at her hands, her face flaming. Baths were never discussed publicly. But then, two days ago she'd never have dreamed it possible for her to be sitting in a bed wearing nothing but a torn shirt in front of two men. Her cheeks deepened in color.

"And move her trunk in here," La Crosse continued. "She'll need fresh clothing." La Crosse reached for his coat, addressing his next order to Bristol. "I want you on deck for the whipping."

"Oh, but . . ." Bristol's heart sank. She was afraid of the men; even in daylight, memories of that rum-soaked brutality had the power to sicken. She wanted the man punished, aye, but she didn't want to face the leers or witness what twenty strokes would do to a human back.

La Crosse ignored her protest, turning to Mr. Aykroyd. "After the lashing we'll have the burials and the sharing-out." His mouth thinned to sarcasm. "Did the plunder have a night visitor as well? Or is the treasure safe?"

Mr. Aykroyd's scars and welts rippled in a smile. "Pirate treasure takes second best to the scent of woman. No one disturbed the guard on the chest."

Bristol listened curiously. She knew the pirate ship had been looted, but she hadn't realized there was a treasure on board.

La Crosse nodded. "Very well." He paused with his hand on the latch. "Mistress Adams, I want you clean and polished for the lashing. I want every man to see you at your best, then decide that no woman is worth twenty lashes, no matter how desirable." He waved Mr. Aykroyd into the passageway, then leaned back into the cabin before closing the door with a wink. "At least most aren't." His smoky eyes swept over the

122

curving shirt. "Some, of course, are worth any price." The door closed.

Bristol stared at the door for a very long while. Personality complexities like those of La Crosse were unfamiliar in her limited experience. She didn't know how to cope. Caleb Wainwright was exactly what he seemed, no more and no less—simple, straightforward, unchanging. Noah didn't flash from one mood to another. Nor did most of the good, uncomplicated people of Salem Village. At least not that Bristol had seen. La Crosse kept her in a state of constant unbalance.

She sighed, her shoulders moving within the large shirt. La Crosse was right to call her a foolish little girl. Bristol suspected uneasily that her Salem Village existence had been a sheltered one, narrow and insignificant against the broader scale of the real world. She pleated the hem of La Crosse's shirt with her fingers. She must mature quickly if she was to survive in this world. She suspected the process had already begun.

Swinging out of bed, Bristol padded to the mirror La Crosse had used for shaving, and she peered at her reflection.

She blinked in dismay. Her hair hung in matted clumps, blood mixing with tiny bits of wood and ash. Beneath a layer of dirt, soot, and dried blood, her face was scarcely recognizable. The swelling near her eye had reached its zenith, and she saw the skin beginning to bruise a blackish purple. The scratch halving her cheek was minor, thank heaven, only temporarily disfiguring; but added to the rest, the scratch aided in making a total mess of her face. Bristol stared into the mirror, her mouth open.

How La Crosse had found anything desirable in that face, she couldn't fathom. Flinging down the mirror, Bristol yanked a blanket from the bed and wrapped herself, sinking into the desk chair. She sipped her tepid beer and glared out the windows at sun-dappled waves.

She remained there until Mr. Aykroyd appeared, followed by several men carrying a wooden tub and buckets of hot water. Behind them, more men deposited Bristol's trunk near the captain's bed. She narrowed her eyes at their rib-nudging leers.

"Out! Get yerselves above deck and back to work!" Mr. Aykroyd growled, and his hand curled menacingly on the hilt of his dagger. The men hastened to obey.

Bristol sank her chin in the folds of the blanket. Knowing how she looked, she couldn't imagine herself in any real danger. Regardless, Mr. Aykroyd positioned himself between Bristol and the men filling the tub. Not until he'd slammed the door behind them did he turn to her.

He shoved his dagger into his breeches and perched on the edge of the desk. And now his blue eyes softened to the gentle look he appeared to save for Bristol. "That be a nasty welt on yer eye," he said finally. A grin deepened the ridges and valleys of his face. "But ye gave better than ye got. Ye clean busted one of the fork prongs. Struck it right into bone, ye did. The surgeon worked the best part of an hour to loosen that prong and dig it out." There was no mistaking the pride in his voice.

Gingerly Bristol traced the ugly swelling near her eye; then a slow responding grin twitched at her full lips. Mr. Aykroyd's news was cheering—maybe she was learning to survive more quickly than she'd thought. "Aye," she answered, allowing a little pride of her own. "Aye, I did do well, didn't I?" She smiled up from the blanket cocoon.

Mr. Aykroyd laughed and patted her shoulder. "Ye did!" He reached into a pocket and withdrew Bristol's pewter mug. "I found this under yer pillow." He set the mug on the desk, and his thick brows met in a frown. "Now, why the long face?" He followed Bristol's yearning gaze. "This little cup?"

Despair settled over Bristol's features. "Aye," she said weakly, her voice thick with home.

Shrewdly guessing her thoughts, Mr. Aykroyd took the cup and turned it in weathered hands. "Ye're homesick, then?" he asked softly.

"Oh, aye!" Forgetting her cheering victory with the fork, Bristol lifted cloudy eyes to Mr. Aykroyd. "So much has happened, and . . . I just wish I could go home!" She swallowed a lump forming in her throat. "Home!" After a pause she asked him, "Have you ever felt like that?"

He laughed and set the cup back on the desk. "Never!" He pointed toward the waves sparkling outside the windows. "That's my home, gel. Always moving, always changing." He studied her in a moment of silence. "But I come late to the sea," he admitted. "Once there be a place I thought of as home."

Bristol remembered the French village of Eze and wondered if this was the home Mr. Aykroyd remembered.

"I learned what I'll pass along to ye. Home is never what ye remember. Once ye leave it, ye'll never find it again. It's gone forever. Remember this: never look back." His blue eyes darkened in intensity. "Home is where the heart is. And, gel, the best advice any man can give is to keep yer heart close to the rest of ye! Let home be where ye are now!" Softening his voice, he patted Bristol's shoulder kindly. "Ye can't go forward if ye're looking back. Ye'll never be happy where ye are if ye're yearning for another place."

Be happy here? Involuntarily Bristol's eyes flicked to La Crosse's rumpled bed. But she couldn't speak of that. She muttered into the edge of her blanket.

"What, gel? Speak up!"

Mr. Aykroyd's concern tugged her heart. "I think it's easier to say than to do. There's so much about here that I don't understand."

"Well, speak out, gel. Some say I listen well." He removed his clay pipe and lit it.

Bristol inhaled a sweet-sour blend of strong tobacco and wondered where to begin. "Mostly it's the captain, Mr. Aykroyd." She drew a breath and spoke in a stronger voice. "I . . . he draws and repels at the same time. I don't understand his attitudes toward things. For instance, when he chose to fight the pirates, doesn't that make him responsible for all the death and destruction?" She looked up, troubled, waiting to be convinced.

Unhurried, Mr. Aykroyd studied the embers in his pipe. Sunlight streamed past the windows to paint his ruined face in tones of burnished gold. "No. Ye be wrong, gel," he answered softly. "Had the captain turned tail and run, the men would have mutinied sure as I be sitting here. Didn't ye hear the cheers when the men knew the *Challenger* would engage? There didn't be one among 'em what didn't hunger for battle as eagerly as Jean Pierre, and that be a truth!"

Bristol listened with doubting ears, but deep inside, she suspected the answer was an honest one.

Mr. Aykroyd waved his pipe. "They be hardly a man on these lanes what don't be nursing a hatred toward Sanchez. Many a mate has sunk to wet sands or escaped with bloody wounds and missing limbs, and all to the cause of Sanchez and that thieving pack of pirates." Mr. Aykroyd leveled a steady gaze at Bristol's intent face. "Captain La Crosse do be a hero for sending that Spanish devil to his grave, make no mistake. And he'll hear a hero's welcome wherever the story's told."

Bristol dropped her eyes. "But Jane . . . and that boy, Master Boyd . . ."

"Aye, tragedies." Mr. Aykroyd examined his pipe, then drew on it, expelling a cloud of acrid smoke. "So long as

Sanchez hoisted canvas, more good vessels than ye could count would have gone to the bottom by his hand. Some would say the saving of further lives is worth most any cost."

Bristol thought about this; then she shook her head and sighed.

"As to other attitudes . . . well, gel," Mr. Aykroyd said gently, "could yer own inexperience be coloring the way ye judge things? Is yer woman softness maybe asking too much from a man's world?"

"Perhaps . . . I just don't know." She sighed again and stood, suddenly anxious for her bath. She felt stiff and cramped and tired.

Mr. Aykroyd touched her shoulder lightly. "One more thing, gel, since we're speaking frank here." He coughed and straightened awkwardly, running a finger around the inside of his collar. He peered into the pipe, not looking at Bristol. "The captain be a fine man." He paused, groping for words. "Captain La Crosse, he don't be making a habit of taking lady passengers to his bed." Mr. Aykroyd cleared his throat uncomfortably. "And if such an occurrence do happen, there shouldn't be no cause for shame to either party."

Astonished, Bristol watched a beet red spread up Mr. Aykroyd's scarred face. And felt an answering heat spring into her own cheeks. Mr. Aykroyd rushed on, stammering.

"Men and women need each other . . . and needing warmth and comfort ain't no cause for shame! It's a hard world, gel. And there ain't no guarantees for tomorrow. Take yer warmth and yer comfort, gel, but do it without guilt. Guilt is good for nothing!" He leaned over his pipe as if the ashes there were the most fascinating item in creation. "I don't be recalling the captain ever taking a lady in here for the night, so if ye be thinking he do seduce everything in skirts, it don't be a truth." Now he lifted embarrassed eyes, glancing at Bristol, then away. "There be something special about ye, gel."

Bristol shifted inside the folds of blanket and studied the floor, her cheeks crimson. But she felt a wave of gratitude that Mr. Aykroyd didn't think less of her. She thought furiously, anxious to divert the subject. "Master Boyd!" she blurted. "Will he be all right?"

Equally relieved to change the topic, Mr. Aykroyd moved toward the door. "He be a mite under the weather, but coming. The tadpole swears an angel helped him through the worst of it. An angel with hair the color of heavenly fire." Comfortable again, Mr. Aykroyd winked broadly. "I swore to the lad I'd seen his angel with me own eyes. I haven't the heart to report his angel is sprouting an eye the color of tar." He grinned, lifted a hand, then closed the door.

Bristol smiled at the trail of smoke he left behind, feeling a rush of fondness for Mr. Aykroyd. Her smile broadened to a grin as she wondered if any of the men guessed at Mr. Aykroyd's soft center. Most likely not. She laughed.

Dropping the blanket, Bristol opened the torn shirt and stepped into the tub. The water had cooled to an inviting temperature, and she leaned back with a grateful sigh, letting the liquid heat soak dirt and tension from her body. "Wonderful," she breathed.

Her eyes were on a level with the desk, and she looked across the room at her pewter mug. Home is where the heart is, Mr. Aykroyd had said. Make a home of wherever you are.

She gazed about La Crosse's cabin, seeing his desk, his books, the table . . . and his bed. Could she ever think of this cabin as home? Not while a breath remained in her body, she thought grimly. Not even temporarily? a wicked little voice whispered in her ear.

Annoyed, she dropped suddenly beneath the water, drowning the voice, and rubbed vigorously at her matted hair as if there were more to wash away than blood and soil.

When La Crosse arrived to escort her above deck, Bristol was clean and polished as commanded. His gray eyes registered approval as he walked around her, inspecting from every vantage. He nodded. "That color suits you, only I'd prefer just a bit lighter shade to match your eyes."

"May I have a glass of wine?" Bristol asked, embarrassed by his frank appraisal and feeling the need of fortification before facing the men above.

"Of course." La Crosse poured two glasses. He gestured toward her eye. "It looks better. Is it, or did you work some sort of feminine magic?" He smiled.

"Both," Bristol confessed. Mr. Aykroyd had sent a bowl of powdered rice, and she'd applied it carefully, thinking all the while how horrified Hannah would be to know her daughter used a cosmetic aid.

La Crosse sipped his wine, watching her over the glass. "Will you take pleasure in seeing Addison whipped?" he asked curiously.

Addison. It made everything worse somehow, to know the man's name. "No," she answered slowly. "Last night I thought I would, but now . . . no, I don't believe so." Perhaps it was a form of growth, but she didn't feel certain a brutal act should be punished by yet another brutality.

La Crosse nodded. "Perhaps the whipping calls up unpleasant memories," he said, keeping his voice carefully neutral.

Bristol looked into her glass, realizing he'd seen the marks on her own back. "Aye," she said, her voice as expressionless as his. She volunteered no explanation; she suspected Sable Horton had told him the story that first day. Regardless, her crime seemed of staggering inconsequence in relation to La Crosse's world. In light of her recent experience, Bristol too now saw her offense as tiny, unworthy of comment.

When he saw she intended no further explanation, La Crosse placed his empty glass on the desk. "You do understand why I want you present?"

"Aye."

"Then we'll make the most of the moment. Your protection depends upon every man seeing and deciding the prize is not worth the punishment. And the prize must be very tempting." La Crosse stepped to Bristol and removed her cloak. Turning her, he untied her apron and tossed it away. He moved back, studying her, and his smoky eyes steadied on the lush outline of her young breasts. He nodded, then reached to remove Bristol's dust cap, his hands tumbling her brilliant glossy hair to her shoulders.

"Please," Bristol whispered. "Must you do this?"

He stood so close that she felt the warmth of his strong body. His hands remained buried in her thick hair, and he stared down into her face with smoldering eyes. "*Mon Dieu,* but you are a beautiful little thing! Innocence clothed in a harlot's body!"

Bristol lifted a pleading gaze. In this moment she despised the curves of her flesh, despised the formation of skin and bone structure that darkened men's eyes. Nervously she smoothed her gown. Because of the harlot's body La Crosse had taken her in the night; because of the harlot's body, a man now faced twenty lashes. As to her innocence, that now lay in question. Hot discomfort flushed her face. Flesh and mind had awakened from childish innocence to stretch toward an awareness of sensual pleasure.

La Crosse laughed and lifted her chin with a finger. He smiled into her eyes, his face inches from her own. "No, little one, I'll not claim the prize," he said softly, misreading her expression. He tucked her arm in his and guided her through the door.

128

A sullen silence pervaded the upper deck. La Crosse led Bristol through a lane of tight-jawed men, taking her to the rear quarterdeck. He led her up the stairs and stopped at the inner rail, releasing her arm when she stood in full view of the lifted faces below.

Bristol steadied her gaze on the far length of the ship. She sensed a difference in the men's stares, feeling menace and resentment mixed with the raw lust she'd felt before. Gripping the rail tightly, she forced herself to look down into those faces, meeting their accusing eyes defiantly. She was blameless. She refused to tremble before their silent animosity.

Her courage rising, Bristol dared a glance at the man who had attacked her. Addison was at the starboard shrouds, barebacked and his wrists lashed to the ropes above his head. Forming a line across the stern, Mr. Aykroyd and the junior officers held swords and daggers at the ready, keeping the men pushed back from their offending mate.

La Crosse waited until the tension and silence seemed explosive; then he moved to the rail and shouted in a heavy, thunderous voice, "This woman was entrusted to my care for safe passage to England. And by God, she shall have it! Look hard and long, mates, and decide for yourselves if betraying a trust is worth the price." He scanned their faces as a hundred pair of eyes swung to Bristol.

Under the weight of their measuring stares, Bristol squared her shoulders and tossed her hair. She lifted her eyes to a sky that had turned leaden and threatening, and she felt a freshening wind tug long strands of red hair into a shining river behind her. If this exhibition would protect her from further attack, she would endure it gladly. The wind molded her dark green gown against her thighs, and she made no movement to minimize the revealing breeze.

La Crosse read aloud the naval precedent sanctioning what was to occur. Then he snapped shut the heavy book and nodded shortly to a man pacing behind the shrouds, a long cat-o'-nine-tails dragging from his hand, whispering along the planks.

The man returned La Crosse's nod, his face grim and set. He pulled off his shirt, oblivious of the sharp chill wind, and Bristol started as his hairy belly and chest and shoulders were exposed to view. The man was massive. He flicked the whip out along the deck with an expert twist of a thick wrist, and his shoulders bulged in a controlled flex of heavy muscle.

"One!" La Crosse snapped, beginning the count. Not a voice murmured. All eyes swung to Addison, lashed to the

129

shrouds. He stood with his legs wide apart and braced, his head dropped between naked shoulders.

The whip played out along the deck, then whistled overhead and bit deeply into the man's back, the tips of the leather thongs curling around his shoulders. Addison's body arched, and a rush of air escaped his lips, but no other sound.

The lack of human voices lent an unnatural aspect to the scene, Bristol thought with a shiver. Overhead, the canvas fluttered with the rising wind, cupping in sharp cracks. Ropes creaked and planking groaned, but not a sound issued from the watching men. Raising her eyes to the darkening gray sky, Bristol imagined she stood on the deck of a ghost ship, empty of humanity but for the phantom voice shouting the count. The whip snapped like a pistol shot, and Bristol heard the grunts of the man who swung it, and she shook off the spell.

Irresistibly drawn, her wide eyes dropped to the man sagging against the shrouds. Addison's back lay open and gushing blood. Now a soft whimper moaned through his lips. Bristol flinched with each heavy swing of the whip. She thanked God she was spared seeing the man's face. As his back turned red and pulpy, Bristol's face whitened to the color of fine ash. Every decent human instinct cried out that this brutality be stopped. Bristol spun and clutched Jean Pierre's arm. "Jean Pierre! Please! This . . . this is . . ."

La Crosse's face was stony, the words of his answer encased in granite. "Stand quiet!" His hard face did not turn from the scene below. "Fourteen!"

Swallowing hard, Bristol turned to the rail. Her snowy face stiffened, and she shivered, whether from the crisp wind or the scene below, she couldn't tell. Several of the younger men turned away. A few slipped to the ship's side and leaned sickly over the water. Those who watched, did so with frozen faces, their jaws knotted and their fists clenching.

Addison fainted before the last three lashes flayed along the scarlet mush of his back. Bristol squeezed her eyes in a prayer of thanks; he'd been spared a small portion of agony. The whipping gave her no feeling of satisfaction. Had her stomach not been empty, Bristol too would have dashed to the rail in sick nausea.

Someone cut Addison's limp body from the shrouds and carried him away. La Crosse tossed a purse to the man wielding the whip, and the man wiped sweat from his forehead and tugged his shirt over a wet, glistening body.

A stool appeared at Bristol's side, and she sank to it

weakly. With gratitude she accepted a tot of rum Mr. Aykroyd pushed into her fingers. The rum burned down her throat, steadying nerves and hands. When Bristol lifted her head, she saw a platform over the railing of the quarterdeck, and silent men were laying a row of canvas-shrouded bodies on the deck—fourteen in all.

While La Crosse read a brief Bible service, Bristol stared at the roped bodies, pondering which might be Jane. Which of those anonymous lumps was Goodwife Jane Able? She drank the remaining rum, wishing she had more. Who would notify Goodman Herman Able? Bristol wondered.

Dully she watched the men lift the bodies to the platform and tilt the boards downward. One by one the pale canvas packages dropped to the water with a distant splash. To her horror, Bristol saw the bodies bobbing on the waves in the ship's trail, silent oblongs of death. It hadn't occurred to her they would float.

Her hand jumped to touch the slash along her cheek. It might have been me, she thought wildly. One of the bodies might have been mine. Her stomach turned.

La Crosse took her arm and helped her from the stool. He peered intently into her face, and she read the concern on his chiseled features, a concern for her alone. "Go below and rest," he commanded softly. "I'll send a tray."

Bristol's insides rolled. She couldn't bear to think of food. Not now. "No . . . maybe later . . . I just . . ."

La Crosse nodded to Mr. Speck, and Mr. Speck and his men closed around Bristol. They marched her through the men toward the stairs leading to the captain's cabin. This time, Bristol felt nothing from the flat faces glancing her direction. Lust and resentment and anger and interest had been whipped away. Those that looked at her reflected indifference, nothing more.

Once inside La Crosse's cabin, Bristol drew an unsteady breath of relief. She felt battered emotionally, glad to be out of the wind and away from the men.

Then she made the mistake of glancing toward the window bank. Outside, an indifferent sea mocked human mortality. A gleeful wave played with the canvas-wrapped toys, tossing the bundles carelessly from crest to crest, throwing them up, then hurling them into valleys of water.

"Sink!" Bristol screamed, covering her eyes. "Sink, damn you!" Not understanding the violence of her fear, she fled to La Crosse's bed. She fell across the sheets, curling into a tight ball. There was no promise for a tomorrow. None. She covered her fiery head with the blankets, afraid to look out the windows.

10

WHILE Bristol hid in fitful sleep, the men above deck shared out the pirate treasure. Later, La Crosse explained the process over a late dinner.

"First the treasure is divided into two equal parts. The first half belongs to the crown." He refilled their wineglasses and cut into a thick slice of roast beef.

Bristol nodded, her face still rosy from sleep. But she felt better; her appetite had returned. The variety of steaming dishes brought water to her mouth and a rumble from her empty stomach. She noticed La Crosse had ordered a dish of orange wedges for her, and she glanced at them with a small smile.

"The second half is portioned out among the men. The captain receives a triple share." He grinned, exposing a row of even white teeth. "The officers each receive a double share, and the men one share apiece."

Bristol felt she'd never been so hungry in her life. She applied herself to eating with single-minded vigor, having difficulty attending to La Crosse's conversation. "What sort of treasure was it?" she asked after popping a pink square of meat into her mouth. Another followed.

La Crosse watched as Bristol's plate cleared, feigning amazement. Smiling, he nudged a dish of corn and red peppers nearer her hand. "Go ahead, finish them. The fresh vegetables won't last out the voyage. Enjoy them while you can."

Embarrassed, Bristol forced herself to eat more slowly. She'd been foolish to refuse her meal tray last night. And fortunate to share the captain's table tonight instead of sitting alone in her own cabin picking at crew's fare. Although she suspected even scouse would be appealing right now. She wondered how long the supply of potatoes would last; maybe the crew wouldn't be having scouse much longer.

She smiled at La Crosse's laden table with sincere gratitude and reached for another helping of rice. "The treasure," she prompted.

La Crosse laughed and sipped a ruby wine. "Sanchez' treasure would gladden the heart of any lady!" The wine sparkle repeated in his smoky eyes. "If you can put down your fork long enough to open a package, I'll show you."

Bristol's eyes lifted in surprise, her fork midway to her lips.

Smiling, La Crosse reached in his pocket and withdrew a thin package wrapped in a square of blue velvet. He laid it at the top of Bristol's plate, then leaned back in his chair, watching her over the top of his glass. His gray eyes danced. "Open it."

Bristol lowered her fork, glancing at him uncertainly. "Is this a gift? For me?" She couldn't think why he'd give her anything.

"Aye. A token of recognition for outstanding courage." La Crosse lifted his wineglass in a toast.

"Courage?" Bristol frowned, wondering if he was making a fool of her. "I've done nothing to merit a gift."

La Crosse's face sobered, and he looked at her over the candle in the center of the table. "But you have. It required courage not to run below deck and hide during the battle. It took courage to defend yourself against me last night." He smiled charmingly. "And who but one of courage would subdue an attacker with a fork? Or stand without flinching from the stares or the whipping?" He looked into his glass and lowered his voice. "And it took courage not to fall on the sword last night."

Bristol gasped. "You knew!" Her fork clattered to her plate, and both hands leaped to her mouth. He hadn't been asleep! La Crosse had watched her. And made no move to interfere! Bristol stared at him, her green eyes wide.

"Of course I knew." He met her stare. "Only cowards fall on swords, Mistress Adams—it takes no courage to die. It takes courage to live. It takes courage to face a life that isn't all we want it to be; it takes courage to overcome the blows fate deals us, to face our fears and shames, our guilts."

Bristol lowered a white face, wadding the square of linen in her lap. "An outward courage." Knowing he'd witnessed that private moment with the sword crumbled her defenses, and the truth spilled from her lips. "Inside, I was frightened.

Everything you mentioned, all those acts you call courageous—they were impulsive reactions. Inside, you wouldn't have found an ounce of courage," she whispered.

Jean Pierre La Crosse leaned forward and pulled her hand from her lap, covering it with his own. "Do you imagine anyone feels differently?" he asked softly. "Do you really believe any of us are brave in our secret hearts? No, little girl, it is not so!" He stroked her hand lightly. "A man who believes himself without fear, who boasts of bravery and courage—that is a foolish man. He courts unnecessary risk and endangers others as well as himself. The truly courageous is one who admits to fear, then overcomes it."

Bristol's green eyes fastened to his.

"Courage is an event of retrospect," La Crosse continued. "We recognize our courage only when a crisis has passed, only when we've conquered the problem and have examined our actions from a distance." His shoulders lifted in an eloquent shrug. "Then, more often than not, we ask ourselves: Was that actually me? Did I do all that?" La Crosse leaned back, releasing Bristol's hand and raising his glass. "It was really you, little one. Really you that faced the fears and conquered."

"I think you give credit where little is due," Bristol answered, not moving. Despite his earnest voice and serious face, she wondered uneasily if he humored her. She had never thought of herself in these terms. Perhaps she'd never before been tested.

La Crosse swirled the wine in his glass, watching the candlelight sparkle through the liquid. "If you see no courage in your actions, perhaps you expect too much of yourself. Or perhaps I don't fully understand your background. In mine, women are generally pampered, pallid creatures. Fragile bits of lace and ruffle much given to fainting and vapors at the first sign of unpleasantness. To discover fire and spirit in a woman is a refreshing surprise." He smiled into his glass. "Certainly worth a small token of appreciation."

Bristol's molded brows lifted. It pleased her to think of herself in this flattering light. But then, she couldn't envision the sort of woman he described. "In Salem Village, fainting is a luxury allowed only during childbirth or extreme shock." Her red curls tossed beneath her dust cap. "And you'll find few New England women to match a description of 'fragile.' There's too much work and never enough time to finish it all. Fragile women wouldn't last a year."

He grinned. "Ah, the hearty stock you colonists are so

134

fond of holding up to the rest of the world." His gray eyes sobered, and he added, "I knew such women in the small village where I was born. My mother was such a one. But the ladies of my adult acquaintance, with one or two exceptions . . ." He sighed and waved his hands. "They are, unfortunately, made of softer goods."

Bristol touched the small package curiously, enjoying the mossy feel of the velvet. But of course she couldn't accept it. She turned her head and frowned at the inky waves outside the windows. No moonlight illuminated the water tonight; instead, dark clouds blotted the sky. A rising swell of sea lifted the ship and dropped it with a none-too-gentle hand. Bristol thought of Jane Able's body tossing in those murky waters and felt a quick pang of regret that she hadn't made a greater effort to know Jane.

La Crosse waited, his lifted brow questioning and his strong face angular in the candlelight. Bristol noticed he too kept a wary eye on the rising sea. Meeting his gaze, Bristol wondered at the brevity of life, the uncertainty of it. Would she one day look back at this moment and regret she hadn't made a greater effort to know Jean Pierre La Crosse?

She sighed, her fingers stroking the blue velvet. Accepting his gift made a beginning. But accepting gifts from men simply wasn't done. Hannah would be appalled if she knew. Bristol shrank from her mother's disapproval. But Hannah was a universe away, in another world, and Bristol's curiosity grew by the minute.

"Now what's wrong?" La Crosse's gray eyes twinkled in amusement.

"Women don't accept gifts from men," Bristol said stiffly. Even as the words left her mouth, she knew how prudish she sounded. And she hadn't meant it like that.

La Crosse waved his arms in a gesture midway between amusement and exasperation. "Where I come from, women expect gifts continually. Mistress Adams, must you make a moral issue of everything?" He paused and studied her pink cheeks. "Bristol . . . this is a simple token. A trinket from the pirates' treasure. I promise you that acceptance compromises you in no way."

Bristol blinked, then almost burst into laughter. She was already compromised! Accepting his gift couldn't possibly compromise her more than she was. Realizing the foolishness of her argument, she gave up and reached for the package, pulling at a thin cord. The blue velvet fell away,

135

and Bristol stared at an exquisite gold chain glittering in the candlelight.

She lifted round eyes. "It's beautiful!" Bristol owned no jewelry other than her brother's death rings—small circlets encasing strands of hair, to be worn as symbols of grief during the mourning period, but not as adornment. She'd never owned anything to be worn just for pleasure.

Smiling, La Crosse rose and reached for the chain. "Lift your hair," he said, and she did so. He dropped the chain over her head and clasped it at her neck. Bristol felt a cool weight against her throat, balancing the warm tingle where his fingers had brushed.

Blushing with a sudden surge of vanity, Bristol stood awkwardly and went to La Crosse's shaving mirror, feeling his delighted grin at her back. She peered into the mirror, admiring the rich golden sparkle of the chain. A look totally incompatible with her white Puritan collar. Disappointed, she looked across the cabin and blurted, "It doesn't look right."

La Crosse laughed and nodded agreement. "I doubt those collars were invented to encourage jewelry. Tuck the chain inside," he advised. "You'll know it's there, and the necklace won't mar the intent of your collar." He shook his head at the folly of women's vanity and poured more wine.

The suggestion was sensible, but Bristol felt loath to hide her first piece of jewelry. She narrowed her eyes at the mirror, wondering how she'd look without the collar. "Aye," she agreed reluctantly, staring into the mirror. "Tomorrow I'll drop it inside." For tonight she'd leave the gold chain outside, regardless of how strange the contrast.

La Crosse gestured her back to the table. "There's still your oranges to finish," he teased.

She'd forgotten. Bristol smiled self-consciously and returned to her chair. The dishes slid on the table as the ship dipped in a sudden lurch. Hurriedly she ate the dish of orange wedges, discovering them to be every bit as wonderful as she'd anticipated. "It's going to storm, isn't it?" Bristol asked uneasily.

"Aye. When I've tucked you in for the night, I'll be going topside." He refilled her glass. "Mr. Aykroyd will come if I'm needed before then."

Bristol set down the empty orange dish and dropped her eyes. "Am I to stay here, then?" she asked in a low whisper. Unaccountably, her heart quickened. She hadn't let herself ponder the arrangements for tonight. But her trunk was here, her pewter cup was here. It seemed she was effectively moved into the captain's cabin.

Watching her, his face expressionless, La Crosse allowed a silence to build before he answered. "That is your decision, Bristol," he said in a level voice. "What happened last night was unavoidable. I do not apologize. External forces were at work, and forces between us. However, what does or does not happen tonight *is* avoidable. Whatever you think, I'm not an insensitive monster." His gray eyes didn't waver. "The choice is yours."

Bristol toyed with the stem of her glass. She knew the right choice. She should smile her gratitude for the meal, stand, and ask to be escorted to the cabin she'd shared with Jane. A lonely cold cabin with a hard cot and Jane's trunk in the aisle—a mournful reminder of the woman who now tossed in a stormy sea.

To choose otherwise rejected her background. She turned the wineglass in her fingers. Since leaving Salem Village, her value system had turned topsy-turvy. Without doubt she knew what a horrified Reverend Parris or Noah or Hannah would say. Bristol's chin rose in inch. Those people were not here. They didn't face the terror of night scuffles in a passageway. They didn't share the fears of a rising storm.

But if she stayed . . . She stole a peek at La Crosse, feeling a rush of warmth in her cheeks. The damage was done; she'd already spent one night with him. Her eyes strayed to the angry sea pounding against the windows, and she told herself her decision was prompted only by a fear of the storm.

"I . . . I'll stay here," she said, embarrassment making her voice weak. Gulping her wine, Bristol refused to meet his stare.

He was silent. When Bristol lifted her eyes, he appeared to be struggling, fighting an inner war. "Decency dictates that I send you back to your cabin. That and . . . other reasons." His smoky eyes were veiled. "But I'm a selfish man, Bristol. I want you here." He watched her. "Just be very, very certain this is your choice. You are free to go; I'll not force you to remain here."

"I don't want to be alone," Bristol answered in a low voice.

"Aye. As you wish." La Crosse spoke softly, but she heard his pleasure. She also heard his deep voice affirm that she'd be committed to more than just comfort throughout a storm. Her heart beat faster, and the scarlet deepened in her face.

La Crosse tugged the rope beside the table and reached to

catch an empty dish before it crashed to the floor. "Will you be uneasy in the dark?"

"What?" Bristol's thoughts had raced ahead to other matters.

"In a storm, there's always increased danger of fire. I'll leave you one candle, but remember to extinguish it when you go to bed." He began stacking the sliding dishes in a tray, and Bristol bent to help.

He would leave immediately, then. To her confusion, a twinge of disappointment welled in her breast. Tonight she'd seen the charming companion Jane had reported. She hid her face by leaning over the table, catching at the chattering dishes.

A sharp rap sounded at the door, and Mr. Aykroyd bustled inside without waiting for La Crosse to bid him enter. Icy pellets stuck to his cap and coat, and sea spray had plastered white wisps of hair to his forehead. Mr. Aykroyd threw Bristol a distracted smile and called out to La Crosse. "She'll be a fair blow, Captain. We're battened down and steady. But I'd be feeling a mite stronger if we'd had more time to make repairs."

All business, La Crosse eyed the bank of windows, measuring the soar of black waves and listening to a scatter of sleet against the panes. "Aye. We'll need sure hands on deck. What's the attitude of the men?"

Mr. Aykroyd smiled, wiping water from his face. "They was a tad surly after the whipping, sir. But the sharing-out eased matters considerably. Your timing could not be better." Admiration underscored his words. Mr. Aykroyd wrung a stream of water from his cap, then shoved it back over the wet glisten of his hair. "They be a sober bunch, but steady and willing."

"Aye. Good." La Crosse pushed his arms into a heavy coat and jammed a cap over his dark hair. "We'll have a look."

She hadn't considered it before, but listening, Bristol understood the sharing-out had been thoughtfully timed to lessen the men's animosity over the whipping of their mate. La Crosse knew his business. Suddenly Bristol felt better, knowing his hand would guide them through the storm.

While La Crosse secured the cabin, Mr. Aykroyd approached Bristol with a rolling gait and an awkward smile. He reached into his coat pocket. "Gel, I've been thinking ... That is ..." He cleared his throat, irritated at his stammer. "I don't be having anyone, and ..."

Bristol watched with a twinkle of amusement; whatever Mr.

Aykroyd tried to say, he wasn't his usual decisive self. She patted his arm encouragingly and smiled.

Mr. Aykroyd cursed under his breath. Then he pulled his hand from his pocket and pressed something into Bristol's fingers. "Here!" he barked. "I don't be much good at speeches, but I want you to have this." Then he abruptly followed La Crosse out the door, bending against a frigid wind blasting down the passageway.

Astonished, Bristol opened her fingers and looked at a tiny cameo. Walking to the candle La Crosse had left her, she held the delicate piece beneath the light. A woman's ivory profile lifted from a jet background, and the entire oval was rimmed by a soft gold frame. The cameo was breathtaking in simplicity and workmanship.

Bristol turned misty eyes toward the cabin door. "I . . . won't . . . cry!" she whispered. Somehow Mr. Aykroyd's gift touched her in ways La Crosse's gold chain had not. No explanations were needed here; she knew Mr. Aykroyd's gift came as a pure expression of affection. An uncomplicated gesture of the heart.

She donned her warmest nightgown and pinned the cameo to her breast, glancing at it frequently while she brushed out her long crackling hair. Tonight, Bristol thought with a smile, she went to bed adorned like a queen, with gold at her throat and gold on her breast. The world was truly an amazing place. Yesterday she'd thought it filled with evil, but kindness and generosity did exist beyond the perimeters of Salem Village.

Bristol blew out the candle and climbed into the captain's bed, but the fury of the storm made it impossible to sleep. The ship pitched and rolled violently, riding giant sea swells, then hurtling down deep troughs. Bristol clung to the bed, her green eyes flaring at unfamiliar noises. Across the room dishes smashed together in the tray and sprays of icy stones peppered the windows. Distant frightening crashes sounded above deck.

For nearly an hour Bristol strained for each terrifying sound, her eyes wide and her clutching fingers aching. The storm was her fault. This was God's anger telling her she belonged in the small cabin she'd shared with Jane. This was God's reminder that it might have been Bristol's body among the canvas shrouds. God's rage tossed the *Challenger* upon furious seas, and that anger was directed squarely at Bristol. Toward her selfishness and vanity, toward her fall from grace, toward a sensual awakening.

Deeply frightened, Bristol fought to remain on the pitching bed while her mind battled concepts greater than previous thought equipped her to handle.

Jagged arrows of lightning hurled toward the waves, flicking the streaked windows in eerie flashes of illumination. They pierced Bristol's thoughts with shafts of iced light.

She smothered a scream. The ship would surely go down! Every person would die! Bristol held to the bed and her terrified eyes swung from side to side. "Wait!" a distant voice called in her head. She heard the voice as clearly as she heard the shrieking timbers of the ship. "Where's your courage? Haven't you battled fear before? And won?"

"Aye," Bristol whispered. She thought of the earlier conversation with La Crosse.

"Will you quiver every time a crisis appears?" the voice taunted.

Bristol's mind steadied, and she shook her head in irritation with the inner dialogue. What were things coming to, that she argued phantom voices in the darkness? But the inner exchange had its effect; anger at herself replaced an incapacitating fear. How could she have imagined herself so important that God followed her every thought and action? And took time to punish those which offended? Did God single her out? A grimace twisted Bristol's mouth while she turned these new thoughts in her mind, her fingers clinging to the bed as the ship rose and dropped.

No. No, of course not. The storm was not her fault. And nothing she did or thought would alter the outcome. A studied calm descended to soothe Bristol's mind even as her body fought to maintain balance.

Aye, if God willed it, the ship would go down, and Bristol Adams would die mid-sea. But then, it might be God's plan that she die on a sunny afternoon, victim of a runaway horse. Or fall prey to a fatal disease. Or, or, or. The point was, it appeared to Bristol, she could not change God's map of her life. But she could live her days with a minimum of needless fears. She could live each day to the fullest.

Had Jane lived each day—really treasured it? Now it was too late, there were no second chances to approach each day as the gift it was.

Bristol stretched out on the bed and forced her tense body to relax, letting herself sway with the ship's roll instead of fighting. She allowed herself the full happiness of being here rather than at the other end of the ship, alone and frightened in the small cabin she'd originally been assigned. If life was

140

so uncertain, she'd try to live hers without fear or guilt or shame. Mr. Aykroyd was right, those emotions were debilitating and erased the simple joys of every day. She would accept God's plan for her, and remember that nothing happened which He hadn't foreseen.

Sometime during the night, La Crosse slid into bed, shivering with wet and cold. Drowsily Bristol turned and offered her warm body to ease the chill of the storm, and Jean Pierre came to her with a soft murmur. While the storm raged and howled, they comforted each other in growing passion.

Once, when lightning cracked the sky and briefly lit the cabin, Bristol opened her eyes to see Jean Pierre bending over her. His face was transfigured, lost in joyful rapture. Bristol closed her eyes and tightened her arms about his neck . . . and followed where he led.

Afterward, they lay in the warmth of each other's arms. Before Bristol's soft eyes closed, she nestled against his solid strength and felt the security of knowing she was where she wanted to be tonight.

Jean Pierre was gone when Bristol awoke to a gray dawn. She stretched and rolled to lay her cheek on his pillow, inhaling the fresh salty scent where his head had lain. Outside the bank of windows, a steady rain pelted the sea. The waves still tossed in anger, but less violently than during the night. She could see the ocean bubbling around raindrops, turning the waters into foaming slate.

Bristol tucked the blankets under her chin and wriggled blissfully into the soft warmth. She felt no urgency to rise. No chickens squawked to be fed, no cows impatiently waited for milking. An empty water bucket didn't beckon, nor a dwindling woodpile. Since boarding the *Challenger,* Bristol had experienced the first idle moments of her life. She stretched luxuriously; it was a wonderful feeling. This must be how it felt to be a true lady, like those in Mother England. She sighed. Best to treasure these lazy moments while she could. She suspected there would be few throughout her lifetime.

A rap sounded at the cabin door, and Mr. Aykroyd poked his head inside. "Ah," he said, a twinkle dancing in his blue eyes. "A lay-abed!" He sounded so like Noah that Bristol stared and had to fight down an urge to offer excuses.

Briskly Mr. Aykroyd carried a tray to the bed. Bristol saw a mug of hot beer and a slice of thick buttered bread. "The captain sent this." Mr. Aykroyd set the silver tray on the bed cover. When Bristol sat up against the pillows, his eyes noted the cameo pinned to her nightgown, and a flush of pleasure climbed the ridges and valleys of his cheeks.

Bristol smiled, glad she'd worn the pin, and reached eagerly for her morning beer. "Ah, it's hot and good. I was just fancying myself a pampered lady, and here you appear to make it true," she teased.

Mr. Aykroyd dropped into a playful bow, surprisingly graceful. "I be at yer service, yer majesty." He straightened with a grin. "I swear, gel. Next ye'll be having an old man jump through hoops!"

They smiled at each other, delighted with themselves. "Was there much storm damage?" Bristol asked. The bread tasted fresh and hot and yeasty.

"Nothing what can't be fixed," Mr. Aykroyd answered, shaking raindrops from his coat. His shrewd eyes studied Bristol, seeing the rosy glow in her cheeks. "Gel, either ye've done some thinking, or ye possess the adaptability of a youth I've long passed." He watched her sipping the beer, propped in the bed, and a spot of color warmed his tired face. "Ye're all right now, with . . ." He patted the bed.

"Aye," Bristol answered calmly, meeting his eyes. She tested her new conviction of living each day fully, without shame, and discovered she could manage with a minimum of embarrassment. The old feelings still simmered inside, but she wouldn't allow any crippling guilts to surface.

Mr. Aykroyd sat on the edge of the bed and took Bristol's hand in his cold fingers. "Now, gel . . ." He frowned. "I advised ye to accept yer human needs and follow where they lead." He peered into her green eyes. "But don't hurl yerself overboard. Retain a little caution. Don't be throwing yer heart into the wind."

Bristol laughed and pressed his hand, rubbing it to restore some warmth. "Thank you for worrying, Mr. Aykroyd, but you needn't. I've thought this out and decided to take each day as it comes. I don't want to be alone. I think . . . I think maybe I'm growing at a faster pace than I can cope with alone. Everything is so new. Does that make sense?" He nodded. "If you're worrying I might . . . might fall in love with Captain La Crosse . . ." Bristol's cheeks heated, and she hurried on. "I know this sounds brazen, but I can stay here without that happening. We're too different."

Mr. Aykroyd opened his mouth to protest, thought better of it, and closed his lips.

Bristol continued. "You're right about people needing each other. I suspect even the captain does." She frowned earnestly into Mr. Aykroyd's intent gaze, remembering how tired and cold La Crosse had been when he returned last night.

Mr. Aykroyd's thick brows met, and he nodded slowly. "Ye're a far piece from home, gel"—both slid a glance toward the pewter cup on the desk—"and sometimes values get twisted in such a circumstance. Sometimes that be growth. Sometimes the turning away breeds a lifetime of remorse. Be certain which it is for ye. I'd not like to see ye hurt."

Bristol squeezed his hand. "I'll be all right," she murmured.

Mr. Aykroyd stared into her emerald eyes for a long moment. Then he smiled and nodded. "I hope so, gel. Now, then . . ." He stood and scooped up the tray of shattered dishes, starting for the door. At the latch he paused. "I'd like to ask a favor of ye."

"Anything," Bristol said emphatically, anxious to repay his kindness and concern.

"Well, I be wondering if ye might knit a wee mitten for Master Boyd's stump. Not a man jack on this ship knows a knitting needle from a powder rammer. They be them what know how to sew, but none to claim knowledge of knitting."

Bristol clapped her hands. "I'd love to! I'm only sorry I didn't think of it myself!" There was yarn in her trunk, and needles.

"The lad would be mighty touched to know his angel did see to his comfort. 'Tis cold outside, and colder still in the holds."

"Thank you for the suggestion, Mr. Aykroyd. I'll begin today!" And she'd fashion new mittens for Mr. Aykroyd, too, Bristol thought, noticing the ragged pair he wore.

She chose dark blue yarn for Master Boyd, wishing she had a lighter, more cheerful color, and spent the day sitting before the rain-streaked window, happily fashioning a rounded cup for the boy's stump. When she finished, Bristol added a band of plain white along the top, then began a matching mitten for the boy's right hand.

La Crosse smiled and lifted an amused brow when he returned, bringing a blast of cold air and a man carrying their supper. "Somehow I don't associate you with domestic virtues." He laughed. "I picture you racing horses, or fighting pirates, or swinging a deadly fork." The man prepared the table, laid out the dishes, and departed with a sidelong glance at Bristol.

She laid down the nearly completed mitten. "Then you know very little about New England women," she responded

143

tartly. "We're creatures of infinite talent and accomplishments." Bristol smiled and took her place at the table, nodding approval at the pink slices of ham and golden mounds of roast pigeon.

La Crosse grinned. "I stand corrected." He touched Bristol's dust cap lightly, removed his coat, and poured them each a generous glass of wine. "To the ladies of New England," he toasted, and drained his glass.

"No oranges tonight?" How quickly she was becoming accustomed to the luxuries of the captain's life.

"Not tonight. There aren't many left; we'll save them for a special treat."

As they ate, La Crosse detailed the storm's destruction and spoke of the carpenters working double shifts to repair storm and pirate damage. It was possible they'd fallen a few days behind schedule; not a serious concern, as ships were scheduled by week, not day. Anything less than a week's leeway would be a nearly impossible schedule to meet.

"So," he ended, pushing away his empty plate, "if you've been concerned that your Aunt Prudence might overlook the *Challenger*'s arrival, you can lay that worry to rest. Your aunt will have someone meeting the Gravesend ferry every day of the week we're scheduled in."

"Someone?" Bristol arched a brow. "You forget my aunt's circumstances. The Adamses don't have a 'someone' to handle such chores for them." Bristol's words carried a bite, but she kept her tone even. "Aunt Prudence will be waiting herself."

La Crosse gave her a level, hooded look. "I'm interested in knowing more about your Aunt Prudence," he said. "Or do you still mean to throw up a wall before all efforts to become acquainted?" He grinned.

Bristol blushed and impulsively tossed a ball of bread at his chest. La Crosse laughed and popped the bread into his mouth.

Hesitantly at first, Bristol spoke of her maiden aunt, telling him the little she knew of Prudence Adams.

"Not an enticing picture," he commented when Bristol lapsed into glum silence. "I can understand your reluctance."

His words were right, but the tone was wrong. Bristol had an idea Jean Pierre didn't see the problem as having the importance she saw in it. "I'll make the best of it," she answered. "There's nothing else to do." Surprisingly, this didn't seem the impossible task she'd once thought. Maybe La Crosse was right. Dealing with an aging aunt wasn't nearly as formidable a task as coping with pirates, storms at sea, night attacks, and boys with one arm.

"And your father," La Crosse pressed. "Is he like his sister?"

Bristol shook her head no, and accepted another glass of wine. Pushing away her plate, she thought how pleasant it was to sit in the warm candleglow with rain pelting the window and pattering cheerily on the deck above their heads. She glanced at La Crosse over the rim of her glass and drew in a tiny breath.

Bright candlelight washed away the small lines crinkling his eyes and emphasized his chiseled good looks. His was not a soft face; there was strength in the chin and jaw, and a hint of cruelty in his lips. But La Crosse owned a face women would admire and men respect. Bristol swallowed and lowered her gaze. "What did you say?" Her mind wandered.

"Your father," La Crosse prompted. Under his interested questioning, Bristol talked for more than an hour, telling him about the Adams family, remembering them with a rush of affection and love. They were distant by half an ocean, and no longer part of her daily life, not included in what she did or thought. With a start, Bristol realized she couldn't have discussed them so dispassionately a week ago.

Seeing her thoughts stray, La Crosse stood and stretched. "It's been a long day" he said gently, extending his hand to Bristol and blowing out the stub of candle.

He led her to his bed and undressed her in the darkness. Bristol buried her hands in his dark hair, feeling her body waken to his sure touch, quivering to life as his fingers brushed bare skin and teased her breath into quickening gasps.

Tonight La Crosse paced the growing urgency. He whispered into her ear, "Shhh. Slowly, slowly, little one." And, submitting to his guiding hands and teaching mouth, Bristol learned there were ways to give pleasure that she never could have imagined.

The rocking ship cradled them, and pattering raindrops serenaded above. And they explored each other's bodies, delighting in their discoveries, seeking to offer ever greater joy, until finally an urgency built in explosive waves and they clung to moist heated flesh, soaring toward a panting release.

Throughout the following weeks, Bristol came to know Jean Pierre's body as well as her own, discovering new delights in each. Often she found herself lifting her head from a lap of knitting or a book Jean Pierre had recommended, and

145

staring out the windows to think: I'm happy. I don't recall ever being so happy. Each time, the realization astonished her.

The pattern of Bristol's life seemed too simple to account for such happiness. She ate, she sewed and read, she slept. Once a week Jean Pierre invited her on deck, under heavy guard, to enjoy a few hours of fresh air and sunshine. But all in all, Bristol's days passed quietly, repetitive in nature, with nothing apparent to spark the happiness glowing on her face and filling her breast.

Lowering a book, Bristol frowned at the sparkling shimmer of waves outside the window, turning the question in her mind. Could it be Jean Pierre himself that fired her happiness? As the weeks had passed, she'd come to anticipate the hours with him with ever greater eagerness. Not only the nights, but also those hours they spent after dinner, talking over the day's events, remembering their past for each other, and enjoying an easy companionship.

By now Bristol knew the tiny French village of Eze almost as well as she knew Salem. She saw the old castle in her mind, pictured dusty sun-dappled lanes. She could see Marie La Crosse in her mind, and feel the young boy's loss at Marie's death. And though Jean Pierre seldom mentioned his English father, a dim outline had begun to form in Bristol's thoughts.

And she had served up her own past as well. Showing him the close-knit, bickering community of Salem Village. Remembering Noah and Hannah and Charity for him.

A sudden thought struck Bristol with almost physical force.

She hadn't thought of Caleb Wainwright in weeks! Not in . . . not in weeks! Her book tumbled unnoticed from her lap. What had happened to her? Bristol rose abruptly from her chair and pressed her hands flat to the glass of the windows, looking out as if she could pierce the distance and see Salem's shores. Caleb! What had made her repress him so totally? Guilt? Shame?

Bristol squeezed her eyes shut and summoned Caleb's face in her memory. A dim blur topped by a head of sandy hair wavered at the edge of her mind, but try as she might, Bristol could not force his face into clear focus.

Disturbed, she sank into her chair. The full impact of betrayal struck her like a blow. Guilt kept her from facing his image, kept Caleb's features out of focus. She reached for her pewter mug, turning the cool metal in her fingers.

She pictured herself running to greet La Crosse when he stepped through the cabin door. She saw herself lifting an eager body to Jean Pierre's skilled touch. She'd betrayed Caleb Wainwright in every possible way, both in body and mind.

Stunned, Bristol stared at her fingers turning white on the handle of the pewter cup. It was time to say good-bye. Really say good-bye. She'd released Caleb to Charity before leaving Salem, but the words were hollow, the gesture only sham. When she'd shouted at Caleb in the settler's cabin, she hadn't meant the words in her heart, it hadn't been her true intent never to see him again.

Now it was. Bristol realized she could never face Caleb again. More important, she didn't love him. Affection, aye, she felt a warm affection for Caleb; he'd been the first man she cared for, and a piece of her would always care. But she did not love him.

Bristol's fiery head rose, and she stared at the waves. In one way she felt as if a weight had been lifted from her heart; in another a new weight had been added. Releasing Caleb left her with . . . what?

Was she in love with Jean Pierre?

A rush of emotion rippled through her small frame. Mr. Aykroyd had warned her not to throw her heart into the wind. And what other wind was there but the whirlwind that was Jean Pierre La Crosse? She couldn't love him! She refused to love him!

It would never work. They were worlds apart in outlook and background. Aye, the evening discussion wove threads through their respective pasts, threads that could possibly be pulled into whole fabric; she understood much of what he was, and he knew her. But could those disparate worlds mesh? Could their understanding of each other's past be brought forward to bear on the present? Bristol didn't know.

She chewed her lip. Sometimes La Crosse whispered into the fragrance of her hair, and the words were in French. But they carried the lightness of endearments, not commitments. Jean Pierre had never spoken of love. He'd promised her nothing. Had not mentioned tomorrow.

Disturbed, Bristol paced the planks of the cabin. Why now? she wondered. Why did these awful realizations rise to haunt her now? And the answer came, swift and certain. Only now had she totally released Caleb Wainwright. And now the voyage was nearly ended.

She searched her memory but found no hint from Jean Pierre of what might follow at the journey's finish. He'd offered no promise to see her again. He'd asked no questions where he might find her in London Town.

147

A core of shocked pain formed in Bristol's heart and grew. Did the hurt mean she loved him? But she couldn't!

Bristol passed a hand over her burning eyes, glad when a knock sounded at the door, grateful to escape a sudden deluge of disturbing questions.

Mr. Aykroyd leaned inside with a smile. "Well, are ye ready for an outing?" His quick eyes scanned Bristol's pale face, and his smile faded to a frown. "What is it, gel? Are ye ill?"

"No." Bristol forced a shaky smile for Mr. Aykroyd. Though it was now spring and weeks past the need for gloves, she spied the pair she'd knitted peeking from his pocket. When she presented the mittens to him, Mr. Aykroyd had stared at the brown yarn for a long moment, his mouth falling open. Then he'd swallowed and rushed from the cabin. Never once had he mentioned the gloves, but they were always with him.

Smiling at the memory, Bristol took Mr. Aykroyd's arm and fondly pressed it. He really was the ugliest man she'd ever seen, Bristol thought with a smile of affection. "I'm thinking about the end of the voyage," she explained, an edge of sadness cracking her voice.

Mr. Aykroyd halted abruptly, and Bristol bumped into his side. He peered down into her face, his blue eyes anxious. "Ye haven't lost yer heart, have ye?" His eyes allowed for nothing but a truthful answer.

"I . . . Maybe . . . I don't know," Bristol replied miserably, dropping her eyes.

"Gel! Don't mistake the minute for the year!" He gripped her arm so tightly it hurt. "This is only a minute! A minute in yer life, and no more. Enjoy it, aye; there's none to know on either side of the ocean that ye've claimed a little pleasure for yerself. No shame in it. But . . ." His eyes bored down intently. "But ye and the captain each have a life waiting. A life of commitments and obligations set in motion long before ye came together. Perhaps obligations that can't be broken."

Bristol stared blankly, trying to sort out what he said. Had La Crosse mentioned her to Mr. Aykroyd? Or . . . A terrible new idea squeezed her heart, and her breath stopped. "Mr. Aykroyd, does Jean Pierre have . . . have a wife?" Was this what Mr. Aykroyd tried to tell her? Her world blackened in front of her eyes. If Jean Pierre had a wife, that would explain why he said little about his current life, but wandered in the past. It would explain why he didn't speak of a future that included Bristol. Why his eyes appeared to sadden at certain moments when he watched her happiness.

Mr. Aykroyd tightened his grip on her arm and tugged her forward. "No," he said shortly. "Jean Pierre La Crosse is not married." He opened his lips, then frowned and clamped his mouth shut, refusing another word.

Bristol's relief was clouded with bewilderment. Why? Why, then, didn't Jean Pierre speak to her of tomorrows?

Mr. Aykroyd deposited Bristol on the rear quarterdeck and stamped away after leveling a hard look at La Crosse.

Jean Pierre lifted an amused brow at Mr. Aykroyd's retreating back. "Did you two have a spat? Neither of you look too cheerful."

"No," Bristol snapped. She turned away from Jean Pierre's grin, angry that her knees went weak whenever she saw him. Confusion swirled in her mind, but since she couldn't possibly sort it out here, not with him standing so close, Bristol pushed the dark questions out of her thoughts. She sighed.

"Come, now," La Crosse coaxed, "it's not a day for deep sighs."

Indeed he was right. Overhead a glorious sky stretched above the masts. The sails strained under a brisk warm wind, cupping full. And Bristol noticed the *Challenger* was making good time, cutting through glassy smooth waters at a smart clip. The day was filled with brilliant colors and tangy salt air to lift her spirits. Bristol could almost taste the promise of early summer.

She looked down the length of the ship and saw that most of the men labored in shirtsleeves; only the officers retained their jackets.

"I have a surprise for you," Jean Pierre announced, taking her arm and leading her to the rail. "Look there." He pointed to the sky, wisps of dark hair blowing about his face.

Bristol shaded her eyes and blinked up at an expanse of blue, seeing nothing but a flotilla of white cloud puffs and a wheeling gull. She looked at Jean Pierre. "I don't see anything . . ." Bristol froze for an instant; then her head snapped up. The bird! She stared at the screeching gull circling in the sky and realized she hadn't seen a bird in nearly two months.

"Aye." Jean Pierre smiled. He extended a spyglass and focused toward a point on the horizon. "Look here and you'll see the shoreline of the Isle of Wight. We've entered the channel."

Bristol looked at him; then she slowly took the glass and

149

held it to her eye. A line of brown appeared in the glass. She stared for several minutes, hardly seeing what she appeared to study so intently. "How. . . ?" She cleared her throat and tried again. "How long before we reach Gravesend?"

Jean Pierre shrugged and accepted the glass, turning to the rail. "Two days. Three at the most. If the wind holds, I'd say two." He trained the glass on the Isle of Wight, not seeing the spasm twist Bristol's pale face.

She sank to her stool and blinked at her hands. Master Boyd had to call her name twice before she looked up. "I brought you a glass of wine, mistress." He smiled shyly, extending the glass.

"Thank you." Bristol managed a weak smile. Master Boyd still wore her blue mitten over his stump, even though Bristol guessed it might be itchy and uncomfortable in the warming weather. "Will you be glad to get home?" she asked, forcing herself to speak.

Master Boyd looked surprised. "Home? This is my home, mistress. With the captain and all the others. They's more family than any I ever had. Me mum threw me away, mistress. Left me for dead on the steps of a great house." He turned to leave.

"Wait!" Startled, Bristol peered into his angelic face; a single blond curl fell across his forehead. "That's terrible! What happened to you?"

"The lady of the house took me in, and the servants raised me. Good to me, they was. When I was old enough, the lady's son took me to sea." He waved the mittened stump toward Jean Pierre. "And I been with him ever since. The captain, he don't try to run me life, mistress. He knows to respect a man." The boy's thin chest swelled, and Bristol hid a smile at the thought of this child fancying himself a man. Master Boyd shrugged small shoulders. "I like the city life for a time; then I have me a hankering for the sea."

Bristol nodded, wondering whose words he parroted—Mr. Aykroyd's? She waved as he scampered down the stairs, returning to his duties as nursemaid to the men ill with scurvy.

A sudden thought nibbled Bristol's mind, and she called out, but Master Boyd had disappeared into the hold. What lady had taken him in? Marie La Crosse? Considering Master Boyd's age and English accent, that didn't seem possible. Yet he clearly had meant Jean Pierre as the lady's son. And that wasn't possible.

Bristol lifted a puzzled glance toward Jean Pierre, watching the wind flutter his collar around his strong face. An hour ago she'd told herself she knew him. But she didn't know him at all. There were so many unanswered questions. She wondered if anyone really knew Jean Pierre La Crosse.

Her sad eyes shifted toward that distant point where the Isle of Wight signaled an ending. The voyage was nearly over. The knowledge weighed against Bristol's heart like a lump of granite.

11

THROUGHOUT the next two days, the last two days, Bristol knew she behaved badly. Emotions ruled her conduct, rather than intellect. She acted impulsively, responding to an ebb and flow of feelings she couldn't fully understand. Unshed tears pricked the back of her eyelids, and she paced the captain's cabin, alternating between anger and despair, made worse because she couldn't pinpoint a focus for either.

Gradually the turbulence of her emotions settled on Jean Pierre La Crosse. The mere thought of him acted to spark a deep anger, the motivation for which Bristol refused to examine in depth. She wanted him to spend every possible moment of their last days with her. Yet when La Crosse appeared with an hour to spare, she lapsed into a sullen, reproachful silence, driving him away.

For the first time since she'd begun sharing his cabin, Bristol turned her back to him in bed. She lay tense and rigid, almost daring him to touch her. And when Jean Pierre lightly stroked her naked shoulder, Bristol shrugged him away with an angry flounce; she squirmed close to the wall and away from his warm body. Jean Pierre hesitated; then Bristol felt him roll on his back, and soon she heard the even rise and fall of his breath. That La Crosse slept while she could not raised a fury in her breast, and it required enormous control not to spin and pound him with her fists.

Instead, she lay stiff as a plank, fighting the sting of tears

151

and promising herself she would not cry. Her stormy eyes stared into the darkness and her mind felt frozen.

After a second day of restless pacing, Bristol collected her scattered belongings and stuffed them into her trunk. She slammed the lid shut and dusted off her hands. But instead of feeling better for her decision, she felt worse.

When La Crosse appeared for the evening meal, Bristol was waiting in the desk chair, holding her pewter cup tightly. She looked up with a pale, stubborn face. "I want to return to my own cabin." A challenge lay in her tone and in her eyes.

La Crosse's smile faded. He stood wide-legged, with his hands fisted on his hips. "Very well," he said thinly. They waited in strained silence for someone to respond to his rope tug.

Refusing to look at him, still Bristol felt his brooding eyes watching her over the rim of his wineglass. She frowned at the cup in her fingers, then pushed the mug deep inside her trunk. She'd expected La Crosse to make her stay; she hadn't thought he'd let her go so easily. The silence in the cabin was thick and stifling. Dimly Bristol understood she had attempted to manipulate a man who would not be maneuvered by ploy. Understanding her mistake, she considered giving up this silly idea and flinging herself into his arms, maybe giving way to the tears just beneath the surface. Did she really want to spend their last night together in the other end of the ship? Alone? Bristol sighed. She'd gone too far. Now her pride wouldn't allow a backing down.

"Will you tell me what this is all about?" La Crosse asked. Bristol heard the thickening of his accent that signaled anger.

"I think you know," she snapped, looking at the darkening waves outside the windows, looking anywhere but into his gray eyes.

La Crosse drained his glass and poured another, slamming the wine bottle against the table. "Why is it women always fall back on that phrase? Why do all of you turn a problem into a guessing game?" His anger exploded into open frustration.

"Is your experience with women so vast, then?" Bristol replied acidly. She sounded petty and waspish and jealous, but she couldn't help herself.

"Aye," he answered flatly, and Bristol flinched. "And experience has also taught that nothing is ever resolved in this frame of mind." He strode to the bed and removed his boots, tossing them to the floor.

Bristol listened to the very familiar sounds with a twist of her heart, but she kept her eyes steadfastly toward the windows. "I think you know what's troubling me, and if you choose not to admit it, that's your right. You're the captain and you can have everything to suit yourself, can't you?" Bristol's hands shook, and she wished she could stop the outpouring of ugly words tumbling from her lips, but she could not. In her own pain, she sought to wound and to hurt him.

Bristol felt his stare. "Aye," he said sharply. "That is right. But I remind you, it is you who refuses to talk."

Neither spoke further, and in the silence, Bristol heard footsteps responding to the rope pull. She stood up, smoothing her apron, angry at the tremble in her fingers. She wished Jean Pierre would take her into his arms and not let her go. Her heart called out to him.

But La Crosse took the chair she'd vacated and bent over his desk, shuffling piles of charts and papers. When the knock came at the door, he lifted a dark face and thundered, "Enter!"

Mr. Aykroyd looked from Bristol to Jean Pierre, and his smile vanished. "Aye, sir?"

Jean Pierre waved his hand. "Take the lady and her trunk to the passenger cabin." Dipping a quill into the ink well, La Crosse leaned over his papers without glancing at Bristol.

Her cheeks flamed crimson. So he would dismiss her like a naughty child without a word of good-bye. She lifted her chin and swept through the cabin door with a grand show of pride—dismally suspecting he hadn't looked up to see it. Mr. Aykroyd followed swiftly, closing the cabin door behind him. His face tightened with concern.

Taking Bristol's rigid arm, Mr. Aykroyd forced her to walk slowly. "Do ye want to talk about it?" he asked.

"He doesn't care about me!" Bristol blurted. She dashed a hand over her eyes and swallowed a persistent lump. "We're almost there, and he hasn't said . . ."

Mr. Aykroyd sighed and shook his head. "Ye're wrong, gel. He cares. More than ye know."

Bristol paused, hope flaring in her damp eyes. "Did Jean Pierre say something to you? Anything?" she whispered.

Mr. Aykroyd patted her fingers awkwardly, gently disengaging her gripping hand. He led her onward. "He doesn't have to say anything, gel. Every man jack on this ship what knows the captain knows he cares for ye. Don't ye recall my telling that he never took a lady to his cabin before?" He pressed her hand and curled it around his arm.

153

Together they stepped onto the deck, brilliant with the reds and golds of a dying sunset. Bristol didn't notice. "If Jean Pierre cares for me, Mr. Aykroyd, then why doesn't he tell me so? Why hasn't he said anything about what happens next? About . . ." Pride held her tongue, and she couldn't go on.

Mr. Aykroyd looked toward the horizon, his thick brows coming together in a fierce frown. "He has his reasons, gel; if ye're meant to know them, ye will."

Bristol lowered her head, feeling rebuked. Mr. Aykroyd had no easy answers; perhaps there were none. Blindly she followed his lead. But her thoughts and heart remained behind in the captain's cabin.

And when they halted in the passageway before her cabin door, Bristol looked at it with dull surprise. She didn't remember walking the length of the ship. At some point she saw that Mr. Speck had joined them; he nodded to her and took up his position in the hallway. Smiling uncertainly, Bristol turned and choked on the stale, musty odor rushing from the cabin when Mr. Aykroyd pushed open the door. She'd forgotten how dank and dark the small cabin was. Mr. Aykroyd lit the wall lamp and paused, reluctant to leave.

"Ye can swallow yer pride, gel, and spend yer last night on board in comfort." His blue eyes worried at her face. "They's no cause to stay here," he added softly.

"Thank you, but I can't . . . I can't go back." Two men shoved her trunk through the door, bumping it against Jane's. Bristol hadn't noticed when Mr. Aykroyd stopped to give the order.

"Well," he said, "if that's the stand ye take." Mr. Aykroyd sighed and tugged a puff of white hair. "Someone'll bring ye a bite soon. But I doubt ye'll take to it." And then he was gone, leaving Bristol alone in the cramped, dim cabin. She looked around, drew a breath, then sank to the edge of her cot and covered her face with her hands.

When the evening meal arrived, Bristol gulped in dismay at the sight of moldy sea biscuit and suspicious-looking salt beef. No wonder so many of the crew were down with scurvy and other illness. How could they eat this? And what did it do to their stomachs? She shoved the trencher away and threw herself on the cot, grimacing at a rock-hard mattress and thin pillow. How quickly she'd grown accustomed to a better way of life.

After a moment, Bristol swung up and opened her trunk, searching until her fingers closed around the pewter cup. Lying back on the cot, she turned the little cup in her hands. What was her family doing tonight? Did they still think about her? Had Noah plowed the fields yet for sowing? Were Hannah and Charity putting in the kitchen garden?

A bitter wave of homesickness weighed Bristol's heart. She felt miserably alone. Rejected and abandoned to a strange country, a new, unknown way of life. After years of warmth and acceptance, the rejection she now experienced brought a new pain. A pain that filled her mind and body with a persistent ache.

Slowly the night passed, filled with sore memories of a small New England house and the people in it. Occasionally her thoughts flew to the man at the opposite end of the ship, but each time Bristol caught herself, she wrenched away from the angry confusion his image stirred. Continually she insisted that she didn't care about Jean Pierre La Crosse; he'd introduced her to the pleasures of the body, and he'd made the voyage a pleasant one by his companionship and charm. That was all. No emotional attachment existed. Bristol sighed, wishing she could convince herself of this. Each time she assured herself that she didn't care about Jean Pierre, the words carried a tinny note of falsehood. And hurt.

Sometime during the long restless night Bristol must have dozed. When she opened her eyes, the wall lamp had been dimmed and someone had removed the trencher of untouched food. Probably Mr. Aykroyd, Bristol thought with a weary yawn. She stretched and wondered what time it was; in the dark, windowless cabin, she couldn't tell if it was day or night.

Standing with a resigned sigh, Bristol brushed the tangles from her long red hair and tied the curls beneath a fresh dust cap. For a moment she considered changing from the clothes she'd slept in, but decided she lacked both energy and interest. Let Aunt Prudence take her as she was—Aunt Prudence didn't promise to be any bargain either.

Mr. Aykroyd unlocked her door and waved two men inside to remove the trunks. "We're nearly in the harbor, gel." He gestured to the men. "Take both the trunks topside."

Bristol blinked, and her heart leaped in her breast. "What time is it?" She patted her pocket, where Noah's purse of coins clinked reassuringly. She couldn't carry her cup for fear of looking foolish, but Noah's purse provided her the link with home she suspected she'd need to endure the day.

"Nearly noon," Mr. Aykroyd answered. "Careful, there!"

he roared at the men, his face darkening. "If either of those trunks gets busted, so do yer heads!"

Noon! Bristol started in disbelief. She must have tossed most of the night, dozing sometime near dawn. And now they were almost to Gravesend. Nervously she smoothed her rumpled gown, seeing the tremor in her fingers. Worries and fears she'd suppressed during the last weeks leaped into her mind with fresh vigor. What was England like? And Aunt Prudence? Would she get along with her unknown aunt? How harsh a woman was Aunt Prudence?

More important, Bristol wondered if La Crosse would appear to say good-bye. She simply could not believe he'd let her go without saying something . . . without telling her they would meet again. She bit her lip. And what would she answer?

The minute Bristol stepped onto the upper deck, she knew La Crosse would have no opportunity to seek her out. The ship vibrated with frenzied activity. Every hand worked with single-minded concentration, guiding the *Challenger* into Gravesend harbor.

Mr. Aykroyd positioned Bristol at the rail near the waist of the ship, leaving Mr. Speck as guard, then hurried to join La Crosse on the forward quarterdeck. Bristol closed her eyes, and her mind threaded through the noise and voices until she found the one she longed to hear. Jean Pierre's strong voice roared orders above the din throughout the ship, and it seemed to Bristol that his accent had never been thicker.

Releasing her breath in a disappointed rush, Bristol understood no farewells would pass between them. She turned listlessly to the rail and looked across the narrowing distance, hearing the leadsman sing out fathoms as the *Challenger* slowly moved into Gravesend harbor. Ships of varying size dotted the water more thickly than Bristol would have guessed possible; the sky was pierced with hundreds of dark masts rocking at anchor. Between ships and docks the waters swarmed with longboats, and the air rang with men's curses and shouts and the noise of penned animals and horses on the wharves and the buzz of hawkers demanding attention for their wares. The dockyard teemed with an amalgam of bustling activities. Rough men with rougher manners crowded the wharves, sweating over heavy nets and barrels of cargo, and here and there disreputable women wove through the mob, wearing hard and used faces and exchanging bawdy jests with the men.

Bristol swallowed and lifted a hand to her mouth, feeling

out of place and overwhelmed. Somewhere a crank whirred and the *Challenger*'s anchor dropped with a splash, striking the waves with sinking finality.

Eager hands spun rope from knots, and the *Challenger*'s longboat splashed into gently lapping water. Next, Jane's trunk disappeared over the rail, swiftly followed by Bristol's. Everywhere her green eyes touched, men hurried to secure the *Challenger*, anxious for shore leave, fresh food, and the beckoning taverns of Gravesend.

Too soon Mr. Aykroyd appeared at Bristol's side, and his hand closed over her elbow. "It's time, gel," he said softly, smiling into her pinched face. Someone threw a rope ladder over the rail, and the men in the longboat below fingered their oars and looked up impatiently.

The color drained from Bristol's face. She spun to scan the familiar decks with a last sweeping glance. But she did not see La Crosse. For an instant she thought she saw a flash of open white shirt and blue breeches on the forward quarter-deck, but when she looked again, no one was there; the fleeting image had been a trick of her yearning imagination. She clasped her hands until the knuckles whitened. He wouldn't let her go without saying good-bye, he wouldn't.

"Come along, gel," Mr. Aykroyd said gently but insistently. He circled her waist and lifted her over the rail. Mr. Speck assisted her into the rocking longboat, and then Mr. Aykroyd slid down the rope ladder and dropped lightly beside her. "I'll be seeing ye safe on the ferry," he said.

In truth, Bristol wondered how she might have managed without him. She'd have been lost and vulnerable on her own. Mr. Aykroyd shouldered a path through the mob, his face and expression discouraging interference. He deposited Bristol in a line waiting to purchase ferry tickets and departed to oversee the loading of her trunk.

Bristol boarded the crowded ferry reluctantly, casting anxious glances over the shifting crowds, looking for Mr. Aykroyd. She didn't think she could bear it if the ferry left without a last word for Mr. Aykroyd.

And it seemed to her the boat made ready to depart. All the wooden benches ringing the sides of the large flat-bottomed ferry were crammed with people. In fact, Bristol realized she'd have to stand for the duration of the six-hour journey.

"At least ye don't be having a lengthy wait for departure," Mr. Aykroyd said when he returned. He cast a threatening eye over the crush of passengers, seeking any faces that might

157

prove offensive. Seeing that most of the passengers were families or persons of quality, he relaxed his fingers on the hilt of his dagger. The nearest faces visibly relaxed, though most continued to stare in horrified fascination at Mr. Aykroyd's battered features.

Bristol smiled faintly, suddenly seeing Mr. Aykroyd as the passengers must, as she had when first they met. Salt-crusted and fierce, he looked more a pirate than had most of Sanchez' men. And Bristol despaired of leaving his comforting affection. "Oh, Mr. Aykroyd . . ." She shook her head helplessly and lowered her face. "Thank you for everything you've done for me. I'll always . . ." His continuing support and kindness had been the pillar she'd leaned on in moments of stress during the past two months.

"Hush, gel, or ye'll have an old man blushing and spoiling the evil image these folks are imagining." He glowered at a nearby woman, and the woman paled and clutched her purse nervously. Mr. Aykroyd gave Bristol a delighted wink and grin. He pressed her hand. "Ye keep yer chin up and yer spirits high," he said, serious again. "Ye'll do fine, gel. Ye have iron in yer backbone." He turned to leave.

"Mr. Aykroyd! Wait!" Bristol's green eyes held a plea. "If . . . if Jean Pierre wants to find me, if he . . . will you tell him that I . . ." Her pride cracked, and a flush of embarrassment colored her pale cheeks.

Mr. Aykroyd stopped her with an enigmatic smile. "Gel, the captain knows where ye'll be. He's known from the first." Then he was gone, his bobbing cap vanishing in the dock mobs.

"Wait!" Bristol whispered, knowing it was useless. What did he mean? Her eyes darted over the crowds, but Mr. Aykroyd had disappeared. She leaned against the bulkhead of the prow and closed her eyes.

Ropes hissed and fell on deck, and the clumsy ferry drifted free of the wharf, wallowing toward open water. Slowly the boat turned in a sluggish current, then rocked forward up the Thames River.

Bristol clutched a metal handle, balancing herself, and noted a few faces watching her with expressions of disapproval. She had an idea her clothing as well as her accent marked her as a colonial. No matter. She dusted her apron and lifted her chin proudly, returning any stares until the unwelcome eyes fell away.

And all the time her racing mind played back Mr. Aykroyd's puzzling words. It was impossible for La Crosse to know where she'd be when she didn't know for a certainty herself. She couldn't recall ever mentioning Aunt Prudence's address. London Town housed over half a million dwellers—Jean Pierre could never find her. In addition, Bristol wasn't certain if Aunt Prudence lived within the city or in a small hamlet outside London. Mr. Aykroyd's words made no sense. Not only that, Mr. Aykroyd had stated that Jean Pierre had known Bristol's ultimate destination from the beginning. It simply was not possible!

She wrestled the mystery until her brain felt numb, and still no answers suggested themselves. Finally Bristol gave it up with a grimace of exasperation. The important thing to remember was that Jean Pierre knew where to find her if he cared to. Or were Mr. Aykroyd's words merely a kindness, an empty assurance to ease her mind? Bristol's leaden heart suspected that if Jean Pierre had intended to see her again, he'd have told her so.

Her chin lifted a fraction. Well, maybe she didn't want to see him again! Bristol ignored the wrench in her heart. Jean Pierre had used her, then cast her off without a word. If he appeared at Aunt Prudence's cottage, she'd slam the door in his grinning face. Whether or not she'd do such a thing, Bristol felt better for thinking it, for reclaiming her pride. After all, Jean Pierre La Crosse wasn't the only tree in the forest; there was still Caleb Wainwright. And never mind that she'd released Caleb and could no longer bring his face into focus; distance did that to memories. Caleb cared for her, and maybe she still cared for him. La Crosse had been but a fleeting experience, nothing more.

A tiny voice in the depth of her mind laughed, bringing an instant frown to crease Bristol's brow.

She abandoned her dead-end thoughts with an effort and tried to concentrate on the passing shoreline, alive with late-spring blossom. She turned her thoughts ahead . . . and found nothing to cheer her. All her dread concerning the character of Prudence Adams returned in force. What sort of life awaited her, Bristol could only guess, and none of her guesses held a shred of appeal. If Prudence's letters were an accurate indication, Bristol could expect to spend a great deal of time in tedious prayer.

A faint, weary smile touched her full lips. She had much to pray about—far more than when she'd embarked on this journey. A ripple of heat passed over her body, and she clasped the metal handle tightly. Nothing could come of tormenting herself with thoughts of La Crosse; she turned a frowning face to the new vistas opening around her.

The Thames narrowed as the ferry pulled closer to London Town, and the waterway choked with coal barges, barking smacks filled with mounds of fresh mackerel, hoys full of produce, and all manner of water conveyances, some of which Bristol recognized and others she'd not seen before. And the nearer they drew toward London, the worse became the condition of the water they traveled.

Bristol pressed a linen to her nose, feeling strangled by the putrid fumes wafting from the waves. The Thames was no better than an open sewer. Garbage, offal, and bloated animals clogged the water with increasing frequency.

Even so—despite the reeking water, despite her pain at each unbidden thought of La Crosse, despite knowing Aunt Prudence's severity awaited—Bristol surprised herself by slowly being caught up in the excitement of approaching the largest, most exciting city in the civilized world. It was an adventure unparalleled in her previous experience.

Her eyes widened and her lips parted in amazement at the enormity of London and its surrounds. Nothing had prepared Bristol for what half a million inhabitants meant in terms of sheer size.

Long before the ferry passed beneath top-heavy London Bridge, a multitude of several-storied houses had been slipping by along the shore, more than Bristol had ever imagined to be in one place. And the industry! A pall of smoky vapor belched from the furnaces of countless brewers, soap-boilers, and dyers, hanging in a dark cloud over miles of the city.

Bristol stared at the fumy overhang in fascinated repugnance, wondering uneasily if the air was safe to breathe and thanking God she arrived in spring rather than in winter. She shuddered at an image of half a million stoves adding coal smoke to the ominous drift. London must be terrible in winter! With a sinking heart she recalled that she'd be here to see for herself.

In fact, she didn't find London all that attractive right now. Exciting, aye; but nice to see and smell, no. The stink around her grew in leaping degrees. Laystalls piled high with dung and human offal dotted the shoreline, and the river was thick and sluggish with malodorous rotting garbage. From the instant the ferry passed the northeastern section of the city, a continuous rain of minute coal particles fell to darken clothing and further poison the air. Bristol's eyes felt gritty, and she glanced down in dismay as her white collar gradually turned sooty and gray.

No one in Salem would believe people lived like this, Bristol thought, recalling the clear water of the Frost Fish River and the pure air of home.

But home hadn't the usual power to distract her now; too many new impressions competed for attention, there was so much to see and marvel at. Bristol stared long and hard at a massive stone building passing on her right, and her eyes lit with recognition. She'd heard of the famous Tower of London from Noah and others but had never expected to see it for herself. Then London Bridge stretched overhead, piled high with two- and three-story houses and snarling with traffic, the noise drifting down to the strangled waterway below.

All around the ferry, small boats vied for space. The river reverberated with a vigorous cursing that would have earned instant punishment in New England, but here no one bothered to take note. Bristol blinked and repressed an urge to cover her ears, hearing unique and colorful swear words she'd not previously guessed the existence of. Nothing whatever seemed familiar. She concentrated on the vast buildings sprawling along the shore, shutting the calls of the rivermen out of her mind. As the ferry approached the city proper, modest homes had given way to enormous formal estates.

Great edifices of stone and brick, some half-timbered, crowded the shore—all of a size to qualify as palaces in Bristol's mind. But she guessed they must be privately owned, as one king surely couldn't own and maintain as many palaces as stretched along the riverfront. One after another, these massive buildings passed, each competing with the next in size and splendor.

Behind the estates rose streets of many-storied tenements, and with a start Bristol realized the tall buildings crowding the skyline cast long shadows. Six hours seemed to have passed in a blink, and the day was waning.

Lines of rope hauled the ferry steadily toward a stone dock, and the ferryman sweated and swore loudly as he negotiated the boat through brown scummy water. The dock lay between two laystalls piled high with oozing human and animal refuse. Bristol choked. A fetid odor stung her nostrils, and she coughed and wiped her eyes.

"You'll get used to it," a nearby woman offered with a slight smile. The shawl over her shoulders lifted in a shrug. "We all have to." She hawked a yellow glob of spittle onto the ferry floor. "It's terrible living here. Terrible. But what's

161

a person to do?" The woman sighed and joined a press of people jostling to depart on the ferry.

Bristol swallowed hard. With a heartfelt wish, she hoped Aunt Prudence waited to whisk her away from the smell and dark overhead cloud and the frightening vastness everywhere she looked. The city towered large, noisy, and sprawling. The houses were monstrous. Even the people seemed larger than life. Everything appeared overwhelmingly outsized. Except Bristol Adams. Bristol felt small and insignificant and lost. She hadn't supposed she'd ever be anxious to find Aunt Prudence, but she was.

Last to disembark, Bristol stepped onto the stone dock, unbalanced for a moment by the firmness beneath her feet. She paused, standing rock-still, and looked ahead at the swarm of people wandering the dock area. Mariners, dockers, hawkers, and oyster women. Brewers and wood mongers. And others whose clothing or bawling voices didn't identify them. Bristol shook her red curls and clenched her fists.

Slowly she advanced into the din and bawdy shouts. She spotted her trunk among a swiftly disappearing pile of luggage, and she walked toward it over a tangle of ropes snaking the ground. Her ears rang with the battering noise, and the stench of London Town burned her nose, thick and offensive.

Pausing uncertainly, Bristol scanned the thinning crowd near the luggage, seeking someone to fit Aunt Prudence's description. She saw no one. Rapidly the passengers departed, along with those who had met them, until only Bristol and her trunk remained in the area roped off for ferry passengers.

Surrounded by rough dock people, Bristol's fresh face and lush figure were as conspicuous as a rose in a bramble patch. She felt the speculative stares directed toward her, and blushed furiously at a barrage of suggestive remarks howled across the raucous noise of the wharf. Hopefully Bristol turned her face back to the ferry, as if La Crosse or Mr. Aykroyd might suddenly appear to smile reassurance and hurry to her aid. But of course there was no one there.

Uneasily she fidgeted beside her trunk, twisting her apron into damp nervous balls. What if Aunt Prudence didn't come for her? What if Noah's letter had never reached London? What if Aunt Prudence were ill? What if, what if, what if! With a rising sense of panic, Bristol turned a host of speculations in her mind, each more terrible than the last. No matter how stultifying life with Aunt Prudence might be, nothing could be worse than being stranded in this vast city alone and knowing no one.

A sudden tug at her sleeve interrupted Bristol's dire thoughts. Relief shining in her eyes, she spun to face a thin little woman, even smaller than herself.

Bristol drew a breath and searched the woman's sour face for a trace of family resemblance. With a sinking heart Bristol decided the woman matched every dismal idea she'd held about her aunt. Fate was yielding up a worse destiny than Bristol had imagined.

The little woman returned Bristol's stare with bad-tempered black eyes, and her thin mouth tightened into a line. She thoroughly examined Bristol's rumpled gown and sooty apron, her expression conveying a disbelief that anyone would dare to appear in public dressed in such clothes. Her own neat gown was fashioned of deepest black from a heavy material Bristol didn't recognize, and a black shawl partially covered iron-colored hair.

"Mistress Adams?" A tart voice framed words that were more an accusation than a question.

Bristol forced her fingers to release the balls of apron. Quite suddenly she remembered that none of the women on the ferry had worn aprons. Or dust caps. Or looked as out of place as she.

"Aunt Prudence?" she whispered in a faint voice.

12

"CERTAINLY not!" the dour little woman snapped. Her thin upper lip curled in disdain and her tone dripped contempt for Bristol's mistake. "Lady Hathaway waits for you by the carriage."

Lady Hathaway? Who was Lady Hathaway? Bristol's wide eyes followed a toss of the woman's iron-colored head.

Away from the noisy activity of the docks stood an ornate carriage unlike anything Bristol could have invented. It looked like a green-and-white house mounted on wheels and decorated with scrolls and swirls.

163

Beside the carriage a large woman shaded her eyes and stared toward them, but from this distance Bristol could distinguish none of the woman's features except a fluff of orange curls puffing from an elaborate headdress. The woman's orange hair added a further confusion. At one time Aunt Prudence had no doubt possessed the Adams fiery hair, but wouldn't she now be gray—at an age past fifty? And what might a fine lady with a personal carriage have to do with Bristol's Aunt Prudence?

The little woman in black ignored Bristol's questions as she might have ignored a troublesome child. She waved a gloved hand and gestured toward a man in green velvet livery who seemed to be waiting for her signal. The man hurried forward, and without a word he and the woman hoisted Bristol's trunk and staggered toward the carriage, grunting and stepping carefully through lines of rope and netting.

"Wait!" Bristol stared after them, astonished that the small older woman had the strength to carry an end of the trunk. Then her senses cleared and she realized they were taking away all her belongings. Bristol lifted her skirts and ran after them. "Wait! Now, see here . . ." But neither paid Bristol the slightest heed, proceeding as if they didn't hear her outpouring of protest.

Bristol halted and sucked in a long breath. Her efforts to wrest an explanation were proving useless. Very well, she thought, narrowing her eyes. It appeared she had no choice but to follow her trunk and submit to Lady Hathaway's curious interest. Bristol squared her shoulders, unconsciously emulating Hannah, and she reluctantly approached the carriage.

The huge woman with bright orange hair lifted a gold-tipped cane and gestured impatiently. Bristol paused and gaped at an intricate arrangement of curls pasted to the woman's powdered forehead. The woman's hair was dyed! Bristol had heard mention of such shocking things, but she'd never expected to actually see dyed hair. And such a color. Bright orange. Beneath the fringe of pumpkin hair lay a round face with generous lips pursed in irritation. The woman's sharp, knowing eyes observed Bristol as acutely as Bristol studied her.

Moving forward, Lady Hathaway advanced upon Bristol like a tidal wave, her silky skirts flowing around her protruding stomach like sheets of water rolling from a ball. She stalked around Bristol, stamping her cane and muttering. "Good God! You're worse than I imagined!" Lady Hathaway's voice emerged from deep in her ample chest, as low-pitched as a man's. She rolled blue eyes to the sky, her heavy jowls working. "That dress is impossibly provincial . . . it must go! And your shoes! A disgrace. You look like a country bumpkin or"—the cane lifted to indicate Bristol's dust cap—"or a servant!" Lady Hathaway turned toward the green-and-white carriage. "Inside! Get inside quickly before someone I know sees us."

Bristol's spine stiffened and her jaw set. What could be keeping Aunt Prudence? Where was she? It looked as if Bristol would have to handle this strange encounter by herself. One thing was certain: she had no intention of going anywhere with this Lady Hathaway—whoever she might be! Warm color sparked Bristol's cheeks, and she planted her feet firmly where she stood, refusing to budge an inch.

"Lady Hathaway . . ." Bristol began. As her anger built, her voice steadied. "While I appreciate your uninvited comments"—her voice clearly stated she appreciated nothing—"I hardly see how my appearance can be a concern to you. Nor my person. I have no intention of entering this carriage or any other. I am being met by my aunt, thank you." As gracefully as she could manage in the circumstances, Bristol sat firmly on top of her trunk lest these mad people attempt to take it again. She folded her arms across her chest and turned her face toward the reeking Thames. Why didn't Aunt Prudence come? All Bristol's previous worries returned in force.

Lady Hathaway stopped midway to the coach and turned around, her mouth opening in a little round circle. Then she clutched her stomach and laughed, an explosive booming sound so like Noah that Bristol swiveled her head and stared.

"At least you have spirit; I like that," Lady Hathaway gasped. She held her jiggling stomach and wiped laughter from her eyes. "You young dolt, *I'm* Prudence Adams. At least I was before I married that old fool Robert Hathaway. Now, come along, enough of this nonsense." She stepped up and thrust her head and shoulders through the carriage door, her enormous bottom hanging outside. "Bridey!" she shouted.

The little woman in black hurried past an openmouthed Bristol and placed her palms upon Lady Hathaway's bottom. Bridey drew a breath and shoved mightily. Lady Hathaway popped into the carriage and fell back against an upholstered seat cushion. She frowned out the window. "Are you addleminded, girl? Come along!"

Lady Hathaway was Aunt Prudence? Bristol closed her mouth and gave her head a curt shake. This strange woman was so unlike anything Bristol had been led to expect that her mind rebelled at the information. She stared in bewilderment at the fleshy face glaring out the coach window and struggled to connect this orange-haired vision with the stern, juiceless sermons Noah received each month. *That* sober writer was Bristol's Aunt Prudence, not this painted, booming mass of silk and ruffles.

Involuntarily Bristol cast a final sweeping glance over the dockyards, a part of her mind still searching for the Aunt Prudence of her expectations.

Lady Hathaway leaned forward and thumped her cane on the carriage floor, and Bristol started and scurried up the steps, taking a seat across from her formidable new aunt. They inspected each other in silence while the driver lashed Bristol's trunk to the back of the coach. Then he and Bridey climbed up onto the driver's seat and the carriage jolted forward.

Lady Hathaway's sharp blue eyes peered from folds of flesh. "What's wrong with you, girl? You're pale as a fish's belly!"

"I . . . this is such a surprise . . . Papa forgot to mention your new name or even that you'd married. He didn't tell me . . ."

Lady Hathaway leaned against the velvet upholstery with a rustle of silk, and she waved a jeweled hand airly. "Well, of course Noah didn't tell you. I never told *him*. Noah Adams is a good man, but such a prig! Ideas of class and so forth. He'd never understand or approve marrying above one's station in life. To Noah, self-interest is the devil's torment, and only community welfare is of importance." Lady Hathaway laughed. "His letters are full of such tripe. Noah always looked at personal wealth like a dire disease to be avoided at all cost—as if the aristocracy was a sort of scab on existence. Does he still hold such outlandish views?"

Bristol nodded slowly, a slight frown creasing her forehead. She felt uneasy, not certain if she was being disloyal to her father by listening to Lady Hathaway's criticism.

Lady Hathaway grinned, the edges of her wide lips disappearing into a wall of cheek. "Well, Lord Hathaway may be an old fool, but he is a very rich old fool." She snorted. "Noah thrives on hard work and noble sacrifice too much to understand the pleasures of an advantageous marriage." She lifted the rings flashing on both dimpled hands and nodded pointedly.

Bristol chewed the inside of her cheek. She felt an urge to

166

defend Noah, but Lady Hathaway had said nothing untrue. The point of unease lay in the fact that Bristol had never before heard her father's opinions presented as a negative.

Sharp blue eyes noted Bristol's distress, and Lady Hathaway waved her sausage fingers, cutting into Bristol's weak protest. "Now, don't misunderstand, dear, there's much to admire in your father. In fact, I admire and respect Noah enough *not* to trouble him with a marriage he'd never approve. I don't wish to upset him."

Recognizing the unmistakable affection in Lady Hathaway's booming voice eased Bristol's mind. She smiled hesitantly. "Perhaps you misjudge Papa, Lady Hathaway. Papa would be pleased to know you're happy and well provided for. I think you might consider informing him; I know he'll want to offer his best wishes."

Lady Hathaway's exploding laugh filled the carriage. "I can't very well do that without compounding the misunderstanding. You see, this deception has been continuing for twenty-four years." She shrugged her shoulders. "How could I guess a niece would one day appear to find me out?"

"Twenty-four years?" Bristol's green eyes widened. "But your letters . . . ?"

Lady Hathaway leaned over the cane, a wicked twinkle sparkling in her eyes. "Once a month I copy Reverend Cornwell's dullest sermon and post it to Noah, shamelessly appropriating the words as my own." Lady Hathaway grinned and gave Bristol a conspirator's wink.

Bristol's mouth opened and closed. She blinked. A twitch began at the corner of her full lips, widening helplessly into a smile. "But that's terrible!" She pictured Lady Hathaway copying the sermons and then remembered Noah earnestly reading them aloud to the Adams family, setting Prudence as an example his girls should strive to follow. A bubble of laughter welled in Bristol's throat. "That's just . . ."

Lady Hathaway nodded happily. "Terrible!" she agreed.

Together they burst into delighted laughter, Lady Hathaway's booming guffaw drowning Bristol's softer voice. Bristol laughed until she felt weak and her sides ached. Aunt Prudence was a flagrant deception, nothing whatever like her letters suggested.

Bristol fell against the velvet seat cushions and held her sides. "I promise your secret is safe, Lady Hathaway." It would be a shame to betray her aunt's secret after so many years. Bristol smiled. Following the shared mirth, it seemed

167

stiff and formal to call the woman Lady Hathaway. Bristol looked at the orange hair and powdered face. "Aunt Prudence," she amended awkwardly.

"Pru. Everyone calls me Pru." Aunt Pru leaned forward and pounded Bristol on the knee. "I like you, Bristol Adams! You're pretty and practical and have a sense of humor, thank God!"

Explanations disposed of, Aunt Pru's deep voice chattered on, remembering Noah and past events, liberally interlaced with local gossip, advice, and an occasional demand that Bristol peer out to see a famous landmark passing the coach window.

"Look over there!" Aunt Pru's jeweled hand tugged Bristol forward. "There's the memorial to the great fire of 1666." Aunt Pru indicated a towering pillar, and Bristol dutifully murmured admiration. "I met Robert Hathaway in the aftermath of the fire. Practically two-thirds of London burned to the ground. You can imagine the confusion! By the time things sorted themselves out, the young fool was enough in love with me not to care that I had no money and no title. Of course, I was younger and considerably thinner twenty-four years ago. Oh, it was quite a mad affair, I assure you. In fact, Robert's father threatened to disinherit Robert if he dared marry me." A note of pride entered Aunt Pru's tone. "Thankfully, the old gentleman died of a seizure before he could arrange a new will." Aunt Pru grinned impishly, and her orange curls bounced around her cheeks. "Love is one thing, but love in the slums is something else entirely. Thank God the old man had the good grace to die when he did!"

Overwhelmed, Bristol nodded with a weak smile. She leaned into the seat cushion and let Aunt Prudence's voice wash over her, focusing on the stream of conversation only when it seemed a fact emerged from the monologue which Bristol should remember. For the most part, she simply stared at her incredible aunt and fought to sweep away all previous notions, trying to think of this woman as her aunt and not a flamboyant stranger. Whoever and whatever Prudence Adams Hathaway might be, Bristol realized she thoroughly enjoyed the woman, was entranced with the strangeness of her. Aunt Prudence appeared to value qualities New England frowned upon, and a suspicion grew in Bristol's mind that her London visit would be anything but what Noah intended.

Glancing at her aunt, Bristol hid a smile behind her hand. Poor Papa would be appalled if he knew how ill-suited his sister seemed for the task of instilling discipline and sober thought into a young girl's mind. Unless Aunt Prudence were other than what she appeared to be, Bristol guessed the trip was not destined to be a lonely exile after all.

"Aha! Now, this is the very heart of London," Aunt Pru crowed, waving at the teeming crowds outside the coach windows. "Here you see the greatest city in all the world! Look outside so you'll have something to describe to your father besides the deceptions of your aunt!"

Obediently Bristol peered from the windows into a maze of crowded lanes. The coach crawled through a heavy, noisy traffic of competing carriages and mounted riders. The lanes were choked and dirty and noisy and smelled of offal and garbage—but above everything hung an unmistakable aura of excitement and bustle.

Hawkers jammed the narrow walkways, holding up their varied wares and singing: "Hot pears and pippins!" "Diddle, diddle, dumplin's ho!" "Sweep here, cheap sweep, here!" "Knives to grind, pretty ladies, knives to grind!" "Secondhand clothes! First is dear, seconds is cheap!" The symphony of the streets rose and fell in jumbled cadence.

Behind the hawkers, Bristol saw a row of beggars lining the sooty shop fronts, being chased away, only to reappear. As she stared, a sightless bundle of dirty rags extended a hand and groped toward the hem of a passing gentleman's finery. "A shilling," the begger pleaded in a professional whine. "One shilling, good sir." The gentleman passed without looking up from the papers in his hand, and the blind beggar clutched toward the next passerby. At his side, a mad-looking woman waved a filthy, mutilated stump and cried, "Shillings! Shillings for them what's poor and unable to work. Shillings!"

Bristol sucked in her breath. No such creatures roamed the lanes of Salem; she'd never seen such persons. Their hollow cheeks and extended bellies and their crust of filth affronted Bristol's sense of decency. How could pedestrians pass so callously? She shivered and turned a pale face to her aunt.

Lady Hathaway shrugged. "It's said they do it to themselves. Whack off an arm or a foot to extract pity and shillings." She sighed and patted Bristol's shoulder. "Don't distress yourself pitying beggars. Look at the fine shops, the grand buildings, the magnificence of the carriages, the . . . Oh, see there! I believe it's the Marquis de Chevoux." Aunt Pru poked her face to the window, peering at a resplendent young man leaning negligently on a diamond-studded cane and chatting with an admiring group. "Yes, it is." Aunt Pru studied the young man thoughtfully, then reversed her instruction and pushed Bristol back on the seat away from the window.

Bristol pulled her mind from the beggars and looked a question at her aunt.

Noting Bristol's arched eyebrow, Prudence leaned back with a naughty grin. "Well! It wouldn't do for the marquis to see you looking like a servant girl. He's one of the season's most desirable catches."

Bristol's face turned a becoming pink, and she felt acutely conscious of her plain high-necked gown of drab gray. It hadn't taken long to observe she was years behind English fashion. She'd seen but one woman on the streets wearing an apron and dust cap, and none with the Puritan collar.

Bristol cast a curious glance at the twin mounds of flesh rounding out of Aunt Pru's low-cut bodice. Without thinking, she touched the high collar of her gray gown; fashion or no fashion, Bristol didn't think she'd be comfortable exposing her own breasts like that. On the other hand . . . She shook her head. Perhaps something fashionable existed midway between her own high collar and Aunt Pru's plunging neckline.

Aunt Prudence leaned over her gold-headed cane and lowered her voice in confidence. "The marquis is a Frenchman, as you've guessed. Frenchmen are fantastic lovers!"

Bristol's mouth fell open, and the blush on her cheeks deepened to scarlet. She felt the gold chain beneath her collar, and a sudden image of Jean Pierre leaped into mind, bringing a warm tingle.

Misunderstanding the sudden heat fusing Bristol's face, Aunt Pru frowned and thumped her cane. "Now, don't be provincial, niece!" She examined Bristol carefully, as if reflecting on Bristol's background; then she continued in a softer voice, "Naturally, I can't expect you to know about French lovers." She cleared her throat and shifted on the seat. "And of course, I myself know nothing from personal experience." An impish glint implied a doubt. "But *rumor* has it that once safely married, a woman can do worse than seek a French lover." She hooted at Bristol's flaming face and pounded her niece's knee. "But first things first. We'll try to keep you virginal until we've made you a suitable match."

"A match?" Bristol repeated weakly. At this point, she couldn't have said which part of Aunt Pru's conversation surprised her more.

"Of course. We can't send you back to that barbaric

170

colony where young girls are whipped for flirting. For flirting!" Aunt Pru sniffed her outrage. "They might as well lash girls for breathing! If you marry here, you can stay here—in a civilized country!" She waved at Bristol's stricken expression. "If you insist on returning, at least you'll return with a wealthy husband and no more ridiculous courtship barbarisms. My dear, New England has reverted to the Dark Ages; I was positively shocked by your father's letters!"

Bristol's expression hovered between amusement and dismay. Glancing out the window at the choking filth, the sooty overhead cloud, and the rows of towering buildings leaning one upon the other, Bristol thought perhaps Dark Age Salem did have a few redeeming qualities. Such as breathable air, clean lanes, and graceful homes of manageable size. And few French lovers.

Aunt Pru's voice rushed on, continuing to arrange Bristol's future. "Keeping you virginal may prove formidable," Aunt Pru mused thoughtfully, clearly relishing the problem. Her knowing eyes swept Bristol's lush figure, stripping away the unsuitable clothing and draping her niece in silks and dropping necklines. "Considering your figure and your face, we'll have to maintain a strict guard at all times." She laughed, pleased by the prospect.

Bristol smiled faintly and lowered her pink face to the hands clutched in her lap. If Lady Hathaway had blithely announced an upcoming journey to the moon, Bristol wouldn't have been more astonished and off balance than she was at this moment. The entire conversation was simply unthinkable; for a few seconds Bristol had actually considered mentioning her lack of virginity. Aunt Pru's breezy, knowing manner encouraged such confidences. And to confess her fall from grace repudiated all Bristol had been taught to revere; she assumed people did indeed commit moral wrongs, but never, never did they speak of them.

Bristol sighed. Lovers. Virginity. Dyed hair and secret marriages. She shook her head to clear it. She felt as if she'd walked into an upside-down world where none of the old rules applied. In a stroke, Aunt Pru swept away the solid values and principles Bristol had believed founded in iron, unquestioned, and transgressed at peril. And if the rules were broken, the actions were hidden and people went on as if the old rules still applied.

But that didn't seem to be Aunt Prudence's world. Seeing herself as her aunt must, Bristol suddenly felt like a dolt, a

171

country fool who might better be tucked away in a village hamlet than sitting in an elegant carriage conversing, however badly, with a powdered sophisticate whom Bristol doubted anything could astonish.

Another stunning fact to emerge from a conversation studded with revelations was that Aunt Pru seemed confident Bristol could be molded into a young lady of this time and place—the country edges could be polished off. An idea about which Bristol didn't feel as certain. Already Aunt Pru foresaw a "suitable match" for Bristol and had jumped past that momentous event to advise a French lover!

Bristol darted a glance from the affable mountain of flesh seated across from her. Aunt Prudence smiled to herself in supreme confidence, obviously plotting the brilliant transformation of her young niece into a dazzling beauty to be slotted neatly into London society.

Well, why not? Bristol asked herself, absorbing some of Aunt Pru's confidence. She peeked discreetly at her ripe breasts pushing the bodice of her drab gown and dared to wonder how she would look if her neckline plunged as drastically as her aunt's. Intuitively she guessed her figure had been fashioned for display. Bristol's spirits lifted. If she must place herself in Aunt Pru's ample hands, she might as well relax and enjoy the experience. She guessed that resisting Lady Hathaway would be like resisting an earthquake—impossible.

Smiling at the image, Bristol leaned against the upholstered seat cushions and turned her eyes to the window. The carriage had left behind teeming lanes and tall leaning buildings, and they turned into Pall Mall, a wide cobbled boulevard faced by impressive estates, enormous sprawls of stone and brick with velvety lawns stretching behind. The coach rocked to a stop before one such palace, and Bristol peered forward to marvel at the sheer immensity.

"Niece!" Lady Hathaway had wedged herself half in and half out of the carriage door. "Come along, girl. Push!"

Dusting off her hands, Bristol placed her palms on Lady Hathaway's swelling bottom as she'd seen Bridey do. She drew a breath and shoved. Resisting flesh conformed to the space available, and Aunt Pru popped through the door, caught by the green-liveried driver, who spun and balanced her expertly.

Aunt Pru smoothed her gown and adjusted her headdress over the orange mound of bobbing curls; then she huffed up three wide steps to a pillared porch. Imperiously she paused

172

and waited for Bridey to dash forward and open heavy carved doors.

Bristol followed more slowly, her eyes wide and incredulous. The towering brick house was undoubtedly the grandest thing she'd ever imagined. When Noah spoke of Queen Mary and King William, it was in a palace such as this that Bristol pictured them. She hid a wry smile. The imposing edifice before her was so far removed from the rural cottage she'd expected, that she found it difficult to reconcile the two pictures.

Inside, a cadaverous man glided silently forward and took Aunt Pru's light cape and folded gloves. Following suit, Bristol allowed him to take her cloak and mittens. He looked at her homespun cloak with a sniff, then glided away like a shadow, disappearing down a long polished hallway.

Bristol thrust her hands in her apron pockets and drew a small breath; she felt overpowered by the massing of ornate detail wherever her eyes fell. The entire Adams house could easily have fit within Lady Hathaway's entry hall. Gilded cupids frolicked around the edges of a lofty ceiling, and beneath Bristol's feet lay a brilliantly colored rug twining with exotic woven flowers. Vases and statues and fresh spring roses overflowed tables against silk-hung walls, and several satin settees had been placed at intervals near doors opening into hallways and other rooms.

While Aunt Pru examined a stack of cards on a silver tray, Bristol wandered about the entry peeking into other rooms. She glanced inside gleaming French windows to see an enormous parlor larger than John Proctor's Salem tavern. She stared at fireplaces dominating each end of the room, and gazed at groupings of delicate furniture, some upholstered, some of polished gently curving wood. Nowhere did she see any hint of a spinning wheel, or loom, or any of the working tools that made a home function.

Such prosaic items must be buried in the depths of the house, Bristol thought wistfully. For an instant she longed to see a bubbling pot or a scarred kitchen table—something homey in a familiar world, something she could touch base with. This luxury and opulence fell so far outside her experience she felt uncomfortable just looking at it. It seemed inconceivable she could ever sit in these massive rooms with any degree of comfort.

Aunt Pru was watching. "Do you like everything? Or is it too bland? At first I tried shades of blue, but last year I changed everything to cream and green." An uncertain note hovered in Lady Hathaway's tone, surprising Bristol. Perhaps more remnants of a humble past survived in Aunt Prudence than showed on the surface.

Anxious not to offend, Bristol nodded and lifted her arms. "Aye." She searched for words. "This is all so . . . overwhelming! I couldn't have imagined a house like this in my wildest dreams!"

Satisfied, Aunt Pru bobbed the orange curls and smiled. "Say 'yes,' don't say 'aye.' 'Aye' is definitely lower-class, dear. You must think of such things now." She started toward a sweep of curving staircase. "Come along, I expect you'll want a rest before dinner. I'll show you to your room, and later, Molly Whitney will help you dress for dinner." Her clear blue eyes slid to Bristol's gown. "You haven't anything . . . more suitable, have you?"

Bristol shook her head, looking at the stern faces framed along the sweep of staircase. Hathaways? Certainly not Adamses; there wasn't a red head among them. Even so, the faces seemed oddly familiar.

Aunt Pru sighed. "I thought not. Well, no matter. I'll arrange a visit to Collette's tomorrow; Collette is my seamstress. And we'll urge her to rush. I'm staging a ball on Friday to celebrate Robbie's return. Collette simply must finish something for you before then."

"Robbie? Has your husband been away?" A bewildering maze of carpeted hallways opened at the top of the stairs, and Bristol waited for Aunt Pru to indicate which they'd take.

"What?" Aunt Pru puffed down a corridor filled with tables and vases and hung with richly framed paintings. "Oh, no, no. Robert's health is poor, he hardly leaves the house anymore. But Robbie! Robbie, on the other hand, is hardly ever here." Seeing the confusion in Bristol's glance, Aunt Pru laughed. "Robbie is our son."

Bristol blinked. The day continued to reveal more surprises. A marriage *and* a son were almost more than she could absorb. "I have a cousin?"

"Yes, but I must confess: he *works*!" Aunt Pru sniffed and lowered her voice as if she confided an embarrassing secret. She frowned. "He insists on it. He's even amassed a fortune." There was a grudging admiration in Lady Hathaway's tone, but she clearly believed there was something disreputable about succeeding in business. "His father and I hope he'll settle down and forget such nonsense once he's married." She sighed. "But that's not likely, considering the girl involved." Aunt Pru pushed open a door near the end of the corridor.

"Never mind that," she said, irritated with herself. "We'll have ample time to lay bare the family concerns when you're rested."

Bristol followed her aunt inside and gasped, her hands rising to her cheeks. Slowly she looked around an enormous room, and her eyes rounded in delight. Shimmering pink silk covered the walls and was repeated on the bed covering and again in the curtains falling from the ceiling to frame the bed. Green damask draperies hung beside tall wide windows, and green carpets were scattered about a polished wood floor. All the furniture was upholstered with cream-colored velvet.

Bristol stopped before a fire flickering in the grate and warmed her back against a chill in the spring night. She looked about the room, admiring everything. Despite the size, glowing candles in silver holders imparted a warmth to the room. More candles than her family in Salem would think to use in a month, Bristol noticed, and all of them good-quality wax, not tallow scapings.

"It's lovely!" Bristol breathed. She stroked the top of a velvet chair hesitantly, trying to picture herself living in this magnificent room.

Pleased, Aunt Pru bobbed her head. "Good. I'm glad you like it. Now, then, dinner is at eight o'clock. You'll have time for a half-hour nap before Molly comes." She pointed to a pink velvet rope near the bed. "If you need anything, just pull that, and Molly or Bridey will appear."

Shyly Bristol lifted her eyes. "I don't think Bridey approves of me."

Aunt Pru snorted. "Bridey Winkle was born hating the world, and she's not seen anything to change her opinion. She disapproves of everyone and everything. But she runs this house with an iron hand, and I couldn't manage without her." Aunt Pru swept off her headdress and rolled her head on a stout neck. "Just remember the blood, dear. Bridey's a servant; you are quality—a lady." Aunt Pru smiled and stepped into the hallway. She bellowed, "Bridey! Where are you? I want help with my . . ." The door closed, cutting her final words.

Carefully, as if she might break it, Bristol eased into a velvet chair and leaned back with a deep sigh of pleasure. It felt wonderful not to be rocking on a ship or ferry, or rattling in a noisy carriage, or forced to think about anything. She doubted she could.

Her mind tilted toward overload with a multitude of new

175

impressions and the staggering information she'd accumulated. Bristol turned a wistful eye toward the pink bed, wondering if she could sleep, even as weary as she was. Too many things clamored for her attention. Her only regret was the lack of someone to share these new experiences.

Stretching in the warmth of the fire, Bristol felt her eyes drift shut against her will. If only Charity were here to share that enormous pink bed and marvel at the blaze of so many candles. Bristol yawned. Her friends in Salem wouldn't believe such luxury existed.

Or believe she could doze instead of exploring her new home. Bristol forced her eyes open a crack. Then she sighed and gave it up. Everything would still be here after a short nap.

At least she hoped this wasn't a dream; Bristol had a guilty suspicion she could easily grow to like this way of life. She snuggled deeper into the soft velvet chair.

Her last sleepy thought was a painful curiosity. Where was Jean Pierre tonight? Was he thinking about her? Did he regret the way they'd parted as much as she? Bristol fell asleep with her fingers tangled in the gold chain at her throat. And his laughing face in her mind.

13

To Bristol's relief, the Hathaways would not dine in the cavernous dining room young Molly Whitney described. Instead, dinner would be served in a more intimate setting—in Lord Hathaway's study, just off his bedroom.

"His lordship be down with gout again," Molly Whitney explained. She shook out Bristol's gowns and carried them from trunk to wardrobe. Sturdy rather than plump, Molly, with her apple cheeks and bustling air, struck Bristol as out of place in sooty London; Bristol could more easily picture Molly as a dairy maid in a fresh country setting.

"I'm sorry to hear of his lordship's gout," Bristol murmured. Sorrier than she could adequately express. She wondered anxiously how a painful case of gout might affect her new uncle's disposition. Uncertain as to the length of her stay in Hathaway House, a recipient of Lord Hathaway's generosity, Bristol fervently hoped his lordship would be in a mood to welcome her. Additionally, she felt decidedly nervous about meeting a real lord of the English realm. Despite Aunt Prudence's description of her husband as an "old fool," Bristol doubted the man could be a fool and still be a lord and amass such wealth as she saw in evidence wherever she looked.

Molly finished unpacking Bristol's trunk and held up the pewter mug. "Where shall I put this, miss?" Her voice was carefully devoid of expression, but Bristol guessed Molly thought the pewter cup a distinct curiosity.

Bristol glanced about the pink-, green-, and cream-colored room filled with exquisite vases and gleaming silver pieces. Her pewter mug seemed a shabby residue of her previous existence. Lifting her chin, Bristol pointed. "Set it on the table near the bed, please." No matter what anyone thought, the mug was *her* shabby remnant, and her only physical link with home. Home. Bristol sighed. Salem Village had never seemed so distant, either geographically or mentally.

Molly placed the mug near the bed and dusted off her hands, dark glossy braids swinging from under her dust cap. "Do that be the onliest one, miss?" she asked doubtfully, nodding toward Bristol's trunk.

"Aye," Bristol replied. And quickly amended her answer to "Yes."

Molly frowned. "But all the gowns . . . they be such dark colors, miss! Do there be nothing gay and cheerful for the supper table?"

"I'm afraid not." Bristol looked at her hands. Even the servants disapproved her clothing. She thought of the hours she and Charity and Hannah had spent carding, spinning, dyeing, and weaving. Bristol's shoulders wilted, and she cast an apologetic glance toward Molly. "What do you think is best?" She stepped out of her rumpled traveling clothes, wishing she needn't wear them ever again. Immediately she felt a guilty pang of disloyalty toward her mother and sister.

"Well," Molly said thoughtfully, "I suppose this one." She shook out the dark green velvet Bristol had worn for the shipboard whipping. Bristol looked at it with a twinge of painful memory. Where was Jean Pierre tonight? Molly's curious voice cut into her thoughts. "Are you one of them roundheads?" Molly asked.

"Roundheads?" Bristol repeated. She didn't understand the term.

"Aye, you know. Roundheads. Puritans. Do you dress so plain because of religion?"

Bristol laughed. "I guess so. That's how everyone dresses in New England." She wondered what Molly wore off duty; the frilly dust cap and white apron over a green low-necked gown suited Molly's rosy cheeks and sturdy figure.

"New England must be a dreary place," Molly commented cheerfully. She dropped the dark velvet over Bristol's fiery head and stepped back to judge the effect.

Turning to a full-length mirror, Bristol saw that her face matched the dismay in Molly's. She saw a drab heavy gown of undistinguished cut. Bristol instantly decided to omit her collar and apron; they would only make it worse. And her dust cap.

"Do you have any jewelry, miss? Something to add a bright touch near the throat?"

"Aye . . . yes." Bristol pinned Mr. Aykroyd's brooch to her shoulder and lifted Jean Pierre's gold chain over the neck of her dress. Her fingers lingered on the cool metal. None of that, she silently chided herself. But where was he . . . where was Jean Pierre . . . would he try to find her? "What do you think?" she asked aloud.

Molly cocked her head and laughed. "I think it be a shame to hide such a figure!" She pointed Bristol toward a chair. "But I imagine Lady Pru will see to that." Molly lifted the wealth of red curls tied loosely at Bristol's neck, judging weight and texture. "We can do something here right now." Molly brushed Bristol's long hair with vigorous strokes, her smooth face creased in concentration.

When she'd finished, Molly gave Bristol a gentle push toward the mirror.

Bristol stared. Her hair flowed from a center part, sweeping high on the crown of her head, then dropping in a shimmer of long gleaming coils. She lifted a hand, but didn't dare touch Molly's artistry. "It's beautiful," she breathed. "I look so . . . different." The arrangement seemed to lift her face, to pare away the rounded youthful look and give greater emphasis to her high cheekbones. Even with the unremarkable dress, Molly had made her appear interesting, more a woman than a young girl.

Pleased and happy with Bristol's reaction, Molly grinned. "I'll show you the way."

Bristol followed Molly's swinging hips through a bewildering puzzle of hallways and into another wing of the vast house, past numerous carved doors and a gallery filled with sharp, chiseled faces. And with every step Bristol's nervousness increased. Would Lord Hathaway like her? Would he resemble the distant, chilly faces of his ancestors?

Halting before a set of heavy double doors emblazoned with the Hathaway crest, Molly leaned forward and rapped sharply. Before the door swung in, she squeezed Bristol's arm and whispered, "Don't worry, you'll like them. They're both dears." Molly then disappeared down the long hallway.

To Bristol's surprise, Aunt Prudence opened the doors herself, resplendent in brilliant blue silk with diamonds and sapphires at her neck and ears. The pumpkin hair teetered atop her head in wide rolls and dripping curls. "Well, don't just stand in the hallway, come inside! Hathaway is impatient to meet you." Aunt Pru led the way into a mammoth bedroom glowing with candles. A small fire snapped in the grate. Spring flowers and gay rugs provided spots of bright color in a green-and-white room.

Aunt Pru nodded approval at Bristol. "Your hair is wonderful—not too elaborate, not too simple, just right!" Her booming laugh rippled the blue silk. "Your dress, of course, is awful!"

Bristol smoothed her hands over the well-worn velvet and managed a nervous smile. "It's the best I have." Hannah's finest dyes and careful needlework counted for little in London Town.

"Well, we'll change that." Aunt Pru waved a glittering hand, her flashing rings catching the light. "Collette expects us in the morning. The woman is magic. More important, she's quick." Prudence leaned to inspect Bristol's necklace and cameo. "Simple, but good," she pronounced, her orange curls wobbling. "Quite suitable for a young girl just beginning her social career."

Aunt Pru advanced toward a door opening into the west wall, her blue silk skirt fluttering behind her. At the doorway she paused and covered her mouth. "If Hathaway isn't feeling well, you and I will retire immediately after dinner." She swept through the door, leaving Bristol to follow in her wake.

Lord Hathaway's study provided a pleasant surprise. It was the only room Bristol had seen that approached normal size, and as such, seemed a mistake in the large house. Immedi-

179

ately Bristol sensed this was the heart of Hathaway House, the core around which all else centered. Dark paneling covered the walls and shone behind rows of books in floor-to-ceiling shelves. At one end of the room, the working portion, stood a cluttered desk and matching cabinet; the opposing end of the study was arranged as a small sitting room, furnished with deep comfortable chairs, a low table, and worn footstools. The chairs and stools were upholstered in faded red velvet showing the effect of much use, and red carpets lay on a polished floor. The overall effect was one of welcome and quiet warmth.

One chair sat very near a cheery popping fire, and from within, a thin man wearing a shawl over an elegant brocade dinner jacket waved Bristol forward. Extended before him, one bare leg rested on a pillow placed upon a low footstool. The foot was swollen, and characteristic of gout, gleamed a shiny purplish red.

"Miss Bristol!" Lord Hathaway greeted Bristol in a strong deep voice belying his fragile appearance. "I'm honored to meet one of my wife's relatives after so many years. Forgive me for not rising." He waved a hand toward his foot. "This is such a nuisance." Nothing in his voice or expression asked for pity; he simply stated a condition.

Perhaps he understated his condition. Bristol stared at Lord Hathaway's arthritic hands and swollen foot with a sympathetic glance; victims of gout suffered excruciating pain. Advancing carefully, she avoided any accidental brush against his leg. "I'm pleased to meet you, Lord Hathaway."

He reached for Bristol's hand and brushed dry lips across her fingers, managing to give the impression of a bow though remaining seated. "The honor is mine. It isn't often I have the pleasure of dining with two lovely women." Clear gray eyes smiled at Bristol. "And please, call me Uncle Robert. I've never before been an uncle, and I rather relish the idea." He waved Bristol into a seat across from him and studied her with an open smile of pleasure. "Pumpkin, you didn't tell me she was so beautiful!"

Bristol blinked. Her aunt qualified in shape and hair color for Lord Hathaway's endearment, but it was startling to hear the term used in the presence of a stranger. With a sudden flash of understanding, Bristol looked into Lord Hathaway's oddly familiar thin face and gentle gray eyes. Lord and Lady Hathaway were doing everything possible to help Bristol feel comfortable and accepted in this strange new world.

Shyly Bristol smiled into Lord Hathaway's aristocratic

face, beginning to relax and shed her apprehensions. Though temporarily crippled, her new uncle had a remarkably strong face, and Bristol sensed Lord Hathaway's strength was without malice, a force to be used in the pursuit of quality and decency. She guessed she would grow to like Lord Hathaway very much.

Aunt Prudence returned from a sideboard with a silver tray of glasses and a bottle of ruby wine. She served her husband, then Bristol. "Now, Hathaway," she said, her eyes twinkling over the rim of her glass, "when have you ever heard me rave over another woman's beauty?"

"Never, Pumpkin, never!" He laughed. "But then, next to your loveliness, few women can be considered beauties." He added gallantly, "Miss Bristol comes close, no doubt because of the family resemblance." He lifted his glass in a toast to Bristol. Laughing, Aunt Prudence nodded and raised her wine.

Watching and listening, Bristol could scarcely contain an amused astonishment. Her aunt and uncle flirted with each other like youngsters in the throes of first passion. Aunt Pru continually leaned to pat her husband's arm, or straighten his shawl, or inquire how he felt; and a flirtatious sparkle danced in her eyes. In the firelight, the rolls of dyed hair looked silky and natural, and Aunt Pru seemed several years younger than she had appeared just hours ago.

In response, Lord Hathaway delighted in his wife. He watched her with pride of possession lighting his gray eyes, and he never overlooked an opportunity to press her hand or offer a compliment that carried a heartfelt tremor of sincerity.

They maintained a running chatter throughout dinner, which was served on lap trays by a number of green-and-white-clad servants overseen by Bridey Winkle. Bridey directed the servants with a dark, tight-lipped expression.

"Cheer up, Mistress Winkle," Lord Hathaway said with a smile. "If you're fortunate, things will get worse. Perhaps the roof will crash in around us."

"Hathaway, now don't tease Bridey. She's had a long, trying day on the docks," Aunt Pru chided him, but her eyes sparkled.

When dinner was finished and dour Mistress Winkle led away the flock of serving girls, Aunt Pru rose and Bristol hastened to follow. But Lord Hathaway waved them to their chairs. "Sit down, sit down. I won't allow you to abandon me," he commanded with a good-natured smile. "Dr. Weede brought my medicine today, and I feel quite up to more wine and conversation." He shrugged off Aunt Pru's frown of concern. "Did you know they make gout medicine from an autumn crocus?" he asked Bristol. "Amazing." He shook a head of graying hair. "Such a small flower can offer such great relief." Aunt Pru sat down, watching him critically, not totally convinced. "But never mind that, tell us about the colonies."

When Bristol had talked for an hour, warming to her subject, she noticed her aunt and uncle exchange a glance of understanding. Lord Hathaway shrugged an apology. He smiled. "Forgive the interruption, Miss Bristol." He patted his wife's hand. "Have your pipe, Pumpkin, we won't shock this young lady more than we have already." Kindly gray eyes crinkled. "Listening to your descriptions, I imagine England seems as different from the colonies as night from day. And I suspect it will continue so for a time."

Bristol nodded and admitted that many of her experiences since leaving home had been startling. She tried not to stare as Aunt Pru prepared two pipes, lit them, and handed one to her husband. Leaning back, Lady Hathaway drew on the second pipe with a noisy sigh of pleasure.

Noticing Bristol's wide eyes, Aunt Pru exhaled a circle of smoke and laughed. "Ah, yes, I'm fond of tobacco. I'm afraid we're exposing our vices." She winked wickedly. "Perhaps you'll acquire a few of your own, living here. I've always thought people really aren't very interesting until they accumulate a few vices."

"Pumpkin!" Lord Hathaway laughed. He turned to Bristol and added seriously, "Pumpkin and I discussed this before you arrived, and decided not to alter our way of life. We come late to the idea of family, but we both feel family is not to be excluded from our lives or treated as guests. We hope you'll come to accept us as we are—blemishes and all."

Bristol's eyes filled with gratitude. While she'd worried about them accepting her, they'd experienced similiar thoughts.

She drew a breath and looked at Aunt Pru's little pipe. "Could . . . could I try it?" Inside, Bristol felt no overwhelming urge to sample the effects of tobacco, but she did feel a compelling need for a gesture showing her willingness to accept and be accepted. Ignoring Aunt Pru's wide grin, Bristol accepted the dainty painted pipe and hoped with all her heart that Hannah never learned of this experiment.

Placing the stem between her lips, she breathed fiery air

into her lungs, erupting in choking coughs and beating frantically on her chest with one hand and waving at a cloud of smoke with the other. If Aunt Pru hadn't grabbed the pipe, hot ashes would have spilled to the rug. Bristol gulped a swallow of wine and wiped at the tears stinging her eyes.

"Remember . . . remember when Robbie tried his first pipe?" Lord Hathaway hooted, trying desperately not to jiggle his tortured foot.

"Yes, oh, yes," Aunt Prudence wheezed, wiping her eyes. "I thought the dear boy would choke to death, like Bristol. What was he then? Sixteen?" She caught her breath and patted Bristol's knee. "I don't believe tobacco is your vice, dear." She chuckled.

Bristol blinked and hiccuped. In the shared laughter, she began to feel a part of them, to feel the beginnings of belonging. "When will I meet Robbie?" she asked, glad of an opportunity to turn the conversation from herself.

Lord Hathaway's eyes lit. "He'll be home . . . when is it, Pumpkin?" Bristol had an idea Uncle Robert knew to the exact minute when his son would walk through the door of Hathaway House.

"Friday. Hathaway, your mind is going, along with your fingers and toes!" Aunt Pru grinned at her husband. "Robbie will be here for the ball, and several weeks afterward." She explained, "Robbie is spending this week with his fiancée's family." A dark cloud crossed her plump cheeks, and the light dimmed in Lord Hathaway's eyes.

Tactfully Bristol looked into her wineglass.

Aunt Pru sighed heavily. "Next month Robbie will marry Lady Diana Thorne." A silence followed her words, broken only by the crackling fire in the grate.

"You may as well explain, Pumpkin, she'll hear it somewhere." Lord Hathaway delivered the advice in a strained voice, tossing off his wine.

As she heaved another great sigh, Aunt Pru's ample bosom rose and fell like a barrel. "Yes, I suppose so. Well. Diana Thorne is a distant cousin of Queen Mary's. And at the moment the queen treasures any family connection—her family is dwindling. I imagine you know Mary overthrew her father for the throne, and she isn't on the best of terms with her only sister, Anne." Aunt Prudence exhaled a furious stream of smoke and waved her wineglass. "These circumstances make Mary particularly vulnerable to requests from anyone claiming a blood relationship, however far removed."

Bristol didn't immediately see how this court intrigue had a bearing on young Robert Hathaway.

Aunt Pru poured more wine and continued the story. "Thus, when Diana decided she wanted to marry our Robbie, and none other, Mary and William summoned Robbie to an audience and . . ."—she exchanged a pained glance with her husband—"and they applied certain pressures to force Robbie into an agreement to marry Lady Thorne."

Bristol's forehead creased in a puzzled frown. "Wouldn't an alliance with the royal house be a privilege?"

Lord Hathaway snorted, and Lady Hathaway erupted in bitter laughter. "Indeed it might, under different circumstances. However, not in this case. Diana's relationship to the throne is a distant one. And Diana Thorne is quite insane."

Bristol started, spilling a few drops of wine. She saw the pain in her aunt and uncle's eyes. "I . . . I'm terribly sorry. But isn't there any alternative? Must your Robbie marry Lady Thorne?"

Lord Hathaway stared at his knotted hands, and Aunt Pru leaned to pat his arm. "Robbie insists. The sovereign's promised to strip Hathaway's title and lands if Robbie refuses. And Robbie won't allow that. We've explained to him that these things are of no importance to us, compared to his happiness." Aunt Pru shrugged heavy shoulders. "We have more than we need to live the rest of our lives in comfort. And any disgrace to the name would certainly be balanced by Hathaway's lifetime of service to the realm." She touched her husband's cheek proudly. "We'd prefer to see Robbie marry a woman he could love and sire children by . . . but Robbie agreed to the royal terms."

Lord Hathaway cleared his throat and directed his gaze toward the flames. "Politically, the marriage is a godsend for William and Mary." He smiled weakly. "Having been in politics all my life, I can see the advantages. It's awkward for the royal family to have a mad cousin on the edges of society no matter how well they obscure the family ties. Once Diana is married, she'll no longer be of such grave concern."

Bristol leaned forward, interested in the story.

In a level voice, Lord Hathaway continued, "William and Mary are new to the English throne, and the crown doesn't rest easy. They have their detractors. And at this moment, there is no heir to inherit, should either of them die. If something happened to William—and it could, as even now he's preparing to sail to Ireland and engage against our deposed King James, Mary's father—Mary would be left to rule

184

alone." His troubled gray eyes met Bristol's. "In that event, claimants would spring forth like mushrooms, fighting to be Mary's heir. Family ties would be minutely examined. At the moment, Diana's relationship is a quiet one, but in the aftermath of tragedy"——he shrugged——"any hint of insanity in Mary's family would rock the British Empire. Those opposed to Mary, and there are many, would use Diana's insanity to cloud Mary's own stability. Such a scandal could topple the throne."

Bristol began to understand. "So the king and queen want Diana married and forgotten? Her ties to the royal house even further diluted?"

"Exactly!" Aunt Pru agreed angrily. "They can't themselves place Diana in an asylum; if word got out, the gossip would be murderous. First Mary takes her father's throne and exiles him; then, if she places another relative in an asylum . . . well, you can imagine what the gossips would make of that. Mary would appear a monster. All of England would fear for Anne's safety, and the country would divide its support between the two sisters. The situation would be explosive." Aunt Pru knocked out her pipe with an expression of hopelessness. "William and Mary seized on Diana's demand for Robbie with an eagerness that would make your head spin! If *he* commits her, that is a different thing entirely——and her connection to the throne can be muddied considerably, once she's married. So . . . in less than a month, Diana becomes Robbie's problem, and she's removed from the monarchy."

Bristol didn't know what to say. Their faces told her nothing would offer consolation.

Lord Hathaway drew a breath. "What a pity Robbie didn't find a lovely girl like Miss Bristol before Lady Thorne set her eye on him," he said with a courtly gesture. "Pumpkin, look at the hair on that girl!" He leaned toward Prudence, adroitly changing the subject. "I recall the first time I saw you, Pumpkin, you wore your hair a lot like Miss Bristol wears hers tonight." His gray eyes swung to Bristol with a faraway smile. "Pumpkin was the loveliest girl I'd ever seen. She was standing in a char of rubble and looking as if she'd lost everything in the world."

Aunt Pru's laugh boomed, and she patted his arm with a coquettish touch. "Hathaway, you old fool, I *did* lose everything in the world! Along with thousands of other Londoners."

"And her eyes were as blue as a spring sky. One look into those bold sad eyes, and I was undone."

Bristol smiled in secret understanding. Suddenly she realized that Lord Hathaway continued to see his wife as Prudence had been when first he met her. He didn't see the mounds of flesh, or dyed hair, or the wrinkles beneath Aunt Pru's coating of rice powder. When he looked at his wife, Lord Hathaway saw a slender young girl of striking beauty, standing amid the smoking ruin of London Town.

Bristol leaned back in her chair, listening with half an ear to Uncle Robert's memories. The day had been long and packed with an array of impressions. Drowsily she watched her aunt and uncle flirt with each other. Her body felt heavy, and her mind drifted. Covering her mouth, she stifled a yawn.

Aunt Pru's sharp eyes noticed, and she laughed. "Hathaway, you're boring this child to tears with ancient memories." She tugged a velvet rope beside her chair. "Molly will take you back to your room, dear. Sleep well; we have a busy day tomorrow." Aunt Pru lifted her face to be kissed, and Uncle Robert held his cheek at an angle suggesting he expected a good-night kiss as well.

Bristol smiled and kissed them both, then followed Molly to her own room. The last thing she heard before leaving was Lord and Lady Hathaway gently arguing the exact color of Pumpkin's hair twenty-odd years ago.

In her room, Bristol stepped out of her gown and slid into the nightdress Molly had laid across the pink coverlet. It seemed an age since she'd boarded the ferry in a place called Gravesend. And a century since she'd flung herself hysterically across Hannah's table, begging Noah not to be sent to a dried-up, juiceless old aunt.

Bristol yawned wearily while Molly brushed out her hair. Aunt Prudence had become Pumpkin, and her aunt's cottage had grown into a mansion. Like visions in a dream: carriages, and servants, and good food and fine wine had appeared as if by magic. And Aunt Prudence had produced a husband and a son, and soon, a mad daughter-in-law.

Bristol shook a head dancing with a whirl of impressions, and a tumble of gleaming curls spilled over the shoulders of her familiar coarse nightgown. She stretched and climbed into a bed as soft as pink clouds. Briefly her hand rose to touch the gold chain at her throat, and she wondered where Jean Pierre La Crosse slept tonight. Did he share a bed with another woman?

Before her mind could respond with more than the beginnings of hurt, Bristol's fiery head sank into the pillow, and she was instantly asleep. Molly Whitney pulled the pink coverlet under Bristol's chin and blew out the candles, then tiptoed from the room.

Bristol awoke feeling refreshed and eager for whatever a day at Hathaway House might bring. For a moment her eyes touched the pewter cup gleaming dully on the bedside table, and she thought about home. About how Hannah would be poking up the kitchen fire and lighting the lamps. Charity would be stretching awake, and Noah would be kneeling for morning prayer.

A few short weeks ago, these memories would have raised a lump to constrict Bristol's throat. But now, her strongest feeling was one of regret that she couldn't write a full account of her experiences. Not without betraying Aunt Pru's secrets. Bristol grinned. She couldn't even mention that Aunt Prudence's hair was as carroty as Charity's; Noah would be astonished, she thought with a small smile.

Padding to the window at the far end of her room, Bristol tugged open the heavy draperies. Outside stretched a manicured park of flower gardens, hedges, and formal arrangements of paths and tree-lined walkways, all part of the Hathaway grounds. And all tinted with the golden mist of dawn. A yawning boy with a mongrel dog at his heels rounded into view, carrying two steaming pails of foamy milk. He disappeared under an overhang of roof.

To the far right, Bristol saw a multitude of outbuildings. Stables, sheds, and barns. Lifting her eyes beyond the gardens, she looked out at rows and endless rows of distant brick houses, funnels of smoke rising from their chimneys toward the dark pall overhanging the city. London—immense, dirty, exciting London Town—awoke to another day.

However, it didn't seem to Bristol that Hathaway House felt any inclination to join the waking city. Finally she pulled the velvet rope, wondering if she'd been forgotten.

Molly pushed inside with a tray of strong English ale, coddled eggs, kidney pie, and fresh raisin buns. "You be an early riser!" She set the heavy silver tray in Bristol's lap.

Bristol's brow rose in surprise. She'd waited two hours before summoning the courage to pull the rope. "What time does Aunt Pru rise?" she asked, sampling a raisin bun.

Molly chuckled and began arranging Bristol's hair. "English ladies prefer to think the sun rises in the middle of the sky—that's where it is when they get up. But Lady Pru left orders to be called earlier all this week. What with the ball to see to, and young Robbie coming home, there's a lot needing done." She smiled. "Bridey said Lady Pru is grumbling like an old bear."

And Aunt Pru was still complaining when she and Bristol at last settled into the carriage and jolted toward Paternoster Row and Madame Collette.

"Uncivilized, that's what this is!" Aunt Pru covered an enormous yawn. "Getting out of bed at such an hour!" She peered into Bristol's fresh face, and her own formed a rueful smile. "I'm not as young as I once was."

Bristol laughed. There was an agelessness about Prudence Adams Hathaway that challenged any attempt to blame attitudes or conditions upon age.

Aunt Pru grinned as if she too understood this, and she then launched into a stream of informative chatter, punctuated by frequent thumps of her gold-headed walking cane.

Bristol learned her wardrobe was henceforth out of her hands and transferred to Aunt Pru's fashionable management. Molly Whitney was assigned the care of Bristol's clothing and personal needs. Servants, Bristol was instructed, were considered family; they could be scolded and ordered about and screamed at and threatened. But never were servants abused at Hathaway House. "It's a limiting restriction, I'll admit," Aunt Pru sighed, "but they're like children. One has a certain responsibility toward them."

Seventy-two servants maintained the house, another thirty-six cared for stables and gardens. Bristol gasped at the number. One-third the people dwelling in Salem Village were required just to keep Hathaway House functioning. For three people. The idea staggered her.

And she had not entirely escaped rules of behavior. Young ladies of quality, as Bristol now was, were permitted to walk on the immediate grounds of their homes so long as they were not exposed to the street. But if Bristol desired to fully explore the three acres of gardens, at least one male and one female servant must accompany her. She could (and would, Aunt Pru promised) attend a large number of hunts, parties, teas, dinners, and the like, but she must always have a chaperon.

"Your chaperon—me—needn't be at your side every minute, however." Aunt Pru grinned. She studied Bristol a moment, then leaned forward and touched her niece's knee, blue eyes narrowing shrewdly. "I have an idea your mind wanders." She watched Bristol stroking the golden chain at her throat. "Perhaps the young man in Salem that Noah mentioned? You're thinking of him?"

A rosy color brightened Bristol's cheeks. "No . . . it's someone else," she blurted.

Aunt Pru nodded wisely, her orange hair threatening to fall from under an important headdress. She studied her niece thoughtfully. "Are you in love with this . . . someone else?" she asked curiously.

"I . . . I don't know." Bristol lifted stricken eyes. "I only know it hurts to think about him. And he's never really out of my thoughts; all the time I wonder where he is and what he's doing, and it feels like something is twisting my heart. It hurts!" She felt ridiculous making this confession, but the words poured from her lips.

Aunt Prudence's booming laugh filled the carriage, and she stamped her cane. "That's love, all right!" She patted Bristol's knee sympathetically. "The only cure is having the man . . . and sometimes that only makes it worse." She chuckled. "I confess you've dashed my hopes at finding you a suitable match. Well? Am I to meet this someone else? Or is he in New England?"

Bristol closed her eyes. She didn't know where Jean Pierre might be now. And if he came searching for her, he'd begin by looking for a Prudence Adams who had not existed for twenty-four years. He'd search London's poorer sections and never think to look among the splendid houses in Pall Mall. "I don't know where he is," she whispered.

Aunt Pru clicked her tongue, but her face brightened as she learned her matchmaking instincts were not to be completely thwarted. "A pity," she murmured insincerely as the carriage rocked to a stop in Paternoster Row. "You must try to put him out of your mind," she advised, and now her voice carried the ring of sincerity. "The best cure for an old love is a new love." Aunt Pru thrust her head and shoulders out the carriage door. "Push, girl!"

Bristol placed her palms on Aunt Pru's wide bottom and popped her aunt through the coach door.

"Careful!" the driver warned, catching Aunt Pru with a deft hand. A stinking river of liquid and solids rained upon the sidewalk, thrown from above. "The mornings are hazardous," he added unnecessarily.

"Disgusting," Aunt Pru sniffed, sweeping grandly through the door of Collette's shop, but not before she had to strike away the hands of clutching beggars. Bristol began to understand why Aunt Pru carried the cane.

189

Inside the shop, Prudence Hathaway proceeded to roll over Madame Collette's shrieks of protest like an advancing tidal wave. "It can't be done," Madame Collette cried, waving tiny hands in the air. "I can't have a gown finished by Friday!"

Aunt Pru calmly removed her gloves and accepted a glass of wine. "Of course you can, Collette, but not if you waste your time arguing." She sipped her wine and leafed through a sheaf of sample materials and colors. "Green is definitely my niece's color, just look at those eyes. But something brilliant and bright and gay!"

"Madam, I am telling you it cannot be done. I won't attempt it!" Madame Collette shouted over her shoulder while she circled Bristol's neck with a piece of string and called a number to an impassive assistant. "It is impossible! Every woman in London wants a gown for your ball, Lady Hathaway. I can't possibly finish in time!" She dropped the string to Bristol's breast and muttered, *"Magnifique!"* and shouted another number, then did the same for Bristol's waist and hips. "I tell you, Lady Hathaway, there is not enough money in England to get this girl a gown by Friday!"

Lady Hathaway drew herself to her full height and looked down her powdered nose at the tiny Frenchwoman. "A gown like you created for Lady Morriston's daughter would be acceptable—only finer, of course."

Madame Collette threw up birdlike hands and a fusillade of French shot past her pursed lips. Surprisingly, Aunt Prudence responded in French as rapid and explosive as Madame Collette's. They marched back and forth across the small shop as the battle of wills ebbed and flowed with much shouting and waving of hands.

At the finish, Lady Hathaway smiled and Collette glared with her fists on slender hips. "It will cost double, Lady Hathaway! Double!"

Aunt Pru grinned and leaned forward from the waist. "In a pig's eye, Collette."

Bristol gasped, not thinking it beyond the fiery little Frenchwoman to eject them from the shop. To Bristol's astonishment, Collette returned Aunt Pru's grin and shrugged with Gallic resignation. They're enjoying this, Bristol realized. She smiled weakly and returned to a low stool to wait and watch and sip her wine.

The ball gown settled, Aunt Pru moved on to arrange the remainder of Bristol's new wardrobe. The contest waged for more than an hour, with both women circling, shouting, drinking wine, and, Bristol suspected, loving every minute. At the conclusion of the negotiations, everything from petticoats to gloves to riding habits to morning dresses to more evening gowns and shawls had been arranged for. Bristol didn't dare calculate the cost.

"Hathaway is paying for everything," Aunt Pru explained when Bristol interrupted with a worried whisper. "He insisted. Dear girl, Hathaway is very rich. And generous. My dear, if a man choses to indulge you, you must always remember to let him do it!" She gave Bristol's arm a squeeze. "Hathaway would be deeply wounded if you refuse his assistance." Her eyes lingered pointedly on Bristol's plain high-necked Puritan gown. "And probably embarrassed. Now, you wouldn't want that, would you?" Happily Aunt Pru returned to shout down Collette on terms of payment.

The rest of the day passed in a blur of errands, most of which Bristol was too weary to recall that evening. What she remembered most vividly was the array of color and material at Madame Collette's, and the feel of Aunt Prudence's massive bottom; Bristol thought she surely had shoved Lady Hathaway in and out of the carriage no less than fifty times. She could scarcely keep her tired eyes open throughout dinner.

"What on earth did you do to her, Pumpkin?" Uncle Robert asked with a cheery smile. "Did you make the poor child carry all the money you girls spent on today's spree?"

"Hathaway, you old fool! You know perfectly well I wouldn't dream of carrying coins!" Aunt Pru fluttered her eyelashes and adjusted her husband's shawl. "Are you warm enough?"

He nodded. "Send the poor girl to bed, then have your pipe and tell me how you bested Madame Collette." Lord Hathaway winked at Bristol. "Your aunt is never happier than when she's beating the French."

Bristol stood, hiding a yawn behind her hand. She tried to thank Uncle Robert for his generosity, but he wouldn't hear of it. He waved a hand. "The pleasure of seeing you as the most beautiful young girl at the ball—besides Pumpkin, that is—will be thanks enough." He pressed her hand as she bent to kiss his hot, dry cheek. "Be careful of young Robbie. Engaged or not, I suspect the rascal is a devil with women." He laughed. "The lad comes by it naturally. So was I before Pumpkin here took me in hand. We Hathaways have a way of losing our hearts to red-haired women!"

Bristol returned the pressure of his fingers and kissed them both good night.

The next days passed in a blink, filled with a dizzying swirl of ball preparations. Bristol followed behind Aunt Pru, up and down stairs, outside, inside, through all the rooms of the house, and with every hour her respect grew for Aunt Pru's sharp eye and gift for organization. Under her direction, an army of green-and-white servants scrubbed a ballroom nearly the size of the Salem Town square, cleaning and scrubbing and polishing and shining. Messengers and delivery men seemed to arrive hourly, mixing with a distinguished flow of gentlemen calling on Lord Hathaway. Sprays of spring flowers appeared in the hallways and entry and festooned the walls. Fresh waxy candles of various scents replaced half-burned stubs. Carpets were dragged away and returned, beaten free of dust. A large red-faced woman wearing a soiled apron and a dour expression appeared at intervals to discuss the mountain of food building in the kitchens.

"That's Maggie O'Hare," Aunt Pru whispered after one encounter when the red-faced woman stamped away, swinging a long ladle like a machete. "A genius, but nasty-tempered. Evil!" Bristol stared with awe at Maggie O'Hare's retreating back. To intimidate Aunt Pru, the woman must be nasty indeed. "Never set foot in Maggie's kitchen," Aunt Pru warned with a light shudder. "I did once, about twenty years ago, and Maggie threw a pot at me." Aunt Pru's blue eyes widened to the size of saucers. "Imagine! Throwing a pot at a lady of the realm!" She shook her pumpkin head mournfully and returned to the voluminous lists. "If I could replace Maggie, I would; I don't know what our kitchen looks like. But the woman can do things with seasonings and sauces that make me the envy of London." Aunt Pru looked up with a weak grin. "Maybe I'll outlive Maggie; then I'll get a peek at the kitchen."

The preparations continued, with Aunt Prudence as field marshal and Bridey Winkle acting as first lieutenant. And at the end of each exhausting day, Bristol and her aunt fell into their chairs in Robert Hathaway's study and repeated the trials and triumphs of the day for his enjoyment.

"And would you believe it, Hathaway, the second-floor mistress announced she couldn't polish the silver on that floor. Couldn't do it!" Aunt Pru shook a mound of orange curls in disgust, slicing into a lump of boiled beef with a tired sigh.

"And why not, Pumpkin? Did you demand a reason?" Uncle Robert's gray eyes twinkled, waiting for the entertainment twenty-four years of marriage had conditioned him to expect.

"Well, of course I did. She said they had plenty of vine-ash to make the silver polish, but . . ."—Aunt Pru paused dramatically—"but they were out of urine to mix the ash with. Imagine that!"

Uncle Robert threw back his head and roared with appreciative laughter, being careful not to move his foot. "Over one hundred people in this house, and no urine?" He scratched his head. "What are we to do, Pumpkin? Serve our guests on blackened silver?" His eyes sparkled.

"Certainly not!" Aunt Pru exchanged a glance with Bristol, and they both giggled. "I had to send out an order that someone urinate at once. Two someones." The giggles exploded into side-aching laughter. "And then . . ." Aunt Pru gasped. "And then . . . no one could do it, so . . . so Bridey Winkle did. Bridey Winkle!"

All three collapsed with mirth. And the evening ended, as they all seemed to, Bristol thought happily, on a tired note of shared affection and laughter.

At last Friday dawned, and Bristol, Bridey Winkle, and Aunt Pru dashed about the house satisfying themselves all was in readiness. Bristol's gown arrived at noon, just as Aunt Pru was preparing to send an outraged message to Paternoster Row. The gown was whisked upstairs to Molly before Bristol had a chance to see it.

"Thank God! I was beginning to imagine Collette would have a revenge on me!" Aunt Pru pulled out a chair and sank into it, careful not to disturb the gleaming silver laid out on the long dining table. "There's time for a nap, Bristol, and I advise we both take one."

Bristol nodded agreement, but her shining eyes indicated she'd have trouble sleeping. This was, after all, her first ball and her first French gown.

Aunt Pru sighed with a smile of understanding. "It will be a late, late night . . . supper at midnight, and I imagine the dancing will continue until dawn." She stood up and stretched, her rounded shape rippling. "I don't know if I'm more excited about the ball or about seeing Robbie." Her weary blue eyes lit from within. "You go ahead to your nap, dear. I believe I'll just check Robbie's room once again. I want everything to be absolutely right."

Bristol yawned despite herself and nodded assent. "I believe I will, Aunt Pru." She hugged her aunt, smelling powder and lavender. "If you need me, just call." She smiled affectionately. "I'm glad Robbie is coming home. I know how much he means to you and Uncle Robert."

As Bristol ran lightly up the curving sweep of staircase, she wondered curiously if the younger Hathaway could possibly be as wonderful as his parents saw him as being. She smothered a yawn. It didn't really matter; she was determined to like him for their sakes.

14

"You look devastating!" Aunt Prudence beamed as Bristol floated down the stairs to take her place in the entry hall beside her aunt.

Bristol blushed with pleasure. She'd just come from Lord Hathaway's study and a flow of extravagant compliments delivered in the old gentleman's gallant style. Unfortunately, Lord Hathaway could not bear any weight on his swollen foot, and he would miss the ball. But he'd insisted on seeing Bristol before she ran downstairs, asking her to turn this way and that so he could admire each cunning tuck of Collette's masterpiece. He praised Bristol's beauty until her face flamed to match her hair.

Collette had designed the gown to sweep over Bristol's shoulders and dip low, displaying a creamy swell of breasts; the gown then draped in to emphasize her tiny waist before flaring out in puffs of brilliant green silk trimmed at bodice and cuffs with lace as delicate as cobweb. Molly Whitney had dressed Bristol's shining hair in soft loops to frame her face, and a flow of curls dropped from the crown of Bristol's head, cascading past her shoulders in a shimmering river of golden red.

When Molly finished, Bristol peeked shyly into the mirror, catching her breath in surprise and delight. The beauty staring from the glass was a woman no one in Salem would recognize. This woman had outgrown the simplicity of Puritan tailoring and wore the low-cut silk gown as if born to it.

If meekness and humility thrived inside that small curving body, no hint glimmered in Bristol's sparkling eyes. The woman in the mirror exuded youthful confidence and eager surety. Anyone observing her would be convinced she knew the power of her rare loveliness.

And tonight, remembering how she looked, hearing the delicious whisper of rich silk, Bristol felt as if she'd been transported into a new, more fitting image. An image always existing just below the surface, waiting to be brought out.

Aunt Pru fluffed Bristol's puffed sleves and fussed over her; a touch here, a tuck there. For herself, Prudence Hathaway had chosen a frothy concoction of pink and mauve. On a less flamboyant personality, such colors might have clashed offensively with the mounds of carrot-colored hair; but Aunt Pru carried the combination brilliantly. She smiled approval at Bristol. "The green exactly matches your eyes, dear, each doing justice to the other." She chuckled proudly. "The men will be fighting to meet you. I've extended last-minute invitations to several interesting young men, with your future in mind."

Aunt Pru's words faded in Bristol's ears, and a buzzing filled her head. She stared at the man striding through the entry door, and her face flamed, then drained of color as a sudden suspicion flashed across her thoughts. Her hand fluttered to a racing heart, and Bristol felt rooted to the floor.

"What . . . ?" Aunt Pru turned to follow Bristol's wide helpless gaze. Then Prudence Hathaway's round face lit with happiness and she ran forward, throwing her large pink-and-mauve arms around the man in the doorway. "Robbie!" she cried. Aunt Pru buried her face in the man's broad shoulder, tears of joy choking her voice.

Jean Pierre La Crosse stared at Bristol over Prudence's shoulder, his gray eyes locking to hers.

Reaching behind her, Bristol's fingers found the edge of a table, and she leaned against it, her hands whitening on the table rim. Shock jolted through her mind. Jean Pierre and Robbie Hathaway were the same person! But that couldn't be! She swallowed hard and tried to drop her eyes, but his flickering stare held her gaze. Dear God, Bristol thought wildly, no wonder Lord Hathaway had seemed so comfortable and familiar from the first. Seeing Robert Hathaway's son, Bristol recognized her uncle's gray eyes, his firm set of jaw and chin, the high aristocratic nose.

Aunt Prudence wiped her eyes and tugged Jean Pierre

195

toward Bristol. "I want you to meet my niece. Robbie, this is—"

"Mistress Adams. We've met, Prudence." Jean Pierre took Bristol's trembling fingers and bent over them. She closed her eyes as his lips brushed her hand, and his warm fingers filled her palm.

Aunt Pru's eyebrows shot toward the curls pasted on her forehead. "You've met?" She turned to Bristol with a delighted smile. "But how? And why didn't you tell me?"

Bristol didn't trust herself to speak. Seeing him so unexpectedly had wildly disturbed her sense of balance. Her knees threatened to buckle, and her mouth had turned to dust. Jean Pierre seemed to fill the large entryway, his vitality and rugged maleness a dynamic force amid the rustle of green and pink and mauve.

"Mistress Adams didn't know we're related, dear Prudence." Jean Pierre's rich deep laugh vibrated along Bristol's nerves. "I brought in the *Challenger*; we had the honor of carrying Mistress Adams as a passenger."

A good-natured frown puckered Prudence's forehead. "But surely the name! We've spoken of little else but Robbie Hathaway since Bristol arrived." She turned to Bristol with a quizzical expression. "Didn't you make the connection with Captain Hathaway?" Prudence smiled in confusion, looking from one to the other.

Jean Pierre laughed and patted Prudence's hand. "You forget everything having to do with business. You know I use mother's name everywhere but here." He lifted her chin. "Would you rather I terminate all business entirely and end your embarrassment, or would it please you more if I used the Hathaway name and informed the world we've become working merchants?"

Prudence contrived to look wounded and flirtatious at the same instant. "You know I'd be disgraced having it known I have a working son. Naturally I'd prefer you end this nonsense!" She grinned. "But since you won't, I admit to seeing your point. Continue with 'La Crosse.' Perhaps no one associates the name with us." She hugged him, oblivious of the fact her niece had not uttered a word. "But what's this about the *Challenger*? What happened to the *Dover Clay*? You took the *Dover Clay* out, didn't you? I couldn't have forgotten that!"

Jean Pierre glanced at Bristol's pale, questioning face, then grinned at Prudence. "A Spanish pirate sank the *Dover Clay*. A very handsome pirate, Pru, you'd have adored him." Aunt Pru's laugh boomed across the entry hall, and she touched

196

her fan to Jean Pierre's arm with an arch smile. "The *Hanover Princess* picked us out of the water."

Aunt Pru's expression was thrilled and a little breathless. "I'm so anxious to hear the details! There'll be no rush at dinner tomorrow; you must plan to tell me everything then!" A sudden thought wrinkled her brow. "Willie Boyd! Is Willie Boyd safe? I'll never forgive you, Robbie, if anything happened to that darling boy!"

Jean Pierre smiled. "He's swapping tales in your own stable right now. And he has a brave story to tell." Jean Pierre's gray eyes looked deeply into Bristol's. "Your charming niece plays a heroic role in Willie's loss."

"Loss?" Prudence demanded suspiciously.

"Willie will tell you about it himself," Jean Pierre answered. He continued speaking, satisfying Prudence as to Mr. Aykroyd's safety and the well-being of such others as she inquired about with much clicking of her tongue.

One by one the mysteries began to unravel. Now Bristol guessed the identity of the great lady who had taken Master Boyd from the steps of her house and raised him. Now Bristol understood how Jean Pierre had known where to find her; Mr. Aykroyd's enigmatic words were explained. Prudence Adams Hathaway was Jean Pierre's stepmother. With a rush of memory, Bristol put the pieces together—and now she realized why Jean Pierre had not hinted at a future. Her hand rose to cover the pain twisting her mouth, and she felt sick inside.

Aunt Pru cast a pointed glance toward the door. "And where is your lady?" she asked with a noticeable lack of enthusiasm.

Jean Pierre's eyes met Bristol's without a waver. "Diana's just outside. Lady Morgan requested a word with her." His face remained carefully expressionless, but Bristol knew her own was not. As the impact of what she'd discovered churned through her mind, her face wore her emotions like a mirror.

Surprise, confusion, despair, wrenched across her features in quick succession. And pain. Pain.

Jean Pierre looked into her stricken eyes, and a hand opened at his side, but he didn't touch her. He smiled then, flashing a row of white teeth. "I hope you'll save a dance for me, Mistress Adams." He turned to Prudence and bowed over her fingers. "Where have you hidden Father?"

"He's waiting for you upstairs. It's the gout again. I know you have to unload the ship and I understand why you spent several days with Diana's family—so many details to ar-

197

range—but you can't imagine how impatient we've been, knowing you're in England and not seeing you!" Aunt Prudence kept Jean Pierre's hand, looking up with love shining in her blue eyes. "Robbie," she said with disarming shyness, "after all these years, couldn't you call me . . . Mother?"

Jean Pierre arched an eyebrow, and a sparkle lit his eyes. "I wouldn't dream of embarrassing you. As soon as you look old enough to have a son my age, I'll call you Mother."

Prudence crowed in delight.

Leaning forward, Jean Pierre whispered something in Prudence's ear, and Prudence laughed wickedly and slapped his arm with her fan. "Impossible!" she shouted, grinning from ear to ear. "You're a devil, Robbie, a wicked child. Now run off to see Hathaway—the old fool's been counting the minutes."

Jean Pierre kissed Prudence's full cheeks and bounded lightly up the curve of stairs past rows of framed ancestors who looked out with his eyes, his mouth, his nose. Bristol lowered her head. For nearly a week she'd looked at those pictures and seen Jean Pierre, and thought the resemblance a product of romantic yearning.

"Isn't our Robbie wonderful?" Aunt Pru smiled, her damp eyes following Jean Pierre until he disappeared at the top of the staircase. "When Robbie comes home, I feel twenty years younger, and Hathaway comes alive."

Bristol stared, trying to focus on Aunt Pru's conversation. She couldn't stop her mind spinning long enough to sort everything out. "I . . . I thought Robbie was your natural son. I didn't realize . . ." she stammered.

Prudence smiled fondly. "I couldn't love Robbie more if I'd borne him. One of the biggest disappointments of my life was the failure to bear Hathaway a child." She looked at her hands, turning a flashing ring. "When Robbie came to us after eight childless years, it was easy to pour all our love into him." She mustered a smile. "Robbie was fourteen when he arrived. A product of a prior indiscretion of Hathaway's. Fourteen is quite a suitable age I've always thought. I've always found younger children to be so . . . sticky. Don't you agree?"

Before Bristol could answer, a tall willowy woman with striking honey-colored hair appeared in the doorway. "Robbie?" she called anxiously. The woman's eyes darted about the entry.

"Lady Thorne . . . Diana." Prudence stepped foward with a gracious smile.

Bristol's heart sank. From a distance, Lady Diana Thorne was breathtakingly beautiful. Past the first bloom of youth, her beauty lay in the ripeness of full blossom. Not before nor in the years to come would the shimmer of loveliness grace her aristocratic features with quite the same lush beauty as she now wore. Her delicately chiseled face showed experience, yet there was nothing jaded or hard in her expression. The pink in her cheeks was the tint of nature rather than artifice. At first glance, Bristol sinkingly admitted Lady Diana Thorne was easily the most beautiful woman she had seen.

But a second glance brought a chill to the heart. There was something in the woman's eyes—something terribly wrong, and a little frightening.

"Robbie? Where are you?" Diana Thorne's whispery voice rose in alarm, and her strange gold-flecked brown eyes scanned the entry hall. Those eyes had a vacant, empty look, as if nothing lay behind them. Or something too wild and deep to risk exposing.

"Diana!" Aunt Pru placed a hand on Lady Thorne's arm. "How stunning you look! Few women can wear scarlet without dimming in comparison, but on you it looks . . ."

Diana Thorne shrugged off Prudence's hand. She stared at Prudence and then at Bristol. And now Bristol saw that Diana's eyes were not vacant at all—they held a mad whirlpool depth unlike anything Bristol had ever encountered. A shudder rippled Bristol's spine. An unnatural strength and passion swirled in Lady Thorne's golden-brown eyes.

"What have you done with Robbie?" Diana Thorne hissed. She clutched her silk cloak in both hands, and her body stiffened, the flesh appearing to harden into ivory-colored marble. "Where is he?" Her voice rose to a sudden shriek, thin and frightened.

Behind Diana, an elegantly dressed couple halted in the doorway and glanced at each other uneasily. Aunt Pru waved them back and cleared her throat. She opened rouged lips. "Robbie's just run upstairs to say hello to his father. He'll return in a moment, dear. Why don't you go on into the ballroom . . ."

Diana's eyes closed, and she swayed on her feet. A thready moan issued from her sensual lips. Then her eyes snapped open and her face contorted in dark fury. "I want Robbie! Where is he?" Her fingers acquired a life of their own, fluttering, flying, clenching, opening, clawing up to scratch pink

199

lines across her milky breast. "Robbie!" she screamed. Her voice soared through the lofty entry hall, echoing panic and rage.

A small dark-clad figure raced past Bristol, and Bridey Winkle dashed up the winding staircase, lifting her skirts and taking the steps two at a time, calling Robbie's name as she went. Aunt Prudence's mouth fell open, and she threw up her pink-and-mauve arms, at a loss as to how to handle the scene unfolding before her.

Diana began to spin, moaning and chanting, "Robbie! Robbie! Robbie!" She turned in slow circles, picking up speed until her scarlet gown billowed around her. Honey-colored tendrils fell from an elegant arrangement and flew about her face. She spun around the entry hall, knocking tables askew and smashing whatever her long fingers touched. Vases and flowers and small statuettes crashed to the floor in an explosion of violence. She hurled a crystal bowl at the wall, sparkling shards spilling down the silk covering. "Robbie! Robbie! Robbie!"

The couple in the doorway covered their mouths, and their eyes widened. Aunt Pru clutched her stomach with one hand and her forehead with the other. Bristol backed against a wall, shrinking from the insane flicker in Diana Thorne's golden eyes.

Diana's cloak spun from bare rounded shoulders as she systematically kicked through the debris, lifting and shattering the few table items remaining unbroken. "Where is Robbie?" she cried, her voice between a chant and a sob. "What happened to Robbie?" She lifted an exquisite Oriental vase over her head and smashed it to the carpet, leaving a spreading wet stain and a scatter of pink roses. "Robbie!" she wailed.

"Diana!" Jean Pierre's rich voice cut through the noise of breaking glass and Diana's labored breathing. He ran down the stairs and enfolded Diana in his arms. She buried her flushed face in his neck, gasping with relief.

"You were gone! I expected you to be standing here, and you weren't! You should have told me where . . ." Her shoulders convulsed and she pressed hard against Jean Pierre, as if she wanted to melt inside him, to become part of his strength and freed from a frightening empty world.

"Shhh. *Calmes-toi. Calmes-toi, chérie.* I'm here now. *Calmes-toi.*" Jean Pierre stroked her honeyed hair, and his deep voice soothed and caressed. "Father asked about you. Will you return with me and brighten an old man's evening?" He lifted her quivering chin and brushed away a flow of tears with his thumb.

"Lord Hathaway?" Diana frowned, struggling to filter her confusion, to summon a logical order. "Yes. Yes, I remember now." Jean Pierre retrieved her cloak, then placed a strong protective arm about Diana's waist and led her gently up the staircase, murmuring close to her ear.

Bristol's breath released in a rush, and she sank abruptly to a satin-covered settee, her feet surrounded by slivers of glass. Lady Thorne was insane. Tensed on the edge of her seat, Bristol watched Jean Pierre and Diana until they disappeared at the top of the staircase; then she turned a dazed stare to Aunt Pru.

Prudence Hathaway waved the couple in the doorway on into the ballroom. She planted her fists on massive hips and surveyed the wreckage around her. "Good God!" Prudence breathed. Bridey Winkle descended the staircase with a battery of servants in tow; she offered glasses of wine to Prudence and Bristol. Aunt Pru nodded gratefully. "Thank you, Bridey. If you hadn't fetched Robbie when you did, I don't know what might have happened." Prudence wilted onto the settee beside Bristol and gulped her wine. "Good God!"

The Hathaways' cadaverous butler ushered two more couples inside, allowing them a brief word with Lady Hathaway before he prodded them toward the ballroom. The guests departed with raised eyebrows and curious glances toward the wreckage and busy servants.

"Make the rest wait," Prudence ordered. She accepted another glass of wine and fell heavily against the cushions of the settee. Her rouge stood in pink circles on her pale face. "Do you know what that Oriental vase was worth? Good God! No wonder William and Mary are anxious to be rid of her! It costs a king's ransom to have her in the house!" Prudence drained her glass and weakly fanned her ample bosom. "Diana's crazy as a bedbug!"

"Does this happen often?" Bristol asked in a hushed voice. The broken pieces of glass disappeared, and new vases and fresh flowers appeared in their place. In a moment only wet stains glistening on the carpet remained to mark the earlier tempest.

"Often?" Aunt Pru shrugged unhappily. "Who knows? I guess we'll discover the answer for ourselves. Robbie and Diana will be living here until they locate a suitable house." Her eyes rounded under folds of flesh. "Think of it—in less

201

than a month, we'll have to contend with Diana every day! Every day!" She shuddered.

Bristol couldn't bear to think of it. She patted her aunt's hands, at a loss for words.

Prudence's worried eyes rose to Bristol, and even the warm candlelight didn't soften the sudden age in her face. "Poor Robbie faces a lifetime of these dreadful scenes." She stared at the glass in her fingers, then sighed and struggled to her feet. "Well. All's calm for the moment. And we are giving a party." She attempted a smile and pinched her cheeks. "Up, girl, and do something with that long face. We don't want anyone seeing us moping here." She handed her empty glass to a passing servant. "The Marquis de Chevoux will be here, and the Duke of Easton, and many more. They must not see you looking glum. Up. Up, now."

Prudence made a few adjustments to Bristol's gown; then her chins rose and her orange head sailed toward the entry door. Lady Hathaway nodded to the butler, and a flood of people poured through the door. Only Bristol noticed the dent in her aunt's usual ebullience; to a casual observer Prudence's enthusiastic greetings and introductions were delivered in her normal style.

For herself, Bristol quickly abandoned an effort to remember the parade of faces and titles passing before her. They were too numerous to recall, and she couldn't settle her mind to the task. She nodded, smiled, and murmured empty phrases to the swell of glittering personages filing past. And her eyes continued to stray toward the staircase.

Jean Pierre. Her heart filled her mouth, and her hands trembled slightly. He was here, in this house. A wheezing blond gentleman lifted her limp hand to his lips, and she muttered a vague distracted acknowlegment of his gushing compliments. Jean Pierre was here. She exchanged bows with an elegant woman dressed in gold satin and sparkling with jewels. Jean Pierre. The woman passed, leaving a faint scent of perspiration and rosewater, and another took her place.

All the while she smiled and bowed and murmured, Bristol's racing mind sifted the information she'd learned in such a rush. Robbie was Jean Pierre. And he would be married in a month. Her lips pressed in pain, and the man before her blinked and muttered a vague apology and moved on. She and Jean Pierre would be living in the same house—with Diana, his wife. Jean Pierre, of the smoldering eyes and strong arms. Jean Pierre, who made music of the night and turned flesh to liquid. Jean Pierre.

There had never been a future with Jean Pierre La Crosse. He'd mentioned no future plans because there could be none. Stunned, Bristol realized what they'd shared on the *Challenger* had been everything to her, but nothing more than a passing interlude for La Crosse.

The full impact of her thoughts bowed her head. Jean Pierre had used her. Used her body to ease the denials of a long voyage. Then he'd discarded her. At no time had Jean Pierre considered a future that included Bristol.

Her face paled, then flamed in shame and anger. Memories of her simple happiness rose to mortify her; memories of shared laughter and quiet touches brought a humiliated quiver to her full lips. Jean Pierre had made a fool of her—a willing fool. How he must have smiled inside when Bristol's eyes lit as he walked through the cabin door! How he must have laughed when she clung to his demanding body and whispered heated words into the hollow of his throat.

Bristol staggered under a dizzy wave of hatred and betrayal. So many nights! So many nights she'd lain awake sorting her feelings for him, being so sure, so careful, before she admitted her love. Love! She'd deluded herself into believing she felt a profound emotion, and worse, that Jean Pierre returned her passion. She'd battled the idea of loving him, but deep inside, she'd known the truth. And all the time he used her!

"Bristol!" Aunt Pru's frown was concerned. "Are you feeling well? You look like death, and you're rocking on your feet." She led Bristol to a settee. "Here. Rest a minute." Pru mopped her forehead and consulted a list she pulled from her waist sash. "I believe everyone has arrived. When you feel stronger, we'll join our guests." Calling the butler and Bridey Winkle, Aunt Pru delivered last-minute instructions.

Both Prudence and Bristol glanced at the empty staircase, then away. "Well," Aunt Pru sighed, "never mind Robbie. We'll have him to ourselves tomorrow. Look here!" She waved a card filled with writing. "This is your dance card, girl! And not a blank space! I think every man passing through the receiving line insisted on a dance with you. You are already a success!" Chuckling gleefully, she ran a jeweled finger down the list. "In two more sets, you begin. I could easily have filled those, but I wasn't certain when we'd finish here." She poked the mound of orange curls and ran a smoothing hand over the layers of pink-and-mauve ruffles. "Come along . . . your future awaits."

Future. Bristol squeezed her eyes shut; then she rose

slowly, tearing her eyes from the vacant staircase. Lilting music drifted from the ballroom, but it sounded flat and distant to her ears. She drew a deep breath, wanting nothing so much as to act as Diana had—smash something and let out the frustration and disappointment and bitter betrayal.

She conquered these feelings with difficulty. Stepping after Aunt Pru, Bristol wrenched her mind to the problem at hand. She'd take one small thing at a time. Drawing a breath, she called to her aunt, "Aunt Pru . . . I've never danced. Is it difficult?" Reverend Parris adamantly maintained dancing was a temptation of the devil. Apparently, Bristol thought listlessly, Aunt Pru's Reverend Cornwell felt differently. Sin appeared to vary depending on geography.

Aunt Pru froze, her large body quivering, and Bristol bounced against her aunt's bottom. Prudence Hathaway turned woodenly and leveled a stare at her niece. "You. Don't know. How to dance?" Glaring incredulity spaced each word. At Bristol's timid nod, Aunt Pru rolled her eyes toward heaven and sank to a nearby settee, looking like a suddenly deflated ball.

"I'm sorry, Aunt Prudence . . . there was never an occasion . . ."

Aunt Prudence stared at the dance card. She fanned her face furiously, blowing wisps of orange into a fuzz around her cheeks. Sitting down, Bristol rubbed her aunt's soft plump hand. Aunt Pru appeared to be in shock. "Aunt Pru? Aunt Pru? I'm sorry, I just—"

"Puritans!" Aunt Pru's heavy shoulders dropped, and she stared into her lap. "I might have guessed." Mournfully she gazed at her niece. "All those lovely young men! And the way they stared at you when they passed through the line!" She sighed and puffed to her feet, squaring her shoulders. "Well. You'll simply have to learn. Just stand in the man's arms and move when he moves. And flirt! Fod God's sake, flirt!" She touched Bristol's back significantly and managed a weak grin. "I *know* you can flirt." The color began to return to Prudence's cheeks. "If you flirt outrageously, perhaps no one will care if you stumble or flop about."

From the corner of her eye, Bristol noticed a flash of red skirt at the top of the stairs. "Aye! I'll flirt outrageously." She tugged Prudence's pink-and-mauve arm, rushing her toward the ballroom. Bristol wasn't ready to face Jean Pierre and his bride-to-be.

But she was acutely aware of him. She knew the exact moment he led Diana into the immense ballroom; she sensed

204

where he stood every minute. Through her unclaimed sets, Bristol circled the ballroom, keeping a distance between herself and Jean Pierre.

"For God's sake, child," Aunt Pru puffed. "Stay in one place for a moment." She fanned rivulets of perspiration leaking down the sides of her face and patted vaguely at her powder. "How can the men find you if you're constantly on the move? This isn't a fox hunt, you know." Pru's eyes yearned toward deep comfortable chairs lining the walls, where aging dowagers chatted and judged the whirling couples. She stopped a servant and snatched a glass of wine from the silver tray. "Ah. That helps." Leaning toward Bristol, Aunt Pru whispered behind her fan, "The man approaching is the Duke of Easton. Rich. Single. Dull as barnwood, but a good catch."

Bristol pulled her gaze from a dark head towering above the other dancers, and she pasted an artificial smile on her mouth. A small rush of breath escaped her lips.

The Duke of Easton bore a startling resemblance to Caleb Wainwright. In the blaze of scented candlelight, the duke's hair gleamed a bright sandy color, and she saw his eyes were a clear pond blue. The duke did not stand as tall as Caleb, nor was his body as muscular—heavy farmwork played no role in the duke's background—but he had Caleb's square jaw and firm chin.

"Mistress Adams?" The duke bowed from the waist, his coat flaring over green satin breeches. He straightened with a bland smile. "I believe I have the honor of this dance." The duke's voice was higher than Bristol had expected, and slightly adenoidal.

Bristol shot Aunt Pru a panicked look.

Prudence held Bristol's card at arm's length and squinted. ". . . Ah, yes, an allemande for the duke of Easton." She smiled coquettishly at the duke and pushed Bristol forward. "An allemande is slow and easy, you'll do fine. Flirt!" she hissed as the duke led Bristol onto the crowded floor.

The Duke of Easton opened his arms, and Bristol walked into them, glancing rapidly at the dignified couples around her to establish procedure. Hesitantly she placed her moist hand in his, and then they were bowing and dipping around the vast room, jerkily at first, then slightly smoother as Bristol tried to adjust to the rhythm and flow of music. Watching the lady on her immediate right, Bristol stepped forward and back, matching her movement to the other woman's. She bumped against the duke's boot, then stumbled and halted near the center of the floor. A lump of angry frustration rose in her throat.

"My fault," the duke muttered stiffly. "I beg pardon." He opened his arms with a graceful flick of his wrists. His square face remained expressionless, but Bristol felt his superiority.

She drew a deep calming breath. Thus far, she'd concentrated so completely on the movements of the dance that she'd taken no opportunity to follow Aunt Pru's advice. Now she did. Bristol presented the duke a dazzling smile and fluttered her long dark lashes. "It isn't your fault at all, sir, but my own." She looked into his startled blue stare, and her own green eyes rounded with a contrived helplessness. "I've never danced before. I should have told you earlier, but I was embarrassed. Thank you for being so patient." She dropped her eyes demurely, letting a sweep of lash shadow her cheek; then she turned as if to leave the floor.

He touched her arm lightly and cleared his throat. "Well," he said in that odd nasal register. "Well. I see. That explains everything." He dipped into a gallant half-bow. "All things considered, Mistress Adams, you've done wonderfully well."

She parted her ripe lips and smiled, lifting a hand to the lace trim at the edge of her swelling breasts.

The duke blinked. "Please allow me to instruct you further." His arms opened, and again he performed that graceful little twist of the wrists, his eyes never leaving her face. Tiny beads of perspiration appeared on his forehead.

Bristol bit her lip to keep from laughing. She saw the gleam in his blue eyes, and she stepped confidently into his arms. She recognized that look, had seen all its various forms most of her life. The duke led her in wide circles around the ballroom, relishing his responsibility as teacher, and maintaining a steady stream of instruction. It was easier this time, and Bristol rewarded him with flashing smiles and liquid glances of manufactured gratitude.

The allemande ended, and the duke reluctantly bowed Bristol to a stop. She discovered herself looking into the grinning face of Jean Pierre La Crosse, standing next to her.

Her face paled. That grin and the dancing eyes above it seemed to guess she'd never danced, knew she'd trampled the duke's boot, understood she felt glassy-eyed with the boredom of dance history and evolution.

Furious, Bristol jerked from Jean Pierre's grin and leveled a brilliant smile at the Duke of Easton. The duke's eyes widened in a stare, and his mouth parted.

And with every slow second, Bristol felt Jean Pierre's eyes;

the nearness of him tensed each nerve and quickened her heartbeat. She favored the bedazzled duke with a seductive sweep of thick lashes and retrieved her fan from the cord at her wrist. With a flirtatious snap she opened the fan and covered the tremble in her lips.

Lady Thorne consulted her dance card and smiled timidly at the Duke of Easton. Her fan touched his arm, and she stepped to his side. "I believe this dance is mine, Charles," she murmured in her whispery voice. At Jean Pierre's side, Diana did not seem tall; only when she stood with another man was her willowy height apparent.

The duke gave his sandy head a shake and looked up from Bristol. Absently he smiled at Diana, but before he led her onto the floor, he turned back to Bristol. "Charles," he called, his nasal voice rising to be heard. "My name is Charles." The swirl of dancers swallowed them.

Bristol's face hardened. Unwilling to look at Jean Pierre, her eyes darted along the walls until she spotted Aunt Pru. Prudence gestured frantically and pointed to Bristol's dance card, while beside her a slender young man eagerly scanned the ballroom.

Jean Pierre bowed in front of Bristol. "Come here," he commanded in a rich low voice.

"No," Bristol whispered. She stared helplessly, wanting to run away, wanting his arms around her. Gray eyes touched her lips, the line of her gown; then his warm arm circled her waist, and he lifted her icy fingers. They swept into the ring of billowing gowns and flaring coats.

The music was a gigue, a lively dance similiar to a jig, and Bristol's heart sank. But Jean Pierre led her effortlessly, as if they'd danced together for years, and in his strong arms, Bristol felt suddenly light and sure of her feet. But inwardly, her nerves quivered and shook, and a fire ignited in the pit of her stomach. Her hatred melted. The scent of salt and fresh breezes filled her nostrils, and had his grip been less sure, she knew she would have stumbled.

But his arm supported her, guided her skillfully, led her once around the room, then out tall French windows onto a stone terrace flickering in torchlight. He danced her across the stones, around large potted rosebushes and into the shadows away from other scattered couples taking the night air.

They slowed and stopped, and Bristol's breath caught in her throat. His arm tightened on her waist, and he drew her trembling body against his lean, hard chest.

A weakness spread through her limbs, and his burning eyes seemed to fill the night sky. Then his hungry mouth crushed her head back in a bruising, searching kiss.

His tongue forced past her lips, and his throbbing erection seared against her body, urgent, demanding. And a familiar fire raced through her flesh, tingling along the nerves, burning in the secret hidden places. Bristol moaned, and her arms lifted. She buried her hands in his dark thick hair, pulling his mouth harder to hers, fitting her heated body into familiar curves and hollows of need.

But a warning flashed white hot across the darkness of her passion. Jean Pierre had used and discarded her. He'd treated her like a dockside whore, ready and available whenever he needed her, no matter the consequence.

Bristol twisted from his arms with a half-sob choking her throat, and her hand flashed, stinging across his cheek. Her glittering green eyes met his stare; then she spun with a strangled sound and gathered her skirts to flee.

Jean Pierre's hand shot forward, capturing her wrist with fingers of iron. "Sit down, little one." The words were gentle, but his voice was commanding. Taking her shoulders, he pressed her firmly onto a low stone wall, then stood wide-legged before her, the moonlight tracing a white line along his jaw. He waited for Bristol's face to calm.

She trembled on the stone wall, panting for breath and battling to control emotions gone wild. Her feelings swung in wide arcs. An hour ago she'd hated him, loathed Jean Pierre La Crosse; and now she'd twined her arms around his neck like a shameless wanton, every inch of her body aching with desire.

Bristol dropped her head and covered her eyes. She felt a pressure behind her lids, felt like crying and screaming and hitting and sobbing and throwing herself into his powerful arms. And nothing would change a thing.

Biting down on her lip, she let the sharp pain under her teeth clear her mind. When she'd composed her face, she lifted her chin, looking at him with hurt and betrayal blazing in her eyes.

Jean Pierre's dark gaze had not moved from her face. In the soft moonlight his eyes loomed dark and compelling, intense and deep. "*Mon Dieu*, but you are a beautiful creature!" he whispered. "You should always wear green, and your hair . . ." The tips of his fingers brushed the silky coil over her ear, his touch as gentle as the warm night breeze. He dropped his hand to the gold chain circling her throat, and his touch brought fire to her neck. "This is too simple. You need emeralds to adorn such beauty."

"Why?" Bristol whispered, her face a study of despair. "Why didn't you tell me?"

He understood. Jean Pierre knelt before her and enfolded her cold hands in his. "I'll answer with a question of my own." He met her searching eyes. "If you had known of Diana, would you have chosen to remain with me in my cabin?" His eyes traced the curve of her full lips, and a flame of desire flickered in the depths of his eyes. Bristol knew he remembered the nights of ecstasy that haunted her dreams.

"I . . ." She closed her lids, blotting out the passion in those gray moon-deep eyes. "No," she whispered. "I would have returned to my own cabin."

"Aye. You would have left me if I'd spoken." His warm hand cupped her chin, forcing her to look into his eyes. "And, Bristol—little one—I want you like no other woman. Can you doubt that? From the moment I found you in the snowbank, no other woman has touched me like you." Gray eyes lingered on her lips, her throat, and she saw his hunger. "Even now . . ."

Bristol dropped her eyes, but she couldn't shut out the heat of his hand on her cheek, she couldn't banish the truth she saw in his face. And she couldn't deny what she felt for him. "Is there any hope that you and Diana . . . ?" Swallowing her pride, she looked at him, a plea in her eyes. And her heart twisted at the strong, unyielding set of his jaw.

"None, *chérie*. The wedding is one month away."

Bristol fought the stone in her throat. "I saw you with her. You're very good." Bitterness iced her voice. "Anyone watching would think you cared for her. They wouldn't believe you wanted anyone else." Jealousy and pain moved across her face.

Jean Pierre looked steadily into Bristol's wounded eyes. "Understand this, little one, I *do* care for Diana. I care very much. Diana has nothing to do with my feelings for you."

Surprise, shock, and anger registered across Bristol's features. She jerked her head to the side and tried to stand, but his strong hands held her on the stone wall. "How can you say that?" Bristol cried, trying desperately to make sense of his words, and miserably failing. "Diana's insane!"

Moonlight chiseled his face, turning his eyes nearly black. "Listen carefully, *chérie*. I've known Diana most of my life; she was not always like this. There is much to admire in her. Like yourself, she is a woman of great courage."

Bristol moaned and shook her head. She tried to stand, but his hands were like granite, pinning her to the wall.

"Aye, courage. Diana cannot help how she behaves, but don't imagine she's unaware, or forgets what she's done when the violence passes. She knows she smashed Prudence's hallway." Jean Pierre's face was tight and sober, his voice low and intense. "And yet, Diana reaches inside and finds the courage to face all those people in the ballroom, knowing they whisper and laugh behind their fans. She holds her head high, and she smiles and hides the pain." He stared deeply into Bristol's eyes. "Aye, pain. Great pain gnaws at those we label crazy. Insane. Mad." He stroked Bristol's cold hands. "Diana is like a crippled animal, limping through a shadowy world peopled with creatures and ghouls you and I cannot imagine. Yet, she's carved a little space for herself. The world she sees terrifies her, but it does not defeat her. And that, my little one, is courage at its best."

Jealousy stabbed Bristol's mind, and raw aching hurt. A great wound slashed across her heart. She'd found him, the one man she wanted, only to lose him.

Now he allowed her to stand, and Bristol rose slowly, clasping her shaking hands. Unable to stop a self-defeating comparison, she contrasted Diana's mature beauty to her own youthful promise. Diana was tall and willowy. Diana had wealth and position. Diana fit into his world. And Jean Pierre had admitted he cared for Diana.

Though Bristol's heart warned against further pain, one last question remained unanswered. She sought the completion of the tragedy; she needed to know if he married one woman while loving another. Bristol stared at moonlight playing across her painted fan, not daring to look at him. "Jean Pierre. I . . . Do you . . . ?"

"There you are!" a booming voice panted. Aunt Pru rounded the potted roses in a flurry of pink and mauve. She halted to catch her breath and waved her fan wildly. "Robbie! I might have guessed it was you who kidnapped my niece!" She blotted her forehead with a bit of lace and nodded at Bristol. "Because it's Robbie, I forgive your disappearance. Robbie has never shown a proper regard for propriety." She turned on Jean Pierre and rapped his arm smartly with the edge of her fan. "This girl's future is in the making, Robbie! And I can't count the men she's jilted while you've kept her here." Aunt Pru waved Bristol's dance card, and a mock frown crinkled her wide forehead. "I told everyone you felt faint and promised them a dance after supper."

Aunt Pru laughed then, and her eyes sparkled wickedly. "I don't know what you did to poor Charles Easton, that stick, but he's been pestering me to strike out names and enter his own. He wants all your allemandes."

Bristol murmured weakly. She'd lost all interest in the dance. Next to Jean Pierre, all other men seemed pallid and uninteresting, dull nerveless creatures without blood in their veins. She tried to imagine kissing Duke Charles Easton, and she shuddered. His lips would be cool and rubbery.

"Now, look at her," Aunt Pru groaned loudly. "She's shivering like a leaf." Aunt Pru leveled a frown at Jean Pierre. "If this child catches cold, Robbie, I'll hold you responsible. It's spring, but there's still a chill in the night air."

Jean Pierre grinned at his stepmother. "If this child catches cold, Prudence, I offer myself as doctor." He let his eyes sweep Bristol's creamy breasts.

Aunt Pru's booming laugh bounced across the stone terrace. "Wicked! What a pity you're too old to spank!" She herded them toward the ballroom. "Diana is looking a bit wild, Robbie. I think she's noticed your absence." Prudence coughed discreetly. "I'd not like her smashing my ballroom as well," she added tartly.

Jean Pierre stepped between the two women, taking their arms. Bristol winced as his arm brushed her breast, and she kept her face steadfastly forward. Jean Pierre said, "Come, now, Prudence. Haven't you ever wanted to toss a vase at the wall?" His voice carried a special teasing quality which Bristol sensed was symbolic of his relationship with Prudence Hathaway.

Aunt Pru grinned. "Of course. Many a time I've wanted to crash a bottle over Hathaway's head." Jean Pierre laughed. "The difference, Robbie, dear, is that I don't. Diana does such things."

Jean Pierre smiled and paused just inside the ballroom doors. He rocked on his heels and examined the ceiling. "I seem to recall an incident a few years ago when a certain well-rounded lady of my acquaintance created a mound of broken pieces from a cabinet of very fine china." He looked down at Prudence with twinkling eyes.

Aunt Pru drew herself up with a sniff, and all her chins quivered with indignation. "That's different. You know how despicable Lady Marlborough is! That silken parlor whore dared suggest I lack background!"

Jean Pierre laughed and kissed Prudence's perspiring

211

cheeks. His face sobered, and he pressed her hands. "Aye, that makes all the difference," he said softly. Bowing to them both, he vanished into the crowd.

"'Yes.' Say 'yes,' not 'aye,'" Aunt Pru muttered absently, her eyes fixed on the spot where Jean Pierre had faded into the dancers. She heaved a massive sigh and squinted at Bristol's dance card. "Somewhere in that crush, a certain Lord Amesley is searching for you. I assure you, dear, it is no loss if he fails to find us. Lord Amesley is fiftyish, married, and passes wind with every other step. Let us hope he overlooks you." She peered at Bristol with concern. "Perhaps you *are* catching cold! You're pale as pudding, and there's no spark in your eyes!"

"I'm fine, Aunt Pru." Bristol's green eyes searched the top of the dancers, finding a dark head and a swirl of scarlet gown. A knife twisted in her heart. "I'm fine," she whispered.

An unpleasant odor assailed her nostrils; Lord Amesley had found her. Bristol hid a miserable sigh and stepped into his arms.

A succession of elegant polished men followed Lord Amesley. They led her around the floor and murmured extravagant compliments above the music. Bristol smiled, flirting automatically, without thought, moving through the motions as if it was second nature to captivate men. But behind the thick sweep of lashes, behind her brilliant smiles, lay a hollow vacancy, a total lack of interest. And always, always, her eyes and her thoughts strayed to a shining dark head topping the others.

It was almost a relief when the Duke of Easton eagerly claimed her for a midnight supper. Bristol accepted his arm with a tired smile. He seated her at an intimate table for two and returned in a moment bearing heaping plates of food. Immediately Charles Easton resumed his lecture on the evolution of folk dance to ballroom dance, delivered in a nasal monotone accompanied by furious blushing and many moist pauses.

Bristol remembered to smile frequently, but her mind wandered toward a laughing honey-colored head bent near Jean Pierre's dark curls. Diana led Jean Pierre to a secluded corner and offered him tidbits from her plate, laughing and touching his shoulder possessively. And Jean Pierre paid her every attention, staring into those golden-brown eyes as if Diana Thorne were the only woman in the room.

Bristol put a hand to her forehead, covering her eyes. Her

temples pounded with the first headache of her life. Seeing Jean Pierre with Diana was a torture past bearing.

Charles Easton smiled uncertainly. "Are you well?" His solid brow creased in concern.

"I'm fine," Bristol answered with a faint smile. It seemed she'd spent the evening assuring people she felt fine . . . and she did not. She'd never felt worse. Wrenching her gaze from that shadowy corner, she stared into her plate, not certain what she was eating. She tried to recall the menu Aunt Pru had labored over so diligently: truffles, pink slices of baked ham, plover tongues, carrots in cream sauce, fresh asparagus (a rare treat), pease pudding, cherry jelly, vanilla pudding, and pistachio cream. The pistachio cream was expected to be the *pièce de résistance,* and all around, Bristol heard appreciative murmurs. But to her the cream tasted bland and uninteresting. As Charles Easton was bland and uninteresting; somehow she stumbled through the supper.

The dancing continued until dawn, when the last happily weary couple yawned good-bye. Leaning in the entryway, Bristol and Prudence watched as Jean Pierre escorted Diana past them toward her family's waiting coach. They both heard his assurances and promises to visit Diana within the week. And listened to Diana's anxious questions. "When exactly, Robbie? I don't like surprises, you know that. What day will you come?" The door muffled Jean Pierre's reply.

"Well." Aunt Pru stretched and covered a gaping yawn. In the first golden streaks of dawn slanting through the windows, Bristol saw that Aunt Pru's powder had streaked and caked; her pink-and-mauve gown hung in limp waves over her rounded stomach, and the orange curls had long since lost any definition—they matted together in a fuzzy pumpkin-colored cap. "I believe the party was an enormous success, don't you, dear?"

Bristol smiled in genuine affection. "It was the most lavish ball I've ever attended."

Aunt Pru snorted and grinned. "It's the *only* ball you've ever attended. Why am I asking you?" She turned toward the steps and kicked off her shoes with a sigh of immense pleasure. She left the shoes where they fell and trudged up the staircase with Bristol following. "I only wish Hathaway might have come downstairs. He was quite a dancer in his day. No one does the minuet like Hathaway!" Aunt Pru yawned again and shook her curls wearily. "What annoys me most about these late nights is that everyone is too tired to gossip, and that's definitely the best part of a party." A naughty sparkle lit her eyes. "Did you see Lord Amesley drop his fork down Lady Battersea's bodice?" Pru laughed and patted Bristol's arm. She offered her cheek for a kiss, then padded down the hallway toward her husband's bedroom. "I'll just peek in on Hathaway; you and I will gossip tomorrow." She yawned and disappeared around a turn in the corridor.

Bristol smiled after her aunt. If Lord Hathaway was waiting for her, and Bristol thought it likely, he'd never see how his wife had wilted as the long evening wore on. Lord Hathaway would see the laughing young girl he'd married.

Still smiling, Bristol bent to remove her own tight slippers, and her eyes looked between the bars of the stair railing. And met those of the man below, standing in the silent entryway, his head tilted to watch her.

Slowly Bristol straightened, her shoes dangling from her fingers, the blood draining from her face. Jean Pierre's eyes smoldered hungrily, and she saw a bulge straining the front of his dark breeches.

She gripped the stair railing. "No," she moaned. Her mind pictured him eating from Diana's plate, laughing with Diana, dancing with Diana. "No! It's too late for us. It was always too late for us!"

His slate-colored eyes seared her breast, her hips, and Bristol watched his breath quicken.

"No," she stammered. "We can't! That's over!" She gathered her skirts and fled down the hallway, stumbling and blinking at tears stinging her lids. She burst into her room and locked the door, falling against it and panting for breath, her heart pounding furiously.

When he came, as she'd known he would, she turned to face the door and laid her cheek against the cool wood, a dry sob on her lips. The latch moved once, then was still. But she felt him in the hallway, sensed his prowling energy beyond the thickness of the door.

Bristol flattened her palms on the wood. "Jean Pierre. Jean Pierre," she whispered, the words choking. When she knew he had gone, she flung herself across the pink bed and buried her face.

If ever she'd doubted her feelings for him, that doubt had burned to ash in the fire of his kiss. Bristol loved him. And the pain was greater than any she'd known.

"I . . . will . . . not . . . cry!" The words tore from between clenched teeth. The bed was large and her body empty, so empty. Angrily Bristol dashed the wetness from her eyes, assuring herself fatigue produced the damp, nothing else.

A warm sun climbed well into the sky before Bristol's hot, moist eyes closed and she fell into a restless, groaning sleep.

15

STILL tired, Bristol yawned while Molly piled her hair high and helped her dress for dinner. Sometime in the last days, Molly had altered Bristol's brown gown, turning Hannah's pattern into something Bristol's mother would never have approved.

"The material be coarse, miss, and my sewing don't be as fair good as what you'll see from Collette, but you'll not be feeling so out of place," Molly explained.

Bristol nodded approval at the mirror, stifling another yawn. Her gown now plunged to expose twin mounds of smooth white breast, and Molly had puffed out the sleeves and pulled in the waist. A panel of gold silk dropped in front and was repeated in gold cuffs and in a narrow golden band circling the drop of neckline. The gown remained simple, but infinitely more fashionable than the original Puritan design. Bristol hugged Molly gratefully. Molly tossed glossy black braids over her shoulders and perched on the arm of a velvet chair, watching Bristol fasten Mr. Aykroyd's cameo to her shoulder. "Did you meet Mr. Robbie last night, miss?"

Bristol didn't look up. "Yes," she answered briefly.

Molly rolled black eyes to the ceiling. "Ain't he something, miss? I never seen a more handsome man—gives a girl the shivers, he does! And a sea captain, miss! Ain't it romantic?" She patted her plump thighs. "I'll wager Mr. Robbie has a thousand tales to tell, not like them dumb stable hands what only yap about horses." She frowned and rubbed her ring finger. "One in particular, that Sam Biddlewell, don't talk about nothing important, just horses this and horses that."

Bristol glanced at Molly and murmured sympathetically. It

215

seemed affairs of the heart didn't run smoothly for anyone. At the door Bristol paused and looked back at Molly's drooping shoulders. "If Sam Biddlewell won't pay you any attention, Molly, find someone who will," she advised tartly. "There's more than one star in the sky!" With a start, she realized the advice would fit herself as well as Molly.

Molly lifted her head with a miserable little smile. "But I only want Sam, miss."

Such was the perversity of the human heart. Bristol pondered Molly's sorrowful words as she hurried to Lord Hathaway's study. Of all the men in London Town, Molly wanted only one.

And Bristol wanted only one.

Pausing outside the study door, Bristol drew a breath and gathered her strength. Inside, she heard Aunt Pru's booming laugh and Uncle Robert's answering chuckle. And then a voice that sent tremors up Bristol's spine—Jean Pierre's rich accented tones. Listening, Bristol sagged against the wall. How would she endure the dinner hours? How could she sit beside him and chat politely and not touch him, not let her heart shine in her eyes?

Somehow she managed. Bristol ate the food on her plate and retained no memory of what she swallowed. She drank her wine and thought it tasteless as water. Keeping her eyes carefully averted, she listened to Jean Pierre's account of the sinking *Dover Clay*, and when he'd finished, she could not have repeated a single word. Gossip of the previous night's party flowed over her without penetrating. Bristol kept her eyes on her wineglass or smiled absently at her aunt and uncle.

But although she dared not glance at Jean Pierre La Crosse, every inch of her body felt him. Her mind was finely tuned to each resonant syllable of his deep voice, every nuance of tone; and each small movement he made vibrated along an inner awareness. When he leaned to pour more wine, her stomach tensed at a faint drift of salt and fresh air. When his fingers played lightly along the stem of his glass, she remembered his hand on her thighs, his skilled fingers cupping her breasts. . . .

Leaning forward, Aunt Pru peered into her niece's face. "Bristol! Where are you tonight? You've scarcely said a word!" Aunt Pru grinned and pounded Bristol's knee. "For the past twenty minutes we've been discussing your triumph last night." She rolled her blue eyes with pleasure and waved her little pipe. "Ah, the conquests!" she crowed. "Charles

Easton is completely undone, and the Marquis de Chevoux refused to leave without arranging a hunt in your honor. Young Lord Babbington was distraught at not being your supper partner, and Viscount Pepperal-Haught insists I bring you to his country house for a weekend." She clapped dimpled flashing hands, nearly upsetting her pipe. "I've longed to see the viscount's mansion for simply ages; Christopher Wren designed it, and everyone says the estate is absolutely magnificent!" Aunt Pru leaned to touch Jean Pierre's arm. "And Bristol and I will need a restful weekend after your wedding, Robbie. Simply everyone of importance is giving you and Diana a party . . . there's hardly a free evening for the next month! We'll all be exhausted! I do hope Collette delivers your cousin's new gowns this week." Aunt Pru tapped her head. "I'll send Collette a note tomorrow!"

Bristol directed her green eyes to her aunt, her every sense feeling Jean Pierre's smoky stare watching above the rim of his glass. "That's very kind of you to think of me when you have so much on your mind," she answered in a faint voice.

Uncle Robert adjusted his shawl and smiled with Jean Pierre's gray eyes. "We're pleased to do what we can, Miss Bristol. Our greatest hope is that you enjoy your stay at Hathaway House." He waved his wineglass and winked at his son. "Robbie, just look at her. Have you ever seen such wonderful hair?"

"*Magnifique,*" Jean Pierre agreed softly, his eyes not leaving Bristol's face. His tone implied more, and an awkward silence followed his comment.

Bristol felt Jean Pierre's eyes touch her hair, brush the creamy swell of her candlelit breasts. Uncle Robert cleared his throat, and Aunt Pru's round blue eyes moved slowly from Bristol to Jean Pierre, a knowing flicker beginning in the depths.

Jean Pierre broke the long pause with a sudden grin toward his stepmother. "Only one woman I know has hair to match Bristol's. And I think . . ." His eyes teased. "Yes, I think the magnificence of the aunt surpasses that of the niece." He lifted his glass and toasted Prudence.

Aunt Pru hooted and preened herself, the uneasy moment ignored. While Prudence and Jean Pierre bantered compliments, Bristol lifted a hand to her pounding temples; the strain of being this close and this artificial filled her head with throbbing tension; her body felt warm and tight. Distraught, she wondered how much longer she must remain before she could politely escape the intimate confines of the study and

Jean Pierre's overpowering male domination. He filled the room with his presence. Jean Pierre sat in his chair with a relaxed elegance, but it was an elegance barely hiding the coiled energy of the man. She felt him drawing her like a powerful magnet, confusing her senses.

As Bristol reached shaking hands for her wineglass, her eyes met Lord Hathaway's thoughtful expression, and she realized he'd been studying her. In that clear gray gaze, Bristol saw a recognition that startled her. Lord Hathaway looked through her role and into her heart.

"Robbie," he said in a musing voice, "Pumpkin has tomorrow afternoon completely filled." Aunt Pru turned toward him in surprise. "I wonder, after church service, if you might do us the kindness of escorting Miss Bristol on a sightseeing tour? With the preparations for the ball, we've neglected to show Pumpkin's niece the sights of London."

Jean Pierre grinned. "I'd be delighted, sir."

"No!" They all looked at Bristol, and a rosy flush climbed her throat. "That is," she stammered, "I don't mind waiting, and . . ." She leveled a helpless appeal toward Jean Pierre, but he leaned back in his chair, the grin widening. Bristol's hand fluttered to her cheek, then to her lap, and back to the pulse thudding in the hollow of her throat. "I'd rather wait until Aunt Pru is free to accompany us."

Prudence Hathaway looked a question toward her husband and read an answer in his steady gray eyes. She shook her orange head at Bristol. "Nonsense! You needn't wait for me, dear. I assure you I have a great deal to accomplish in preparing for this wedding. After all, the queen will attend." She rolled her eyes and fanned her chest. "The details! You can't imagine! And Diana's mother is as addle-brained as . . . That is, old Lady Thorne is worse than no help at all!" She patted Bristol's arm. "If you're concerned about the lack of a chaperon, I assure you no one will whisper at an outing with your own cousin."

Bristol met Lord Hathaway's calm eyes with a plea in her own, but his knowing glance didn't waver. She felt manipulated and beaten. To insist on a chaperon now would cast undue importance on the event. Looking at Uncle Robert's face, Bristol suspected he hoped her charms would sway Jean Pierre from a wedding no one wanted. And deep inside stirred a tiny rebellious hope of her own. And this despite her knowledge the wedding would not, could not, be canceled. Jean Pierre was a man of his word. The wedding would occur as scheduled.

Even so, tremulous hope and half-formed plans interfered with her sleep, leaving her tired and nervously excited when she awoke the next day. Reverend Cornwell's sermon washed over her fiery head.

Prudence, Jean Pierre, and Bristol attended services in the Tri-Trinity Church where the most Reverend Mr. Cornwell bludgeoned his congregation with uninspired exhortations to tread the paths of righteousness. Aunt Pru diligently bent over her lap desk, scribbling notes for the monthly missle to Noah and casting broad winks in Bristol's direction. Bristol returned the winks with an absent smile; her mind centered on a dark head across the aisle.

Alone. This afternoon they would be alone, and when she thought of it, her stomach tightened and her heart rolled in her chest. What would he say to her? And she to him? What could they talk about? Her green eyes clouded. Jean Pierre would marry another woman. There was nothing to say but good-bye.

A grimace of quiet pain pinched Bristol's expression, and she sought another topic to focus her thoughts. Reverend Cornwell couldn't hold her attention, or anyone's, Bristol decided with a small sigh. The congregation was crowded with nodding heads.

In Salem, a tithingman would have rapped those drowsy heads with a long hard pole. But English custom regarding the sabbath had proved as different from Bristol's experience as everything else since she'd left Salem's shores.

The congregation slept undisturbed. And the leisure-loving English restricted their preachers to half a day, using Sunday afternoon for idle pleasures.

Aunt Pru had been appalled to hear sober New Englanders spent their entire sabbath sitting in hard-backed pews in unheated meetinghouses. "Barbaric," she pronounced with a sniff. "I see no reason why pews should not be upholstered. And half a day of prayer and goodness is enough for anyone!"

At last the sermon ended, and Aunt Pru paused to invite the insipid Reverend Cornwell to Hathaway House for Sunday luncheon and a chat with Lord Hathaway.

"The reverend's impossibly dull," Prudence whispered to Bristol before Jean Pierre hefted her bottom into the carriage, "but Hathaway insists on a weekly tot of religion, gout or no gout."

During an uncomfortable ride, Reverend Cornwell squatted on the carriage seat next to Bristol, his bandy legs too small

219

for a pear-shaped body. "I can't understand it, Lady Hathaway," he complained. "Each time you find enough brilliance in my sermon that you're moved to take notes, it seems a greater number than usual fall asleep in the pews! I've observed this phenomenon for years!" He chewed on a ragged thumbnail and stared at Prudence with troubled eyes.

Not daring to glance at her aunt for fear she'd explode into giggles, Bristol cast a quick look at Jean Pierre. He met her sparkling eyes with a grin of understanding, and they both felt a need to turn suddenly, peering out the windows with feigned interest, unable to look at Prudence or the reverend. Bristol's chest convulsed with hidden laughter, and her breath rushed past her lips in small choking gasps. She lifted a hand to the throat of her high-necked gown.

Aunt Pru pressed the dyed curls pasted to her forehead. She looked at the carriage roof. "I can't condone such rudeness, Reverend Cornwell." Her deep voice sounded strangled. Prudence cleared her throat with a booming sound midway between a guffaw and a cough. "I've always found your sermons to be most . . . ah . . . useful. Unique, in fact." She coughed energetically into a square of linen, looking helplessly at Jean Pierre and Bristol's averted heads. "Your sermons are the best of their kind I've ever heard."

Reverend Cornwell turned brooding eyes to the windows and chewed his other thumb. "I've always thought so myself, Lady Hathaway, but it seems you're one of the few in my flock to appreciate a good sermon."

"Oh, I do, I do." Aunt Prudence collapsed into a spasm of coughing, strangled shrieks emerging from behind the balled linen.

Reverend Cornwell stared, then looked toward Bristol and Jean Pierre's blank faces with an expression of puzzlement. Neither moved to assist Lady Hathaway, so the reverend leaned across and pounded her broad shaking back with the heel of his hand. "Are you all right?" he inquired anxiously, his glance sliding to Lady Hathaway's purse. The Hathaways had proved exceedingly generous over the years.

"Yes, yes," Prudence gasped, puffing for breath.

When the carriage finally halted and the reverend and Aunt Pru stood outside, Aunt Pru adjusted a mound of orange curls and pushed her head through the carriage door, her breath still unsteady. Her blue eyes sparkled wickedly. "Will you two join us? I'm certain the reverend has some memorable words to inspire our luncheon." She made a face.

Bristol's green eyes danced above the edge of her fan, and

she hid a smile while Jean Pierre leaned out the window to call, "Please accept our regrets, Reverend. *C'est dommage!* It's a pity, but we have an urgent engagement. Had my cousin and I known . . ." He shrugged elegantly, conveying the impression he would gladly have canceled anything to share the preacher's company had he but known of the opportunity in time.

Reverend Cornwell puffed out his chest and bowed stiffly. "Of course, if you must go . . ." His voice trailed in obvious disappointment. He nodded to Bristol's partially hidden face peeking through the window. "It is an honor to meet you, Mistress Adams. And I must add that it is refreshing to meet a young woman of modest demeanor. So many young ladies feel it necessary to wear gowns cut to their navels, exposing their . . . ah . . . exposing a lot of . . . ah . . ."

"*Décolleté?*" Jean Pierre offered, a grin spreading across his chiseled face.

The reverend looked flustered. "I don't speak French, sir, I don't know what you mean."

"Breasts!" Aunt Pru shouted, hefting her own massive bosom under the reverend's nose. Her face darkened, and she snorted. "Breasts, Reverend, breasts!" She pulled his arm and yanked him up the steps. Blushing furiously, the reverend stumbled after her, his bandy legs threatening to crumple at any minute.

"Driver!" Jean Pierre called. "For God's sake, get us out of here!" He looked at Bristol and burst into uproarious laughter. "Breasts!" Jean Pierre shouted.

Dropping her fan, Bristol clutched her aching sides. "Your sermons are the best of their kind," she quoted, wiping her eyes.

"I've always thought so myself!"

"Unique!"

The carriage rattled around a turn, and laughing, Bristol threw out a hand to steady her balance. Her knee rocked against Jean Pierre's leg.

It was as if a brand of fire seared her flesh. She gasped and looked into his eyes, the smile fading from her lips. His smoldering stare riveted her to the seat. Neither of them moved.

"Bristol . . ." His rich accent caressed her name, and his eyes darkened to slate.

Eyes that seemed to swirl with molten gray mist probed emerald-green ones. Bristol wet a suddenly dry mouth and felt the rapid increase of her heartbeat. She tried to drop her

221

eyes, but his intense stare would not release her. Her knee trembled against his tensed leg, and she felt her face pale to the color of snow. Weakness spread through her limbs, and her stomach fluttered. "Jean Pierre," she whispered. "Oh, Jean Pierre." She heard the anguish in those strangled words.

His eyes traced the curve of her lips. "I think of you always," he said softly. He didn't move to touch her, but Bristol felt his leg against hers, sending waves of electricity through her body.

"Please, we can't . . . we must forget . . ." Disconcerted, she looked at the scar her fingers had tenderly mapped, the lips her own had clung to. "I . . ."

His voice was low and intense. "I want you every waking minute. I think of you lying sweet in your bed, and I must fight not to smash your door and take you." His eyes flickered with passion and his face was hard as granite, but his voice remained soft. "Take you and make you call my name."

Bristol buried her face in her hands. Blood roared in her temples, and her body burned with familiar fires. "Stop! I can't bear it. Oh, Jean Pierre, I can't bear it!"

"Look at me," Jean Pierre commanded quietly. "Look at me, Bristol, and tell me you want me too. Tell me you lie in your bed and think of me."

"I can't! This is wrong! I . . . I can't!" She shook her head in despair, refusing to lower her hands and look at him as he wanted. He asked nothing but the truth, but she couldn't say the words. Their relationship had to end. Must end. Jean Pierre would marry in a month; it was madness to continue. A dry sob escaped her lips.

Outside the carriage drifted sounds of a spring afternoon: coach passengers calling to one another, drivers cracking whips and cursing, iron wheels rattling, laughing pedestrians taking the air. Inside, a strained silence held two people in a capsule.

Finally Bristol lifted her face and pushed back the tendrils of hair dropping from her combs. She chewed her lip. Jean Pierre's face was composed and coldly distant. "My apologies," he said formally. "As you know, I don't push myself on unwilling women." He stretched and arranged himself in an elegant sprawl, careful not to brush her skirt. "And I apologize for appearing outside your door. It won't happen again."

Dear God, help me through this moment, Bristol thought desperately. "Jean Pierre, it isn't that. Please try to understand!" She wrung her hands and felt her heart cracking into little pieces. "The way I was raised . . ." Her hand rose in a helpless gesture. "What happened on the *Challenger*—that was . . ." She wet her lips and swallowed the knot in her throat. She tried again. "But to continue with no possibility of a future, that makes me . . ."

He glanced toward the sunny window. "There is no need to explain, Bristol."

Moisture stung her lids, and she clasped trembling hands in her lap. "But I need to tell you . . ."

Hard gray eyes swung to fix on her face. "I've made a mistake, Mistress Adams, and I have apologized. Nothing more need be said." Ice chilled his words.

Bristol's lashes brushed her cheeks, and she sagged against the seat cushion. "Oh, Jean Pierre," she whispered through bloodless lips. Her arms ached for him, and her body felt as heavy and as hollow as her heart.

Breaking an uneasy silence, Jean Pierre slid to the window, and his rich voice began an impersonal commentary on the sights warming in spring sunshine. Dully Bristol followed his words, nodding and murmuring in a disinterested voice as the carriage rumbled through the lanes of London, past St. Paul's Cathedral, past the Royal Exchange crowded with Sunday idlers. Jean Pierre took her to Newgate Prison and insisted she tour the Museum of the Royal Society.

Bristol marched through the museum listlessly, ignoring the people around her, staring at the displays without seeing. The tanned skin of a Moorish warrior made no impression, nor did a piece of bone voided in Sir William Throgmorton's urine. Bristol lacked the interest to inquire who Sir William might be or might have been.

She felt alive only when Jean Pierre's guiding hand lightly touched her elbow, and then her head spun dizzily with need. She wanted to turn and step into his strong arms. But to what purpose, her mind despaired, to what end? Their relationship led nowhere. Had ended before it really began.

"Please," she asked quietly when the carriage pulled from the museum, "may we go home now?"

"There's another place I want you to see."

They rode without speaking until the coach stopped before massive Bethlehem Hospital. Jean Pierre paid a two-penny entrance fee and led Bristol into the dark, depressing interior.

Uneasy, Bristol stared at dank stone walls and fouled floors. She darted a questioning glance toward Jean Pierre's impassive expression, then sighed. His face was set and firm, telling her nothing.

A weary guide dressed in soiled tunic and dirty breeches herded the crowd together, then removed a torch from a bracket and set off down a reeking hallway. Bristol didn't want to follow, but Jean Pierre's hard face moved her forward. He nodded curtly, and reluctantly she trailed the others.

In the darkness of a narrow corridor, an uncomfortable silence hushed the crowd. Ladies drew long skirts close to their bodies with fearful glances toward sounds of dark scrabbling. The corridor was inky. Filth and excrement oozed underfoot, and Bristol's cloth slippers slid and grew damp. Only Jean Pierre's firm fingers burning on her waist kept her from fleeing back in the direction they'd come. Every breath filled her nostrils with a terrible stench.

Bristol cringed in the darkness. Before the hallway opened into a dark cavernous room, she heard the shrieks and howls of human agony. Frightened, she searched Jean Pierre's face, but she couldn't determine his expression in the deep gloom. Of all the places in London, she couldn't understand why he'd chosen to bring her here, to this evil-smelling blackness. Her mind rebelled, and her stomach heaved at the odor of rotting filth. Echoing screams and wails curdled her blood.

When the silent group moved into a huge room, Bristol gasped and ducked her head. In the dark recesses of a high roof, a flutter of bats screamed and swept through the upper reaches, some diving toward the crowd below. Several ladies dodged and cried out before again lapsing into expectant silence. The guide lit more torches, bringing a welcome flicker of illumination. Assured, comfortable once more, the sightseers moved to a wall of iron bars and peered inside with relieved whoops of laughter and pointing fingers.

Bristol hung back in shock and revulsion, her heart pounding painfully in her breast. But Jean Pierre's fingers bruised around her arm. He pulled her forward.

People were behind the iron bars. Some were chained to the wall with heavy cuffs chafing their arms or legs, others wandered aimlessly across fetid straw, staring blankly at the sightseers and flickering torchlights. Many rubbed their eyes against the unaccustomed brightness.

Sickened, Bristol stared helplessly at a man standing against the wall, chains circling his legs. Systematically the man pounded his forehead against the stones, blood gushing down his face and soaking into a tattered shirt. He seemed unaware of the blood. At his feet a filthy woman wriggled in the stinking straw and cackled to herself. Seeing the row of

224

onlookers, she hiked a ragged skirt to her waist and drew bony knees to her chest. She dropped her knees wide with a lewd grin and began to stroke the bush of louse-infested hair between her legs. The crowd hooted and laughed. The woman hurled a handful of urine-soaked straw at the bars.

Bristol turned away, sick to her stomach, but Jean Pierre's fingers bit into her shoulders and pulled her up, forcing her to see the display of human misery.

Near the bars close to Bristol a woman rocked on her heels, oblivious of the screams and laughter echoing in the cavernous room. Beneath the dirt and scabs crusting her face lay hints of a once-great beauty. She'd fashioned her arms into a cradle, and vacant eyes stared into the empty nest; she rocked her arms and made thin crooning noises in the back of her throat, lost in a distant world. Hovering above the squatting woman stood a deformed mockery of a man. His matted hair swung beneath a huge mountain of flesh rising from his shoulders, and spittle dropped in a glistening thread from the corner of his lips. He hopped back and forth on spindle legs, dirty hands pulling and stroking a thin white worm sticking rigidly from a hole in his breeches.

As Bristol's hands tensed on the bars, the man shrieked and fell upon the crooning woman. He ripped up her skirts, and his hand smashed across her face, knocking her to the straw; he jumped on her and thrust the worm inside her body, making gobbling noises with his mouth. The woman lay as she'd fallen, her legs limp, and she stared blankly at the deep blackness above, crooning softly to herself and rocking her cradled arms.

Bristol's head dropped and her mouth soured with nausea. Then suddenly she felt herself being ripped from the bars, seconds before a howling man fell against the spot where she'd stood. Skeleton arms reached through the bars, missing Bristol by inches. The man grinned through rotted black teeth, and his fingers opened and closed near her breast.

Bristol pressed against Jean Pierre's strong chest, and his arms folded around her, guiding her across a slippery floor, away from the leering, screaming man. The man pushed against the bars, shouting, "God has given me dominion over all women! Come to your master!" Bristol stared in horror as the man tore down his breeches and waved a huge scabbed and oozing penis through the bars. "Here is the staff of life! Your salvation!" The crowd roared with laughter, and the man hopped down the bars toward a more appreciative audience. He lunged hard against the bars and urinated, straining

225

to hit the women. They cried out in laughter and backed from the hissing yellow stream. Frustrated, the man screamed and spun from the bars; he directed the bubbling river over a woman laying rigid in the straw. The woman didn't move or protest or halt an anguished howling she aimed steadily toward the stone walls.

"Oh, dear God," Bristol breathed, squeezing her eyes shut. But nothing could blot out the flesh-crawling shrieks and howls. Or the putrid smells and laughing catcalls of the sight-seers.

Jean Pierre's hands shook her shoulders. Cupping her chin, he lifted Bristol's ashen face. Her lips were inches from his, and she felt his warm breath on her cheeks. She looked at him resentfully, her eyes stinging, trying to understand and failing.

"Can you hear me? Bristol, listen to me! Try to hear what I tell you, try to understand! This is Bedlam. Do you know the term?"

She shook her head. Her eyes centered on the intensity of his face, the one sane point of focus in this room. Bristol longed to step into his arms and bury her face in his neck; she wanted him to take her away from this godless, evil darkness. She wanted the strength and hardness of his body to shut out her thoughts. It was impossible to have guessed this mockery of life existed. She didn't want to know of it.

"Bedlam," Jean Pierre continued, his voice rising above the screams and wailing, his eyes relentless and insisting. "The insane are imprisoned here. When relatives tire of making excuses for them, when their behavior can no longer be tolerated, when their care becomes too great a burden—here is where they are sent. Abandoned to darkness and filth and the additional torment of each other. Displayed like the animals they become, to anyone with a two-penny price. Look at them!" His powerful hands spun Bristol toward the bars and the blank howling faces distorted in torchlight. A rat ran over the feet of the crooning woman coupled to the hunchback.

Bristol wrenched her face to the side. Sick, her stomach knotting, she finally understood what her eyes saw, understood why he had brought her here. Tearing from Jean Pierre's hands, she stumbled toward the yawning darkness of the corridor. Immediately Jean Pierre caught her arm and steadied her, guiding her through the malodorous muck underfoot, leading her out to a lane bathed in the warm golden tones of sunset.

Bristol sucked deep breaths of London's poisoned air into her lungs, thinking it fresh in comparison to what lay buried in the stone building at her back. Sober and quiet, Jean Pierre lifted her into the Hathaway coach and took the seat facing her.

"Without this marriage, Queen Mary ultimately will have to send Diana to Bedlam," he said quietly as the carriage pulled into a Sunday traffic of sedan chairs, hackneys, and other coaches emblazoned with crests and scrolls. "Mary will have no choice."

Bristol shuddered. "Couldn't the queen lock Diana into a comfortable private residence instead? Provide her with a . . . a keeper and a decent surrounding?"

Jean Pierre shook his head. "There's danger to the throne in an arrangement like you suggest. Once Diana was locked away privately, her madness would become a secret of greater importance than Mary can afford. Keepers can be bribed. Secrets have a way of becoming public. But in Bedlam, every second person claims high connections. And none are taken seriously; it's considered a symptom of the delusions. In Bedlam, Diana could claim to be Mary's sister if the notion struck her, and no one would pay the slightest attention." His eyes darkened. "In other words, the best way for Mary to protect this secret is by not allowing it to become a secret. Do you see?"

Miserably Bristol nodded. "But wouldn't it be difficult for Mary to explain Diana's disappearance if she committed Diana to Bedlam?"

"Nothing could be simpler. A death is announced, and some poor wretch is spared the potter's field and given a quiet but decent burial while Diana disappears into the blackness of insanity, registered under another name." He shrugged. "No one would believe her if she insisted her name was other than what appeared on the register."

Bristol closed her eyes.

Jean Pierre continued quietly, "And without this marriage, a fine old gentleman will be stripped of lands and title, rewards he has earned by a lifetime of service to crown and country." Jean Pierre spoke flatly, no emotion in his voice. "Now do you understand that my marriage has nothing to do with you?"

Bristol's emerald eyes filled with anguish, and she looked at him across the small space. The sun's dying rays slanted past the window, painting his face in golden shadow. Her heart twisted.

"And you? Will you ultimately have to send Diana to Bedlam?"

"Never!" His face hardened. "Never. She may one day have to live an isolated life, but she'll not live it like an animal."

They stared at each other in the golden light of a dying day. "I love you," Bristol blurted. Dropping her face into her hands, she whispered, "I love you."

The carriage rattled through the lanes, the driver's whip cracking above the horses' heads, his shouted curses mingling with those of other drivers.

When Jean Pierre spoke, his voice was hoarse and pained. "I respect your beliefs, little one, and I admire your strength. When I look at you, my resolve crumbles and I want you. No matter what my desires would do to your life." His gray eyes burned into hers. His jaw tightened. "Keep your door locked, Bristol . . . you must have the strength for two."

The coach rocked to a halt before Hathaway House, and the driver sprang to open the door, stepping back respectfully. Jean Pierre dropped to the ground, and his powerful hands reached to circle Bristol's waist. He lifted her from the door of the carriage and held her against his body for an instant before he set her on the ground, so close she felt a beckoning heat. Hands remaining on her waist, he stared soberly into her green eyes. "My door is always open," he said softly. "If your conscience allows it, come to me. Come to me, Bristol."

Bristol stumbled from his arms and ran up the stairs, fleeing inside and dashing up to her room. Throwing herself on the pink bed, she hid her face in handfuls of soft spread and felt the torments of a breaking heart.

Later, she ordered dinner in her room, unable to bear the thought of sitting politely near Jean Pierre in Lord Hathaway's study. She lacked the strength to hide her feelings in idle chatter, to resist if he followed her from the room.

Tonight she drank her wine from the pewter cup, but even this talisman of staid New England values brought her no relief. Her body ached for Jean Pierre. When they were on the ship, she'd conquered her background and her guilts. But now . . . The lax attitudes of London society could not obliterate a lifetime of indoctrination. She could not go to him, could not vanquish an overpowering sense of sin, could not compromise herself in a situation that led to damnation and ruin.

But when she blew out her candles and lay sleepless in the large lonely bed, Jean Pierre's image rose to haunt her, and her body betrayed her need. Every nerve longed for his touch; her thighs and stomach tensed with desire. Bristol ran shaking hands over her long nightgown. "Jean Pierre." Beneath sweating palms, her nipples rose, remembering his lips. Bristol tossed upon the rumpled bed in tortured longing.

Finally she kicked out of the sheets and paced her room, stopping at the back window to throw open the draperies and stare out at a warm, scented night. A lover's moon gentled London rooftops and shaded the Hathaway gardens into secret trysting hollows.

Then a movement in the shadows caught Bristol's attention, and she lowered her troubled eyes to a slender figure, the face lifted. With a cry of misery Bristol twisted from the window and ran to her bed.

How could she endure this? How could she withstand this terrible burning passion? Would the fires of hell be any worse than the torture of wanting him and knowing the hopelessness of it? Could the sin of action be any worse, any more damning, than the torment of intense desire? She moaned and writhed on her tangled sheets.

Then she whispered his name and swung down from the bed. She ran to the window, calling under her breath, "Jean Pierre. Jean Pierre."

But he was gone. Only dappled moonlight shone where he had stood. Slowly Bristol stumbled back to her bed, a sob breaking against her throat.

16

JEAN Pierre did not reappear in the garden beneath Bristol's back window. Or if he did, he arrived after Bristol abandoned her vigil. She could not get him out of her mind. The days passed in a blur of misery; Bristol alternated between moods of despair and periods of flushed hyperactivity. Nothing helped. Always she felt the bittersweet ache of loss.

To occupy her mind, she threw herself headlong into Aunt

229

Pru's activities. Together they called on England's aristocratic women and received visits from these haughty ladies in return. And wherever they called, Jean Pierre's upcoming marriage found a place in the conversation. There was no escaping his name, his memory—no possibility of forgetting her pain for even the space of an afternoon.

Nearly every night, parties were held to honor the engaged couple. However, if the truth were known, invitations were prompted more from a respect for the Hathaway name rather than any joy in the upcoming nuptials. Court gossip being what it was, few of England's reigning families remained unaware of the circumstances leading to the wedding. But under William and Mary's somber rule, parties were not encouraged, and a legitimate excuse found a ready welcome. The invitations were issued.

Bristol accepted them all. In part she was relieved to escape the intimate dinners in Lord Hathaway's study; but her heart yearned for those rare moments of Jean Pierre's company. If she understood she could not run from him forever, or from herself, no trace of such knowledge suggested itself in her behavior.

She danced beneath the glittering chandeliers in London's finest houses and flirted desperately with the men who vied to fill her dance cards. She swirled in their arms and laughed at their witticisms and indiscriminately encouraged their attentions with a nearly hysterical need to fill an aching emptiness.

All the while knowing such was impossible. No matter how vast the ballrooms or how large the dining areas, Bristol knew where Jean Pierre was at every moment. And each night she waited in gathering tension for that magical moment when he bowed over her trembling fingers and claimed his dance. For the length of one allemande, Bristol lost herself in the strength of his arms, grew warm under his intense gray eyes, and felt weak at the touch of his firm guiding fingers on her waist.

For Bristol, the evening ended when Jean Pierre returned her to Aunt Pru's side. The remaining hours crawled by, dull and long, an unending duty to be endured. And the pain of watching Jean Pierre with Diana Thorne sliced through her heart like a sword.

Every empty day brought the wedding nearer. Nothing Bristol did eased her anguish. She played with Willie, the calico cat young Master Boyd had presented her when he called. She walked in the Hathaway gardens. She went riding with new friends. She accepted dinner invitations from the men who clamored for her attention. Nothing lessened the bitter ache in her heart. Not even hiding in her room, trying to bury her thoughts by writing long letters home.

At first, letters from home had produced a wave of homesickness, but gradually the packets elicited a lesser reaction. Problems on the Adams farm seemed distant and unreal—part of a life that no longer affected Bristol. Being nearly two months in transit added to an impression of growing unreality.

Bristol read of New England's last snows while sitting beside an open window fragrant with the scent of lilac and June breezes. Charity wrote of tender buds beginning to open on the rosebushes when Bristol had only to lift her head to see waves of summer blossom and miles of billowing trees in full green leaf. The problems of downed fences and wandering livestock and the endless details of Salem's ongoing squabbles seemed small and insignificant when Bristol compared them to the scope of her own experience, or to conversations of court intrigue and Irish battles and the recent French invasion of the Channel.

Nonetheless, she commented on every incident mentioned in her family's letters, pausing to gaze at her pewter cup and to smile when Willie batted a paw at her moving quill. Bristol filled pages with her flowing script, telling Charity of the local flowers and describing the sights of London for her parents. Aunt Pru remained shadowy in Bristol's letters; she didn't mention Jean Pierre or Lord Hathaway at all. Nor the numerous balls she attended, or the beautiful gowns Collette had created.

As safe topics dwindled, Bristol began inserting bits of Reverend Cornwell's sermons, always with a guilty twinge of remorse. And always her fingers longed to pen Jean Pierre's name, to pour her frustrated love onto the blank pages.

Thankfully, Jean Pierre was now seldom in residence; little chance existed of meeting unexpectedly in the corridors. The *Challenger* was being heeled and scraped and refitted in Gravesend and new cargoes had to be arranged, all claiming much of Jean Pierre's time and attention. La Crosse Shipping, Jean Pierre's company, had purchased additional ships in Jean Pierre's absence, and these needed to be inspected and made ready for sea duty. A multitude of details had accumulated while Jean Pierre captained the *Challenger*. His company suffered his absences. The cost of sailing the seas, of momentarily escaping the duties of a large business, were timely and demanded long hours on his return.

231

Bristol couldn't write to her family of such matters. Her letters kept her day-to-day life in shadow, vague and indefinite. And slowly it began to seem as if Salem were a faraway place she'd read of in a vividly written book. Interesting but dreamlike. Her own life lay here, in Hathaway House, with Aunt Pru and Robert Hathaway . . . and Jean Pierre.

"Sorry to interrupt, miss, but it's time to dress for dinner." Molly bustled into the bedroom and pulled open the wardrobe doors, selecting a golden-red gown the color of Bristol's hair. She shook it across the bed and bent to find matching slippers. "His lordship be feeling somewhat improved, and they're planning to eat in the dining room. There be fresh vegetables tonight, Bridey said."

Bristol laid the quill in its slot and folded her letter. She preferred Lord Hathaway's study to the vastness of the dining room. However, downstairs meant she'd not have to sit close to Jean Pierre, and it also meant Uncle Robert's gout had improved to the point of bearing some weight on his foot.

Improved or not, tonight Uncle Robert was uncharacteristically testy. He sipped his wine near an enormous buffet, looking over the green-and-cream room with an expression of distaste. "I almost relish a swollen toe," he grumbled. "Then we can avoid this cavern!"

Seating herself at one end of the long polished table, Aunt Pru glared at her husband with a wounded look. "What's wrong with this room? I thought you liked what I'd done with it." She nodded curtly at an army of waiting servants, and they entered carrying heaping platters.

Lord Hathaway took his seat. "I do, Prudence, I do." He shouted down the length of the table, peering past elaborate candelabra and bowls of flowers. "But it's big! Everything in this house is four damn sizes too big! Look at us," he fumed, "strung out like coins in a pauper's purse! We can't possibly have a conversation!"

"We're here to eat!" Aunt Pru snapped. "We can talk later, and hopefully without profanity!"

"Well, I like to eat in my study. There dinner is pleasant, and not a bloody formal affair!" Uncle Robert scowled at his plate.

Jean Pierre leaned forward and rapped his knife against his glass. "Come, now, this isn't like either of you. May I propose a toast?"

Uncle Robert and Aunt Pru raised their glasses, glares still pinching their faces. Bristol turned an expectant gaze toward

Jean Pierre, hoping he could ease the tension. The wedding was tomorrow. The closer the wedding had drawn, the more her aunt and uncle had found fault with everything around them. Both became irritable and easily upset by small annoyances they would have overlooked a short time ago.

Jean Pierre rose from his chair and inclined his dark head toward the door. Bridey entered and placed packages in Lord and Lady Hathaway's hands. "Please accept these gifts as small offerings of my appreciation for your tolerance and acceptance of a situation I know you both find difficult. I hope the love and friendship we've shared through the years will continue to grow and expand to include the woman I bring you as my wife. Diana needs your care and understanding."

Bristol's eyes filled, wavered, and she dropped her gaze. Jean Pierre's rich, deep voice continued, expressing his affection for his father and stepmother. At the conclusion of his speech, Aunt Pru rushed to enfold him in a massive lavender-scented hug, and Lord Hathaway blew his nose.

The remainder of the meal passed in fond silence. Not until they assembled in the parlor for sherry did the tension again make itself felt.

"Pumpkin . . ." Uncle Robert began. Bristol read censure in his clear gray eyes, the first she'd seen since her arrival. "It seems an unnecessary cruelty to restrict Miss Bristol's cat to one room. We've all enjoyed hearing of Willie's exploits, but I have yet to glimpse Willie himself."

Aunt Pru bristled. Without providing a reason, she'd requested Bristol to keep the cat in her bedroom and refused Willie the run of Hathaway House.

"Nor have I enjoyed the honor of meeting the wonderful Willie," Jean Pierre teased. He extended a glass of sherry to Bristol, his fingers brushing hers with a jolt of heat. For an instant their eyes met, then slid away.

"That cat is not worth seeing," Aunt Pru insisted stubbornly. "It has no breeding whatsoever—it's a stable cat, a mixture of questionable parenthood!"

The men laughed, and Bristol managed a weak smile, uncomfortable with the commotion Willie evoked. "If you find Willie objectionable, Aunt Prudence, I'll . . . I'll return him to Master Boyd." Bristol stared into her glass. In the last weeks she'd developed a deep affection for Willie, undistinguished as he was. He purred across her desk while she wrote letters, amused her by chasing strings of yarn, and curled at the bottom of her bed while she slept. But she would willingly relinquish Willie if Aunt Pru would smile again and be happy.

Prudence Hathaway sighed, not relishing her role as villain. In her generous heart, she suddenly recognized Willie was not the true issue. She'd allowed herself a transference of feelings, a rejection of the newcomer. But it wasn't Willie that she rejected; it was the idea of Diana Thorne. Aunt Pru patted Bristol's shoulder. "No. No, dear. Keep Willie, and you may let him out of your room on occasion." A deep sigh fluttered the lace at her bosom. "You can't return him to Willie Boyd now; young Willie would be crushed. He was so pleased you named that silly cat in his honor." She shrugged at Robert and Jean Pierre, and a hint of her old sparkle gleamed in her eyes. "Keep him. Regardless of his parentage."

"Well," Uncle Robert said when politics and fashion had been exhausted as topics, "have business and being the toast of London kept you two from getting acquainted?" A hint of disappointment and faint hope lay in his tone. As if to say that even now, as late as it was, there still was time for his son to find someone else.

Not trusting herself to answer, Bristol turned large green eyes to Jean Pierre. But Jean Pierre's mood had darkened as the evening progressed; he lacked the will to keep the conversation light and impersonal. His brooding eyes shot a tremor through Bristol's heart. "My cousin avoids me." He made no attempt to soften the bluntness in his voice.

Aunt Pru lifted her hands, and Lord Hathaway's sad eyes steadied on Bristol's pinkening face. "A pity," he murmured, and drained his glass.

Bristol looked from one to the other. "I . . . it isn't that I . . ." There was no possible way to finish the stammering sentence. She did avoid him. Only by escaping him could she make life tolerable. Seeing Jean Pierre only intensified her pain, her loss. Even with limited exposure to his strength, his face and eyes, his overwhelming maleness, she still couldn't sleep, couldn't eat. Jean Pierre haunted her thoughts and heart.

Aunt Pru broke an uncomfortable silence by announcing what each thought and no one wished to mention. "Well, the wedding is tomorrow." She blinked into space. "This is our last night alone together. Tomorrow evening, Robbie, we'll welcome Diana into our midst." An awkward pause followed her sigh.

Lord Hathaway cleared his throat, and he arranged his

face in lines of interest. "Have you given thought to a wedding trip, Robbie? Has Diana found a house for the two of you?"

Jean Pierre swallowed the last of his sherry and poured another. He answered evenly, his face impassive. "I suggested we visit Eze, but Diana finds no charm in small villages. Perhaps we'll visit Paris in the fall."

Bristol looked at her hands. She would have loved Eze. She would have loved being with Jean Pierre wherever they went.

Jean Pierre's slate-colored eyes steadied on his parents. "I'm grateful for your hospitality in opening Hathaway House to us. Actually Diana hasn't yet begun to look for a house. The wedding has kept her in a state of"—he searched for a suitable word—"excitement. I've discouraged her from looking until after the wedding." He shrugged. "Perhaps I'll be able to help then. Diana shrinks from the chore."

"I see," Lord Hathaway said weakly. Aunt Pru pushed at a limp orange curl, her eyes troubled. Lord Hathaway patted his wife's hand and looked at his son. "You are welcome here for as long as you wish, Robbie, I hope you understand that."

Forcing a smile to her wide lips, Aunt Pru abruptly changed the subject. "Are you wearing the green silk, Bristol? All the ladies will be on display. I think the green silk shows you to best advantage."

Bristol nodded and set her glass on a table lest her shaking hands snap the stem. Tomorrow. Jean Pierre would be lost forever tomorrow.

As if by prearranged signal, they all stood simultaneously, self-conscious smiles on their faces. Aunt Pru feigned a yawn. "Well," she murmured, "I think an early night best. Unless . . ." She looked at them hopefully. "Unless anyone is interested in a game of ombre?" Aunt Pru loved cards, particularly if a few coins were wagered on the outcome. She shrugged at the refusal she read in their eyes. "I guess not. Ah, well, we can all use the rest. Tomorrow will be a long day." She accepted her husband's arm and turned toward the door. Bristol hastened to follow.

"Bristol?" Jean Pierre's accented voice carefully held no expression. "Would you honor me with a small moment? I have a gift for you too."

Aunt Pru nodded happily, her orange curls bouncing. "I'm so relieved, Robbie! I can promise you Bristol has worked as hard as anyone on the wedding details. She cataloged the gifts filling the East Room." Prudence smiled and touched the sparkling diamond buckle she'd insisted on wearing immediately upon unwrapping it. "I did thank you, didn't I, Robbie?"

Jean Pierre smiled and kissed her cheek. "Several times, Prudence."

"Yes. Well." Aunt Pru returned to her husband, who was limping badly, and Bristol heard them arguing about Willie all the way up the staircase.

Alone with Jean Pierre, Bristol sank uneasily to the edge of her chair and watched him close the French doors. Her heart raced and she felt the rapid rise and fall of her breast. She hadn't allowed herself to be completely alone with him since the visit to Bedlam—since she'd confessed her love. Her mouth dried and she knew her heart lay exposed in her eyes.

Without speaking, Jean Pierre turned and stared across the room, his smoky eyes narrowing and falling from her lips to the throbbing hollow of her throat, then to the sweet curve of her breast. "*Mon Dieu*," he whispered hoarsely, "every time I see you, you're more beautiful!"

"Please, Jean Pierre! You only torment us both." Bristol's voice was no louder than a whisper, and she lowered her eyes in pain. A familiar weakness spread throughout her body. He'd never been as handsome as tonight, on the eve of his wedding. Jean Pierre's candlelit face seemed all angles and seductive shadows; black breeches and a maroon jacket fitted his hard body to perfection, and the frothy white lace at his throat emphasized dark hair and deep eyes.

He crossed to a sideboard and stood with his back to her while pouring them each fresh glasses of wine. "You do avoid me," he said softly, walking toward her.

Bristol didn't take the glass, didn't dare risk touching his hand. He placed the wine on a table near her chair and lifted his glass to his lips, watching her with moody eyes.

Bristol plucked at her skirt. She wished she had the willpower to rise and leave this impossible situation. But she could not. "I'm sorry," she whispered through parched lips. "I . . . you don't know how difficult . . . " Her voice trailed.

"Don't I?" he asked. His accent thickened with passion. "Do you realize how difficult it is to stay away from you? To respect your feelings and beliefs?" His dark gray eyes burned into hers. "Do you know I still pace the corridor before your door and battle myself? How easy . . . how easy to break past and take you! Can you guess how your face tortures me? How memories eat my mind?" His voice lashed across the room, harsh and deep.

"Oh, Jean Pierre!" Bristol breathed. She closed her eyes

236

and clenched her fists. "We can't go on; please understand!" She stood then, her knees uncertain and weak. "Tomorrow you'll be married. Married!" She stared hopelessly into the face she knew so well, and her cheeks drained of color. "It's adultery. People are hanged for—"

"In New England!" he said, his eyes not leaving her face.

Bristol's shoulders dropped. "Adultery is adultery anywhere in the world. Does it matter if the noose tightens on flesh or on conscience?" Her eyes beseeched him. "No matter our feelings or our desires, there's nothing left for us. Nothing!"

"There is tonight," he whispered, staring into her eyes. "We have tonight, little one. Tonight adultery does not enter the question."

An anguished sound broke past her lips, and Bristol swayed on her feet. She wanted him with every beat of her heart. "It's the same thing as adultery," she moaned. "No, Jean Pierre, we can't. It's over!" Gathering her skirts, she blindly dashed past him and ran up the staircase. She knew if she remained another instant, she'd fling herself into his arms.

Her room looked barren and empty. Taunting moonlight streamed past the windowpanes to remind her of a moon-washed captain's cabin. Her bed sat cold and large, a symbol of memories gone. Bristol passed a shaking hand over her eyes and fell into a velvet chair. She stood and paced to the window, then to the fireplace, then again to the window.

After an hour of aimless wandering, she remembered the gift he'd mentioned. What would she answer when Aunt Pru inquired? It didn't matter. Nothing mattered but him—the man she'd fled.

Angrily she pulled off the golden-red gown and dropped it in a puddle at her feet. For a moment the pale lushness of her young body gleamed in the mirror, and she stared at herself, trying to see what Jean Pierre saw. Warm breath rushed past her parted lips, and she turned away with a groan, hurrying into a soft nightgown of Collette's creation. A white floating mist with delicate foaming lace at cuffs and plunging neckline. She loosened the curls on her head, and a sensuous weight tumbled about her shoulders and down her back. She stood in front of the mirror and knew she'd never been more beautiful.

And for nothing. For no one. No one would see the gown cling and flow, only to mold and shape once more. No one would stroke the silky gloss of curls falling across her breast. Jean Pierre's husky voice echoed in her thoughts: "We have tonight, little one." Tonight, but no tomorrows. Bristol's head

237

dropped. No tomorrows. Never again. Never to taste his lips, to experience the ecstasy of his arms and mouth and teasing hands.

A sound wrenched past her throat, and her hands rose in fists against her cheeks. "I can't!" she whispered. "It's damnation!" But her body moved forward on shaking legs. It's wrong. Wrong! she thought wildly as she watched her fingers reach for the latch.

And finally: I love him, as she trembled in the dark silent corridor before his door. Her conscience blazed and melted away. As if in a dream, she touched his latch, her hand moving slowly, her heart violently hammering.

The door was open. It swung in, and she stood framed in the doorway, her eyes wide and helpless.

Jean Pierre lay against a mound of pillows, still dressed in shirt and breeches. One candle burned near his bed, and he held a wineglass in his hand. Smoky eyes met hers. "I've been hoping," he said softly. Putting down the glass, he opened his arms. "Come to me. Come to me, my love."

Bristol felt faint; her legs refused to move. She held to the door for support, staring at him. Instantly Jean Pierre was at her side, sweeping her into powerful arms. His lips crushed hers in a savage kiss of need and passion denied too long.

And when his bruising mouth released her, Bristol buried her face in his neck, inhaling the scent of salt air. "I love you," she whispered. "God forgive me, I love you."

He moaned, his voice hoarse. Then he laid her on his bed and stood over her, his eyes devouring the lines of her quivering body. His hand touched her breast, and he pulled the white gown down and away, sucking in his breath as the candlelight warmed her trembling flesh.

An explosive urgency sparked between them. Bristol lifted her arms while he tore at the string of his breeches. "Jean Pierre . . ." she breathed, eager, needing, anxious with the fervid demands of her body.

They came together violently, wild with each other, blind to everything but their need. Jean Pierre's fingers bruised her tender flesh, his plunging body rose above her. And Bristol met each fierce thrust with a searing fire of her own, urging him closer, deeper, harder, until each shook with sensation and rapture.

Spent and gasping for breath, they lay tangled in each other's arms. When their breath had slowed, Jean Pierre leaned above her and tenderly cupped Bristol's face in his hands. He stared down into her soft eyes. "I love you," he

238

said simply. His lips traveled her eyes, her cheeks, her swollen mouth. "Why does one woman enflame the body and travail the mind? Is it the curve of lips?" He kissed her gently. "Or the spirit behind the brow?" His mouth brushed her forehead. "The carriage of your wonderful body, or the luster in those green eyes?" His lips found the hollow of her throat, and Bristol felt the velvet strength of his erection growing against her inner thigh.

She moaned, feeling her body respond as his teasing mouth closed over a rose-tipped nipple. "Jean Pierre . . ." she whispered, embracing his name, calling to him again and again. She guided him down, down. As his tongue moved over her moist silky skin, he groaned and whispered in French Bristol did not understand. But she understood the meanings in her heart and in the heat of his hands as he teased open her legs and made circles on her belly with his tongue. And then his dark head moved lower yet, and she whimpered and lifted to him, falling back into the pillows with a strangled cry of bliss.

They made love throughout the moonlit night, unable to quench the fires of urgency and passion. And when they rested, Jean Pierre's arms circled her and he murmured into her ear, and they drank wine and touched each other with embraces born of loss.

"I would stop the dawn if I could," he said, tenderly brushing a long strand of red hair from her cheek.

"There is tonight," she whispered. And reached for him again.

Tints of gray and faint pink shaded the sky when Jean Pierre gently lifted her exhausted body and carried her slowly through the dim hallways. Bristol clung to his neck, her face hidden against his shoulder and covered by a tangle of damp hair. She didn't let herself think past this moment. It was enough to be with him now, to feel his powerful arms holding her, to smell their musky scent, and to know he loved her.

Jean Pierre laid her tenderly in the pink bed, and his lips lingered at her mouth. "Sleep well, my love, my little one," he murmured in a hoarse whisper.

"I love you. Oh, Jean Pierre, I love you!" For an instant the drowsiness cleared, and she stared up into his sober face with her heart shining forth in green splendor.

Gently he brushed her cheek; then he placed something on her bedside table. And he was gone.

17

ALTHOUGH Aunt Pru had sent scores of invitations for the lavish wedding reception, both civil and religious services were small, attended only by family and close friends. Reverend Cornwell officiated at the Tri-Trinity chapel, where Bristol found it less shattering to focus her attention on the reverend than to look toward Jean Pierre and Diana. Arriving direct from the magistrate that married them, the couple knelt at the altar and received Reverend Cornwell's blessing with bowed heads.

Bristol listened to the reverend's monotone with a weary, disbelieving mind. She welcomed her exhaustion; it insulated her from the pain of watching another woman wed the man she loved. With every aching breath Bristol wished herself anyplace on earth but here in this unyielding pew, seeing, listening, and feeling a cake of ice encase her heart.

It didn't seem possible the man at the altar had left Bristol but hours ago. Yet her pale cheeks and the violet shadows smudging her eyes were proof of their night together.

Valiantly Bristol struggled to push those memories into a separate room of her mind. A secret room to be closed and forgotten until she could examine it without the bitter agony of loss. Bristol chewed the inside of her cheek and wrung her hands in her lap. If she failed to submerge her memories, her emotions, life would be intolerable.

She sighed. Even with the best intentions, reminders of their relationship would exist; Bristol couldn't banish them all. Her hand crept to touch the emeralds and diamonds lighting her throat. Earlier this morning, when she'd unwrapped the package at her bedside, she'd discovered these magnificent gems: perfect for her green silk gown—and a wildly generous gift.

Aunt Pru had arched a brow in breathless admiration, having immediately noticed the jewels against Bristol's milky-white bosom. "From Robbie?" she asked needlessly. And her thoughtful blue eyes searched Bristol's tired face. Then her pumpkin curls had bobbed in a quick headshake, as if speculation added complications too unsettling to bear close scrutiny.

Beside Bristol, Aunt Pru puffed up and heaved a sigh; with a start, Bristol realized the religious service had ended. She straightened her shoulders and mentally stiffened her courage. Then Bristol joined the short line of well-wishers, her feet dragging.

She advanced in the line with downcast eyes and managed to offer her best wishes without meeting the gaze of either bride or groom. Bristol knew if she looked into Jean Pierre's eyes, her heart would shatter.

Thankfully, the reception was crowded and noisy with festive gentry. Occasionally Bristol noticed a guest pause and regard the newlyweds with a curious eye, as if wondering why Lord Hathaway's heir had chosen as he had; but good breeding decreed that no mention of Diana's eccentric behavior be uttered aloud. Aristocratic peccadilloes were politely ignored and consigned to the dust bin of memory unless further erratic conduct brought previous acts to mind. Which frequently occurred in the instance of Diana Thorne Hathaway, some whispered—most guests were not so ill-bred as to make like comments in public.

"But they're thinking it, I know they're thinking it." Aunt Pru fidgeted nervously. She mopped her powdered forehead and glanced over the gardens bright with flowing gowns and satin breeches in colors to rival the brilliant beds of June flowers. "I keep worrying Diana will do something terrible." Aunt Pru wrung dimpled hands. "I wish Mary had attended the reception." England's young queen had graced the religious service but offered regrets for the reception. "Why Diana's mother doesn't stand by her side and calm her, I can't guess. Lady Thorne's been dealing with Diana for years. I'd think her more qualified than I in soothing our bride through this long day. But she's left everything to me!" A servant passed along the terrace with small iced cakes and glasses of champagne. Aunt Pru accepted one of each, but ate her cake with little evidence of pleasure.

Bristol peered over her fan at a sallow, aging woman reclining in the shade of a leafy oak. "I think Lady Thorne may be ill, Aunt Pru. She doesn't look at all well."

Aunt Pru shaded her eyes and scowled at the thin, tired woman beneath the tree. "If Lady Thorne dies and leaves me alone with Diana, I shall never forgive her!" Prudence grinned weakly at her niece. "And Lady Thorne strikes me as spiteful enough to do it."

Bristol's smile faded as she spied Duke Charles Easton threading through the crowded gardens, coming toward her. Her shoulders lifted in a delicate sigh. More than ever he reminded her of Caleb Wainwright. His sandy hair tousled in a slight breeze, and his face was a freshly scrubbed pink. He wore an expression of bland cheerfulness that was almost doltish in his single-minded intent to claim Bristol's company.

Watching the duke, comparing him with Caleb, Bristol wondered how she could possibly have once imagined herself in love with Caleb. She hoped Caleb Wainwright had forgotten her and found someone else, for if fate could snatch Bristol from the Hathaway gardens and instantly deposit her on Salem's soil, she knew she'd never again be romantically interested in Caleb Wainwright, if for no other reason than that Caleb would always remind her of Duke Easton. She hid a contemptuous twist of lips behind the spread of her fan.

"Bristol!" Charles Easton bent over her fingers, his wet lips cool and rubbery on the back of her hand. "I've never seen you more beautiful!" He spoke in an irritating nasal tone. "I daresay there's a melancholy softening in your eyes and . . . yes, I believe a touch of sadness becomes you." A red flush climbed his neck. "May I dare to hope that sorrow will ease now that I've found you?"

Bristol was glad the fan hid her expression. Exhaustion made her irritable. For an instant she was tempted to tell him how boring he was, how she suffered his company and fought to keep from yawning in his cheerful bland face.

But of course she did not. Sighing, she accepted his arm and listened with half an ear to his brimming summer plans. Bristol nodded absently, realizing she'd need Charles Easton. To remain in Hathaway House with Jean Pierre and his bride would be a torment. She'd need outside activity. Either that or surrender her own sanity. Besides, Charles Easton was no better and no worse than the others paying her court.

Louis Villiers, the Marquis de Chevoux, rescued her from Charles, clasping her arm possessively and contriving to brush her breast; he detailed a round of parties and hunts and river picnics and country outings he hoped she'd grace with her presence. Then came young Lord Babbington with his summer arrangements, no less ambitious. A succession of men appeared to beg her company for upcoming events, and Bristol discovered she needn't spend a single painful day at Hathaway House unless she wished it.

Her green eyes swept across the expanse of lawn and tables and chattering guests. Even at a distance she felt Jean Pierre's slate-gray stare. She felt him in her heart and in her very soul. Dropping her chin, she closed her eyes. Please, God, I'm trying to follow the right path. I won't seek him again. But help me! Strengthen my resolve! Help us to live in the same house without betraying our feelings, without dishonoring ourselves.

For today, she'd borne all she could. Pleading an indisposition, Bristol retired early, before the toasts to the newlyweds began in earnest. But weary as she was, sleep didn't come readily. She tossed in her bed listening to the music and laughter drifting through her windows, and she tormented herself, wondering about that moment when Jean Pierre would lead his bride to their newly finished quarters in the hallway next to her own.

The next morning, Bristol looked for the answer she both dreaded and longed to know. And a dagger pierced her ragged heart. Diana's face was glowing and radiant when she joined Aunt Pru and Bristol at their table on the terrace. Before lowering a pale face, Bristol noted Diana's perfectly fitted gown of rose-colored moiré and thought miserably that Diana had never looked so lovely or so happy.

"Good morning, dear." Aunt Pru greeted her new daughter-in-law with a wide smile. She looked past the battery of servants cleaning the party debris and waved toward blue skies and banks of flowers creeping over low stone walls. "It's such a glorious day, I decided we'd breakfast outside and take the morning air."

"Indeed," Diana agreed in her whispery voice. "Glorious!" Her golden-brown eyes turned inward, and Bristol wondered if Diana referred to the day . . . or the night.

Clenching her hands in her lap, Bristol worried that the smile on her lips looked as ghastly as it felt. "Good morning, Diana," she murmured haltingly. "May I pour you some ale?"

Diana's eyes widened curiously, as if seeing Bristol for the first time, and unconsciously Bristol shrank from the strange flicker she saw there. Diana's gaze abruptly narrowed. "You didn't stay for my party," she said icily, her smile vanishing. She stared at Bristol, sunlight turning her eyes a tiger gold.

Uneasily Bristol glanced at Aunt Pru, but Prudence leaned to the flower centerpiece, examining it in absorbing detail.

243

"I'm sorry, Diana, I wasn't feeling well." In the silence, Diana's golden eyes didn't move; clearly she expected a less feeble answer.

Bristol bit her lip and stumbled on. "I . . . I'd stayed up very late the night before the wedding, and I . . . I was simply exhausted." Still Diana's golden eyes stared. "And . . ." It was one of those awful moments that stretched into eternity.

Diana smiled. "What an odd coincidence. Robbie mentioned that he too didn't sleep the night before our wedding." Diana sat gracefully and arranged her rose-colored skirt with care.

Bristol's jaw tightened, and she felt herself staring at Diana's finely molded face. Diana could not possibly know anything about Jean Pierre and Bristol. Bristol told herself that her own guilty mind manufactured suspicion where none existed. Still . . . Bristol felt those strange golden eyes swirl and narrow when Diana's gaze flicked toward her.

Diana folded a linen across her lap, and her lips curved in a lazy, satisfied smile. "Fortunately, Bristol, Robbie was able to overcome his fatigue."

Bristol started and gripped her napkin with both hands. Jean Pierre and Diana. Would he have stroked Diana with the same sensual touch Bristol knew so well? Had he teased Diana to whimpering madness like . . . ?

Aunt Pru cleared her throat. "Try the poached eggs, Diana, they're excellent if I do say so."

Diana glared at her plate, a frown pulling her delicate brows together. "I don't eat poached eggs." Her whispery voice rose on a note of suspicion and ire.

"Oh?" Aunt Pru responded weakly. "Well, then. Well, then. Perhaps you'll enjoy the sausage. No one turns a sausage like our Maggie."

Diana rolled the sausages across her plate with the tip of a slender finger. She shuddered and shook honey-colored curls. "I won't eat sausage," she announced flatly. Her mouth thinned.

Aunt Pru shot a worried glance toward Bristol; they both saw the angry flush turning Diana's cheeks to crimson. Bristol quickly offered a basket of raisin buns. "These are wonderful," she said, her voice too loud. "And there's quince jelly if you like." She realized she was holding her breath.

Slowly Diana looked from Bristol to Prudence. "I eat one meal only,'" she hissed in an icy whisper. "I eat a slice of ham, carrots, and a dish of vanilla pudding." Her voice climbed rapidly until she was shouting into their astonished faces. "I told you! I know I did!" Abruptly Diana jumped from the table, her face dark and mottled. "Who prepared this death plate? Who tries to poison me?" The golden eyes narrowed in wild and dangerous rage, and Diana snatched up her plate, running from the terrace into the house.

For a breathless moment neither Bristol nor Aunt Pru moved. They stared toward the tall French doors through which Diana had disappeared. Then Aunt Pru came to life, struggling frantically to rise from her chair. She huffed toward the doors, moving faster than Bristol had yet seen her do. "My God! Diana's going to the kitchen! We have to stop her!"

Bristol lifted her skirts and dashed after her aunt. They rounded the hallway toward the kitchen in time to see a flash of rose as Diana stormed into Maggie's domain. "Oh, dear heaven," Aunt Pru gasped. She drew a breath and pushed through the door behind Diana, Bristol at her side. Aunt Pru halted, and fluttering hands leaped to cover a rounded mouth. Bristol stared.

Diana crossed the kitchen in large angry strides, and as Bristol and Prudence skidded to a stop by the door, Diana hurled her plate at Maggie O'Hare's feet. Food and slivers of china exploded over Maggie's shoes. "I won't eat poison! I demand my usual meal, and I want it now!" Diana's eyes spun golden fury, and her whispery voice jerked to a shriek.

First Maggie stared incredulously at the mess soiling her shoes and hem; then her heavy red face deepened to purple. "Poison?" she screamed. "You dare call *my* food poison?" Maggie's fists tightened on wide hips, and a weighty ladle twitched in her fingers. "You be getting your high-and-mighty arse out of my kitchen! And now!"

"What?" Diana shrieked, her voice cracking with rage. "Nobody talks to me like that!" Her tall body shook, and her hands opened and closed at her sides, balling the rose moiré into wrinkled clumps.

"Diana, no!" Aunt Pru whispered, her face as frozen as those of the servants standing stiff and horrified in the large warm room.

"How dare you burst in here and insult my food! This is my kitchen! You hear that?" Maggie advanced a step and thrust her angry purple face inches from Diana's. Her features congealed into those of a furious gargoyle, and the ladle came up threateningly.

Diana fell on her. Screeching and clawing, Diana sank

taloned hands into the tangled mat of Maggie's gray hair, and kicking feet shot from under the rose-colored gown. Maggie's fist struck hard at Diana's ribs, and the ladle thudded painfully in a series of raining blows. But Diana had the strength of ten; Maggie's bulk offered no obstacle, nor did Diana appear to feel any of Maggie's heavy blows. Handfuls of hair flew over the fighting women.

"Oh, my God!" Aunt Pru breathed. She sagged against the wall. Passing a hand over her eyes, Prudence shut out the appalling sight. But not the sounds. They screamed and hissed like clawing cats.

Bridey Winkle slowly lowered the cup of ale she'd held midway to her lips since Diana burst through the door. Bridey was first to recover her senses. She dashed across the room, shouting to the men for help, and Bridey thrust her small dark body between the scratching, kicking women.

"Oh, God," Aunt Pru repeated again and again as Diana blacked Maggie's eye and kicked Bridey Winkle in the stomach. Maggie's ladle cracked heavily across Diana's jaw, and a bright slash of blood opened along Diana's cheek.

"Oh, God," Aunt Pru moaned, her fingers digging into Bristol's arm. Bristol didn't notice. She leaned against Aunt Pru, her green eyes wide and horrified.

Chaos had invaded Hathaway House.

Later, after Diana had been carried to her room, kicking and screaming, and Dr. Weede had departed after administering a sedative, Aunt Pru gulped a glass of strong ale and stared miserably at Bristol. "I didn't think to ask her about food preferences. It was thoughtless of me . . . unforgivable! This is all my fault!"

"Nonsense, Aunt Pru!" Bristol drew deeply from her own glass. If she was as chalky as her aunt, neither of them looked well. "You couldn't have guessed this would happen."

After a pause, Aunt Pru shrugged and favored Bristol with a weak grin. "Well, at least I've discovered what the kitchen looks like." Her tone sobered, and she added, "Now, if Bridey can only persuade Maggie to stay on. Do you think . . . ?"

"Yes, of course." Bristol patted her aunt's round arm, feeling drained and disturbed. "Maggie's been with Hathaway House too many years to leave."

"I don't know," Aunt Pru answered uncertainly. "Once Maggie threw a pot at me; she said if anyone ever came into her kitchen again . . . Did I tell you?" she asked in a distracted voice.

Gently Bristol turned Aunt Pru toward the stairs. "Yes, you told me. Ask Bridey to cancel the carriage, Aunt Pru, and lie down. We can make calls tomorrow."

Aunt Pru's troubled blue gaze met Bristol's, and she paused with a hand on the railing. "That's good advice." Silently they climbed the winding staircase under the eye of Hathaway ancestors. Aunt Pru stopped. "Diana pulled out Maggie's hair! And blacked Maggie's eyes!" She waved flashing plump hands in a gesture of bewilderment. "And Bridey's limping, and Diana is black and blue and has a cut on her face. Whatever will Robbie and Hathaway say when they return from their ride? They leave for a simple trip to the doctor's and come back to—"

"Shhh." Bristol kissed her aunt's wilted cheeks. "It isn't your fault! Everything will seem better after a rest."

"I hope so," Aunt Pru said emphatically, turning toward her bedroom. Then she predicted in a dark voice, "But I have an idea this is only the beginning."

Prudence was correct. As summer passed, Diana's behavior worsened. At Charles Easton's river picnic, she upset the tables and threw hampers of food into the Thames when it was discovered her vanilla pudding had been forgotten. No one could poison ham and carrots and vanilla pudding. How this might be so, Diana never explained, and no one asked. She exposed a breast at the Globe Theater and screamed abuse at horrified patrons. She whipped two carriage horses so severely one later had to be killed. She tormented her personal maid until the young girl packed her few belongings and ran away from the security of a much-needed job and lodgings. When the message arrived that Diana's mother, Lady Thorne, had died, Diana erupted into a three-day rage of such weeping violence that at the finish, not a stick of bedroom furniture remained whole or usable.

She soiled herself at Louis Villiers' dinner party. An invisible rapist chased her sobbing through Lord Babbington's garden. She set fire to the skirt of a flirtatious duchess who dared cast a seductive eye toward Diana's exhausted husband.

Something had to be done.

When the rainy season arrived and summer leaves crisped to orange and red, Jean Pierre agreed Diana could no longer be allowed outside Hathaway House. A house of Diana's own was out of the question; she couldn't be left untended. Jean Pierre remained the only person capable of soothing Diana's rages, and he too became a prisoner in Hathaway House, unable to leave lest his absence bring on Diana's terrors and incite her to fresh violence. His employees and business acquaintances came to Hathaway House when Jean Pierre was needed . . . and they came by appointment only.

Watching a man of such great physical energy pace the halls like a caged animal wrenched Bristol's heart. Throughout the dismal summer, she'd accepted whatever invitations came her way, regardless of who tendered them. And yet, wherever she was, with whomever, her heart lay absent from the many garden parties, theater engagements, dinner parties, and float picnics up the Thames and away from the stink of London. Her mind and emotions remained behind, in Hathaway House, with a troubled man who daily grew more tense and strained as he futilely attempted to cope with his wife's demands.

And as autumn tinted the countryside and the social season drew to a reluctant close, Bristol discovered more and more of her evenings free to be spent with her adopted family. By October, when chill blinding fog made outings impossible, London society ground to a standstill. Only a fool would venture into the fog, inviting carriage collisions, or robbery by highwaymen, or the near-certainty of becoming lost and stranded in thick obscuring London fog. All across the city, people huddled before dirty coal fires and made do with each other.

At Hathaway House, this created a greater tension than in most of the grand mansions along Pall Mall. Lord Hathaway's cozy red-and-wood study became the scene of hurried unpleasant dinners instead of the laughing, affectionate intimacy Bristol recalled so fondly. Nearly every night, Diana found an excuse to disrupt the meal. Often Jean Pierre had to carry her from the room.

"I waited and waited!" Diana complained. "Who was that man you spent all afternoon with?" She stared up from her platter of ham, her golden eyes demanding.

Patiently Jean Pierre met the golden swirl of accusation in his wife's eyes. He touched her arm briefly. "You remember Mr. Aykroyd, Diana. He's helping to run my company during my . . . during our vacation."

Bristol's pale cheeks brightened. "How is Mr. Aykroyd? I'd so much like to see him! The next time he plans to visit, would you tell me?"

Aunt Pru chuckled. "You've been too busy to see anyone! Mr. Aykroyds asks for you every time he calls. And each time, you've been out . . . breaking hearts!" She smiled

248

proudly. "Which, confidentially, I think I've enjoyed more than you have." She fluttered her lashes at Lord Hathaway in an attempt to flirt. But the mood wasn't right, and it didn't quite work.

Lord Hathaway smiled at his wife in strained affection and adjusted his gouty foot carefully. "Poor Pumpkin! You enjoy the gowns and parties and flirtations so much. What a pity you don't have a daughter of your own." Distress leaped into his eyes, and he flicked an embarrassed glance toward Diana. "That is, I mean to say . . ."

Jean Pierre took up the conversation smoothly. He looked soberly at Bristol, and her heart melted. His hollow gray eyes were deeply shadowed, and the lines in his face had intensified. "Nothing would please Mr. Aykroyd more, Bristol. The next time he—"

Diana scowled at them both and cut into Jean Pierre's conversation. "How is it *she* knows this Aykroyd person, and I, your wife, do not?" Her fingers whitened on the edges of her lap tray.

All eyes dropped to the tray, and Bristol held her breath. Diana had destroyed more meals than she'd eaten in this room.

Gently Jean Pierre pried his wife's fingers from the tray, and he spoke quietly. "You do know Mr. Aykroyd, *chérie*. The man with the scars?"

Diana's brow wrinkled, and she thought furiously, the process almost visible to those who watched. When she nodded and relaxed into her chair, a collective sigh blew through the study. "Yes." Diana smiled. "I remember now."

And one more scene had been averted. But only for tonight.

With the winter snows, Diana became acutely aware of her lack of freedom; she demanded to go out, and if her plans were thwarted, a fury erupted. It became a normal part of their lives to watch deliverymen carrying new furniture up the staircase. Winter also signaled a change in Diana's diet. For no apparent reason, Diana sent word to Maggie (through Bridey Winkle) that her new menu would be a piece of boiled beef, one turnip, and pease pudding every meal—every day. Bridey coaxed Maggie into this concession, and Hathaway House laid in a supply of turnips. Everyone in the house wondered at the change, and no one dared risk asking Diana.

Mercifully, there were periods of calm. To the vast relief and great astonishment of everyone, sometimes days passed when Diana behaved as sanely as anyone, appearing for meals lovely and perfectly composed. On these occasions, Diana revealed a delightful charm, which had the effect of making her bad periods all the more shocking by contrast. But when Diana felt well and serene, dinner reverted to a gay and laughing affair, and often the family played basset or ombre well into the night, with Diana a cheerful and graceful partner.

"I'm afraid the men have bested us once again," Diana said. She looked at the cards spread on the table, then dancing eyes peeped over her fan. "Gentlemen, we bow to your superiority."

"As it should be, ladies." Jean Pierre grinned. He divided the wager between himself and his father.

Aunt Pru squinted in a narrow stare. "Are you really going to take our coins?"

"Now, Pumpkin . . ." Lord Hathaway smiled. "You'd take ours if you won."

Aunt Pru sniffed. "Well, of course, but that's different." She looked into an empty beaded reticule. "You've taken all my coins; it's time to quit," she said with a pout.

Bristol started to rise from the table, but Diana's whispery voice stopped her. "Oh, but this is such fun." Diana's golden-brown eyes held a charming appeal. "Couldn't we have one more game . . . we'll play for kisses." Her silk fan fluttered, and she glanced up at Jean Pierre and Lord Hathaway with a teasing smile.

Lord Hathaway bowed from the waist, favoring his leg. "How can any gentleman refuse such a tempting offer?" He winked at Jean Pierre. "We accept."

For an instant Jean Pierre's eyes touched Bristol's; then she looked away. "I believe I'll sit out this hand," she said faintly.

Diana caught her fingers. "Oh, no, you must stay, we need you." She smiled up at Bristol, her face rosy with pleasure. "Please, Bristol, we can win this time, I just know it." Everyone laughed.

"Thank you, but I . . ." Bristol stopped at the sudden swirl in Diana's eyes. "Please, Diana, I'd rather not."

One of the cards crumpled in Diana's fist, and the mood suddenly changed. In the silence, Diana stared down at the ruined card; then her head slowly rose and she looked at all of them, her eyes pleading. "What's wrong with me?" she whispered. "I didn't mean to tear the card. Something happens in my head, and I . . ."

"*Chérie,* don't think of it now," Jean Pierre said, kneeling at her side. "Enjoy your evening. Here . . ." He reached for the cards. "I'll deal."

Before he rose, Diana laid her palm gently against his cheek. "I'm sorry," she said in a low voice. Her glance included them all. "I'm sorry that I ruin things sometimes. I don't mean to."

Lord Hathaway cleared his throat. "We know," he said gruffly. "Now, then, if I'm to win a kiss, we must begin."

Diana smiled gratefully. "Perhaps I'll find you irresistible enough to give a kiss no matter who wins!" The color returned to her cheeks and a lovely smile lifted her lips.

During such evenings, Bristol suffered deep pangs of crippling jealousy. She tormented herself wondering about the significance of Diana's dewy glances toward Jean Pierre, agonized over each touch, and wondered if Jean Pierre made love to his wife when Diana was well. Ruefully Bristol admitted that at her best, Diana was as lovely a woman as ever graced a drawing room.

Bristol decided, ill or well, it was best to avoid Diana—peace of mind for both women seemed to demand it. Often, when Bristol hid herself in her room, Willie purring in her lap, she worried which was worse, watching Jean Pierre's torment when Diana lapsed into a lengthy spell, or enduring the moist radiance in those golden eyes when Diana seemed well. Bristol rubbed her temples and shoved at a lock of shining red hair. Daily her own position grew more impossible.

She felt like a child craving sweets who is forced to gaze upon a sugary confection every day, all the while knowing the impossibility of ever tasting it. She was so close to Jean Pierre . . . and yet a universe away. Sometimes his gray eyes touched hers, and hunger and yearning slumbered there. Sometimes, when he didn't know she saw, Bristol felt him watching, and she had to leave the room lest she run into his arms. When they accidentally brushed, a wave of dizziness flooded her body, and she had to catch the nearest item for support.

Stroking Willie, Bristol leaned her head against the chair back and watched fat, lazy snowflakes drift past her bedroom window. Willie yawned and nested into her lap. Smiling down at the warm ball curling into her skirts, Bristol thanked God for Willie. All the frustrated love and possessiveness she repressed, she'd lavished on Willie. She knew she'd spoiled the cat outrageously. But Willie was her salvation. Willie was something to write about in her letters home; Willie amused her when she hid in her room. Willie belonged to her.

251

Bristol sighed and reread the latest letter from Hannah. The events described had happened months ago. Hannah's cramped pages told of the labors of fall harvest and the trials of putting up winter supplies. Noah wrote the harvest was better than expected; he'd slaughtered eight hogs this year. Charity glowingly told of crisp New England autumn, and Bristol detected an unaccustomed lightness in Charity's broad script. Idly she wondered at the new happiness in Charity's words.

Dropping the letter beside her chair, Bristol absently scratched Willie's ear. A sudden storm of homesickness broke across her thoughts, as severe as anything she'd experienced during the first days on board the *Challenger*. She clearly saw the Adamses' modest house and Noah's ripe fields; she imagined the smells bubbling from Hannah's autumn pots. Bristol saw the brilliant fall colors and pictured friends and neighbors gathering for the hog slaughter and the celebration that always followed.

And all of it had happened two months ago—old news before her eyes read it. The new year was only a few days away, Salem's harvest a thing of the past. She swallowed a bitter lump and her green eyes settled on the pewter cup across the room. Molly had placed a sprig of red heather in the cup, and Bristol suddenly saw it as a fitting combination. The heather and the pewter cup symbolized her life. She was a blend now, her old existence joined to a new. And she didn't feel as if she belonged in either world.

She felt at loose ends. Her admirers braved fog and cold to call at Hathaway House, and even though Bristol flirted automatically, there was a vacancy behind her sweep of dark lashes. None of the men meant anything to her—in Bristol's mind they were identical, interchangeable pieces. As long as Jean Pierre La Crosse occupied the same world as Bristol, as long as his strong male dominance haunted her dreams, there could be no other man. She resisted seeing anyone, went out reluctantly. And she avoided Jean Pierre as well—her pain was too great.

Black braids swinging, Molly poked her apple cheeks around the door. "Hungry?" She bustled into the room and waved two fingers, her signal to Bristol that the house seemed quiet. "I think Mrs. Diana be good tonight, but it be iffy." Molly assisted Bristol into a blue wool gown and dressed her hair. "Bridey said she don't be certain. Mrs. Diana threw a perfume cask against the wall, then wouldn't let Bridey clean the mess for over an hour. Stinks bad in there." Molly shrugged. "But when Bridey went to dress her for dinner, Mrs. Diana be smiling."

"Thank you, Molly. Sometimes it helps to know what to expect." Before leaving for Lord Hathaway's study, Bristol leaned back into the room. "Let Willie out after his dinner, will you? He could use a bit of exercise—he's been cooped up in here all day."

"Aye, miss. Willie do be a favorite of mine, but I wish you'd have named him Sam." Molly's eyes sparkled, and she touched a small band of braided hair she wore on her finger. "Sam do be the loveliest name!"

Bristol smiled and closed the door. At least Molly made progress with her Sam. Perhaps there was hope for the human heart.

But for her own? During dinner, Bristol cast small quick glances at Jean Pierre, wondering if he remembered, if he ever thought of the moments they'd shared. Yes. His eyes told her so. How might the two of them have responded if . . . ? But "if" was a fruitless game. There were no "ifs" in life, only harsh realities.

Slowly Diana lowered her fork, and an instant tension sparked the study. She leveled a whirling golden stare at Bristol. "I don't like the way you're looking at my husband," she hissed. Everyone recalled the duchess's flaming skirt. Aunt Pru and Uncle Robert stiffened, and Bristol heard their intake of breath.

Spots of color dotted her cheeks, and Bristol's food turned sour in her mouth. "I . . . I'm sorry to offend you, Diana, I assure you that was not my intention." Her voice sounded hollow and unconvincing.

The golden eyes flickered, and Bristol's blood chilled. Diana smiled, and the smile was more terrible than her rage; her golden eyes pierced to bone. "I don't like you," Diana said deliberately, coldly, testing the words on her tongue.

Jean Pierre's laugh sounded hoarse and strained. "Now, don't tease our little cousin, *chérie*. What has she done to offend? Bristol hides in her room with her books and her cat. The only time she appears is when Charles or Louis or James or one of the others appears in the parlor with yet another desperate plea." He attempted to make a joke of it, but Diana's stare didn't move from Bristol's face. Swiftly Jean Pierre removed the tray from Diana's lap.

Not an instant too soon. Diana jumped to her feet and turned on her husband; splotches of color darkened her face, and her fists clenched at her sides. "And you, Robbie? Do

253

you make desperate pleas for her too?" Diana whirled toward Bristol, her pale mottled face ugly with hatred. "Whore! Don't you think I know where he goes at night?"

"No, Diana, we haven't—"

Diana screamed, "Do you think me so stupid I can't read your eyes when you signal each other?" Passion soared in the whispery scream, and Diana shook violently. Her angry eyes swept from side to side, seeking a weapon.

"Robbie!" Lord Hathaway gripped his wife's hand, and they both looked toward their son, fear jumping in their eyes.

Jean Pierre moved quickly. He scooped Diana into powerful arms and strode from the room. They heard her shouts and obscenities until Jean Pierre carried her from hearing.

Aunt Pru fell back in her chair. No amount of rice powder or artful cosmetics could halt the ravages of the past months. Her eyes were old and helpless. "What are we to do?" she whispered. "That poor demented creature is making us all miserable!" She stared at her limp hands, twisting the rings on her fingers. "And Robbie! I can't bear to think of Robbie. He's covered with scratches!" She dropped her face into her hands.

Staring into the fire, Lord Hathaway nodded soberly. He too had aged since spring; seldom did he leave his study, even when his foot could bear weight. "Robbie. Have you noticed the weight he's lost, Pumpkin? And so haggard!" The fire snapped in false cheeriness. "Mr. Aykroyd confessed Robbie's business suffers from his absence." A deep sigh emerged from Lord Hathaway's brocade jacket. He adjusted his shawl and patted his wife's hand. "We knew it wouldn't be easy, Pumpkin," he reminded her softly.

A long silence lengthened before Bristol released her breath and looked up at her aunt and uncle. "I think perhaps it would be best if I took future meals in my room. I upset Diana." She rose and smoothed her skirt, unable to meet the sorrow in their eyes.

"Bristol . . ." Aunt Pru reached a hand to her. "We hardly see you as it is. Must you hide in your room?"

"You're as much our family as anyone here, Miss Bristol." Robert Hathaway's attempt at gallantry was English valor at its best. "We'd like you here with us."

Bristol bit her lip and directed her eyes toward the fire. "I . . . there is a grain of truth in what Diana thinks," she blurted in a low voice. "If Jean Pierre and I . . ." She couldn't go on.

"We know," Lord Hathaway responded quietly. Bristol

turned to him with a sigh; it didn't surprise her. No censure lay in his kind voice, only a deep sympathy. "We'd hoped something might come of it before the wedding, but Robbie is not a man to back from a commitment." He shrugged, and compassion clouded his eyes. "This must be terribly hard on you both."

Bristol raised her white face to the ceiling and blinked rapidly at the moisture filming her eyes. I won't cry! she vowed fiercely. When she could master the quiver in her voice, she whispered, "I look at him, and my heart breaks." She wanted to promise them she'd never do anything to disgrace their house, but she could manage no more. Clutching her blue skirt, she ran from the study and sought the cold solitude of her room. Surely, she told herself, things could not get worse.

In the morning, she found Willie. He'd been carefully laid before her bedroom door, his neck twisted to face backward, his eyes grotesque in death. His four severed paws lay in a neat row beneath his opened belly. Willie's tail was stuffed in his mouth.

18

PROTESTANT England did not celebrate Christmas; the day passed like any other, quiet and unremarked. Instead, the populace reserved their winter frustrations, their pent-up tensions, for an explosion of rejoicing on New Year's Day. Despite a bitter cold and a leaden sky, joyful bonfires appeared throughout the city and dotted the countryside. Those that could, exchanged small gifts and prepared a bountiful table. Church bells pealed from every belfry, and the snow-packed lanes rang with a jingle of sleigh bells as sleighs and carriages dashed about the city filled with laughing, shouting celebrants.

The merry sounds penetrated Bristol's closed windows, but they did not reach her thoughts. She sat before the fire in her bedroom staring dully at the flames, acutely conscious of the empty hollow in her lap where Willie should have been. Leaning her glossy curls against the chair back, Bristol closed her eyes. Tears would not restore Willie to life. Tears would not summon his warm weight to her lap. Though she repeated these words until they whistled in her head, still her eyes felt gritty and her throat tensed with unshed tears.

A week had elapsed since Bristol found Willie outside her door and had run screaming down the corridor. A bitter week during which she'd refused to leave her room, refused to admit anyone but Molly and Aunt Pru, and refused to examine the stack of invitations for New Year's Day. Bristol saw nothing to celebrate in the dawning of 1691, no reason to dash about in the snow at the side of someone she cared nothing for. Listlessly she stared into the flames until Molly knocked at the door.

"They be a visitor asking for you," Molly said, leaning into the room, her black braids swinging. Her eyes measured Bristol with concern.

Bristol returned her gaze to the fire. "I don't want to see anyone. Send them away."

Molly chewed the tip of a braid and frowned. "I do wish you'd reconsider, miss. I don't be wanting to tell him anything. He be a fierce man; I don't be liking the looks of him."

Bristol didn't move or look from the flames.

"Bridey said this man comes often, and he do be a friend of the family . . . but he looks to me more like a pirate, miss." Molly shuddered. "All them scars! I don't know what he be wanting with you."

Bristol's fiery head snapped up, and her expression glowed with more animation than she'd displayed all week. "Mr. Aykroyd!" she cried. "Oh, Molly, it must be Mr. Aykroyd!" She jumped up and peeked hurriedly into the mirror, pushing impatiently at her hair. "Molly, tell him . . . no, no, never mind. I'll tell him myself." She fussed with her gown, then rushed past Molly, a smile for the amazement on Molly's face. She patted Molly's hand and hastened down the corridor; if there was one person who might cheer her, it was Mr. Aykroyd.

Bristol ran into the downstairs parlor and threw her arms around his neck. Then she leaned back and smiled into Mr. Aykroyd's beaming face. He truly was the ugliest man . . . and the dearest, she thought affectionately. "You look so . . . different." She smiled. This was the first time she recalled seeing him without a knit cap; his thinning white hair was plastered neatly across his ruddy forehead, making him seem

256

not quite as tall as she remembered. And he wore clothing Bristol had never expected to see him wear, looking cramped and ill-at-ease in his formal attire, as if afraid he might burst the seams of satin breeches and a fitted frock coat.

Mr. Aykroyd looked down at himself and shrugged. Then he grinned, rippling the scores of ridges and valleys pocking his weathered face. "Ye look a mite different yerself, gel." Blue eyes glowed appreciatively. "More mature somehow, and thinner in some spots, rounder in others."

Bristol laughed and sat down, patting the settee beside her. Molly's hair arrangement added an illusion of sophistication, and the gray wool gown she wore was nothing similiar to the drab Puritan designs she'd worn on board the *Challenger*. Of finest quality, this dress dipped to display a generous cleavage and molded her small waist. Blue ribbon threaded the sleeves and sash, and the soft material clung to her body when she moved. "I'm a lady now," she teased, "a grown woman of high quality."

Mr. Aykroyd smiled and nodded; then he sat gingerly on the edge of the settee, careful lest he soil or break it. Fishing in his pocket for the clay pipe, he cast a guilty glance at the parlor doors. "Do ye think Lady Pru will mind a pipe?" he whispered.

Thinking of Aunt Pru's dainty pipe and the enjoyment she derived from it, Bristol shook her head with a smile. "No, Aunt Pru won't mind in the least."

In a moment Bristol inhaled a pithy blend of sweet and sour, and suddenly she realized how very much she'd missed Mr. Aykroyd. "I'm glad to see you," she said simply, squeezing his hand.

"Well, I be asking after ye, and each time ye're out gadding with a duke or a lord or a marquis or some such." He smiled, his blue eyes examining her face. "It seems ye've taken London by storm, not that I ever harbored a doubt."

Shaking her curls, Bristol laughed. "London has taken me by storm." They gazed fondly into each other's smiles. "How have you been?" Bristol asked softly.

Mr. Aykroyd sighed and tugged a lock of white hair, disarranging the careful combing. "As good as any salt can be when the sea calls and hears no answer." He glanced into the clay pipe. "The captain and me, we be together a lot of years . . . and I tell ye frankly, this isn't one of the good times." A disgusted snort blew out his lips. "They be a widow in South-wark what cast her eye on me and my house. If captain don't put to sea soon, the widow will be planting her spring garden outside my kitchen door!" Bristol laughed and clapped her hands. Mr. Aykroyd scowled. "It ain't good to put a seagoing man in the way of plump widows! And it ain't good for a seagoing man to be heading up a business!"

"Both Jean Pierre and Uncle Robert say you've been wonderful. Jean Pierre couldn't manage right now without your help." Bristol hid a pang of emotion at the mention of his name. "It's been . . . difficult for him."

Mr. Aykroyd met her eyes with a shrewd nod, and Bristol dropped her face. "I know what it's been for the captain. Now, tell me how it's been for ye," he said gently, and drew on his pipe. He leaned back on the settee, his eyes on her face.

Bristol drew a breath. "Oh. Well . . . it . . . it's been wonderful!" Color flushed her cheeks with rosy warmth. "Just look around us." Bristol waved at the opulent room. "Could you dream a parlor like this, even if you tried? I never expected such . . ." He watched her, holding the bowl of his pipe. "And my room! Mr. Aykroyd, you should see my room! It's huge, and all done in pink, and . . ." He said nothing.

Bristol drew another breath and failed at a smile. "The parties!" she rambled desperately. "I've been to so many parties and I've danced out my slippers, and I've chased a fox and gone to picnics along the river." Her voice sounded brittle, artificial, and she wished he'd say something, anything. "I have more gowns than I can count, and . . . and I never do any hard work. Aunt Pru says ladies don't do hard work." She shifted her eyes from his steady clear gaze. "I've had dance lessons and voice lessons. Aunt Pru says my voice . . ." The babble died on her lips. She stared into the silent sympathy in Mr. Aykroyd's eyes and knew he saw past the unconvincing falsity. He saw the truth.

"Oh, Mr. Aykroyd," she whispered. "I'm so miserable!"

Taking her hand, Mr. Aykroyd leaned forward; he tilted his head, trying to meet her downcast eyes. "Some say I do be a good listener," he reminded her softly. Settling back on the cushions, he drew on his pipe.

And a torrent of words burst from Bristol's heart, responding to the kindness in his tone and the understanding in his caring eyes. "I had a cat . . . Willie . . . and, Mr. Aykroyd, I loved Willie more than anything! He sat . . . and when I wrote letters, he . . . And he was mine! Only mine! I took care of him . . . I did everything for him . . . and Willie loved me, too, Mr. Aykroyd, I know he did . . . he slept on my bed, and . . . he'd curl in my lap for hours . . . and there was never enough stroking and petting to please him. I wish you could have seen him, he was so . . . I knew all his habits, just where he liked to be scratched, what he liked best to eat, the spots he favored." Mr. Aykroyd watched intently, seeing the pain mar her lovely features.

"I loved Willie!" The longer Bristol talked, the more difficulty she had with the words. Her throat tightened, and her chest felt like iron bands circled it. The words came hard. "And then . . . and then, Diana . . . Diana took Willie away and she . . . and she killed him! A little at a time! She destroyed my Willie! It was Diana!" Bristol covered her face, and her body shook. "I don't know what to do! I'll never see Willie again, never hold him again . . . and it hurts so much!"

As Bristol fought to control the sting behind her lids, Mr. Aykroyd expelled blue jets of pungent smoke toward the ceiling. Finally he put the pipe in a crystal bowl and wrapped his large hands around a knee. He waited silently until Bristol dropped her fingers and looked toward him with reddened eyes. "Gel," he said gently, "we're not talking about a cat named Willie." He read the shocked expression in her wide green eyes, and he reached for her hands. "Gel, ye're talking about the captain." He went on, speaking quietly, his eyes on Bristol's chalky face. And his understanding put Willie's death in a bitter new perspective.

When he finished, Bristol closed her eyes and swayed on the settee. He was right. She sensed it deep inside. She'd made Willie a surrogate, a vessel for the frustrated love she felt for Jean Pierre. And when Diana destroyed the surrogate, Bristol had clashed head-on with a personal misery she'd been too proud to acknowledge.

"Jean Pierre is lost to me, isn't he?" she whispered through bloodless lips. "Really and completely gone, with no hope."

"Aye," Mr. Aykroyd answered, his eyes on her face.

Bristol tilted her head toward the ceiling, watching it swim through a fog of moisture. "What can I do?" Each word weighed heavily with despair.

"Well, now, gel, they's a story ye might find a wee interest in hearing." Mr. Aykroyd glanced at her, then leaned into the settee and centered his gaze on the fire in the grate. "Once, me and the captain put into an island for supplies. A jewel of an island she was, with proud, fine-looking people. While the boat be loaded, the head man of these people walked the captain and me on a tour of his island. In due course, we came to a long spit of sand and rocks. Beyond the spit was a stretch of sea, wild and foaming, and past that, on the other side, just close enough for the eye to see, lay another spit leading to another island."

Bristol lowered her eyes from the ceiling, and gradually, as she listened to his deep soothing voice, her hands dropped the bit of lace she twisted and lay quiet in her lap.

"Captain and me, we started out on the spit to examine that piece of wild sea, but the head man, he said no. A man, Kemane Hano, stood on the spit preparing to swim to the other island, and Kemane Hano must not be disturbed. Well, the captain and me, we looked long and hard, but all we be seeing was sand and rock and some scattered bones."

One hand still clasped his knee; a cloud of sweet-and-sour smoke obscured his face. Mr. Aykroyd's blue eyes looked into the distance of memory, and when he took up the tale, it was as if he returned from a faraway place.

"Kemane Hano, the head man told us proudly, set out years before to swim the wild sea and explore the neighboring island. No one had ever done this before. The village gave feasts in his honor, and Kemane Hano strode out to the end of the spit, walking tall and confident. But when he reached the end of the spit, he saw what the captain and me saw when we explored that spit later. A deep channel ran there, wild and fast and filled with jagged rocks. If Kemane Hano wasn't smashed on those rocks, he would surely be swept out to sea. Either way, to enter the water was to die."

Mr. Aykroyd turned his eyes to Bristol's pale face. "So Kemane Hano stood on the spit. He could not go forward, and his pride held him from going back."

Logs fell and resettled in the grate. Outside, distant sleigh bells sounded above the faint murmur of voices deep within the house.

Finally Bristol broke the silence, her voice low and troubled. "Why didn't the villagers call him back instead of leaving him to starve?"

Mr. Aykroyd sucked on his pipe. "It's possible they didn't be knowing about the channel. It's possible they salvaged Kemane Hano's pride by pretending he waited while he prepared for the swim. It's possible they refused to acknowledge his failure; they still see him there today. Whatever the reasons, Kemane Hano perished rather than admit his mistake and call for help."

Bristol slowly turned the story in her mind. "Are you telling me to go home? To return to New England?" she asked in a low tone. She thought of writing, of asking Noah if she could come home now; and she felt a stirring demon of pride.

"Gel, I don't be telling ye what to do. It's not my place to make yer decisions." He stared into his pipe bowl. "But aren't ye standing on a spit like Kemane Hano? Ye can't go forward."

When she didn't answer, he added softly, "And like him, unless ye do something soon, ye're in danger of perishing."

Bristol blinked. "Perishing?" Personal danger jolted through her mind.

Mr. Aykroyd's face hardened. He said soberly, " 'Tis a new idea to ye, gel, but not to some in this house. Think! Think of yer cat! The hand that turned against yer Willie could as easily turn against ye."

Bristol gasped. Her green eyes widened and paled to jade; she stared at Mr. Aykroyd, dry lips falling open. "Diana?" she whispered.

"Aye, gel. Diana. Who do ye suppose she imagines as the greatest threat to her happiness? As the obstacle in her path? Yer dead Willie tells ye the answer." Mr. Aykroyd's blue eyes measured Bristol through a cloud of fragrant smoke. "Think on it, gel, think on it. And remember: them what is touched with madness don't reason like ye and I. Don't be fool enough to believe ye can outguess them or hang yer own morality on they shoulders. Ye can't."

Bristol wet her lips and closed her hands, feeling a tension along her stiffly erect body. "I . . . You've given me much to think about, Mr. Aykroyd. I thank you."

"Don't be taking too long about yer decisions, gel. Them what know ye, don't like to see ye hurt." Embarrassed, he rose to his feet, and Bristol stood also. Mr. Aykroyd pressed her hand and managed a grin. "They be a selfish reason here as well. If the tensions ease in this house, mayhaps I can move the captain back to sea and save me own house from the widow."

Bristol's full mouth curved in a wobbly smile, and she clung to his hand. "Mr. Aykroyd . . . you've been a true friend, and I . . ." A mist clouded her vision.

"Now, gel, don't be turning sentimental on me." He smiled below an infusion of color darkening his mapped cheeks. He patted her fingers awkwardly. "Bad enough the widow oozing sweetness on me. Now, don't ye be starting too."

"Well, maybe the widow would be good for you," Bristol

teased. Pushing aside the new disturbing thoughts, she concentrated on leaving him with a smile. She abandoned an effort to thank him; it wasn't necessary. The undercurrent of affection ran strong and swift between them, and Bristol realized it had no need of words.

A crimson flush climbed Mr. Aykroyd's scarred face. "Now, what would a good woman like the widow want with an ugly old salt like me?" he muttered.

Bristol kissed his cheek and smiled into his eyes. "You. Just you. And she'd be fortunate indeed to have you."

He shoved his pipe into his coat pocket and frowned at the floor. "The things what fall out of yer mouth, gel! No wonder ye've taken London in hand. Ye could charm the barnacles off a bow!" He grinned down at her. "Best forune in 1691."

"Best fortune, Mr. Aykroyd."

From her front bedroom window Bristol watched his hired carriage until it disappeared in the snow-studded traffic jamming Pall Mall. A light fall of snow thickened as she stood at the window, hissing as it struck the panes.

Bristol cleared a circle on her steamy window and gazed into the lane below. Lights appeared on the sleighs and carriages; snow obscured the festive bonfires. The traffic diminished, and deep resonant peals from the church steeples sounded muffled beneath the thickening fall of snow.

Sighing, she let the curtains drop. Bristol had no desire to watch the merrymakers. Crossing the room, she sank into a chair before the fire and stared into the flames. Occasionally her green eyes strayed to the pewter cup on her desk, and she considered rising and fetching it. But she didn't. Today she resisted the idea of home, of Salem. In her aching heart, Bristol knew Mr. Aykroyd had planted the seeds of her solution, and in the end, she'd do as he'd gently suggested. She saw nothing else for herself.

But not yet. Later, she told herself, later this week she'd write to Noah. By the time Noah's answer reached her, she'd have been in England nearly a year. Maybe her family waited to hear she was ready to come home.

But was she? Bristol wrestled the question through a solitary dinner and again as she sipped a glass of sherry by the fire. The answer was an unqualified no! She'd never be ready to leave London, not so long as a single shred of hope remained that Jean Pierre and she . . . But no hope remained. There had never been a basis for hope. Bristol's fingers tightened on the stem of her glass. And yet . . . while here

262

she could at least see him, hear his voice, exchange a few hurried words. And sometimes when their eyes met . . .

But were stolen words and fleeting glances enough to build a life upon? Bristol knew she couldn't continue as she had during the past year. Charles Easton pressed for a commitment; Louis Villiers pressed for a commitment. And considering either was unthinkable. But to refuse . . . Then the invitations would slowly dwindle. And as time passed and she continued to refuse the offers for her hand . . . what then? Would stolen words and fleeting glances be enough? Was she destined to become a faint shadow seeking such vague assurances? A troubled spirit nourishing on yearning stares and accidental touches? Could Bristol Adams be satisfied with melting slivers of an elusive whole? Living but a fragment of life?

No.

Bristol shivered despite the crackling logs in the grate. No, she could not. Living such an empty life, she'd become the dried-up, juiceless virago she'd once supposed Aunt Pru to be.

Pressing a weary hand to her temples, Bristol leaned back in the chair. There was no choice. Not really. For her own sake, for the sake of the people in this house, Bristol understood she must leave and deal with the loss as best she could. No matter her pain; the pain of remaining would be worse.

A quiet knock sounded at her door, and thinking it Molly come for the dinner tray, Bristol called, "Come in."

"Thank you, Bristol, I feared you wouldn't see me."

At the sound of Jean Pierre's deep voice, Bristol jerked to her feet, droplets of sherry sparkling across her fingers. She lifted a hand to her mouth, her anguished stare meeting his. For a moment she couldn't believe it was really Jean Pierre and not a vision her own longing had created.

"Jean Pierre?" Bristol stared, shocked at his appearance. Aunt Pru had reported Diana's behavior following Willie's death as worse than anything prior, but Aunt Pru had been purposely vague regarding the effects on Jean Pierre.

Bristol clearly saw the terrible cost of his marriage written on Jean Pierre's features. His eyes stared from dark sockets, and his face was thinner than Bristol remembered. His cheeks were hollowed and gaunt. No hint of his former arrogance shone in a weary stance; he stood like a man tired of existence. Strands of gray lightened his brow. The gray must have been there for some time, Bristol thought wildly, wishing it so; she simply had not noticed before. "Oh, Jean

Pierre," she breathed. The full impact of their situation saddened her low voice.

"I brought you a New Year's gift," he said crossing the room and stopping before her. Bristol hadn't thought to light any candles. But the firelight was enough to illuminate the deep fatigue in his face, the dull exhaustion in his eyes.

Bristol longed to reach a hand to that tired face. Instead, she looked down and said, "I have nothing for you."

Jean Pierre smiled, his expression strained. "Good, little one. It's better that way." He winced at the hurt in her green eyes, then looked at her again with an attempt at his old challenge. "I have your gift, but you must find it." He held his arms away from his body.

Bristol stared at the firelight flickering upon his face, resisting his game. Suddenly she realized this was the first moment they'd spent alone together since his marriage. High color warmed her cheeks, and her body tingled with the nearness of him. She felt the tension in her stomach.

Turning aside, Bristol drew a shaky breath. To search his pockets was out of the question—impossible; it was wrong of him to ask it. Touching broke the unspoken rules. The rules that made their life possible, endurable, at Hathaway House. She knew—utterly believed—if they once broke the rules, their lives could never again be the same; life would be unbearable, worse than the torment they now experienced, a thousand times worse.

A small mewling noise sounded from the opening of his dark buff coat, and a tiny orange head emerged near Jean Pierre's shoulder. Black button eyes blinked once and darted back inside the coat.

Bristol gasped. She lifted her eyes to Jean Pierre's smile, then stared again at his coat. A fluffy orange ear and one dark eye peeped back at her from the ruffles of Jean Pierre's cravat. He reached inside then and withdrew a ball of orange fur. "Shhh. *Tranquille, petit chat,* this lady will love and care for you. Quiet, now." He placed the tiny hissing kitten on Bristol's shoulder.

Small needles clung to her gown, and an orange ball burrowed into the hollow of her neck, the little body trembling with fright. Bristol murmured soothingly and stroked quivering orange fluff; the kitten scarcely filled her hand.

She looked past the fur tickling her chin and felt a scald behind her lids. Swallowing hard, she managed to say, "Thank you, thank you. I love him already."

Jean Pierre's lips rose in a tired smile of pleasure. "His

name is Seven." He laughed at the expression on Bristol's face. "The little cat was already named, but perhaps he'll not mind a new name if you prefer." Jean Pierre reached and ran a finger down the kitten's spine. Bristol felt the heat of his hand radiate against her cheek. They looked at each other across the small space separating them.

"Oh, Jean Pierre," Bristol whispered helplessly. She could never afterward recall who moved first; they came together as naturally as two people who had never been apart. His arms folded around her, and she pressed her cheek against his broad chest. He leaned his head against her hair. They stood in quiet closeness, taking warmth and comfort from each other, feeling no need for words.

Not until Seven exhibited a tentative urge to explore did they step apart. Bristol smiled uncertainly and turned to her bureau to make a temporary home for Seven. She felt shaken by a deep sense of shared intimacy. Behind her, she heard the clink of glass as Jean Pierre poured sherry for them both. He waited while she transferred a pile of frothy underthings and gently placed Seven on an old shawl in the drawer.

"May I sit with you for a little time?" he asked.

Bristol's heart moved in her breast, hating that their situation was such that he must ask her permission. "Of course." She returned to her chair, sitting where she could see Seven's orange head peeping above the drawer. For the first time in her relationship with Jean Pierre La Crosse, she felt a lessening of the tensions between them. She didn't sense the familiar challenge and a need to meet that challenge. Watching his gaunt tired face in the firelight, she felt only a deep tenderness and a love that flowed beyond the demands of flesh.

Jean Pierre leaned his dark head against the velvet chair back. "It's quiet here." He sighed. "Quiet and clean and peaceful."

He felt it, too. Bristol observed his body slowly relaxing and realized how tensed he'd been, as if primed to instantly respond to sudden danger. Perhaps he was, she thought sadly, her eyes deepening to emerald. "This week has been bad, hasn't it." She stated a fact.

Jean Pierre ran his hands over his eyes, and stretched his neck against his fingers. "Willie's death was . . . as hard on Diana as on you, though expressed differently. For her, it was an act to be forgotten by further violence, by larger, greater emotions to obliterate the one at base." He closed his eyes. "There's no point in relating the events of this past week, it would only upset you. I'm glad you kept to your room."

Seated in the chair across from him, their feet almost touching, Bristol folded her hands in her lap and watched the shadows moving about his tired face. An understanding welled in her heart. The companionship of loving was as great a part of men and women as any instant of ecstasy in one another's arms; perhaps, she thought, the companionship was the more important of the two. She remembered seeing Noah, worn and battered from a day's struggle in rocky fields, sit quietly in her mother's company and later rise refreshed. She pictured Aunt Pru, tired and wilted from her parties, turning toward Lord Hathaway's room instead of her own. And Lord Hathaway, tenderness in his eyes despite the agony of a gouty foot. And now Jean Pierre had come to her.

Quietly Bristol rose and knelt by Jean Pierre's side. She laid her cheek on his thigh and offered her nearness for his comfort. Jean Pierre's hand dropped to her head, and he stroked her hair with long gentle movements.

"I love you, Bristol," he said in a low voice. "You are the one shining truth in my life, the island of sanity I cling to." A short, bitter laugh escaped his lips. "I, who have never clung to any person, to any thing." His hand caressed her hair, the silky strands rising under his fingers. "I cling to you. I think of you when all around is black; I see the softness in your eyes, and I know there is still beauty and meaning in the midst of chaos."

Hearing his words, listening to his low quiet voice, Bristol understood she could not leave Hathaway House. The letter to Noah would never be written. Knowing Jean Pierre loved her would be enough; knowing he needed her would sustain her life.

She lifted her head and gazed deeply into his steady, serious eyes. "Where is Diana now?" she asked, her heart glowing on her face.

He stared, and she saw he understood. "No, Bristol. I would not ask it of you. I know your beliefs, the guilts and torments you would suffer."

She almost smiled; what guilt, what torment could be worse than the pain she lived each day? Looking at the firelit ridge of scar along his jaw, she lifted her fingers. Her eyes saw the tightening of his lips and the hurt in his dark eyes. "Where is Diana now?" The quiet passion of both lay in her voice.

He closed his eyes, then opened them and searched her

266

face. "Asleep. Dr. Weede left an hour ago. He bled her and sedated her." His voice dropped to a hoarse whisper.

Rising, Bristol took his hand in both of hers and guided him from the chair. She looked up and showed him the love shining in her soft green eyes. "Please," she said. "I love you."

She led him to the bed, and he followed with wooden steps. She undressed, and he watched without moving. Then her fingers trembled at the fastenings of his coat, his white shirt, his cravat. She fumbled with the string at his waist and pushed him gently to the bed while she pulled away his breeches. At last he was naked. She touched his lean hard chest in wonder.

Jean Pierre caught her hand. "Bristol," he said in a husky groan. "Don't do this. Stop while we still can. This is no good for you." He turned his eyes from her body glowing in the firelight.

"Jean Pierre," Bristol whispered. "My Jean Pierre." Her fingers pressed him back; then she lay beside him and lifted on an elbow to kiss his eyelids, the line of his jaw, the corner of his lips.

He tried once more. "Bristol, I'm too exhausted to be strong for you." He captured her hands and stared into her eyes. "I'm a man, little one, not a saint; I can't resist much longer. Take this moment and cover yourself!"

She stopped his words with a kiss, tender, clinging. Then she ran her fingers across the dark hair curling on his chest, and felt him shudder. She looked the length of his naked body and drew in her breath. Cupping his face in her small hands, she smiled into his dark, troubled eyes. "I do not take an unwilling man," she teased softly, smiling at him.

She smelled the freshness of his hair, buried her hands in the dark curls tied at his neck. She laid her cheek against the crisp hair covering his chest, so different from the rest. And his hands moved over her satiny body with joy and astonishment, with the wonder of love. Seeing her as if for the first time, as she saw him.

Then he moved over her, slowly, unhurried, and he brushed long hair from her cheek. "I love you," he said. Intensity quivered in his hard face, his eyes, his voice. "I love you, little one."

He entered her as his lips met hers, and they moved together in a new rhythm, quietly, deeply, building a gentle symphony of tender touches and soft murmurings. And this time, as she soared toward climax, it was not the crashing ending of before, but a shared intimacy of expanding bliss taken togther.

"Bristol, *chérie* . . ."

"Shhh. Rest now, my love, my Jean Pierre. Rest now."

And he slept, finding the first peace in weeks, sleeping with his dark head cradled against the fullness of her breast, pillowed in her love.

She guarded him through the deep snowy night, leaving but twice. Once to bring Seven into the warmth of their bed, and once to add logs to their fire. Her arm went to sleep, and fiery needles shot up to her shoulder, but she did not move, would not disturb his rest. Only when faint light struggled against the cold black outside the windows did she look from his face and allow herself to stir. Gently she shook his naked shoulder, her fingers stroking his smooth, muscled skin. "Jean Pierre," she whispered, kissing his forehead, his eyelids.

Gray eyes opened, and he looked up with a clear gaze. She saw that his face looked less tight, less strained. "*Chérie*. Little one." He reached for her. "I can't bear to leave you." His arms tightened, and he pulled her close against his body, warm with sleep. "I cannot leave you," he murmured, his voice thickening. His kiss was urgent and demanding. And his body awakened and found her ready for him.

Later, when he'd slipped from her room, Bristol lay in the suddenly empty bed, the taste of his kisses still burning on her swollen lips. She turned her face into the bed linen and inhaled his male scent, the smell of love and salt and perspiration. Jean Pierre. Placing her body where he had lain, pressing her face into the pillow his head had touched, with his scent lingering in her nostrils, and Seven pressed into the hollow of her waist, finally Bristol allowed herself to sleep.

When she awoke late in the morning, she couldn't be certain what time it was. The sky was dark and heavy with thick falling snow. She dressed and stood at her front window, peering down toward a lost ground. Up and down seemed indistinguishable in the white blur. A flash of red caught her attention for an instant, but vanished before Bristol could be certain she'd seen anything. Perhaps someone braved the storm, though she couldn't imagine anyone so foolish. Bristol stretched and yawned; she drew a heart on the clouded window and smiled at herself, at her lightheartedness. Today, she thought, she'd think only happy thoughts, treasure her memories of the night. Returning to her chair by the fire, she settled Seven into the nest of her lap.

She'd nearly fallen asleep, a smile on her full lips, when a violent pounding jerked her rudely awake. Hastily placing Seven in the bureau drawer, Bristol ran to throw open her door.

Diana leaned in the doorway, her golden eyes wild, her crimson cloak swirling. Tendrils of honey-colored hair streamed down the shoulders of a snow-dusted cloak and flew about her face. "Robbie!" she cried. "Robbie's been hurt . . . a terrible accident . . . he's calling for you. Come quickly!" Diana turned and raced down the corridor, not waiting to see if Bristol followed.

Bristol's face froze, and her heart stopped. She felt the color blanch from her cheeks. Jean Pierre hurt? For an instant she swayed dizzily; then she snatched up her green cloak and flew out her door, dashing down the hallway and tumbling down the stairs, taking them two at a time. She ran past Bridey Winkle and pulled frantically at the heavy double doors in the entry.

"What . . . where are you going?" Bridey's dour face stared in disbelief. "It's a blizzard out there!"

"Jean Pierre! There's been an accident! He's hurt!" Bristol pounded the door in frustration. Would it never open? "Damn!" The door burst open, and Bristol dashed outside, her thin at-home slippers skating across snow and ice. Slipping and sliding, Bristol descended the stairs to a coach she could barely see in the curtain of snow. A driver Bristol didn't recognize assisted her up, and Diana's strong hands pulled her inside and out of the blinding swirl of snow.

"Go!" Diana shouted to the driver.

Before Bristol leaned against the seat cushion, she saw a spill of light as the house doors opened and a figure ran out on the porch. She couldn't make out who it was. Bristol clasped her hands together and caught her breath. She absolutely would not feel guilty about not waiting for anyone else. Jean Pierre was hurt; he needed her.

She closed her eyes, struggling for breath. Where was he? What had happened? The snowstorm blanketed the carriage windows, and Bristol could see no more than a few feet past the panes. She wondered how on earth the driver would manage to get them through the storm.

"Diana, where are we going? What happened? How badly is he hurt? What . . . ?" Bristol stopped and sucked in her breath at sight of Diana's face.

Diana leaned against the cushions, a strange satisfied smile curving her lips. In the gray half-light of the storm, her eyes

269

glittered tiger-gold and icy. "You'll see," she purred, and the whispery voice sent a chill up Bristols spine.

A thousand questions sprang into Bristol's mind. And looking at the odd smile twisting Diana's mouth, Bristol felt a leap of alarm. She peered down at her hands, away from those golden eyes. She'd forgotten her gloves, and already her hands felt cold and were turning pink.

Her mind spun. Jean Pierre hadn't left Hathaway House in weeks—why now, in the midst of London's worst winter storm? And Diana—had Diana been out too? Had she been with him? Bristol rubbed her hands nervously. Bridey Winkle knew everything that occurred in Hathaway House—why had she looked so surprised? And why wasn't Aunt Pru with them? And where was Benton, the regular coach driver?

Bristol cleared her throat and glanced uneasily at the vacant white windows. She blew on her fingers.

Diana laughed. Her own gloves were fur-lined and warm; she wore fur-topped boots and a thick wool jacket beneath the crimson cloak. "Cold?" she inquired pleasantly, and Bristol stared in horror at the blaze in Diana's eyes, the triumph. Diana Thorne Hathaway wore insanity like a perfume; it rose up from her and permeated the coach.

"Oh, Diana . . ." Silvery vapor clouded Bristol's lips, but no sound emerged. She tried again. "Please, Diana . . ."

Diana smiled.

Swallowing hard, Bristol rubbed her pink hands together. Her feet were cold and rapidly numbing. "I know you don't mean to, but you're frightening me." Bristol spoke as if to a child, quietly, calmly, praying her thudding heart and shaking hands didn't betray the growing fear tightening her stomach.

Diana smiled and said nothing.

Drawing an icy breath deep into her lungs, Bristol tried to control the frightened quiver in her voice. "Please, Diana, let's go back." Diana smiled and stroked her cheek with the fur on her glove. "He's not hurt, is he, Diana? This is just a little game, isn't it?"

That awful golden stare turned Bristol's knees to jelly, and she dropped her gaze. She saw there was no point in trying to reason with Diana; she'd see the ride through, it couldn't go on forever. Diana would have her joke; then they'd go home. Bristol stamped her heels on the carriage floor, feeling a tingle like needles shoot through her feet. Her toes stung and her hands felt like chunks of ice. She wished she'd thought to change shoes and snatch up her gloves. But of course she hadn't. Thinking Jean Pierre needed her, she'd flown from the house without thinking. Without thinking.

And she couldn't think now. Fear crouched at the edges of her mind, whispering terrible possibilities. "Are we going much farther?" Bristol asked haltingly. This was a cruel joke; it was so cold inside the coach. Bristol stared at Diana's smile, and her heart lurched in her breast.

"Oh, I don't think it will be much farther. Anytime now, I should think." At last Diana moved her golden empty stare from Bristol's face and directed a lazy glance toward the frosted white windows.

"Diana," Bristol whispered, her voice fading behind a mist of vapor. Her jaw knotted, and she shook her head, trying to clear the terrible thoughts. Fear rose in an icy wall. Why had Diana brought her out into this storm?

The answer came swift and certain. Diana was insane; Diana did not function with the same reasoning and motivations as other people. Bristol glanced quickly at the blank windows. Quietly, forcing her voice to sound reasonable and light, she attempted a smile. "Diana, Jean Pierre will be very angry when he discovers what you've done. If we go back now, right now, I promise not to mention this." Bristol rubbed her stinging fingers, feeling the false smile on her lips stiffen and freeze.

Diana laughed, and the whispery sound curdled Bristol's blood. Lifting a wooden stick, Diana rapped the roof of the carriage. "Robbie will never know, little cousin." The carriage rocked to a lurching stop. "Your journey is ended." Silent snow enfolded the coach.

Diana shoved the carriage door open to a whirling white world, sightless and deadly. Bristol could see no more than three feet, four at most. A thick white curtain enveloped London. And muted silence hung over the frozen lane.

Bristol's eyes flared. The fear was no longer a dormant thing, but real, a force gnawing her mind. Growing, sapping her strength. "Diana, no!" Her voice emerged strange, not like her own. Outside, the snow fell in a solid blanket, like an icy white shroud. And it was quiet. "Don't do this," Bristol pleaded. "Don't!" Her voice came in choking vapory gasps.

Diana's mouth smiled above glistening teeth, and she laughed. Her golden eyes spun wild and mad. "Out! Get out!" Warm silvery vapor hid the terrible smile for a moment, but only a moment. Then Diana's strong hands shot forward, and she dragged Bristol from the seat.

"No!" Bristol screamed, finding her voice. "Help! Help

271

me!" She fought Diana in the small cramped space, but she knew from the first it could be no contest. Diana was larger, heavier, warmer, and Diana had the strength of the insane.

Bristol clung fiercely to the edges of the door, her cold fingers slipping, slipping. Desperately her eyes beseeched in a last appeal. "Please, Diana, I beg you! Don't! I beg you, don't do this!" Diana's fur-topped boot struck Bristol's chest and knocked her out of the doorway.

Sprawling, gasping for breath, Bristol landed hard in the packed snow of the lane. Her bare fingers clawed in the snow, seeking purchase, and she scrambled to her feet, but thin slippers slid on hidden ice, and she toppled to her knees. "No! Oh, dear God, no!"

Laughter, wild and exhilarated, spilled from the coach interior; then the door slammed and a whip cracked. The carriage vanished into a white wall.

And then there was only deep frozen silence.

19

NUMBING cold bit through her thin cloak and penetrated her flesh. Bristol swayed and took another step. She placed one foot before the other, and then again. She could no longer feel her feet; she may as well have been barefoot for all the protection of her satin slippers. Lifting a hand, she wiped snow from her face and blinked dizzily at the lane before her. Fresh snow had nearly filled the carriage ruts. The trail she followed would vanish entirely in minutes.

Bristol bent her head against the icy pellets stinging her cheeks. She pushed her red hands under her arms, seeking warmth. Never in memory had she been so desperately cold. But never had she ventured outside without adequate protection. She stamped her feet, hoping to restore the circulation. Snow clung to her skirt, weighing her hem down, heavy and wet.

Think! She had to think! But her mind felt as numb and frosted as her cheeks, as her hands, as her sliding feet.

A patch of ice skated out beneath her, and she fell hard, her raw hands plunging through the snow, scraping against small rocks and gravel. She sat where she'd fallen, staring at her hands, at lines of slowly welling blood. She scarcely felt the sting of the scrape.

Slowly, slipping on the ice, Bristol struggled to stand. And fell once more. This time she made no attempt to rise. It was hopeless. She settled in the snow and watched fresh flakes drift over the billowed spread of her green cloak. How long she'd been walking, she could only guess—it felt like an eternity, but she knew it couldn't have been more than a few minutes. Her hands and feet itched. She rubbed her nose, blinking at a painful tingle.

"Stand up," Bristol commanded herself. "Keep moving." But she did nothing. An odd, pleasant warmth seemed to envelop her. Why should she move when it was so quiet and peaceful where she sat? And anyway, where could she go? She had no idea where she might be, in the country or in the heart of the city. Dark shapes loomed on either side, they might be trees or houses. She should have investigated earlier when she had the strength instead of doggedly following the carriage tracks. Now she didn't want to move, no longer believed she could. The snow was too thick to battle; she couldn't see a few feet past her nose. This thought struck her as funny, and she touched the icy tip of her nose and smiled.

She looked into the swirling blizzard, not bothering to brush away the snow clinging to her lashes. There were thoughts she should be thinking, words of contrition her faith demanded. She had not lived a blameless life.

But Bristol's sluggish mind veered from the concentration required to detail her offenses out loud. God already knew. After all, her sins had been programmed into her life; all she'd done was follow the path. She frowned. Maybe that wasn't good enough. Maybe one was supposed to fight destiny. She lifted a pile of snow and watched it trickle through her red fingers.

Her mind wandered. Pity the papists, she thought. A frozen Catholic's God would require a full confession here on earth before the gates of heaven swung open. Death was less of a worry to Protestants. Protestants knew from the beginning that the gates of heaven were firmly closed. Only saints gained entrance. And Bristol was no saint.

It was so cold. She shivered. "I'm going to die," she whispered. Her lips were stiff. But she wouldn't die with fear in her heart and a whimper on her tongue. And that surprised Bristol a little. Now that she faced death, it wasn't as terrifying as she'd always imagined.

Was that courage? Once she and Jean Pierre had discussed courage. Her snowy brows met in dim concentration, but she couldn't remember the conversation about courage. She did recall Jean Pierre had thought her brave, and she wouldn't disappoint him. She'd not die with frozen tears on her cheeks. Life had given her much to be thankful for. And she'd lived long enough to know a woman's rapture. Bristol yawned, glad now of the warmth tingling through her body.

Jean Pierre had needed her, and she had responded. A violent fit of shivering quivered through her small frame. There was no way to have foreseen Diana's cruelty; Bristol's mind did not function in that manner. If she had the moment to live again, she'd do as before—run to fill Jean Pierre's need, real or imagined. Her teeth chattered uncontrollably. She stared into the shimmering white curtain as if she might see him just beyond the icy fall. "Jean Pierre," she murmured, her lips barely moving. "I love you."

Bristol tilted her head and listened, but she heard no answer, only the peculiar stillness of falling snow. It didn't matter as much as she'd thought it would. Nothing really mattered. She yawned, her hand bumping against her wooden lips. Bristol stared at her red fingers in surprise. A tiny giggle escaped her lips.

It was time to sleep now, to curl into a ball and doze for a minute or two. She felt an itching, burning in her toes and fingers; her face hurt. A small inner voice vibrated with warning, but Bristol ignored it. She wished she were home, in her bed in Salem Village. She felt sleepy and warm, almost burning, too warm almost. And so sleepy.

20

SOMEONE was hitting her. Methodically slapping her burning cheeks back and forth, calling her from the edges of a deep sleep. "No," Bristol murmured drowsily, "don't. Just let me sleep." She tried to pull away from the stinging slaps, but she felt strangely weak, and the slaps followed where her head turned. It seemed as if she moved in slow motion, hearing the sound of the slap before she felt the stinging jerk of her head.

"No. Please," she protested. Her lips stung, her hands and feet burned unbearably; her entire body tingled as if a thousand needles pricked her skin.

"Well, now. She do be coming around." A harsh croaking wheeze spewed gin fumes against her cheeks. "Get her a tankard of warm whiskey and pail of warm water." The voice paused, then roared, "Move, woman!" Someone tapped across a wooden floor, and the slaps continued.

In a moment the footsteps returned and a woman curved Bristol's icy fingers around a mug. Bristol thought she'd never felt anything more wonderful. Her eyes fluttered, and she bent her head, lifting the mug to her mouth. Choking and coughing at the fiery whiskey, she caught her breath and swallowed again, letting the welcome heat curl in her stomach. Everything rushed in on her—Diana, the storm, falling—and then a sense of release, of letting go, and . . .

But she wasn't dead. She wasn't dead! Bristol glanced up from the edges of a warm tattered blanket. Blinking rapidly, she stared around her. She was in a small room with one wide window looking out at the raging storm. A glowing coal stove threw sulfurous fumes as well as soot and heat into the air. A scarred settle leaned against one wall; a long table flanked by benches nearly filled the room. Despite the white glare from the window, the room appeared dark and dingy. Small and used, smelling of poisonous coal, perspiration, and gin.

Ending her rapid survey of the room, Bristol turned her eyes to the man squatting before her stool. Red eyes sunken in fleshy hollows returned her stare. Once, years ago, that face might have had character, a certain dignity even, but now it wallowed in the ravages of strong drink and bitterness. Tiny purple veins crisscrossed sagging cheeks, mapping a life of poverty and ruin. The puffy, twisted nose gave testament to years of brawling.

The man stood, and his knotty hands fisted on the hips of a muscular body gone to slack. "Well, now," he repeated, and Bristol read a flicker of calculation in the reddened eyes. He coughed and spit a glob of dark phlegm against the stove. It bubbled and dried with a hiss. Bristol lowered her eyes. Even though he stood a few feet from her, she could smell the heavy sweetness of gin. "Let's have a look at ye, girlie."

"Leave her a bit longer, Cutter, can't you see she ain't right yet?"

Bristol lifted her eyes to the woman. Thin, rawboned, the woman stood a full two inches above the man's dripping cap. She might have been thirty, she might have been fifty—it was a face that had been old at childhood. The forehead protruded, the chin receded, and hair of uncertain color strayed from a bun at her neck. But her dark eyes were kind when she leaned to help Bristol lift the cup of whiskey. "Here, a tot more. Do your hands still sting?"

"They're better now." The whiskey burned down her throat. "Who are you? Where did you find me?" That wasn't right. She should begin by thanking them. "You saved my life. I can't thank you enough." The coal stove threw off a stifling heat, and even though she still felt a chill deep in her flesh, Bristol shifted beneath the blanket and let it slip from her shoulders.

The woman smiled, a tired worn smile. She sat on a bench at the table and jerked her thumb toward the man. "He found you. Cutter Rumm." She lifted an expressionless face to the man, then back to Bristol. "He went out to buy more gin and found you in the lane. Managed to get you and two bottles back here without breaking either." Her thin mouth twisted.

Easily, without moving his body, the man flicked his hand out and slapped the woman's face. Hard. She made no sound, didn't lift a hand to the red mark flaming on her cheek. "And ye'll be happy for them bottles come dark, slut." The lack of passion in his voice alarmed Bristol more than his anger would have. Violence without passion chilled the blood.

She swallowed another draw of whiskey, willing her body to thaw, to function. The sooner she left this dark place, these two people, the better. "Mr. Rumm, I thank you for saving my life." She forced a smile to her warming lips, but she didn't meet his eyes.

"The question, now, is what to do with ye." He sucked a long pull from a gin bottle, and his shrewd little eyes slowly moved across Bristol's face, stopping at the blanket opening with a speculative stare.

Instinctively Bristol tightened her fingers on the blanket. "I hope you'll see fit to extend your help further, Mr. Rumm, and assist me home."

He laughed, a rasping abrasive sound. "Ye hear that, Kitty? She hopes I'll 'extend' my help and 'assist' her further." He drank from the bottle, wiping his stubbled chin with the back of his hand. "Now, don't she talk pretty. A regular toff she be." He hawked another glob at the stove and leaned against a wooden counter. Rows of nearly empty bottles stood on sagging shelves behind. "They be money in this business, Kitty, I smell it." He stared at Bristol. "Stand up, Queenie, and let us have a look at ye."

Bristol's fingers tightened around the mug, and she cast a frightened glance at the woman. "Do it," Kitty said in a low voice, not meeting Bristol's eyes.

Slowly, her aching body protesting, Bristol stood.

"Drop the blanket."

The blanket fell near her feet.

"Now the cloak."

Bristol hesitated, her mind racing. Frantically she inventoried her person. She had no purse, was wearing no jewelry. She had nothing to offer the man to take her home, nothing with which to tempt him.

He laughed. "Now, there, Kitty me girl, is how a woman ought to look." He reached a hand toward Bristol's breast, missed, and tried again. This time his bruising fingers squeezed her flesh. She cried out and stumbled back a step. His hand slapped across her face as dispassionately as earlier he'd struck the woman called Kitty. And as hard.

Bristol reeled, nearly falling over the stool. She felt her cheek beginning to swell. Deeply frightened, she looked at them both, blinking at a film of pain. Cutter Rumm was very drunk; she couldn't believe she hadn't noticed earlier. "Sir. Mr. Rumm." Bristol steadied her voice, keeping her tone deceptively calm as the woman had done. She seized on his earlier words. "My family will pay you, pay you well, if you

277

take me home." Sensing pleas would go unheard, she deliberately fought any hint of begging. Instead, pretending this was a normal situation, she returned to the stool and folded her hands in her lap. She would not, absolutely would not, raise her hands to cover the exposed mounds of breast pushing at her low neckline. She knew that to do so would only distract the man's sodden brain.

He shifted against the counter and drank from the bottle. "Pay me to return ye." Gazing at the ceiling, he turned this in his mind. Kitty sat absolutely still, her face blank and waiting.

"Yes, sir." Eagerness lightened Bristol's voice. "They'll pay well to have me back. Very well!"

His small red eyes lowered and settled on her face. Perhaps he wasn't as drunk as she'd thought. "If they be so anxious to have ye back, then how comes it to happen someone threw you out in the snow? And where do these fine folk live, anyways?"

Bristol's mouth suddenly went dry. How could she explain it so he could understand? She answered the easiest question first. "Hathaway House in Pall Mall."

Cutter Rumm slapped his knee and howled in laughter. "Pall Mall! Ye hear that, Kitty? Pall Mall!" He swept the snow-wet cap from his head and threw it across the room, exposing thin graying hair. "Ye expect us to believe the rich toffs in Pall Mall drove all the way down here to throw ye out in the worst storm in ten years . . . and they'll be paying a ransom to get ye back?" The laughter died from his eyes, and they glittered dangerously. "I don't be knowing yer game, Queenie, but ye ain't dealing with no fools! Nobody on Pall Mall be paying a cent for ye. More likely, ye be some whore's serving wench what did wrong. Instead of putting a blade to yer throat like decent folk would do, she pushed ye out to freeze."

"No." Bristol choked. Her heart fluttered and seemed to stop. "No, please listen . . . I can explain." Words babbled past her lips, a stream of words, words of explanation, words of desperation, words that sounded too fantastic, too contrived to be true.

At the finish, when the rambling speech died on her lips, they looked at her in disbelieving silence. Kitty's eyes softened dreamily. "Cutter, what if all that be true—fires in every room, plenty to eat every day, servants and fine gowns . . ." She looked at Bristol's soaked skirt and took the hem between her thumb and forefinger. "I never seen anything

278

this fine up close," she murmured. No envy lay in her voice; such a miracle lay beyond envy; she felt the cloth and admired it.

"If it be true." Cutter wheezed and snorted. He waved the bottle, nearly empty now. "A crazy lady! Running out in a blizzard dressed like that to help the crazy bitch's husband! Dead cats and a spinster aunt married in secret!" He glared at Kitty, and involuntarily she drew back, dropping Bristol's hem. "Kitty, if ye believe this slop about lords and fine ladies, ye're as batty as Queenie says that crazy woman is!" He finished the bottle and tossed it behind the counter, where it shattered in a tinkle of glass. "No, they's no coins to be made hiring a wagon and riding to Pall Mall. Like as not get a knife in the ribs for bringing back the trash they threw out." He stared at Bristol. "*If* that part about Pall Mall was true at all."

Bristol's green eyes pleaded. "Oh, please."

Cutter Rumm pushed from the counter and weaved toward Bristol. He stopped, panting gin into her face, and he blinked at the wide green eyes, at her hair, down the front of her trembling breasts. He tried to thrust a finger between her breasts, missed, tried again and missed. Giving it up, he laughed. "I know what ye be good for, Queenie. And it'll bring a shitpotful of coins into this house!" Swinging toward Kitty, he grinned, showing a broken row of black teeth. "Know what I mean, slut? Queenie here will earn more than ye ever brung in a year of street work."

Kitty's thin face remained expressionless. She met his red eyes with a steady blank stare. "And what if she's telling the truth, Cutter? What if a fat ransom is waiting in Pall Mall?"

Bristol interrupted, her voice rising in hope at Kitty's support. "I've told the truth, Mr. Rumm, I swear it!"

Kitty's flat voice spoke again. "You'll never claim that purse if you put her on the street. Rich folks ain't paying for damaged goods, Cutter. More likely they'd hang your head on a pike."

He looked unsteadily from one face to the other, confusion dimming his eyes. "Shut up! Both of ye! Ye're making me head spin. I need to think this out!" He half-fell, half-sat on the bench at the table and rested his chin in his hands. "Get me something to eat, and bring me another bottle."

Obediently Kitty rose and brought another mug and more gin. She gestured for Bristol to follow, and disappeared through a door at the rear of the room. Bristol cast a despairing glance from the muttering man to the darkening window.

Night was falling. Cutter Rumm was too drunk to take her anywhere, even if the snow had stopped, which it had not. Fighting her fright, battling a rising sense of panic, she hastened through the door after Kitty.

The room beyond was small, dirty, and cramped. The only thing in its favor was a log fire in the hearth, less stifling than the coal fire in the outer room but also less generous, obviously for cooking, not for warmth. Kitty leaned over the flames, ladling a thin lumpy stew onto a cracked wooden trencher. She waved Bristol to a wobbly stool near the hearth. "Sit and rest." She returned in less than a minute, a grim smile on her face. "He won't eat it, but he likes the smell, and sometimes, when there's meat, he'll chew a piece." Her mouth twisted. "Not that there's ever much meat. You feel any better? You want some food?"

Bristol's skin continued to tingle and itch, but she sensed no permanent damage had been done, thank God. To her surprise, she felt a rumbling of hunger, even though Kitty's stew looked less than appetizing. Bristol thought of Maggie O'Hare's rich thick stews and lowered her face in shame. Kitty offered to share what they had. "Yes, please," she murmured.

Kitty filled two trenchers and took a stool near Bristol. They ate in silence, and Bristol tried not to think about the origin of the limp vegetables floating on her trencher. They appeared neither fresh nor wholesome. She lifted the spoon to her lips and swallowed.

Kitty scraped the scant leavings back into the pot over the fire and dropped the trenchers into a tub of cold greasy water. Sighing, she arched her spine against her hands and sat down. But before she could speak, Cutter Rumm's voice roared from the front. "What kind of hellhole is this? Get your arse in here, slut, and light me a candle! Who are you to leave a man to eat in the dark?"

Scrambling from her stool, Kitty snatched two stubs of tallow and hastened into the front room. Bristol heard the sound of a heavy slap, and when Kitty returned, one cheek blazed.

Saying nothing of her swelling face, Kitty sank to her stool and gazed into the small dying cook fire. "He'll never let you go," she said in a low voice. "Hope kills. Don't hope. He won't never let you go."

Bristol wrung her hands. Calm, she told herself, quelling the rising frenzy in her mind. Calm, be calm. There was a way out of here, she simply had to find it. Steadying her voice, she looked at Kitty's sloping profile. "I told the truth. When my aunt and my . . . cousin discover I'm missing, they'll be frantic. I know they'll pay well for my return." If only she'd tucked a few coins in a purse! Then she could hire a hackney and go home herself. She couldn't bear to think how totally dependent she was upon the two people in this house. So completely at their mercy.

"Cutter ain't going to believe your story," Kitty said. She turned sad eyes toward Bristol's ashen face. "It's easier not to." Kitty looked at Bristol's gown and the damp remnants of a once-elegant coiffure; she shook her head. "Cutter's mind is gone to gin. By the time he decided there might be truth in what you said . . ."

Bristol closed her eyes, and it was an effort to keep her voice steady and low. "But, Kitty, what has Mr. Rumm to lose? Couldn't he take me to Pall Mall and discover the truth for himself?"

Kitty stared. "What has he got to lose? The hire of a wagon, for one thing. Look around you, miss; do you see any evidence of extra shillings? And suppose this family of yours—not parents, mind you, but an aunt and an uncle and a cousin—what if this family thinks you're worth a whole lot less than you think you are? They might pay, aye, but will they pay as much you'd earn for Cutter if he keeps you here spreading your legs for coins over the next few years?"

"Spreading my . . . Oh, dear God!" Bristol's face turned chalky. She swallowed, her eyes not leaving Kitty's sad, sober face. "Oh, Kitty, please help me! I have to get home!"

Kitty's scraggly brows rose in horror. "Me? Go up against Cutter?" She shrank on her stool. "No. Don't go looking to me for help. He'd kill me." Her eyes shifted to the fire, the tub of greasy water, the floor. "No," she whispered. "I'm sorry, but whatever Cutter decides . . . you and me, we got to live with it."

"He'd *kill* you?"

"In the blink of an eye! He don't be called Cutter for nothing; ain't nobody quicker with a knife." Kitty watched Bristol's shudder of revulsion. Softly she added, "Aye, it's not a pretty world down here. But was yours better? Wouldn't a blade have shown more mercy than leaving you to freeze to your death?" Her thin hand touched Bristol's drooping shoulder.

Looking into the small fire with dull eyes, Bristol asked, "Can you at least tell me where I am?"

"Almsbury Lane."

The name meant nothing. Bristol might have been a short distance from Pall Mall, or she might have been in another country. She didn't know. "Is it too far to walk?" she asked.

Kitty laughed. "Queenie, you wouldn't get a hundred paces before somebody grabbed you. Maybe someone who'd give you a worse life than you'll have here." She pointed to Bristol's slippers. "And how far do you think you'd get wearing them? They's ready to fall off your feet now." She shook her head. "No, there's no possibility to walk."

Bristol dropped her head in her hands. She'd wakened this morning feeling safe and happy, secure and loved. Now . . .

Kitty watched her. "I'll do all I can to make it as easy as possible," she said kindly. Her bony shoulders rose in a shrug. "You'll adjust. We all do what we have to." Sighing, she stood and yawned. "Maybe you'll be more cheerful in the morning." Her voice indicated she didn't believe this any more than Bristol did. Kitty waved toward a door at the back of the kitchen; then she scattered the logs in the hearth to save the bits of wood. The flames flickered out, and instantly both women felt cold.

Bristol would have to stay the night; there was nothing else to do. Reluctantly she followed Kitty into a tiny chill room containing two straw pallets, a slop basin, and four wooden pegs holding a change of clothing. Kitty waved a stub of candle toward one of the pallets. "That's Cutter's, but he don't use it. He'll pass out over the table or curl up on the floor beside the stove. You can use it." She snuffed the candle, and Bristol heard her lie on the straw.

Kitty spoke from an icy darkness. "One more thing. They's a wooden bat beside the pallet. It's for the rats. Filthy things!"

Slowly Bristol approached Cutter's pallet, her ears straining for the noise of scrabbling claws. She lowered herself to the straw and found a thin blanket, which she pressed around her body. The straw stank, and in five minutes she was covered with bites, scratching and hearing minute rustlings within the pallet.

Blinking rapidly, her throat burning, Bristol feared she'd finally lost the battle not to cry. "Tears won't help!" she whispered between clenched teeth. Biting back ready tears, she stared into the cold darkness with moist eyes. She wasn't frozen in the snow; she wasn't dead. A roof lay over her head, and there was food in her belly.

There had to be a way out of this; there had to be! And she'd find it. She'd bide her time and find the way. The important thing was not to panic, not to make foolish mistakes. Plus, she reminded herself, they'd be searching for her. Jean Pierre, and Aunt Pru, and Uncle Robert—they wouldn't rest until they found her.

But they wouldn't know where to begin. Where to look. And they might easily assume she'd died in the storm. Bristol tossed on the rustling straw. If she allowed such thoughts, she was defeated. She'd block the negatives; she'd key on the hope that they were searching for her.

A loud slam sounded from Kitty's side of the small room, and Bristol sat up, her heart leaping into her mouth.

"Damn!" Kitty hissed. "I thought I killed it!" Bristol heard the wooden bat drop to the floor.

Frantically Bristol spun and dug her fingers between the straw and the wall until her hand closed around a wooden bat. She hefted it reassuringly, suddenly glad to have it. Dear God, how could she hope to sleep! So many worries whirled in her brain. And rats! The tension of listening, waiting, made her head ache.

"That's mine! Touch it again and I'll knock yer beastly little head off!"

Bristol's eyes snapped open; she peered through the darkness. "Kitty?" she asked uncertainly.

"No, it weren't me. That's Mrs. Pudden."

"Who?"

"Mrs. Pudden," Kitty whispered. "Behind the wall. On the other side."

Mrs. Pudden's voice screamed, as clear as if she stood in the room with Kitty and Bristol, "I warned ye!" Then came the crack of a heavy blow and a child's shriek. Other shouts lifted, and a baby's thin wail rose and fell.

Kitty clicked her tongue. "Poor thing. She's got it bad, Mrs. Pudden does. Her and eleven brats in two rooms." A note of pride lightened Kitty's whisper. "Leastways me and Cutter got three rooms and just the two of us."

Bristol was appalled to think eleven children and their mother lived in two rooms as tiny as this. She listened to the ongoing battle behind the wall and tried to imagine the fracas. "How do they live? Is there a Mr. Pudden?"

Kitty chuckled. "Maybe once. Who knows? The men come and they go. They bring Mrs. Pudden a few shillings, but they bring the brats, too. The oldest is thirteen."

Bristol tried to imagine it. "How does she possibly take care of them all?" Behind the wall Mrs. Pudden screamed and something flew at the wall.

"Them above nine works the streets. Rosie, she's the eight-year-old, Rosie watches over the rest when Mrs. Pudden goes to the streets herself. Which ain't as often as she'd like. Most times, Mrs. Pudden catches a baby, then she and Rosie takes in washing and sewing. They make do, like us all."

An image of New England children rose in Bristol's mind, pink cheeks, well-fed, well-clothed. Not like she pictured the children beyond the wall. New England children attended dame schools and learned a trade. None she'd heard of lived twelve people to two rooms. "What do these children do on the streets?"

Kitty's voice was surprised. "Why, they beg or steal, of course. Sometimes the twelve-year-old brings home men, when she's lucky. But Charlene's as plain as the bottom of a slop basin; the pickings ain't good for her, poor child."

"Little children . . ." Begging, stealing, whoring. Bristol shook her head. Worlds within worlds. She hadn't realized this world existed side by side with the opulence of Hathaway House. She hadn't thought of it.

Kitty seemed to sense what Bristol was thinking. "It ain't so bad as you might think. Mrs. Pudden's done what she can to give the kids a chance in life. She blinded the oldest. Shrewd she is, that Mrs. Pudden, she only blinded one eye so's the family don't feel no burden having to lead him around." Bristol gasped and covered her mouth. Her stomach rolled.

Kitty continued. "She took the arm of one and the foot of another. Now she has a board strapped to the baby's head. Heard some newfangled idea you can deform a head while it's still soft." Kitty chuckled. "You ever hear of such a thing? Seems to me the old way is best—hit 'em hard. But they's still time if the board don't work."

Bristol bit down on her thumb. She had to escape this place! A terrible thought stunned her mind. The Puddens, Kitty, all the others that lived in these cold, crowded tenements—they would never escape. She thought about that. "Kitty?" Bristol whispered, glad the other side of the wall had quieted. "Kitty, come with me. I know my aunt will find a place for you. Come with me."

Kitty didn't answer for so long, Bristol wondered if she slept. Then Kitty whispered into the darkness, "I can't go nowhere. I couldn't leave Cutter."

Bristol had forgotten the drunken man in the front room. "He's your husband, then?" The idea was repulsive. And she didn't think Aunt Pru would find a place for the likes of Cutter Rumm.

Kitty laughed softly. "Husband! Cutter Rumm bought me off me mum when I was ten. Good thing, too. Mum seen I weren't going to be handsome enough to work the streets, and she give me two days to get out of her rooms." Bristol felt rather than saw Kitty's shrug. "Mum got a few shillings, and I got a roof and a full belly for the last fifteen years."

Bristol blinked and lifted on an elbow, peering through the cold gloom. It was impossible for Kitty to be only twenty-five; she looked older than Hannah.

A little defensively Kitty added, "Cutter weren't always a drunken wreck. Ten years ago, when he were still in the mines, before the dust got him, before his lungs give out, well, Cutter Rumm walked with the best of 'em. That he did!" Her thin chest rose in a wistful sigh. "That he did."

Easing back on her pallet, Bristol stared into the blackness. She scratched her neck and arms, and felt stirrings in her hair. Kitty's life seemed so hopeless, without a hint of promise or hope for the future. But Kitty's voice didn't beg pity; Kitty didn't find anything extraordinary in the lives she'd recounted. And that was more shocking to Bristol than any outrage would have been. A deadened acceptance of the unthinkable. Bristol shivered.

"Queenie?" Kitty murmured after a long silence.

"'Bristol,' please."

"I . . . I'm glad you're here . . . Bristol. It's real nice having a woman to talk to." The words were shy and hesitant.

Bristol could think of no answer. She didn't want to be here. Not as a companion to poor Kitty, and not as a . . .

The flicker of a candle appeared suddenly at the door of the room. Bristol rose on her elbows and sucked in her breath. Her green eyes widened in fright.

Cutter Rumm swayed in the doorway, the candle under his chin lighting an evil leer.

21

"If you damage her, Cutter, you'll never get the ransom! You'll never see a penny if she's raped." Kitty's voice shot through the darkness, calm and steady.

Above the candle, Cutter's red eyes flicked toward Kitty, then back to Bristol. Bristol held her breath, not daring to move.

"There ain't no hurry, Cutter. She ain't going nowhere. She'll still be here when you've had a chance to make up your mind."

"Shut up," he roared. "Shut up! I can't think with yer voice yammering in me face." His eyes swung from Bristol and glared at the pale thin shape on Kitty's pallet. Lurching, he stumbled toward Kitty and fell heavily beside the straw. "Ye know what I be wanting. Hike up yer skirt and open yer legs!"

Without a word Kitty lifted on the rank straw, and Bristol saw a flash of thin bony legs. Cutter grunted, and his fingers scrabbled at the opening of his breeches. Across the narrow space separating the pallets, Kitty's expressionless dark eyes met Bristol's. Then her hand reached, and she pinched out the candle, plunging the small room into darkness.

Weak with relief at her escape, Bristol lay back on her pallet. A few feet away, she heard the thumpings and panting grunts of a joyless coupling. Kitty made no sound.

Bristol turned her face to the wall and closed her eyes, wishing she could shut out the sounds. Kitty had saved her this time, but could she continue to do so? Long after Bristol heard Cutter's wet snore, she lay tensed against the wall, her fingers curled on the wooden bat.

By morning the snow had thinned and stopped, leaving London smothered in a shroud of deep white. Before dawn, coal carts plunged through the drifts, delivering welcome heat to the mansions in London's fashionable areas. Soon other wagons and drays and carts and coaches appeared in the lanes. London began to dig out, to resume the business of life halted by the storm.

In Almsbury Lane, the Pudden children followed the coal carts, catching lumps that fell from the rattling black mounds, thrusting thin arms into the snowy street, searching for bits and chunks that dropped. Few coal carts paused long in Almsbury Lane; business was poor here, the coins scarce.

What this section of town couldn't steal, they bought by the piece from the coal hags, blackened old women with exhausted cold faces who hung yokes on their shoulders and sold what they could from the buckets swinging at the ends of the yoke. It was a rare customer who purchased more than a handful of lumps.

Bristol watched a coal hag's seamed face lift in gratitude when Kitty bought half a pail of the damp coal. Kitty counted halfpennies into the woman's pocket and shut the door.

Leaning over his morning ale, Cutter sat at the table running a scarred thumb across the blade of a knife. "I'll find that money, slut." He coughed and spit toward the stove, missing by a wide margin.

"Aye," Kitty answered placidly. "That you will."

"It be mine."

"Aye, that it is."

He glared at her and stabbed the knife point into the table. "I could beat it out of ye," he growled.

"Aye, that you could." Gingerly Kitty pried the stove open with a stick of wood and threw a handful of coal on the embers.

Listening, Bristol decided the conversation had a deadened familiarity to it, as if each spoke a role they'd played until it no longer held meaning.

She stared out the window, watching the Pudden children race up to the coal hag and grab at the lumps in her buckets. Her green eyes peered up the lane, watching it come to life. Now the storm was over, Jean Pierre would come looking for her. How long, dear God? How long before he found her? Would he find her?

After a night of worried thinking, she cherished no illusions about her situation. She couldn't depend on Cutter Rumm to take her back; she saw that. And to attempt it on her own was impossible. She had no money to pay a hired cab, and her slippers were ruined. She couldn't walk barefoot in the snow, and the clogs Kitty lent her weren't designed for lengthy walking. Plus, she had no idea which direction to go. And no knowledge of how to cope on the streets, a different world from any she'd known.

Cutter snarled, as if sensing her thoughts, "Into the kitchen with ye; ye can help Kitty ready things for the regulars. They'll be coming now the snow's stopped. Ye might as well be useful whiles I'm deciding about ye."

Kitty smiled and shook her head. "Cutter, look at them hands. She ain't done no work." Her smile vanished at sight of his face. "I reckon she can learn." Dodging Cutter's slap, Kitty scurried toward the kitchen with a quick wave for Bristol to follow.

Bristol edged past Cutter and hastened into the kitchen. "I grew up on a farm, Kitty, I can work," she whispered. In fact, she thought it might take her mind off the panic threatening to strangle her. It would be good to lose herself in something besides the icy fear clamping her chest.

Kitty looked at the fine wool gown and Bristol's smooth hands. She shrugged apologetically. "You don't look like you ever used them hands for more than waving a fan."

Together they cleared the skimpy remains of a sparse breakfast, and Kitty whispered answers to Bristol's questions.

"I hide the coins . . . if I didn't, Cutter would give everything to drink, and then how could we eat or keep warm?"

"Where do the coins come from?"

"This here is a pub." Kitty chuckled at the look on Bristol's face. "You was unconscious when Cutter carried you in. I guess you didn't be seeing the sign. This is the Royal Rumm."

Kitty seemed to expect a comment, and Bristol searched for something to say. "It . . . that's a nice name," she offered lamely.

Pleased, Kitty nodded. "I thought of it," she admitted with a note of pride. "It brings us a bit of money, and sometimes, when one of the regulars has a bit extra"—she shrugged—"I can take him in back and earn a tot more." She spoke matter-of-factly, perhaps a bit wistfully, as if she wished more of the regulars had money to spend on a woman. But it was the money that was of interest, not the regulars.

When the kitchen was in order, though not what Bristol thought of as order, they filled available containers with snow and set the pots before the hearth to melt. As it melted, they poured the water into a crock and gathered more. "I'm hoping to collect enough for cooking and enough left over for a wash," Kitty said timidly. She fought with herself. "You can have first wash if you want, and I'll take second."

"Thank you," Bristol said. It didn't look to her as if Kitty had taken time for a wash in a long while—she didn't think she'd want to go second. Being poor was a circumstance a person couldn't help, but being clean . . . "Isn't there a well nearby?" She couldn't help a note of disapproval in her voice.

A faint pink flush appeared on Kitty's cheeks. "They's a well, but it's more than a mile distant. A long ways to carry buckets." Now it was Bristol's turn to blush. She'd made too hasty a judgment; this was not a world she knew. "The Thames is a nearer walk," Kitty said, looking at her hands. "But a person would be a fool to wash there. Come out worse than you went in."

Bristol remembered the putrid brown scum coating the Thames. "Kitty, I'm sorry," she said in a low voice. She stirred the stew pot, embarrassed to look at Kitty. Her stomach clutched at a closer examination of the pot's contents.

Kitty touched her shoulder. "We do the best we can."

Next they cleared the shattered gin bottles behind the front counter, wiped off the table and benches, and made a desultory sweep of the muddy floors. The phlegm-crusted stove they left alone. Soon the first of the regulars trudged through knee-deep snow to appear at the door. Others followed, until seven men hunched over the table, smoking, shouting, and buying ale or gin.

Bristol heard the drunken voices, but she didn't see the speakers. During the night, Cutter had decided Bristol was to remain hidden until he'd made his decision regarding her future; would he sell her favors or take a chance on a generous ransom? Until he made his choice, Bristol was to work in the kitchen while Kitty tended the men. Though he wanted no one to know of her presence, still Cutter couldn't resist positing a hypothetical problem to his regulars, and Bristol listened as she worked, hearing them argue what each would do if he stumbled across a finely dressed lady tossed out in a snowstorm.

Rumm and two others weren't certain, but the consensus seemed to be that returning such a treasure would be folly. Far better to keep the girl and earn as much as possible until her youth and beauty faded—a rapid consequence of such a life.

Bristol's heart sank, and she bent over the tub of oily water with a pang of fright. She ran a rag over the trenchers and stacked them to one side, wishing the kitchen had a window. With all her soul she wanted to look outside and see Jean Pierre. She needed a miracle.

At the moment, all she had was a filthy kitchen. Bristol didn't fault Kitty; she saw the demands of the men left Kitty no time for women's work. But Bristol had time. Time she needed to fill until Jean Pierre found her.

Drawing a determined breath, Bristol cast a hard eye around the room. She squared her shoulders and rolled her hair into a bun at her neck. There was a soiled apron forgotten on a back peg, and she tied it around her waist. She decided to begin with the floor, and took Kitty's hoarded water without a twinge of remorse. If she had to live here awhile, she refused to live in filth. Hannah Adams had not brought up her daughters to tolerate filth. If Bristol had to live here . . . She wrenched her mind from that thought and dropped to her knees and attacked years of accumulated dirt with a fury that would have gladdened even Bridey Winkle.

Later, when Kitty dashed into the kitchen for a hot flip iron, her thin lips rounded in surprise. She stared at a circle of clean floor, the planks gleaming white next to the untouched blackness of the rest. "Bristol! This is . . . this is wonderful!" Kitty's eyes moved to the dwindling supply of fresh snow water, and a flicker of disappointment appeared.

Bristol's mouth set, and she looked up defensively. "First the house, then us!"

Kitty scratched a trail of bug bites along her neck. Then she chuckled. "Good. I'll bring in more snow."

"I'm waiting, slut!" Cutter's wheezing shout rose over the babble of the regulars. "This flip won't heat itself and no customer's going to drink it cold!"

Kitty's mouth thinned, and she grabbed up the flip iron and ran back into the front room. Bristol cringed at the sound of a heavy slap. Then Bristol settled her knees on the rutted floor and scrubbed hard, as if that inch of planking was the most important thing in her life.

Thus passed the first day in a chain of weeks. Bristol worked in the kitchen, her patch of white floor widening until a generation's dirt disappeared, and Kitty dashed back and forth to fetch flip irons, or clean mugs and trenchers, or bread, or whatever the men demanded. Kitty kept the snow pails filled, gathering water to meet Bristol's needs, and collected pennies from the men—spending them as quickly as they came in. Kitty bought liquor and coal and cooking wood and bits of meat and packets of flour and limp vegetables when she could get them, and precious oil for the one lamp in the house. And both women worked until dark shadows lay in permanent shadings under their eyes.

At night, when the regulars returned to their cheerless cold rooms, Bristol and Kitty cleaned the front pub room, washed the trenchers from the day's use, mended their own clothing and Cutter's, and visited softly while they wove candle wicks and dipped new candles. Always with an ear cocked to the drunken ranting issuing from the coal-warmed front room.

Two pairs of women's hands made a vast improvement over one pair. Slowly the worn planks of the house took on a respectability they hadn't known in years. A warm, mellow wood emerged from walls never scrubbed in their long history until now. Kitty and Bristol tore down the shredded rags next to the front window and made curtains from Bristol's green cloak (her cloak was too thin to wear outside for more than display, and she couldn't leave the Royal Rumm in any case). The pub room looked better than it had in living memory.

But it was the kitchen that benefited most from an extra woman in the house. Gleaming pots appeared where once had been lumps crusted with grime. It was discovered the fire burned hotter and better when years' accumulations of ash were cleared away and saved to make lye in the spring. Brown crocks turned white under Bristol's scrubbing, and they shone on clean shelves. Candleholders were freed of wax, and one was discovered to be of silver which they sold for a handful of coins and celebrated by buying extra food. When Bristol poked up the fire in the mornings, she looked around her with a grim smile of satisfaction. Even Hannah would find no fault with this kitchen; everything gleamed.

However, it wasn't Bristol's fetish for cleanliness that Kitty most appreciated, but Bristol's talent for cooking. They quickly discovered Bristol was a far better cook than Kitty would ever be. In her heart, Bristol felt no particular pride in this; she suspected Kitty never had the time or the ingredients with which to learn any culinary skill. Whatever the reasons, Bristol could turn bits of food into savory stews and inventive pies, and Kitty could not. The kitchen became Bristol's unquestioned domain, and once she had it cleaned, she filled her long days learning to stretch their supplies and turn poor-quality food into something nourishing and palatable.

Even Cutter showed a renewed interest in his suppers under Bristol's deft hand. Her failures earned her hard slaps from a quick hand, and twice Cutter took after her with his knife, affronted by something on his trencher he didn't like. Each time, Kitty's calm voice intervened to confuse and halt the lurching attack. Kitty was somehow able to reach into

291

that gin-fogged brain and inject a grain of reason, a service she also performed on those occasional nights when Cutter appeared at the door of the bedroom, roaring and stumbling and pulling at his breeches. True to her word, Kitty did all her limited circumstances would allow to ease the burden of Bristol's existence in the Royal Rumm.

Bristol and Kitty kept Cutter in a state of drunken confusion as to the number of passing weeks. Kitty continued to soothe and assure him there was no hurry to announce any decision. There was no rush to begin selling Bristol to the regulars or to anyone else, Kitty insisted. As the appearance of the Royal Rumm had improved, so had the number of customers. They had more coins now than ever before; there was no hurry for Bristol to earn more.

Cutter pulled at the bottle, listened, blinked his bleary red eyes, and spit bloody phlegm at the stove. Occasionally, when the gin ran low, he'd sway and roar that it seemed Queenie had been with them for months. Then Kitty would refill his glass, nod placidly, and agree it often seemed that way to her as well. "Odd, isn't it?" she said, dismissing his questions.

From the first, Kitty took the hardest tasks on herself. She always worked the front room, dealing with the raucous men, within easy reach of slaps and blows. It was Kitty who emptied the slop basins and cleaned the spit-globbed stove and pub floors. And it was Kitty that coaxed Cutter from Bristol's pallet and took him into herself, suffering his thrusts and grunts in silent submission.

She asked nothing in return. Only a roof over her head and food in her belly. And the wonder of Bristol's companionship, unique in Kitty's experience.

For both women, the high point in a long exhausting day came during those quiet moments in front of the dying kitchen fire, when they rested on low stools and spoke softly of the small events which made up their day. And gradually Bristol began to fit into a new hard life.

By now she knew all the Pudden children by sight, most by name, and she greeted them warmly when they appeared to sell the stolen items that kept the Royal Rumm functioning. She and Kitty talked through the wall to Mrs. Pudden and shared the triumphs and tragedies of that family, worrying over them and interested in them. Now the coal hag had a name to go with her wizened face, and though she never saw them, Bristol could distinguish the voices of the regulars and knew which name matched which voice and discussed them with Kitty as if she'd known them always.

Which was also how she came to view Kitty—as if she'd known Kitty all her life. In some ways Bristol felt closer to Kitty than she had to Charity. Living in two small rooms, they had no secrets and no privacy; they shared everything by necessity, including a common fear of Cutter and the struggle for day-to-day survival. Such bonds were strong and exerted a leveling effect.

It wasn't long before the details of Kitty's life lost the power to shock or appall. Bristol now accepted the facts of grinding poverty as matter-of-factly as Kitty; it was her life too. She listened to accounts of Kitty's early years with murmurs of interest but not pity; no matter what horror Kitty recounted, they saw worse on the streets every day, heard more terrible stories through the walls.

For her own part, Bristol talked about the Adams farm and her life from the time of her arrival at the Royal Rumm. The months at Hathaway House stayed buried in a separate part of her heart. Though Kitty's curiosity was boundless, Bristol gently turned aside the questions. To pull up that life and examine it, even for Kitty, would have been unbearably painful. And she knew what Kitty would have said: "Let it go. Don't hope. Hope kills."

Without hope, Bristol's life would have been unendurable. To face the weeks flying past, she clung to her slender faith and couldn't bear to subject her thoughts to Kitty's sad comment: "Hope kills."

Deep inside, she feared Kitty might convince her, and then how could she go on? So Bristol hugged her inner thoughts to herself, and fed the faint hope, keeping it alive.

And all her hopes centered on Jean Pierre. Bristol had accepted the reality of her situation and no longer plotted impossible escapes. Once, to her shame, Bristol had lain awake several nights planning to steal Kitty's small hoard of coins and dash out to find a hackney cab. But hackneys didn't frequent this section of London. And in the end, she'd realized she couldn't have taken the money anyway. That small pile of silver (Bristol was now privy to the hiding place) was all that stood between the Royal Rumm and freezing. Or starving.

Still, her stubborn heart would not give up. Somehow, some way, she would leave the Royal Rumm. Deep inside, she refused to accept that God's plan was for Bristol Adams to live out her life in a pub kitchen. If she ever allowed herself to believe differently, Bristol felt she'd go mad.

It was difficult enough to stay sane with the constant hard

293

slaps, the bleakness of living, and the fear of the nights. The cold and hunger and rats and the constant itching from heaven knew what bugs. No joy existed in this world, only days that were less bad than others.

Sometimes, sweating in the kitchen, her hands plunged in bread dough or up to the elbows in greasy water, Bristol yearned for a window. She thought it would ease her mind enormously if she could glance outside and see other people. It would give her secret hopes a focus.

But the only time Cutter granted her the privilege of looking out the one window was when the weather turned cold and snowy and the regulars didn't come. Then she invented tasks in the front room, frequently lingering by the window and dreaming of seeing Jean Pierre's hard strong face in the swirl of flakes.

"He'll come," she whispered fiercely. Against all odds. "One day he'll come."

Cutter's hand lashed across her cheek, leaving a flaming imprint. "Get ye into the kitchen and help Kitty." He wrinkled his veined nose in revulsion and spit on the floor in disgust. "Smell that? Smells like she be cooking rat turds! Ye're the cooker person. Get yer arse in there!" He flipped his knife and dug the tip into the scarred table, glowering into his cup of gin.

Reluctantly Bristol turned from the window and hastened into the kitchen, so accustomed to heavy slaps that her hand no longer rose to her cheeks. Pausing in the doorway, Bristol smiled at Kitty, who labored to push a paddle through a boiling pot. Bristol's nostrils crinkled in distaste. Cutter was right, the smell was terrible. "In the name of heaven, Kitty! What are you cooking?" The odor had a vaguely familiar scent, something Bristol hadn't noticed in antiseptic Hathaway House, but went further back. To home. Now, what . . . ?

Kitty laughed. "Have you gone daft! It's the rags!" She smiled at Bristol's blank face. "The rags! You know." Kitty pointed to her lower body. "The monthly rags." Pausing, Kitty wiped a hand across her perspiring forehead. She frowned at Bristol's odd expression. "You know," she said thoughtfully, "I don't recall you using any since you got here."

Abruptly Bristol sat hard on a stool, her hands clutching the sides until her fingers turned white against the wood. Of course. The smell was the boiling rags. In Hathaway House Molly whisked away such necessities and folded clean ones in their place. But at home, every month she and Charity and Hannah had . . .

Bristol's face turned white. Stunned, she stared up at Kitty, her green eyes round. Her lips moved, but no sound emerged. "Kitty," she whispered, her heart racing, her mind counting, "I . . . I . . ."

Kitty's hands rose to her mouth, and her dark eyes widened.

"Kitty, I think I'm pregnant."

22

THEY talked of little else. When Kitty ran into the kitchen during the day, she and Bristol exchanged whispers about the baby. They discussed pregnancy and babies at night when they fell on their straw pallets, and they planned and speculated until they dropped into an exhausted sleep.

Bristol passed through the weeks in a daze, concentrated on the miracle taking place in her body. She developed a habit of touching her stomach, marveling at its new contours. She began snatching brief rests throughout the long days, sitting for a moment and gazing into the hearth. More and more her thoughts turned to Hathaway House, and memories she'd carefully and deliberately hidden in a remote corner bubbled to the surface.

With each vivid memory, each life contrast, the need to escape built, until Bristol felt wild with frustration. She considered every scheme. For the thousandth time she tore apart the Royal Rumm searching for a scrap of paper on which to scribble a message. But as she'd known before the search began, no paper existed. Nightly she and Kitty plotted how they might extract a halfpenny from their handful of coins, but a halfpenny squandered on paper meant the sacrifice of wood or coal or food or liquor. All of which were needed for survival. And even had they dared, neither could think of a foolproof method of contacting someone without Cutter being aware.

When finally Bristol accepted the impossibility of sending a message to Pall Mall, she decided her only hope was to escape.

"Kitty? Kitty, are you asleep?" she whispered. Casting a quick glance toward the door, Bristol reached to shake Kitty's thin shoulder. "I'm going to leave. I have to go."

Kitty gasped and bolted upward in the darkness. "Oh, Bristol, I don't know . . . he'll . . . Cutter might . . ."

Bristol's voice begged understanding in tones of anguish. "I can't have my baby here, I just can't! Help me, Kitty, please tell me how to find Pall Mall!" Her fingers found Kitty's hand, waiting for an answering squeeze.

Kitty tensed, straining toward Bristol's pallet. "When would you go?"

"Tomorrow night. Here's my idea . . ." Her whisper rising excitedly, Bristol detailed her careful plans.

Kitty listened in silence, her lack of comment saying more than any words. "I don't know," she answered finally. "I think you underestimate Cutter." Kitty sighed heavily. "But I'll do what I can."

The next day passed with agonizing slowness. Listening from the kitchen, Bristol decided the regulars would stay forever—the day had no end. Each time Kitty rushed into the kitchen, Bristol deviled her for weather reports (cold but clear), Cutter's state of mind (nasty but normal), and how Kitty progressed in getting Rumm very very drunk (coming along as planned).

When at last the kitchen fire burned low and no sounds had emerged from the pub room for more than an hour, Bristol and Kitty looked at each other.

"I'll miss you," Kitty whispered, moisture sparkling in her lashes. She tied her shabby gray cloak under Bristol's chin and exchanged sturdy worn shoes for the clogs Bristol wore.

Bristol swallowed an unexpected lump. Taking Kitty's hands, she stared into the woman's thin face. "I won't forget you," she whispered urgently. "I'll send money and food and clothing." Her eyes probed Kitty's. "Are you sure you won't change your mind and come with me?"

Kitty shook her head and wiped her eyes with the back of a hand. "I can't, Bristol. He . . . well, you know." Sweeping Bristol into an awkward hug, Kitty pressed four coins into her hand. "Go to Mercy Lane, turn right until you find Linton Way, then walk left for about a mile. There's hansom cabs there, and one'll take you to Pall Mall." She held Bristol at arm's length and blinked rapidly. "Good luck."

Not trusting herself to speak, Bristol fiercely hugged Kitty, then tiptoed to the kitchen door. Inside the pub room, her eyes swept the cherry glow of the coal stove and Cutter Rumm's hunched figure snoring over the table. With a deep shivering breath and a last excited glance toward Kitty, Bristol stepped into the room.

She moved silently, gliding between Cutter Rumm and the stove. Lightly she touched her stomach, pulling the cloak tightly around her body. She would make it! For the baby's sake, for her own sake, she would make it. Weeks ago she hadn't known enough to survive the streets, but now . . . now she understood how to blend into the night scene; she'd overheard Mrs. Pudden discuss it often enough. Dressed as she was, Bristol would pass as a prostitute seeking a late escort; no one would bother her with any problems she couldn't handle. She fervently hoped. And with the coins Kitty had stolen, Bristol had even a better chance. Home! Her pounding heart skipped a beat. She'd make this up to Kitty—the coins came at a dreadful cost.

Slowly, ever so slowly, Bristol slid the bolt on the door, listening with each taut nerve for a break in Cutter's snore. Then her fingers dropped silently to the latch, and she closed her eyes as she applied a slow pressure. In another minute she'd be outside and speeding toward Jean Pierre. Dear God, how she longed for him!

The door clicked open, and Bristol screamed.

A knife appeared from nowhere. One minute there was quiet darkness, the next second a knife quivered in the splintered door, pinning Bristol's sleeve above the latch. She screamed as the blade scraped her wrist, opening a wet stain on her cuff.

"Going somewhere, Queenie?"

Eyes wild with fear, Bristol darted a glance over her shoulder as Cutter stumbled up from the table. Her mind shrieked with silent outrage and disappointment too vast to bear. Jerking her sleeve, she ripped free of the knife and clawed at the heavy door.

But Rumm's large hand slammed it shut, and a wave of gin fumes crashed over Bristol's face. Brutal hands caught her bleeding wrist and twisted her hand up into her line of vision.

"See this here cut, Queenie?" Rumm's voice wheezed danger. "It could as easily been through yer wrist as well as

297

beside it. Coulda gone through yer ribs as well." Small red eyes glittered. "If'n ye ever try this again, I'll kill ye."

Shaking, tears wetting her cheeks, Bristol tried to yank free. "Please, please let me go. I beg you. Please let me go!" But she knew he wouldn't, knew it by the rage deep in his eyes.

"This here might help ye remember who decides what in Cutter Rumm's place. Ye'll go if and when I say so." His hand lifted then, as rough and heavy as a club, and he beat her. Beat her with drunken calmness, beat her until the red glow of the coal stove flickered in and out in crazy patterns, beat her until Bristol fell to the floor unconscious.

Two painful weeks elapsed before the last purple bruises faded and Bristol could walk erect without wincing. At last the utter futility of escape sank home, and with it came a deep despair.

Night after night she tossed on her pallet, sleepless, listening to Kitty's thin chest rattle and remembering how close, how close she'd been to escape. Her fingers still felt the forbidden latch; she had actually tasted the free air outside. And it all had come to nothing.

Turning her drawn face into the hollow of her arm, Bristol forced her thoughts to the baby, attempting to lift her spirits. And as always, a flame of joy lit the tiny room, filling it with needed warmth. Jean Pierre's child! She nourished Jean Pierre's baby beneath her heart. When Bristol allowed herself to experience the soaring glory of her pregnancy, an outpouring of emotion nearly strangled her. She could believe her love sped to Hathaway House and touched the spirit of Jean Pierre. Surely he sensed her calling; he would come for her. This was her only hope.

But shifting in the darkness, her wooden bat tensed in her fingers, sometimes a tiny voice crept past Bristol's carefully guarded defenses. What if Jean Pierre did not come? A black chill enfolded her heart. If he hasn't found me after all this time . . . will he ever? The floodgates of her mind opened to despair, and there followed grim days when she wondered if she'd ever regain her shaky confidence.

Somehow she always did.

However, as Bristol's stomach slowly grew beneath her marveling fingers, she found it more and more difficult to banish the doubts. She'd fed on hope for months, and might have continued to do so indefinitely. But time was passing, and it was no longer enough to simply bide her time; there was more than her own future at stake.

Unless she wanted her baby born into this dismal tenement, this life where hope killed, she had to find a way out. Soon. Even if it meant risking another beating. Cutter Rumm was a drunk, not a fool. Already she'd had more time than she had any right to hope for. When he noticed Bristol's blossoming stomach, Cutter would realize she had been at the Royal Rumm for a long time. He'd know she and Kitty had tricked him, had cost him the coins Bristol might have earned in the back room.

"Bristol, he won't let you keep it. Cutter will kill that baby the minute it's born," Kitty whispered, setting a flip iron in the fire to reheat. "There's no money for a baby." They discussed this endlessly. And found no solution.

Bristol's hands tightened on the trencher she scrubbed. Had the platter been of china, it would have splintered into fragments. Her mouth clamped in a determined line. "He'll have to kill me first."

Kitty's laugh was harsh. "Do you think he won't?" Her sad dark eyes rested on Bristol's face. "Then there'd be one less mouth to feed instead of two more."

"If he tries to hurt my baby, I'll kill him, Kitty, I swear it!"

Kitty shook her head, limp tendrils of hair falling from the bun at her neck. Killing Cutter was too ridiculous to merit comment. "Suppose," Kitty whispered after a quick glance toward the door, "just suppose Cutter lets the baby live. Then what?"

Bristol's mouth relaxed, and her eyes turned inward, looking where Kitty could not see. The child would have Jean Pierre's gray eyes and strong features. Maybe the Adams red hair. "I'll raise him, Kitty, and I'll love him," she whispered fiercely. "And Jean Pierre will find us."

Kitty's eyes turned sorrowful, and she smothered a sound with her fingers. "Hope . . ." she began, but the expression on Bristol's face stopped the words on Kitty's lips. Instead she patted Bristol's chapped red hands. No good would come of this baby. There could only be heartache ahead. All Kitty could do was prepare Bristol for the worst; sometimes that helped when the worst came—as it always did. "Bristol. You know you can't raise a healthy child down here. Have you . . . ?" Kitty faced away from the pain she knew would convulse Bristol's expression. "Have you thought about maiming the child? What you'll choose and how you'll do it?"

Bristol's face pinched and her flashing eyes fixed on Kitty. "Don't you ever say that again!" she hissed. "My baby will never be maimed! Never!" Her body shook with the horror of it, and the Pudden children paraded through her mind, crippled, blinded, deformed, addle-minded. "Never!"

Placidly Kitty watched her. "You may not have any choice," she murmured sadly. She pained and hurt along with Bristol. "Cutter will do it for you. He might let the baby live if he sees it's able to earn."

Shaking, Bristol ran a wet hand over her eyes. She was wrong to be angry with Kitty; none of this was Kitty's fault. Maiming was the way of life down here, all Kitty knew. Returning to the tub of dirty trenchers, Bristol whispered, "I can't. I'd rather see my baby dead than tortured."

Death was not out of the question. Kitty presented this possibility for Bristol's consideration. They discussed it through the wall with the ever-pregnant Mrs. Pudden. "Ye can visit the witch in Hector Street," Mrs. Pudden suggested. "Sometimes it works and sometimes it don't. How far along do ye be?"

"Three months, I think, maybe more." Bristol's stomach wrenched. She felt nauseous even discussing this.

"Would it hurt?" Kitty asked the wall, her dark eyes on Bristol.

Mrs. Pudden's rough laugh exploded. "Well, of course it hurts! I nearly bled to death last time." Her voice soared triumphant. "But I got rid of the brat."

"Isn't . . . isn't that murder?" Bristol inquired faintly. She asked herself why she continued this conversation. She could never rid herself of Jean Pierre's baby. Already she adored it.

Kitty's eyes widened across the space between their pallets, and Bristol heard Mrs. Pudden's astonished pause. Finally Mrs. Pudden found her tongue, and her voice was unpleasant. "Ain't it murder to push a brat out in the streets to starve or freeze? They hung Mrs. Tepeck's eleven-year-old boy for stealing a heel of week-old bread! Now, that's murder. Best be rid from the womb than bring 'em out to be killed." And that was that, in Mrs. Pudden's mind. She refused further discussion; Bristol was clearly as mad as any of the lunatics in Bedlam if she endured a pregnancy without at least one honest attempt to rid herself of it.

Bristol and Kitty lay sleepless in the darkness. "Oh, Kitty, I'm so scared sometimes," Bristol admitted. "I want this baby so much, but I don't want it born here. I want it safe!" She blinked at the ceiling. "I want to go home!" Touching her stomach, she swallowed hard and fought the scalding tears behind her lids. "I want to go home!"

Reaching across the darkness, Kitty squeezed Bristol's hand and held on. "Just do the best you can; it's all any of us can do."

And Bristol took one day at a time, fighting not to worry too far beyond the concerns of the moment. Sometimes her fingers lingered at her stomach, and her heart gladdened with a happiness that lifted her above her surroundings. Other days, she felt a desolation of crippling dimension. She buried herself in the routine of daily life, taking comfort in a dull sameness that allowed her to daydream the best possible futures.

And she felt the changes in her body with a mixture of fear and joy. Fear of Cutter's reaction; joy in the knowledge she carried Jean Pierre's child. This growing link to Jean Pierre was living evidence of their love, a cherished proof of the joy and tenderness they had found in each other.

Watching Bristol's expressive face glow in the firelight, Kitty lowered her sewing to her lap and sighed. "I know what you're thinking," she said. "Jean Pierre." By now Kitty knew the full tale. She fixed her sad eyes on Bristol. Bristol had worn that inward look from the moment they finished the day's tasks and took their stools before the fire.

Smiling, Bristol kept her thoughts to herself. But she felt his name on her lips, his image behind her eyes. Jean Pierre would come. Every day she sensed this more strongly. Hope had jelled into conviction. She could not have explained the difference, but it was there. Jean Pierre was coming. All Bristol had to do was wait.

Kitty shook her head, and her thin lips pressed together. In her view, often expressed, Bristol built toward a crippling disappointment. The pregnancy had catapulted Bristol into a dangerously unreal world. Kitty's shoulders rose and fell in a sigh. It did no good to speak of it. "Are you warm enough?" Kitty glanced to where Bristol sat in chemise and petticoat near the fire.

"Aye." Bristol's gaze swung from the flames and settled on the gray gown in Kitty's lap. "I can do that, Kitty, you don't have to." Jean Pierre's eyes were nearly the color of the gown. Bristol stared at the fabric, mesmerized by it.

Kitty turned the material in her fingers, letting out the waist. Smiling, she looked up and bit off a thread. "I want to do something," Kitty answered. "Besides, I like the feel of the cloth."

Bristol returned the smile and nodded. The gray gown had stood her well. She worked, lived, and slept in it. A cloth

301

of lesser quality would long ago have shredded to ruin. As it was, the gown had been patched in many places, and was soiled and stained beyond repute. Anywhere else, a gown in such tatters would have been consigned to the rag bin. Here, it still was grand enough to wear and hold one's head high.

However, it wasn't long after Kitty's ministrations that the gown once again felt tight at Bristol's waist. She paused in her chores, floury hands plunged in bread dough, and glanced down at her thickening stomach. She'd need to let out the gown again. Her brows met in a frown of careful thought. If she snipped a length from the curtains they'd made out of her cloak, perhaps she and Kitty could design a panel that could be loosened from time to time without having to take the entire waist apart. She decided to ask Kitty's opinion the first chance she had.

"I wonder . . ." she began when next Kitty dashed into the kitchen.

Kitty paid no attention; her face was pale and sober. "Bristol!" she whispered breathlessly. Kitty's elbow swept the lump of dough to the floor; she paid it no heed.

Bristol's eyes widened in surprise. She glanced from the floor to Kitty's flushed face and hot eyes. "What . . . ?" She couldn't recall Kitty ever showing a disregard for food. Bending, Bristol reached for the dough, but Kitty's thin fingers clamped onto her arm, gripping painfully.

"Shhh." Kitty hissed. *"Listen!"* She hauled Bristol across the kitchen and paused beside the pub door. Men's voices rose from inside.

"What?" Baffled, Bristol stared at Kitty, but Kitty shook her head furiously and pressed a finger across Bristol's lips.

"I tell ye, Cutter, it's uncanny, it is. Just like that 'hypothetical' story ye spun us some months back." Bristol glanced at Kitty, and her green eyes flared. It was Billy Tuffin speaking; she recognized the rasp of cheap whiskey grating his voice.

Kitty waved a hand, tense and anxious. "Just listen!" she begged in a nervous whisper.

Cutter's voice wheezed over Billy's. "I don't remember no story!" He spit toward the stove, still glowing hot, although a warm April breeze fluttered the green curtains at the window.

The men laughed. "Ye wouldn't recall yer own name, Cutter Rumm, if'n it weren't painted on the sign outside yer door!"

Cutter growled, and someone laughed and told him to put away his knife.

"Yessir," Billy Tuffin continued, "they's all in an uproar about it over to Stoneridge Lane. Big reward, me cousin said. Men stopping house to house offering a bag of coins for information about a grand red-haired lady lost some months now."

"A grand lady? Down here?" The voice of Cod Meeker dismissed the possibility. "Only grand lady ever stopped in Almsbury Lane was the one in Rumm's sotted imagination."

Billy Tuffin's rasping voice took on a calculating edge. "Well, the lady they's offering the reward for disappeared in a snowstorm about the time of Cutter's tale." He drank noisily. "Sorta makes ye think, don't it?"

Voices erupted, shouting to be heard, asking about the reward.

In the kitchen, Bristol went limp against the wall, a rush of breath escaping her lips. When she opened her eyes, they blazed like green jewels. She stared at Kitty without seeing. "I knew he wouldn't give up," she whispered hoarsely. "I knew it!"

In the front room, the shouts and arguments quieted to hear Cutter's explanation. "There ain't no grand lady here!" he insisted. The watching faces hooted in doubt.

Cod Meeker voiced the suspicions of all. "Maybe aye and maybe no. We all know you got somebody hid in that back room. It ain't Kitty baking these loaves! That slut ain't never baked a loaf what be this light and tasty in her whole miserable life!"

Voices agreed. "Maybe them men what be asking would pay dear to know about Cutter's tale and his hidden woman."

"Aye," the regulars chorused. One voice rose above the others. "And maybe them what asks will wonder why a certain Cutter Rumm ain't come forward on his own. Maybe them men will shove Cutter's knife up his arse!"

The men roared with appreciative laughter.

Bristol's eyes swam with relief. She was saved! Her baby was safe! One of the regulars would tell the story to claim the reward. She threw her arms around Kitty, tears of happiness sparkling like diamonds in her lashes. She didn't see Kitty bite her lip in worry.

Cutter's snarling wheeze lifted above the laughter. "I tell ye my woman ain't been here more than three weeks at most! And she ain't no grand lady! Ain't no one going to pay a farthing to hear about no common trollop. And that's all she be!"

"Then why the mystery?" a voice demanded. Others

303

agreed. "Show her to us!" they shouted, and banged their mugs on the table.

Undecided, Cutter sucked on a rotted tooth and scowled. Then he staggered up from his seat on the bench and yelled toward the kitchen. "Queenie! Move your arse in here. Now!"

Bristol wiped floury hands on her apron, her heart hammering against her ribs. Yes, yes, yes! Luck was with her. Let the regulars see, let them remember! And please God, let them tell the men who searched for her! With a confident smile for Kitty, Bristol hastened into the pub room.

Cutter snatched her arm and dragged her to the front near the stove. "There!" he shouted. "Do this be a grand lady?"

The regulars stared. They examined the long red curls tied in a tangle at her neck, and the floury streak across her cheek. Their eyes slowly traveled past her soiled apron to the patched and stained gown and the clogs on her bare feet. Their thoughtful stares missed nothing; Bristol felt like a cow offered for auction. They saw the bruises of Cutter's slaps and her rough callused hands and broken nails. They studied the violet shadows beneath her eyes and the rows of bug bites flaming her neck and arms.

"Ye're right." Billy Tuffin sighed. "That don't be no grand lady."

Bristol's head jerked up, and her eyes rounded in sick dismay. Waves of heat flowed from the stove, and a trickle of sweat rolled down the neck of her gown. She battled a leap of panic and a fainting sensation of heat and disbelieving eyes. "I . . . Listen . . ." Cutter Rumm's fingers crushed into her arm, and his bleary eyes flickered dangerously.

Bristol's eyes silently pleaded with the regulars. She wet her lips. If they didn't believe she was the lost lady of the snowstorm, they would say nothing, would not tell the searching men.

Sick, Bristol swayed on her feet and battled a scream of desperation welling in her throat. Surely God wouldn't be so cruel as to extend this thread of hope, then snatch it away. She blinked at Cutter, a frantic appeal in her eyes, all the while knowing the futility of begging. She read what he was thinking, and her heart dropped.

Cutter stood in deep foggy thought. Gradually his belligerent snarl relaxed. The full import of his momentous good fortune slowly penetrated a sluggish mind. Greed had frozen his ambitions; which path to take had confused him beyond action. Now, however, the decision had been made for him, and his mushy brain need struggle no longer. If the regulars didn't believe this was the lady being sought, then neither did Cutter Rumm. She had lied. He was no man's fool. The men searched for someone else; anyone could see she wasn't any grand lady. Knowing this finally freed Cutter Rumm to begin amassing his fortune. His little red eyes glittered. A man with two women to sell and a pub in front—that man need bow to no one. Realizing this, Cutter felt almost as fine as when he'd swung a coal pick and done honest work. He'd been a man of labor then, respected, a man to reckon with. Cutter thought furiously. They'd all seen her now; why wait?

"I been saving her for a special offering, and this here looks to be it," he wheezed happily. Behind his veined cheeks and broken nose, his mind already heard the clink of coins. Red eyes shrewdly totaled the room; Cutter would make more today than in a week of selling watered ale and gin. "Who'll have her first? I guarantee she's worth every coin ye can beg or steal!" He winked lewdly, hinting that Cutter Rumm didn't offer what he hadn't first sampled himself.

Deep silence greeted his words. Puzzled, Cutter frowned and swayed on his feet. He read disgust and rebellion in the eyes of his regulars. Sucking his bad tooth, he returned their stares. Then he gripped Bristol's chin, his fingers digging against her cheeks, and he peered into her suffering face.

"What be the matter with ye, men? This here is a passable wench! Are ye too gin-soaked to see it?" Baffled, he glared from one hard face to another.

Finally Cod Meeker spit at the stove and rose to leave. "I'll not be sitting in the company of a degenerate, Cutter Rumm. And I'll not suffer more insult." His stony eyes settled on Cutter's knife. "If ye leave yer knife and want to step outside, I'll show ye what I think of this business."

Cutter's blank red eyes moved over the other faces in growing bafflement. Two more customers stood to depart. "Never thought I'd see the day," Billy Tuffin rasped. "We ain't much, Cutter, but we ain't animals. Like some I could name." He spit on the floor. "We still got a shred of dignity." He followed Cod Meeker to the door. "We don't dig in a hole what's already planted. We ain't sunk so low as to defile motherhood. And you ain't never going to see one of us offering the likes for sale." The door slammed behind them. Others nodded agreement and followed.

"Motherhood?" Cutter shrieked in disbelief. His fingers clawed into Bristol's arm, and he spun her violently, his narrow eyes staring at her belly, finally seeing what the others had noticed immediately. Gaping, unable to accept what his

305

own eyes confirmed, Cutter's face collapsed. The regulars silently filed past, casting looks of disgust and censure as they moved out the door. One spit, narrowly missing Cutter's boot.

Helplessly Cutter watched them leave, and his eyes slitted in rage and frustration. His fortune vanished before his eyes. The toffs wouldn't pay for her, and the regulars wouldn't pay. Maybe his regulars would be back; maybe they wouldn't. One thing was certain—Cutter Rumm had been played for a fool. Somebody had to pay.

Bristol read his thoughts as clearly as if he'd screamed them aloud. "No," she whispered from lips turned to ash. "Please! No!" She stepped backward, her face turning the color of paste, her eyes huge and terrified.

"Cutter!" Kitty screamed from the kitchen doorway. "Cutter! No!"

Cutter Rumm heard nothing but a roar of fury whistling through his brain. He advanced on the object of his devastation, of his ruined hopes, of his humiliation. And his heavy hand slashed across her face, splitting Bristol's lips. It wasn't enough. He hit her viciously.

Pain exploded in Bristol's head. She staggered under his blows, tasting a rush of blood. Still he came. She cried out and covered her head with her arms. But her head was not the focus of Cutter's rage. His knee smashed into Bristol's stomach, and she screamed and clutched her sides. White-hot pain doubled her in half, and dark bile flooded her mouth. He was everywhere, a spitting demon with hammering fists and feet, smashing, hitting, kicking with limitless fury.

Frantically Bristol tried to twist away, to protect her stomach. But the demon followed, relentless and shouting. Hair tore from her scalp as he caught her and hurled her into the table edge. Her eyes puffed shut beneath crushing blows raining down on her head and body. She bent, wild to shield the baby, and Cutter kicked her upright, his boot burying itself in the soft hill of flesh below her waist. Something ripped and broke and tore free in a blinding wrench of agony. Something wet and sticky flowed down her legs.

When it was over, finally over, Bristol curled on the planks in a bright puddle, barely conscious. Both eyes swelled shut; she could not force them open. Above her wheezed a labored panting, and somewhere she heard Kitty crying, a thin hopeless wail of utter wretchedness.

There was not an inch on her body that didn't cry out in pain. But the agony in her mind dimmed all else. Blindly her fingers crept to the blood flow between her legs, and a howl

306

of animal pain shrieked past the broken lips. She screamed, "No! No! No!" The anguished sound faded to a series of thready whimpers. "Nononononononononono . . ." Bristol struggled to pull herself up, half mad with the need to find his knife and go after him. Her weight fell on aching wrists. Something snapped, and her mind exploded into darkness.

23

PAIN. Savage ripping pain. It tore at Bristol from within and without. She didn't remember where she was; the pain created a black universe of its own. She could open her eyes to a slit, but when she tried to turn her head, she fainted. Darkness rose like a veil, fell and rose again. Agony pervaded her thoughts, waking and in a faint. Pirates swarmed through her mind and tortured her body. She stood in Salem Town square bending under agonizing lashes that went on and on. Cutter Rumm's fist appeared as a tiny dot and rushed toward her face, growing until her brain swelled with it, and she relived a hundred vicious blows, felt his fist hammering her eyes, her splitting lips, raising knots on her face and head and body. Excruciating. Ferocious. Pain.

Fever raged through her flesh, and slurred words of delirium cracked open her lips. Odd combinations of people appeared in a gray mist; snatches of conversation drifted in and out of her mind. Hannah and Kitty, Charity and Aunt Pru. Goodwife Martha Cory and Uncle Robert. Reverend Parris and Mr. Aykroyd. They disappeared if she stared long enough through the pain-blind narrows of her eyes. Dead faces hovered in the fog, relatives and neighbors whose names she'd forgotten; they appeared and disappeared in a dizzying swirl.

Sometimes when the pain was almost more than she could bear, Bristol felt a gradual detachment from her feverish body. She floated near the ceiling and grieved for the broken doll groaning on her pallet. At such times, her heart ached in sorrow for that writhing young girl whose life trickled steadily from between her legs. She floated and watched and felt it would be a blessing to reach out and snip the thread and let go—simply drift away. She cried out in protest when a brutish pain yanked her back into purple flesh.

Someone placed a cloth across her swollen eyes, a cloth soaked in a foul-smelling concoction. She screamed and fainted when her lips were sponged. A crude splint made of kindling wood appeared on her left wrist. Packing to stanch the flow of blood separated her thighs, and she felt the rags chill and turn soppy.

Voices rose and vanished. She heard the murmur of the regulars in the pub room, and listened to Reverend Parris thunder from Salem's pulpit. Someone wept continually. A man's voice asked about a lady lost in a snowstorm, and Cutter's angry shout sent him away. Hannah whispered to Bristol, telling her to stand tall and hide her suffering. She heard brawling children, and Mrs. Pudden's shouted advice. Kitty whispered; Diana screamed. They all roared through her mind in a knifing hurricane of sound and disconnected phrases.

Bristol Adams knew she was dying.

In a clean bed, with adequate care, with a reason to defy the hovering specter, she might have lived. But on the filthy stink of a rotting pallet, in the desolate landscape of Almsbury Lane . . . with her baby gone and life draining from her thighs . . . and with no hope . . . no more hope . . . Bristol's exhausted mind gave up. Her will to live ebbed and waned.

A face wavered above her. "Swallow," Kitty begged, tears streaming down her thin cheeks. "You must eat." Carefully Kitty eased a spoon past Bristol's scabbed lips and tilted cool soup to fall into Bristol's throat.

Choking and gagging, Bristol emerged from a blinding red fog and swallowed. She tried to focus on Kitty's face, tried to understand why Kitty tormented her. But she swallowed; swallowing hurt less than strangling.

"Again," Kitty insisted, and the spoon clicked against Bristol's teeth. "That's good. Now, again."

Bristol opened burning dull eyes and shuddered at the hope behind Kitty's tears. Kitty rested a chapped palm against Bristol's cheek. Then she wiped a hand across her own nose and dashed tears from her eyes. Again she took up the spoon.

"No more," Bristol croaked. Kitty placed her ear near Bristol's dry puffed lips.

"Oh, Bristol," Kitty cried. "You have to eat! If there's any hope at all, you have to eat!"

Darkness hovered at the edge of Bristol's vision, but she gathered her strength and managed to speak before a black wave rolled over her mind. "Hope kills!" she rasped. And surrendered to the savage pain.

Time lost all meaning. She might have lain on the pallet for hours or an eternity. Time narrowed to the space between labored, agonized breaths. Pull the air in, let it out, try not to scream. How much better not to take that next gasping breath, to sigh and rest and end the pervading, terrible, killing pain. But the body was a machine built to betray the brain; the next breath continued to come. It didn't matter. Soon Bristol felt the life force seeping, leaking from her body. Soon she would sleep, and sleep would offer peace, freedom from hurting. Freedom from the people trying to keep her alive, trying to prolong the torment.

"Open yer eyes, Queenie," a woman's voice insisted. "Come along, now, open yer eyes." Bristol felt a gentle tapping on her cheek, stubborn, not going away.

"Please . . ." Vacant green eyes slowly cleared to a glassy stare. Bristol peered at a pasty moon face fading in and out above her. "Who . . . ?"

A bony arm, surprisingly strong, dug through the straw and circled Bristol's shoulders. She nearly fainted at the pressure on her back. "Come on, now, come on." The woman grunted, puffing stale gin and leeks into Bristol's battered face. She hefted Bristol into a sitting position.

Red dots exploded on a black field, faded, then appeared again. Bristol watched them. "Please, let me alone, I . . ." The few words exhausted her strength, and Bristol sagged against the woman's arm, gathering her weak energy for another attempt at reason. Why was the woman doing this to her?

"All right. Rest a minute." The woman squatted, rocking on her heels beside Bristol, her arm supporting Bristol's spine.

The voice . . . Bristol's slack mind searched to place it. Mrs. Pudden! Speaking sapped too much strength, but her green eyes spoke through the slits.

"Ye want to know about Kitty," Mrs. Pudden whispered, her button eyes darting to the door and back. "Kitty went to save ye. I hope to God she'll be back soon." Again she shot a look toward the door and the distant sound of voices. "Now, we have to get ye ready."

"Ready?" Bristol's stiff mouth formed the words, but no

sound emerged. She didn't understand what Mrs. Pudden said; she wanted only to lie down. If she lay very still, sometimes she didn't hurt so much. Sitting was agony. She cradled the splinted wrist in her lap, and a thin reedy sound broke past her lips.

"Stop that," Mrs. Pudden hissed. "Aye, that's better." She tied Bristol's blood-matted hair with a torn strip of rag, then reached into a pot and gently washed Bristol's face. Next she tried without success to clean some of the blood from Bristol's tattered skirt. Mrs. Pudden frowned. "Nothing for it there. Not so long's ye're still flowing." She peered into Bristol's white face and sighed. "Ye're a mess, darlin', but it's the best we can do." She glanced toward a dim light in the doorway, and she cocked her head, straining toward the voices in the front room. "Soon," she muttered. "Surely it'll happen soon." Mrs. Pudden's moon face measured the weaving, gasping girl bleeding into the straw. "Ye best be who ye say ye are . . . for the sakes of us all."

Nothing Mrs. Pudden said penetrated, nothing made any sense. All Bristol wanted was to close her eyes and sleep. The endless sleep. She felt heavy, so heavy, she could not have lifted an arm. Keeping her weighted eyelids open seemed an enormous effort.

Suddenly an explosion of noise erupted from the front room, and Mrs. Pudden drew in a sharp breath, her dark button eyes glued to the door. Shouting, shrieks, the sound of overturning furniture and splintering wood. Then a man's form loomed in the doorway, tall and lean, a sword swinging from one hand.

Bristol tried to look up, but she could not; her head felt too heavy to lift. She tried to concentrate, seeing a man's breeches and hose and silver buckles on fine boots. It made no sense. Cutter didn't own silver buckles. Cutter didn't wear hose.

"My God! Bristol!"

Jean Pierre's voice. Bristol groaned and wished for more pain. Pain of the flesh was easier to bear than the tricks of the mind.

Powerful arms carefully lifted her from the straw. And Bristol's head fell against a broad shoulder, too heavy to move, too weak to resist. The man shifted her to one arm, her weight no greater than a child's, and his fingers whitened on the hilt of his sword.

Gasping with pain, Bristol forced open her eyes and saw Mrs. Pudden's wide-mouthed stare. Bristol's gaze shifted, and a pale ridge of scar came into focus along the man's jaw. Her cry of joy nearly strangled her. It wasn't another formless vision! Jean Pierre had come! He'd come, like she'd always believed he would.

Jean Pierre's lips brushed her hair. "A little longer, *chérie*, my love, my little one. Endure a little longer, then you can rest and grow strong." He strode from the tiny malodorous bedroom and carried her into the pub room. Bright light filtered past the front window, and Bristol turned her face into his chest, away from the glare. He'd come! Her head fell limp on Jean Pierre's shoulder, and a tide of blackness threatened. But she ground her teeth together and bit at her mangled lip, forcing herself to remain conscious.

The pub room was crowded. Four of Jean Pierre's men held the regulars at sword point in a huddled corner. The regulars clutched each other, and their gin-reddened eyes focused past the men, on Cutter Rumm. Cutter hunched over the table, blinking rapidly at his outspread hand. His knife had been driven through the palm, pinning his hand to the wood. At Rumm's side, Mr. Aykroyd stood, his cutlass pressing across the bowed back of Cutter's neck, a thin line of pink opening beneath the blade.

"Please, sir," a woman's voice screamed. "You promised you wouldn't kill him if I told you!" Kitty cowered near the wooden counter, her pleading dark eyes fastened to Jean Pierre's savage granite face.

Jean Pierre hesitated, the sword twitching in his fingers. His icy face contorted in hatred, and he spit violently in Cutter Rumm's face. Cutter did not move. Cutter's eyes didn't leave the knife quivering up from his palm.

The blade in Mr. Aykroyd's hand increased its pressure. "What be the order, Captain?" Mr. Aykroyd's voice was as hard and ugly as his face. Blue eyes dipped to Bristol's still form, and his face turned wild with fury. The line under the cutlass deepened and turned red.

Kitty screamed. "You gave your word!"

Jean Pierre's stone frozen eyes didn't leave Cutter Rumm's face. "Look well, little one," he said softly, and not a man heard that hiss from hell that didn't feel a chill of terror race up his spine.

Cutter wet his lips, and his red eyes shifted from Jean Pierre to Mr. Aykroyd. He swallowed.

"No one touches this woman," Jean Pierre spit, his voice brutal with rage. His lips curved in a terrible smile that did not reach his eyes. "I'll have the hands that did this!" He

311

nodded to Mr. Aykroyd, and his flat gray eyes savaged Cutter Rumm's face.

It happened fast. Mr. Aykroyd slammed Rumm's other arm on the table; then his glittering cutlass rose and dropped, and Cutter Rumm's hands, severed at the wrists, lay on the stained table. Cutter's blank eyes stared at his lifeless hands, at the gush of red pumping from his wrists. Somewhere a woman's keening wail rose.

Jean Pierre raised his arm, and the tip of his sword dug beneath Cutter Rumm's chin, opening a dripping cut. The sword pulled Cutter's face up, and Jean Pierre's eyes seared down into that terrified gaze. The sword shuddered in Jean Pierre's hand and held. His face was something no one in that room would ever forget. Jean Pierre's jaw knotted and turned white; then he lowered the sword and rushed Bristol to a waiting coach.

Although she tried, Bristol could never remember the ride to Hathaway House or what happened immediately after. Scattered images appeared and vanished. Dr. Weede arrived, departed, and arrived again in bewildering sequence. Aunt Pru hovered near the bed, wringing plump hands, her face pale and pinched with anxiety. Aunt Pru's posture was the same, but her clothing flashed past in different colors, different designs. Molly bustled in and out, paused by the bureau, then seemed to reappear near the window or at the end of the bed. Uncle Robert's thin aristocratic features floated overhead, only to black out and appear somewhere else. The only constant in a confusing pain-ridden parade was Jean Pierre.

Each time Bristol's eyes fluttered open, Jean Pierre was at her side. Other faces came and went, but his always met her eyes first, his warm fingers clasping her hand.

Then finally the day came they'd prayed for.

"I love you," Bristol whispered. And there was no agony in her smile. Her emerald eyes glowed clear and aware.

A hoarse cry broke from Jean Pierre's lips and he buried his face in her waist, his arms circling her. "Thank God! Thank God!" Bristol lifted her hand, surprised to discover herself still dangerously weak, and she stroked his dark hair. When his head rose, the gray eyes were unashamedly moist. The fingers he reached to her cheek trembled. "Several times we thought . . ." he croaked, his voice catching in his throat. Warm fingers traced her cheek, her lips, her brow. Bristol took his hand and held it to her breast. Though her heart ached at the exhaustion thinning his face, she smiled.

"I love you," she murmured, her eyelids dropping. "I love

you." When she slept, it was a normal sleep, without the fiery pain hammering her ribs, without visions of delirium tossing her mind.

Her recovery was slow. May turned to June, and June blended into early July before Dr. Weede judged it safe for Bristol to leave her bed and begin the gradual process of resuming her life. Even then, he insisted on frequent rest and bed directly after dinner.

As Bristol regained her physical strength, her mind also strengthened, and she fought to sort out the past months.

Jean Pierre laughed. "Whoa. One question at a time. Before you reach the last one, I've forgotten the first." Tonight he wore a billowing blue shirt open at the throat. A gleam of moisture shone on his skin; even with the windows wide, London sweltered in July heat until long after dark. "You're certain I'm not tiring you? You don't want me to leave? I'm concerned you overdid it with your walk in the gardens."

Bristol smiled and rested against the pillows mounded at her back. "I don't want you to leave."

"Well, I'm tired, if anyone cares," Aunt Pru snorted. She lowered her embroidery hoop and crossed her arms. Yawning, she wriggled her bulk against a velvet cushion, then looked toward Bristol's bed with an impish grin. "I'm sure you two won't miss your chaperon if she takes a short nap."

They smiled at her, and Aunt Pru's chins bobbed toward her ample breast. The months since Jean Pierre's marriage, the months of Bristol's disappearance, had taken their toll. A stranger would have guessed Aunt Pru older than her mid-fifties, would have seen immediately the tensions and strains.

From the bed, Bristol watched her aunt doze, and her green eyes softened with affection. A gentle snore lifted Prudence's powdered row of chins; then they settled once more.

When sunset had turned the bedroom to a mellow golden glow, Bristol looked up at Jean Pierre, and her questions reformed. During her slow recovery, the family had steadfastly kept upsetting topics away from her. Now she felt the need of answers.

Quietly, holding her hand in his, Jean Pierre told how Bridey had raced up the stairs to tell of Diana and Bristol dashing out into the blizzard; how he waited, pacing frantically until the coach returned—without Bristol. Servants had carried a raving Diana upstairs; Jean Pierre dragged the driver to the stables. Before the man died, Jean Pierre learned the coach had driven east. The driver didn't know how far or where he'd stopped. But it was a beginning, a place to start. Then came the months of searching, of not giving up—someone had to have seen her, had to know if Bristol Adams was dead or still alive. Then one day Kitty appeared at the servants' entrance with her tale of a brutal beating. Kitty told them Bristol was dying, that she had lost the will to live. Kitty told them where to find her.

"Prudence ordered bolts of cloth for Kitty," Jean Pierre added, "and baskets of food every week. That and the purse I sent should make her life easier."

Bristol nodded, thinking what a difference those items would mean in Kitty's life. She and Jean Pierre sat quietly, holding hands and listening to the soft sounds of Aunt Pru's sleeping. After a while Jean Pierre lit a candle and placed it near the bed. He glanced at Bristol, and she met his eyes with a reassuring smile. It hadn't upset her to talk about the ride, Kitty, and the Royal Rumm. It all seemed so long ago. Safe in the pink bed, with Seven curled against her waist and Jean Pierre's warm fingers pressing her hand, the past seemed like a distant country; unpleasant, but a place to be discussed without pain.

"Where is she now?" Bristol asked.

Understanding, Jean Pierre said, "Diana?" His eyes pained and grew dark. He looked down at Bristol's hand in his fingers. "Dr. Weede supplies us with a ready amount of laudanum. Diana spends her days floating in a world half between sleep and wakefulness." Lifting his dark head, he gazed at the dying rays of sunset. "Some days she lies quietly in bed. Others . . . Occasionally she howls at a wall. Sometimes she crawls on the floor and cries like a child. She can stare at an object for hours without moving. Someone must be with her always." He sighed. "She was left alone twice. Both times, she did damage to herself. All we can do is try to let her know we care."

Bristol shuddered. Where did Diana's mind go when it left her vacant and blank? For a moment Bristol remembered the wretches in Bedlam, and then she squeezed Jean Pierre's hand. Wherever Diana's mind wandered, her body was safe and clean and protected. Bristol no longer felt any animosity toward Diana for throwing her into the snowstorm; one might as well blame a baby for crying. Diana could not help what she was.

Jean Pierre and Bristol relaxed in comfortable silence, watching the room darken. Seven yawned and adjusted himself into Bristol's side. Her hand idly stroked his ear.

She felt Jean Pierre's smoky eyes loving her face, and she lifted a hand to touch his cheek. He kissed her palm, heedless of Aunt Pru. Smiling, Bristol inclined her curls toward the sound of snores and withdrew her hand. Her fingers dropped to the soft fabric of a summer nightgown, and she felt the expanse of flat stomach beneath. For a moment the smile froze on her lips and horror leaped behind her eyes.

Jean Pierre's sober gaze measured her expression. "Bristol, my love," he said in a low voice. "Can you talk about it now?"

Stricken, she lifted tortured eyes to him. They had not spoken of the baby, not mentioned the loss of life's dearest treasure. She looked down at her hand, the palm flat against her stomach. "I lost our baby," she said in a dull voice. "The baby died."

Gently he took her hand, lifting it from her stomach and pressing it to his cheek. "Yes." The pain in his voice matched the pain in her heart.

Bristol's throat worked. Her eyes stung and burned. From the first, she'd wanted his baby like she wanted breath. And when the baby died, she'd lost a piece of herself.

"Perhaps it would help, little one, to let the tears come."

"No!" She wiped a hand across her eyes. "Jean Pierre, my dearest love . . . I want to tell you, but . . . I can't bear to talk about . . . It was . . ." She'd loved that tiny growing life so deeply, so hard. "I . . ."

"Shhh." His strong face paled, and Bristol saw something in his slate eyes she'd never seen there before. "I know. There is no need for words. I know."

Bristol stared into those flinty eyes and knew he did understand. She turned her face toward the dark windows. Her pain was of such a depth, such a dry hot intensity, that tears could never bring relief.

Jean Pierre cupped her chin in his hand and lifted her face to meet his eyes. "Listen to me, little one," he said, his voice low and intense. "I love you like life itself. You are safe now. You will always be safe with me. I won't let anyone hurt you ever again." His smoky eyes burned into hers. They stared at each other; then his mouth moved to cover hers.

"Arghhh . . ." Aunt Pru yawned and stretched. "Did I nap long? Did you miss me?"

Hastily they broke apart and looked at each other. Then they laughed and called Aunt Pru to the bed for a three-handed game of ombre.

Soon Bristol's strength had returned until it seemed she

315

couldn't possibly have been so desperately ill. Cards and invitations arrived daily from friends rejoicing at her reappearance and recovery, and hinting for an explanation of her absence. Many, like Charles Easton and Louis Villiers, had doubted Aunt Pru's story of an extended illness from the beginning.

Bristol shuffled the cards and invitations and frowned. Though it was obvious she could pick up a varied and demanding social life if she chose, Bristol saw no point in doing so. It didn't seem fair to Charles and Louis to keep them dangling with unfounded hope. Nor was it fair to herself. Why immerse herself in a tide of parties and courtships when she neither welcomed nor enjoyed the company of other men? It all led nowhere, and she was not the person she had been.

Bristol felt at loose ends. She didn't know what direction her life was meant to take. And she felt it to be only a matter of time before she and Jean Pierre came together. Each tried to deny it. Neither wanted to dishonor the Hathaway name; neither wanted to betray their beliefs. They tried to convince themselves they could build a relationship based on loving companionship. But the physical magnetism between them was too strong. Their eyes met, their fingers brushed, and a smoldering passion ignited.

Bristol saw it in Jean Pierre's brooding eyes, and she felt a familiar fire whenever she looked at him. She couldn't be in the same room with Jean Pierre without feeling a tingle of response to the call of his body. How long could fragile intentions withstand the craving needs of flesh?

Then Hannah's letter arrived. And the torment of indecision was swept away by a new pain.

Dear Bristol,

There's been an accident. A hired man was guiding the plow and Noah was walking alongside throwing stones out of the path. He fell beneath the blade and his legs are gone. William Griggs comes by every day and doctors as best he can, but he doesn't give much hope. Come home. Your father regrets sending you away and now admits it. Noah wants you home, Bristol. He wants to make peace with you before he dies. He suffers for what happened. Please hurry. Prudence tells us you have been very ill and unable to write. I hope you are well enough to travel now. Come quickly, daughter, there is little time.

Your affectionate mother,
Hannah Adams

White-faced, Bristol extended the terse letter to Aunt Pru. While Prudence read, Bristol slowly gazed around her bedroom with a numbed expression. Papa. She couldn't imagine this bedroom vacant; she thought of it as hers. Papa wanted her home, and he was sorry he'd sent her away. This room was more hers than anything she'd known before; the desk, the bed, the chair by the fire—they held so many memories. Papa wanted to make peace with her before he . . .

Aunt Pru gasped, and quick tears sprang into her eyes. She folded Bristol against her massive bosom. Inhaling the light scent of lavender, Bristol met Jean Pierre's smoky eyes above her aunt's shoulder.

She was going home.

24

IMMEDIATELY Prudence dispatched a lengthy letter to Noah, and in it she promised Bristol would sail on board the *Princess Anne*. Bristol scribbled a quick note, adding that the *Princess Anne* departed England ten days from the date of her letter.

Those ten days were the most frantic in Bristol's life. She and Aunt Pru paid a hurried call to Paternoster Row and cajoled Collette into creating a wardrobe of Puritan gowns, collars, aprons, and petticoats. Grudgingly Collette agreed, but only with the proviso that Bristol never wear such abominations in London Town, and that Bristol never admit such horrors were sewn in Collette's shop. Next, Bristol and Aunt Pru shopped for plain sturdy shoes and handkerchiefs devoid of decoration. They bought unadorned shawls and unbeaded reticules and plain white dust caps. They had two strong trunks delivered to Hathaway House.

The shopping trips were dismal, quiet outings, totally dissimilar to previous excursions. Aunt Pru wept continually, and Bristol couldn't speak past the constant lump clogging her throat.

Gossip being London society's favorite pastime, word traveled quickly, and a deluge of farewell invitations arrived hourly at the house in Pall Mall. Lord Pepperal-Haught hosted a lavish dinner-ball in Bristol's honor, the first and last invitation she accepted. Too much wine soured the dispositions of the Duke of Easton and the Marquis de Chevoux; tempers flared and each accused the other of stealing Bristol's affections. An embarrassing argument erupted, noisy with shouts and threats. To the dinner company's horror, it ended with the duke and the marquis squaring off in the gardens, their swords poised, and a drunken Jean Pierre roaring a challenge for the victor. Only the cool intervention of Lord Hathaway prevented a scandalous disaster.

The following day Bristol received both Charles Easton and Louis Villiers privately, and endured distressing scenes with each as she firmly and irrevocably declined their pleas for marriage.

Every day more personal items disappeared into her new trunks, and gradually the pink bedroom lost its sense of being uniquely Bristol's and assumed a vacant, impersonal look. To Bristol's dismay, most of the things she'd accumulated during her year and some months in England could not be kept. There was no place for luxuries in staid New England. She assembled the gifts and trinkets from her host of admirers and presented them to the servants, seeing that Molly and Bridey received first choice and the most pieces. Bristol kept Mr. Aykroyd's brooch and the gold chain from Jean Pierre; she could bear to part with neither.

For two days Bristol composed a speech for Aunt Pru and attempted to deliver it when she presented Aunt Pru with the emerald-and-diamond necklace and eardrops Jean Pierre had given her on the eve of his wedding. But Bristol's carefully prepared speech crumpled in the face of Aunt Pru's streaming eyes, and the women fell into each other's arms. The English language didn't possess words strong enough to convey Bristol's gratitude and love. She doubted any language did.

Then suddenly everything was packed, all the last-minute chores complete. It was time to leave.

Bristol's trunks were loaded on the Gravesend ferry, the

good-byes had been said. She stood outside the Hathaway coach and met Uncle Robert's sad eyes through the carriage windows. "We shall greatly miss you, Miss Bristol," he said gravely. Aunt Pru shrieked and fell across the cushions looking ill. Lord Hathaway leaned to touch her arm. "Now, Pumpkin, you can see the girl is suffering, give her a smile."

Aunt Pru's tearstained face appeared in the window; she held a linen to her swimming blue eyes. "I can't bear it. I simply can't bear it!" Her chins wobbled and she summoned a ghastly parody of a smile. "Come back! Come back and bring Charity and Hannah and . . . and Noah! But come back!" Her face collapsed. She held Seven's orange head to the window, hiding her own face.

Seeing Bristol's chalky expression, Jean Pierre stepped forward and firmly cupped her elbow. He turned her away from the carriage and guided her over ropes and netting, past barrels and piles of cargo littering the docks. Raucous noise surrounded them, and hot August sun drew a hideous stench from the rotting laystalls enclosing the wharves.

By the time they boarded the ferry, Bristol had nearly conquered the scald threatening her eyes and the quiver in her hands. She pressed a linen to her nose against the stench burning her nostrils and breathed through her mouth. She and Jean Pierre paused at the rail of the flat-bottomed ferry, and Bristol directed her eyes to the green-and-white coach at the edge of the pier. An orange mound leaned from the window and waved a bit of lace.

Gently but firmly Jean Pierre led her from the rail and toward seats in the shade of the bulkhead. They sat down, not speaking. Slowly the unwieldly ferry lumbered from the docks and sought a sluggish brown current. On either side, London slid away, giving place to a summer countryside baking in August heat.

The ferry rode low in the water, crowded with travelers, some holding wicker baskets upon their laps, other waving limp hands before irritable faces and complaining loudly of the heat. Their eyes slid to the elegant, commanding man who escorted what looked to be a servant girl, or perhaps one of those roundheads from the colonies. Pretty she was, but so out of fashion. Yet plainly the man adored her; his lack of manner and decorum was shocking; the two might have been alone, for all the notice the man paid watching eyes. After a time, the observers lost interest. They dozed in the heat and tried to breathe the fetid river air without retching.

Bristol toyed with the edges of her new white apron. She'd

319

noticed the sharp glances dismissing her clothing, and she smiled at her lap, thinking of Collette. The ferry passengers couldn't know the high-necked brown gown and square white collar felt as strange to her as it looked to them. This morning Molly had dressed Bristol's glossy red hair in the style she'd worn when first she arrived in England—parted in the center, with long curls tied loosely at her neck. A dust cap with a dainty lace edge (Aunt Pru had insisted on the lace) rested on the back of her head. Bristol felt uncomfortably out of place and out of balance, like a ghost who is suddenly returned to unfamiliar flesh.

Jean Pierre startled her when he spoke near her ear. "You look very young and very innocent." He smiled. "More like the girl I pulled from a snowbank than the sophisticate that brought London to its knees."

Bristol didn't look at him. "I feel neither young nor innocent," she said in a low voice. "I feel ancient. Tired and empty." It was true. She hadn't slept well in days. And her heart bled at the decisions she'd made during those hot, sleepless nights. Decisions that sucked away life; decisions she'd known for a long time must be made.

"Look at me," he commanded softly.

Unable to disobey that tone, not wanting to look into those cherished gray eyes, Bristol lifted her head.

Jean Pierre read her face, and his smoky eyes darkened with pain. "You're not coming back," he said flatly.

"No," she whispered, her eyes pleading. She reached into her apron pocket and withdrew the pewter cup, the only thing she owned that was hers alone. Silently she placed it in his hands.

He held the cup between his fingers and stared toward the shoreline, his jaw knotting, his face hard. "I came to you last night. Your door was locked."

"If I'd opened my door to you . . . I could never leave you." She saw his face glittering through a mist of unshed tears.

Jean Pierre looked at her, and she saw every detail of his strong loving face, a face that would haunt all the days of her life.

"I love you," he whispered. "I love you enough to let you go. My Bristol. My little one." He stared at the distant shore and then back. "Yet I'm selfish enough to want you with me. To sentence you to a half-life, to expose your reputation to ruin and ridicule. My selfish needs would keep you with me, in the shadows, always."

320

A sob rushed past Bristol's lips, and she buried her face in shaking hands.

His accent thickened with emotion. "I never met Noah Adams, and I wish him no hardship. Yet some sliver of decency is glad of his misfortune, grateful that Noah Adams saves you from my selfishness by calling you home. For no other reason would I let you go."

Bristol's shoulders trembled, and she squeezed her eyes shut, leaving damp traces where her lashes brushed her cheek.

"I love you," he continued quietly. "I battle myself for your sake. I want you like a dying man wants life. But I love you enough to want more for you than I can offer. Somewhere, my little one, a brighter life waits for you, a life without guilt or shame. A life with the honor that shines in your spirit." His hand lifted her chin, oblivious of disapproving stares. "I love you enough to give you honor at the cost of the only thing in life I hold dear."

She met his burning stare, her face twisting. "I love you more than anything else in this world," she whispered.

His eyes made love to her. "I know," he answered in a hoarse voice.

Then, there was nothing to say. They passed the remaining ferry journey in aching silence, each agonizingly aware of their thighs touching on the cramped bench, of heartbeats tuned as one. It was almost a relief to disembark at Gravesend and step into the longboat of the *Princess Anne*, one of Jean Pierre's ships.

Straining backs bent to the oars and threaded the longboat through a multitude of schooners and small boats bobbing in the harbor. Then Mr. Aykroyd was assisting Bristol onto the rolling decks of the *Princess Anne*. He beamed down at her, his blue eyes sparkling. " 'Tis a fine day for a sea voyage, gel." Bristol pressed his hands and tried to smile. The result was disastrous.

"Mr. Aykroyd will accompany you and see you home safely," Jean Pierre said.

"I'm glad to see you," Bristol murmured. But neither her voice nor her face expressed gladness at anything.

Mr. Aykroyd looked shrewdly from one to the other; then he shook his white head and tactfully withdrew.

Jean Pierre took Bristol's arm and guided her silently down the length of the ship. Around them, men swarmed in the rigging and shouted and hauled and packed and stowed, engaged in the frenzied activity of preparing to get under way.

Heavy clouds of sail dropped from the yards, and the *Princess Anne* shuddered and creaked as a breeze snapped the canvas and strained at the anchor.

Pushing open the door of the captain's cabin, Jean Pierre led Bristol inside. A robust man with ruddy complexion and thinning hair looked up from the desk with a surprise that quickly turned to obeisance. He sprang to his feet, almost bowing. "Mr. La Crosse! What a pleasant surprise!" He peered behind Jean Pierre. "And this is the young lady that—?"

"Get out."

The captain's eyes widened. "I beg your pardon, sir?"

"I said get out!" Jean Pierre roared. "Leave us!"

The captain of the *Princess Anne* flushed and hurried out the door without a backward glance.

They stared at each other, punishing themselves with hungry longing. And then Bristol ran into his arms, and he held her as if his life depended on her heartbeat pounding against his.

"God help me," Bristol cried, "I cannot bear this!"

"Tonight," he said, and his voice was dull and expressionless, "tonight I shall get very drunk and buy a red-haired whore and I will pretend that she is you. I will imagine her skin is as silky and soft as yours, that her mouth and body welcome me with the sweet sensuality that is you. I will touch her and I will feel you beneath my hands. I will enter her, and it will be your voice that calls my name." His arms tightened around her. "And all the time," he whispered hoarsely, "it will not be you. It will never again be you."

"Dear God," Bristol moaned against his chest. Her hand flew to touch his face; then his urgent lips met hers in a crushing, aching kiss. She clung to him desperately. Never again. His hands burned on her trembling body. Never again. His lips tasted of salt and heat and desire. Never again.

And then he was gone.

With a wrenching sob Bristol fell into the captain's chair, feeling as if a monstrous wind had pulled the life from her body. She stared out the window with blank eyes; she was numb and empty, a hollow thing with no spark. Above deck a grating squeal shuddered through the ship, and the anchor slowly rose, sucking foam and weed. The leadman's voice sang out fathoms, and voices shouted from the high rigging. The *Princess Anne* turned in the current. Slowly she moved out of the harbor, regal and proud, her masts stretching toward a cloudless sky.

They had nearly approached the open sea before Mr. Aykroyd appeared to fetch her. He stepped into the darkening cabin and placed a gentle hand on Bristol's shoulder. "Captain Kelling do be needing his cabin," he said in a quiet voice.

Bristol stumbled to her feet, and her wild eyes met his. Then Mr. Aykroyd opened his arms and pressed her head against his shoulder, unable to withstand the anguish on that small lovely face. They stood in an embrace for a long moment; then he patted her shoulder and placed his arm around her waist, leading her up the stairs and through the rocking ship toward the stern.

The quarters prepared for Bristol's return trip were wholly unlike the tiny dark cell she'd long ago shared with Jane Able. Jean Pierre had put the ten-day departure time to good use, ordering quarters for her as commodious as possible. Three rooms had been joined into one, and a supply of fresh oranges was stacked along the wall behind her trunks. The cots had been removed and a real bed bolted to one wall. She sank to the edge and felt a soft mattress beneath the pink spread. She'd been provided a desk and two upholstered chairs and a wardrobe for her clothing. It almost looked like a bed-sitting-room combination. And empty. Dear God, it was empty.

"Do ye feel like a bit of company, gel?"

Bristol started; she'd forgotten Mr. Aykroyd. She shook her head, red curls sliding across her back. Hoping he understood, she looked up. "No, thank you, Mr. Aykroyd, not right now."

A grim smile shifted the scars along Mr. Aykroyd's cheeks. "Well, ye'll be having it just the same." He sat down in one of the upholstered chairs and fished in a pocket for his clay pipe. "Ye ain't the only soul feeling a little dismal just now." He gave her a sly wink. "Mayhaps someone here is missing a certain plump widow." Bristol's eyebrows shot up, and the beginnings of a real smile tugged the corners of her full mouth. "Where's yer manners, gel? Ye ain't even inquired about my most interesting social life!" His blue eyes twinkled, and Bristol laughed.

The weeks passed quietly, one day blending uneventfully into the next. Three weeks out, the *Princess Anne* ran afoul of a raging squall, but Bristol tied herself into the bed and slept through the worst of it. She'd come too close to dying to fear it any longer. If she died in the squall, she would have lived the best of her life; no woman could hope for a greater love than had been hers. And the pain of it was with her constantly.

Mr. Aykroyd was a godsend. Without him, Bristol thought, she could not have endured those first terrible weeks of lonely adjustment. He read aloud while she sewed, he taught her two-handed card games. "Which ye are to put out of yer head the instant we land. Those Puritans have no call to cards. They clamp heads in pillories for less." Bristol smiled; Mr. Aykroyd never seemed to recall that Bristol herself was a Puritan.

She wrote a hundred letters to Jean Pierre and crumpled each into wads which Mr. Aykroyd fed to the fish—accompanied by a stream of muttering and many sad shakes of his head. She ate plum duff and scouse and complained with Mr. Aykroyd about the quality of the fare. He teased her about her dust caps and plain gowns; she teased him about the widow lurking in Southwark. They strolled on deck and he explained the workings of the cannon and showed her how to tie various knots.

And one day a brown shimmer appeared on the horizon, and soon after, the *Princess Anne* trimmed sail and maneuvered through Salem's difficult harbor mouth.

Mr. Aykroyd leaned on the rail and looked across the water toward the low wooden houses of Salem Town. Behind them, they heard a loud whir and the anchor splashed into the waves. On the distant hills, many leaves wore October's colors; the countryside blazed with orange and red and gold.

"What do ye be thinking?" Mr. Aykroyd asked softly, measuring the pale anxiety in Bristol's expression.

She stared toward the shore. She'd forgotten the splendor of New England autumns. And how small and squat Salem was compared to the bustle and business of London. From this distance Salem Town looked rather quaint and pastoral. Lazy puffs of dust trailed carts and wagons in the lanes; three cows grazed along the city shoreline. The air tasted sharp and clean; the only refuse and debris lay close to the wharves, quickly dispersed to the open sea.

A stranger seeing Salem for the first time would not imagine the dissension and suspicion underlying the wholesome appearance. But Bristol Adams was not a stranger. This was home. She knew of the problems masked by Salem's sleepy appearance; what she might have wished to forget, Hannah's letters had kept alive. All the problems flooded Bristol's mind, petty volcanic problems. This world was as different from London as mud was from marble.

"I'm thinking that . . . that I wish I could return with you," she whispered through pale parched lips. "I'm afraid it won't be like I remember . . . I've forgotten so much." She glanced at her soft smooth hands. Within a week calluses would appear; her hands would be rough and red the rest of her life. Once again, the world, with Bristol in it, seemed to turn upside down, and everything was different.

She blinked rapidly. Somewhere, maybe on the wharf, maybe at home in Salem Village, Noah was waiting for her. What would they say to each other? For an instant time spun backward and her father's weathered face rose in her mind's eye. She saw him bouncing her on his knee, red hair peeping beneath a cap, his green eyes, so like her own, crinkled and dancing with laughter. The child she had been shouted with delight and buried her face in his leathery-smelling neck.

Then time rolled forward, and her vision cleared and focused on the distant dock. There was no mistaking the ramrod-erect posture of her mother, and Charity's carroty hair catching the afternoon sun. Suddenly, all the years of family enveloped Bristol, and her heart yearned toward them. She wanted to hurry, to run, to clasp them tight to her heart: Hannah, Charity, and most of all, Noah. She'd sailed from home with hard thoughts for her father, and he'd ended by sending her to the greatest adventure of her life. She'd resented the whipping, the exile, and refused to admit she'd earned both; Noah had done only what community rule demanded. It was Bristol who had broken the law. A wiser heart quickened with urgency—she had a peacemaking of her own to offer. She would take her father's work-battered hands and beg forgiveness for the trouble she'd brought him, the worry she'd caused, the resentment she'd harbored in her heart.

Her eyes moved along the shore. This was her home. She would build a life here, in the healing shadow of her family, the people she loved and who loved her. An ease of mind she hadn't experienced in months descended like balm to soothe her troubled thoughts. She was coming home! For the first time during the voyage, she began to believe she would be all right.

Mr. Aykroyd read it in her face. He patted her shoulder and reached for her hands. "Gel, 'tis easier to part here. Them Puritans don't take to men and women kissing, and I'd be proud if ye feel an urge to kiss this old cheek when ye're ready to leave." Bristol returned the pressure of his fingers and felt a sudden sting behind her eyes. "I think ye'll not be

325

going back to England." He saw confirmation in her green gaze before she dropped her head. "And it may be that yer ship and mine, they won't pass again." He swallowed and waited a moment before continuing. "But I want ye to know . . ." His voice sounded peculiar. "I want ye to know that if ever I'd been blessed with a wee daughter, I'd have wanted her to be like ye."

Bristol flung herself into his arms and kissed the scarred and ruined cheek. "I'll never forget you," she whispered fiercely. "Never!" Then she stumbled blindly down a rope ladder, and rough hands pulled her into the longboat. She lifted her face, and her green eyes told him good-bye.

"Go with God, little gel!" he shouted across the water.

Bristol lowered her face and gripped the edges of her apron. The oars bit into the water, pulling her away from one life and into another.

She climbed rickety stairs to the wharf, and for an instant her eyes swung to the *Princess Anne*, her proud masts rocking against the blue sky. A lone figure stood at the railing.

Drawing a deep breath, Bristol resolutely turned her back and looked toward Hannah and Charity. She started toward them, first at a walk; then she was running. And her eyes searched the wagon behind them, seeking Noah, looking for her father.

Then she saw their faces, and a cry tore from her lips. Bristol Adams had come home. But she'd arrived too late.

25

FROM the moment Bristol left Salem, a part of her had longed to return, had yearned for home. And now that she had come back, part of her still searched for the home she remembered. To her bewilderment, Bristol didn't feel as if she'd found her home.

Nothing was the same; nothing was as she remembered. The Adams house seemed smaller, shabbier, and the outbuildings more in need of repair than she recalled. Noah's fields appeared to have shrunk. The safe familiarity she longed for was missing.

However, the greatest changes lay within the house. Mild, amiable Charity had become distant and withdrawn, encircled by a hard shell Bristol could not penetrate. And Noah's death had cleaved Hannah in half. This Bristol understood, for she herself felt less than whole with Jean Pierre forever gone. She watched her mother with a sympathy born of secret understanding.

Hannah's energy had diminished to listlessness; a stoop frequently curved the famed erect posture. She turned inside herself and often stared at nothing for hours. Values Hannah had treasured for over fifty years suddenly seemed of questionable merit. She'd buried five sons and one husband. Her two daughters were grown and of marriageable age. Of what earthly use was Hannah Adams? Hannah felt it a gross unfairness that God had not taken her along with Noah; she found no reason in continuing when she'd outlived her usefulness. Staring into the future, Hannah foresaw an immediate need to sell the farm; she could not manage all the work herself. And then what? Was she destined to become a burden, to live in the households of her daughters when they married?

"Neither of us has a husband on the horizon, Mama," Bristol gently chided. She glanced quickly at Charity, realizing she didn't know if this were true or not for her sister. Hannah didn't respond. "And if you came to live with one of us ... well, an extra pair of hands would be welcome." Bristol recalled the difference an extra woman had made at the Royal Rumm, and for a moment she considered telling Hannah. But a delicate shudder moved her shoulders, and she pushed those thoughts from her mind. "Don't think of it now," she added. "It's time to get ready for the sabbath services. Nothing needs deciding this minute."

"But soon." Hannah sighed, rising from the table. She paused at the door of the bedroom she'd shared with Noah, and she straightened her spine as if it required courage to enter that room.

Bristol watched with a sore heart. Her mother had aged greatly since Bristol left Salem. More gray silvered the chestnut in Hannah's hair, and her vitality seemed to be leaking away. Overburdened eyes squinted from a worn face, and she no longer attempted close work.

Bristol's mind followed her mother. Her voice was distracted when she spoke to Charity. "Are you ready for services?"

"Aye," Charity snapped. "We don't need you ordering us about. We managed fine before you came home, you know."

Bristol's green eyes widened, and they stared at each other. This was Charity? Shy, diffident Charity? Bristol stammered, "I'm sorry, Charity, I didn't mean . . ."

Charity covered her eyes, and her shoulders caved around her thin chest. "No, no. It's me that's sorry." She sighed and frowned into the fireplace. "Forgive me, Brissy, I . . . I have a lot on my mind."

In the last year, Charity had filled out, and although her figure would never approach the lush curves of her sister, she wore a woman's body. And the face of a freckled child. But an unhappy, sorrowing child. The open, readable face Bristol remembered was gone.

Hannah reentered the kitchen adjusting a plain shawl. "Aye," Hannah said tartly, and her lips thinned, "I guess you do hold much on your mind, missy." Her faded eyes moved to Bristol, explaining. "She and that Parris bunch were seen dancing in the woods. Dancing!" Hannah's expression hurt to see. "Maybe now you've come home, Bristol, you can talk some sense to her."

Confused, Bristol shook the red curls tied at her neck. That "Parris bunch" had also been the Adams bunch when she left.

Charity glared up from the fire, her pale eyes sparking resentment. "We weren't dancing, Ma. We were skipping!" She lifted a plea to Bristol. "Is skipping so terrible?"

Before Bristol could frame an answer, Hannah cut in. "Tell Charity skipping or dancing or whatever . . . tell her it's wrong! She knows it is! But they must have their sport! Their amusement!" Disgust pinched Hannah's voice. "This community was not founded on sport! What would happen to the common good if everyone decided they needed 'amusements'?" She spit the words. "I ask you that, missy, what would happen if decent people threw aside their work and demanded sport?"

Hopelessness settled like a mask over Charity's tight features. "You just won't understand."

Uneasily Bristol cleared her throat. "I'll fetch the wagon," she said, and fled the tensions in the kitchen. Outside, she breathed deeply of crisp chill air. A bank of clouds covered the eastern sky, and Bristol frowned, hoping it didn't signal snow.

As she harnessed the horses and hitched up the wagon, Bristol tried to sort through the changing relationships she'd returned to find, and she sought to determine what her own role would be. Obviously a person who had danced through two pairs of slippers in one night could not chastise another for mere skipping. On the other hand, dancing was not shameful in London; here it was. It seemed to Bristol that one must play by the rules wherever one happened to be. Or was that just an excuse?

She sighed. Every day in Salem seemed less appealing than the last. During the three days she'd been home, Bristol had listened to a seemingly endless stream of news updating the lives and affiliations of neighbors and residents. The news was not encouraging. Everyone seemed as angry and upset as Charity.

The story best typifying this upset was Hannah's account of Ann Putnam Senior's attempt to hold a quilting bee, usually a happy, gossipy event much anticipated. But before the bee date arrived, regrets poured in, and finally the bee had been canceled. Martha Cory could not be seen with Rose Kenneth, as their husbands were recent enemies; several ladies refused to sit in the same room with Parris supporters; if Rebecca Nurse did not attend, then Elizabeth Porter refused to attend; Elizabeth Proctor declined, wondering why she'd been included in the first place; Hannah Adams refused to enter the home of a woman who allowed her daughter (Ann Junior) to skip and thus exerted a bad influence on Charity; if Bridget Bishop attended, those who objected to the tavern owners along Ipswich Road would not; if Bridget was excluded, no others from Ipswich Road would attend. And on it went.

Salem had splintered into smaller and smaller cliques, until it became impossible to hold a large gathering with any hope of success. Someone was certain to be abrasive and offending in his views, inciting a brawl and further dividing the groups on yet another issue.

Seeing it fresh, it appeared to Bristol that everyone hated everyone else. She understood Hannah's concern for the common good; the common good appeared severely threatened. The problem, as Bristol perceived it, was that the doctrine of common good had eroded to a point where each person thought solely of himself. Neighbors had become people viewed with suspicion and distrust. Someone must be found to blame for the dissension and grumbling discontent in the village. Pointing fingers abounded.

Bristol pondered this while she drove to the meetinghouse, the reins rough and unfamiliar in her smooth hands. Perhaps if she'd not been away, perhaps then the changes would have occurred gradually enough to escape notice. As it was, a pattern opened before Bristol and revealed disturbing alterations to the village life she remembered.

As Bristol understood from Hannah, the animosity between Salem Village and Salem Town had escalated to eruptive bitterness. Salem Village wanted free of Salem Town, but the town would not permit it. Salem Village desired a township in its own right, craved freedom from town taxes, town law, town watches, town supervision and interference. Commercial Salem Town had little understanding or tolerance for the very real problems of rural Salem Village. Compounding the issue were the merchants along Ipswich Road; though geographically within Salem Village, most felt a far greater kinship with the profit philosophies of Salem Town. The Ipswich Road people supported Salem Town. And the majority of villagers hated them for it. This schism fatally weakened village petitions for autonomy.

Further disrupting village harmony was the familiar sour note of Reverend Parris. On this issue, many Ipswich Road people aligned with villagers they opposed in the fight for autonomy. The parish council, now composed of anti-Parris people, including some that lived along Ipswich Road, had voted to refuse the reverend further payment of salary. They fervently hoped Samuel Parris would go away, taking all the controversy with him. Instead, the reverend and his dwindling supporters gave every sign of preparing to wage a grim political battle to replace the council.

Frenzied counts were taken among the population by both sides, seeking to solidify their position. This placed many villagers in an awkward position. Some did not support Reverend Parris, but did not support the council either. They broke into a new and vocal grouping. As did those who supported Reverend Parris and supported the council on all but the Parris issue. As time passed, these four groups experienced altercations and reformed into still smaller, angry units.

Local politics degenerated into a bewildering maze for newcomers. The same people shifted into different alliances on different issues. Only the outcome of these passionate upheavals could be seen with any clarity.

Great political frustrations translated into bitter personal hatreds. Each group—and there were many—blamed another group for village problems and tensions. Each angry person within each angry group passionately desired changes and improvements they were not getting. Someone blocked the way; someone was at fault. But placing blame was a sly business. To acknowledge another group as having the power to cause all this misery and upset was to declare one's own group powerless. This, no one wished to admit. Thus frustrations and tempers built and built, with no acceptable outlet.

People turned on one another in rage. They might have their hands tied on the larger issues, but not the small ones. If a lifetime neighbor's fence encroached, one had the power and the duty to see it removed, stone by offending stone. If the neighbor dared point out the fence had stood as it was for thirty years, no matter. Remove it! And we'll see you in court if need be.

If babies died or livestock froze or crops failed, the disaster was too great for frustrated hearts to bear. It was bad enough to watch the community turn on itself like a ravening animal, but to believe God punished the villagers as well—that could not be borne. Something or someone else had to be at fault. And the ruined farmer looked desperately to his neighbors, wondering how they'd managed to kill his livestock or to blast his field—and why. And he lashed out in revenge.

Bristol's head spun with such stories; she'd heard them again and again since her return. The slightest offense was enough to create a lifelong enemy. The entire village fumed and smoldered.

Before sabbath services began, the Adams women visited Noah's grave, and Bristol grieved silently before a simple freestone marker, wondering what position Noah had taken in the village disruptions. How had his sensible practicality fit within the sparring groups?

Try as she might, Bristol couldn't summon a clear image of her father. When she stared at the mounded earth, isolated pictures flashed through her mind, but most came from distant childhood. She blinked and choked on a lump in her throat. Keenly, Bristol felt Noah's absence. She wished with every breath that she could make up for the worry and heartache she'd caused him. Wished with all her heart she might have pressed her face into that leathery neck and whispered, "I love you, Papa," just once.

Blinking hard, Bristol bent and placed a spray of bright autumn leaves below the gray stone. After a moment, she followed her mother into the meetinghouse.

Sliding into place beside Charity in the children's pew and waiting for Reverend Parris to begin the text, Bristol immediately noticed the deep quiet of the room. She remembered loud chatter and friendly greetings. Now the villagers held themselves in stiff silence, their cold faces toward the front, indifferent to who walked down the aisle or who filled the seat beside them. Uneasily Bristol smiled at Mary Warren and felt a pang of surprised hurt when Mary tossed her head and looked away, no trace of a smile on her lips.

"What's wrong with Mary?" Bristol whispered to Charity behind her hand.

Charity pulled her gaze from the men's side of the room and lifted a surprised brow. "Mary works for John Proctor—in his tavern. You know that. *We* don't have anything to do with the Ipswich Road people."

"*We* used to be friends with the Proctors and the Warrens," Bristol answered dryly.

Impatient, Charity frowned. "That was before."

"Before what?"

Charity's hands fluttered. "Oh, I don't know. Just before. Before everybody started fighting." Her eyes flicked to the men's side; then she leaned to whisper into Abigail Williams' ear. Abigail listened, giggled, and whispered into Ann Putnam Junior's ear. Ann smiled and whispered back.

Bristol sighed. It appeared she'd made an enemy of Mary Warren without even being here. The idea seemed so outrageous she was tempted to laugh. But she didn't.

Automatically Bristol's eyes strayed to the men's side, and she discovered herself looking for Caleb Wainwright. He wasn't among the men. The knowledge had no effect on Bristol one way or another. She felt neither disappointed by his absence nor happy to avoid a confrontation. Merely indifferent.

Covering a yawn, she wished the services would begin. Abigail Williams tossed herself about on the pew and whispered loudly, and Bristol decided a year and a half had done nothing to improve Abigail's disruptive temperament. She could understand why Hannah disapproved of the girl. A year and a half had, however, added greatly to Abigail's appearance. Her apron and long collar did nothing to hide a woman's figure blossoming beneath—and a bold challenge sparked her blue eyes, unusual in a twelve-year-old.

Watching the three girls, Bristol decided only Ann Putnam Junior looked as she had when Bristol sailed. Though the same age as Abigail, and though both were blond and blue-eyed, there the resemblance ended. Ann possessed the translucent face and eyes of a visionary; she had a look of permanent innocence. That quiet Ann could be so in the influence of impish Abigail Williams remained a mystery to Bristol. Perhaps Charity bridged the gap. It seemed to Bristol that Charity's diffidence aligned with Ann, and Charity's new-found resistance to authority would delight Abigail. Bristol shrugged; it was none of her affair.

Still, she was relieved when the service began and the girls settled into the pew. But her relief was of short duration. Quite simply, Reverend Parris' thunderous text frightened Bristol. He didn't preach, he ranted; he shouted and screamed and purpled in the face. Once Samuel Parris had preached that New England was the promised land, God's haven for his saints. But now Reverend Parris' promised land had drastically narrowed in scope. Perhaps God-fearing souls were safe within the walls of the meetinghouse (a far smaller area than all of New England), and then again, perhaps not. Evil stalked even the village meetinghouse and imperiled all within. And here the reverend's flushed face looked betrayed, angry, and puzzled that it could be so.

That it undeniably was so went unquestioned. According to Reverend Parris, Satan, in all his treacherous guises, could count a large portion of villagers as his own. Many, he shouted, had signed the dread book and now served Satan as their master instead of looking to the clergy for leadership. These disciples of evil tormented the good folk of the village, making lives miserable and wretched and filled with dissent.

The parishioners nodded emphatic agreement, and some leveled dark stares of accusation at one another. They knew as well as the preacher that servants of Satan lived within the village. Hadn't they suffered for it? No one was safe anymore. The only solace in an evil world was the safety of one's own hearth. It was a sorry time in the history of man when a person couldn't count himself safe from evil even within the house of God.

At the noon break, Bristol stumbled outside for a deep breath of cold fresh air. She felt bludgeoned and wary of the people around her. Which were the servants of Satan? Realizing what she'd just thought, Bristol gave herself an irritated shake. What was she thinking? She'd known these people all her life—they were good decent people. Not evildoers, or witches, or malicious imps, or plotters of some dire misfortune aimed at innocents.

Setting her mouth, Bristol strode firmly to Mary Warren and took her arm with a forced smile. "Hello, Mary."

Mary Warren drew back as if she'd been stung. But Bristol held to her arm. "What are you doing?" Mary gasped.

Bristol's voice pleaded. "Mary, we used to be friends!"

Mary shook off Bristol's hand. "No more," she snapped. "Your family are friends with the Wainwrights, and we don't speak to people who claim other people's pigs as their own." She started to turn aside, her face flushed and angry.

It was layer on layer of confusion. "Who, Mary? Did my family claim Warren pigs?" Bristol lifted a hand in a helpless gesture. "All the pigs root in the forest, it's easy to lose one . . . that doesn't necessarily mean someone stole it. But I'm sure Mama will make it right if such a thing did happen."

Mary hissed. "The *Wainwrights* took our pigs!" She nodded fiercely. "Mark my words, you'll rue the day your family took up with a Wainwright." She leaned and whispered into Bristol's dust cap, "If you want my opinion, I think old man Wainwright signed the devil's book before he died." Bristol gasped. "*They* didn't lose their harvest this year, but the Haversacks did!" Mary's eyes glittered triumphantly. "How do you explain that? The fields are side by side!" Having made her point, Mary flounced away.

Bristol stared after her. Had the whole community gone mad? Bristol looked around in disbelief. Instead of separating into two groups, one to the reverend's house, the other to Ingersoll's tavern, now families ate their lunch from hampers in their wagons, or beside the lane, or at a corner of the meetinghouse. A few families banded together, but most sat in isolated groups, eating quietly and ignoring the people around them. Bristol looked toward Hannah for guidance; she felt as if she stood on the moon, for all her knowledge of local custom and the welcome she felt.

Hannah marched firmly across the lane and into Ingersoll's tavern. Bristol and Charity followed. A wry smile played across Bristol's pink lips; apparently the Adamses turned their backs on the reverend's table, but at least they weren't yet reduced to eating their Sunday lunch from the back of a wagon.

The afternoon service was as black and frightening as the morning's had been. When Bristol reeled outside at its finish, she felt she wouldn't trust a neighbor to fish her from a pond if she were drowning. She struggled with these new attitudes, finding them repugnant and distasteful. Her eyes frowned toward Hannah talking in the doorway with Reverend Parris; she wished Hannah would hurry. Bristol wanted to go home.

She needed to think about what she'd seen and heard and try to regain a sensible perspective.

The moment Hannah climbed up on the wagon seat, Bristol flicked the reins and shouted to the horses. They rode in silence until the Adams gate came into view. Then Hannah swiveled to address both Charity in the straw behind and Bristol on the high seat. "Reverend Parris is coming by in about an hour. I want you both to see the parlor is dusted and made ready."

The girls nodded. Confused, Bristol glanced at Hannah. "Mama, wouldn't it have been easier to speak to the reverend at his house? While we were right there?" Bristol saw by Hannah's tight face that such a visit was out of the question.

"No," Hannah said shortly. She cast a meaningful glare toward Charity, quiet behind them. "I won't set foot in a house that shelters Abigail Williams! Skipping! Mark my word, that girl's no good!" Hannah sniffed. "Besides, that Tituba person makes me nervous. It's not natural the way all the young girls flock to that woman!"

Bristol started. She hadn't thought of Tituba in more than a year. ". . . and the one who is not, shall stand in dark flames. . . ." Bristol's skin rippled in a sudden chill. Perhaps Hannah was correct; there was something odd, something not right about Tituba.

Bristol smiled slightly as she turned the horses toward the barn. Now she was doing it. Harboring dark suspicions on the flimsiest of evidence. Whatever side one took on the Reverend Parris issue, Bristol gave him grudging credit for an improved sermon deliverance. She didn't recall ever leaving Sunday meeting with a single memory of what had been said. Yet today Bristol felt she could quote the reverend verbatim. His text and sermon had left her deeply shaken.

Later, watching the reverend settle into a stiff, seldom-used chair in the Adams parlor, Bristol realized Reverend Parris was a disturbed man. He'd lost weight, and while the pompous superiority would never fade from his features, it appeared diminished. He had the air of a man who has tried and failed and can not fathom what went wrong.

Samuel Parris had arrived in Salem Village expecting to assume spiritual and community leadership, only to discover half the population did not want him there at all, and the half that did had approached nearly every available minister in New England before reluctantly settling for Samuel Parris. When the respect and leadership Samuel Parris had expected were not forthcoming, he had demanded it . . . and then his troubles began in earnest. His battle to assume his rightful place, to walk in the gentle glow of God's approval, had been lost inch by painful inch. Until now he was reduced to begging for his salary and stepping among people who met his gaze with flinty eyes. Like those of Hannah Adams, who reminded him his troubles extended even into his own household. Naturally he'd punished his niece Abigail and his daughter Betty for the skipping episode. But the punishment had not been satisfactory. Both girls exhibited a peculiar relief rather than penance, causing him to wonder what crimes they hid in addition to the skipping.

Samuel Parris agonized inside. How many supporters the skipping incident had cost, he couldn't guess. He spent hours contemplating the problem, for Samuel Parris had a mind for petty concerns—the larger issues, he scarcely saw. The disintegration of Salem Village was occurring before his eyes, and he did not see it. What he saw was that people like Hannah Adams no longer extended their support; and this, Samuel Parris considered an abominable unfairness, as that chit Charity Adams had been skipping right along with Abigail and Betty and the others.

He sighed, seeing again the taloned claw of Satan behind this matter. Gradually the reverend had come to understand that Satan and Samuel Parris engaged in hand-to-claw battle, both on issues of personal concern and in the matter of village souls. A battle it seemed no one appreciated but himself.

He blinked and tugged his thoughts to the Adams parlor and the business at hand. Here, at least, he entered into a mission of trust and importance. His chest puffed, straining the cloth of his waistcoat.

"As you know," he began, looking soberly at Hannah, "it was my privilege to guide Noah Adams through the last dark days and assist him home."

"Aye," Hannah answered sourly, her expression leaving an abyss of doubt as to the reverend's helpfulness. Even Charity grimaced and turned a pale freckled face toward the plank floor.

Samuel Parris frowned at the three women. He directed his gaze to Bristol, who watched him with a careful measuring stare. Bold chit! "Before Noah passed to his reward, he entrusted me with letters to you each." Now he had their full attention, he noticed with a grim smile. He seized the advantage, delivering a mini-sermon on the values of trusting one's minister. And paying his salary.

"Give me the letters," Hannah interrupted, extending her hand.

Reverend Parris drew himself up and shot her a reproving glare; then he gave it up. Slowly he withdrew three packets from his coat. He tapped them against his palm. "I need tell you I am privy to the information in these letters." He paused; allowing them time to realize Noah had shown the respect of confiding in his spiritual leader. "And I am prepared to discuss a certain issue and initiate immediate action." Reluctantly Samuel Parris relinquished the letters. Then he settled back and waited as each woman broke a seal and began to read.

Bristol's fingers trembled as she opened the thick sheaf of papers and smoothed them on her lap. That her father had expended his last strength to pen his thoughts to them touched her deeply. More than ever, a sore heart wished she had arrived home in time, wished she might have held his hand and been with him. Bristol focused on the first page, and Noah's voice spoke to her.

Daughter,
As ye can see by this scrawl, it doesn't go well for me. William Griggs, who admits he's lost more patients than he's healed, doesn't give me much hope or time. And I'm not prepared to die until the loose ends are tied. Bristol, girl, I was wrong to send ye away. I've pondered it in life and on my deathbed, and I've seen the error of my thinking. I misinterpreted the providences regarding ye, and for this I have tormented myself and ye. I beg yer pardon. All the providences pointed ye toward Caleb Wainwright. I see this clearly. And from the wisdom of my deathbed, I wish to put it right.

Bristol swallowed and closed brimming eyes. The papers shook in her fingers. She sensed it would be best to fold the sheets and not read on. But of course she couldn't do that.

Young Wainwright has made a point of honor to call here at least once a month during the entirety of yer exile. I confess to my shame that I received the lad coldly and threw him off the Adams property when first he showed his face. But in the last six months I have come to see Wainwright's value and to appreciate his dogged tenacity. I now see that only my foolish pride has stayed my hand from calling ye home. In death I give ye what

I denied ye in life: it is yer father's dying wish, made from the sanctity of his deathbed and witnessed by none other than an ordained minister of our Lord, that ye, Bristol Ellen Adams, wed Caleb Wainwright.

Stunned, Bristol blinked and stared at the words. She rubbed her temples and met the affirming nod of Samuel Parris. This wasn't possible, she thought wildly. Deathbed wishes were serious, binding events; to refuse was nearly unthinkable. But . . . dear God! She returned her eyes to the pages, shaking her head to focus on the heavy scrawl.

Young Wainwright showed the sense not to discuss ye on his visits. But I have now talked a marriage with him, and he do give his word. The lad admits he's been waiting for ye to return. He confesses he feels morally bound to ye until ye either wed him or release his obligation.

Bristol understood her father would have interpreted Caleb's statement to refer to the whipping. But in her heart, Bristol knew Caleb's reference was to the settler's cabin and what happened there so long ago. In another lifetime. A sense of unreality numbed her mind.

Wainwright further agrees to see to the welfare of yer mother and sister when ye are wed. I'd not like to see Hannah wed again and put a man free on the acres I gave my legs and life for. But I know she can not work the fields herself. I am advising yer mother to sell my farm, but the coins won't last forever. I go to my reward content that yer mother won't be forced door to door on the dole like that nasty-tempered ingrate Sarah Good. Hannah and yer sister will have a roof and a full belly with ye and Wainwright.

Bristol's dazed eyes lifted to Hannah and Charity, both bent over their own letters. Tears slid down Hannah's wrinkled cheeks, and Charity's face was pale as chalk, her freckles standing in sharp relief. Bristol drew a shuddering breath. Not only had her own future been arranged, but she was now responsible for the care of Hannah and Charity as well. Their future was linked to her own, and all of them depended on Caleb Wainwright. She lifted the letter toward a candle for more light, and read on.

Do not think I soften out of humility brought about by my coming death. I do not hand ye yer dearest desire from a need to leave this world on good terms with ye. That is a truth, aye, but more, I impress on ye that I see the match between ye and Wainwright as God's will, hitherto misinterpreted by his humble servant Noah Bains Adams. This marriage be God's will, and the last dying wish from the deathbed of yer loving father.

The letter continued, filled with fond memories and a stiff attempt to express love by a man awkward with expressions of verbal affection. Bristol read the first half again, hoping she'd dreamed her father's last wishes. She had not. The second reading was as clear as the first.

Reverend Parris cleared his throat discreetly, and Bristol started. They all watched her. "Are you prepared to discuss the arrangements?" Samuel Parris asked.

"Mama, do you know what is in my letter?" Bristol's voice emerged in a strangled whisper.

Hannah mopped her streaming eyes. "Aye," she answered quietly. Tenderly she folded her own letter and slid it into her apron pocket. "I hold no objection; it was your father's wish."

Charity sat like white stone, her eyes blank and fixed in space. Alarmed, Bristol wondered what might have been in Charity's letter to produce such a stricken expression. Then her mind returned to the coming hurricane of events.

Reverend Parris rubbed his palms together, assuming an air of brisk efficiency and usefulness. "The first banns will be read at Thursday town meeting, and I'll order a notice for the publishing post." No question existed but that the wedding would occur. "I've taken the liberty of scheduling the services of a magistrate for November 1." He stood, his mission completed. "I would be pleased to attend a wedding party and extend my blessings," he added hopefully.

Bristol watched, her mouth opening, then pressing into a distressed line. Everything was happening so fast! One moment she was free to contemplate her life at leisure; then, in a stroke, her future had been carved in granite. All arranged and neatly complete. With difficulty she centered her eyes on Samuel Parris. "Mr. Parris, wait!" Her hands rose and fell. "I . . . Will you be seeing Caleb? I mean, before the first banns are read out?"

Affronted, Reverend Parris sniffed. "Of course, Mistress

Adams, I needn't be reminded of my duty. The young man will be duly informed."

"Would you ask Caleb to call here immediately . . . before the banns are read? I would appreciate it if you would deliver that message." Her thoughts spun in wide arcs. "I . . . we . . . there are matters to discuss," she finished lamely.

Reverend Parris drew himself to a frosty height. "It is my duty and my obligation to render what assistance I can to my flock." Grandly he swept from the house.

For a moment a heavy silence stifled the parlor. Then Bristol's despairing eyes swung toward her mother. "Oh, Mama, I'm to be wed!"

Charity toppled from her chair in a faint.

26

ODDLY, no one had asked for a detailed accounting of Bristol's stay in London. At first she felt an outpouring of relief; English pleasures were New England sins. Then Bristol experienced a mild sense of surprise, and finally disappointment. Many times she would have enjoyed remembering Aunt Pru and Uncle Robert aloud. Jean Pierre she didn't allow herself to think about.

This lack of interest baffled Bristol immediately following her return; then gradually she understood the villagers could not turn aside from their own urgent problems long enough to examine the concerns of others.

Therefore Bristol felt no real surprise when Caleb's questions were as shallow as the rest had been.

"Did you visit the Tower of London?" he inquired politely.

"Aye." It was all the answer required; he didn't probe for further elucidation.

They sat facing each other in the Adams parlor, both stiff and uncomfortable. Whenever Bristol glanced at Caleb Wainwright, she thought of the Duke of Easton. But Charles Easton would have turned up his aristocratic nose at the leather coat and breeches Caleb wore. And she noticed Caleb's sandy hair was thicker and longer than Charles's, more unruly. Also she remembered Charles Easton as shorter and less muscular than the man sitting across from her. But the resemblance was startling nonetheless. Bristol sighed. Thinking of Charles and how he'd bored her, then drawing parallels with Caleb— it was not a good beginning.

She slid a look toward Caleb from beneath her long lashes and tried to approach this first meeting from another angle. Instead of comparing him to Charles, she compared him to the Caleb she remembered. And decided this was not the same man she'd left behind.

The simple, open features Bristol recalled had matured into an honest strength. A man had emerged from the clay of young adulthood. Though Caleb clearly felt ill-at-ease, he didn't shrink from the conversation as he might once have done; he sat in his chair with the expression of one determined to see an awkward business through.

"Did you see London Bridge?" he asked next. Pond-blue eyes touched her face, then moved away, and Bristol realized he saw changes in her as well.

"Aye," she answered, impatient with this inane exchange. She wondered if he would ask about every London landmark he'd heard of. Nervously Bristol smoothed her skirt and waited for his next question. Today she'd chosen a white blouse with billowing sleeves. A dove-colored bodice ended in twin points above a skirt the shade of rich brown earth. She pushed a glossy wisp of red hair beneath her dust cap and wondered for the hundredth time if she should have chosen a plain cap instead of the frilled one.

Silence filled the uncomfortably chill parlor, and both studied their hands. Then they both spoke at the same moment.

"I think we . . ."

"There's something . . ."

Caleb smiled, the first time he'd done so since arriving, and Bristol felt a little better. Returning his smile, she lifted a hand and deferred to him. "You first."

Instantly his strong square face sobered. Unable to remain seated, he stood and approached the window, judging a light dusting of fresh snow with a farmer's eye for moisture. He turned then and met her eyes directly. "You know of course that Noah desired us to wed."

341

"Aye. But, Caleb, there are things I think you should know . . ."

He lifted a large work-hardened hand. "In a moment, Bristol. First, it's important that you understand how I feel." Gazing toward the frozen mud in the lane, he gathered his thoughts. "I am willing to wed you. I gave my promise long ago, and I"—a flush of red lay heavy on his neck—"I ruined you for marriage to anyone else. My responsibility is clear."

Bristol's cheeks flamed, and she clutched her hands in her lap. Listening, she heard nothing tentative in this new Caleb. Hints of strength in the boy had hardened in the man.

"It's our duty to marry. This length of absence brings changes; I'm not what I was, nor, I suspect, are you." He studied her from the corner of his eye, seeing a glint of sorrow in her green eyes, a new womanly confidence in her posture. "Some of the changes, we can see. Others will appear as we . . . as we live together on a daily basis. It's important you understand that I accept whatever changes there may be. I'm prepared to wed and provide you and your family a decent home."

Bristol lifted her eyes. "Before you make further commitment, Caleb, there are . . . things you should know." She intended to tell him about Jean Pierre and the baby. Whether to tell him she still loved Jean Pierre, she hadn't yet decided upon. Bristol drew a breath. "There is a man in—"

Caleb cut into her words. "Bristol . . . no." He returned to his chair and leaned forward, hands on knees. Serious blue eyes probed hers. "A year and a half is a long time. I know things happened to you. You may even have felt strongly toward . . . toward someone. But you came home. And if you're willing, we'll wed. I believe if our marriage is to have any hope of success, we must put the past behind us. Our lives begin now. Here today. Whatever happened before this minute is not important, not anymore. Talking about the past will only pain us both."

Dropping her gaze, Bristol stared into her lap. Instinctively she sensed the wisdom in what Caleb suggested. What good would it do to talk of pirates and beatings? What good would it do him to know another man had held her, another man's seed had grown for a brief time in her body? He was right. Such knowledge could only pain them.

"Bristol, I'll never ask you about anyone else. I don't want to know." He looked away, and his jaw knotted. "And I don't want you to ask me."

Surprised, Bristol lifted her head. It hadn't occurred to her

342

that Caleb too might harbor ghosts. He'd returned to the window, and she couldn't see his expression.

When he turned, his face was composed. "Is that agreed?"

Bristol nodded slowly. "Aye," she murmured. "Caleb . . . I . . ." Bristol swallowed, wondering how best to phrase this. "You're right. People change. Things happened, and . . . and I'm not the foolish young girl I was. And you aren't . . ." She stopped and drew another deep breath. "What I'm trying to say is that the new people we both are shouldn't be held to the promises of the children we were. What happened that day in the settler's cabin . . . it isn't enough to build a life upon. You owe me nothing."

He stared at her, shocked.

Bristol's hands fluttered, and her eyes begged for understanding. "We're different people now. I know you don't wish to discuss the time between, and I'll respect that. But, Caleb, that time did pass, things did happen, and they left a mark on us both. We aren't the children of the settler's cabin, we're adults now." She stopped. Reading the appalled censure in his eyes, she knew she hadn't reached him.

"Bristol," he said in a low tone, "you have changed in ways I wouldn't have believed possible."

"That's exactly my point," she said helplessly.

"Listen carefully. Though your attitudes may have altered, for whatever reason, attitudes in this community have not." He continued to stare. "Honor and duty are still revered here. Responsibility and obligation aren't taken lightly. They remain the measuring sticks by which a man judges his life. The settler's cabin *did* happen. And I am responsible. I know my duty. This is—"

"Caleb, I seduced you."

His cool gaze didn't flicker or move from her face. "I am responsible," he repeated. "In addition, this marriage is Noah Adams' dying wish. A man's last wish merits respect, and I gave Noah my word. Finally, there is the common good."

Bristol blinked. "The common good?" she asked weakly.

Again he stared. "Aye. Of course. What if everyone behaved as we did?" His sturdy cheeks pinked. "Then refused to accept responsibility for their passions. How long do you imagine this village would remain a decent and godly place to live? What sort of community are we building here if a man turns his back on his duties and obligations?"

Bristol suggested no answers; she had none. Except . . . in her heart she knew this marriage was wrong; they were miles

343

apart in viewpoint. But for Caleb, not to marry would be a worse wrong.

She remained in the cold parlor long after Caleb's horse passed through the gate. It was settled, then. They would marry. And neither had mentioned the word love.

Slowly Bristol's thoughts moved backward, and her fingers rose to touch the gold chain beneath her blouse. Her emerald eyes dulled. She mourned Jean Pierre La Crosse. Now she let herself remember, allowed a brutal craving to tear at her heart. And when she'd recalled every whisper, every caress, she felt drained and empty. And filled with longing for him. Let go, she admonished herself. Let go and get on with the business of building a life.

And how better than to marry Caleb Wainwright? Staring at the window, now dark, she listed the reasons why she should marry Caleb. First, it would help her forget Jean Pierre—at least she prayed it would. Marriage provided a direction to her floundering life. It was her father's last wish. The union would guarantee Hannah and Charity a home.

Against these reasons lay a desire not to be pushed into a new life. An inability to ignore her love for Jean Pierre and a lack of feeling for Caleb Wainwright, plus a nagging worry that something simmered just below the surface which she could not see, concerned Bristol greatly. If she could discover a valid reason to defy her father's last wish and escape the marriage to Caleb, Bristol knew she'd seize it eagerly. She examined her thoughts again and found no loopholes.

Face blank, she unclasped Jean Pierre's gold chain. It piled heavy in her palm, catching what light remained in the room. Bristol stared at the gold links for a long moment, remembering; then she dropped to her knees and carefully pushed the fine chain through a wide crack in the planking. Her fingers shook, and her shoulders dropped. In time, maybe she could forget; maybe she could feel an affection for Caleb Wainwright. Her sore heart did not believe it.

Later, Hannah asked, "Did you work out the details?" She placed a trencher of venison stew before Bristol and Charity, then took her place at the table after a long squinting glance at Noah's empty seat.

"Aye," Bristol answered listlessly. She had no enthusiasm for discussing her conversation with Caleb.

"Did he mention his house?"

Bristol spooned a chunk of venison. "No. He didn't."

Hannah blinked in surprise. "Caleb built the third-largest

344

house in the village. And he has two bond servants. You're catching a well-to-do husband, missy!"

Charity choked on an odd sound and pushed from the table. "Excuse me, Mama, I don't feel well." She fled into the bedroom and slammed the door.

Hannah squinted and shook her head. "I don't know what's gnawing at Charity. Lately she's been . . ." At a loss for words, Hannah waved her spoon.

They ate in silence. Bristol swallowed automatically, and her eyes returned time and again to the closed bedroom door. For several days, since the reading of the letters, Charity had barricaded herself in the bedroom when she wasn't needed for chores. She'd dismissed the fainting incident by saying she didn't feel well, and in truth she looked ill. But Bristol had an uneasy feeling there was more to it.

She continued to be bewildered by the changes in Charity. That her sister was unhappy could be seen by anyone, but Charity withdrew into a wall of distant silence and refused any attempts at real conversation.

Bristol tore a piece of bread and turned the problem in her mind. Something must have happened during her absence to produce Charity's marked character change. But what? Charity, meek, sweet Charity, had been content and even happy when Bristol left for England. Bristol clearly recalled seeing Charity's face shine with happiness not a week before she sailed.

Her spoon clattered and dropped to the floor. Caleb! Bristol had given Caleb to Charity! Was that it? What had resulted from those few minutes of foolish conversation?

Troubled green eyes stared at Hannah. "Mama . . . when Caleb visited here, what did he do?"

Hannah shrugged and watched Bristol retrieve her spoon. "I don't recall. Talk mostly. Crops, livestock, rain. The usual things."

Bristol leaned forward. "Mama, did Charity talk with Caleb? Alone?"

"Well, of course. Charity was a great help—this was before she went hard to handle. She'd sit for hours with Caleb and make conversation until Noah came. Caleb always seemed to arrive when Noah was busy."

Bristol stared at her trencher. Aye. It could be. She peered into Hannah's puzzled frown. "Mama, think carefully. Could there be . . . an affection between Caleb and Charity?"

"Aye, I'm sure they like . . ." Hannah's squint widened as she understood. "No! Absolutely not." She stared at Bristol.

345

"No," she repeated more slowly. "I believe I'd have noticed if there were. No."

Bristol wasn't convinced. Later, when she crawled into bed next to Charity, her mind continued to worry disturbing possibilities. Charity's erratic behavior would be explained if . . .

"Charity?" Bristol looked sadly at the carroty curls spread across the pillow next to her own. "Charity, are you asleep?"

"I'm not now," Charity's muffled voice sighed.

Bristol lifted on an elbow and gently touched her sister's shoulder. "Charity, could we have a talk? A real talk?" Charity didn't respond. "We used to share things. Can't we be friends again?" Bristol heard the bewilderment in her own voice.

Charity hesitated, then rolled to face Bristol. "What do you want to talk about?" she asked cautiously. The timidity once marking Charity's speech was gone, replaced by a new sullen tone as alien to Charity as a second nose would have been.

But this was a beginning. Bristol snuggled beneath the quilt and peered into Charity's face, so pinched and miserable. "I want to talk to you about Caleb." Charity's face tightened, and she started to roll away. "Wait! Charity, listen! Please listen!" Bristol found Charity's hand under the quilts and hung on. "I think maybe there's something between you and Caleb. And if that's true, then I won't marry him!" Charity froze, her face blank, her pale eyes staring. "Charity, I know what it's like to love and be frustrated in that love. I . . ." Bristol pleaded, "Charity, please! Talk to me!"

A variety of emotions flicked across Charity's face. Surprise, hope, suspicion, elation, disbelief. And finally despair. An angry despair. "Are you giving Caleb to me again, Bristol?" she spit. " 'Here, Charity, you can have him until I'm ready to take him back.' Is that it, Bristol? You want more time? Do you want to make him suffer before you settle for him?"

Appalled, Bristol drew back. It was like watching a lovable kitten turn into a snarling tiger. "You don't understand. I only want what's right for—"

"Oh, I understand, all right. Caleb makes do with me until he learns you're coming home. Then he vanishes. Vanishes! And I . . ." Her voice broke on a sob.

"Charity, please listen! Something happened long ago, and because of it Caleb believes he has to marry me. He has to! His honor won't let him tell you the reason, but we can work this out, if . . ." Bristol saw Charity wasn't accepting what she said. "If you want him," she finished lamely.

"The reason? Oh, aye, I know the reason." Charity's voice rose on an ugly sound. "Can you 'work out' Papa's death wish? Can you 'work out' the expression in Caleb's eyes when he heard you were coming home? Can you?" She sat up in bed, her thin body shaking.

Bristol wrung her hands. "Charity, I'm sure you misinterpreted Caleb's expression."

"Now you're telling me what I saw!" Charity sneered. "Well, I don't want any more of your generosity, and I don't want Caleb Wainwright!" Bristol gasped at the expression in Charity's eyes. "All my life I've taken your castoffs! I got the clothes you'd outgrown, the shoes that no longer fit you. I took the caps and collars and aprons and vests you grew tired of! And I even took Caleb when you cast him off!"

Bristol stared in shock. She'd had no idea Charity felt like this.

"Well, dear sister, you can't cast off Caleb this time!" Charity's taunting voice rose between a sob and a shout. "Even if you wanted it and I wanted it and . . . The fact is, you cannot!"

"Charity, I—"

"By now every person in Salem Village knows what was in our letters. Do you think any of them would look at us again if we ignored Papa's death wish? We'd be silenced! No one would talk to us! And could I live with myself or you with yourself if Papa's last wish was ignored? No! So don't tell me it can be worked out. It can't, and you know it!"

"Charity, please . . ."

Charity's reedy voice broke. "And Caleb!" she whispered, her glassy green eyes staring from hollows. "Caleb is willing."

Bristol's tone was desperate. "Charity, Caleb thinks he *has* to marry me! That's why he's willing. He doesn't understand there's a choice! Before I left, he and I—"

"Stop!" Charity hissed. "Just stop! *Caleb is willing!*" Her pale eyes swam with hurt and betrayal. "Don't you see what that means?" Her teeth bared and she trembled with emotion. "Just leave me alone!"

"Charity . . ."

"*Alone!*"

Bristol stared at the betrayed passion in her sister's eyes, and her heart felt as if someone had wrung it. Had she once imagined Charity lacked spirit? How wrong she'd been!

Bristol slid from the quilts and quietly moved her things into Hannah's room. Hannah blinked up from her pillow in surprise, then shifted to make room, and her faded eyes filled with gratitude. It was lonely in Hannah's bed. She patted Bristol's hand and rolled over, sleeping better than she had in weeks.

Bristol, however, could not sleep. She lay for hours listening to the silent house. And thought of the tangled emotions in these small rooms. She'd been wrong to think her problems would end if only she came home. Coming home had opened new problems. And she foresaw more along the path providence had decreed for her.

Bristol Ellen Adams and Caleb Jonathan Wainwright were married November 1, 1691.

Caleb drove them over the snow-rutted roads to Salem Town, where a self-important magistrate pronounced the words making them man and wife. No rings were exchanged, no kiss shared. Silently they rode back to the Adams house, where Hannah had prepared a wedding feast for a small knot of well-wishers.

"There would have been a larger group," Hannah assured Bristol anxiously, "but so many are fighting . . ." She ran a hand over her graying chestnut hair. "We were lucky to find this many willing to share the same house with each other."

"It doesn't matter, Mama. I don't care," Bristol answered truthfully. She smiled and nodded automatically, walking through best wishes and political discussions and gossip like a person sleepwalking. Nothing seemed real. Any minute she'd wake in the pink bed at Hathaway House and discover this was all a dream. Her green eyes settled on Caleb, standing across the kitchen frowning at Reverend Parris. He was a stranger. Fighting a sense of panic, Bristol realized she'd married a stranger.

Caleb Wainwright had never danced or held cards in his large hands. He'd never read anything but the Bible and Baxter's *Call to the Unconverted*. Caleb had never stood on the rolling deck of a sailing ship or traveled farther than Boston. He saw no reason to do either. He didn't hunt for sport or waste time on picnics, parties, or idle pleasure. The concept of pleasure for its own sake baffled him. He'd never attended a theater performance and would have been appalled to realize he knew someone who had. Work was Caleb's life.

Everything Bristol had learned to enjoy would have shocked her new husband. His grim confidence would have evaporated in a flash had he suspected how unappealing his world was to his new bride.

Neither displayed any urgency to begin their new life together. They lingered until the guests covered yawns and wondered aloud how late it was. Until Hannah's rum punch dwindled to levels no hostess liked to see. Until Reverend Parris tactfully drew the bridegroom aside and whispered in his ear.

Only then did the newlyweds reluctantly move toward the door.

"Mama . . ." Bristol clung to Hannah, not wanting to leave the home where she'd grown up. Not wanting to be alone with Caleb.

Hannah absently patted Bristol's shoulder, watching a scramble for cloaks and hoods from the corner of her eyes. She looked tired. "Can you manage for Caleb and the hired hands until Charity and I arrive?" she asked, returning to Bristol with practical matters.

Bristol remembered cooking for a roomful of pub regulars. "Aye, Mama, I can manage."

Already Hannah had an offer for Noah's farm, and she and Charity would join the Wainwrights as soon as the Adams house was packed. They were all beginning a new life.

A life Bristol felt distinctly uneasy about. Sitting beside Caleb on the high wagon seat, she pictured the rooms she'd just left, the rooms she'd loved from her birth. Bristol blinked and sat a little straighter. She suddenly realized Charity hadn't offered best wishes. As small as the Adams house was, Charity had managed to keep a group of people between the newlyweds and herself. The irony of the situation struck Bristol like a blow. Once she too had hidden in corners putting space between herself and the man she loved.

Looking up at the night sky, Bristol watched flakes of quiet snow dance out of the darkness. Somewhere up there, she imagined an indifferent God yawning. The older she got, the more difficult it became to believe God really cared for individual destiny. Heresy crept through Bristol's mind. What if God did *not* plot each person's life in advance? What if the providences pointing lives along certain roads . . . what if they were but figments of vivid human imaginings? What if the tangles of the human heart were not God's plan, but simply the result of frail humanity struggling alone? Staying doggedly on an imagined pathway long after reason demanded differently.

It would be a colossal jest on mankind. Bristol's lips curved in a near-hysterical smile. What an enormous joke if she, Goodwife Wainwright, sat here as a result of Noah misinterpreting a providence that didn't exist. Her eyes sparkled with unshed tears. What a gigantic mockery. All the lives, all the . . .

"Are you warm enough?" Caleb's low voice startled her. "We're almost there."

"Aye." Bristol shivered beneath the lap robe, but she didn't complain. She'd never again complain about cold.

Caleb drew a frosty breath and began speaking. "We're passing Wainwright fields now." He waved toward the flat darkness on both sides of the wagon ruts. "I guess you know Pa died while you were away, so there's more land than you know about. All this is . . . ours." Caleb continued to speak, his tone warming with enthusiasm as he talked of his fields, his barns, the house he'd built, the plans he held for expansion. As he talked, Bristol began to realize the full extent of his holdings. And to understand why he would have been foolish to relinquish his inheritance as she'd asked of him that long-ago day. Her face flamed with ancient embarrassment. She'd been selfish and unreasonable and so young. Tonight she felt a million years older than that girl.

Caleb guided the horses past a split-rail fence and down a narrow lane to a large house surrounded by numerous outbuildings.

He carried her trunk into the kitchen and adjusted an oil lamp. After a brief tour he asked, "Do you like it?" and Bristol heard his pride and the hesitant appeal for her approval.

"Aye," she answered sincerely. The house was three times the size of the Adams house. The parlor, though not yet furnished, was large and heated by a coal stove. The kitchen wasn't as organized as it would be, but it was of generous size and had two large windows. The buttery was well-stocked and large. More than enough space had been provided in a wing off the kitchen for spinning wheel and loom and churns and storage bins and worktable and all the sundry items needed to run a home smoothly and self-sufficiently.

Three bedrooms lay behind the kitchen, drawing heat from the chimney housing. Hannah and Charity could each have their own room until the children started to come. Bristol's mind jerked from that thought with a spasm of pain.

Slowly she followed Caleb into a bedroom slightly larger than the others. He pushed her trunk against a long blank wall and straightened. Their eyes met and slid away.

Nervously Bristol toyed with the string of her hood. She'd dreaded this moment from the instant she finished reading Noah's letter.

Caleb drew a breath, and she noticed he was slightly

drunk. His words slurred. Staring at her with a moody expression, he whispered hoarsely, "Dammit, Bristol, this is our wedding night."

"Aye." Her mouth worked, but no sound emerged. She cleared her throat.

He waited, but when Bristol didn't move, he pulled off his clothes and dropped them in a pile. When she lifted her pink face, Caleb was in the bed, his smooth naked chest showing above the quilts in the light of an oil lamp. His brooding eyes almost accused, watching her from an expressionless face.

Haltingly, moving with wooden steps, Bristol turned her back and quickly undressed, feeling his eyes on her, feeling shame heat her cheeks. If God was merciful, the ground would open up and swallow her. If Bristol Adams' peace of mind counted for anything in the scheme of things, God wouldn't let this happen. So strongly was she wedded to Jean Pierre in her mind, that crawling into that bed was a sin of greatest magnitude, an adultery, a hideous betrayal.

"Turn around," Caleb whispered in a husky, blurred voice.

Heart aching, she did as he demanded. Her hands moved to cover her nakedness and failed.

Caleb stared and wet his lips. "I never saw a naked woman," he said, his breath coming faster. "You . . . you're beautiful!" His whisper turned to a croak. Wide blue eyes swept over her body, hungering at the pale-rose-and-cream breasts, pausing to wonder at the red wedge between her shivering legs. Desire colored his eyes opaque.

Bristol saw, and she shuddered. Caleb didn't see Bristol Adams Wainwright; he saw woman. A naked stranger. A vessel to relieve a man's urges. Suddenly Cutter Rumm leaped into her thoughts, and Bristol's mouth twisted in revulsion.

Caleb tossed back the quilts and reached for Bristol's hand, pulling her into the bed. She looked down at him, jolted by the smooth hairless body that was not Jean Pierre. Repelled by rough exploring hands that belonged to a man she didn't know. She turned her face aside, away from the rum-scented lips that moved over her mouth with blind passion.

She stared into Caleb's face as he lifted over her, searching for something familiar. There was nothing. Groans exploded in her ear; then he pushed hard into her unresponsive flesh. Once, twice, then large hands clamped on her shoulders and he cried out.

In less than three minutes it was over.

When Bristol heard the even rise and fall of his breath, she crept into the icy room and found her nightgown. She couldn't bear to wake naked beside him. Then she eased onto the bed and rolled to the edge. Eyes stinging, Bristol stared into the darkness.

If only she'd never known the touch of a man skilled in love . . . if only she could somehow bury her memories. If only she could endure the emptiness she suspected was in store. If only.

This was a terrible mistake. Lying rigid in the cold night beside her new husband, Bristol understood she should never have returned to Salem Village. Half a life was a thousand times better than no life at all. She'd thrown away a great love, and married a man she could never love.

Never again would she run to a door with joy shining in her eyes. Never again would her heart pound at the sound of a man's thickening whisper. Never again would she experience a woman's ecstasy.

She'd been a blind fool.

"Oh, Jean Pierre." Her mournful whisper cracked with the agony of a broken heart.

27

NEW Year's Day dawned cold and clear. An ideal day for sleigh rides and rosy cheeks and laughter. A day to sled in the lanes, listening to iron runners squeak across the fresh snow pack. A day for visiting and wishing friends and neighbors a prosperous 1692.

But few Salem Villagers left their houses.

Martha and Giles Cory would have welcomed visitors to break the tedium of each other's company. Giles repaired harness and Martha read most of the long day. Occasionally Martha lectured Giles on how he might improve himself and strive toward the perfection she herself had achieved. Giles ignored her. He was too old to mend his ways. He didn't bother telling Martha to shut up; he knew she wouldn't. Martha believed it her purpose in life to reform all who came within reach of her tongue. Giles considered this damned annoying. The rest of the village considered it meddlesome and outrageous. Few visitors called at the Cory house in the best of times.

In Ipswich Road, John Proctor hung a "Closed" sign on his tavern door and sat in the pub room before a small fire. He thought about his wife. Elizabeth displayed every sign of being infected with the village madness. She'd nailed a horseshoe over the tavern door, and John wouldn't be surprised if she'd buried an iron knife in front of the steps. She'd allowed Reverend Parris' sermons to frighten her out of her wits. John went over the bitter argument he and Elizabeth had had last night. John Proctor did not believe in horseshoes or iron knives or garlic in the windows or the Lord's Prayer written in one's shoe. He didn't believe any of these precautions would deter Reverend Parris' witches and demons, because John Proctor did not believe in the existence of such things. Evil existed, aye, but it wasn't anything supernatural. Generations to come would look back at the New England colonies and smile at the quaint superstitions their ancestors had lived by. John believed this implicitly. Witches tearing a community to fragments? Witches blasting fields and souring milk? Murdering babies and leveling curses? Ha! John Proctor stared into the fire. He thought his was a lone voice. He recalled the witch conversations he'd overheard in his tavern. John Proctor was a worried man.

Three miles farther along Ipswich Road, Bridget Oliver Bishop had also closed both of her taverns. The only holiday business she might have expected were the young men of the village sneaking in to play the forbidden shuffleboard. Bridget allowed the game because the young men bought drinks while they played. That the villagers hated her for contributing to the corruption of youth bothered Bridget Bishop not at all. She leaned over a table, her sensual face set in concentration, and she pushed goat's hair and hog bristles into the poppet she was making. Then Bridget took up bits of cloth she'd carefully gathered and fashioned tiny garments for the doll. No, Bridget didn't care what people thought. But when certain men lusted after her, then snubbed her when their wives appeared—that made Bridget angry. Very angry. She muttered a few words and smiled at the poppet. Then Bridget Bishop drove a sharp silver pin through its leg.

Sarah Good was scarcely aware it was New Year's Day.

All the days were dismally alike to her. She led her five-year-old daughter, Dorcas, up the ladder into old Goody Osburn's hayloft, and she buried Dorcas and herself in warm straw. It was bitter cold in the barn, but better than being out in the snow. Sarah unwrapped a piece of cloth containing a slice of mince pie and two meaty venison bones. A savage frown turned her face ugly. The old bitch could have given more; it wouldn't have killed her! Sarah felt a surge of hatred. She hated all the people that gave her charity. Once she'd had as much as anyone; once Sarah Good had been as fine a woman as any of the high-and-mighty bitches in this village. But when you marry, you climb into a man's cart; if his cart rises up the hill, you do too; but if it slides downhill, the road falls out from under you. And you're reduced to begging door to door for food and shelter. Well, she had her pride. Sarah might beg, but she wouldn't bow her head, she'd never grovel. Sarah gave Dorcas a venison bone. Dorcas worried her. The little girl was pathetically eager to please, desperately anxious for approval. Sarah didn't give a damn for approval and made no effort to please. If she wanted to please, she'd leave Salem Village; she knew all the sanctimonious bitches wanted her to. The good ladies of the village stared at Sarah like she was a slap in the face to the common good, like it was Sarah's fault she had to beg door to door. Common good—it made Sarah want to throw up. And because they wanted to be rid of her, Sarah Good vowed she'd never leave. She'd rub their self-righteous faces in common good!

A few miles from old Goody Osburn's hayloft, one of the few happy New Year's celebrations was taking place in the home of Rebecca and Francis Nurse. Rebecca sat in the midst of her laughing, teasing family, bouncing a grandchild on her knee, or perhaps a great-grandchild—it was hard to keep track. Her dried-apple face smiled and bobbed, enjoying the warmth and good smells bubbling from the hearth. Rebecca couldn't hear well enough to make out everything being said, but she smiled when her family did, looked pensive when they did, which wasn't often. Beaming at her gathered family, Rebecca felt content and pleased with herself; when she passed to her final reward, all these pieces of herself would live on to show she'd come this way. At three score and ten years, she doubted she had many years left to enjoy. But dying didn't frighten Rebecca; she believed her soul would join the saints in a heavenly home. Never in all her years had Rebecca told a single lie, and not once had an unkind word escaped her lips. It was an achievement to take pride in. She watched a chubby three-year-old pull up on her knee, and she smiled.

In the home of Reverend Samuel Parris, Tituba and Elizabeth Parris prepared the holiday meal. Abigail Williams approached her uncle in his study and flounced into a chair. After a moment Samuel Parris looked up from his sermon preparation and frowned. "What is it?" he asked coldly. Reverend Parris disliked interruptions, and the girl knew it. To his astonishment, Abigail expected to discuss witchcraft with him. He sent her packing with a stern lecture on children keeping their place. He reminded Abigail that children's opinions were of no interest to anyone, were totally without value. Her chatter was a waste of an adult's time, and worthless. Watching Abigail's angry retreat, Reverend Parris scowled. He fervently hoped the girl would marry soon and leave his household. He was sick of her demands for notice and attention. Reverend Parris shook his head and returned to his papers. The idea—paying attention to a twelve-year-old chit like that! What was the world coming to?

Ann Putnam Junior had no time to think of attention or idle discussions. The responsibility for the holiday meal fell on her young shoulders, and she was hard at work, always with an ear cocked toward the bedroom for her mother. Ann Senior was having another bad spell. Ann Junior understood. Life had not been kind to Ann Senior. Ann Senior's mother had cheated Ann of her rightful inheritance, leaving her wild with hope for her husband's inheritance. But Thomas Putnam's stepmother had persuaded Thomas' father to alter his will on his deathbed—Thomas and his brothers received nothing. Twice Ann Senior had been cheated by older women she trusted; the lesson was not lost on her. Age turned women into harpies, instruments of hurt and deprivation. Ann Senior wondered about other old women in the village; she'd lost many babies, and she just knew the old women were somehow responsible. She lay in bed and opened her Bible at random, swinging down her finger for chapter and verse. The verse did not apply. Ann Senior searched for the verse that read: "Ann Putnam Senior, yer babies are dead and yer fortune is gone. And these people are to blame . . ." And then a list of names. Ann Senior could guess which names would appear, but she wanted it confirmed by another source. The Bible would be best, but any source would do. In the kitchen, Ann Junior stirred the pots, and a tear slid down her pale cheek. She wanted so much to help her mama; she would do anything to help Mama. She wanted Mama feeling good again, smiling again. She hadn't seen her mama smile in years. Every night Ann Junior prayed God would deliver the names to her Mama. Then everything would be all right.

Seventeen-year-old Mary Warren wanted her life to be all right too. And she knew what it would take. John Proctor. But standing between herself and John Proctor was his wife, Elizabeth. Mary glared at a trencher of holiday food and pushed listlessly at it with her spoon. Her father shouted at her to eat or leave the table. She stared at him from sullen eyes. Mary would rather have spent the holiday with the Proctors, where she worked as a tavern wench, but Proctor had sent her home. Mary's father reached across the table and slapped her. Her mouth opened, and Mary's heart beat faster; she felt a tingle between her legs. Her father spit in disgust. Twice Mary had driven John Proctor to a fury of impatience and he'd struck her. Both times Mary nearly fainted with rapture. She'd looked into John Proctor's eyes just as he hit her. She knew he returned her sick love, she just knew it. If only there wasn't Elizabeth Proctor . . .

In the Wainwright household, New Year's Day passed quietly. Hannah read her Bible in her room and Charity hid in hers. Bristol sewed and listened with half an ear to her husband's ambitions for the coming year. She sighed silently. Their two months together had quickly settled into a dull routine oddly reminiscent of her life at the Royal Rumm. A drudgery unlightened by hope. Add slaps, she thought miserably, and she could easily have imagined herself in Almsbury Lane.

Life patterned into hours of exhausting labor, living in a household strained by tensions and darkened by a suspicion that happiness was an ever-elusive goal. As the weeks had passed, Bristol gradually came to understand that Caleb's image of her was frozen in time. He still saw her as the selfish girl who had threatened his inheritance—as an impulsive child pressing a foolhardy elopement. His mind lodged firmly on these impressions and could not be swayed, nothing Bristol did or would ever do could alter Caleb's ancient ideas of her. They were cast in iron. In two months of marriage he'd paid but one compliment: "At least you don't giggle and make light of things anymore."

Bristol had stared in astonishment. Then realized she hadn't laughed since their marriage. It seemed a very long time. A time of work and worry.

The largest worry in Bristol's life was Hannah. When the Adams farm sold, another vital chunk of Hannah Adams died. The values Hannah most treasured in life were being stripped from her. Watching Hannah Adams was like watching years flash by; every week she looked six months older. Unless something was done, and quickly, Bristol suspected Hannah would not live out the year. But what?

When Bristol wasn't concerning herself with Hannah's ebbing energy, she worried about Charity. Poor miserable Charity. Charity fled the Wainwright farm on the flimsiest of excuses or hid in her room. When Charity made a reluctant appearance, her pale green eyes shone like wet stones, hard and as grim as the line of her lips. Charity suffered. It tugged Bristol's heart to watch Charity enact the misery Bristol had endured living with Jean Pierre and Diana. Charity avoided Caleb whenever she could, and when they were forced together, she kept her sad face to the floor and seldom spoke.

Bristol watched with sorrowing eyes, and she longed to tell Charity that Caleb's advances to her were infrequent and unsatisfactory—she recognized the agonized question in Charity's eyes. But Bristol could do no such thing. Sex was a topic no decent woman ever mentioned. So they stumbled along, and the tensions grew.

Midway into a cold January, a letter arrived from Aunt Pru. Bristol turned Aunt Pru's creamy envelope between her fingers, and a solution began to form in her thoughts. If she could convince Hannah to visit London, she suspected her mother would find a renewed interest in life. In the Wainwright household, surrounded by gloomy attitudes, Hannah had scant chance to recover her vitality. But at Hathaway House, bombarded by Aunt Pru's infectious cheer . . . The longer Bristol pondered the idea, the more valid it appeared. She tore open Aunt Pru's letter and eagerly scanned the pages.

And fell into a black pit from which she never wanted to surface. Aunt Pru congratulated Bristol on her marriage in listless terms. Further reading revealed why. Diana had crawled out on the roof in a raving haze of drugged insanity. And she jumped. Diana Hathaway was dead. Jean Pierre had returned to the sea; he was free.

Bristol Adams Wainwright was not.

Numb, her face a tortured mask, Bristol slowly folded the letter and dropped it onto the fire. She watched it curl into ash from blind, beaten eyes. Fate was life's greatest enemy; a cruel, sadistic trickster. Jean Pierre, her dearest Jean Pierre. She staggered into the bedroom she shared with Caleb and fell across the quilts. She stared unseeing at the heavy ceiling beams. Oh, God. How different life would have been, married to her Jean Pierre; the difference betwen a rag doll and a living woman.

It wasn't that Caleb Wainwright was a bad person, her blunted mind admitted. He was not. Caleb was a good man, well respected, flourishing, and a decent husband if not warm and loving. But a distance existed that could never be bridged—a gap forever keeping Bristol and Caleb strangers. A distance created by the fact that each of their hearts belonged elsewhere.

Seeing Caleb and Charity together told Bristol all she needed to know about Caleb's heart. He and Charity were more alike in outlook, more compatible, than Caleb and Bristol could be in fifty years of trying. Caleb and Charity fit together like . . . like . . . Bristol and Jean Pierre.

Bristol turned her hot, dry face into the pillow and felt a giant hand squeeze her heart.

Then sudden urgent fingers tugged her shoulder, startling her from a vacant, empty world. Bristol sat up, her dead eyes staring at Charity. Immediately Bristol forgot her own troubles. "Charity! What is it? What's happened?"

Charity wrung her hands, and her freckles leaped from a paste-white face. Her eyes were wild. "Oh, Brissy . . . oh, Brissy . . ." Her voice rose in a reedy wail.

Frightened, Bristol pulled Charity to the edge of the bed and gripped her icy hands. "Charity! What is it?" Charity's eyes rolled like terrified pale marbles; she shook all over.

"Oh. Oh. When Mama finds out, it will kill her! This on top of everything else!"

"Is it Caleb, Charity? Has something happened to Caleb?" Bristol bit her lip. She'd never seen Charity like this. The girl hovered at the edge of hysteria.

"It was innocent, I swear! We were just having a bit of sport."

"Shhh. Everything will be all right. Just tell me what happened!"

Charity's voice cracked in panic. Tears rivered down white cheeks. "The worst part is, we don't know for sure if he saw us. Or what he'll do! I just know he saw us, I know he did! Oh, Brissy, help me! Help me!"

"Charity," Bristol said, her voice sharp. She pulled Charity's hands from her face and forced the sobbing girl to meet her eyes. "Slowly. I want to help, but I can't until I know what's happened. Slowly, now. Start at the beginning." Bristol couldn't imagine what might have occurred to produce the terror and fear in Charity's crumpled face, in her posture, in the wild rolling eyes.

Then, as the story poured past Charity's frozen lips, Bristol did understand, and her own cheeks drained of color.

Several of the village girls had met in the Parris kitchen. They badgered Tituba for stories; then Ann Putnam Junior had begged Tituba to look into the past and name the people who had hurt Ann's mother. But Abigail objected and turned the direction of the conversation. Eager to marry and escape the confines of the reverend's house, Abigail demanded the girls cast fortunes to reveal their future husbands. Charity seized on the idea, as did Mary Warren and the others.

Under Tituba's direction, they began. Each broke an egg white into a glass of water and chanted a spell Tituba taught them. Slowly the egg white formed into a symbol of their future husband's profession.

Mary Warren swore she saw a row of pub kegs in her glass. Poor frightened Betty Parris insisted she saw nothing; she was ten years old, so this surprised no one. Abigail Williams thought the experiment a failure; she saw so many images forming and reforming, she could make sense of none. But Charity. They all watched in growing horror as the clear shape of a coffin appeared in Charity's glass. They stared in fascinated shock . . . and did not hear Reverend Samuel Parris' steps until he was in the kitchen nearly on top of them. Reverend Parris glanced at the girls sitting in a circle on the floor, paused, frowned, then returned to his study.

"Oh, dear God," Bristol breathed, her heart pounding.

"Aye! Aye!" Charity tore at her hair, distraught.

"Did the reverend say anything to you?"

"No. But that isn't his way, Brissy. He'll ponder it before he denounces us. It was that way with the skipping!"

Bristol's cheeks felt as snowy as Charity's. "Witchcraft," she whispered. "He'll accuse all of you of practicing witchcraft."

Charity shrieked and covered her face. "Aye! It'll kill Mama, Brissy! It will just kill her!" She clasped Bristol's hand in a painful grip. "It was all innocent, Brissy, I swear it! We didn't mean any harm. When that coffin appeared, I . . ." She shuddered and broke into fresh sobbing.

Automatically Bristol patted Charity's cold fingers while her mind raced. "Wait, Charity, wait. Let's think this through." Her brow contracted in fierce concentration. "It's possible he didn't see you." She held up a hand, stopping

Charity's protests. "This wouldn't be the first time Samuel Parris missed something right under his nose. Or maybe he saw but didn't understand what you were doing." She thought hard. "In any case, Reverend Parris won't do anything immediately, maybe not at all. No, listen to me! Think what a position this places him in! He's been preaching witchcraft—but in his own kitchen? With his niece, his daughter, and his servant at the center of it? He'll believe, and rightly so, that if the story comes out, he'll lose what little credibility he has left. He might even worry that he'll be blamed for every misfortune in the village . . . that some will think he's a witch too."

"Oh, Brissy, Mama will hear of it . . ."

"He'll have to wrestle hard with his conscience. Denouncing all of you won't be easy for him. At least this gives us some time to think.'

Charity despaired. "But in the end, he'll denounce us, Brissy! You know he will. Witchcraft is all he's talked about for months! He sees Satan everywhere! Then Mama will—"

"Charity! We have to stay calm!" Bristol caught Charity's fingers and pulled them from the carroty hair. Clenching her hands, Bristol forced herself to remain steady while her thoughts ran pell-mell through a whirling mind. One thing at a time, she cautioned herself, take one problem at a time. First . . . Hannah. Bristol agreed with Charity; a thing like this after Noah's death, after selling the farm, after Charity's rebellion, would finish Hannah.

"Abigail promised she'd think of something . . . but what? What? There isn't anything . . ." Charity's voice rose in a thin frightened wail, and she began to shake again. Crimson blotches appeared on her face and arms; her neck flamed white and red.

"I think we can prevent Mama from hearing about this, Charity," Bristol said slowly, "but I'll need your help."

Hope blazed in Charity's fear-soft eyes. "Anything! I'll do anything. But what, Brissy, what can we . . . ?"

Quickly Bristol outlined a plan; they'd convince Hannah to visit Aunt Pru. The weather was the worst of the year for travel, and getting Hannah to leave immediately would be a serious obstacle. Charity clung to the idea. She would have agreed to anything.

As soon as Charity could control the shaking in her hands, they approached Hannah's room and put forth the suggestion. Hannah stared from one tight, pale face to the other. "Are

360

you both mad? Why should I risk my life to visit England? I don't want to leave home."

Bristol drew a deep breath; she understood about home. She also understood suddenly how far she'd strayed from her Puritan background. She was about to lie, and felt no regret for it. But lying didn't come easy. "Mama"—she arched her eyebrow in what she hoped was an expression of surprise— "Have you forgotten? Papa always wanted you to meet his sister and see his birthplace."

Hannah squinted. "I don't recall that." Her brow knit. "No," she said slowly, "I don't recall that at all."

"I do, Mama," Charity said quickly. She still looked terrible. "Every time we received Aunt Prudence's letters, Papa said he wished you could meet her." This was true.

"And visit the family home," Bristol added. This was not true. She looked away, hating to take advantage of Hannah's confused mental state, but convinced the trip was Hannah's only chance for survival. "I'm surprised you don't recall . . ." Her words hung in the air, a gentle reproach.

Hannah's faded eyes sharpened. "Well, now that you bring it to mind, perhaps I do remember." Her pride rose to ease the deception of her daughters.

"Aye." Bristol immediately strengthened the suggestion in her mother's mind, remembering aloud conversations that never occurred.

Hannah frowned, her efforts to remember painful to watch. "Aye, I suppose so, I don't recall exactly, but if you say so, I guess . . ." It didn't enter Hannah's mind that either of the girls lied. Lying cast the soul into eternal fire. In Hannah's mind, no one lied. It was inconceivable.

"Perhaps in the spring . . ." she murmured reluctantly. Bristol and Charity exchanged glances. Then Bristol patted her mother's work-red hands and withdrew to the kitchen, glad she didn't have to be present for the next part. What they were doing to Hannah left Bristol feeling sullied and dirty.

Part two of the plan was up to Charity. Charity was to strongly hint that Hannah was a burden on the household. Neither girl had the slightest doubt this terrible suggestion would impel Hannah to depart immediately. The methods they were using would be difficult to live with.

But the plan worked. Hannah lifted a quivering chin and agreed to sail within the week. A long, heartbreaking week for all.

Thinking she was unwelcome in Bristol's house aged Hannah overnight. It was an old woman they put aboard the Dutch trader *Bredene*. A frightened old woman who never had sailed before and who was thrown off balance by Bristol's news that the Prudence Adams Hannah had always thought of as a spinster of modest means was in reality married and wealthy. A deceptive stranger. Hannah boarded the *Bredene* wearing a crisscross of fear and confusion on her weathered face.

She didn't understand any of this. Not Prudence Adams, who was suddenly Prudence Hathaway (Bristol refused to answer questions, just smiled and said, "You'll see"), not the rush, not the strain in the Wainwright household. Despite Charity's hints that Hannah burdened the house, Bristol had been heartbroken to release Hannah instead of relieved to be rid of a burden.

Hannah suspected there was more to her trip than met the eye. But she felt too old, too exhausted, to sort it all out. She'd go to England. What else could she do? Besides, her Noah had wished it; both Charity and Bristol said so.

Bristol and Charity waved from the docks, not looking at each other, ignoring the sparkle of tears on their lashes. "I feel terrible!" Bristol whispered when the *Bredene* swung toward the harbor mouth and dropped sail. One glance at Charity's face stopped the words on her lips. She placed an arm around her sister's heaving shoulders.

"I'll never see Mama again!" Charity sobbed.

"Nonsense." Bristol smoothed Charity's orange curls. "Mama will come home. And the visit will be good for her. Aunt Pru is the best thing we could hope for Mama." In her heart, Bristol believed this utterly.

She helped Charity onto the wagon seat and turned the horses toward Salem Village. Charity wept hysterically, giving vent to the pent-up emotions of a difficult week. Each time a knock sounded, or a horse passed in the lane, Charity had started violently, and her face turned to white stone. She expected an enraged population to mob the house and drag her out. Salem smoldered with fear and frustration, and no one held any illusions that all that was required was one spark to ignite an eruption of violence. Charity and Bristol both walked in fear, knowing a handful of foolish girls might well provide that spark.

Glancing at Charity's tear-streaked face, Bristol sighed. She was deeply worried. Twice Charity had ridden in to the reverend's house for a hurried secret conference with the other girls involved. Each time Charity had returned home on the verge of nervous collapse. All the girls hung at the fringes of hysteria, terrified and cowering under hideous speculations of what would happen when the reverend denounced them. That he would, none of them doubted. Soon his conscience would compel him to root out the evil in Salem . . . and in his own house. It seemed a miracle that he'd delayed this long. Frowning, Bristol wondered if Samuel Parris had actually seen what the girls did. But of course he had—they were all so certain. Hadn't he?

"Abigail will think of something," Charity promised Bristol. Her teeth chattered in fright and desperation. She wrapped icy hands about her ribs and shivered. "Abigail will think of something!" Charity clung to this thought with savage hope. Abigail was strong; Abigail was clever. Abigail would think of something.

Abigail did.

28

By February 1, everyone in Salem knew of a strange affliction bringing down the village girls. It began in Reverend Parris's house. Little Betty Parris took to her bed and cowered there nearly comatose with fear. Villagers flocked to see, and reported the child shivered and cried out constantly: "No! Oh, no! See the coffin! . . . Oh, no! . . . He saw us! He saw us! The punishment . . . oh, it hurts, it hurts!" Everyone tried without success to penetrate the girl's ravings, tried to coax an explanation for the odd phrases. But no one reached that small frightened mind, not even her parents. In fact, it was noted the reverend especially seemed to drive the girl deeper into her terror instead of bringing her relief.

Immediately after seeing Betty's torment and the attention it brought her, Abigail Williams developed the same symptoms. She too writhed on her quilts and ranted about coffins and someone seeing and someone practicing painful punishment on her flesh. If anyone noticed the slight alteration in phrasing, no one attached any importance to it. That "he" became "someone" wasn't nearly as noteworthy as Abigail's behavior. Everyone agreed Abigail's symptoms were more serious and far more interesting than Betty's.

As a curious audience swelled in number, Abigail's erratic actions increased in intensity and frequency. Often she jumped from her bed, red and white weals covering her face, arms, and neck, and she jerked about the parlor like a puppet on a string, knocking over furniture, smashing into walls, and attempting to throw herself into the fireplace.

Fortunately, someone was always near the hearth to prevent a tragic injury to the poor demented girl. That she was demented, no one could question. People in their right minds did not dance or lift their skirts to an indecent height. And once Abigail rubbed lewdly against two of the men. Demented behavior for certain. Occasionally she flew about the room like a dervish, and some observers swore her feet didn't touch the floor. She made gargoyle faces at the audience and spoke streams of nonsense words, and sometimes doubled over in pain, screaming, "Someone is hitting me! Someone is tormenting me!"

Speculation ran high as to the cause of the girls' strange illness. Some believed both had mysteriously gone insane; others maintained it must be a new disease; still others hinted at darker suspicions.

Martha Cory carefully observed the phenomenon and pronounced it a fake. "The girl makes a fool of herself to get attention," Martha announced flatly. "This is just a new sport for her." Martha Cory washed her hands of the spectacle and went home, unaware that Abigail overheard the unflattering remarks.

But fakery and insanity were quickly ruled out as the affliction spread. Ann Putnam Junior next fell prey to the strange disorder. She twisted across her bed in a feverish sweat of obvious terror. Her blue eyes rolled back in her head, and she tightened into a fetal curl. Occasionally she jerked into other strange positions, her limbs drawing into rigid, awkward configurations. While neighbors gaped, Thomas Putnam tried to straighten his daughter's arms and legs, but had to quit for fear he'd break bones as stiff and unyielding as iron. Ann Senior tended the girl, beside herself at this new calamity to strike the Putnam household. "Who does this to you?" Ann Senior begged. "Tell us the names of those who torment you!" But Ann Junior only wept and groaned, and flaring hives erupted on her rigid limbs. Ann

Senior frantically scanned the arriving crowds, searching faces for any trace of guilt or satisfaction. Whoever worked this evil on her poor little Ann would surely show something in their expressions. Of course she found what she sought.

Next, the Putnams' maid, Mercy Lewes, began similar ravings, and after her, Elizabeth Hubbard, the niece of Goodwife Griggs.

When Mary Warren fell into a fit in the midst of John Proctor's tavern, the villagers' attitudes changed abruptly from curiosity to cold fear. What was happening? Where would it end? They stared at their own children and hugged them close, feeling a chill tighten around their hearts. Abigail, Betty, Ann Junior, Mercy, Elizabeth, and now Mary Warren. Mary had taken one look at Reverend Parris stepping through the pub door and begun frothing at the mouth and throwing herself about the tavern much as Abigail was doing in the parsonage. Mary, too, like all the rest, shouted of coffins and men trapped in water glasses and a painful punishment. Observers stared. Similarities impossible to ignore were emerging from the girls' howling mouths. The same affliction attacked them all. John and Elizabeth Proctor carried Mary in to bed, and Elizabeth Proctor took on Mary's chores. "I don't mind," she said tartly. "I've been doing that lazy jade's chores all along." But Elizabeth didn't look pleased, nor did John as his customers silently slipped away.

Finally, Charity Adams collapsed, falling into bed with chills and fever and glassy-eyed terror. Sometimes she shouted and raved, other times she lay like a corpse, staring white-faced at a point near the ceiling. That she experienced pain, no observer doubted. Painful rashes spread across her face and body, her limbs froze in rigid, contorted postures or melted limp and rubbery. Mysterious marks flared upon her flesh, and Charity doubled over in cramping groans. Not even Bristol could penetrate Charity's disconnected ravings. When Bristol tried, she felt as if she talked to a wall.

"I'm at my wits' end," Bristol admitted to Caleb, pushing a spill of hair under her dust cap. "I can't reach her!"

Caleb stamped snow from his boots and sat at the table. Accepting a mug of steaming beer, he took a swallow and stared into the fireplace. "I'm worried," he said quietly. "Do you know what they're saying in the village?"

"Aye. Rebecca Nurse stopped in to ask if there was anything she could do to help. She told me . . . Rebecca said they're talking about witchcraft." Bristol's eyes strayed to the cloves of garlic hung in her windows. She shuddered. "Do you think . . . ?"

Caleb glanced at her briefly; they seldom exchanged a direct look. "I don't know what to think," he said, his square face sober and troubled. "I laughed when your mother hung the garlic in the windows and nailed the horseshoes over the doors. But now . . ." He drained his mug and set it on the table. "Now, I just don't know."

In the following silence, they heard Charity sobbing in her bedroom. "It hurts! Oh, it hurts!" Caleb ran a shaking hand through a shock of thick sandy hair.

Shyly Bristol touched his wrist. It was the first physical contact they'd had in weeks. Distracted, Caleb smiled absently and withdrew his fingers, pouring a fresh beer. "Did William Griggs come here today?"

"Aye." Embarrassed, Bristol busily stirred a stew bubbling over the fire. She didn't mind their lack of touching, welcomed it in fact, but to offer sympathy and be rebuffed brought a flush of color to her cheeks. Even though she knew he wasn't aware of what he'd done. Part of Bristol's mind was glad of the problems in the village, even those with Charity. It took her mind from the dismal marriage she'd made, from taunting thoughts of Jean Pierre's freedom and her own lack of it. Bristol kept her mind firmly on the problems at hand; if she dwelt on Jean Pierre, Bristol thought her despair would drive her mad.

"Well? What did Griggs say?"

"What? Oh." Bristol shrugged wearily. "What is there to say? Goodman Griggs is as baffled as anyone."

Perhaps William Griggs was more puzzled than most. He called on all the girls daily, trying everything modern medicine had to offer. Nothing helped. Not tonics, not plasters, not prayer. In fact, when Reverend Parris prayed over the afflicted girls, everyone present had to cover his ears at the resultant howling. All agreed the reverend's presence made an impossible situation worse. The reverend—who had forgotten the girls sitting over glasses in his kitchen, if he'd ever noticed them at all—grew more frantic by the hour. Only one thing shrank from the holy word of God. Evil. Satan. And those afflicted by Satan's touch.

And it had all begun in the reverend's own house. For Samuel Parris, life assumed a ghastly hue. Answers hovered in his mind, answers he didn't dare examine too closely. There had to be other explanations. There had to be!

The town council called a special meeting, demanding a

full report on the situation from William Griggs. Reluctantly William Griggs admitted he knew of nothing in the field of medicine to account for the girls' affliction.

"Exactly what does that mean?" an angry voice shouted.

William Griggs exchanged a worried glance with Reverend Parris. He shifted uneasily. "It means . . . I think this is a problem for the clergy, not the medical profession." His eyes slid from Samuel Parris as he passed the ball into the reverend's court. The men stared and waited. William Griggs shrugged and looked over a room filled with tense, anxious faces. "In my opinion, what we have here is multiple malefic witchcraft . . . the evil hand."

The crowd sucked in their breath, and for a moment no one spoke. An expert had finally uttered aloud the thoughts of many. The meeting room exploded. It required a full twenty minutes before Reverend Parris was able to establish a loose order. "Wait!" he cried. "Wait! Before we lose our heads, let me assure you, the clergy has not been idle! We are already taking steps!"

An angry voice rose above the others. "More prayer? No more words, Parris! I don't give a piss for more words!"

"This all started in your house! That's what prayer gets you!" another accused. "We want action!"

The anti-Parris faction roared to their feet, and only John Walcot's militia prevented Samuel Parris from being rushed. Tonight the fears and frustrations of the village centered on Samuel Parris, regardless of political leanings. The trouble had started in his house; he must somehow be responsible.

Shaken, Samuel Parris continued, surrounded by a ring of Commander Walcot's men, "I've met with the ministers of Salem Town, Andover, and Beverly. These are learned men, leaders of the community," he pleaded. "They know what we're facing, and they all counsel patience. Before we leap to conclusions, let us wait and see how the afflictions develop!"

"We've seen enough already! Why should we listen to ye?"

A note of desperation crept into the reverend's tone and expression. "We'll pray and fast and—"

"If yer prayers don't protect yer own house from Satan, how will them prayers protect us?" The man waved his fist. "Step aside, ye insignificant fart, and let us handle this our own way! We know what the cause is, we don't need no waiting!"

"Aye!" the crowd roared.

"We'll find the witches!"

"Aye!" came an affirming shout.

367

"And we don't need no pompous dirt bag telling us what to do! Not when his own household offers fertile ground for Satan's stroke!"

"Aye!" the crowd screamed.

"Please," Reverend Parris shouted, watching his career disappear in smoke. "Let us use reason! Show caution in this matter! William Griggs admits he doesn't know for certain! He only offered an opinion. An opinion, not a fact! We must tread carefully!" His words of restraint came too late; his sermons had not prepared the ground for patience.

The last of the reverend's words drowned in hoots and catcalls. Only when Thomas Putnam stood, did the room quiet. His daughter was one of the afflicted, as was his maid; he had a right to be heard. Thomas Putnam had slept little in the last days; his eyes were shadowed, his ruddy face tired and worried. "As you all know, I keep a godly house." Murmurs of assent greeted his opening words. "And you also know, my house has suffered more than most."

"Aye," the crowd agreed. With both a daughter and a serving wench down, and a nervous wife, Thomas Putnam did indeed have his hands full.

Slowly Thomas glanced over the room, meeting the eyes of friends, neighbors, enemies, and political opponents—all united for once in a terrible cause. He nodded to Caleb Wainwright, Giles Cory, John Proctor, Francis Nurse, Abel Gardner, Nathaniel Ingersoll, and many others. "Right or wrong, I've been a Parris supporter—though I am no longer." Deep silence met his words; no voice interrupted. "Whether or not you believe Samuel Parris qualifies to be our leader, in this instance his advice is sound. Witchcraft is a serious allegation. With serious consequences. If Satan stalks the village, godly folk will find and vanquish him—"

"Aye!" a hundred voices shouted.

"—but if we make a mistake . . ." Thomas looked about the room, and eyes dropped under his sober, steady gaze. "Then we ourselves become the tool of Satan. We must act rationally. Think on that, neighbors."

They did. And a few heated brains cooled.

"We must act with restraint and caution. Listen to our chosen leaders. Let them discuss and watch and decide what happens here. John Hale of Beverly and John Higginson and Nicholas Noyes of Salem Town are good men. No one here will dispute that." No one did. Only Reverend Parris looked grieved at the respect and admiration in Putnam's voice. "Let those men have their say."

Someone spit. "Put two ministers together and they'll not agree on the time of day!"

Thomas Putnam nodded agreement. His face darkened, and he turned toward Samuel Parris. "That's right. So here's the offer I make you and the ministers. One week. All of you decide within one week what hurts our children, or we'll find the answers ourselves." His voice broke. "And I'll move heaven and earth to get the witch responsible! One week. Do you hear me? One week, and that's all!"

"But . . ." Reverend Parris stepped forward.

The crowd shot from their seats and carried Thomas Putnam on their shoulders to Ingersoll's tavern, where they drank into the night and discussed a variety of plans. Few cherished any hope the collective ministers would solve the problem or even come forth with a reasonable line of action.

Later, as she listened to Caleb's account of the meeting, a line of anxiety deepened between Bristol's brows. The village had come together on one issue, but the meshing of minds was prompted by violent tempers and a common growing fear. The fragmentation continued to exist, as Bristol perceived it. Court suits were in progress, enemies still sought to wound each other, large and small problems continued to rage. A picture of hot underground flows appeared in Bristol's mind, bubbling lava streams meeting in one boiling caldron, then exploding under pressure into a million shattered pieces. She shivered.

"I think it's right to wait and see," Bristol offered, dropping her nightgown over her curls, her spine turned toward Caleb.

"I just want Charity to be herself again," Caleb answered in a muffled voice from the bed.

"Aye," Bristol said quietly, conscious of Charity moaning in the room next to theirs. She lifted the quilts and slid into bed. She held her breath, hoping Caleb wouldn't reach for her. Sometimes when he'd been drinking, he sought release with her body. When Caleb panted over her, Bristol felt an aching emptiness of despair. The follies of the human heart . . . the misery of error.

After a moment she heard Caleb's steady snore. Gratefully she turned her back to him and slept.

Regardless of the meeting consensus, not everyone in Salem Village possessed the patience to wait while the ministers deliberated. Mary Sibley, a young village matron, suggested they end the suspense immediately. She suggested a witch cake be baked to break the girl's silence. It would free their tongues to name their oppressors if they were indeed be-

369

witched. She led a group of frightened angry women to Tituba, who all agreed had the magical expertise to bake such a cake, and they presented Tituba with urine they'd collected from the afflicted girls. They shouted down Tituba's nervous protests, then waited silently while Tituba mixed the urine with rye meal and baked the cake. One of the women brought forward a black dog, and Mary Sibley forced the cake into the dog's throat. They all stood back to watch. If the dog suffered torments by ingesting a cake baked from the girls' urine, it would constitute positive proof of the girls' bewitchment and consequently free their tongues.

The dog vomited over the snow and ran howling toward the woods.

The village had its proof.

And the witch hunt began in earnest. Frightened people dashed back and forth, in and out of the village center. They were afraid to be isolated in their homes, afraid to be out among possible witches. The town market sold out of garlic and horseshoes within an hour; everyone copied the Lord's Prayer and wore the scrap of paper near his skin. No one met another's gaze directly for fear of a hex. The witches had to be found. And quickly.

To no one's surprise, Ann Putnam Senior assumed a position of leadership in the relentless push to wrest the names from the girls. Before the village could rid the community of evil, they needed the names of Satan's disciples.

Ann Senior appeared at Bristol's door, fresh from the parsonage, where she'd interrogated Betty Parris and Abigail Williams. Her pretty, vacuous face was flushed with victory, and she led her followers into Charity's room and leaned over Charity. A triumphant glitter lit her blue eyes.

"Charity?" Ann's soft voice was insistent. "Charity? You can talk now, your tongue is released from the devil's hold."

Uneasy and frightened, Bristol watched from the end of Charity's bed. The women crowded around Ann Senior, and all stared intently at Charity. Charity lay twisted in a grotesque posture. Her right elbow nearly touched her chin; her left elbow strained toward her ribs on the right side. Both legs curled at odd angles. Bristol utterly believed Charity incapable of assuming such a tortured position had the girl been in her right mind. She looked at the women bending over the bed and wondered if one of those wild faces could be responsible for . . . Pearls of sweat broke along Bristol's pale brow. Disconsolate, still she attempted a shred of objectivity. But she felt herself being swept up in the village hysteria: it had to be witchcraft. There was no other answer for the girls' torment.

"Charity," Ann Senior coaxed softly. "Tell us who hurts you . . . tell us who does this to you." She pushed at the carroty strands falling over Charity's face and looked into glassy green eyes. "Is it Sarah Osburn, Charity? Is it that old hag Goody Osburn?"

Charity's eyes disappeared; only the whites showed, and her tongue leaped nearly to her chin. The women gasped, but Ann Senior didn't blink. Her own daughter acted this way too.

"Abigail Williams said she saw a yellow dog with two legs and furred wings and a head like a woman's. She said that hellish creature turned into the shape of Goody Osburn. Did you see it too, Charity? Did you?"

At the mention of Abigail's name, Charity's eyes rolled forward and fixed on the face above her. "Abigail said . . ." Charity's voice emerged a croak, scarcely recognizable.

"Aye," Ann Senior soothed. "You saw Sarah Osburn's shape, didn't you? Goody Sarah Osburn torments you, doesn't she?"

Bristol realized she was grinding her teeth. Her knuckles whitened on the brass bedstead. She hadn't seen Sarah Osburn in years; the old woman had been bedridden since she retired from midwifery. Bristol's eyes widened; hadn't Sarah Osburn assisted at several of the stillbirths Ann Senior had suffered?

"It is Goody Osburn tying you in knots, isn't it, Charity?"

Charity's wild eyes swung around the row of expectant faces. "Aye!" she gasped. "Aye! Sarah Osburn twists me up and hurts me!"

Ann Senior's face flushed with victory, and her eyes lifted to those of the women. Then she bent again. "Who else, Charity? Who else torments you?"

Bristol swayed at the end of the bed. Sarah Osburn! Who could imagine it? And Sarah turning into a yellow dog with the head of a woman . . . Eyes wide with terror, Bristol jerked her attention back to the scene at the bed.

"I don't know! I don't know!" Charity moaned. But all who watched noticed her limbs begin to relax and unwind from the torturous position.

"Is it Sarah Good, Charity?" Ann Senior suggested. Her eyes blazed, and all the women tensed. There wasn't a woman present who had not extended pity and welfare to

371

Sarah Good, and not a one had heard a proper thank-you. "Does Sarah Good hurt you?"

Slowly Charity's arms dropped to a normal position across her thin chest. "Aye," she whispered, seeing the approval in the faces above her. "Aye," she said. "Sarah Good torments me something terrible!"

"There's a good girl," Ann Senior crooned. "Soon this will all be over and you'll feel well and strong again. We just need to confirm one more. One more."

"More?" Charity breathed. She blinked the wet glass eyes and tried to read the faces above her. Dark freckles popped over her face like tiny raisins in paste.

"Tituba," Ann Senior questioned softly. "Doesn't Tituba hurt you too?"

"Tituba!" Bristol gasped. She simply could not think Tituba guilty of hurting the girls. Scaring them, aye, but hurting them? Tituba worshiped little Betty Parris; it was unthinkable she would injure the child in any way.

But it was true. Charity's croak confirmed it. "Aye."

A flood of memory overcame Bristol, and she began to shake. Who but a witch would have gone into the trance Bristol witnessed? Who but a witch could have known about Bristol and Caleb in the settler's cabin? Who but a witch would have dared utter such dark words as Tituba had muttered that long-ago day? It had to be true!

"Brissy?" Charity found her sister's face among the others and lifted weak arms.

Bristol hurried around the bed and cradled Charity's head to her bosom. Rocking, she patted Charity and whispered, "Shhh. Shhh. Rest now. Everything is going to be all right."

At first it seemed that it might be. Charity joined Bristol and Caleb at the dinner table that night, the first time in ten days. Her eyes were clear. She felt weak and admitted to a strange drained feeling. "Maybe it's over now," she said, sipping her beer with shaking hands.

Caleb toyed with his food, pushing chunks of ham around his trencher. His wary eyes brooded. "Charity . . . did you really see those things? A yellow dog with wings and the shapes of Sarah Good and Tituba?"

"Are you saying I didn't?" Charity flared. Pale eyes met his, a challenge in the depths, and her thin lips pressed in a stubborn line. "Do you make light of the suffering I've endured?" She paused. "At the hands of the witches?" Softly her tone suggested he questioned the validity of any suffering not caused by him. Anger foamed at the edge of her voice.

Worried, Bristol put down her spoon and watched the hostility leap between them. She'd never heard Charity be sharp with Caleb, nor Caleb question anything Charity did. Something was coming to a head here that Bristol did not fully understand. Caleb faced a crisis of belief; Charity sensed the beginning of a fresh betrayal.

"Caleb," Bristol hurriedly interjected, "Charity didn't hurt herself! And she wouldn't lie! Surely you aren't suggesting . . ."

"I'm not suggesting anything!" Caleb answered shortly. His thoughtful stare centered on Charitys white face. "I just wonder if someone else didn't put suggestions in her head. Like that crazy Ann Putnam Senior. Ann has sought a focus for her hatreds and frustrations for years. Could she be using you, Charity? Could all of them be using you for their own reasons?"

Shocked, Bristol stared at her husband. "Caleb, everyone knows Ann has been . . . upset for a long time. But you're saying she's malicious, that she's evil! That simply cannot be true!"

Momentarily Caleb's eyes flicked to Bristol, then back to Charity's stony resentment. "I think," he began slowly, "that Ann Senior truly believes what she's doing is right. I believe her intentions are not evil, but possibly the tool of evil. I'd not like to see Ann's desires projected onto others."

Caleb and Charity stared at each other; an implication hung in the suddenly chill kitchen. It seemed to Bristol that sparks of tension flew between them.

Abruptly Charity jumped from her chair, the quick movement overturning her mug of beer. "I know what I saw," she hissed, her eyes glassy marbles of loathing. "I know what I felt, and I know what I suffered." Those terrible eyes didn't leave Caleb's face. "And if ever again you call me a liar . . . you will suffer for it."

They stared at Charity with open mouths—this wasn't the Charity Adams either of them knew. This was a person they could believe was indeed possessed. Whatever Charity might once have felt for Caleb Wainwright, now there was only hatred blazing in those glittering glass eyes. Her emotions had congealed into a cancerous lump of frustration, betrayal, and now hatred. Caleb had scorned her feelings once too often.

Caleb started to rise, but the expression on Charity's face halted him. "You will suffer for it," she repeated, spacing the words. For an instant an expression strange to the face of an unmarried girl in Salem flitted across her pinched features.

Power. Charity had a power, and seeing Caleb Wainwright's ashen face, she knew it. Whirling, she ran into her bedroom and slammed the door behind her.

Neither Bristol nor Caleb moved. They stared at Charity's door in shocked silence, each struggling with strange new thoughts. Then Bristol cleaned Charity's spilled beer. When she finished, she fetched the jug from the hob behind the hearth and poured a fresh hot beer for Caleb and herself. Her hands trembled.

"What's happening to all of us?" Bristol asked in a low voice. She sat down and pushed away her cold supper.

Caleb stared into his mug. "I honestly don't know." He took a long pull from the foaming glass; then his troubled gaze met hers. "I agree with John Proctor, Bristol. I can't believe in witches." Bristol gasped, but he went on as if talking to himself. "I can't believe some person muttering a chant over a soup pot can affect my harvest or the health of a baby or whether or not person A will love or hate person B." He directed his eyes to the flames. "I can't believe these girls are tormented by something invisible. I believe in what I can see."

Bristol twisted the edges of her white apron and closed her open mouth. Stay reasonable and calm, she told herself. "But, Caleb, if witches didn't exist, why would our government legislate against them? Why would reasonable men make laws against something that doesn't exist?"

Caleb turned his mug in damp circles on the table; he stared into the fireplace. "John and I discussed that. Government is made up of men. Even educated men make mistakes."

Bristol leaned over her glass. "Can the Bible be wrong too, Caleb? In Exodus it says: 'Thou shalt not suffer a witch to live.' Did God make a mistake too, Caleb? Are you claiming that?" Her voice climbed. This conversation frightened Bristol. She wondered if he was closing his mind, refusing to face the situation.

He looked into the flames, turning his mug on the table.

"Caleb, listen to me, please!" Bristol stared into his strong set face, and dots of color jumped into her cheeks. "I know that things haven't been . . . all they might be between us, but . . . don't put this question of faith between us as well. Every family in the village needs unity now, like never before. Please. Let us agree to see Charity through these terrible times with compassion. Whatever you . . . whatever you believe, Charity *has* suffered, and she needs our support and our

. . ." She almost said "love"; then Bristol blushed and altered her thought. "She needs our support and our help."

"A man must follow his conscience, Bristol."

In the silence, Bristol felt a hysterical urge to laugh. Aye. Oh, aye. Wasn't their marriage proof of Caleb's conscience? As if proof were needed. This talk made her feel giddy and out of touch with reality.

He continued, "The legislature can be wrong—*is* wrong. And, aye, the Bible can be wrong too." He directed a plea to his wife. "The Bible also is interpreted by men." Looking away from Bristol's horrified expression, he returned his eyes to the fire. "I'm a simple man, Bristol. I'm good with my hands and the soil. I'm not good at putting ideas and feelings into words."

"Caleb . . ."

"When this is finally over, I . . . I want to send Charity to Hannah in England. I'll talk to her about it when she's calmer." He didn't look up, but Bristol saw a climb of red rising along his neck. He spoke so softly she had to lean forward to hear. "I think you've guessed that . . . that you and I can't build a life with Charity sharing this house. She and I . . ." His voice trailed. "I just think it would be best." Standing, Caleb stretched and yawned and moved toward the bedroom. Passing, he touched Bristol's hair, his fingers clumsy and awkward with the gesture.

Bristol sat without moving until she heard the squeak of the mattress sagging beneath his weight. Then she rose and cleared the table. Caleb had staggered her tonight. First in his disbelief in witches, then with his tentative effort toward affection. She dropped dirty trenchers into a tub of melted-snow water.

"You cast the seeds, now you must reap the harvest," she whispered to herself. She'd agreed to this marriage; she must do her part to make it work. But Bristol's heart held no enthusiasm for the task. Deep inside, she admired Caleb's resolve. Even feeling as Bristol guessed he did for Charity, he had the strength of conscience to make an honest effort with Bristol. He'd looked squarely at their situation and made a decision. Charity must leave. Without seeing Charity every day, without Charity in the next bedroom . . . maybe Caleb believed he could build a life with Bristol.

Bristol didn't feel as certain. Jean Pierre didn't live in the next bedroom, she didn't see him every day, but he stood between Caleb and Bristol as surely as if he lived in the house. She paused, her hands in the tub of water, her shoulders drooping, and she stared at the soft blue wall in front of her. Jean Pierre. Oh, dear God, how she longed for him during the endless cold nights. How she missed his laughing gray eyes and his teasing grin. No matter how cruel the world might seem, Jean Pierre had always been able to coax a smile to her lips and offer her a fresh perspective.

How would Jean Pierre La Crosse view what was happening in the village? With a sinking feeling, Bristol suspected he too might dismiss the idea of witchcraft. The thought made her uneasy. But Jean Pierre was not a simple man unused to voicing ideas. He would be able to explain his reasons and present them so logically that she too would see things as he saw them. Had the conversation tonight been with Jean Pierre, Bristol knew she would not now be feeling so frightened and alone.

After drying her hands, Bristol hung her apron on a peg in the buttery, then sank to the table, holding a last mug of warm beer between her cold fingers. She stared into the embers dying below a row of gleaming pots. With all her aching heart she wished she were half a world away from Salem. Fate had played a game with her life.

If only she'd known of Diana's death before she wed Caleb. If only she'd written Noah that he'd been right in the beginning: she and Caleb were not meant for each other. If only. The old familiar hopeless game of "if only."

If only the witchcraft furor were really over.

But it was only beginning.

29

On February 29, 1692, Sarah Good, Sarah Osburn, and Tituba were arrested. Tempers in the village ran high. These were the hags responsible for torturing the village girls and doing heaven knew what else. Not a person in Salem Village had not suffered mysterious misfortunes at one time or another. Gossip flew and speculation built by the hour; which of the witches had caused which calamity? How deep did the evil strike? For a time there was talk of a lynching party, but cooler heads prevailed and it was decided to wait and see what happened.

The following day, Jonathan Corwin and John Hathorne, distinguished members of the upper house of the legislature, arrived at the village meetinghouse to examine the accused. The makeshift courtroom was packed. People jammed the pews and lined the walls and shivered on the outside steps.

As family of an afflicted girl, Bristol and Caleb had no trouble gaining entrance. Finding a seat was another matter. They crammed into a center aisle and stood packed tightly, but with a better view than they'd first expected. If Bristol held her neck just so, she could see between the heads in front. The scarlet robes of the examiners lay in clear sight, and she had a fair view of the stools where the girls would sit. It looked as though she'd have a partial lane of sight for the accused.

John Hathorne and Jonathan Corwin solemnly took their seats behind the high dais, and their sober faces stared over the packed room. At the proper moment, they nodded and armed guards escorted the girls to a spot just below the dais. Bristol noted with surprise that the ranks of afflicted girls had now swollen to include Ann Putnam Senior, Mary Walcot, and two young married women she knew but slightly.

Conscious of numerous staring eyes, the afflicted girls filed importantly to their row of stools and demurely seated themselves. Bristol thought they could easily have been mistaken for a female choir, sitting gracefully and waiting for the moment they would be called on to perform. All were neatly combed, dressed in their sabbath best, and they sat with hands folded primly in their laps.

Bristol released a silent breath of relief. She'd lain awake most of the night fearing today's examinations might turn into a debacle. And she didn't want Charity subjected to that. Regardless of today's outcome, Bristol whispered a prayer of grateful thanks that Hannah was not here to see Charity held up to public inspection. It would have embarrassed and humiliated Hannah.

One of the guards roped off an area to serve as the prisoner's dock, and the judges appointed Goodman Cheever as court recorder. Then the examiners pronounced all in readiness, and Judge Hathorne nodded for the guards to bring out the first prisoner. Everyone craned his neck, and the girls glanced up with flushed faces and excited eyes.

The guards escorted Sarah Good into the dock. She stared about her, an ill-tempered expression tugging down the corners of her mouth.

All hell broke loose.

Screaming. Shrieking. Howling. Falling. Fits and frothing. Hysteria and convulsions.

Abigail Williams shrieked and fell on her knees, clutching her throat. Her face contorted, and her tongue burst from her mouth. Her blue eyes bulged. "She's choking me! Make her stop! Save me! Help!"

Ann Putnam Junior stared at Abigail's crimson, strangling face, and she too screamed. "Aye! Oh, make her stop!" Ann's angelic face froze in horror, and she cried, "Oh! Oh! Tell her to stop! Please make her stop! The witch pinches me all over with fiery claws!" Ann toppled from her stool and rolled on the floor, desperately beating at an invisible tormentor with both small fists.

Several of the girls crawled behind their stools, hiding and wailing and sobbing frantically.

Ann Putnam Senior jerked to her feet and quivered in violent shudders. A mask of fear and loathing twisted her face. "Now she's floating near the rafters!" Her shaking finger soared, and every eye stared up at nothing. "Oh! Oh, look! She's flying down to hurt us!" Ann Senior covered her head and crashed to the floor, writhing and screaming.

The others took up the cry, howling and shrieking and crawling on the floor. They yelled and wept and screamed and beat at themselves and each other. Some dared terrified peeks between their fingers at an astonished Sarah Good; then they fell over in fresh agonies.

John Hathorne and Jonathan Corwin stood behind the dais and peered down at the frenzy with openmouthed amazement. They could scarcely believe what their eyes saw and ears heard. No one could. The girls in full cry were shocking, horrifying.

Jonathan Corwin's mouth worked, and he pointed at Sarah Good, but the noise was so overpowering no one heard what he yelled. John Hathorne purpled in the face, attempting to shout above the unbelievable din. Finally a guard touched Sarah with the tip of his lance and directed her attention to the judges. She read their lips: "Look away! Turn your eyes away from them!"

Sarah's mouth clamped in a line of disgust; then she turned slowly, crossed her arms on her chest and stared at a distant wall.

Almost instantly the girls quieted, and a collective sigh of gratitude blew through the room. Everyone stared. The girls lay about the planks like discarded dolls tossed by a careless hand. Nearly all were drawn into torturous postures. A few continued to weep quietly, but aside from an occasional moan or isolated yelp, they were still.

A solid block of faces swung from the stricken girls to Sarah Good. Sarah stood in a posture of supreme contempt, her stony eyes on the far wall.

Judge Hathorne cleared his throat and straightened his scarlet robe. "Look at the children," he commanded in a strained tone. He clearly hated the idea of a repetition, but nothing could be left to chance—he had to be certain what caused the hysteria.

Sarah shrugged and turned, her glance full of disdain.

Again the cacophony erupted. Screams, tears, howls, and violent thrashing across the floor. Some shook in brutal spasms, others turned rigid as stone. They flopped about the planks like fish out of water.

The judge cupped his hands around his mouth. "Look away!" he shouted. "Look away from them!"

Toward the middle of the meetinghouse, Bristol lifted her hands and pressed them over her ears. All around her, others did the same. She didn't dare look at Sarah Good for fear a scream would burst from her own lips. A need to scream seemed to build inside, and she had only to scan the crowd around her to see others feeling the same pressures she did.

Standing on tiptoe, Bristol searched the melee for Charity. Charity sat on the floor, her feet straight before her, her hands buried in her carroty hair. Charity's cap had disappeared, and her hair tumbled loose around her face. She might have been a statue carved of white marble. Or a mute, oblivious of the spectacle around her. She didn't move, didn't blink. The only sign of life was tears streaming from her wide, staring eyes and dropping in wet circles on her collar. It looked as if she'd been struck deaf and dumb.

Eventually the judges restored a ragged order and seated themselves behind the dais. Jonathan Corwin blinked repeatedly, as if trying to rouse himself from a dream. He opened his lips, then shook his head and deferred to Hathorne.

Judge Hathorne drew a breath and folded his hands before him. He leveled a measuring glare at Sarah Good. "Sarah Good, what familiar do you keep?" Everyone knew witches kept familiars to do their foul work. And everyone whispered this was a fine opening question.

"None," Sarah spit, her voice as waspish as her face. No hint of humility bowed her head. She met the judges' eyes with a bold gaze.

"Have you made a contract with the devil?"

Sarah laughed. "Of course not! What an idiotic question!"

Judge Hathorne glared. "Why do you hurt these girls?"

"Girls? Didn't I see Ann Putnam Senior and a couple more who aren't 'girls'? A couple of them bitches are almost as old as I am—they aren't girls no more!"

Hathorne ignored her outburst. "Why do you hurt these girls?" he repeated.

Sarah's lip curled. "I don't hurt them. You see me standing here, don't you? Did you see me go anywhere near them?" Her eyes flashed. "This is all ridiculous. I scorn it!"

"Did your shape torment them?"

"My shape?" Sarah laughed again, a nasty sound. "The only shape I got is the one you're looking at!"

Angry, Judge Hathorne leaned over the dais and directed the girls to look upon the prisoner and determine if this was the person who hurt them. They screamed and covered their eyes and refused to look.

"I order you to look at Sarah Good!" Judge Hathorne roared.

Fearfully they peeked. And fell shrieking into each other's arms, sobbing with pain. "Aye!" they chorused. "She hurts us. Oh, make her stop!"

Sarah looked away with a snort of contempt, and matrons passed among the girls, pulling them up on their stools. Judge Hathorne stared hard at Sarah Good. "Do you still deny what you do? Tell us the truth! Why do you torment these poor children?"

"Children, my arse!" Sarah glared at the judges. "I don't torment anyone."

The judge lifted his hands. "Then who does?"

"There was two more arrested besides me," Sarah muttered sullenly. "Ask them." She scratched her arm, and immediately the girls set up a howl, grabbing their arms and screaming that Sarah Good's shape scratched them.

When he could again be heard, Judge Hathorne persisted stubbornly. "Who torments the children?"

"You know so much," Sarah yelled spitefully, "you tell me!"

"There'll be respect in this courtroom," the judge admonished sharply. His narrow eyes swung from Sarah to the guards, making his point. "Now, tell us who torments these children!"

Sarah sighed and shrugged. "Well, it isn't me. Maybe that stingy old bitch Goody Osburn."

The crowd gasped at hearing Osburn accused by one of her own kind. No one doubted Sarah Good's guilt; they saw it clearly.

The questioning continued, relentless and stubborn. And aside from occasional outbursts from the girls, a pin could have been heard, had one dropped. The audience did not cough or shuffle. They gaped and listened and scarcely dared to breathe.

Judge Hathorne probed, and Sarah Good responded with abuse that worsened as the hours passed. She began to understand the full extent of her peril, and her answers lagged, rambling through a litany of complaint and self-pity.

At last came the conclusive test. Judge Hathorne leaned over the dais, his face weary. "Sarah Good, can you recite the Lord's Prayer without faltering? Perfectly?"

The packed room sucked in their breath and strained to hear Sarah's recital.

"Of course I can. What a stupid question!"

"Then do it!"

Sarah sighed. "If I must, I will." She paused and drew her brows together in an ugly frown of concentration.

"What? Speak louder!"

"Yea, though I walk through . . . let's see . . . I will fear no . . ." She stopped and frowned at the planks. "I can do it! . . . Our Father what are in heaven . . . no . . . Our Father who be in heaven . . ." Beads of sweat rose on Sarah's furrowed brow. As well as anyone, she knew no witch could repeat the Lord's Prayer without error.

"When is the last time you dared defile the meetinghouse by attending sabbath?" Judge Hathorne's face fired with a victorious flush.

Sarah wiped her palms on a dirty skirt. Her eyes flicked this way and that. "None of the village bitches give me and Dorcas anything good enough to wear to meeting. We can't go in rags, can we?"

Triumphant, Judge Hathorne banged his gavel. Sarah Good was dragged away and bound over for trial.

Bristol and Caleb followed a silent crowd through the slushy lane and into Ingersoll's tavern for lunch and hot cider. Once inside, the voices came to life, buzzing over the large warm room. The Wainwrights found a small table near a larger one where the girls were fed trenchers of stew and mugs of steaming ale.

Bristol and Caleb faced each other over the table, listening to the shouted opinions filling the tavern. "Good riddance!" sounded again and again. Few would be sorry to see Salem Village rid of its beggar. "I just knew it!" someone stated loudly. "Why, I remember once when she came begging at our door . . ." Everyone had a story to prove Sarah Good's guilt as a witch.

Bristol abandoned an effort to force down the food on her trencher. She looked into Caleb's tight, worried face. "You don't agree with this, do you?" she whispered, after checking to be certain no one could overhear.

Troubled, Caleb stared at his wife. "Do you? Can you believe in two Sarah Goods? One standing before your eyes, another as an invisible fiend choking and torturing?" He shook his head, and his jaw clenched. "I can't. I think Sarah goes to prison not for witchery, but for begging an existence at the doors in this village."

Shocked, Bristol gasped. "Caleb, you can't mean that!"

He leaned over the table and lowered his voice. "Look at them." He inclined his head toward the long table of laughing girls. "Do they look tormented to you? I think not. They're having a grand time! In their whole lives, no one has taken seriously a single word from their mouths. Now everyone in this community hangs on each phrase like it was gospel! No queen was ever as lofty as Charity when those men came to take her statement. You saw her . . . she enjoyed it! She loved having them eager to hear everything she said."

Bristol blinked at her hands. If she were totally honest with herself, she'd have to admit she'd experienced the same uneasy feeling as Caleb when she listened to Charity give her statement. The entire business confused and frightened Bristol.

A bell rang summoning them back to the meetinghouse for the afternoon session. But before leaving Ingersoll's, Bristol stopped at the girls' table and leaned over Charity. "Are you all right?" she whispered anxiously.

Excitement blazed in Charity's eyes. "Did you see us, Brissy?" she inquired breathlessly. "Did you see how the witch made me dumb?"

"I saw!" Abigail laughed. Immediately she mimicked Charity. Abigail clutched her hair in both hands and made her face go blank and staring. All the girls laughed. Mary Walcot banged her mug in appreciation and agreed Charity had looked just like that.

Charity turned back to Bristol with a smile. Her face glowed. "I hope you have a good place to see from," she said.

"I . . . we'll wait for you when it's over," Bristol croaked. Her lips felt stiff. Stumbling, she caught up with Caleb, and they entered the meetinghouse.

When the girls had been led inside and settled on their stools, Tituba followed the guards into the dock. She created a sensation.

First, little Betty Parris had to be restrained from running to hug her cherished Tituba. Seeing this, some immediately doubted Tituba had hurt anyone. Reverend Parris led his daughter from the courtroom, his face flaming with embarrassment. Betty did not reappear.

During the delay, it was noted the antics of the afflicted girls lacked the power of the morning's demonstration. Some whispered the girls' lunch sat heavy on their stomachs; others wondered if Tituba might be innocent.

"Why do you hurt the children?"

"I don't hurt the children. I love the children. They try to make me, but I don't do it." Tituba's chocolate eyes stayed carefully away from the girls. She knew the procedure.

"Who tries to force you?"

"The man who made me sign the book."

Pandemonium broke across the courtroom. Tituba's statement was tantamount to a confession, and instantly a chill fear charged the atmosphere. The girls went berserk with screaming and convulsions; their eyes rolled in their heads, their tongues burst from their lips. Several women in the audience fainted and had to be carried out. Everyone's heart hammered wildly.

Tituba continued. Aye, she admitted signing a contract with the devil; aye, she'd attended witches' covens. She served a black man that appeared sometimes as a hog or a large dog, and sometimes as a red or black rat. She attended ritual gatherings by riding a stick through the air.

Judge Hathorne looked ill. The room was still as death. "Do you hurt the children?"

Tituba's wounded eyes leaped in her dark face. "No, sir. I never did. I love the children, I swear it." She appealed to a stunned audience, who dropped their eyes in fright as her gaze passed over them. "I didn't do it. They said to hurt the children, or they'd hurt me. But I wouldn't. No, sir!"

"Ann Junior testified someone tormented her with a knife last night. Did your shape try to cut off her head?"

"Ann?" Horrified, Tituba wrung her hands and shook her head. "No! No! Osburn and Good, they said to do it, but I said no."

The crowd gasped and swayed. At last it was confirmed; a confessed witch named the others.

Judge Hathorne glanced at Goodman Cheever, who wrote furiously. "Are you getting all this?" Goodman Cheever nodded without looking up. Judge Hathorne studied his notes and returned to the witch. As much as possible, he avoided meeting her eyes. "Did you pinch Elizabeth Hubbard this morning hard enough to leave bruises?"

"A dark man's shapé brought her to me and made me pinch her. I didn't want to."

"Who does these terrible things—is it you or the shape in which you serve your evil master?"

"My shape. Not me; my shape."

Judge Hathorne mopped his head and glanced at Jonathan Corwin. Corwin scribbled notes. Hathorne continued. "Does Sarah Good, whom you have named a fellow witch, does she have a familiar?"

"Aye. She has a yellow bird who sucks between her fingers."

"Does Sarah Osburn have a familiar?"

"Osburn has a yellow dog. Abigail Williams saw the creature. It has wings and a woman's head, and it turns into Goody Osburn. She has another hairy thing with only two legs. You can ask Abigail."

Abigail Williams confirmed it.

"Did you hurt the Currins' baby?"

"Goody Good and Goody Osburn told me they hurt the Currin baby, but I did not. No, sir."

The damning testimony went on with continuous outbreaks from the girls. At Tituba's confession, their sluggishness had disappeared, and they exhibited genuine terror, cringing and screaming if her glance grazed past them. Several bowed their heads and wept and appeared to be frozen in trance states.

Calmly Tituba continued to answer questions throughout the afternoon. She freely confessed to being a witch and hinted she'd been one long before coming to New England. She admitted to consorting with witches and the devil himself, to having signed the damning roll call. The detail she offered was convincing. She resisted suggestions that she had or was now hurting the children, but she had no qualms about blaming Goody Osburn or Sarah Good.

"Who else?" Judge Hathorne demanded. "Do other witches foul the village?"

Tituba closed her eyes and rubbed her temples. "Darkness on the land."

In the audience Bristol shivered, and icy bumps rose on her skin. She'd heard those words before.

"I can't see anymore. I'm blind now." Tituba's grizzled head shook in puzzlement. "I try to look at . . . like I used to . . . but I'm blind now. It doesn't work anymore."

"Explain that."

Tituba couldn't. "I'm blind now."

The guards led her away.

And brought old Goody Osburn into the courtroom. Obviously ill and totally baffled at what was happening to her, Goody Osburn blinked at the girls, and her toothless mouth fell open. No one had bothered to tell her about anything like this. They'd lifted her out of her sickbed and brought her here to witness a marvelous event, and seeing the girls, Sarah Osburn decided she wouldn't have missed it for the world. It was a display, a demonstration of some kind, she thought. Goody Osburn cackled and grinned and tried to clap her hands, but the pain in her chest didn't allow for much of that. Two men sitting high behind a counter shouted at her, but she paid them no mind. The girls were much too entertaining; Goody Osburn wanted to watch them. Ann Putnam Senior was rolling on the floor and falling over like a hog. Goody Osburn yelled a greeting. She'd helped deliver a couple of Ann's babies, both dead. Goody Osburn had heard a couple of Ann's babies lived, and maybe one of those howling mouths belonged to Ann's daughter. But all the maids looked alike to Sarah Osburn, especially screeching and thrashing around like that. They were sure all having a good time of it. Old Goody Osburn only wished she didn't feel like she was going to die any minute, or she'd have jumped right in and rolled around with them.

The guards carried her away, cackling and pointing and smacking her lips over her gums.

No one spoke as the crowd filed outside and walked toward their wagons. They needed time to sort out what they'd seen and heard. Everyone felt drained and empty, yet tense at the same time.

John Proctor paused at the Wainwright wagon, where

Caleb and Bristol waited for Charity. "It's a travesty, Wainwright," John Proctor said in a low voice.

"I don't understand why that crazy old woman confessed." Caleb removed his hat and ran a hand through his sandy hair. He stared at the reins in his fingers, then looked down to meet Proctor's concerned frown. "Why did she invent all that foolishness?"

John shrugged. "Who can say?" He glanced at Bristol's white face, wondering how freely to speak. "Maybe Tituba actually believes she's a witch. Maybe her nightmares are so vivid she believes them. Maybe she's making a kind of sacrifice, hoping it will all end here."

Bristol drew a cold breath and forced her hands to release clumps of apron. "Then you don't think this is over?" Inside, she felt pulled in different directions. She'd grown up accepting the reality of evil, of witchcraft, of a devil always on the prowl. What John and Caleb believed sounded dangerously like heresy. Bristol's mind was keen and open to progressive thought, but this—to doubt where there seemed no doubt— she found this a hard idea to accept. And if they were right, then what did that mean about the courtroom scene she'd just witnessed?

"No, Goodwife Wainwright, I do not think the witch hunt has ended." John Proctor spoke quietly, with chilling conviction. "We've rid ourselves of a begger, a sick old woman, and a storyteller who entrances our girls from their chores." He paused, his eyes straying to the village cemetery. "But how long before someone wishes we could remove other people as easily?" He looked from Bristol to Caleb. "How long before politics enter the issue? How long before someone sees witchcraft, not as the cause of his troubles, but as the solution?"

Caleb's face drained of color. "As a way to settle personal animosities," he added.

"Exactly." John's eyes grew thoughtful as he watched Charity climb into the wagon bed and take her stool on the straw. High excitement glowed on Charity's cheeks, and she waved gaily to the other girls joining their families. Mary Warren jumped into the back of John Proctor's wagon and turned her face toward him. "Exactly," John muttered softly, and walked away.

During the next two weeks, Bristol decided John and Caleb were wrong. If the rest of the village was anything like the Wainwright farm, all was quiet. Perhaps too quiet, Bristol thought uneasily, but she didn't ascribe the lull to witchcraft.

Caleb worked outside regardless of weather, fixing fences,

tending the animals, overseeing the work of the bond servants, repairing harness, chopping wood, and seeing to all the myriad chores required to sustain a large farm. Inside, Bristol had little difficulty keeping up with her work, even when Charity didn't feel like helping. Which was often lately. Bristol fell behind in spinning and weaving, but New England women were always behind in spinning and weaving.

What worried Bristol more than the household tasks was her sister. For several days following the examination, Charity had seemed in a state of high exhilaration. Long after everyone was usually asleep, Bristol heard Charity wandering about the house, and Charity had been first to rise. They discovered her dressed and combed and preparing breakfast before the first cock crowed. This lasted nearly a week; then Charity appeared to wind down, and she took on a dull look. Now she seemed at loose ends, unsure what to do with herself.

"Are you feeling well?" Bristol asked, looking at Charity drooped over a mug of cooling beer. She had to repeat the question.

"What?" Charity glanced upward, and Bristol noticed dark shadows beneath her pale eyes. "Oh. Aye, I'm fine."

Bristol finished gutting the hares she planned to roast for supper and held the carcasses over a candle to singe the hair. Wrinkling her nose at the smell, she slid another glance toward Charity. "You look tired."

Charity's brooding eyes watched Bristol turn the hares. "Did Caleb tell you he's sending me to England after the trials?" Her voice was harsh and abrupt.

Carefully Bristol avoided meeting Charity's eyes. "Aye. He thinks you'll be happier there."

Charity flared. "Who gave Caleb Wainwright the right to decide what will make me happy?" Her voice lashed out. "He hasn't guessed right about that yet!" Staring into her beer, Charity blinked back sudden tears. "I don't want to leave here any more than you did! I'm old enough to make my own decisions about my own life!"

Putting the hares on the table, Bristol wiped her hands on her apron. She searched for the right thing to say. "I think I know how you must feel—" she began.

"No you don't!" Charity's eyes flashed and her lips trembled. "Everybody thinks they know how I feel or what's best for me or how I should behave. But none of you do! It's easy for you, Bristol. Now that you're married, you can come and go as you please. People pay attention when you say

387

something. You have what you want." She didn't see the quick spasm of pain shadow Bristol's face. "But you've forgotten how it feels always to be treated like a child. And never, not ever, have you known what it's like not to have a man waiting for you."

"Charity . . ."

"You were always the pretty one. You always had a choice. You've never had to worry about being a thornbark. But what about me?" Her voice caught on a sob. "There's no one anxious to court Charity Adams! I *do* have to worry about being a spinster, because the only man I ever . . ." Charity stared at Bristol; then her mouth snapped shut. She dropped her head.

Bristol sank to a chair and leaned her elbows on the table, the hares forgotten. "Oh, Charity," she whispered sadly. "Everything is such a mess, isn't it?" Tilting back her head, Bristol stared at the ceiling as if she might find some answers there. "You don't know how I wish things were different. And I can't begin to explain, because you and I have drifted so far apart. I doubt you'd really hear anything I wanted to tell you."

"Nothing you said would change anything, would it?"

After a moment Bristol sighed and answered. "No. No, I can't change anything for you, or for me, or for . . ." Her voice lapsed into silence.

"It doesn't matter," Charity said bitterly. They sat in a pocket of quiet; then, surprisingly, Charity reached out and touched Bristol's hand. "I don't blame you, Brissy," she said in a low voice, not looking at her sister. "I did at first, and . . . sometimes I . . . but deep down, I know it isn't your fault." Her voice hardened. "I know whose fault it is. You warned me."

Bristol shrank from the hatred in Charity's face. "Oh, Charity, don't do this. Don't turn your feelings into hate!" Bristol swallowed and hesitated at the expression in her sister's eyes. "I don't mean to tell you what to do," she stammered, "but we both know hatred is wrong. Maybe if you talked with Reverend Parris . . . maybe he could counsel . . ."

Charity laughed, a pained unpleasant sound. "Him? He'd lecture me on how the village has done wrong to him, and then the next day everyone in Salem would know my troubles." She shook her head, the orange curls too bright against her face. "No, Brissy. I'll find the answers myself."

Sighing, Bristol decided she might as well be talking to a stranger for all the resemblance this young woman had to the

Charity she'd known all her life. Wearily Bristol pushed up from the table and began scraping fur off the hares.

"I'm just . . . just bored, maybe," Charity said in an indifferent voice, changing the subject. A little color returned to her cheeks. "For a while life was interesting. All those people coming to the house, all the excitement, and I felt . . . important!" She looked away from Bristol's horrified stare. "Well, you know what I mean."

"No," Bristol answered slowly. "No, I don't think I do."

Charity's thin shoulders lifted in a shrug. "Oh, you know. For a while people listened to me." Her eyes shone. "Like I mattered. Like someone cared what I thought and felt."

"I care what you think and feel, Charity." But watching her sister, Bristol knew that wasn't enough. There was only one person Charity wanted to have notice. Bristol's heart went out to the girl, and with it, a feeling of impotence. There was nothing she could do to help ease Charity's misery. Nothing anyone could do.

"I know, but . . ." Charity let the sentence die.

Bristol threaded a spit through the hares and placed them above the fire. Conscious of Charity hunched over the table, she assembled water, flour, lard, salt, and began mixing pie dough. When the silence became awkward, Bristol looked up and suggested, "Why don't you take old Brown out for a ride? He could use the exercise, and you might like some fresh air."

"There's no place to go."

With Tituba in the Boston jail awaiting trial, the girls had lost their meeting place.

Bristol searched her mind. Hurriedly she wrapped a wheel of cheese and placed it beside Charity. "Would you take this to Martha Cory, then? I promised it to her."

Charity eyed the package, and her lip curled in distaste. "How can you say you care about my feelings and then sentence me to Goody Cory's? Can't you guess how she'll lecture me? Goody Cory would find fault with a saint!"

But she went. Bristol watched from the window as Charity trotted old Brown past the house. Her emerald eyes darkened. She decided Caleb was right about Charity. The best thing for the girl would be to put her on the first ship for London. But they couldn't do that until after the trials. And no trial could be held until the new governor arrived from England—sometime in May, the gossips said. Two months distant.

Dropping the curtain, Bristol returned to her pies. What

worried her was Charity's hatred for Caleb. Charity had allowed a frustrated love to clot into betrayal and loathing. Anyone could see her heart was eaten with black emotion.

But surely, Bristol thought sadly, surely they could manage to live peaceably for two more months. Caleb did all he could to avoid provoking Charity, and Charity kept to her room. Bristol felt like an uneasy buffer between the two.

On the one hand, she didn't want Charity to leave, didn't relish being alone with Caleb and the changes he'd hinted would occur. But neither did Bristol want Charity to remain with them. She saw what this strain was doing to her sister, turning her from a sweet, loving girl into a hate-filled harpy. In London, Aunt Pru would open her house and her heart to the wounded girl and provide her everything a young woman could wish—dances, pretty gowns, a constant supply of suitable young men. Aunt Pru would build Charity's confidence, help her see what a pretty girl she was.

Bristol turned the spit over the hearth and set out trenchers, spoons, condiments. Nodding to herself, she decided to take Charity aside tonight and tell her everything about London. She'd tell Charity all the details no one had asked to hear, all the pleasures and pastimes so frowned upon in Salem Village. Thinking it over carefully, Bristol realized the time was right now; Charity would welcome hearing of these diversions and might even alter her position about leaving Salem when all the new daring experiences were detailed. No one could be bored at Hathaway House. And who could tell what beauty might emerge after Collette and Molly finished with Charity?

Hathaway House. Bristol stared at the pewter cups on her shelf. With one missing. Then she shook her long hair forcefully. No, there were things about Hathaway House she wouldn't be able to speak of. The pain. . . . But she'd tell Charity what she could.

Bristol didn't have the opportunity.

Charity returned as Caleb and Bristol and the two servants were sitting down to eat. She reeled through the buttery door, her eyes wild and rolling in her head. Tearing her hair and frothing at the mouth, Charity crashed to the floor in a violent fit.

It had started again.

30

Martha Cory's examination took place March 21, 1692. She steadfastly maintained she was a saint, and proved it to her own satisfaction by offering tart comments on the idiocy of the proceedings.

But Martha's commentary was far overshadowed by the maelstrom her glance effected on the girls. They screamed in anguish and jerked up their sleeves to show teeth marks where Martha Cory's shape chewed their flesh and punctured their skin. Faced with conclusive evidence, Judge Hathorne bound Martha Cory for trial and committed her to the Boston prison.

On March 23, 1692, Dorcas Good, Sarah Good's five-year-old daughter, was cried out upon and examined. Eager to please, the waif willingly confessed to being a witch. "Aye." She beamed. "Mama made me sign the book, just like you said." Careful probing elicited the damning evidence that Dorcas kept a snake as familiar, suckling it from her little finger. She held up her hand, delighted with the sensation she caused. With such a concrete confession, the court had no choice but to send the child to jail.

Neither Martha nor Dorcas eased the girls' torments; their agonies continued. And built toward a subtle but conclusive contest. Thus far, all those cried out upon had fit the label of village misfit; now the girls tested the strength of their afflictions. They turned in fury upon old Rebecca Nurse, accusing Rebecca of inflicting fresh pain on their bodies and spirits.

The community rocked to its foundations. Cheerful, kind-hearted Rebecca Nurse enjoyed the respect and admiration of nearly all villagers regardless of political affiliation or group loyalties.

An incredulous judge queried the girls individually, a startling departure from previous procedure.

"Charity Adams? Does this woman torment you?"

391

Biting her thumb, Charity glanced at Rebecca's dried-apple smile and dropped her head. She gave no answer.

"Ann Putnam Senior?"

Ann Senior jumped from her stool, wild eyes rolling. Screaming and weeping, Ann Senior swore Rebecca Nurse had appeared in the night and brutally beat Ann as she tried to sleep. Judge Hathorne blinked. "This old woman who uses a cane to stand—she beat you?"

Ann bent double with pain, panting and gasping. "Aye! Her shape has the strength of ten! See it even now!"

Judge Hathorne's jaw knotted. His stare swung to Abigail Williams. "Abigail, are you tortured by Goody Nurse?"

"Aye!" Abigail cried, covering her eyes. Her blossoming body shuddered in sensual ripples of fear. She pulled her skirt over her head, and a matron rushed forward to tug it back in place.

Peering desperately at her wailing mother, Ann Junior shouted, "Goody Nurse hurts me too! Oh, the pain, the pain!"

Helplessly Judge Hathorne shrugged toward Rebecca Nurse, who strained to hear what was said. "You see the accusations? What do you say to it?" he shouted above the noise.

Ann Senior kicked her heels on the floor and pointed, her face ugly. "You came last night and brought the black man with you and asked me to tempt God and die! You tried to force me to eat and drink of damnation!"

A matron shouted into Rebecca's ear; then Rebecca shook her head no, and a quavering smile curved her lips. "You're mistaken, dear," her soft voice answered. "I'm sure you mean well here, but you're mistaken." She reached a shaking veined hand as if to help Ann to her feet, and all the girls erupted into hideous shrieks and howls.

"Stop that!" Judge Hathorne thundered.

Instantly the girls fell silent and gaped up at the judge, their mouths open. They cast uneasy glances among themselves. Never had the judge ordered them to silence. They stole quick peeks at the audience, sensing the sympathy for Rebecca Nurse. And an angry suspicion toward themselves.

Bristol's heart surged with sudden hope. Perhaps . . . please, God . . . perhaps the cycle would break here. No one could possibly believe little Rebecca Nurse guilty of a single unkind deed. Bristol clutched Caleb's arm, and she glanced at him, her emerald eyes confident.

Reading her expression, Caleb moved his head in a barely

perceptible negative shake. "Hathorne's challenged them," he said in a low voice, his eyes worried.

The girls understood; they accepted the challenge with vengeance. Those sitting mute broke into piteous cries. Mary Walcot, who at first refused to name Goody Nurse as her assailant, now identified Rebecca positively. Elizabeth Hubbard wept and screamed and danced in pain, displaying sets of raw teeth marks along her arms. Mary Warren howled like a banshee. Shrieking in pain, her eyes rolling, Charity Adams sobbed that Goody Nurse strangled her. Abigail Williams jerked in spastic twitches, and everyone saw a rash of pin pricks appear on her legs. Screams and howls shook the rafters.

When he could at last be heard, Judge Hathorne wiped his face and reluctantly leaned over the dais. "If you are guilty, you would do well to confess and give glory to God."

Confused, unable to hear clearly, Rebecca turned her small, wrinkled face upward. "But I'm as innocent as a newborn babe." She blinked and frowned down at her shaking hands clutching the cane. "I don't feel well. I've been sick for several days," she offered, as if that explained everything.

Judge Hathorne mopped his neck. "Maybe you aren't a witch but have been tempted that way?" he asked hopefully. "No."

A Mrs. Pope who had joined the shifting number of afflicted girls fell into a grievous fit, and the others followed.

The judge ignored them. "Do you think these girls are suffering or pretending to suffer?" he shouted at Rebecca.

The crowd sucked in its breath, and the girls doubled their howling and screaming and teeth marks and puncture wounds. Whenever Rebecca moved an arm or an eyebrow, the girls sobbed and clutched their own arms and faces, yelling that Goody Nurse's shape brutalized them. Abigail and Ann Junior foamed at the mouth and thrashed in violent fits.

"I don't know, sir. I wouldn't want to comment on it," Rebecca answered, watching the commotion with a baffled frown.

The judge wet his lips and stared down at the girls. He flicked a glance at Rebecca Nurse, leaning on her cane, then again looked at the agonies below his dais. Sighing, he banged the gavel. He saw no option but to hold Goody Nurse for trial.

Staggered, Bristol moved from the courtroom in a trance. If Rebecca Nurse could be held for a witch, then no one was safe. Not for one second did Bristol imagine Rebecca guilty.

Suddenly she found herself seriously considering the arguments John Proctor and Caleb presented against witchcraft. She climbed onto the wagon seat and slid a glance toward Caleb's sober profile. He sat stiffly, his lips in a tight line, his jaw knotting and releasing. She noticed his knuckles turn white against the reins. If Caleb was right . . . if Rebecca wasn't a witch . . . if none of them were witches, then what in God's name was this all about?

Swiveling on the high seat, Bristol settled her troubled stare on the top of Charity's head. Sport? Did they do it for sport? Bristol shivered. No, she couldn't accept that. Then what? Attention? No! It couldn't be. Bristol turned back on the seat. But . . . Rebecca Nurse? A witch? Bristol felt sick.

That night, for the first time in her marriage, Bristol crawled beneath the bed quilts without reluctance. She faced her husband and gazed into his steady eyes. "Caleb?"

"Aye."

"Hold me." Bristol could not quit shivering. "Please hold me."

Caleb opened his arms, and she burrowed into his broad warmth. They nestled in the darkness, close yet still alone. Gradually his large body absorbed her chill of fear and bewilderment. Then his words frightened her again.

"It won't end," he said bluntly against her hair. "If they can send Rebecca to prison, their power is limitless. Any name suggested to them is in danger. The village now has a perfect tool to exact revenge, to punish hatreds and political frustrations."

"Dear God," Bristol breathed. She wished he was wrong, but deep inside, she sensed the truth of what he said.

"How did we let this viper loose?" An agony thickened Caleb's voice. "How can it happen? These are good people! Decent people! But did you see their faces? I can't make sense of it in my mind." His arms tightened around her. "Why are the girls doing this? Why are we allowing it?"

Both of them whispered, conscious of Charity on the other side of the wall. Neither had spoken to her during the ride home, and Charity hadn't appeared to notice. She drifted in a world of her own making, unreachable, outside rational understanding.

"Caleb?"

"Aye."

Then he understood. And he responded to her need for human warmth. His large calloused hands closed over her breasts, and Bristol covered his fingers with her smaller ones and pressed against his touch, feeling her nipples harden. "Slowly," she whispered, turning to meet his mouth. "Make it last."

Whether he followed her direction, or whether he too needed to prolong the touching, tonight Caleb displayed a tenderness and consideration in their lovemaking he'd not shown before. Bristol didn't find the release she sought, but tonight it didn't matter as it had in the past. The gentle contact with another human being was what both desperately needed, and they found it. For the first time, they slept in each other's arms.

And forgot the tormented girl listening beyond the wall.

Twenty-two people were accused in April. Thirty-nine more went to jail in May. Among them was Elizabeth Proctor, triumphantly accused by Mary Warren. When it was determined Elizabeth Proctor was pregnant, Mary Warren fainted with shock. In a rage, she cried out on John Proctor, her sick love turning to hatred. Both John Proctor and his pregnant wife were carted to Boston prison, bound over for trial.

The Proctors were among friends. Bridget Bishop, Ann Pudeater, Alice Parker, George Burroughs, and scores more from the surrounding towns of Ipswich, Beverly, Andover, and Salem Town. Especially the hated Salem Town. During the examinations, people constantly approached the stricken girls, slyly whispering in their ears. Soon after, someone else found himself accused of malefic witchcraft. Often this new witch held anti-Parris convictions, or lived along Ipswich Road, or sat on the voting committee of Salem Town.

No one dared question the validity of the girls' testimony or inquire how the girls knew names of people they'd never met. To question called attention to oneself, and it was better not to attract the girls' attention.

Everyone feared the afflicted girls and politely shunned their company—and hoped to God the girls didn't know him by name. Clearing the Bay Colony of witches was important, aye, but in the furor, mistakes could be made.

News of what happened in Salem Village spread throughout the colony like a poisonous miasma. Curiosity seekers rode to observe the examinations—and often heard their names cried out, riding a cart to prison instead of returning home. To the delight of whispering enemies.

The jails filled, and the General Court of Massachusetts ordered a public fast throughout the colony, hoping a day of prayer would quiet the spreading terror. Witches leaped behind every shadow. No one felt safe. People boarded themselves behind doors and whimpered in their sleep. Evil overran the colony; some swore God had forsaken New England.

Not a soul felt safe from peril, nor would until the new governor arrived and ordered the trials to begin. Every day a delegation met ships arriving from England, praying Governor Phips would be on board. The jails were overflowing. The witches were chained and guarded, but who knew what horror might occur with such massed evil concentrated in one spot? The colony's peace of mind demanded the trials begin at once. Lives and crops were at stake.

Governor Sir William Phips arrived May 14 and found himself badgered for a trial date before he stepped off the ship. Responding immediately, he appointed a special court of oyer and terminer and commanded the trials to commence.

"Thank God!" people breathed in the lanes. "Now we can purge the witches! We can hope again!"

However, in some cases events had already been set in motion that neither the governor, nor fate, nor hope could alter.

On May 14, 1692, Charity Adams stared into the crowd, then fell into a fit and cried out the name of Caleb Wainwright as her tormentor. The other girls added their shrill cries to the accusation. Charity slid to the floor in a blatantly sexual posture and shrieked that Caleb Wainwright violated her. His shape drove her to rapturous agony, she screamed, his ice-cold member penetrated her virginal thighs.

Bristol gasped, and her eyes widened until they hurt. Her hands jumped to her mouth, smothering a scream. People backed away from her and Caleb, curling their lips in fear and disgust. Neighbors pushed their women behind them and shoved away from a man they'd known and respected all their lives. Until finally Caleb and Bristol formed an isolated pocket within the crowd. "No!" Bristol whispered, shaking her head. "Oh, no!"

Caleb stood like a man of stone. He watched Charity thrusting her hips off the floor, and his square face looked sadder than Bristol had imagined a human face could be. Deep pity blunted his blue eyes . . . and something else. Bristol covered her face with her hands. Caleb loved Charity. Even now, he loved her. His heart shone on his face, in his eyes, in the way his shaking hands yearned toward her. Caleb Wainwright stared at the tormented creature writhing on the planks . . . and he forgave her. He loved her; if anyone was to blame for what happened, it was he.

"No, Caleb!" Bristol clawed at his arm, reading his face as surely as if he'd spoken aloud. "Tell them she lies! Tell them you don't violate her! Tell them it isn't true!"

He stirred and blinked down into Bristol's white face. "Isn't it?" he asked softly through bloodless lips. "Is lust of the heart any less damning than the deed?" His face crumpled and his eyes turned black. "I'm sorry, Bristol. I've made a terrible mess of things, haven't I?" Then his eyes fastened on Charity until the guards rushed in and led him away.

Bristol pushed from the courtroom, trying to follow, but the guards turned her aside and chained Caleb in a cart with many others. Heart pounding, Bristol could only stand in the dusty lane and watch the cart jolt down the path. When it disappeared, she ran toward the wagon, not waiting for Charity, and she whipped the horses savagely, racing them toward home. Home? Bristol had no home; she who treasured the thought of home, who longed for home, had none. This vile land seething with evil was home to no one. God spit on this land.

She left the wagon and horses for the servants and ran inside the house, where she paced like a crazed person. Caleb would be released. Aye. No one knowing Caleb Wainwright could believe he was a witch. But she recalled neighbors drawing back, expressions of revulsion and fright pinching their faces. Dear God! But when they thought about it, they'd remember Caleb as a man of honor. A man who lived to perform his duty and obligations in a decent, upright manner. But so did Rebecca Nurse, and Mary Easty, and Dorcas Hoar, and Mary Bradberry, and all the others now in prison.

Bristol attempted to pour a mug of rum, but her fingers shook so badly she spilled more than entered the cup. Hurling the cup against the wall, she sank to the table and dropped her head. Nearly a hundred were in prison now. So many. Were they all like Caleb? Was there a single practicing witch among them? Caleb. Oh, dear God!

She pounded her fists helplessly on the table. Surely no one would testify against Caleb; he had hurt no one. Charity would not continue with this. Would she?

Unable to remain seated, Bristol flew into Charity's room and threw her sister's belongings into a trunk. It was unthinkable that she and Charity continue living together.

Charity had to be insane; it was the only explanation. As

insane as Diana Thorne had been, as insane as any wretch howling in Bedlam. Charity lashed out to punish, to hurt as she believed herself to have been hurt. She wanted Caleb to suffer as she suffered.

Bristol dashed off an angry note telling Charity she was no longer welcome in the Wainwright house. Pausing, she bit the end of the quill. Where would Charity go? Well, Bristol recalled bitterly, Charity wanted to be in charge of her own life, let her find shelter on her own.

Folding the scrawled letter, Bristol tossed it inside the trunk and slammed the lid. She ordered one of the servants to deliver the trunk to the village meetinghouse.

But that night she couldn't sleep; the house was terribly quiet. Her husband languished in Boston prison. She had no idea where her sister might be. And Bristol grieved for them both. For the follies of the human heart.

Caleb deserved none of this; he'd only done as his conscience demanded. Bristol groaned and beat at her pillow. And Charity. Poor demented Charity was her blood, her flesh; and she'd refused Charity shelter. Closed her door on her own sister like Charity was an abomination.

Moaning, Bristol tossed on her bed and stared hotly into the darkness. Silence closed around her, heavy and accusing. "Oh, Mama," she whispered to the ceiling. "What would you do? What would you advise if you were here?"

Throwing back the light quilt, Bristol padded into the kitchen and lit a candle. She tugged her writing desk before her and dipped the quill.

Dear Mama,
    I've put this off too long.

Shivering, Bristol paused with the quill over the page. How did one speak of the unspeakable?

Events are happening, Mama, terrible things, which I know I must tell you. . . .

At dawn, Bristol folded a thick pile of pages and addressed them. One of the servants carried the letter to Salem Town for posting. She watched the man disappear down the lane, wishing she could retrieve the letter. But better for Hannah to hear the news from her than from a well-meaning friend. Silently Bristol bowed her head and thanked God Hannah

398

was far away in England, and not here to see what was happening to her family, to her friends and neighbors.

For the next two weeks Bristol remained near the house, not venturing past the Wainwright gate. She cleaned everything twice and spent hours planting herbs and vegetables to complete her kitchen garden. She'd hoped constant work would keep her mind from events in the village, but it did not. Every day the servants brought home news of more people accused, more people carted to the packed jails in all the surrounding towns.

"Some say Mistress Charity do be one of the worst afflicted."

Bristol swayed and held to her hoe for support. She could never recall the servants' names. One was Booker and the other Clem, but she couldn't seem to sort out which was which.

"Mistress Charity be tormented as bad as Mistress Williams and Mistress Putnam," Clem or Booker said. "The poor child do suffer greatly." His eyes darted to a horseshoe nailed above the buttery door. "Them things don't work, Goody Wainwright, you ought to know that. If it was me, I'd hang more garlic."

Bristol's eyes snapped open, and she glared at him. "Get out of my sight," she hissed. "Get out! Now!"

Surprised, he blinked, then scurried toward the barn. Bristol passed a shaking hand over her eyes and dropped the hoe. Stumbling into the house, she dipped a ladle of spring water from the bucket and dashed it over her face.

He probably hadn't meant anything, she told herself with a sigh of despair. The servant hadn't meant that horseshoes didn't keep Caleb from the house. Bristol felt a hysterical urge to giggle and realized she was coming apart. How funny. Did anyone notice how many accused witches kept all the recognized witch protectors in or on their houses? Did horseshoes and garlic and iron knives and all the rest—did they work on strangers' houses but not on the witches' own houses? Black suddenly became gray, and white bled into red. And what did the pussycat say to the queen?

"Crazy! I'm going crazy," Bristol blurted to the fireplace. She staggered through a door and lay on a bed, realizing it was Charity's small brass bed. Bristol stared around the empty room, stripped of all reminders of her sister. What had Charity thought when she lay in this bed hearing murmurs from the bedroom beyond? What agonies had this room known? What misery? A dry sob burst from Bristol's throat, and she rolled from the bed as if it seared her flesh. She stumbled into the kitchen and stared at the rows of shining pans and pots, the stocked larder, the carefully proportioned rooms and softly painted walls. Caleb had built this house. But for whom? Who was meant to use all the items so lovingly fashioned by his hands? That bucket. That churn. The table and chairs he'd made during long winter nights. Who had been in his mind? And what had happened to Caleb Wainwright's dreams?

"Oh, God, *what happened?*" Bristol fell on her knees and clasped her hands in front of her face. "Please, God . . . please, God . . ." She tried to pray, but the only words to pass her white lips were, "Please, God. Oh, please, God."

She thought she would go mad, but somehow she stumbled through the days until Caleb's trial. When she heard Bridget Bishop and Caleb Wainwright would be the first, she agonized over the news, wondering if it had any special significance. Would the judges proceed slowly at first, or be merciless? Would friendly faces fill the jury, or men with grudges to settle, scores to even?

On the morning of June 2, hollow-eyed from lack of sleep, Bristol dressed carefully, knowing many eyes would watch her. She selected a lightweight summer gown of simple design and wore her plainest collar and white apron. Looking in a hand mirror, Bristol noticed that even her hair, dressed in a severe bun at the neck, appeared dull and lifeless. Her starched white collar seemed to pull the color from her cheeks and the life from her eyes. Or perhaps a look of slack fear had lain there always. Today it felt as if it had.

Though she left the house early, by the time she tied her mare in front of the meetinghouse, the courtroom was packed.

"Excuse me," Bristol said, pushing against a wall of people. "Let me through, please!"

"Well! Who do you think you . . . ?" Then she was recognized, and a lane opened as if by magic. When the crowd closed behind her, Bristol stood near the front of the room.

Though all the windows were wide, the room steamed hot, stinking of sweat and sour body odor tinged with fear. Bristol felt a sheen of perspiration break over her skin. She sensed the body heat of those in front and to her sides, but she didn't glance at anyone. Instead, her eyes fixed on the men whispering and smiling in the jury box—the men whose opinions would alter destiny.

When she thought she would faint unless she could gulp

one deep cooling breath of fresh air, William Stoughton, chief justice of the court of oyer and terminer, finally entered and rapped the court into session. A hush of expectation settled over the mass of people, and most forgot their discomfort in anticipation of the drama unfolding before them.

As guards led Bridget Bishop into the dock, Bristol studied the man who would have such impact on so many lives. Justice Stoughton wore a dark skullcap over shoulder-length hair partially masking a high brow and triangular face. Beneath a long sharp nose, thin lips clamped in a line, and his large moist eyes grew sober as matrons positioned Bridget's arms straight out from her body. Judge Stoughton was an imposing man; his voice matched his physical appearance.

"You are not to move, Bridget Bishop, or in any way torment the good people of this court," the voice commanded, accustomed to unquestioning obedience.

Bridget shrugged and appeared uninterested, but none could overlook dark stains spreading beneath her arms. The woman poured nervous sweat.

Next, the girls were ushered into court, and each took an oath that the prisoner at the bar was the one afflicting her. Bristol's darting eyes fastened on Charity, praying the girl would glance up. But Charity sat on her stool demurely, hiding her expression by staring into her lap. Bristol bit into her thumb to keep from crying out. Bristol's heart bled: Charity Adams suffered.

Deep inside, Bristol couldn't believe Charity had any comprehension of the evil she wrought. Charity could not have changed that much. And she looked so pretty and young, so innocent, in a pale yellow blouse and brown laced vest over a matching skirt. Her carroty curls hung past her shoulders in long neat coils, framing her face. That tormented childlike freckled face!

It was impossible to think Charity could allow the madness to continue. Charity would halt Caleb's trial, Bristol assured herself. When Caleb took his turn in the dock, Charity would rise and recant her accusation. She would! Bristol swallowed hard and blotted her forehead. With great effort she swung her attention from her sister to the questioning.

Witness after witness offered testimony above the howls and screams of the girls, and the evidence mounted against Bridget Bishop. Within minutes the girls' careful grooming vanished. Their hair flew in damp tangles about wild faces, they clawed their clothing, bite marks reddened their arms, and hives flared on their bodies. Only Mary Walcot retained

401

any composure; she remained on her stool, quietly knitting a blue vest, her needles making a homey clicking sound incongruous amid hell's cacophony. The jury agreed Mary Walcot had been struck deaf and dumb; the witch sucked away the girl's senses. Oblivious of the discussion, Mary Walcot ignored the thrashing storm at her feet.

She was the only person in the room to do so. Abigail, Ann Junior, and Charity Adams suffered so terribly, several times the judge was forced to halt testimony and ask matrons to assist the girls and offer them relief. He made each girl approach Bridget and grasp her hand, sending the devils back into Bridget's body and temporarily out of her own. His voice and attitude indicated Bridget Bishop's case did not go well.

Indeed it did not. Poppets had been discovered in Bridget's basement—with shiny pins stuck through them. They created a buzzing sensation when presented into evidence. Bridget hotly denied knowing of their existence—an obvious lie. Next, several men testified the buxom Bridget had appeared during long winter nights and lain on top of them, squeezing the breath from their bodies. Bridget shouted that these men lusted for her, and better they on trial than she. Then a man shivering with fright swore he'd seen Bridget turn into a black cat, then a monkey, and finally into herself once more. When she'd observed him watching, she'd lifted her skirt and exposed her bare backside to him. Bridget denied knowing the man at all, even though everyone knew he was her nearest neighbor and the two had been battling a boundary dispute for years.

Final testimony came from the matrons. They swore Bridget Bishop did indeed have a "preternatural excrescence" on her body. There was a wart inside her left thigh where she suckled her familiar.

"That's a damned lie!" Bridget screamed. "Who among you does *not* have a wart or a mole somewhere on your body?"

Judge Stoughton silenced her with an icy glare, and nodded for the guards to drag her away. He cautioned the jury to keep silence until the day's end, and he recessed the court.

Gleefully the girls danced outside for their lunch, and Bristol watched Charity's flushed, excited face until the girl passed from view. Bristol's heart dropped to her knees. Charity appeared as exhilarated as the others, swept with power and the glories of attention. They skipped to their noon meal as if they hadn't a care in the world.

The jurors, most of whom remained in the courtroom, wore different expressions. A few looked ill; all wore the sober faces of men charged with a serious, distasteful duty. They turned the testimony in their minds—the poppets, the witnesses, Bridget's flagrant lies—and none observing could doubt the eventual verdict.

An icy knot of fear formed in Bristol's heart and grew. Despite the sweltering heat, her hands turned chill. By the time the guards pushed Caleb into the dock, she shook with dread and misgiving. Seeing his face drove a spear of cold fright into her brain. Caleb cherished no hope; none whatsoever. Bristol read it in his dead eyes, in the listless obedience as he allowed the guards to position his arms out from his body. She saw dark smudges beneath his eyes and knew he hadn't slept. It appeared to Bristol he'd already lost weight. But it was the obvious loss of all hope that turned Bristol's palms clammy.

The girls filed into the courtroom, once again freshly groomed, and each swore Caleb Wainwright threatened their lives and precious souls. For an instant Caleb's steady sad eyes met Charity's and their gaze locked. Then he turned his face in despair, and his square jaw knotted. Charity's head jerked and her pale eyes narrowed.

Watching them, Bristol twisted her hands and bit her lip until she tasted blood. What had they said to each other in that long glance? What had they asked that neither could give?

The proceedings began, and for an instant Bristol's heart leaped with new hope. Charity remained on her stool, her head bowed, and she didn't react to the shrieking and convulsions foaming around her.

Then, almost as if she moved in a dream, Charity's arms lifted and crossed her breast. She began swaying to rhythms deep within her mind. Her pale face opened like a rose and her expression was that of a woman eagerly welcoming a lover. Charity's lips parted, her thighs relaxed. Slowly her head fell back, exposing a milky column of throat, and a hoarse moan broke from her lips. The screams and wails called to her in a seductive siren song. Hands slid to cup her small breasts, and she dropped from the stool, groaning on the floor, her body thrusting and opening in sexual rapture.

Gagging, Bristol tore her eyes away. Bile choked her throat. Her hands leaped to her lips, pressing back the brackish liquid flooding her mouth. Hating to look, unable not to, she swung her eyes toward Caleb.

He stood like granite, arms outspread, his legs wide, and he watched Charity's virginal plunging with dying eyes, eyes that wept inside. Those eyes burned into Bristol's soul, blue wells of unimaginable sorrow.

The testimony began. The jury heard of pigs that disappeared beneath the witch Wainwright's evil eye, crops that withered in fields Caleb Wainwright passed, a baby that sickened and died after Caleb Wainwright visited the parents' house. They made note that no tears wet his eyes, and heard of a mark on his calf which the devil had cleverly disguised as an old scar.

At last the jury drew together for deliberation, and everyone in the packed courtroom held his breath and strained to overhear. In less than twenty minutes the foreman stood and announced a verdict. Both prisoners were returned to the dock.

"Proceed," Judge Stoughton commanded.

"We the jury find both Bridget Bishop and Caleb Wainwright guilty of malefic witchcraft as charged."

The room stunned to silence and all eyes riveted on Judge William Stoughton. He nodded and folded his hands.

"Let it be posted: Bridget Bishop and Caleb Wainwright shall be hanged by the neck until dead on the morning of our Lord June 10, 1692."

The room spun in exploding sound, and dots the color of blood swam across Bristol's vision. She stared toward Charity, seeing the girl jump to her feet and stare openmouthed in chalky disbelief.

Then a black wall crushed over Bristol, smashing her to the floor.

31

WHEN a matron helped Bristol sit up, nearly everyone had fled the courtroom. A few remaining jurors whispered in sober tones near the front of the room, and an old man pushed a birch broom along empty aisles.

"No!" Bristol screamed, still hearing Judge Stoughton's voice echoing in her head. "No! No!" She covered her eyes.

The matron studied Bristol's ashen face and signaled the jurors. "I think we got another one down with the affliction." She leaned above Bristol, her face sly and knowing. "Is it Goody Barnes that hurts you, dearie? It's Goody Barnes, isn't it? That nasty bitch thinks she's better than the rest of us. Is it Goody Barnes who hurts you?" she coaxed.

Appalled, Bristol stared into the woman's eager flushed face. She scrambled to her feet, and gathering her skirts, she dashed out of the meetinghouse, running blindly and gulping deep breaths of cool evening air. She ran without knowing her destination, ran until her chest hurt and her feet stumbled and her mind could think only of protesting muscles and nothing else.

Finally she bent against a stone wall, panting and sucking air into burning lungs. Insane! It was all insane! Slowly her vision cleared, and she recognized the stones beneath her fingers. The cemetery wall. Jumping back as if the rocks were hot lava, Bristol rubbed her temples with shaking fingers.

No. No. No! Madness laughed through her head. Caleb. It was unthinkable! Her shocked mind shied away and bounced back. She could not accept that they'd judged him guilty; but they had.

She shook her head back and forth, long hair tumbling from the bun at her neck. Then Bristol flung the red strands from her face and stared upward at stars beginning to pierce a dark sky. She raised her fists. "Where are you, God? Why have you turned away from us?" She screamed the words, her body shaking violently. "Where are you? Help us!" Her voice split. "Oh, God, help us!" she moaned.

There was no answer. Only a buzz of crickets and the rustle of night animals. And distant hysterical weeping. The wrenching sobs shot into Bristol's mind like bullets of agony. From somewhere, someone screamed a greater anguish than her own. Bristol turned away, stumbling in the deepening darkness, embarrassed that she and the unseen stranger intruded their grief on each other. Then she halted. Her skirts swept about her shoes, and her face froze.

Slowly, unwillingly, Bristol retraced her steps and entered the shadowy cemetery, following the sounds of hysteria and knowing in her heart what she would find. In the dim light of a half-moon Bristol located the pale oblong of Noah Adams' stone. She sagged against the gray freestone and made herself look down. A tormented figure sobbed beside the sunken rectangle.

"Charity," Bristol whispered, her voice dull and dead.

Charity's head jerked up, and her face was terrible to see. Tears cut muddy tracks down her cheeks; her eyes were wild and foaming with animal torment. Her yellow blouse hung in tatters, and strands of hair flew about her cheeks. Both hands held clods of earth from Noah's grave.

"I didn't mean it!" she screamed, her voice as wild and demented as her face. The clods broke in her fists, and she flung herself across the grave. "I didn't mean it to go this far," she sobbed, beating her forehead against the ground. "I never thought they'd find him guilty! Never!" She doubled in agony and curled into a screaming ball, rocking and holding her sides. "I love him! Oh, God, I love him! I love him!"

Bristol knelt, her knees sinking into soft summer earth, and she gathered Charity into her arms, cradling her like a small child. "Shhh. Let's go home now, Charity." Bristol's heart felt like a deadweight in her chest. "Shhh. Let's go home." She pulled Charity to her feet.

Charity walked like an old, old woman, bent in the middle, shuffling blindly, and moving where Bristol guided. Bristol took her home and laid Charity in the narrow little bed. Throughout a long terrible night Bristol held Charity's icy hand and watched her with vacant, stinging eyes.

"I love him! I love him and . . . oh, God . . . I've killed him! I don't know what happened . . . it was like a dream and . . . I've destroyed what I love most!" Charity's sobs tore her chest apart, ripped her throat raw, and flayed Bristol's senses until she quivered with savage pain. All through the night Charity screamed and sobbed and moaned and tormented them both.

Toward dawn Charity dropped into a feverish sleep, and Bristol dozed in a chair, her mind black with nightmares. When they woke, it began again.

Bristol bowed her head under the torrent of poisonous guilt and agonized love. Her brain felt as if it had been scooped clean and replaced with crawling worms. Darkness and horror chased through her mind—and deep heartbreaking pity for the demented creature in the bed.

How they endured the next days, Bristol never remembered. She bathed Charity's wild, twisted face and forced food between her lips and never dared leave her sister's side. She didn't wonder what the servants thought as they went about their chores listening to the shrieks and moans echoing through the house. She didn't care that the kitchen fire died out for the first time in her memory. She didn't give a moment's thought to whether or not Charity was missed in the village. Nothing mattered. Nothing. The world as they'd known it was ending. Not with rejoicing and blazing glory as all had expected, but in a shroud of black, smothering evil.

Then finally the fire in Charity burned itself out, leaving an empty husk where once a bright young girl had been. Her pale, swollen eyes gazed up at Bristol. "It's tomorrow, isn't it?" she croaked in a raw voice.

"Aye," Bristol said. She stared at the wall, unable to face the expression on Charity's gaunt, hollowed cheeks. Her throat worked and she gripped Charity's hand.

"Go to him," Charity urged, her eyes begging. "He'll need someone tonight." Her thin childlike form scarcely rippled the summer blanket. "And tell him . . . tell him I love him," she whispered. Two large tears hung on her lashes like jewels.

Bristol nodded, her heart in ashes.

She rode into Salem Town and found the sheriff's house and the makeshift jail behind it. Dirt-crusted lanterns lit the edges of a wooden enclosure, throwing weak shadows into the night. Bristol knocked at the sheriff's door, her hand moving in slow motion as if it didn't belong to her. She felt surprised when George Corwin responded.

"I've come to see my husband, Caleb Wainwright," she said in a flat, expressionless tone.

Sheriff Corwin studied her, still chewing a bite of supper. "Aren't you one of Noah Adams' girls?" he asked, looking at the red wisps curling from under her dust cap.

"Aye."

407

He nodded. "I thought so." He shifted on the porch, his dark eyes looking troubled. "I don't know the procedure on this sort of thing. Nobody told me. We haven't hanged anybody in a long time; a man forgets."

"Please," Bristol said simply, her green eyes filling.

He watched her and chewed at his thumbnail. Then he pushed open the door and waved her inside. "Aw, hell, I knew your pa and I've known Wainwright all his life. I guess it wouldn't hurt anything." He led Bristol into a small neat parlor and lit a candle. "Wait here." A woman peeped from the kitchen, and Bristol heard a murmur of low conversation; then all was quiet.

In a few minutes George Corwin returned with Caleb. "Now, you can't stay long," he warned Bristol, but his voice was kind. His eyes strayed to the open windows and back to Caleb.

"I'm not going anywhere, George," Caleb said quietly. He wore a rough workshirt open at the neck and soiled brown breeches. There was a tear in his left stocking.

"Just the same, I believe I'll leave the door open," George Corwin said with an apologetic shrug. "You understand." They heard him walk down the hall and into the kitchen.

Neither moved. They looked at each other across the small parlor. Bristol's heart squeezed in her chest. He looked exhausted, dark circles stained his eyes, and a calm resignation dulled his expression. She realized he'd come to terms with dying. And this hurt most of all—that a vital strong man in the summer of his life should be resigned to dying. Bristol dropped her white face, and her shoulders heaved.

"Don't, Bristol," he whispered. Then his arms were around her, holding her against his chest, comforting her. Above her shining head, his lifeless eyes stared out the window. "I've made such a mess of so many lives," he murmured.

"It isn't your fault," Bristol cried. She gripped his arms and stared up at his pale face. "Things just . . . just came together wrong! You did what you had to do!"

Gently he pressed her head against his shoulder so she wouldn't see his face. And she recognized his deep need for touching, for the solid warmth of another living, caring human being. "No, Bristol," he said softly, "I forced my own ideas of duty onto those around me. And I hurt so many." He stroked her hair. "You were right that day when you tried to tell me." Beneath his coarse shirt, Bristol felt his heartbeat, strong and steady. One after the other. He lifted a long red curl and pressed it to his cheek, closing his eyes and trying to imprint the silky feel of a woman's hair on his mind for all time.

"Oh, Caleb!" His arms tightened around her, and they stood in clinging silence, holding to the warm life in each other.

"Excuse me."

Reluctantly Bristol stepped from his arms and cast a resentful glance toward the door. Caleb stiffened at her side.

Mopping his brow and tugging his vest, Samuel Parris strode into the parlor. The reverend blew out his cheeks and sat on the edge of a high-backed chair.

"On this important night, I have come to offer my spiritual guidance," he announced solemnly.

Caleb stared. "No," he said quietly. Bristol moved to the window, wishing for a cool breeze, wishing Samuel Parris would vanish. She turned and glared at his clouding face.

"Caleb," Parris admonished, leaning forward, "I've come to pray with you." He saw the rejection in Caleb Wainwright's expression. "It isn't too late to confess and save yourself," Parris wheedled. "You don't have to hang!" Samuel Parris mopped his brow again, looked at the wet linen, and stuffed it into his pocket.

Caleb laughed, a short bitter sound. "There's nothing to confess. I'm no more a witch than you are, Parris."

A sly look narrowed the reverend's eyes, and he darted a quick look toward Bristol. "I think you miss my point. You don't have to hang—*if you confess.*"

"If I lie, you mean?" Caleb's face darkened. "This is the spiritual guidance you offer? A suggestion that I condemn my soul to hell for lying?"

Reverend Parris jumped to his feet and paced the room. He jerked the linen from his pocket and wiped his forehead. Then he stopped and stared hard at Caleb. "Just tell the truth," he begged, but a desperation in his tone suggested otherwise.

"The truth by whose definition? I've told the truth! I can deny being a witch a thousand times and no one will believe. But if I confessed just once, everyone would believe. That's the truth, isn't it?"

Bristol looked at Reverend Parris. Surely he knew what Caleb said was true.

Samuel Parris wrung his hands. "But you'll die! Don't you understand that yet? Tomorrow morning you are going to be hanged unless you confess!" He wadded the linen into a ball and rolled it across his brow. "How did this happen? How did it go so far?"

Caleb exploded. His face twisted and his large hands opened and closed. "You," he spit. "You are the greatest single cause of what's happening in Salem Village!" Reverend Parris gasped and drew back from the accusation on Caleb's face.

"I never . . . my career . . ."

"You came to a village with mild problems and you created bitter divisive controversy. Instead of healing the breaches, you caused more, you whipped the populace into a fury of hatreds and frustrations. You encouraged an atmosphere of fear and mistrust and inflamed the villagers against one another!"

Samuel Parris' face drained of color. "No!" he whispered.

"When Betty and Abigail began raving, you allowed the witchcraft interpretation to protect your own self-importance. You couldn't afford another skipping incident, could you? Better to have them possessed by Satan than to have snickers over the antics in your own home. You didn't want anyone whispering that Samuel Parris couldn't even control the children in his own house." A charged quiet choked the room. Then Caleb sank to the edge of a chair, and his head dropped between his shoulders. "How do you live with yourself? When you see the evil you helped to cause, how do you live with it?"

"No!" Samuel Parris screamed. His face was ashen. "You're all witches, it's true! You deserve to die! May your rotted souls burn in a fiery hell!"

George Corwin ran into the room, a napkin in his hand. "What's going on here?" he shouted.

"Leave us," Caleb said, looking at Samuel Parris. "And may God have mercy on you."

Corwin stared at the white faces in the room; then he escorted the reverend none too gently from the house.

Over his shoulder Samuel Parris screamed, "You'll roast in Satan's fires! Do you hear me? You'll be buried in unhallowed ground! All of—" The door slammed.

George Corwin pushed his head into the parlor, his face red and angry. "Five more minutes. That's all!" He disappeared.

"Parris knew," Bristol said dully. "For an instant he knew."

Caleb glanced up from the chair and ran his hands through thick sandy hair. "By the time he stepped through the door,

410

his justifications were made. His image intact." Wearily he stood.

They stared at each other and knew there was nothing more to say.

"Thank you for coming, Bristol."

"Oh Caleb, I . . ."

His jaw knotted and he stared past Bristol, out the open window. "How is she?" he asked softly.

Bristol swallowed the stone in her throat. "She . . . she loves you, Caleb."

He closed his eyes and swayed. Then he looked at Bristol. "Will you give her this?" He withdrew a thick letter from his pocket.

"Aye," Bristol whispered. She wished to God he didn't have the tear in his stocking. Running into his arms, she hugged him fiercely, pressing against his heartbeat. "Caleb! Caleb! Lie to them! Tell them what they want to hear!"

"I can't, Bristol, you know that." Gently he held her away from him and brushed a strand of hair from her eyes. "You were always so beautiful." He smiled. "I'm sorry for the pain I caused you. Once you started to tell me about a man. Maybe . . ." His voice trailed.

At the door, Bristol paused for a last look, seeing him through a blur of tears. He was tired and soiled, and there was a tear in his stocking.

"Help her, Bristol. She'll need your strength."

Choking, Bristol ran outside and jumped blindly on her horse. Giving the mare its head, she let it run. They were nearly home before she could begin to think. Facing Charity was a task she dreaded like nothing before in her life.

Charity threw open the door and clutched Bristol's hands. "Did you see him?" Frantic eyes searched Bristol's face. "How did he look? Is he eating? Can he sleep? Does he have a Bible? Are they hurting him? Did you tell him that I . . . ?" Charity leaned dizzily and lifted a hand to her eyes. "God in heaven, Bristol! *Tell me!*"

Bristol opened her mouth; then, unable to speak, she mutely extended Caleb's letter. Charity stared at it; her trembling hands reached out. The agony on Charity's face was too much to bear. Bristol shoved the letter into the girl's hands and ran into her bedroom.

She flung herself across the bed and threw an arm over her eyes, steeling herself for that moment when the silence ripped into screams and animal misery.

But it did not. When next Bristol opened her eyes, Charity

was bending over her, gently shaking her awake. "It's time, Brissy." Charity spoke in a calm, sweet voice from another era.

Bristol struggled from the fog of deep sleep. Rubbing her gritty eyes, she blinked again at Charity. "Charity?" Charity was neatly gowned, her orange hair washed, brushed, and tied beneath a plain white cap. But her face—it was the Charity of old, before life went sour. Her face was soft and open, the dusting of freckles giving her a radiant innocence.

Charity helped Bristol sit up; her eyes were shadowed but clear and steady. Any hint of stridency had vanished from her voice, leaving her tone quiet and almost shy. She touched Bristol's cheek. "I'm going ahead now. They'll be moving Bridget and Caleb from the jail to the hill. It may comfort him if I'm beside the cart." Dumbly Bristol nodded. "You dress and come when you can. I'll meet you at Gallows Hill."

"Charity . . ."

Suddenly Charity leaned forward and swept her sister into a tight embrace. "Thank you for understanding! Always remember, Brissy, I love you!"

Charity was gone before Bristol's mind could focus. She jumped from the bed and ran to the window, pulling back the curtains in time to see Charity galloping down the lane astride Caleb's gelding, Exodus.

Hurriedly Bristol dashed water in her face, dressed, brushed out her long curls, and ran to the stables. The servants had her little mare waiting, and Bristol mounted, bending over the mare's neck and digging in her heels.

Gallows Hill was ringed with wagons, horses, and quiet people. They waited in silent groups, no taunting or jeering as occurred in the town-square punishments. Bristol tied the mare and stepped forward. A path opened for her, until she stood at the outer rim of the hill, staring up at the trees capping the rise. From a thick branch two nooses swung in a lazy breeze. Ladders waited beneath.

Wide eyes dry, her face stone white, Bristol stared at the hemp nooses. And waited. Long before anyone saw the cart, iron wheels squeaked into an unnatural silence, and they heard a patient clop of horse's hooves striking puffs of dust from the ground. Bristol knew if she turned, she would see an advancing red cloud. But she did not turn.

After what seemed an eternity, Reverend John Higginson and Reverend Nicholas Noyes, both of Salem Town, entered her line of vision, leading Bridget Bishop and Caleb Wain-

412

wright to the top of the hill. Samuel Parris was nowhere to be seen.

Bristol watched Caleb climb the hill, and her green eyes sparkled with unshed tears. Never had he looked so tall, so straight and decent and good.

A small cold hand slid into hers, and Bristol felt Charity at her side. Their shoulders touched and they leaned on each other.

Sheriff George Corwin positioned Bridget and Caleb beside the ladders and knelt to bind their hands while Reverend John Higginson delivered a brief sermon. His sober voice caried easily above a soft rustle of tree leaves. A drift of honeysuckle scented the air; not a cloud marred the perfect blue sky.

Behind the reverend, Bridget Bishop lifted her chin and defiantly studied the crowd. Caleb Wainwright stood tall as a ship mast, his eyes on two leaning heads.

Reverend John Higginson closed his Bible and stepped to one side. "Bridget Bishop, do you have any final words?"

Bridget moved forward and thrust out her shapely bosom. She wore the scandalous red bodice that had provoked so many frowning whispers over the years. Slowly her dark gaze scanned the crowd, stopping here and there. Several men shifted and dropped their eyes from her stare. "I have nothing to say." Bridget laughed.

"Caleb Wainwright, do you have any final words?"

Remaining beside the ladder, Caleb lifted his head and spoke in a strong, quiet voice. "I am innocent of any wrongdoing and have never willingly harmed anyone. I pray that a wronged populace will regain its senses before others stand where I stand today. I ask God to grant that ours is the last blood shed on this account. And I ask God to forgive those who act from ignorance." His steady blue eyes moved over the silent listeners. Then he bowed his head and repeated the Lord's Prayer perfectly.

The crowd strained to hear, then exploded into shouting. Some charged the hill. Only the intervention of the clergy prevented them from rushing the sheriff and freeing Caleb.

An esteemed Boston preacher, Mr. Cotton Mather, whipped his white horse back and forth along the base of the hill, driving people back. "Hear me," he shouted. "These persons have been tried in a court of law and judged guilty! We must obey the law! We cannot allow anarchy here!"

The confused mob shouted and waved their fists. "He said

413

it right!" they yelled. "No witch can speak the Lord's Prayer without mistake!"

Reverend Mather's face was as troubled as theirs, but he stubbornly stuck by the law. "Maybe we didn't hear correctly," he roared. His horse pushed them down the hill. "Regardless, *this is the law!* These two have been sentenced to hang, and they must hang!" His commanding voice rang across the mob and drove them back. "We cannot and must not take the law into our hands! We are civilized, not barbarians! Let the law do its work!"

The crowd reluctantly gave way beneath his authority. Cotton Mather trotted his horse to the side and nodded up at Reverend Higginson, who looked in turn toward Sheriff Corwin. For a long tense moment George Corwin did not move. The crowd held its breath, and hundreds of hearts beat as one.

Then Corwin swung toward Caleb and Bridget, his face blank. "Up the ladders," he growled in a low, harsh voice unlike his normal tone.

They mounted the ladders. Bridget's face mocked the world. Caleb's eyes remained fixed on a carroty head until a black hood dropped over his face. The sheriff tightened the nooses, forcing both heads into an unnatural angle. George Corwin drew a deep breath, swallowed, and kicked the ladders away.

A wind seemed to rush down the hill, sucking out breath and icing the flesh. No one moved. All eyes sickened at the bodies jerking below the tree limb. At last the black dance ended. The bodies stilled and hung limp, turning slowly in the summer breeze.

And not a person dared breathe. They waited, their eyes fixed and expectant. Any second the two dangling bodies would drop to the ground and jump up chuckling. Then everyone would sigh and go home. But they didn't. The bodies hung heavily, both necks at a twisted, awkward angle. A dark stain appeared on the front of Bridget's skirt.

"Mama, I want to go home," a child's voice whined.

Bristol pulled her eyes from the empty, dangling bodies and searched the crowd for the child who cried out. It seemed desperately important to identify that child. When again she turned a glittering stare toward the top of the hill, both bodies had been cut down. Two men bent over Caleb and gripped the noose halter. They dragged him to the side of the hill and pitched his body into a shallow grave, then shoveled it over. They spit and walked away.

Sick inside, Bristol reached for Charity, but Charity was gone. She rocked dizzily on her feet. Caleb's chin protruded from the dry red dirt. And one hand and part of a knee.

Around her the crowd melted backward. Women coughed, men cleared their throats. And the justifications began. Tempers flared. Emotions too complex to understand twisted the hearts and reasoning of shocked minds. "Good riddance!" a voice said loudly, and murmurs of agreement rose in a troubled hum.

Suddenly Bristol could not endure another single second. She whirled and ran, bumping into people, crashing against horses and wagons, and finally she fell panting against a tree. Leaning on the rough bark, she bent and vomited until her stomach cramped, until her throat burned raw and acid stung her mouth and eyes.

A man's lace-cuffed hand extended a damp cloth, and she accepted it gratefully, pressing the wet linen over her burning face. Strong fingers closed on her arm and led her around the tree trunk, away from staring eyes.

"Are you all right?"

Recognizing the Boston preacher's resonant voice, Bristol lowered the linen and fell against the tree. Her dull eyes stared up at Mr. Cotton Mather. The people had tried to save Caleb, and this man had prevented them.

Cotton Mather's sober dark eyes didn't flinch from the condemnation in her stare. "I'm sorry," he said simply. "It's a terrible thing when one of our loved ones is—"

"Don't say it!" Bristol rasped. Her throat felt like raw meat.

"I believe you mistake what I intended to say," he answered in a low, gentle voice. "It's terrible when one of our loved ones is dead in the prime of life."

"You could have saved him, and you did not!"

He frowned at the ground. "Widow Wainwright . . ." he began, and Bristol jerked as if he'd struck her. "I . . . I'm sorry. Whether or not I agree with the law's conclusions, I believe law is what separates us from the pagans. We must obey our laws! Salem is a tinderbox. If tight control is not kept . . ." His shoulders lifted in a worried shrug, and his youthful face creased in deep concern. "The entire colony could blow up in our faces. Can you understand that? We're sitting at the edge of a holocaust."

Bristol's shaking hands rose and covered her eyes. "But they're dead!" she whispered. "Dead!" She lowered her hands

415

to her mouth. "Can you believe they were really witches?" Her swimming eyes clouded with despair.

He searched her face as if deciding how freely to speak. "I don't know. I believe in the existence of witchcraft and in evil as real as the tree at your back," he answered slowly. "I also believe frightened people are capable of grievous error." He lifted his eyes toward the hill and the pieces of rope fluttering from a thick tree limb. When he continued, Bristol felt he spoke to himself. "It is the evidence I question, the lack of concrete proofs that lead us into error. How can we accept testimony from one possessed by the devil? Can we trust the devil to speak truth through the mouths he controls? And can we hold a flesh-and-blood person accountable for the actions of his shape? Do the children cry out the true names of their tormentors, or does the devil work his evil by putting false names on their lips?" He seemed to have forgotten Bristol. "I believe in witches, but I see no fair or accurate method to prove witchcraft without a confession freely given."

"If the clergy believes as you, then why . . . why don't you halt these egregious trials?" Transfixed, she stared at him.

Cotton Mather blinked as if suddenly remembering he had an audience. "Not all the clergy believe as I do. And while the present laws are in force, we must live with them." He took her icy fingers and pressed. "What I sought you out to tell you is that many are working to change the laws. Any changes will come too late to help you and your family, but they may come in time to save others similar suffering. I believe it better that a thousand witches go free than to have one innocent person hang."

"It's too late for that," Bristol moaned. "Innocents have already died here!"

His dark eyes pained. "If I can do anything to ease the suffering of you or your family, please call on me."

Bristol's heart lurched in her breast. Family. Wildly she peered past his shoulder. Where was Charity? Charity needed her now like never before; they needed each other. Without another word, she pushed past Reverend Mather and ran to the base of Gallows Hill. Nearly everyone had gone. "Have you seen Charity Adams?" she asked a man standing frozen, staring at the tree atop the hill. He didn't answer. She grabbed a woman's arm. "My sister! Have you seen Charity Adams?" The woman shrugged and walked away.

Alarmed, Bristol chewed her lip. She swung into the mare's saddle and flew toward home. Home. Of course that was where Charity would go; she wouldn't display her grief in public.

Bristol burst through the door and knew instantly the house was empty; it had that peculiar silence of empty rooms.

She waited all afternoon, and still Charity did not appear. Night deepened and the hours passed. Frantically Bristol paced back and forth through the rooms, picking up items and letting them fall. Where was she? Where was she! Throughout the slow silent hours, Bristol reviewed every word, every tiny gesture Charity had made today. She'd been so elated to see Charity restored to her old self that Bristol hadn't questioned the reasons for the change. Charity should have been beside herself with anguish, but she'd been outwardly calm—inwardly peaceful. Why? What had happened? What had released Charity's agony?

Toward dawn, Bristol sank into a chair and rubbed her aching temples. *Where was Charity?* What was her state of mind? What was she thinking? Bristol leaned her head against the top of the chair. This was getting her nowhere. She'd have a mug of hot beer to steady her nerves. By the time she finished a mug, the sun would be up. If Charity hadn't ridden through the gate by then, Bristol would go for help.

She stood and passed a weary hand across her eyes. Exhausted, she'd bent to the hearth before she remembered the beer would be cold; they'd let the fire die out. Her eyes stared at a pile of fine white ash for several seconds before she registered what it was. Then her green eyes focused on a browned curl of paper. A scrap of letter that hadn't burned:

> . . . forgive you, my darling, but I worry that you will not forgive yourself. . . .

Bristol screamed. In her heart she knew. Oh, God, she knew! She knew where Charity had gone!

The mare's pounding hooves made an eerie sound in the empty predawn lanes, and Bristol felt a surge of relief when the mare turned into freshly seeded fields and raced toward the forest edge. They entered the shadowy thicket, and Bristol found a hidden pathway, overgrown with summer foliage, gray and dim in the feeble light.

"Hurry," Bristol urged, her teeth chattering. "Hurry!" She kicked hard at the mare's flank.

Her heart jumped to her mouth, and she felt lightheaded when the mare skidded into the clearing. Early pink touched the tumbling chimney of the settler's cabin. A chill iced Bristol's flesh as she spotted Exodus, still saddled, nibbling at the encroaching forest.

"Charity!" Bristol screamed, her feet running before they touched the ground. It was quiet. So terribly quiet. "Charity!" Bristol raced across the sagging porch and burst through the door.

She stopped, her skirts billowing out in front of her. Then she crashed to her knees, clutching her stomach and staring up in sick horror.

Charity swung from the rafter, turning slowly.

She had thrown a rope over the sturdy ceiling beam. Below her dangling feet, a stool lay on its side. Bristol looked at the stool. A C was carved in the top—not an old C, but a fresh one, perhaps a year old. C for Charity.

Slowly Bristol raised her eyes; she could not look away. One of Charity's shoes had fallen off, and her stockinged foot seemed so small, so vulnerable. Her fingers were curled like a child's. And for once, Charity's freckles were unnoticeable; her face was swollen, infused with blood. Her pale blind eyes stared into eternity.

Bristol pitched forward into the black dirt.

32

THEY brought Charity home, quiet men from the village, and laid her out on the kitchen table. "No," Bristol said politely, there would be no public service. "No," she said, she didn't need or want help. "No," she repeated, no cemetery plot, she'd bury Charity at home where she could tend the grave herself. "Thank you and good-bye."

When they left, she washed the body, moving like a person in deep wooden shock. It took a long time to work the rope loose from Charity's neck. Then she dressed Charity in her finest gown and best linen apron and wove white roses in her hair.

Bristol did not hurry. It was late afternoon before everything was exactly right and she'd done all she could. Then she removed Caleb's musket from above the hearth and carefully loaded it. She poured herself a tall mug of straight rum and marched out to the barn.

The men, Clem and Booker, straightened in surprise when she entered the musty-smelling building. She ignored them and seated herself on a mound of sweet hay. Carefully she set the rum in the straw beside her and raised her knees, resting the musket there. She aimed it at the two servants.

"I want two caskets," she said evenly.

"Ma'am? Two?"

"Two. Build one for my sister. Build the other for a man six feet tall."

Clem and Booker exchanged uneasy glances. "Well, uh . . ."

"Do it, or I'll blow you to hell."

They stared at her calm white face and looked hard at her finger curling on the trigger. "Aye, ma'am."

It was full dark when they finished, and Bristol's mug was empty. She stepped them into the house at gun point and ordered Clem to pour rum all around. They sat outside on the porch, drinking and listening to the night. She kept the musket on them.

The moon had dropped when Bristol prodded them awake with the musket barrel. "Come on. We're going now."

Reluctantly they hitched the wagon and climbed on the seat. Bristol stood behind them in the straw bed, the musket inches from their heads. They cast terrified looks at each other, both knowing where they were going. She didn't have to tell them.

For a few minutes she thought she'd have to shoot them both. But they stared into her narrow eyes, then drug their feet up Gallows Hill.

"Don't make me, Goody Wainwright, please don't make me," Clem pleaded, looking down at the shallow grave and the pieces of flesh protruding above the dirt.

"I can't!" Booker begged, a sob in his throat.

"Get him out of there, or I swear I'll kill you both."

They looked at each other desperately, neither doubting she'd do it. Booker sobbed, and Clem shuddered uncontrollably. "It ain't natural!" he cried. "The devil will get us sure!"

"Maybe," Bristol snapped. "But right now you have to worry about me." Her finger tightened on the trigger. "Get . . . him . . . out . . . of . . . there!" She stepped back and aimed, and her finger quivered.

"We're doing it! We're doing it!" Sobbing openly, frightened nearly out of their wits, the men brushed the dirt from Caleb's body; then she threatened them down the hill to the wagon. They laid Caleb in the straw bed and drove her home, the musket steady at the back of their necks.

"What if somebody sees us?" one of them asked, shivering. The horses made a lonely flesh-creeping sound in the dark dead lane.

"Are you gonna let us live?" the other one whispered.

Bristol didn't speak, not a single word, until the wagon creaked to a halt before the barn. "Over there. Under the oak tree. Dig."

Golden rays of dawn glowed across the treetops before they finished the graves and fell exhausted against the oak trunk. They stared at her like she was a demon escaped from the pits of hell.

"Get up," she ordered. The three of them went into the barn and returned with the coffins. She watched as they lowered the caskets into the open holes. "Now, bring my husband."

Clem stopped beside the wagon, his face set in stubborn fatigue. "No, ma'am. This is it. I ain't going to touch him again. That there is a witch. I ain't going to do it!" he balked.

She lowered the musket and blew off the tip of his left shoe. Before either of the tired, stunned men could react, she dropped the spent gun and reached under the straw in the wagon and withdrew the loaded musket Caleb kept hidden there. She aimed it at their chests. "Dammit, now you move!"

Clem howled and stared at his bloody shoe. "My Gawd, she shot off my big toe! Look at that! Most of it's gone!"

"The next ball goes between your eyes unless you put my husband in his grave!"

Grunting, they carried Caleb to the grave and lowered him into the coffin. Clem trailed bloody footprints in the dust.

"Now my sister." They fetched Charity, and Bristol watched through narrowed eyes. "Be careful!"

When they'd finished, they stood in shuddering quiet, the open graves behind them.

"If I hear one word, a single word, about what happened here tonight, I'll shoot you down like dogs," she said in a steady voice. "It may take the rest of my life, but I will find you and I will kill you." They believed it. "I never want to see either of your faces in this county again." They nodded crazily. Bristol tossed a bag of coins at the feet of each.

"Now, get out of here. You may both take a horse, but not Exodus or old Brown. Any of the others."

They raced for the barn like the devil nipped their heels, and in a few minutes they flew past the house and vanished down the lane.

Bristol waited until the noise of horses' hooves faded, then slid into the graves and placed a spray of summer flowers in the hands of Charity and Caleb. She didn't look at their faces; she wanted to remember them as they'd been, not as they looked now. She smoothed Charity's apron and adjusted Caleb's leg so the tear in his stocking did not show. Then she lowered the coffin lids into the holes and nailed them shut.

Exhausted, Bristol dragged across the yard and into the house. Already the sun was hot, and wet rings circled her arms. For a moment she sat at the kitchen table and rested. She felt tired and empty.

But she couldn't stop, not yet. After dashing her face and neck with cool water, she collected a broom and a sharp knife and returned to the open graves. Filling them was hard. Blisters bubbled up on her palms, broke over the shovel handle, and reformed. At the finish, she thought she would faint. Her arms felt like lead, and her back ached as if she would break in two.

Before sitting for a brief rest in the leafy shade, Bristol stamped up and down over the graves, packing the dirt. She shoveled more dirt and packed that. The graves might sink as they settled, and she didn't want that to happen.

In the barn she found a wheelbarrow and used it to carry away the extra dirt, scattering it about the barnyard. The sun hammered at her head, and the entire upper part of her gown was soaked through with perspiration. A buzzing roared in her ears, and only sheer determination kept her on her feet and moving. She didn't know how much time she had. And oh, God, she was tired!

Finished with the extra dirt, she returned to the graves and swept all traces of loose soil out of the grassy cover beneath the oak. Then she took the knife and walked into the pasture. She hacked out a piece of sod here and another there, not taking them from the same spot. Loading the pieces in the wheelbarrow, she pushed back to the graves. Working painstakingly, she trimmed the sod and fitted it together like a puzzle over the raw dirt of the graves.

At last it was done. Bowing her head, Bristol stood between the graves and quietly offered a prayer for them both.

"God bless you and keep you," she whispered at the end. "And may you find each other in heaven."

She stepped back, swaying with fatigue, and critically examined her handiwork. Unless someone stood exactly over the spot, the graves were unnoticeable. She'd fitted the sod tightly, and in a few weeks nature would complete the task. Only Bristol would know the graves were there.

Satisfied, she returned the wheelbarrow to the barn, put away the wagon, fed the animals, swept out tracks and footprints, and picked up her broom and dulled knife. Both hands were bloody and swollen; gripping anything sent waves of pain up to her shoulders. She dragged herself to the house.

Inside, Bristol stripped off her wet ruined gown, wanting a bath more than anything. She sat on the edge of her bed, telling herself she'd rest for just a moment, then carry in water for a wash. But she sagged backward and fell instantly asleep.

When she woke, the heat of the day had passed and the slant of mellow shadow streaking the planks told her it was early evening. Bristol pulled into a sitting position, scrubbing at her eyes. Even with sleep, she still felt tired, and muscles she hadn't known she had, ached and protested each movement.

The buzzing continued to hum inside her head, and for an instant she wasn't certain whether she'd heard a knock or imagined it. Tying a wrapper around her waist, she walked slowly down the hallway.

A thin man with shifting eyes and a weasel face stood on the porch; another rode through the gate. Bristol combed her fingers through her hair and pulled the wrapper together at her breast. "Think, think," she whispered to herself, but her mind seemed wrapped in insulation. Her body walked, her puffy hands moved, but her mind didn't seem part of anything she did.

"What is it?" she said.

The man's eyes lifted from her breasts. "You the Widow Wainwright?" He leered.

Bristol cringed.

He unrolled a length of poster, his eyes flicking to her breasts and the satiny gleam of moisture on her skin. "This here's a legal notice," he announced. He waved it briefly in front of her face, then nailed it to the side of the door.

"What?" Bristol gasped. If only her brain would wake up! The paper looked fuzzy. "What are you doing?" How dared he drive nails into Caleb's house?

"Your husband is an executed felon. Everything he owned now belongs to the state." The weasel face smiled in satisfaction; all was right in the world. "You got ten days to vacate the premises." He licked his lips. "If you got no place to go, dearie—"

"Get out," Bristol choked. A tide of panic tightened her throat. Where could she go? With no money and no family, where in God's name could she go? A sense of despair cluttered her mind, and her eyes hardened at the injustice of it. Green flint stared over the farm Caleb had loved. Gone. All gone.

The man leaned his elbow against the door. "Now, I could—"

"You heard the lady, get your slimy butt out of here!" Sheriff George Corwin slid off his horse and walked up the porch steps. He stared hard at the weasel-faced man.

"I'm only doing my job," the man whined.

"Do it somewhere else." George Corwin kicked the weasel-faced man over the side of the porch and growled down at him. The man scrambled up from his knees and ran toward his horse. "Ten days!" he called over his shoulder. "You got ten days!"

Bristol closed her eyes. "Thank you," she said softly to George Corwin. She leaned against the doorjamb, feeling two hundred years old. Old and burned out. Where would she go? She didn't have money for ship passage, she didn't even have enough actual coins for more than three days at one of the inns.

Sheriff Corwin fidgeted on the porch, turning his hat in large hands.

"I'm sorry, Sheriff, my mind is . . . Would you step inside and share a cup of cider? It's cool."

"Well . . . uh . . . the truth is, Goodwife Wainwright, this isn't a social call." An uncomfortable red darkened his face. "Fact is, I have to arrest you."

Bristol stared, and her heart fell to her knees. But it wasn't really a surprise; nothing could be. "Witchcraft?" she whispered when her stiff lips would move.

Corwin nodded. "The girls say you witched Charity to death and, uh . . ." He shifted his bulk and glanced briefly at her swollen hands. ". . . and there's a second count of bodysnatching."

Bristol nodded slowly. She'd known it might happen, else why had she taken such pains to hide the graves? She stood in the doorway, not moving.

423

"I know it's a shock," Corwin said smoothly, not looking at her hands again. "But Wainwright's body is gone." He ran a finger around the inside of his collar. "Lotta folks want a decent burial for their loved ones . . . however, I sure don't see any grave around here." He didn't look.

Instead he met Bristol's vacant eyes with an expression of sympathy, and she wondered if George Corwin believed in witches. She suspected a tug-of-war played in his head.

His hat circled in his fingers, and he stared out at the barns and pastures, the fields thick with young shoots of summer wheat. "I told you I knew your pa," he said quietly. "Not a finer man born than Noah Adams. I served with him in the militia, back in the early days. I'm glad he isn't here to see what's happened to his family, to this county."

"You're only doing what you have to," Bristol said, guessing his thoughts.

Heaving a massive sigh, he met Bristol's eyes. "We have to go, ma'am," he said.

"Aye." Bristol shook her head, wishing the buzz would go away. Stepping toward him, she wondered if he would tie her hands.

"Maybe you'd like to change out of that . . ." Corwin's big hand indicated the wrapper. No surprise showed in his ruddy expression; he'd done this before, he knew what arrest did to people's minds.

"Aye," Bristol agreed, her voice blunted. But she didn't move. She looked at him to tell her what to do.

Corwin opened the door and guided her inside. He sat at the kitchen table and waited while Bristol entered the bedroom and dropped a gown over her head. When she came into the kitchen struggling to fasten her collar, he gently pushed away her puffed hands and fastened it himself. Then he suggested she might want to take a few things.

"Aye," she answered, returning to the bedroom. Picking up her hairbrush, she turned it in her fingers, trying to think what to do with it.

George Corwin took the brush and laid it on the bed. "Maybe a change of . . . ah . . ."

She understood and lifted fresh underclothing from her trunk. He turned his back. "You might want a dress for the examination . . . ?" Of course he was right. She chose a light summer green—someone had once mentioned she looked especially well in green, but she couldn't think who might have said so. Folding the gown around her underthings, she handed the bundle to the sheriff, who then laid it on the bed.

Gently he suggested stockings, apron, collars and ". . . something for your hair, those little caps." She laid them out. "I think it might be wise to include a cloak," he added, dropping his eyes. "We don't know how long you'll be gone."

It was late June, and surely she'd be home in a few days. But Bristol humored him by laying a heavy cloak on the bed. She waited, unable to decipher what came next.

Corwin spied a large tapestry bag on a peg and packed her belongings; then he went to the barn and saddled Exodus for her.

It all seemed like a dream. When she awoke the following morning in the jail behind George Corwin's house, she had only fuzzy memories of how she came to be there. It didn't seem real. But the jail was very real. Bristol swallowed and looked around her. Thank God her mind was beginning to thaw.

Goodwife Corwin, a plump little woman with kind eyes, brought Bristol a warm mug of beer and helped tie Bristol's hair at the neck. Her hands were better this morning, but still puffed and awkward to use. Goodwife Corwin shook out the light green gown. "George thinks it best to leave immediately—to escape the worst of the heat." The little woman helped Bristol dress.

The eight-mile ride to the packed village meetinghouse passed more quickly than Bristol would have liked. The lanes were tree-lined and shady, and a scent of warm earth and wildflowers filled her nostrils in a heady blend. They met other constables escorting other prisoners along the road. Had the faces not been so pale and grim, Bristol might have imagined they rode to a summer picnic. Except, she remembered, few New Englanders indulged in such frivolities as picnics and social outings. Their minds centered on darker pursuits.

Her heart sank at sight of the crammed meetinghouse. People spilled from the door and into the lane. Already they mopped slick brows, and dark stains wet their clothing. Everyone agreed it would be another scorcher; they blamed the witches for a lack of cooling rain. Unless the witches were stopped soon, the crops would burn in the fields. People would go hungry come winter.

Sheriff Corwin led Bristol up the steps and inside. Shuddering faces paled and drew away from her in fear and awe. They stared until her green eyes met theirs; then they hastily dropped their gaze before she could work an evil eye on them. Seeing their blatant fear, Bristol felt a hysterical urge to laugh. It was so ridiculous—so absolutely, terrifyingly ridiculous! If she were a witch, she'd hex them all and simply walk away. Why did no one think of this? Hysteria bubbled in the back of her throat, and she halted before a vaguely familiar woman whose name she couldn't recall. "Boo!" Bristol hissed. The woman leaped back, and her eyes rolled up in a pasty face. Bristol laughed.

"Don't do that," George Corwin snapped. "Get hold of yourself!" His grip tightened painfully on her arm, and he gave her a rough shake. "You need your wits now as never before," he said gruffly. "Fear works in their favor. Your fear as well as theirs!"

She slid a look at his ruddy perspiring face and wished the world was made up of George Corwins. She knew he was right; she was being foolish. But her mind felt detached from her body, out of control. Bristol was terrified.

A guard took her from the sheriff and pushed her into the dock. Everything was familiar; simply a new perspective. A matron lifted Bristol's arms out from her body. "Don't move, don't fidget, don't torment the girls," the matron said in a bored voice.

Bristol turned her head and stared at the afflicted girls. She didn't care that a staggering volume of noise immediately erupted, or that Judge Hathorne purpled in the face yelling at her to look away. She wanted to see them, to see her accusers.

The girls were in full cry. One of their own was dead, and the person they blamed stood in the dock. Their screams and howling rocked the room and roared through Bristol's head. Her mind ached with the screeching, pounding noise. But she did not drop her eyes. Her mind fastened on small details, and these tiny observations seemed vitally important.

In honor of Charity's murder, Mary Walcot temporarily had put aside her knitting and joined the others convulsing on the floor. Bristol noticed Mary now worked on a scarf—the vest must be finished. This seemed terribly significant. The scarf would be brown and gray, not colors Bristol would have chosen. Ann Putnam Junior wore her hair parted in the center today instead of to the side, and this too appeared urgently important. Mary Warren had sewn a new blouse. Mercy Lewes wore her hair loose, but it didn't detract from the beginnings of a dark growth along her upper lip. Elizabeth Hubbard's earlobes didn't match, and Bristol wondered how she'd overlooked noticing this previously.

And Sable Horton had joined the accusers. Bristol stared at the pretty dark-haired widow rolling about the planks. It was fitting somehow. Sable Horton had been present the day her adult life began, the day she met Jean Pierre. Sable Horton should be here the day her adult life ended. Thinking of Jean Pierre steadied Bristol's mind, and she looked away from Sable, coolly deciding Abigail Williams was the one to watch for detail.

Abigail attracted every eye: hers was by far the most grievous affliction. She frothed at the mouth and her tongue protruded to astonishing lengths. She tore out hunks of hair and writhed in spectacular convulsions. Bristol's detached mind wondered how it was possible to tear out hair day after day and have any left. Curious, Bristol watched with a sharp eye. She saw Abigail's teeth snap; then the girl's arm rose for the audience to see. The crowd gasped at flaming teeth marks and shrank from Bristol in fright and revulsion.

Bristol smiled. It had happened so fast and could be seen only from where she stood. The mystery of bites and scratches and punctures was solved—only, she realized it hadn't been an enigma for some time. Only Ann Junior produced marks that seemed impossible to self-inflict. Ann, the quiet visionary.

An image of nesting baby birds rose in Bristol's mind. Could an adult bird identify a specific cheep with the gaping mouth that produced it? She doubted it. But she stared at the open howling mouths and tried to pluck a voice from the din to match. The swirling, pounding noise was too great; she couldn't do it. Rough hands clamped the sides of her face and forced her eyes from the girls. Judge Hathorne screamed at her, and she noticed a tic in his left cheek.

Her examination began.

33

THE courtroom was hot; unlit candles in wall sconces sagged and lost shape. Trickles of sweat ran between Bristol's breasts and down her ribs. Her arms felt as if they weighed a

427

hundred pounds each, and she didn't know how much longer she could hold them out. As the pain in her trembling muscles increased, it became more and more difficult to concentrate on the judge's questions.

Judge Hathorne paused and shuffled through the papers on his dais. He glared at Bristol from beneath heavy brows. "Did you witch to death one Charity Adams?" he repeated. A chorus of screams broke from the afflicted girls, and he stared them into moaning quiet.

"No, sir. I did not." Bristol didn't remember how many times she'd answered this question.

"Did your shape inflict harm on Charity Adams?"

"No."

"Tell the court again how Charity Adams died."

Bristol stared, her eyes flickering resentment. They'd examined it again and again. And each time stabbing pain stung her heart. Yet, even with the endless repetition, she understood the full impact of Charity's death hadn't fully penetrated. A portion of her brain closed off the knowledge; she felt if she allowed herself to look into her emotions, to deeply examine Charity and Caleb's deaths, her mind would fly off in darkness and never return.

"My sister took her own life," she answered dully.

Judge Hathorne's cheek jumped in regular spasms. He leaned forward with the crucial question. "What drove an innocent young girl to suicide?" he demanded. "Unburden your black soul and tell this court the truth!"

Closing her eyes, Bristol shook sweat from them. Her arms quivered; she could have sworn heavy stones hung from her wrists. "Charity did not confide in me."

"Tell the truth! Why did Charity Adams die?"

No possibility existed for the truth. If Bristol hinted at Charity's remorse, her love for Caleb, village gossips would feast for months on vicious speculation. She would not do that to Charity and Caleb's memory. But she couldn't lie, either. Better people than she had stood in this dock and resisted damnation. And so would Bristol. It seemed the most important goal in her life—not to lie. Bristol's hot eyes flicked to Goodman Cheever furiously filling pages with testimony. What was said here would be preserved for history; she'd not disgrace the Adamses or the Wainwrights by having history remember her as a liar.

"Tell us the truth!" Judge Hathorne shouted, his tic jumping wildly. "You tempted Charity Adams to her death! Your shape seduced her to fashion a noose and drape it about her neck! Your wicked familiar kicked the stool out from—"

"No! No! No!" Drops of sweat poured from her forehead and salted her eyes. "Please, sir, may I wipe my forehead?" She would have given ten years of life to rest her arms for one minute.

"No!" The judge nodded to a matron, who reached a desultory swipe across Bristol's streaming face. The girls snickered, and all made a show of wiping their brows. They seemed the only people in the hot jammed courtroom not running with sweat.

Judge Hathorne fired question after question after question. They swooped down at her like flaming arrows. Arrows to pierce all the nightmares of her life. "No," she cried again and again. If she didn't lower her arms, she would faint. Spiraling dots swam before her eyes. Her arms quivered and jerked and sank against her will. The strength to hold them up vanished. The girls noticed and went crazy, weeping and beating at Bristol's tormenting shape.

Immediately Judge Hathorne positioned guards on either side of her. They didn't dare touch a witch, but it was safe to extend their lances. The lance bottoms were a thousand times better, but still agonizing. Her arms tingled and shook and felt like lumps of rock attached to her body.

"The truth! Everyone knows you refused your sister shelter. You took her life as well, didn't you? Tell us the truth! She exposed your husband as a witch, and you lusted for revenge. Isn't that true!"

"I've told the truth. I'm innocent of witchcraft."

The judge paused. "Sable Horton swore in her statement that you appeared in the forest wearing the white shape of a snow creature and tried to force her to sign the devil's contract. What do you say to it?"

Bristol fought a war in her mind. She knew her case was lost; what did it matter if she indulged herself? She gave in. "Who? I don't recall anyone named Sable Horton. Is she that loose whore from Salem Town that meets men in the forest?" God forgive my petty vengeance, Bristol thought.

Sable Horton went crazy, flopping from her stool and screaming abuse at Bristol. Despite her aching arms, despite the sweat blurring her vision, despite knowing her case was lost, Bristol turned and smiled sweetly as the matrons dragged Sable from the room. A small insignificant victory, but no large satisfactions were left.

When Judge Hathorne restored order, he mopped his brow

and pronounced Bristol bound for trial on witchcraft. She felt no surprise; the outcome had never been in doubt. He pulled his wet scarlet robe away from his neck. "Count two," he read. "Bodysnatching."

A ripple of delicious horror shuddered through the audience. No one would have departed if the village blazed in ruin. They stared with fascinated loathing. Dead bodies were all corrupt, but a witch's dead body retained the seeds of evil. To touch one without immediate purification with holy water was to court death and certain rot of flesh and soul. They'd never before seen anyone who dared steal a witch's body.

Feeling the weight of their condemnation, Bristol shook as a deep anger formed and swelled in the pit of her stomach.

"Did you take the witch's body from Gallows Hill?"

"Caleb Wainwright was not ever a witch!" Bristol's answer rang strong and clear. Her eyes flashed toward Goodman Cheever rapidly recording her words.

Hathorne's left cheek blurred in spasms. "Wainwright was found guilty of malefic witchcraft under due process of law."

"The law is wrong. He was innocent."

"He was pronounced guilty by a jury of his peers!"

Bristol's eyes hardened to green jade, and she refused to yield. "He was innocent! My husband was no more a witch than I am! Than you are! He was good and decent! Caleb Wainwright had more compassion and humanity than anyone in this room!"

The judge jumped to his feet, his left cheek jerking. "I'll not tolerate insolence," he bellowed. "Further arrogance will earn you severe punishment!"

A brackish clot knotted Bristol's chest. She didn't relish the idea of punishment, but neither would she bow to his threat. "My husband was no witch," she whispered stubbornly. "And neither am I."

Judge Hathorne glared down at her, making a supreme effort at patience. Slowly he sank to his seat. "If you are not a disciple of the devil, then how do you explain the evil possession you work on these girls?" He waved toward the base of the dais.

Mary Walcot knitted placidly. One of the younger girls picked her nose. Two lay on the floor serenely humming and examining their skirt hems. Abigail combed Ann Junior's hair. One or two whispered and giggled.

At the sudden pause in testimony, they froze and glanced up at the judge. Instantly they fell into fits of screaming and howling.

430

When order was effected, the judge lifted a bushy eyebrow. "Well?" he asked, his point made.

Bristol couldn't believe his blind conviction. "There is evil in this courtroom," she agreed in a low voice. "But it is not wrought by any standing in this dock. History shall judge who perpetrated the evil here. History will see with clearer eyes than any alive today!" A deep hopelessness belied her impassioned words.

Judge Hathorne purpled in rage. He swung toward Goodman Cheever. "Strike that blasphemy from the record!" he shouted. He leaned over the dais, and Bristol knew he would have struck her if he could have reached that far. "Did you steal the witch's body from Gallows Hill?"

It was useless to argue.

"Tell us the truth!"

"Aye."

Shocked silence greeted her answer. Then a rush of breath hissed from the massed audience. Women toppled over like rag dolls. Hideous heat bounced from the walls and struck in waves.

"I took my husband home and I gave him Christian burial as befitted the decent life he'd led."

Even Judge Hathorne stared in horror. The girls reached new heights of shrieks and spasms, but no one noticed. Every eye stared at Bristol as if she was a creature composite of all the grisly monsters in hell's blackest cavern.

"The witch must be dug up and moved from sweet ground," the judge croaked. "His flesh will poison good earth. A witch's corruption is fit only for barren soil." He wet his lips and blotted a streaming face. "Where is he . . . buried?"

"I won't tell you."

"In the name of God the father, redeem yourself and confess the witch's unholy grave! I order you to reveal where he is buried!"

"Do whatever you will to me, but I'll never tell you!" Bristol's teeth ground together, and she spit the words. Ten days, she prayed, with rain, maybe a week. And the fertile sod would knit together. They would never find Caleb and Charity. More time would be better, dear God, but three days will do.

"We will find the witch," Judge Hathorne shouted hoarsely. The left side of his face moved with a life of its own. "We'll find his corrupt body and throw it in a barren ditch."

"No . . . you . . . won't."

He studied her, his hands clamped to the edge of the dais.

431

His glare tracked the flow of sweat dropping past her flinty eyes, settled on her quivering, aching outstretched arms. A small satisfaction played at the corner of his lips. He folded his hands and leaned on the dais. "You claim you are not a witch," he stated in a purring tone.

"Aye, I am not."

"You are rational enough to agree your sister and your husband are both dead."

"Aye."

"Do these deaths disturb you?"

She stared up at him, and her mouth fell open. He was insane. They were all insane. Nothing else could explain what they did and said. "I . . . I can barely endure the pain of thinking about it," she whispered.

"And yet"—he glanced at the expectant audience, snapping out his trump card—"yet not a tear wets your eye." He smiled softly. "Can you explain that? How is it you present yourself dry-eyed in the face of multiple tragedy?" Now he allowed a full smile, and triumph glittered in his narrow eyes.

Hopeless, weary to the point of collapse, she answered. "Long ago I took a vow not to cry. Tears change nothing. Will weeping bring my sister back to life? Will tears restore my husband's good name?"

"Witches cannot cry," he stated flatly. "Confess the truth! Unfetter your soul! It wasn't a personal vow, was it?" His voice soared and swooped. "It was Satan! Satan stole your tears when you signed the contract to serve him as your master!"

"No."

"Confess!" he screamed.

Bristol shook her head and dropped her eyes from the expression on his purple face. She felt sick and beaten.

His voice droned on and on. Then finally it was over. Judge Hathorne ordered she be tried on both counts. And mercifully, they released her arms. Bristol staggered at the sudden rush of blood needling up her arms.

A guard prodded her outside and shoved her into a cart; many of the crowd followed, hurling abuse and small stones. Someone knelt to bind her wrists.

Sheriff George Corwin pushed the man aside. "I'll do that," he said. He loosened the rope so it wouldn't cut into her flesh. While he retied her wrists behind her back, he talked. "I'm sorry," he said in a low voice. "It couldn't have gone any other way, you know that."

"Aye."

"The judge ordered me and a bunch of my men out to the Wainwright place immediately."

Bristol squeezed her eyes shut and dropped her head. So she wouldn't have the time she needed. It had all been for nothing.

Corwin finished and stepped around the cart where she could see his face.

He fanned his hat in front of perspiring cheeks. "I'll be directing the search," he said, studying the clear hot sky. "Telling the men where to dig. And where not to dig. I'd hate to tear up a fine place like Caleb's farm any more than we have to. So . . ." His eyes swung from the sky and bored into hers. "So, if there's a flowerbed or some special spot you wouldn't want disturbed, I'd try to respect that."

Her heart jumped, and Bristol stared deeply into his steady eyes.

"But now's the time to say so."

Bristol bit her lip. If she was wrong . . . She swallowed a knot of uncertainty. The suspicion and mistrust had to end somewhere. "I . . . I've always favored the grassy rise beneath the oak tree, Mr. Corwin. I'd hate to think of it being dug up." Emerald eyes beseeched.

He nodded and settled his hat on the back of his head. "Sounds like a nice shady spot to sit and direct the operation," he said, turning toward his horse.

"Mr. Corwin!" He looked over his shoulder. "Thank you . . . for all that you . . ."

He smiled and tipped his hat. "Once your pa did something for me," he said. "Good luck to you."

Bristol braced herself as the cart bucked forward, raising clouds of choking red dust. There were still people in the world whom the madness had not touched, she thought gratefully. In the sheriff's position, he could make the nightmare a little easier for those who passed through his hands.

Nothing could ease the horror of Boston prison.

34

AFTER five bone-jarring hours on the road, Bristol almost felt grateful when the cart turned into Prison Lane and rattled toward a wooden enclosure rising out of early darkness. The night was warm and moonlight shimmered across the waves in Boston harbor. Standing in the cart, Bristol yearned toward the distant water. Somewhere out there, across that gigantic sea, her Jean Pierre lived and breathed. Knowing it, thinking of him, gave her a tiny sliver of courage to cling to. She had known love, and if her life ended tomorrow, no one could take that from her. Jean Pierre had been the reality of her life; not this. As she watched the dark prison draw nearer, she prayed he would never learn her fate.

The jail perched on a grassy hill outside of Boston Town. A cluster of log sheds formed the core, and around it lay a yard fenced by high wooden slats. Originally built to house no more than forty, now the prison swelled with nearly two hundred accused witches awaiting trial. Prison personnel could not cope with the sudden influx.

Harried officials directed a daily building program, adding pens to the main enclosure as quickly as they could be thrown together. The makeshift pens were unsatisfactory, unwieldy, unsanitary, and difficult to police. Additional guards had been posted to oversee the pens, but they resisted patrolling the poorly lit enclosures. The men weren't easy at guarding witches. God only knew what this conglomeration of evil might do to a man. They avoided contact with the hags and warlocks whenever possible.

Consequently, the prisoners suffered an appalling lack of everyday necessities. They ate swill. None were healthy. All were filthy. Lice and dysentery were facts of everyday life. Fresh water had to be hauled from Boston and was considered a luxury. Sewer facilities were nonexistent.

Bristol had heard the prison described as "a grave for the

living," and as the cart stopped and she stared around her in the dim light, she decided the description had been kind. A fetid stench assailed her nostrils, and a deep rancid layer of muck crusted the ground. Dark shapes lay wedged together in a ring around the inner enclosure; even witches had to sleep, but nothing said they needed better than dirt for a mattress, or had to have shelter. Moans sounded everywhere, and pleas for assistance, but the guards remained in the log sheds, refusing to respond.

A weary man with hard eyes and a grim mouth met the cart and stared at Bristol by the light of a stained lantern. "Another one," he stated sullenly.

The cart driver stretched his neck and rubbed cramped muscles. "Count your blessings, Kingston, you coulda had three. The others went to Andover."

"Son of a bitch!" Kingston spit in the dirt. "This means some sorry sod has to stay up all night!" He glared at the driver as if this inconvenience was his fault.

The driver shrugged. "Get her outta the cart, will you? I want to go home."

"So who doesn't?" Kingston gripped Bristol's arm and dragged her from the cart. He shoved her ahead of him toward one of the log sheds. "You got the papers on her?" he asked the driver. The driver tossed over a thick packet and rattled out the gate.

Inside the log hut, a group of men sat in a circle drinking from battered mugs. They glanced up without interest as Kingston led Bristol past them and into a dark empty room. He placed a candle on the room's earthen floor. "You're to remain here for twenty-four hours," he said, pushing her down into the dirt.

Bristol's tongue flicked out and licked dust from her lips. Her stomach growled. "Mr. Kingston?" she asked timidly.

"What?" He frowned at her, about to close the door. Bristol noticed a peephole cut in the upper half.

"May I please have a drink of water and could you untie my hands?"

"No." The door started to close.

"Mr. Kingston!" He glared back into the room, angry now. "Please," she begged. "Why am I in here?"

"You all ask that, and you all know the answer. You do it to harass us!" He slammed the door.

After a moment a wary eye appeared at the peephole, watching her. Bristol stared at it a moment, then looked away. Her mind raced, turning the question, trying to think of anything but thirst and hunger. Of course. Familiars. A familiar had to feed from the witch's body once in each twenty-four-hour period. Part of jail processing was obviously to collect evidence for the trial. Bristol squirmed near the wall and leaned her spine against the logs. A twenty-four-hour rest would be wonderful; her eyes closed.

Instantly the watching eye blinked out and a violent pounding erupted against the door. The eye reappeared. Each time Bristol's head nodded toward her breast, the door shuddered beneath a shattering pounding noise. Sleeping was not allowed.

The hours passed, and eventually she wished with all her heart for a familiar to appear. She ached all over and felt bone-weary. She wanted nothing more than to stretch out in the dirt and sleep. Forget everything and sleep. No sooner had the wish crossed her mind than the door crashed open and a man bolted into the room. He raced to a far corner and stared in triumph at a small brown spider. "Here it is!" he sang out.

"So?" an indifferent voice called from the next room. "Kill it and go to bed. We're sick of your complaints!"

The man lifted his boot and ground the spider into the dirt with a shiver of fear. He snatched up his foot and rapidly examined himself to see if he'd acted before the familiar witched some part of his body into a hairy monstrosity. Weak with relief, he turned to Bristol and prodded her to her feet. He muttered to himself, "Off to the examination room, then the damned report, and then to bed."

This time she knew better than to risk anger by asking what the examination room was. The man shoved Bristol into a small room with a cot along one wall. He lifted his leg over the cot and kicked an old woman out of a whimpering slumber. "Here's another one," he said. "I'll be just outside if you need help with her."

The old woman rubbed her eyes and nudged a bundle of rags sleeping beside her. Both women pulled to their feet, grumbling and carping at each other and Bristol. "Take your clothes off."

Mutely, heart thudding, Bristol turned to show her bound hands. One of them cut the ropes. Slowly she undressed, her face red and her eyes blunted.

They examined her inch by inch. "Bend over." Bristol did as they demanded, wishing God would strike her dead. The indignity, the humiliation of it, was more than she could bear. She wasn't surprised when they found what they sought.

"Look here," one of them cackled, pointing to the faint ridges on Bristol's back. "A familiar's feeding tit if I ever saw one!"

"Please, once I was whipped, that's—"

"Shut up."

Next they took a knife, sharpened to a fine thin point, and began pricking her all over. They started at her toes and worked up, raising fiery needles of pain. Bristol flinched and cried out and tried to twist away, but the strongest held her while the other dotted the knife point across her skin.

Unable to resist, incapable of fighting them, she went limp. Her body sagged. Every sense felt deadened by exhaustion. Her mind seemed wrapped in cotton.

"Here it is!" the old woman crowed. "See?" She touched Bristol's hipbone with the knife point. Bristol didn't react. Had she not been watching, Bristol wouldn't have known the old woman pricked her. She decided they could have broken both legs at this point and she would have felt nothing.

"That's it, all right, the devil's mark. Dead flesh."

Mercifully they put away the knife and threw her clothes at her. The younger of the two returned to the cot and rolled near the wall. The older one waited until Bristol dressed; then she kicked open the door. "She's got it, all right," she shouted at the man. "On the back and on the hip, just here." She drew a circle on her own hip to show him.

He nodded. "Write it up and I'll be back."

The old woman shook her head. "Write it up yourself, you lazy slug. You know I can't do letters." She slammed the door.

Muttering beneath his breath, the man jerked a lantern from a peg and gave Bristol a vicious kick out the door. She sprawled in the muck, curling into a ball and covering her head.

"Get up," he screamed. She scrambled to her feet, her eyes wide and frightened, and he shoved her through the darkness, down a lane of packed bodies, and out the gate. They marched through meadow grass and finally halted before one of the wooden pens. He unlocked the gate and hurled her through, locking it behind her. When his grumbling mutter faded, Bristol looked around.

Beneath a starry, moon-bright sky, she saw row upon row of jammed sleeping bodies. The seeping ooze of a dung hill glittered at the end of the pen. The stink was unbelievable.

"Bristol Adams?" a soft voice called nearby. "Bristol Adams Wainwright? Is it you?"

"Aye," Bristol answered in a loud whisper. A shape rose from the sleeping bodies. "Rebecca!" Bristol ran forward and dropped to her knees beside the old woman. Rebecca Nurse squeezed to one side and made room; then she pressed Bristol's fingers.

"I can't say I'm glad to see you; not here." The woman's cheerful little face split into a thousand wrinkles around a smile. "Are you hungry?"

Bristol nodded.

"I'm afraid the water's gone until tomorrow." Rebecca lifted a filthy apron and rummaged in the pocket. She produced a crust of bread and a chunk of moldy cheese. "My granddaughter bribed the guards to get this in. I save it for newcomers. It isn't much, and this is the last of it. But everyone's so hungry after the familiar room. Were you in the full twenty-four hours?"

"Shouldn't you be sleeping?" Bristol whispered loudly near Rebecca's ear. She had to repeat it.

Rebecca chuckled and patted Bristol's hand. "At my age, a person doesn't need much sleep. Besides, I'll be sleeping plenty before too long." She watched Bristol wolf down the food. Between bites, Bristol told of the empty room and the spider. Rebecca smiled. "That's nothing. You are looking at the worst witch of all time. Oh, aye." Her button eyes twinkled in the starry light. "When I went in, it started to rain—the last good rain we had before this dry spell. And every stray cat and dog and mouse and frog in Suffolk County wiggled into that room. All of them wringing wet and looking for a dry spot. Near scared the life out of that young man." She shook her gray head and chuckled.

That Rebecca could retain any good humor at all in this foul place astonished Bristol. Soon, however, the smile faded from those wrinkled old lips, and Rebecca spoke of sadder events. Old Goody Osburn had died in the prison. Others they both knew were very ill. Elizabeth Proctor feared for her unborn child, as the food was poor and maggoty and the water often went bad before fresh was hauled to the prison. Rebecca feared little Dorcas Good's mind had gone; the child suffered greatly. She'd heard rumors that torture was practiced in the men's pens, and both men and women were kept chained. Rebecca lifted her skirt and showed Bristol her own shackles.

In the morning two guards arrived and locked iron cuffs around Bristol's ankles, the cuffs attached to a length of chain soldered to eight-pound iron balls. Bristol could walk only by

438

bending and carrying the balls. Using this method, she could hobble about, bent at the waist. She soon discovered that trying to drag the balls only flayed the ankles.

By daylight, the pen was hideous. A square of fenced misery and offal. That humans could survive such conditions was a staggering idea. But they did, and Bristol gritted her teeth and vowed she would too.

On Rebecca's advice, Bristol claimed an area of fence. When guards dragged away a woman there, Bristol slid immediately into the narrow spot, marking it as her own by tearing a scrap of skirt and nailing it to the fence with a sliver of wood. The benefits of a fence position were instantly obvious. It was difficult for the sightseers standing on benches behind the fence to hurl refuse at anyone directly beneath the fence. Also, the wooden slats provided a backrest and offered shelter from a boiling afternoon sun. Those without a fence place sat in the middle of the compound and served as target for the sun and curious onlookers. These women glared at Bristol, angry and resentful that a newcomer had beat them to the fence spot. Bristol returned their stares and thanked God for Rebecca.

Rebecca proved invaluable by helping Bristol and other newcomers adjust to the hardships of prison life. If the food wouldn't stay on their stomachs, Rebecca teased them about being too fat. When the water didn't arrive on schedule, Rebecca suggested a rain dance and coaxed a smile. As layer upon layer of dirt and mud accumulated on Bristol's skin and clothing, Rebecca congratulated her on looking like a fresh arrival no longer.

In July, Rebecca Nurse was hanged. Along with Sarah Good and three others.

Bristol spent the day in quiet prayer and hopelessness. She leaned against the fence and stared at the iron cuffs banding her ankles. Rebecca Nurse dead. How did rational minds accept such an atrocity? Her eyes strayed to Rebecca's fence spot, already claimed by a new haggard face. But Bristol saw Rebecca there, and her throat ached.

By the first week in September, Bristol came to understand none of them would leave the prison alive. Those who did not die here, died at the end of a rope.

Five more had been hanged in August, including John Proctor. Elizabeth Proctor escaped hanging only by reason of pregnancy; she'd been tried, and when the baby was born, she would hang.

Despite the hangings, the likelihood of dying in prison was

far greater than dangling at the end of a noose. The trials progressed slowly. At the present rate of trial sittings, Bristol calculated it would be years before the pens cleared of witches.

Looking over the crowded desperate women, Bristol swallowed hard and wondered if she could survive these conditions for years. In her heart, she doubted it. Summer had been appalling; winter would be deadly. That they had managed to endure the blistering summer was credit to the hardiness of humanity.

The pens were open sewers, an invitation to rats and maggots and giant mosquitoes that raised welts the size of shillings. Breathing the foul stench burned nostrils and lungs. All thought of modesty disappeared within hours; no privacy existed of any kind. Two buckets of sour water were allowed every other day and vanished instantly. No one bothered to give the women provisions for monthly needs; they caught the curse and had no way to blot the flow or clean themselves. Lice foraged in hair and clothing. They fought like animals for moldy bread and scraps a dog would not have touched.

When rain fell, everyone rejoiced—for a short time. They stood in the compound and scrubbed weeks of crust and filth from their bodies and tried to wash the clothes they wore. Then they lay down in the mud to sleep, and it began again, the cycle of dirt and bugs and dysentery and hopelessness.

Quickly they became the animals most of the populace believed them to be. When they spoke of it, and they did endlessly, they felt anger and bewilderment at their treatment, at the terror in eyes which slid away from direct contact. Yet, sometimes they stared at each other and saw what others saw—and fear leaped in their own eyes as well. They'd entered these gates as clean, responsible human beings and had become ragged hollow-eyed creatures of hell, willing to claw a neighbor for a scrap of food or a bit of space. Any could have served as model for a sketch of the worst features associated with witches.

"Care for company?"

Bristol looked over her shoulder as Divinity Cooper lowered her iron shackles with a sigh. Hurriedly Bristol buried a bone she'd stolen from the community pot. "Aye, sit down." She patted flat the earth next to where she hid her treasures and settled her back against the wooden slats. "Is there anything new?" It was the standard greeting.

"No." The standard answer. Divinity crossed her legs and

settled carefully within the perimeters of Bristol's rectangle of space. A skirt hem on a neighboring patch was enough to instigate a scratching, howling fight. Divinity closed her eyes and let the autumn sun warm a muddy face.

Guiltily Bristol fought with herself. Should she offer to share the bone or not? Three weeks ago Divinity had nursed Bristol through an attack of dysentery . . . but Bristol's stomach felt as if it gnawed itself. She'd keep the bone. She sighed. "Divinity, I have a bone; come back tonight."

Divinity smiled and nodded, knowing the battle Bristol had lost; they all waged such wars. "Thank you," she said formally. "Hester Ellison told me they tortured two more men yesterday. Tied their necks to their heels until blood ran out of their noses and mouths."

Bristol looked up, interested. "I didn't hear that. Was it anyone we know?"

Divinity shook her head, her stiff matted hair not moving. "I don't think so. At least no one I know."

They sat quietly, looking at each other and wondering for the hundredth time what the other would look like cleaned, rested, and well-fed. Divinity's round eyes peered from a face crusted with grime and dried mud. Bristol knew her own face looked the same. She glanced at their fouled skirts and tried to decide what the original colors might have been. She couldn't remember. Each scratched her head and body while they visited; it was as natural an action as breathing.

"Did you hear Phillip English escaped again?" Bristol asked.

"No!" Divinity's eyes sparkled; escape stories were the essense of life. "How?"

"Same as before. Bribed a guard. He got his wife out, too; she was in the North pen." Here, as everywhere, money made all the difference. With money, extra food could be had, a second cup of water. And with enough money, escapes could sometimes be arranged.

Divinity's eyes took on a dreamy cast. "Someday a tall, handsome man will look over the fence, see me, and bribe the guards to let me out." Like Bristol, Divinity had no family, no one to care that she was in prison.

Bristol laughed. "Divinity, this man of yours needs to be a witch himself to see anything worth saving! He'll have to use magic to see past all that." She waved at the tatters Divinity wore over months of dirt. It occurred to Bristol that she hadn't the remotest idea of Divinity's hair color.

441

Divinity sniffed. "My dear, I shall simply cast my best hex, and he'll instantly see what a treasure I am." She grinned.

"Cast a spell to call up a rescuer for me too." Bristol laughed as Divinity picked up her iron balls and hobbled across the compound to her own piece of fence.

Bristol had met Divinity Cooper at one of the prayer meetings Reverend Cotton Mather regularly held for the witches. Neither attended much anymore. Prayer wasn't likely to alter their predestined paths, and too long an absence could cost their fence spots. They'd seen many a woman return from a lengthy prayer meeting, a glow of peace on her muddy face, only to discover she had to claw someone out of her place. Peace and screaming didn't mesh well. The Boston preacher didn't miss either Bristol or Divinity—his prayer meetings were well attended despite the cost.

"Anything new?" Bristol asked automatically when next Divinity visited Bristol's rectangle.

"Aye."

Bristol's head jerked up at the unexpected answer.

"They *pressed* a man to death!" Divinity's round eyes stared. She rocked back on her heels and awaited Bristol's reaction.

Bristol's mouth opened and closed. "Pressed a man to . . . to death?" Would the horror never end? She scratched her ribs and stared into Divinity's mud-dark face.

"Aye. Name of Giles Cory. I never met him, but I knew his wife, Martha Cory." In the past they might have complained of Martha's sharp tongue, but Martha Cory had been hanged last week. They said nothing. "Goodman Cory wouldn't plead guilty or not guilty, so they put a heavy rock on his chest to make him plead. But he wouldn't. They kept adding big stones until he . . . until he died."

The two girls stared at each other, trying to imagine what it must be like to feel life slowly crushed from the body, stone by stone. Bristol shivered. Man's inhumanity to man could never be understood.

"It took three days for him to die," Divinity added hoarsely.

Bristol closed her eyes. "It's time to stand up," she said, changing the conversation. If they didn't stand often, rise out of the hobbled position, eventually they wouldn't be able to straighten at all. They'd seen it happen to others. Both girls rose, holding their popping spines and groaning. Upright, they could see Boston harbor, sparkling in fall sunshine and dotted with rocking ship masts.

442

"Did you ever sail on one of those?" Divinity asked, her eyes yearning toward the tall ships. Always the romantic, Divinity envisioned a trip on a sailing ship as a glorious experence.

Bristol smiled sadly. "Aye," she murmured in a soft voice. "Once . . . a long time ago in a better life." All the ships resembled the *Challenger*. Indulging a moment of foolishness, she let herself think one of them might be Jean Pierre's ship. Bristol's smile turned wry, and she shook her head. She was becoming as wishful as Divinity.

A rotten egg sailed over the fence and smashed against Bristol's shoulder, emitting a foul, noxious odor. Both girls instantly dropped to their knees and crawled nearer the fence, out of the sightseers' range.

"It gets worse every day," Divinity complained.

Bristol scooped a handful of dirt and scrubbed it into the ooze dripping down her arm. It helped some. "Sometimes," she muttered in a low voice, "I worry that the good citizens will storm the prison and murder us all."

"I know," Divinity answered, watching a rain of eggs pelt the center of the enclosure. "They've only managed to hang nineteen so far." Her voice was bitter. "The law isn't killing us fast enough; there are still hundreds alive."

Bristol's hollow green eyes watched two women cover their heads and duck behind a dung pile. "How long do you suppose New England will be patient? How long before they decide to forget the law and hurry things along themselves?"

Guards chased away the angry, frightened people hurling garbage at the witches. Then they unlocked the gate and stood just inside the pen. One of them glanced down at a piece of paper. "Bristol Wainwright! Bristol Wainwright!"

Bristol and Divinity stared at each other. Divinity's dirty fingers covered her mouth, and her eyes grew to saucer size. Both knew the procedure. The women were called out, cleaned some, and the next day were taken away to trial.

And no one yet had survived a trial. All had been hanged.

35

THE same old woman who weeks ago had pricked Bristol with the knife led her into a room containing a wooden tub filled with water. The old woman pushed Bristol into the tub and gave her a perfunctory scrub with stinging lye soap. At the finish, the old woman tossed a handful of clothes toward Bristol and ordered her to dress.

The clothes were neither new nor very clean, but compared to her own filthy rags, they were queenly raiments. The old woman eyed Bristol fleetingly and pronounced her satisfactory. Apparently it wasn't necessary to attack the embedded dirt beneath Bristol's nails, or curl her hair, or tend to the red rashes of bug bites. So long as she wasn't offensive to the nostrils of judge and jurors, she would do.

Guards returned her to the pen with instructions to practice standing in order to endure tomorrow's long journey to Salem Town.

Bristol walked to her rectangle of space and leaned against the fence, her heart still thudding. From the moment they'd called her name, her nerves had tingled in fear and dread. How did one adjust to dying? She'd faced death before—but it was never acceptable.

Uneasily she scanned the compound, seeing that the women avoided her as if she carried a fatal disease. Their eyes slid toward Bristol, then dropped away. Bristol Adams Wainwright was a dead person; they all knew it. Only Divinity Cooper offered comfort.

Divinity settled beside Bristol, and together they watched the sun disappear in a blaze of reds and purples. A glitter of stars appeared overhead. "I'll miss you," Divinity said. A rustle of women adjusting themselves in sleep whispered through the night.

"I hope your tall, handsome man finds you," Bristol answered. Leaning forward, she placed her small hoard of treasures in Divinity's lap. She had one limp carrot, a ragged piece of shawl, and a battered shilling which had been bequeathed to Bristol in similar fashion.

Divinity accepted the items with tearful gratitude. "Thank you."

Although neither could think of anything to say, Divinity remained. No words would ease the fright and hopelessness in Bristol's heart, but it helped not to be alone.

In the restless silence, Bristol's thoughts ranged through a panoply of years. She recalled herself as a child, as a young adult, and examined the woman she'd become. People whom she'd known and loved paraded through her mind, and she longed toward each, saying good-bye. One face surfaced again and again, but she couldn't bear to bid it farewell. Not yet. Not until the very last.

"Divinity? Are you awake?" Bristol asked softly.

"Aye."

"Once, Divinity, I knew a very special man. His name was Jean Pierre La Crosse, and I loved him as life itself, and he loved me . . ." Her story spun into the starry night. Bristol talked to the distant white twinkles, and Divinity listened, understanding Bristol's craving to speak his name, to summon his image . . . to say good-bye in her own way.

When Bristol's voice trailed, both girls sat quietly. Then Divinity pressed Bristol's hands. "You've been luckier than most," she said. "You've had a great love. Which is more happiness than most here have had." She didn't speak with envy; Divinity uttered a simple truth.

"I never told anyone this," Bristol said in a low, thick voice. "But . . . I never gave up. Deep inside, I always thought that somehow . . . somehow Jean Pierre and I would find each other again. When Caleb died . . . God forgive me, for a while I hoped that maybe . . . you see, I've never imagined growing old without seeing Jean Pierre at my side." She remembered that she would not live to grow old. "Somehow I thought we'd age together, surrounded by children with gray eyes and red hair." Her head dropped. "Oh, Divinity, I love him!"

Divinity squeezed her fingers and gently tugged Bristol to her feet. "Come on, it's time to stand and stretch."

They gazed toward Boston's moonlit harbor, both thinking of sea captains and great loves. And because she'd talked about him, in every dark ship on the water Bristol saw the *Challenger*. Neither girl noticed a glow behind them until Bristol yawned and turned back toward the fence.

"Divinity!" Bristol's fingers clawed at Divinity's suddenly rigid arm.

"Oh, God!" Divinity breathed. "It's happening!" Her eyes rounded in fear.

A long line of flickering torches advanced on the prison, bobbing up Prison Lane from the town proper. Bristol and Divinity distinctly heard a low rumble of angry shouts and the sound of horses.

Dropping to her feet, Divinity wrestled frantically with the iron cuffs circling her ankles. A sob burst from her lips. "They'll kill us!" she cried. "They'll kill us all!" One of the sleeping women lifted up and yelled for Divinity to be quiet.

Bristol knelt beside Divinity, her mind racing. "They can't kill us all! We're too many!" She clapped a hand over Divinity's whimpering mouth. "Listen to me! Someone will see the torches. Someone will send for Reverend Mather. Even now he's probably gathering men to help us." Was that true, or had Boston exploded in witch fever as Salem had? "I've seen Cotton Mather handle a mob before. He'll help us; he believes in the law."

"We're the closest pen, they'll take us first," Divinity wept.

First one woman overheard and looked for herself, then another. News spread through the compound like wildfire, and the women woke screaming. The pen erupted into a madhouse of screeching, terrified women. They sprang from their cramped spaces and ran forward, forgetting the iron balls shackling their feet. Many pitched forward into the muck.

Bristol jerked up, blood pounding in her ears. The other pens woke, and screams blew through the prison like a wind from hell. In front of the jail, the torch line broke into two groups, one racing to subdue the guardhouse, the other . . . the other running toward them. Bristol spun and stared in terror as the gate crashed inward and torches and men spilled into the pen. For an instant they halted, taken aback at the massing of devil's hags screeching and cowering from the light. Then the men flooded into the pen. The women shrieked and tried to run and could not.

Bristol's hands leaped to her mouth. Several women were clubbed to the ground like helpless animals at a slaughter. Others huddled against the fence, covering their heads and screaming for mercy.

The men dashed through the enclosure, bending to unlock iron bands with keys mysteriously produced. Brutal kicks herded the women out the gate.

Relentless hands bruised into Bristol's skin, holding her while another man opened the cuffs on her ankles. Throwing aside the chains, he turned to Divinity. Divinity sobbed and begged, but her cries went unheard in the explosion of noise and screams and shouts. Viciously the men booted both girls into the stumbling crowd of women streaming from the gate.

Outside, men circled the women, prodding them with sharp lances into a terrified knot. Others drove stakes into the meadow grass and piled faggots at the bases.

"Burn the witches!" impatient voices shouted. "Burn the hags of hell!"

Divinity clung to Bristol's arm, sobbing, her body shaking uncontrollably. The women wept and pleaded and screamed for pity.

In the midst of the wailing terrified women, Bristol stood like a frozen statue. Her body quivered in violent spasms, but her mind felt apart. Her death was preordained. Dying no longer frightened her. Burning did. To hang was terrible, but it was also quick; burning was not quick. Eyes wide with horror, she stared at the men stacking dry wood at the stake bases, and her mouth fell slack.

Finished, the men whirled and ran toward the circle of women. Brutal hands flew into the ring and dug into flesh. Bristol felt herself yanked forward. Divinity and five others were pulled out next, all whimpering and falling, weak with terror.

Three men half-carried, half-dragged Bristol to the last of the stakes. They hurled her against a wooden pole and lashed her arms behind her. A cord circled her waist, and another cut into her throat, binding her to the stake. "Please," she whispered, her voice a terrified croak. "Please."

They didn't hear. They ran on to the next stake, cutting lengths of rope to bind Divinity.

Bristol's head sagged against the pole, and she peered toward the night sky, hidden by bright torchlight. A cracked voice floated across her mind: " . . . and the one who is not, shall stand in dark flames. . . ."

"But not the others," Bristol prayed through bloodless lips. "Please, God, save them. Help us, Father, help us!"

Her brimming green eyes looked desperately to the town in the distance, and a flutter of hope quickened in her breast. Tiny dots of light wound toward the prison. Another line of torches streamed up from the harbor. But they were so far away.

The men in the clearing ran back and forth, flickering

torchlight illuminating their faces. Seven women were lashed to the stakes. More men searched the meadow floor for additional poles. The remainder gathered behind a man who obviously led the mob; they looked to him, waving swords, muskets, and hissing torches.

The leader stepped forward, a tall man in somber Puritan dress with a face that twisted in fear and loathing. He waved a worn Bible in the night and lifted his voice. "Thou shalt not suffer a witch to live!"

"Aye!" roared the voices. A lone shout lifted. "No sermons, Hacker, get on with it!"

"Aye!" came the chorus. "Burn them! Burn the witches!"

Hysterical, Bristol stared toward the dots of light in the distance. "Hurry!" she urged. "Hurry!"

"Have you anything to say?" the leader cried in a parody of legality.

Goodman Hacker earned a torrent of scorn. "Never mind that!" "Burn them!" "Set the torches!"

A dark-haired woman tied to the first stake screamed, "I curse you! God will give you blood to drink! God will curse your babies and the seed of their seed!"

The men gasped and drew back. Then the mob surged forward, and only Hacker's hasty intervention prevented them from tearing the woman from the stake and killing her with their bare hands.

"Hear me!" Goodman Hacker shouted, running up and down before the line of stakes. "Hear me! They will all die! Blood will cleanse Boston of evil, but blood washed in fire! Blood shall not stain our hands!" He pulled the men from the woman. "Colter! Light the fire on this one! Now!"

The man called Colter began with the cursing woman. He thrust his torch deep within the pile of faggots and held it there. Then he ran down the line. The bound women screamed, and their eyes bulged toward the curls of smoke drifting at their feet and hems. The circle of women awaiting their turn at the stakes covered their eyes and shrieked. They held to each other and watched Colter pausing at each pole, then running forward.

Colter shoved his torch against the wood at Divinity's feet, ignoring her screams; then he raced toward Bristol. For an instant he stopped and stared into her panicked, pleading gaze. This one was cleaner than the rest; he could see what she looked like. "You're beautiful!" he breathed.

"Please," Bristol said. Her lips framed the word, but only a croak emerged.

"Colter!"

The man gave his head a shake, looked about him, then bent with an angry glare. He plunged the torch into the wood at Bristol's shoes.

A panting silence hung in the clearing of men and whimpering women. All eyes fixed on the gray curls of smoke fogging the women's feet. In the distance came faint shouts and the pound of horses' hooves, but no one turned to see.

Then the wood about the feet of the cursing woman caught with a soft burst of flame, and a hoarse cheer broke from the men's throats. All down the line of stakes, fire blossomed in orange balls around the base of the stakes.

Above a hurricane of fear roaring through her mind, above the crackling whisper of flame, Bristol heard Divinity scream—a long hopeless wail that pierced the autumn night. It went on and on and on. A wavering curtain of heat shot up from the fire nibbling Bristol's feet, and she blinked at the men's eager contorted faces through a wave that shimmered and moved.

One or two of the men seemed to suddenly realize what they did, and they sank to their knees with pale sickened expressions. But the mob didn't see; they waved their fists and shouted triumph until their throats rasped hoarse.

Scorching heat flickered against Bristol's cheeks, and her hands at her back grew hot and tingled. By straining at the cord around her neck, she could glimpse the woman tied to the first stake. The cursing woman's skirt caught fire with a soft poof, and flame raced up the oily rags. Her wide mouth opened in a shriek that clawed along mind and flesh.

Frantically Bristol twisted and jerked at her ropes. Her fingers scrabbled at the back of her skirt, pulling it up in clumps, trying desperately to keep her hem from the licking flames. Fire caressed her shoes, and slowly the soles charred and blackened. Heat scalded into her toes and calves and penetrated her hysterical mind. She saw the first woman's hair explode in a fiery halo around her face. Bristol screamed, a long mindless shrill of sound.

When her eyes snapped open, it was as if her scream had blown the men backward in a giant wind of anguish; they ran and scattered. Foaming horses poured into the clearing, and the women's screams mingled with a clash and ring of swords meeting swords, of musket fire flashing deadly light. Men from the harbor spilled into the clearing. Fighting, shouting, screaming people ran everywhere.

It could all be seen by the light of the burning witches. A

smell of charred flesh wafted outward in nauseating oily drifts. The first woman blackened on the stake, her white boiled eyes the only dots of color to mark where her head had been. Divinity's skirt ignited in a flaming column, and the girl screamed in a voice of madness.

Bristol leaned her head against the stake, screaming through cracked lips. Fiery fingers began to stroke her hem, dived, flickered, and suddenly flamed her skirt in a circle of orange horror. The fire raced up her body, seeking flesh and hair and bone.

A tall powerful man broke from the shouting, slashing mob and raced behind Bristol. His sword flashed down the stake, and hand and waist and throat cords fell away. He drug her from the flames and threw her into the dirt, rolling her back and forth. Smothering hands beat at her body, at the smoking ends of her hair. And she screamed when his hands touched her lower legs, the raw burned flesh.

Her clothes ripped from her body, still smoking, and a man's cloak dropped over her chemise and charred petticoat. Bristol pulled to her hands and knees and lifted her head. She shook tears of pain from her eyes and tried to see clearly. "Oh, God," she whimpered. It couldn't be. "Jean Pierre?" Her whisper was disbelieving. "Is it you? Is it really . . . ?"

He bent, and she saw his face in the blazing firelight. The firm jaw, the ridge of scar, the finely molded nose . . . and his hard smoky eyes. Pain and joy washed across her mind in red waves.

Jeane Pierre's powerful arms swept her into an embrace and held her against his chest. "Little love! Tell me you'll be all right!" His hand stroked her hair, touched her face, turned her eyes to meet his.

Bristol's arms flew around his neck, a cry broke from her lips. "Jean Pierre! Jean Pierre!"

The intense gray eyes closed for an instant. "Thank God!"

Her trembling fingers leaped to touch his face, his hair, his grim mouth, the scar she knew so well. Hysterical laughter welled in her throat. How was it possible? Maybe she'd gone mad with pain and terror. But no, the muscles rippling beneath her fingers belonged to no other. Whimpering, she buried her face in his neck and clung to the smell of salt and sea and man.

"You're safe now, little one. Safe." Tenderly he lowered her to the meadow floor, and her hands moved over him, reassuring herself, not wanting to let him go.

He caressed her cheek, his gray eyes flickering. "God, how

I've longed for you!" he whispered. Then he was running toward the crush of swords and shouting, his blade in his hand.

She'd believed she remembered everything about him, but she'd forgotten his fluid grace of movement, the easy confidence, and the power in his face, his stance. Bristol pulled into a sitting position and dashed tears of pain from her eyes. She found him in the slashing swirl of firelit bodies, his shoulders straining, his face hard and concentrated. Thigh muscles bulged, his arm rose and struck metal, lifted again and sliced into flesh. Bristol buried her face, then looked again. He was still there, fighting, shouting, living. As she watched, another man stepped free for an instant, saluted her with his sword and a scarred grin, then whirled back into the fight. Mr. Aykroyd.

Bristol's heart soared in joy. She could have watched them forever, her eyes shining with love, but she remembered Divinity. On hands and knees, wincing and groaning, she crawled to the crumpled, charred heap that was Divinity. Divinity was hurt, hurt badly, but the girl was alive. Bristol gentled Divinity's head in her lap, lifting the girl so Divinity could see the fight. Divinity's eyes rolled up, glazed with pain, and she ran her tongue over ash-flecked lips. "Will they burn us again?" she panted.

"No," Bristol soothed, pushing matted hair off Divinity's brow. "No, everything will be all right now."

And she believed it would be. Bristol's feet throbbed and flamed, her hands were black in spots. But she scarcely noticed. Her eyes followed a white shirt weaving and slashing through the mob. The men from town flooded into the clearing, and Bristol saw Reverend Cotton Mather plunge into the foray atop his white horse. Bending under the force of additional men, the mob gave way and gradually retreated into the darkness. Muskets fired from a greater distance.

As suddenly as it had begun, it ended. The clearing was littered with wounded men from both sides; others milled about aimlessly, swords swinging from their hands, their eyes turning again and again to the charred black things hanging from the first two stakes.

Guards rushed into the clearing, freshly released from the captured guardhouse, and their eyes widened in sick horror at what they saw. Rapidly, voices raw with shock, they rounded up the women and led them back to the pen.

"No! Not this one." Jean Pierre's steely eyes fastened to

451

those of Captain Kingston. Jean Pierre's hand tightened on the hilt of his sword, and his legs bent and tensed.

"They all go back," Kingston whispered. His face drained of color, and he knew himself outclassed. But he stepped back, positioning for battle. He hefted his sword, testing the weight, readying himself.

A knife appeared in Kingston's back, and Mr. Aykroyd's voice hissed softly, "I think not. We saved yer incompetent arse from more trouble than ye've got already. Ye'll have plenty to answer here as it is. We'll take these two women as our prize."

Bristol stared up from where she held Divinity, and saw the indecision on Kingston's pale face. Even with Jean Pierre's sword at his chest and Mr. Aykroyd's knife at his back, the man displayed a stubborn courage.

Cotton Mather spurred his horse toward the conflict. "Kingston!" his authoritative voice cut through the tension. "Release these women into Captain La Crosse's care. I'll take the responsibility." He reined his horse and peered down at Kingston. "I have it on good authority that three days hence, the governor will adjourn the court of oyer and terminer. These two would eventually have gone free anyway."

Kingston's eyes found Bristol, and she saw in his glance that the termination of the court would not have come quickly enough to save her from the rope. Slowly Kingston moved his eyes from Jean Pierre's narrow stare to Reverend Mather. "It's on your responsibility."

"Aye." Mather watched Kingston walk away; then he extended his hand to Jean Pierre. "Thank you, Captain, my men wouldn't have arrived in time. Is this the young lady you've been negotiating for?" He smiled at Bristol.

"Aye."

Mather lifted the reins. "It's been a pleasure having you in my home, La Crosse. If you lay anchor in Boston again, my wife and I would be pleased to have you and your lady stay with us."

Jean Pierre bowed from the waist. "*Merci*. Please extend my thanks to Goodwife Mather for her hospitality."

Reverend Mather tipped his hat and rode toward a group of men knocking over stakes.

Dropping to the grass beside Bristol, Jean Pierre stared deeply into her wide shining eyes. "I've come for you," he said softly. Gently he moved Divinity's head, then gathered

452

Bristol into his arms. Their knees sank in the meadow, and he held her tightly to his heart.

Mr. Aykroyd drove his cutlass into the grass and knelt beside them. His scarred face split into a grin. "I swear, gel! Ye best marry the captain quick. I never did see anyone get into such messes on their own." He shook thin wisps of hair and smiled. "Ye're the most disaster-prone gel I ever did see! And look how ye're dressed! A man's cloak and yer underthings! Didn't I teach ye anything?"

Bristol smiled, her green eyes luminous. "God in heaven, but I'm glad to see you both!" She reached a hand to that dear ugly cheek.

He covered her hand with his own. "Little gel, ye—" A flash of orange exploded at the edge of darkness, and Mr. Aykroyd's expression froze. The sound of a musket shot floated into the night. Instantly Jean Pierre jumped forward, catching Mr. Aykroyd before he crashed over Bristol. "No!" she screamed, her eyes blank and rejecting.

Bristol clawed herself up over him, her hair falling against his cheek. A ragged wet flower opened on his lower chest. Bristol's horrified eyes lifted to Jean Pierre, seeing his expression harden to stone. "Speak to me!" she cried, turning back to Mr. Aykroyd. "Oh, God, no! Speak to me." Her fingers flew over his face, his shoulders, his arms.

"Well, if that don't beat all!" Mr. Aykroyd stared up indignantly. He pushed up on an elbow, touching his side and staring at the blood on his fingers. "The fighting was over. *Over!*" He looked from Bristol to Jean Pierre, then back. He grinned. "Hurts like hell. But at least it ain't my face this time."

Jean Pierre's tight expression relaxed. Winking at Bristol, he bent to help Mr. Aykroyd sit. "That's good. We'd hate to see your beauty marred."

Mr. Aykroyd's grin widened. "They's a widow in Southwark what feels the same." He tore his shirt and wadded the material against his wound. Then he looked at Bristol's frozen face, and his eyes softened. "It's all right," he said gently. "I've come through worse than this. I plan to bounce yer babies on me knee."

Her hand shaking violently, Bristol reached out and touched his lips, then his hair and his cheek. She buried her face in her hands. "I thought . . . oh, dear God, I thought . . . I just couldn't bear it if . . . not you! I . . ."

Her shoulders convulsed; then Jean Pierre was lifting her,

453

cradling her in his strong arms, pressing her face into his shoulder.

And the tears came. A wet torrent scalded down her face. Tears gushed from her eyes, and deep shuddering sobs tore her throat. Hot burning tears, the tears she'd repressed for so long—they streamed and flooded and poured from her eyes and heart. She could not stop. Her shoulders heaved in deep racking spasms, and her breath choked in wet gasps.

Jean Pierre sank to the autumn grass, and they remained on their knees, clinging to each other. "If Mr. Aykroyd had died . . ." Bristol sobbed, gasping and strangling. Her fright opened the floodgates of her heart. "So many died! Charity, and Caleb, and Papa, and Rebecca, and Martha, and John Proctor, and all the rest! And our baby! Oh, Jean Pierre, our little baby!" The tears she'd stored in some secret core burned down her cheeks in aching painful sobs, a torrent of anguish. Her throat swelled raw, and her chest convulsed. And still the tears rivered down her cheeks in needed release. Cleansing, healing tears.

Holding her quivering wild body, Jean Pierre kissed her hair, her flowing eyes, her moaning lips. His strong arms circled her, and she wept until each shuddering breath was agony and her throat felt like fire.

When she began to quiet, Jean Pierre pressed her limp body against his hard warm chest, listening to her weak sobbing. "We'll sail at dawn," he murmured against her hair. "I'm taking you home to England, my little Bristol."

She stared up with swimming vision, meeting those deep gray eyes. "Please. Can we leave now? Tonight?"

Jean Pierre glanced over her head at the dying embers of seven fires, and his eyes steadied on the shadows of the pens. Mr. Aykroyd groaned. Then Jean Pierre gently brushed her wet cheek with his thumb. "The *Challenger* sails tonight, my love."

36

INSIDE the captain's cabin, Bristol leaned forward in the desk chair and wearily listened to frantic sounds from above deck. She heard men's shouts and running feet and a snap of night breezes in yards of dropping canvas. Rope groaned and animals bawled and someone loudly cursed. And over it all she heard a deep vibrant voice shouting orders. A longing for him welled in Bristol's throat, a longing embedded in her very soul. She felt a dizzy surge of wild joy.

"Bristol?"

Bristol turned to the bed, where the ship's surgeon labored, rubbing ointment into Divinity's raw, charred flesh. "Aye?" Bristol answered, feeling a stab of guilt at her happiness when Divinity suffered so greatly.

The *Challenger*'s planking shuddered as wind cupped unfurling canvas and swung the ship toward the open sea.

"Bristol! We're on a ship, aren't we?" Divinity whispered through cracked lips, and tears of pain leaked down her muddy face.

Bristol hobbled to the bed and knelt beside Divinity, taking her hand. She smiled. "Aye, you're going to have that ship adventure you wanted. We're sailing to a new life, Divinity, where it's clean and fresh for us."

Divinity's eyes darkened. "So many died," she whispered. "So many." Her eyes closed.

Bristol's heart rolled, and she clutched the surgeon's shoulder. "Is she . . . ?"

The man glanced up and shook his head. He called for two men to move Divinity into a passenger's cabin. "No, she's fainted. Best thing for her right now. She'll have a limp, but she'll live." He pressed Bristol firmly to the edge of the bed. "Let's have a look at your feet."

The surgeon salved her feet and legs with something to suck the fire away. It felt wonderfully cool. She could walk—not well, but she could walk into Jean Pierre's arms when he came for her. And by then she'd found the pewter cup on his desk.

"You kept this," she marveled, turning the little mug in her fingers. She remembered all the times she'd held this mug to her breast, drawing comfort from its memories of home. Home.

"Aye," he answered, "it was something of you." Gray eyes caressed her face. His hand gently lifted her chin. "I love you, Bristol. When I learned you had married, I nearly went mad thinking of you and another man . . . It was then I decided to come and take you. Husband or no husband, you belong to me. You're mine." His gray eyes smoldered into hers, and a heated knot flamed in Bristol's stomach. The fingers on her chin tightened. "Was he . . . was he good to you?" Jean Pierre murmured in a husky voice.

"Someday, my love, my Jean Pierre, someday I'll tell you about Caleb Wainwright. But not now; not now, my dearest."

Warm lips crushed her mouth, and her arms rose to circle his neck, pulling him closer. When Jean Pierre released her, she trembled in his arms, shaken with the desire his touch awakened in every hidden part of her body.

"It's nearly dawn," he said gently. Lifting her, he carried her upstairs to the afterdeck. Overhead, the canvas fluttered; below, foamy black water lapped the ship.

Jean Pierre held her to his chest, so close she could feel the steady warmth of his heartbeat against her spine. His cheek rested atop her hair, and they stared into a solid wall of black. Black sea, black sky, black land.

Footsteps sounded across the planking, and Mr. Aykroyd stood beside them. He cleared his throat and touched his side gingerly; then he handed Bristol the little pewter cup. His eyes met hers. "Home is where the heart is," he said gently.

Bristol stared at him; then, understanding, she stepped to the rail and dropped the cup, listening to the distant splash below.

"Don't look into the darkness of the past, my little love," Jean Pierre murmured softly. He turned her from the curtain of blackness toward a first glow of sunrise streaking the eastern sky. "Look forward." One hand swept across the faint pink horizon, the other found her waist. "Out there is England. And the rest of our lives."

Bristol's eyes rose from the dawn glow, and she gazed up at his strong profile—at the man who gave her life meaning.

Mr. Aykroyd lit his pipe and stood by her side, his hand on her shoulder. "Home," he said quietly.

Bristol's eyes closed in silent gratitude. Her arms went around their waists, and she hugged them both. Then she lifted tear-bright eyes to the sunrise, and her lips curled in a rapturous smile.

She had finally come home.

ABOUT THE AUTHOR

Maggie Osborne was born in 1941 and grew up in Kansas and Colorado. After attending Ft. Lewis Junior College in Durango, Colorado, she worked on a newspaper and then as a stewardess. She currently lives with her husband, a manager with State Farm Insurance, and her son in Colorado. In addition to community activities, her leisure projects include painting and renovating old houses with her family. She is the author of *Alexa,* another historical romance also available in Signet.